THE

PORTABLE

MAUPASSANT

*Edited, and with
an Introduction, by*

LEWIS GALANTIÈRE

NEW YORK

THE VIKING PRESS

1947

PUBLISHED BY THE VIKING PRESS IN JANUARY 1947

PUBLISHED ON THE SAME DAY IN THE DOMINION OF CANADA

BY THE MACMILLAN COMPANY OF CANADA LIMITED

Grateful acknowledgment is made to Alfred A. Knopf, Inc. for permission to utilize the Maupassant translations by Ernest Boyd and Storm Jameson in the books *The Novels and Tales of Guy de Maupassant* and by Ernest Boyd in *The Collected Novels and Stories of Guy de Maupassant*. For this volume Lewis Galantière has edited and revised their translations in part.

PRINTED IN U. S. A.

BY THE COLONIAL PRESS INC.

To Ernest Boyd

THE CONTENTS

CONTENTS

THE PORTABLE

MAUPASSANT

EDITOR'S INTRODUCTION

MAUPASSANT, though a very great writer, does not appear at first blush to have been an interesting person. He had of course emancipated himself from certain conventions, and he possessed a sharp intelligence of a skeptical and negative kind; but his pleasures were without distinction and his opinions without originality. A child of his age, he had read out of school a little Herbert Spencer, the shorter pieces of Schopenhauer, a book on ant-life, and not much else. He made trips to Italy and North Africa, but for his health and out of restlessness, not out of either intellectual or esthetic curiosity. Fashioned by elders who had inherited from the Romantics a contempt for the bourgeoisie, influenced by those two tender, disillusioned giants, Flaubert and Turgeniev, pursued by illness throughout the last twenty of his forty-three years of life, it was in the nature of things that his occasional reflections should be somber, world-weary, and often platitudinous. Thus he was able to write solemnly: "Absolute truth, the naked truth, does not exist"; or, "Selfishness is the source of all passion and all delight"; or, "When prostitutes marry they soon develop into ladies"; or, "I cannot help despising thought when I see how impotent it is."

We have only to look twice at any artist to see that profundity of thought is no more necessary to the cre-

1

ation of a work of art than to the building up of a great industrial enterprise. Works of pity and terror and even comedy can be written by men who enunciate such commonplaces of disappointed optimism as these; can be written, indeed, on these very premises. Starting from tawdry philosophic principles, Maupassant wrote stories in which men and women are shown to be animated by the impulses implied in those principles: selfishness, envy, vanity, greed, cruelty, moral apathy. Observing men and women with a terribly penetrating eye, apprehending their motives with a terribly alert intuition, writing with unblinking clarity of vision, Maupassant paints a picture of society which, in his greater tales, is not distorted and is troublingly credible. But what makes those tales great is that in them, and perhaps without being aware of it, he gives the lie to his announced principles. In "Story of a Farm Girl," or in "The Return," for example, he adds an ingredient that nullifies his boast of indifference—the divine salt of his unacknowledged charity, his pity. True, he never promises justice, he never supposes redemption; but he recognizes the presence of the inextinguishable spark of goodness in this mankind that he affects to despise, and he is moved by it. It is this that makes him a great writer. For what matters in a work of literary art is the emotion and attitude of the writer, not the emotion and attitudes of the people he portrays. What counts is the values cherished by the artist, not the values cherished by the characters. And the difference between the artist as artist and the artist as man is that (in the example of Maupassant) the values in the light of which he writes are higher than the values in the light of which he lived. Meanwhile, belief in the existence of evil (or evils) is not a bar to creation, it is on the contrary the condition of creation. And philosophic error has no more to do with art than with soap-making.

We do not possess all of Maupassant's private papers. The best of his biographers, Ernest Boyd, says that his mother "saw to it that as much of his correspondence as possible was destroyed," and doubtless she burned other useful documents as well. We know, meanwhile, that he was morbidly disinclined to let anything about himself be made public, even threatening suit against a publisher who had inserted a portrait of him in a book, and demanding that the entire edition be called in. But we do possess, apart from the tales and novels, two aids to the formation of an estimate of his character and opinions—such letters as exist, of which a representative selection is here offered in English for the first time, and a savagely frank diary he wrote up in April 1888, whose most revealing pages are to be read in this volume under the title, "On the Water." Nobody can pretend to know Maupassant who has not read this sad and noble journal of a materialist. His ideas about his craft are vigorously set forth here in the "Essay on the Novel," originally a preface to *Pierre et Jean;* but, unlike Flaubert and Henry James, this was not a subject on which Maupassant liked to dwell. When, in the spring of 1891, towards the premature close of his brief and brilliant career, Jules Huret sought to interview him for the *Echo de Paris,* Maupassant said to him coldly: "Literature? Sir, I never speak of it. I write when I am in the mood, but I never talk about it."

Maupassant's letters are of intense psychological interest by reason of the paradox they present. On the one hand they give off the impression of a morally sympathetic person—earnest, industrious, and fun-loving in his younger years; deeply honest and free from cant in his later years (his thirties, alas, were his "later years"). On the other hand they display so stubborn a will to eliminate everything emotional and spiritual from his personal relations and to confine such experience within the boundaries of his creative expression, that they seem to be written out of a desiccated heart. Except for Flaubert, and his mother and brother, it would appear that Maupassant never loved any human being. His relations with other people seem to have been a matter of either sensation or calculation. There is in his letters rarely the expression of an idea, hardly a single inquiry about his correspondent's welfare, or a note of affection—always excepting the letters to his mother, and the deeply moving letter to Turgeniev on Flaubert's death. He is ceaselessly concerned with himself; and from the moment success comes to him, he has, one would say, only three preoccupations: his health, his literary properties and earnings, and his relations with women—*le contact de deux épidermes,* as Chamfort defined it.

And yet, Maupassant is not to be condemned out of hand. In the brief span of ten years this man produced nearly three hundred stories (some of them running to fifty or sixty pages), six novels, a number of travel books and plays, and a steady flow of newspaper and magazine articles. It is true that half the tales, more or less, are brief anecdotes and are written according to fixed and simple formulae; but the other half are quite simply masterpieces, as witness the extraordinary variety of "best" and "favorite" stories chosen by critics for comment and by editors for compilation these fifty years past. All the novels, meanwhile, like the great tales, are solid if limited commentaries on society and searching analyses of the movements of the human heart—which is to say, works that cruelly empty a writer of his emotional substance. There is, I believe, no avoiding the conclusion that a creative effort of such sustained intensity must exhaust the emotions and dull the sensibilities of the creator to the point of unsociability, leaving him incapable of giving himself to men and women in any other fashion—wherefore incapable also of receiving from them anything else than their admiration. This is painfully corroborated in the Maupassant-Bashkirtseff correspondence, printed here in full. We may, if we choose, see in Maupassant's letters to the Russian girl pure vanity and boorishness; I see in them a weariness of the spirit that is very sad. The applause of the world is a thing for which the artist is likely to pay with something more than the simple strain of creation. The ivory tower is a lonely place, and the notion that the artist chooses it in the lightness or the presumptuousness of his heart, is a vulgar error. He is locked up in it by a force stronger than himself.

II

Born near Dieppe, in Normandy, on August 5, 1850, brought up by a strong-willed mother whose husband lived a separate existence in Paris, Maupassant had in most respects a normal middle-class childhood. (Whether or not the Maupassants, who sprang originally from Lorraine, were marquesses of the Holy Roman Empire, seems not to be decided: Guy de Maupassant never used the title.) He swam, fished, sailed, attended both Church and lay schools, and when time came for him to embark upon a career, this step too was taken in the manner customary in his class. "The conquest of Paris," Boyd writes, "was an adventure undertaken in a spirit of the utmost caution and without undue risks." Not a garret in the Latin Quarter, but a minor clerkship in the Ministry of the Navy was found for him in March 1872. It was a dull career, beginning in the printing-supplies room and ending in the accounts section.

At twenty-two, Maupassant was a short, sturdy, ruddy-faced provincial with a broad forehead, fair brown hair and mustache, and good manners. He was silent in the company of his elders, but seems to have been healthily boisterous among his comrades. The family had little money, and this young civil servant, like any other, saved his coppers for week-end outings. His recreations were purchasable women, walking-tours, and rowing on the river, for which sport he had such a passion that he took lodgings at first out of town, on the banks of the Seine, where in fine weather he rose at dawn to wash down his boat and take a turn at the oars before appearing at nine o'clock at the Ministry. He overexercised like an ambitious Yale man and boasted of his prowess with women like a Balkan chieftain pretending to read law at the University of Paris. Most people seem to have found him attractive in his younger years.

Maupassant's studies had—it was inevitable in that age—been on the classical side, and already in school he had begun to write verse of a comic-erotic sort. Literature, meanwhile, was not a career likely to dismay his watchful and ambitious mother. With her late brother, Alfred Le Poittevin, she had grown up in the company of Flaubert and of the scholar-poet of Rouen, Louis Bouilhet. Le Poittevin's stout soul and noble wit are sufficiently indicated in this sentence from a letter he wrote on his death-bed: "I have reached the point of seeing the things of this world only by the gleam of the terrible torch that is lighted for the dying. But I must tell you that that figure of speech is not mine, it is Saint-Simon's; and the torch is not terrible." Bouilhet, who had spent ten years studying Chinese in order to translate Chinese poetry, and who wrote Latin verse with ease, was a charming poet in his own tongue, particularly successful in the vein of classic Molièresque satire. His last years were spent as Librarian of his native city, and when Madame de Maupassant put her son in the Lycée Corneille at Rouen, she took him round to call on her childhood friend. Bouilhet liked the youth and taught him French versification. It was presumably from him that Maupassant received the impulse to devote himself to writing, and it is certain that his first ambitious efforts underwent Bouilhet's scrutiny and had the advantage of his counsel.

He worked two years with Bouilhet, and it is clear that he was a competent versifier by the time he settled in Paris. Here his mother placed him under the protection of Flaubert, who wrote to her in February 1873, "I have wanted for a month to tell you how fond I have grown of your son. You cannot imagine how charming, intelligent, sensible, good-humored, and amusing I find him." Flaubert received on Sundays in his flat, five flights up in the rue Murillo, where a silk tablecloth was flung over the desk to hide his "work in progress" from prying eyes. In the rue Murillo Maupassant was introduced into the company of Turgeniev, Zola, Taine, Edmond de Goncourt, Daudet, and other great men of the day; and here too he met the younger writers who were beginning to enjoy a reputation that has not in every case survived to our time: Huysmans, Henry Céard, Léon Hennique, Zola's shadow Paul Alexis, and Gautier's son-in-law Emile Bergerat.

As he had been Bouilhet's pupil in Rouen so he became Flaubert's pupil in Paris. In the celebrated preface to *Pierre et Jean* Maupassant says: "For seven years I wrote verse, I wrote tales, I even wrote a villainous play. Nothing of this remains. The master read it all; then, the next Sunday while we lunched together, he would give me his criticisms. . . . 'If you have any originality,' said he, 'the essential point is, bring it out; if you have none, you must acquire it.'" How acquire it? "'When you pass a grocer sitting in his doorway, a concierge smoking his pipe, or a cab-stand, show me that grocer and that concierge, their attitude and their whole physical aspect, including, as indicated by the skill of the portrait, their whole moral nature, in such a way that I shall never mistake them for any other grocer or concierge; and by a single word give me to understand wherein one cab-horse differs from fifty others.'"

This was the lesson of the master, and although it would be foolish to deny that Maupassant did magnificently acquire, and even deepen, that originality of vision which Flaubert drummed into him, it would not be absurd to guess that this vision of the artist was not his native possession. Maupassant was in his nature a calculating Norman with a quick, ordinary mind and a talent for storytelling. What he got from Flaubert was not merely method, but literary refinement and insight into the human heart. Without Flaubert he would have written stories, but those stories might have been coarse and undiscriminating.

Maupassant's own ideas of his art, meanwhile, were clearly borrowed from Flaubert. Speaking for himself, and not for his master, he writes: "Whatever the thing we wish to say, there is but one word to express it, but one verb to give it movement, but one adjective to qualify it. . . . Give us fewer nouns, verbs, and adjectives with almost inscrutable shades of meaning, and give us a greater variety of sentences, variously constructed, their parts ingeniously fitted together, sonorous in tone, and with cunning rhythms. Let us strive to be

faultless stylists rather than collectors of rare words."
What is this but pure Flaubertian doctrine? Flaubert
used to say: "Let us absorb the objective and see that
it circulates in our being." Maupassant wrote about his
method: "I subject myself to a kind of invasion, I am
penetrated by what surrounds me. I impregnate myself
with it, I submit myself to it, I bathe in the environing
influences." This is but another way of reciting the
master's lesson. Flaubert wrote in 1876 to his friend
Mme. Roger des Genettes, about one of his own great
stories: " 'Un Coeur simple,' is very plainly the tale of a
humble existence, the life of a poor country girl, devout
and mystical, loyal without fervor, as tender as new
bread. She loves successively a man, her mistress's children, a nephew, an old fellow she looks after, and her
parrot. When the parrot dies, she has it stuffed; and
when she herself lies dying she confuses the parrot with
the Holy Ghost. There is nothing ironic in this story,
as you seem to think; on the contrary, it is very sober
and very sad." He adds, as Maupassant would never
allow himself to do, "I seek to melt the reader's heart,
to make sensitive souls weep, being one of them myself"; but the rest, the attitude to the subject, the elements of the story selected for emphasis, the insistence
upon the absence of irony, all these were bequeathed
by the author of *l'Education sentimentale* to the author
of *Une Vie*.

For seven years, then, Maupassant passed his days
in a government bureau, his evenings under the lamp,
and divided his Sundays between Flaubert (who spent
only a few months of the year in Paris) and the river.
He found it hard to obey Flaubert's injunction to refrain from rushing prematurely into print, and he seems
never to have been at peace for a moment, harassed
by ill-health, worrying ceaselessly about the exiguity of

his income, badgering Flaubert (with success) to arrange for his transfer to a more agreeable post in the Ministry of Education, trying here and there to establish a connection that will allow him to write criticism. At the end of a half-dozen years he had the satisfaction of seeing a one-act play performed without other remuneration than applause and the promise of lighter duties at the Ministry. In 1879 Flaubert agreed to let him take his verse to Charpentier for publication, and in April 1880 the volume, *Des Vers,* made its appearance. But something else had happened in March 1880 of infinitely greater importance: in a volume by a half-dozen hands, entitled *les Soirées de Médan,* Maupassant had published his first great story, "Boule de Suif," its title derived from the nickname given the roly-poly prostitute who is its heroine.

This volume was the materialization of an idea launched by Zola when he was entertaining its contributors at his house at Médan, on the outskirts of Paris. He had written a story on the Franco-Prussian War, the classic "Attack on the Mill." Two of his guests, Huysmans and Céard, had written stories on the same theme. All three were objective and original tales of a sort then not common about a war in which one's own country had so lately been engaged. To his other guests, Maupassant, Hennique, and Alexis, Zola proposed that they too write on this subject and that the six tales be brought together and published under a title that would suggest storytelling round the evening fire. "For us," Maupassant wrote to Flaubert, "the advantage was that Zola's name would sell the book." And pretty much as Flaubert had once protested to Mme. des Genettes that "Un Coeur simple" was without irony, so Maupassant now explains that *les Soirées de Médan* possesses no hidden significance: "In bringing out this book we had no anti-patriotic intent; in fact we had no particular intent at all. We simply sought, each of us, to strike a truthful note about the war, to strip it of the kind of jingoism preached by Déroulède, and to get rid of the fraudulent enthusiasm that up to now has seemed to be considered a necessary ingredient in every tale about a pair of red pants and a musket."

Flaubert had the inexpressible joy of seeing the fledgling he had so lovingly trained, take to the blue like an eagle. "I am impatient to tell you," he wrote to his *bien aimé disciple*, "that I consider 'Boule de Suif' a *masterpiece*. Yes, young man, neither more nor less; done by the hand of a master. It is very original in conception, very clearly visualized, and excellent in style. I am enchanted. . . . You may be sure that this little tale will *survive*. What marvelous mugs, those mugs of your bourgeois! And not one of them muffed! Cornudet is immense—and true. The nun scarred by smallpox is perfect. The poor prostitute weeping while Cornudet hums the 'Marseillaise' is sublime. I could hug you for half an hour. Really, I am really happy! . . . I have put down on a scrap of paper my schoolmasterly comments. . . ."

We may say without malice and as plain fact that for Maupassant to begin his career with a story of a prostitute was entirely in character. At twenty-nine years, he was still immature enough to take pleasure from an evening in one of those provincial *maisons de tolérance* that used to serve the small-town leading citizens as club, and where a game of cards with one's pals was a stronger attraction than the lavish hospitality sold by the gold-toothed, black-stockinged inmates. And yet, already in "Boule de Suif" we see that the literary values instilled in him by Flaubert are a more powerful influence than the values he pursued in his non-literary existence. Maupassant neither leers at his subject nor moralizes about it. The woman, Boule de Suif, is certainly not made glamorous in the style offered to our eyes by the most sex-ridden community in the world, the American advertising trade; nor is she presented as a "good girl gone wrong" and a "victim of society." She is a human being in a fix and is not helped out of it by the respectable company in which she finds herself running away from the Prussians. "La Maison Tellier," which followed immediately, is coarser in conception, dependent for its initial impulse on what we have learned to call a "gag"; but here too the subject is raised above the level of anecdote by the prodigious insight with which the day of the Confirmation is narrated.

III

The year 1880 marked the turning-point in Maupassant's life. In May, the great-hearted Flaubert died, and though the pupil was deeply affected by the master's death, he was now well able to make his way without the master's guidance. His life thereafter is an almost monotonous record of popular success attended by disease and slowly cumulating insanity. Stories and articles were begged of him by a daily press that traditionally offered literary fare to its readers. He joined the list of those French writers who, as the custom then was, furnished fiction for publication in Russian reviews prior to its appearance in France. And every book publisher, it goes without saying, sought Maupassant for his list. In January 1881 he brought out his first collection of tales under the title *la Maison Tellier.* In 1882 he published *Mademoiselle Fifi,* a second collection. In 1883 he produced both a volume of stories and a novel, *Une Vie;* in 1884, three volumes of stories; in 1885, again both a book of tales and a novel, *Bel Ami;* and so it went for ten years through 1890, the last year of publication during his lifetime, when the inferior novel, *Notre Coeur,* and the still brilliant stories contained in *l'Inutile beauté,* appeared. So numerous were his stories, so wide was their dissemination in the periodicals of the day, that from 1883, when he began to publish a novel a year, critics virtually stopped reviewing the books in which his shorter pieces were collected.

The young French writers of the 1880's inclined at first to make room for Maupassant; but when they saw that he held himself aloof, saw that he disdained their "schools" of psychology, magism, symbolism, and the rest, and that he broke no new ground but was instead a mere continuator and adapter of that esthetic of realism which Flaubert, the Goncourts, and Zola had taught the great public to accept, they attacked him. When, in 1886, five young rebels published a directory of four hundred names which they called *Petit Bottin des Lettres et des Arts,* Maupassant was one of only three writers against whose names they set the letters, N.C., for *Notable Commerçant,* "notorious tradesman," of course. A gibe reported by Jules Huret in 1891 went to the effect that Maupassant's ideal for the writer was "to get the Louvre and Bon Marché department stores as his publishers." The Symbolists, adopting the tone of the academicians whom they also despised, called him an "absurd and bestial erotomaniac, a kind of lubricious traveling salesman." The established critics had meanwhile moved in the contrary direction. They had begun with warnings that "the public is already tiring of these ugly delineations of scabrous subjects," and that "it is not necessary to trail one's pen through evil haunts in order to be a man of talent." They ended shortly by asserting that "what charms us most in this work *(Une Vie)* is precisely those pages that a mother may permit her daughter to read." Sarcey, who wrote the first of the "warnings" cited above, was soon declaring that "in his most daring pages and most wanton scenes, Maupassant still respects his pen"; and Albert Wolff, author of the second "warning," was to praise Maupassant's gift for "leading the reader to meditate" upon life. Actually, once their fears for *la jeune fille française* were stilled, there was little in Maupassant's writing to give umbrage to the guardians of order and authority. He neither professed nor expressed political views. He was not a practicing Christian, but neither was he anti-clerical. And he who had begun by despising the *Revue des Deux Mondes* finally published *Notre Coeur* in that fortnightly magazine which was the organ of the French Academy, itself the stronghold of the Church, the Army, the Nobility, and the Royalist Party.

The young writers who called Maupassant a businessman were not libeling him, as his letters reveal. He was always in complete possession of his subject, he wrote with great facility, and when, as it were, orders were received, he filled them promptly, as Buloz said of George Sand, "with the punctuality of a notary." He was indifferent to the opinion of his readers (they would take what he offered them) and he was not above warming up a cold dish. Again and again, he rewrote and republished the same story, and not always at different lengths to suit different markets. When he determined to prove that he was a novelist as well as storyteller, he incorporated three published tales into his first novel and he repeated the process in later novels. Nobody was ever more expert, more professional in the preparation of copy for the printer.

IV

Critics have tended to group Maupassant's stories in social categories: the peasant, the prostitute, the government clerk, the country squire, the petty bourgeois, the Parisian clubman, and so on. These categories and others are represented in the present volume; and as Maupassant dealt with very nearly all of them year after year, and wrote as well at the beginning of his career as at its end, this is perhaps as good a plan as any for the presentation of his work. For critical purposes, I find that his stories distribute themselves geographically, so to say. Those whose scene is Corsica or North Africa go to the bottom of the list (there was room for none here); much higher marks are given to the Parisian subjects; and the highest price is set upon his scenes of life in Normandy, that province whose hills, woods, hedges, ponds, and seacoast he so much loved, and whose peasants, squires, townspeople, and fisherfolk he knew so well.

Claude Morgan, a writer emerged from the French Resistance, recorded in his diary of captivity in Germany: "To recapture the feeling of France, I am re-reading Maupassant. No writer is more essentially French." What is "essentially French" in Maupassant is not at all his concern with love, harlotry, and crass materialism, nor his clubman aspect, but the passion he feels for his native province. It is one of the distinguishing marks of the professional classes of France to this day, that they never lose touch with their native countryside. An American writer, or surgeon, or banker who makes a success of a career in New York is lost to the plain, the mountain, or the seacoast where he was born. He goes home for Christmas or a funeral;

but it is no longer his home, he spends no time there, he cuts himself off from intimacy with farmers, villagers, mountain folk, or fishermen; and if he sends down roots, he sends them down in the shallow soil of Westchester, or Long Island, or suburban Jersey. Not so the Frenchman. Normandy, Alsace, the Béarn; Touraine, Lorraine, the Beauce; Brittany, Burgundy, the Camargue—these regions where men plough the earth, trim the vines, dry the nets, herd the flocks, are as dear and familiar to the lawyer, the professor, and the literary critic of Paris as the streets and squares of the city; and it is because of this that France possesses, in the eyes of her sons, a personality that we who are masters of a continent cannot sum up in the words "the United States." Not only Lamartine and Hugo, not only the Fromentin of *Dominique,* but the greatest of the French naturalists had a feeling for the earth that was almost pantheistic. They resembled Wordsworth and Hardy, not the light-hearted listeners for the first cuckoo of spring. Human nature was for them not pretty, but overwhelming. Their characters were not detached from the earth but rooted in it. We have only to read one of these stories to understand why Millet should have been Maupassant's favorite painter: again and again, both painted the same scene with the same intensity.

"I love this land," Maupassant wrote, "and I love to live in it because my roots are here, those deep and delicate roots that attach a man to the land where his fathers were born and died, attach him to the thoughts men think, the food they eat, the words they use, their peasant drawl; to the odors that rise from the soil and the villages and linger in the very air itself. I love the house in which I grew up and from whose windows I see the Seine flowing the other side of the road, past my garden, as if flowing through my own acres; the great wide river bearing its many ships downstream to Le Havre while below me lies the broad city of Rouen with its countless blue roofs and its forest of Gothic steeples whose bells sound in the blue air and waft to me their gentle and distant droning."

The priest in *Une Vie*, transferred to a different parish, speaks in his way to the same effect: "It's a wrench, Mme. la Comtesse, it's a wrench, I can tell you. I've been here eighteen years. Oh, I don't say the parish brings in much. It's a poor place. The men—no, you couldn't call them very religious. And the women, well, nobody could say they behaved properly. As for the girls, they get married in church, all right, but only after they've made their pilgrimage to Our Lady of the Great Belly; orange blossoms are not at a premium in these parts. And yet, I love the place."

Here, in the words of Father Picot, we have the essence of Maupassant's enduring work: love of place, recognition of human frailty, economy of statement, and readiness not to sit in judgment upon men—implied compassion. The fact that he deals with scabrous subjects is quite beside the point. Every writer deals in his fashion with secret or indelicate subjects, and each reader is free to decide whether he prefers the treatment that consists in declaring jauntily, "In the spring a young man's fancy lightly turns to thoughts of love," or prefers Maupassant's way of saying the same thing about the influence of nature upon physical longing in the delicate scene of Jeanne's surrender to her husband on a Corsican hillside. As long ago as 1888, when he had to write very cautiously for his English and American readers, Henry James had this to say about

Maupassant: "It is easy to exclaim that if he judges life only from the point of view of the senses, many are the noble and exquisite things that he must leave out. What he leaves out has no claim to get itself considered till after we have done justice to what he takes in. It is this positive side of M. de Maupassant that is most remarkable—the fact that his literary character is so complete and edifying." Another critic, Professor F. C. Green,[1] observes shrewdly: "His men and women are all secretly haunted by the fear of public opinion. They surrender without a struggle to their weaknesses and abandon themselves furiously to their lusts or mean ambitions. Yet all are convinced that outside the pale of society there is no salvation, no peace of mind, no true existence." Thus, if a moral is wanted, Maupassant the amoralist appears to provide it. It was Goethe who said that although we are not permitted to demand that the artist work with a moral purpose, yet a work of art never fails to have a moral effect.

v

Maupassant's life affords a clear but by no means singular instance of the literary effect exercised by non-literary causes. The fact that his mother and father lived apart from the time he was a child, and the disease that attacked him in young manhood and killed him in middle-age, were no less influential than the tutoring of Flaubert in shaping his career.

His father, Gustave de Maupassant, has been de-

---

[1] To readers who would like to look at Maupassant in the French, I commend the selection made by Professor Green under the title Choix de Contes, published by the Cambridge University Press. The essay placed at the head of that collection, written in English, is the best introduction to Maupassant that I know.

scribed as "fascinating and a fascinator" of women. This quality, or more properly, its too frequent demonstration, was resented by Mme. de Maupassant with rather more energy and pride than we are accustomed to find in her age. If I have read her character aright, she did not wait to be deserted by her husband, but sent him away, and herself brought up Guy and his younger brother, Hervé. Guy seems nevertheless to have been allowed to see his father from time to time, and that he saw him with a sharp eye we gather from this fragment of a letter written to his mother when he was nine years old: "I was first in composition. Mme. de X. rewarded me by taking me to the circus. It seems she rewards papa, too, but I don't know with what." Not even Henry James's Maisie could have written more to the point. Guy was brought up in his mother's skirts with a whole series of classic results. He never married. He never fell in love. He never made an intimate friend after he left school. He never took another confidante than his mother. He never wrote a story of a happy marriage.[1] More curious than these commonplaces is the great number of tales he wrote of fatherless little boys, some adored and spoiled by men not their fathers, others cast off or brutalized by men who are their fathers. Psychoanalysts can tell us, doubtless, whether this is to be taken as meaning that he longed secretly for the affection of his own father (with whom he seems to have been on good enough terms) or whether what it indicates is a childish dream that he was the product of an adulterine union of his mother and a sort of fairy prince, and was intermittently engaged in "finding" his "true" father. Whatever the case, the history of Maupassant,

---

[1] A story does exist in which a husband asserts that his marriage is a happy one.

which has never been systematically explored, contains matter for inquiry by persons possessing more than a layman's knowledge of these things.[1]

As for his disease, we know that his brother died insane at the age of thirty-three, and that his mother, though physically sound and a woman of powerful will, was a neurasthenic. She refused to acknowledge the truth about her younger son, and insisted that Hervé had died of "sunstroke." Everything points to the likelihood that she took advantage of Guy's reverence and love to force him to share her mental suffering from the time he was very young; and this subject, their respective bouts of gloom, must have been a constant element in their correspondence. Certainly he, on his side, hid nothing of this sort from his mother; and we find him, already at twenty, writing to her in this vein: "My long solitary evenings are sometimes terrible. You too must have gone through gloomy periods during the long December and January nights."

That Maupassant was powerfully built, insistently athletic, a first-rate swimmer and sailor and a good shot, is as well known as his overindulgence in women. Edmond de Goncourt records that when Maupassant's health was gone, in November 1890, the younger man said to him as they strolled beside the Seine, "It was rowing on that river that brought me to the state I am

---

[1] In 1906 a reporter for the Paris daily, l'Oeuvre, offering evidence which M. René Dumesnil calls "disturbing," asserted that Maupassant had had three children by a woman of Strasbourg, born respectively in 1883, 1884, and 1889. I have not been able to inquire further into this. A lady close to Maupassant wrote a book about their relations; but it does not disprove the notion that there was more of Cressida than of Troilus in him. The kind of tie that bound him to a woman is suggested in the book of his valet, François Tassart, who, referring to Maupassant's last lucid year, 1891, bemoans the visits of "the beautiful wicked lady, the vampire, who is doing my master so much harm."

in today." Confessions of excessive athleticism are too rare for this one to be disdained; there ought to be more of them for the good of mankind; but this cannot, unfortunately, be taken as the sole cause of Maupassant's derangement of mind. Exactly what his illness was, remains unknown. It is usual to assert that he was syphilitic. Given his private life and the state of medical science in his time, the conjecture is credible; but I am not aware that it has ever been established beyond doubt. In the letters that we possess there is a single mention and dismissal of such a suspicion—though the many eminent physicians who examined Maupassant diagnosed enough other ailments to furnish a scenario for a new Molière or Bernard Shaw. It is interesting meanwhile that a parallel case is to be found in American literature in the person of one of our greatest historians, Francis Parkman. Like Maupassant, Parkman loved the out-of-doors. Like the Norman squire, the Boston Brahmin drove himself physically, so that he could say of his first attack of illness, "All collapsed, in short, but the tenacious strength of muscles hardened by long activity." Like Maupassant's disorders, Parkman's centered in the eyes, then brought on unbearable headaches which led to pain-filled, sleepless nights, to rheumatism, and to "feelings of mental confusion and disorder." In Parkman's immediate family as in Maupassant's, the medical record was troubling. Like Maupassant, Parkman was treated unavailingly for both mental and physical ailments that remained inadequately diagnosed. Only the suspicion of syphilis is missing.

The repeated attacks of temporary blindness, the megrims, the wretched weariness that invaded him, and the inhalations of ether to which he became addicted for relief, had for our purposes two effects. They deepened his pessimism and they led to hallucinations which be-

came the material of a succession of tales of terror that
mark his whole career, from "l'Horreur," a poem written
in 1869 in imitation of Poe's "Raven," to "Qui Sait?" the
last story he ever finished. Those tales have been greatly
admired by the medical profession, and a Russian specialist, writing in the *Archives d'Anthropologie Crimi-
nelle* in 1904, has gone so far as to class Maupassant with
Dostoyevsky in this domain, calling them "two masters
who have contributed the most precise observation and
the most brilliant analysis of sick souls and brains." For
my part, I find hallucination dull as a subject of literature: the specimen here included is offered only by
way of rounding out the representative character of this
volume.

The influence of disease upon Maupassant's attitude
to the world is another and more interesting phenomenon. From the beginning, he adopted the pose of total
objectivity, of "indifference" (his great word), and he
convinced both his contemporaries and later critics that
this attitude was inherent in his being. "I never knew a
man so indifferent to everything," his sometime companion, Henry Céard, said. "He never needed to detach
himself from anything because he was never attached to
anything," Faguet wrote. This was indeed his doctrine,
and it sprang from the formal teaching of Flaubert. But
formal teaching is to be distinguished from the temperament of the writer, and it can be shown in multiple
examples that Maupassant was, no less than his master,
a tender and not a tough soul. Again and again, at the
end of his tales of wretchedness, he sums up the moral
and emotional sense of his story in a sentence that is like
a sigh of compassion, of infinitely gentle comprehension.
Again and again, though without overt moralizing, he
castigates cruelty, shatters complacency, moves the
reader's heart. But under the influence of disease, the

pretense of indifference became irritated cynicism and was transformed into authentic morbidity. By 1884 the unhappy Maupassant had begun to believe what he wrote to Marie Bashkirtseff: "I am indifferent to everything and I spend two thirds of my time being profoundly bored. The third third I spend writing lines that I sell as dearly as possible while regretting that I have to practice the abominable trade. . . . There is nothing that I desire and nothing that I look forward to. As for regretting what I have no power to change, I'll wait to do that when I am doddering." Four years later, in 1888, he is doddering—and regretting. In *Sur l'eau*, he rages at himself and at the human race: "How blind, how drunk with pride, how stupid a man has to be, to think of himself as anything else than a beast barely superior to other beasts!" But while he rages, he also regrets: "Happy are those whom life satisfies, who amuse and interest themselves, those who are content with life." Raging and regretting, he is forced finally to yield to the truth, to face himself; and he admits what he has so long, so stubbornly refused to admit: "I am of the thin-skinned." He is of the thin-skinned exactly as Flaubert is of the "sensitive souls." It is the thin-skinned who are the realists: the thick-skinned write magazine verse.

And thus the flaming meteor sinks and is gone. In mid-1891 Maupassant can no longer hold a pen. At forty years, he is not a skeptic, not a moralist, he is a despairing and a dying man. Ten years before, he had been a clerk in a government office with small prospects and limited ambitions. In ten years he had become a writer of universal fame to whom Dumas could say with perfect sincerity, "You are the only author to whose books I look forward with impatience." He had a yacht in the Mediterranean, a large house on the Norman coast, a luxurious flat in Paris. Critics praised him, men admired him, women worshiped him. And in his anguish he sat writing his epitaph: *J'ai tout convoité sans jouir de rien* —"I have coveted everything and taken pleasure from nothing." On New Year's Day 1892 he tried to cut his throat with a paper-knife. He was removed from the Riviera to Dr. Blanche's private asylum in the Passy district of Paris. After eighteen months of physical debilitation and gibbering insanity, he died there of general paralysis on July 6, 1893.

I regret, as much as anybody can, the omission of certain great stories from this volume. Room had to be found, however, for the best of Maupassant's six novels and for certain capital documents—the letters, the pages from *Sur l'eau*, the essay on the novel—from which this book takes its particular character. I am aware also that tales have been included which some may consider to have been too frequently reprinted already: "The String," "The Necklace," "Boule de Suif." To have left them out would in my view have been sheer affectation.

LEWIS GALANTIÈRE

THE PEASANTRY

STORY OF A FARM GIRL

Because the weather was very fine, the people on
the farm had hurried through their midday meal in
order to get back to the fields.

The servant, Rose, remained alone in the great
kitchen, where the fire on the hearth was dying out
under the large pot of hot water. From time to time she
ladled out some water, and slowly washed her plates
and dishes, stopping occasionally to look at the two
bands of light which the sun threw onto the long table
through the window, and which showed the defects in
the pane.

Three venturesome hens were picking up the crumbs
under the chairs, while the smell of the poultry yard,
and the warmth from the cow-stall came in through the
half-open door. A cock was heard crowing in the distance.

When she had finished her work, wiped down the
table, dusted the mantelpiece, and put the plates on the

high dresser, close to the wooden clock, that stood loudly ticking, she drew a long breath. She felt oppressed, without exactly knowing why. She looked at the black clay walls, the rafters blackened with smoke, from which spiders' webs were hanging amid red herrings and strings of onions, and then she sat down, overcome by the stale emanations that rose from the floor, on which so many things had been continually spilt. With this there was mingled the pungent smell of the pans of milk, which were set out to raise the cream in the adjoining dairy.

She wanted to sew, as usual, but she did not feel up to it, so she went to get a breath of fresh air at the door. As she felt the caressing light of the sun, her heart was filled with sweetness and a feeling of content penetrated her body.

In front of the door a shimmery haze arose from the dunghill. The fowls were lying on it; some of them were scratching with one claw in search of worms, while the cock stood up proudly among them. Every moment he selected one of them, and walked round her with a slight cluck of amorous invitation. The hen got up in a careless way as she received his attentions, bent her claws and supported him with her wings; then she ruffled her feathers to shake out the dust, and stretched herself out on the dunghill again, while he crowed, counting his triumphs, and the cocks in all the neighboring farmyards replied to him, as if they were uttering amorous challenges from farm to farm.

The girl looked at them without thinking. She raised her eyes and was almost dazzled at the sight of the apple-trees in blossom, which looked a little like powdered heads. Just then a colt, full of life and friskiness, galloped past her. Twice he jumped over the ditches, and then stopped suddenly, as if surprised at being alone.

She also felt inclined to run; she felt inclined to move, to stretch her limbs, and to relax in the warm, breathless air. She took a few undecided steps and closed her eyes, for she was seized with a feeling of animal comfort; and then she went to look for the eggs in the hen loft. There were thirteen of them, which she took in and put into the sideboard; but the smell from the kitchen disturbed her again, and she went out to sit on the grass for a while.

The farmyard, which was surrounded by trees, seemed to be asleep. The tall grass, where the yellow dandelions rose up like streaks of golden light, was of a vivid green, fresh spring green. The apple-trees threw their shade all round them, and the thatched houses, on which grew the blue and yellow iris flowers with their swordlike leaves, smoked as if the moisture of the stables and barns were coming through the straw.

The girl went to the shed where the carts and traps were kept. Close to it, in a ditch, there was a large patch of violets, whose scent was perceptible all round, while beyond it, the open country could be seen where crops were growing, with clumps of trees in the distance, and groups of ploughmen here and there, who looked as small as dolls, and white horses like toys, that seemed to be pulling a child's cart, driven by a man as tall as one's finger.

She took up a bundle of straw, threw it into the ditch and sat down upon it; then, not feeling comfortable, she undid it, spread it out and lay down upon it at full length, on her back, with both arms under her head, and her legs stretched out.

Gradually her eyes closed, and she was falling into a

state of delightful languor. She was, in fact, almost asleep, when she felt two hands on her bosom. She sprang up with a bound. It was Jacques, one of the farm laborers, a tall powerful fellow from Picardy, who had been paying court to her for a long time. He had been looking after the sheep and, seeing her lying down in the shade, he had come stealthily, holding his breath, with glistening eyes, and bits of straw in his hair.

He tried to kiss her, but she gave him a smack in the face, for she was as strong as he. He was crafty enough to beg her pardon; so they sat down side by side and talked amicably. They spoke about the weather, which was favorable for the harvest, about the season, which had begun well, about their master, who was a decent man; then of their neighbors, of all the people in the country round, of themselves, of their village, of their childhood, of their recollections, of their relations, whom they would not see for a long time, perhaps never again. She grew sad as she thought of it, while he, with one fixed idea in his head, rubbed against her with a kind of a shiver, overcome by desire.

"I have not seen my mother for a long time," she said. "It is very hard to be separated like that." And her gaze was lost in the distance, towards the village in the North, which she had left.

Suddenly he seized her by the neck and kissed her again; but she struck him so violently in the face with her clenched fist, that his nose began to bleed, and he got up and laid his head against the trunk of a tree. When she saw that, she was sorry, and going up to him, she said, "Have I hurt you?" He laughed. "No, it was nothing"; only, she had hit him right in the middle of the nose. "What a devil!" he said, and he looked at her with admiration, for she had inspired him with a feeling of respect and of a very different kind of admiration, which was the beginning of real love for that tall, strong wench.

When the bleeding had stopped, he proposed a walk, as he was afraid of his neighbor's heavy hand if they remained side by side like that much longer; but she took his arm of her own accord, in the avenue, as if they had been out for an evening walk, and said, "It is not nice of you to despise me like that, Jacques." He protested, however. No, he did not despise her. He was in love with her, that was all. "So you really want to marry me?" she asked.

He hesitated, and then looked at her sideways, while she looked straight ahead of her. She had plump red cheeks, a full, protuberant bust under her loose cotton blouse, full, red lips, and her chest, which was almost bare, was covered with small beads of perspiration. He felt a fresh access of desire, and putting his lips to her ear, he murmured, "Yes, of course I do."

Then she threw her arms round his neck, and kissed him for such a long time that they both of them lost their breath. From that moment the eternal story of love began between them. They played with one another in corners; they met in the moonlight under a haystack, and gave each other bruises on the legs with their heavy nailed boots underneath the table. By degrees, however, Jacques seemed to grow tired of her; he avoided her; scarcely spoke to her, and did not try any longer to meet her alone, which made her sad and anxious; and soon she found that she was pregnant.

At first, she was in a state of consternation, but then she got angry, and her rage increased every day, because she could not meet him, for he avoided her most carefully. At last, one night, when everyone in the farmhouse was asleep, she went out noiselessly in her petticoat, with bare feet, crossed the yard and opened the door of the stable, where Jacques was lying in a large box of straw, over his horses. He pretended to snore when he heard her coming, but she knelt down by his side and shook him until he sat up.

"What do you want?" he then asked her. And she, with clenched teeth, and trembling with anger, replied, "I want . . . I want you to marry me, as you promised." But he only laughed, and replied, "Oh! If a man were to marry all the girls with whom he has made a slip, he would have more than enough to do."

Then she seized him by the throat, threw him onto his back, so that he could not disengage himself from her, and half strangling him, she shouted into his face, "I am in the family way! Do you hear? I am in the family way?"

He gasped for breath and was nearly choked, and so they remained, both of them, motionless and without speaking, in the dark silence, which was broken only by the noise that a horse made as he pulled the hay out of the manger and then slowly chewed it.

When Jacques found that she was the stronger, he stammered out, "Very well, I will marry you, if that is the case." But she did not believe his promises. "It must be at once," she said. "You must have the banns put up." "At once," he replied. "Swear before God that you will." He hesitated for a few moments, and then said, "I swear it, by God."

Then she released her grasp, and went away, without another word.

She had no chance of speaking to him for several days, and as the stable was now always locked at night, she was afraid to make any noise, for fear of creating a scandal. One morning, however, she saw another man come in at dinner-time, and so she said, "Has Jacques left?" "Yes," the man replied; "I have taken his place."

This made her tremble so violently that she could not unhook the pot; and later when they were all at work, she went up into her room and cried, burying her head in her bolster, so that she might not be heard. During the day, however, she tried to obtain some information without exciting any suspicions, but she was so overwhelmed by the thoughts of her misfortune that she fancied that all the people whom she asked laughed maliciously. All she learned, however, was that he had left the neighborhood altogether.

II

Thereafter a life of constant misery began for her. She worked mechanically, without thinking of what she was doing, with one fixed idea in her head: "Suppose people were to know."

This continual feeling made her so incapable of reasoning, that she did not even try to think of any means of avoiding the disgrace she knew must ensue, which was irreparable, and drawing nearer every day, and which was as sure as death itself. She got up every morning long before the others, and persistently tried to look at her figure in a piece of broken looking-glass at which she did her hair. She was very anxious to know whether anybody would notice a change in her, and during the day she would stop working every few minutes to look at herself from top to toe, to see whether the size of her stomach did not make her apron look too short.

The months went on, and she scarcely spoke now. When she was asked a question, she did not appear to understand, but she had a frightened look, with haggard eyes and trembling hands, which made her master say to her occasionally, "My poor girl, how stupid you have grown lately."

In church, she hid behind a pillar and no longer ventured to go to confession, as she feared to face the priest, to whom she attributed superhuman powers which enabled him to read people's consciences. At meal times the looks of her fellow servants almost made her faint with mental agony, and she was always fancying that she had been found out by the cowherd, a precocious and cunning little lad, whose bright eyes seemed always to be watching her.

One morning the postman brought her a letter, and as she had never received one in her life before, she was so upset by it that she was obliged to sit down. Perhaps it was from him? But as she could not read, she sat anxious and trembling, with that piece of paper covered with ink in her hand; after a time, however, she put it into her pocket, as she did not venture to confide her secret to anyone. She often stopped in her work to look at those lines written at regular intervals, and which terminated in a signature, imagining vaguely that she would suddenly discover their meaning, until at last, as she felt half mad with impatience and anxiety, she went to the schoolmaster, who told her to sit down, and read to her, the following:

My Dear Daughter: This is to tell you that I am very ill. Our neighbor, Monsieur Dentu, has written this letter to ask you to come, if you can.

For your affectionate mother,

CÉSAIRE DENTU,

Deputy Mayor.

She did not say a word, and went away, but as soon as she was alone, her legs gave way, and she fell down by the roadside, and remained there till night.

When she got back, she told the farmer her trouble. He allowed her to go home for as long as she wanted, and promised to have her work done by a cleaning woman, and to take her back when she returned.

Her mother, who was dying, breathed her last the day she arrived. Next day Rose gave birth to a seven-months' child, a miserable little skeleton, thin enough to make you shudder. The infant seemed to be in constant pain, to judge by the anguished way in which its poor little hands opened and shut, hands as thin as a crab's legs; but it lived, for all that. Rose said that she was married, but that she could not saddle herself with the child, so she left it with some neighbors, who promised to take care of it, and she went back to the farm.

From that time there arose in her heart, which had been wounded so long, something like brightness, a mysterious love for that frail little creature she had left behind her. But there was fresh suffering in that very love, suffering which she felt every hour and every minute, because she was parted from her child. What pained her most was a mad longing to kiss it, to press it in her arms, to feel the warmth of its little body against her skin. She could not sleep at night; she thought of it the whole day long, and in the evening, when her work was done, she used to sit in front of the fire and stare intently into it, as people do whose thoughts are far away.

People began to talk about her and to tease her about the lover she must have. They would ask her if he was tall, handsome, and rich. When was the wedding to be, and the christening? And often she would run away, to cry by herself, for these questions were like the pricking of a needle, they hurt her. In order to forget them, she began to work twice as hard; and still thinking of her child, she made up her mind to save money for it.

She determined to work so that her master would be obliged to raise her wages.

By degrees, she almost monopolized the work. She persuaded him to get rid of one servant girl, who had become superfluous since Rose had taken to working for two; she saved money on bread, oil, candles, on the feed, which they gave to the fowls too extravagantly, on the fodder which had been wastefully flung to the horses and cattle. She was as miserly about her master's money as if it had been her own, and by dint of making good bargains, of getting high prices for their produce, and by matching the peasants' tricks when they offered anything for sale, she was at last entrusted with the buying and selling of everything, with the overseeing of all the farm hands, and with the provisions necessary for the household, so that in a short time she became indispensable to him. She kept such a strict eye on everything, that under her management the farm prospered wonderfully, and for five miles round people talked of "Master Vallin's servant," and the farmer himself said everywhere, "That girl is worth more than her weight in gold."

But time passed by, and her wages remained the same. Her hard work was accepted as something that was due from every good servant, and as a mere token of her good will; and she began to think rather bitterly, that if the farmer could put two or three hundred francs extra into the bank every month, thanks to her, she was still earning her two hundred and forty francs a year, neither more nor less, and so she made up her mind to ask for an increase of wages. She went to see the master three times about it, but each time she talked about something else. She felt a kind of immodesty in asking for money, as if it were something disgraceful; but at last, one day, when the farmer was having breakfast by himself in the kitchen, she said to him, with some embarrassment, that she wished to speak to him particularly. He raised his head in surprise, with both his hands on the table, holding his knife, with its point in the air, in one, and a piece of bread in the other, and he looked fixedly at the girl, who felt uncomfortable under his gaze, but asked for a week's holiday, so that she might get away, as she was not very well. He acceded to her request immediately, and then added, in some embarrassment himself:

"When you come back, I shall have something to say to you, myself."

III

The child was nearly eight months old, and she did not recognize it. It had grown rosy and chubby all over like a little bundle of living fat. She flung herself on it as if it had been some prey, and kissed it so violently that it began to scream with terror, and then she began to cry herself, because it did not know her, and stretched out its arms to its wet-nurse as soon as it saw her. But the next day, it began to get used to her, and laughed when it saw her, and she took it into the fields and ran about excitedly with it, and sat with it under the shade of the trees. Then, for the first time in her life, she opened her heart to somebody; she poured out her troubles to her baby, told him how hard her work was, her anxieties, her hopes, and she quite tired the child with the violence of her caresses.

She took the greatest pleasure in handling it, in washing and dressing it, for it seemed to her that all this was the confirmation of her maternity. She would look at it, almost astonished that it was hers, and she used to say to herself in a low voice, as she danced it in her arms, "My baby, this is my baby."

She cried all the way home to the farm. She had scarcely got in before her master called her into his room, and she went, feeling astonished and nervous, without knowing why.

"Sit down," he said. She sat down, and for some moments they remained silent, in some embarrassment, their arms hanging at their sides, as if they did not know what to do with them, and looking each other in the face, after the manner of peasants.

The farmer, a stout, jovial, obstinate man of forty-five, who had lost two wives, evidently felt embarrassed, which was very unusual with him, but at last he made up his mind, and began to speak vaguely, hesitating a little, and looking out of the window as he talked.

"Rose," he said, "have you ever thought of settling down?" She grew as pale as death, and, seeing that she gave him no answer, he went on, "You are a good, steady, active and economical girl, and a wife like you would make a man's fortune."

She did not move, but looked frightened; she did not even try to comprehend his meaning, for her thoughts were in a whirl, as if at the approach of some great danger; so after waiting for a few seconds, he went on, "You see, a farm without a mistress can never succeed, even with such a servant as you." Then he stopped, for he did not know what else to say, and Rose looked at him like a person face to face with a murderer, ready to flee at the slightest movement. He waited nearly five minutes, then he said, "Well, what do you say?" "Say to what, master?" And he said, quickly: "Why, will you marry me, good Lord!"

She jumped up, but fell back onto her chair as if she had been struck, and there she remained motionless, like a person overwhelmed by some great misfortune. After a bit the farmer grew impatient, and said: "Come, what more do you want?" She looked at him almost in terror; then suddenly tears came into her eyes, and she said twice, in a choking voice, "I cannot, I cannot!" "Why not?" he asked. "Come, don't be silly; I will give you until tomorrow to think it over."

And he hurried out of the room, very glad to have got the matter over, for it had worried him a good deal. He had no doubt that next morning she would accept a proposal which she could never have expected, and which would be a capital bargain for him, for in this way he bound a woman to himself who would certainly bring him more than if she had the best dowry in the district.

Neither could there be any scruples about an unequal match between them, for in the country everyone is very nearly equal; the farmer works as hard as his hired men do, who frequently become masters in their turn, and the female servants frequently become the mistresses of the households, without its making any change in their lives or habits.

Rose did not go to bed that night. She lay down, dressed as she was, on her bed, and she had not even the strength left in her to cry, she was so thoroughly overcome. She remained inert, scarcely knowing that she had a body, and with her mind in pieces, as if it had been taken apart with one of those old-fashioned instruments used for re-stuffing mattresses; only at odd moments could she collect fragments of her thoughts, and then she was frightened at the idea of what might happen. Her terror increased, and every time the great kitchen clock struck the hour she broke into a perspiration of fear. She was losing control of herself, and had a succession of nightmares; her candle went out, and then she began to imagine that someone had thrown a spell over her, as country people so often fancy, and she felt a mad inclination to run away, to escape, to flee before her misfortune, like a ship scudding before the wind.

An owl hooted. She shivered, sat up, put her hands to her face, into her hair, and all over her body, and then she went downstairs, as if she were walking in her sleep. When she got into the yard, she stooped down, so as not to be seen by any prowling ruffian, for the moon, which was setting, shed a bright light over the fields. Instead of opening the gate, she scrambled over the bank, and as soon as she was outside, she started off. She went on straight before her, with a quick, elastic trot, and from time to time, unconsciously, she uttered a piercing cry. Her long shadow accompanied her, and now and then some night bird flew over her head, while the dogs in the farmyards barked as they heard her pass; one even jumped over a ditch and followed her and tried to bite her, but she turned round at it, and gave such a terrible yell, that the frightened animal ran back and cowered in silence in its kennel.

Now and then she crossed a family of young hares gamboling in a field, but when the frantic fugitive approached, like a delirious Diana, the timid creatures scampered away, the mother and her little ones disappearing into a burrow, while the father ran at full tilt, his leaping shadow, with long ears erect, standing out against the setting moon, which was now sinking down at the other end of the world, and casting an oblique light over the fields, like a huge lantern set down on the ground on the line of the horizon.

The stars grew dim and the birds began to twitter; day was breaking. The girl was worn out and panting, and when the sun rose in the purple sky, she stopped, for her swollen feet refused to go any farther. She saw a pond in the distance, a large pond whose stagnant water looked like blood under the reflection of this new day, and she limped on with short steps and with her hand on her heart, in order to dip her legs in it. She sat down on a tuft of grass, took off her heavy shoes, which were full of earth, pulled off her stockings and plunged her legs into the still water, from which bubbles rose here and there.

A feeling of delicious coolness pervaded her from head to foot, and suddenly, while she was staring into the deep pool, she was seized with giddiness and with a mad longing to throw herself into it. All her sufferings would be over, over forever. She no longer thought of her child; she wanted peace, complete rest, and to sleep forever. She got up with raised arms and took two steps forward. She was in the water up to her thighs and she was just about to throw herself in, when sharp, pricking pains in her ankles made her jump back, and she uttered a cry of despair, for, from her knees to the tips of her toes, long, black leeches were sucking her life blood and swelling as they adhered to her flesh. She did not dare to touch them, and screamed with horror. Her cries of despair attracted a passing peasant to the spot. He pulled off the leeches one by one, applied herbs to the wounds, and drove the girl to her master's farm, in his gig.

She was in bed for a fortnight. As she was sitting outside the door on her first morning out of bed, the farmer suddenly came up and planted himself before her. "Well," he said, "I suppose it's settled, isn't it?" She did not reply at first, and then, as he remained standing and looking at her intently with his piercing eyes, she said with difficulty, "No, master, I cannot." He immediately flew into a rage.

"You cannot, girl; you cannot? By God, you'll tell me why you cannot!" She began to cry and repeated, "I cannot." He stared at her and then exclaimed, angrily,

"I suppose you have a lover?" "Perhaps that is it," she replied, trembling with shame.

The man got as red as a poppy, and stammered out in a rage: "Ah! So you confess it, you slut! Who is the fellow? Some penniless, half-starved ragamuffin, without a roof over his head, I suppose? Who is it, I say?" And as she gave him no answer, he continued, "Ah! So you won't tell me. . . . Then I'll tell you; it is Jean Baudu?" "No, not he," she exclaimed. "Then it is Pierre Martin?" "Oh, no, master."

Angrily he mentioned all the young fellows in the neighborhood, while she denied that he had hit upon the right one, and every moment wiped her eyes with the corner of her big blue apron. But he still tried to find it out, with his brutish obstinacy, and, as it were, scratched her heart to discover her secret, just as a terrier scratches a hole, to try and get at the animal which he scents in it. Suddenly, however, the man shouted, "By George! It is Jacques, the man who was here last year. They used to say that you were always talking together, and that you thought about getting married."

Rose was choking, and she grew scarlet, while her tears suddenly stopped, and dried up on her cheeks, like drops of water on hot iron, and she exclaimed, "No, it is not he, it is not he!" "Is that really a fact?" The cunning peasant, who had partly guessed the truth, now asked; and she replied, hastily, "I swear it; I swear it to you. . . ." She tried to think of something by which to swear, for she did not dare invoke sacred things, but he interrupted her: "At any rate, he used to follow you into every corner, and eat you up with his eyes at meal time. Did you ever give him your promise, eh?"

This time she looked her master straight in the face. "No, never, never; I solemnly swear to you, that if he were to come today and ask me to marry him, I would have nothing to do with him." She spoke with such sincerity that the farmer hesitated, and then he continued, as if speaking to himself, "What, then? You have not had *a misfortune,* or it would have been known, and as it is of no consequence, no girl would refuse her master on that account. There must be something else at the bottom of this."

She could say nothing; she had not the strength to speak, and he asked her again, "You will not?" "I cannot, master," she said, with a sigh, and he turned on his heel.

She thought she had got rid of him altogether and spent the rest of the day almost tranquilly, but as worn out as if she, and not the white horse, had been turning the threshing machine all day. She went to bed as soon as she could, and fell asleep immediately. In the middle of the night, however, two hands touching the bed woke her. She trembled with fear, but she recognized the farmer's voice immediately when he said, "Don't be frightened, Rose; I have come to speak to you." This astonished her; but when she felt him getting into bed she understood what he was after; and being quite naked and still drugged with sleep, she felt herself helpless in the presence of his desire, and began to tremble violently. She certainly did not consent, but she resisted weakly, herself struggling against that instinct which is always strong in simple natures, and very imperfectly protected by the hesitant will of inert and feeble creatures. She turned her head now to the wall and now towards the room, in order to avoid the attentions which the farmer tried to press on her, and her body writhed under the blanket. Whereas she grew weaker with the fatigue of the struggle, he grew more brutally insistent under the urging of desire. With a sudden movement he pulled off the bedclothes; then she saw that resistance was useless. With an ostrich-like sense of modesty she hid her face in her hands, and ceased to struggle.

They lived together as man and wife, and one morning he said to her, "I have put up the banns, and we will get married next month."

She did not reply, for what could she say? She did not resist, for what could she do?

IV

Rose married him. She felt as if she were at the bottom of a deep pit from which she could never get out, and all kinds of misfortunes remained hanging over her head, like huge rocks liable to crash down at any moment. Her husband seemed like a man she had stolen, and who was bound to find it out. And then she thought of her child, who was the cause of her misfortunes, but who was also the cause of all her happiness on earth, and whom she went to see twice a year, though she came back more unhappy each time. Gradually she grew accustomed to her life, her fears were allayed, her heart was at rest, and she lived with an easier mind, though still with a vague terror floating in her mind. Years went by, and the child was six. She was almost happy now, when suddenly the farmer's temper grew very bad.

For two or three years he had apparently been nursing some secret anxiety, he seemed to be troubled by some worry, some mental disturbance, which was gradually increasing. He would remain at table a long time after dinner, with his head in his hands, sad and devoured by sorrow. He always spoke sharply, sometimes even brutally, as if he bore a grudge against his wife, and at times he would answer her roughly, almost angrily.

One day, when a neighbor's boy came for some eggs, and she spoke very crossly to him, as she was very busy, her husband suddenly came in, and said to her in his unpleasant voice, "If he were your own child you wouldn't talk to him like that." She was hurt and did not reply, and then she went back into the house with all her grief awakened afresh. At dinner, the farmer neither spoke to her, nor looked at her, and he seemed to hate her, to despise her, to know something about her secret at last. She quite lost her head, and did not dare remain alone with him after dinner. Instead, she hastened to the church.

Night was falling; the narrow nave was in total darkness, but she heard footsteps in the choir; the sexton was preparing the tabernacle lamp for the night. That spot of trembling light, deep in the darkness of the arches, seemed to Rose her last hope, and with her eyes fixed on it, she fell on her knees. The chain rattled as the little lamp swung up into the air, and almost immediately the small bell rang out the *Angelus* through the increasing mist. She went up to him, as he was going out.

"Is Monsieur le Curé at home?" she asked. "Of course he is; this is his dinnertime." She trembled as she rang the bell of the priest's house. The priest was just sitting down to dinner, and he made her sit down also. "Yes, yes, I know all about it; your husband has mentioned the matter to me that brings you here." The poor woman nearly fainted, and the priest continued, "What do you want, my child?" And he hastily swallowed several spoonfuls of soup, some of which dropped on to his greasy cassock. But Rose did not dare to say anything. She got up to go, and the priest said, "Courage. . . ."

She returned to the farm without knowing what she was doing. The farmer was waiting for her. The farm hands had left during her absence. She fell heavily at his feet, and shedding a flood of tears, she said to him, "What have you got against me?"

He began to shout and to swear: "What have I got against you? That I have no children, by God! When a man takes a wife, he doesn't want to be left alone with her until the end of his days. That's what I have against you. When a cow has no calves, she's not worth anything, and when a woman has no children, she's not worth anything either."

She began to cry, and said, "It's not my fault! It's not my fault!" Her tears and her words softened him, and he said in a gentler voice, "I don't say it is, but I don't like it, all the same."

v

From that day forward, she had only one thought; to have a child, another child; she confided her wish to everybody, and in consequence of this, a neighbor told her of an infallible method. This was, to make her husband drink a glass of water with a pinch of ashes in it, every evening. The farmer agreed to try it, but without success; so they said to each other, "Perhaps there are some secret ways." And they tried to find out. They were told of a shepherd who lived ten miles off, and Vallin one day drove off to consult him. The shepherd gave him a loaf on which he made some marks; it was kneaded with herbs, and both of them were to eat a piece of it before and after their caresses. They ate the whole loaf without obtaining any results from it.

Next, a schoolmaster unveiled mysteries and processes of love unknown in the country, but infallible, so he declared; yet none of them had the desired effect.

Then the priest advised them to make a pilgrimage to the shrine at Fécamp. Rose went with the crowd, prostrated herself in the abbey, and mingled her prayers with the coarse supplications of the peasants around her. She prayed that she might be fruitful a second time; but it was in vain, and then she thought that she was being punished for her first fault, and she was seized by terrible grief. She was wasting away with sorrow; her husband also was aging prematurely and wearing himself out in useless hopes.

Then war broke out between them; he called her names and beat her. They quarreled all day long, and when they were in bed together at night he flung insults and obscenities at her, panting with rage, until one night, not being able to think of any means of making her suffer more, he ordered her to get up and go and stand out of doors in the rain, until daylight. As she did not obey him, he seized her by the neck, and began to strike her in the face with his fists, but she said nothing and did not stir. In his exasperation he knelt on her stomach, and with clenched teeth, and mad with rage, he began to beat her. Then in her despair she rebelled, and flinging him against the wall with a furious gesture, she sat up, and in an altered voice, she hissed, "I have had a child, I have had one! I had it by Jacques; the Jacques you know. He promised to marry me, but he left without keeping his word."

The man was thunderstruck, and could hardly speak. At last he stammered out, "What are you saying? What are you saying?" Then she began to sob, and through her tears she said: "That is the reason why I did not want to marry you. I could never tell you, for you would have left me without any bread for my child. You have never had any children, so you cannot understand, you cannot understand!"

He said again, mechanically, with increasing surprise, "You have a child? You have a child?"

"You know you took me by force. I didn't want to marry you," she said, still sobbing.

Then he got up, lit the candle, and began to walk up and down, his arms clasped behind him. She lay cowering on the bed and crying, and suddenly he stopped in front of her, and said, "Then it is my fault that you have no children?" She went on sobbing and he resumed his pacing of the floor; then, stopping again, he continued, "How old is your child?" "Just six," she whispered. "Why did you not tell me about it?" he asked. "How could I?" she replied, with a sigh.

He remained standing, motionless. "Come, get up," he said. She got up with some difficulty, and then, when she was on her feet, he suddenly began to laugh his hearty laugh of his good days, and seeing how surprised she was, he said, "Very well, we will go and fetch the child, since you and I can't have one together."

She was so scared that, if she had had the strength, she would assuredly have run away, but the farmer rubbed his hands and said, "I wanted to adopt one, and now we have found one. I asked the priest about an orphan, some time ago."

Then, still laughing, he kissed his weeping and agitated wife on both cheeks, and shouted out, as if she were deaf, "Come along, mother, we will go and see whether there is any soup left; I shouldn't mind a plateful."

She put on her petticoat, and they went downstairs; and while she was kneeling in front of the fireplace, and lighting the fire under the pot, he paced the kitchen with long strides, and said:

"Well, I am really glad of this: I must say I am glad; I am really very glad."

THÉODULE SABOT'S
CONFESSION

WHENEVER Sabot came into the public-house of Martinville, a roar of laughter went up in anticipation. The fellow was as good as a play. He had no love for parsons, not he! He ate them alive.

Sabot (Théodule), master joiner, represented the radical party at Martinville. He was a tall, thin man with a sly, gray eye, hair brushed onto his temples, and a thin mouth. When he said, "Our holy father the wash-out" in a certain way he had, the whole company yelled with laughter. He was careful to work on Sunday while mass was going on. Every year he killed his pig on the Monday in Holy Week, so as to have black pudding till Easter, and when the priest passed he always said merrily:

"There's the fellow who's just been swallowing his God out of a pint-pot."

The priest, a stout man, also very tall, feared him for his chaff, which won him many supporters. The Reverend Maritime had a diplomatic mind, and liked subtle methods. For ten years the struggle went on between these two, covert, bitter, and incessant. Sabot was on the town council, and it was thought that he would be made mayor, which would certainly constitute the definite defeat of the church.

The elections were about to take place, and the re-

ligious party in Martinville trembled for its security.
One morning the priest went off to Rouen, telling his
servant that he was going to the archbishop's palace.

Two days later he returned, looking joyful and triumphant. Next day everyone knew that the chancel of the
church was to be restored. His Lordship had given six
hundred francs towards it out of his own pocket. All the
old deal stalls were to be removed and replaced by new
ones of oak. It was an important job of carpentry, and
by evening everyone was talking of it.

Théodule Sabot did not laugh.

When he walked through the village next day, neighbors, friends and enemies alike, all asked him jestingly:

"Is it you who's to do the church choir?"

He found nothing to answer, but his heart was black
with rage.

"It's a fine job," they added unkindly. "Must be two
or three hundred francs profit in it."

Two days later it was known that the work of repair
was to be entrusted to Célestin Chambrelan, the joiner
at Percheville. Then the rumor was denied, and then it
was announced that all the church pews were to be
replaced as well. It would cost quite two thousand
francs, and they had appealed to the government for the
money. There was great excitement.

Théodule Sabot could not sleep. Never, within the
memory of man, had a local joiner executed such a task.
Then the story ran that the priest was heartbroken at
having to give out this work to a joiner who was a
stranger to the village, but that Sabot's opinions were a
barrier that prevented the contract from being entrusted
to him.

Sabot knew it. At nightfall he betook himself to the
rectory. The servant told him that the priest was at
church. He went there.

Two lay sisters, sour old spinsters, were decorating the altar for the month of St. Mary, under the direction of the priest. He stood with his enormous stomach in the middle of the choir, superintending the labors of the women who, perched on chairs, were arranging flowers round the shrine.

Sabot felt uneasy there, as though he had entered the house of his deadliest foe, but his avarice spurred him on. He came up cap in hand, taking no notice of the lay sisters, who remained motionless upon their chairs, stupefied with amazement.

"Good evening, parson," he stammered.

"Good evening, joiner," replied the priest without turning his head, engrossed in the work at the altar.

Sabot, who had rather lost his bearings, found nothing more to say. After a pause, however, he added:

"You are making preparations?"

"Yes," replied Maritime, "we are drawing near to the month of St. Mary."

"Right, right," said Sabot, and was silent.

He was by now anxious to leave without speaking at all, but a glance at the choir restrained him. He saw that there were sixteen stalls to be repaired, six on the right and eight on the left, the vestry door occupying two places. Sixteen oak stalls were to be had for three hundred francs at the outside, and with a little good management a clever workman could make a clear two hundred francs on the job. He managed to stammer:

"I've come for the work."

The priest looked surprised.

"What work?" he asked.

"The work to be done," murmured Sabot, now quite desperate.

At that the priest turned and stared at him, saying:

"Do you mean the repairs to the choir of my church?"

At the tone adopted by the priest, Théodule Sabot felt a shiver run up his spine, and once more he suffered a violent longing to slink away. But he replied meekly:

"Yes, your Reverence."

The priest crossed his arms on his broad paunch, and said as though thunderstruck with surprise:

"And you . . . you . . . you, Sabot . . . come here and ask me that! . . . You . . . the only infidel in my parish. . . . Why, it would be a scandal, a public scandal. His Grace would reprimand me; I might even lose the parish."

He paused for a few seconds to regain his breath, then proceeded more calmly:

"I quite understand that it pains you to see a job of such importance entrusted to a joiner from a neighboring parish. But I cannot do otherwise, unless . . . but no . . . that's impossible. You'd never agree to it, and without that . . . never."

Sabot was now looking at the ranks of pews running right to the west door. Mercy! was all that to be restored?

"What must you have?" he asked. "It can't do any harm telling."

"I must have overwhelming proof of your good intentions," replied the priest firmly.

"I don't say," murmured Sabot, "I don't say but what an understanding mightn't be come to."

"You must communicate publicly at high mass next Sunday," announced the priest.

The joiner felt himself growing pale and, without answering, asked:

"And the pews, are they all to be done too?"

"Yes," replied the priest with emphasis, "but later on."

"Well, I don't say," replied Sabot. "I don't say. I'm no atheist, I'm not; I've no quarrel with religion. What upsets me is the practice of it, but in a case like this I dare say you'd not find me obstinate."

The lay helpers had descended from their chairs and were hidden behind the altar; they were listening, livid with emotion.

The priest, perceiving that he was victorious, became familiar and jolly at once:

"Splendid! Splendid! Now that's very sensible of you, very sensible. Wait and see."

Sabot smiled uncomfortably, and asked:

"Can't this here communion be put off for a bit, just a little bit?"

But the priest resumed his severe expression.

"From the moment that the contract is given to you, I must be certain of your conversion," he said, then continued more mildly:

"You'd better come and confess tomorrow, for I shall have to examine you at least twice."

"Twice?" repeated Sabot.

"Yes," said the priest with a smile. "You see, you need a thorough cleaning, a complete wash. I expect you tomorrow."

"And where'll you do it?" asked the joiner in dismay.

"Why . . . in the confessional."

"What? . . . In that box over there in the corner? Now look here . . . I don't like your box a bit."

"Why not?"

"Why . . . why, I'm not used to it. And I'm a bit hard of hearing too."

The priest showed himself accommodating.

"Very well. Come to my house, to my study. We'll get it done there privately. Does that suit you?"

"Oh, that'll suit me all right, but that box of yours, no!"

"Well, tomorrow then, after the day's work, at six o'clock."

"Right! right you are. That's settled. See you tomorrow, parson, and damn the man who goes back on a bargain."

He held out his huge rough hand, on which the priest let his own fall with a loud smack. The echo ran along the vaulted roof and died in the distance behind the organ pipes.

Throughout the following day Théodule Sabot felt uncomfortable. He suffered an apprehension very like the fear one suffers before having a tooth out. At every moment the thought flashed across his mind: "I've got to confess this evening." And his harried soul, the soul of a not very strongly convinced atheist, was sorely troubled before the vague, powerful terror of the divine mystery.

As soon as his work was over he went off to the priest's house. Its owner was waiting for him in the garden, reading his breviary as he walked up and down a small path. He seemed delighted to see him and welcomed him with a hearty laugh.

"Ah—here we are, then! Come in, come in, Monsieur Sabot; no one will eat you."

Sabot entered the house first.

"If it's all the same to you," he faltered, "I'd like to see my little affair through at once like."

"At your service," replied the priest. "My surplice is here. One minute, and I'm ready to listen to you."

The joiner, so distressed that his mind was a blank, watched him put on the white garment with its pleated folds. The priest signed to him:

"Kneel down on that hassock."

But Sabot remained standing, ashamed at having to kneel.

"Does it do any good?" he stammered.

But the priest had become majestic.

"Only upon the knees," he said, "may the tribunal of repentance be approached."

Sabot knelt.

"Recite the Confiteor," said the priest.

"Eh? . . ." asked Sabot.

"The Confiteor. If you no longer know it, repeat one by one the words I am about to utter."

And the priest pronounced the sacred prayer in a slow voice, scanning each word for the joiner, who repeated it after him.

"Now confess," he said.

But Sabot said nothing, not knowing where to begin.

Then the Reverend Maritime came to his aid.

"Since you seem to be rather out of practice, my child, I will question you. We will take the commandments of God one by one. Listen to me and do not distress yourself. Speak very frankly and never be afraid of confessing too much.

" 'Thou shalt worship one God alone and adore Him with all thy heart.' Have you loved anyone or anything as much as God? Have you loved Him with all your soul, with all your heart, with all the strength of your love?"

Sabot perspired with the effort of thought.

"No," he replied. "Oh, no, your Reverence. I love the good God as much as I can. Oh, Lord! Yes, I love Him all right. As for saying I don't love my children, no. I can't say that. As for saying if I had to choose between them and the good God, as for that I won't say. As for saying if I had to lose a hundred francs for love of the good God, as for that I won't say. But I love Him all right, that's quite certain. I love Him just the same."

"You must love Him more than anything," said the priest gravely.

And Sabot, full of good will, declared:

"I'll do my best, your Reverence."

" 'Thou shalt not take the name of the Lord thy God in vain,' " resumed Maritime. "Have you occasionally sworn oaths?"

"No—oh, no, not that! I never swear, never. Sometimes, in a moment of hot temper like, I may say 'God blast.' But I never swear."

"But that is swearing," said the priest, and added severely, "don't do it any more. I pass on to the next: 'Thou shalt spend the Sabbath in serving God devotedly.' What do you do on Sundays?"

This time Sabot scratched his ear.

"Well, I serve the good God in the best way I can, your Reverence. I serve Him . . . at home. I work on Sundays. . . ."

The priest magnanimously interrupted him:

"I know you will behave better in the future. I pass over the three next commandments, as I am sure you have not sinned against the two first, and we will take the sixth with the ninth. To proceed: 'Thou shalt not take another's goods, nor retain them wittingly.' Have you ever in any way taken what did not belong to you?"

Théodule Sabot was indignant:

"Certainly not! Certainly not, your Reverence! I'm an honest man, that I swear. As for saying that I've not once or twice taken an extra hour over a job when I could, as for that I won't say. As for saying that I've never put a few centimes on to a bill, only a few centimes, as for that I won't say. But I'm not a thief, oh, Lord, no!"

"Taking a single centime constitutes a theft," answered the priest severely. "Don't do it again.—'Thou shalt not bear false witness nor lie in any way.' Have you told lies?"

"No! that I haven't. I'm not a liar; that's one of the things I pride myself on. As for saying that I've never told a tall story, as for that I won't say. As for saying that I've never tried to make another fellow believe what wasn't true, when it suited me, as for that I won't say. But as for being a liar, well, I'm no liar."

"You must keep a closer watch upon yourself," said the priest simply. Then he pronounced: 'The works of the flesh thou shalt not desire save only in marriage.' Have you ever desired or possessed any woman but your own wife?"

"No!" cried Sabot sincerely. "Certainly not, your Reverence! Deceive my poor wife? No! No! Not so much as with the tip of my finger, and no more in thought than in deed. I swear that." He paused for a few moments, and then continued in a lower voice, as though a sudden doubt had assailed him:

"As for saying that when I go to town I don't ever go to a house—you know what I mean, a gay house— and fool about a bit and have a change of skin for once —as for that I won't say. . . . But I pay, your Reverence, I always pay; and if you pay, that's that, eh?"

The priest did not insist, and gave him absolution.

Théodule Sabot is at work on the repairs to the choir, and goes to communion every month.

ROSALIE PRUDENT

THERE was in this affair an element of mystery which neither the Jury, nor the Judge, nor the Public Prosecutor himself ever quite fathomed.

The girl Prudent (Rosalie), a maid employed by the Varambot family, of Mantes, became pregnant unknown to her employers, was brought to bed during the night in her attic bedroom. She killed and buried her child in the garden.

It was the not uncommon story of a servant's infanticide. But one fact remained unexplained. Search of the girl Prudent's bedroom had led to the discovery of a complete set of baby clothes, made by Rosalie herself, who for three months had spent her nights cutting out and sewing them. The grocer, from whom, out of her own wages, she had bought the candles burned in this long labor had come forward as witness. Moreover, it was known that the local midwife, whom the girl had informed of her condition, had given her all instructions and practical advice necessary in case her time happened to come at a moment when no help was at hand. She had further sought a place at Poissy for the Prudent girl, who foresaw her dismissal, since the Varambot couple took questions of morality very seriously.

The man and his wife were present at the assizes: an ordinary provincial middle-class couple of small means, very angry with this slut who had defiled their house. They would have liked to see her guillotined on the spot, without a trial, and they overwhelmed her with malicious evidence that in their mouths became veritable accusations.

The accused, a fine, strapping peasant from Lower Normandy, rather refined for her station, wept incessantly and made no reply.

There was nothing for it but to suppose that she had committed this barbarous act in a moment of despair and madness, since everything pointed to the fact that she had hoped to keep and rear her child.

The Judge made a final attempt to get her to speak, to wring a confession from her. He urged her with the utmost kindliness, and at last made her understand that these men come together to judge her did not wish for her death and even pitied her.

Then she made up her mind.

"Come," he asked, "tell us first who is the father of this child."

So far she had obstinately withheld this information.

She answered suddenly, staring angrily at the employers who had spoken with much malice against her.

"It was Monsieur Joseph, Monsieur Varambot's nephew."

The couple started violently and cried out with one voice: "It's a lie! She's lying! It's a vile slander!"

The Judge silenced them and added: "Go on, please, and tell us how it happened."

Then she poured out a sudden flood of words, comforting her hitherto constrained heart, her poor, lonely, bruised heart, spilling out her grief, the full measure of her grief, before the severe men whom until this moment she had looked upon as enemies and inflexible judges.

"Yes, it was Monsieur Joseph Varambot, when he came on leave last year."

"What does Monsieur Joseph Varambot do?"

"He's a corporal in the artillery, Sir. He spent two months in the house, you see. Two summer months. I didn't think anything of it, I didn't, when he began staring at me, and then saying sweet things to me, and then coaxing me all day long. I let myself be taken in, I did, Sir. He kept on telling me that I was a fine girl, that I was nice to look at . . . that I was his sort. . . . I liked the way he talked; for sure I did. What'ud you expect? You listen to these things when you're alone . . . all alone . . . like me. I'm alone in the world, Sir. . . . I've no one to talk to . . . no one to tell about things that vex me. . . . I haven't a father, or mother, or brother, or sister, no one. I felt as if he was a brother who'd come back when he began talking to me. And then he asked me to go down to the river bank with him one evening, so we could talk without being heard. I went. I did. . . . How did I know what I was doing? How did I know what I did after that? He put his arm round me. . . . I'm sure I didn't want to . . . no . . . no. . . . I couldn't. . . . I wanted to cry, it was such a lovely night . . . the moon was shining. . . . I couldn't . . . he did what he wanted. . . . It went on like that for three weeks, as long as he stayed. . . . I would have followed him to the end of the world . . . he went away. . . . I didn't know I was going to have a baby, I didn't . . . I didn't know until a month after."

She broke into such a storm of weeping that they had to give her time to control herself again.

The Judge spoke to her like a priest in the confessional: "Come now, tell us everything."

She went on with her tale:

"When I saw I was pregnant, I went and told Madame Boudin, the midwife, who's there to tell you I did, and I asked her what I ought to do supposing it happened when she wasn't there. And then I made all the little clothes, night after night, until one o'clock in the morning, every night; and then I looked out for another place, for I knew quite well I'd be dismissed, but I wanted to stay in the house up to the very last, to save my bit of money, seeing I hardly had any and I had to have all I could, for the little baby. . . ."

"So you didn't want to kill it?"

"Oh, for sure I didn't, sir."

"Then why did you kill it?"

"It's like this. It happened sooner than I'd have believed. The pains took me in my kitchen, as I was finishing my washing-up.

"Monsieur and Madame Varambot were asleep already; so I went upstairs, not without trouble, dragging myself from step to step. And I lay down on the floor, on the boards, so I shouldn't soil my bed. It lasted maybe an hour, maybe two, maybe three—I don't know, it hurt me so dreadful; and then I pressed down with all my strength, I felt him coming out, and I gathered him up.

"Oh, I was so pleased, I was. I did everything that Madame Boudin had told me, everything. And then I put him on my bed. And then, if I hadn't another pain, a mortal pain! If you knew what it was like, you men, you'd think a bit more about doing it, you would. I fell on my knees, then on my back, on the floor; and I had it all over again, maybe another hour, maybe two, all by myself, there . . . and then another one came out . . . another little baby . . . two—yes, two . . . think of it! I took him up like the first and laid him on the bed, side by side . . . two. How would I be able to bring up two of them, now? Two children. Me that earns twenty-five francs a month. Tell me, how could I? One, yes, could be managed, with scraping and saving, but not two. It made my head go round. I didn't know what I was doing, I didn't. And do you think I could choose one rather than the other?

"I didn't know what I was doing! I thought my last hour had come. I put the pillow over them, without knowing what I was doing. . . . I couldn't keep two . . . and I lay down again on top of it. And then I stayed there tossing and crying until I saw the light coming in at the window; they were dead under the pillow for sure. Then I took them under my arm, I got down the stairs, I went out into the kitchen garden, I took the garden spade, and I buried them in the ground, as deep as I could, one in one place, the other in another, not together, so that they couldn't talk to each other about their mother, if little dead babies can speak. I don't know about such things.

"And then I was so ill in my bed that I couldn't get up. They fetched the doctor and he knew all about it. That's the truth, your Honor. Do what you like with me. I'm ready."

Half the jury were blowing their noses violently to keep back their tears. Women were sobbing in the courtroom.

The Judge questioned her.

"Where did you bury the other one?"

"Which did you find?" she asked.

"Well . . . the one . . . the one who was in the artichokes."

"Oh. The other one is under the strawberries—at the edge of the well."

And she began to sob so dreadfully that her moans were heartbreaking to hear.

The girl Rosalie Prudent was acquitted.

THE DEVIL

The peasant stood facing the doctor across the dying woman's bed. The old woman, calm, resigned, quite conscious, looked at the two men and listened to their words. She was going to die; she made no complaint, her time had come; she was ninety-two years old.

The July sun poured through the window and the open door, its blazing warmth falling over the floor of brown earth, whose surface was worn into gentle undulating hollows by the sabots of four generations of countryfolk. Smells of the fields came borne on the scorching breeze, odors of grass, grain, and leaves crisp in the blaze of noon. The grasshoppers kept up their ceaseless sound, filling the countryside with a thin, crackling noise like the rattle of the wooden crickets children buy at fairs.

The doctor, raising his voice, said:

"Honoré, you can't leave your mother all alone in this state. She will die at any moment."

And the peasant repeated dejectedly:

"But I've got to get my wheat in: it's been out too long. The weather's just right, I tell you. What d'you say, Mother?"

And the dying old woman, still in the grip of Norman avarice, said "Yes" with eyes and face, and gave her son leave to get his grain in and to leave her to die alone.

But the doctor grew angry and said:

"You're nothing but a brute, do you hear! And I'll not let you do it, do you understand! If you must get your wheat in today of all days, go and fetch Mother Rapet, I say, and make her look after your mother. I insist on it, do you understand! And if you don't obey me, I'll leave you to die like a dog when it's your turn to be ill, do you hear?"

The peasant, a tall, lean man, slow of gesture, tortured by indecision, between fear of the doctor and the ferocious passion of the miser, hesitated, calculated, and stammered:

"What'll she want, Mother Rapet, for looking after her?"

"How do I know?" the doctor cried. "It depends on the length of time you want her. Arrange it with her, dammit. But I want her to be here in an hour's time, do you understand?"

The man made up his mind:

"I'm going, I'm going; don't get angry, doctor."

The doctor took himself off, calling:

"Now you know, mind, what you're about, for I stand no nonsense when I'm angry."

As soon as he was alone, the peasant turned to his mother, and said resignedly:

"I'm going t'get Mother Rapet, seeing t'man says so. Don't worry yourself while I'm gone."

And he went out too.

Mother Rapet, an old washerwoman, looked after the dead and dying of the village and the district. Then, as soon as she had sewn her clients into that sheet which they can never throw off, she went home and took up the iron with which she smoothed the garments of the living. Wrinkled like a last year's apple, malicious, jealous, greedy with a greed passing belief, bent in two as if her loins had been broken by the ceaseless movement of the iron she pushed over the clothes, one might have thought she had a monstrous, cynical love for death-throes. She never talked of anything but the persons she had seen die and of all the kinds of death at which she had been present, and she talked about them with a wealth of minute detail (which was always the same) the way a hunter talks about his bags.

When Honoré Bontemps entered her house he found her getting blue water ready for the village women's handkerchiefs.

"Well, good evening," he said. "You all right, Madame Rapet?"

She turned her head to look at him:

"Same as always, same as always. What about you?"

"Oh, I'm getting on fine, I am, but mother's not."

"Your mother?"

"Yes, my mother."

"What's the matter with your mother?"

"She's going to turn her toes up, she is."

The old woman drew her hands out of the water: bluish transparent drops rolled to the tips of her fingers and fell back into the bucket.

She asked with sudden sympathy:

"She's as bad as that, is she?"

"T'doctor says she'll not last through the afternoon."

"She must be bad, then."

Honoré hesitated. He considered various ways of approaching the proposal he meditated. But, finding none of them satisfactory, he broke out suddenly:

"How much d'you want to look after her for me

until she's gone? You know I'm not rich. I can't even pay for so much as a servant. That's what has brought her to this pass, my poor mother, overmuch worrying, overmuch hard work. She worked like ten men, in spite of her ninety-two years. They don't make 'em like that now."

La Rapet replied gravely, "I've two charges, forty sous a day and three francs a night to the rich; twenty sous a day and forty a night to t'others. You can give me twenty and forty."

But the peasant reflected. He knew his mother too well. He knew that she was tenacious of life, vigorous, and sprung of hard stock. She might last a week in spite of the doctor's opinion.

He spoke resolutely:

"No. I'd rather you had a sum down, to do the whole job. I've got to take a risk one way and the other. The doctor says she'll go any minute. If that happens, you win—and then I lose. But if she holds out till tomorrow or for longer, I win and you lose."

The nurse looked at the man in surprise. She had never yet treated death as a gamble. She hesitated, tempted by the thought of making a lucky bargain. Then she suspected that she was being tricked.

"I'll not say one way or the other until I've seen your mother," she replied.

"Come on, then, and look at her."

She dried her hands and went with him at once.

On the way not a word passed between them. She walked with a hurried step, while he stretched his great limbs as if he had a brook to cross at each stride.

The cows, lying down in the fields, overpowered by the heat, raised their heads heavily, lowing faintly as the couple passed, as if asking for fresh grass.

As he drew near the house, Honoré murmured:

"Perhaps it's all over after all." His unconscious wish spoke in the tones of his voice.

But the old woman was far from dead. She was lying on her back, in her wretched bed, her hands outside the purple calico counterpane, fearfully thin hands, knotted like the talons of some strange beast, or like a crab's claws, doubled up by rheumatism, fatigue and the daily toil which had been her lot. Mother Rapet went over to the bed and considered the dying woman. She felt her pulse, touched her chest and listened to her breathing, asked her a question to hear her voice in reply, then, having looked at her again for a long time, she went out, followed by Honoré. His conviction was strengthened. The old woman would not last out the night. He asked: "Well?"

The nurse answered: "H'm. She'll last two days, p'raps three. You can make it six francs, the lump sum."

He cried out at that:

"Six francs! *Six* francs! Have you lost your wits? I swear she won't live more than five or six hours—no longer."

They argued for a while, both very obstinate.

At last he had to give way, the woman was on the point of going, time was passing, and his wheat couldn't be got in without him.

"All right," he said. "Six francs, all told—including the washing of the corpse."

"Done! Six francs."

He went out with great strides towards his grain, which lay on the ground under the fierce sun that ripens the harvest.

The woman went back into the house.

She had brought her sewing, for when she was

tending the dying or dead, she worked unceasingly—
sometimes for herself, sometimes for the family, who
employed her in this double task for an extra fee.

All at once, she asked:

"I suppose you've seen the priest at any rate, Mother
Bontemps?"

The old woman shook her head; and Mother Rapet,
who was pious, got up with alacrity.

"Good God! Is it possible? I'll go and fetch M. le
Curé."

With that she ran to the presbytery in such haste
that the urchins in the market-place, seeing her hurrying thus, thought some accident had happened.

The priest came out immediately in his surplice, preceded by a choir boy who rang a little bell to herald
the passing of God through the calm, brilliant countryside. Men who were working a long way off took off
their great hats and stood without moving, until the
white robe disappeared behind a farm; the women who
were gathering the sheaves stood upright and made
the sign of the Cross; some black hens, terrified, flew
along the ditches with a wild, jerky gait to a hole well
known to them, where they disappeared hurriedly; a
colt tethered in a field took fright at the sight of the
surplice and started running round and round at the
end of his rope, throwing his hind legs high in the air.
The choir boy in his red skirt walked quickly and the
priest, with his head drooping slightly on one side and
crowned with its square biretta, followed him, murmuring his prayers as he went; last of all came old
Rapet, all bowed down, nearly doubled in two as
though she were trying to walk and prostrate herself at
the same time, her fingers clasped as in church.

Honoré, from the distance, saw them pass. He asked: "Where'st agoing, Father?"

His hired man, quicker-witted than he, replied: "He's taking the Sacrament to your mother, bless you." The peasant was not at all astonished.

"That's all to the good, anyhow."

And he went on with his work. Mother Bontemps made her confession, received absolution and was given communion; and the priest went home again, leaving the two women alone in the stifling bedroom.

Then Mother Rapet began to think about the dying woman, and wondered whether she was going to last much longer.

The day was drawing in, fresher air blew in sharp gusts: a two-penny colored print, held by two pins, fluttered against the wall; the little curtains at the window, once white but yellowed now and spotted with flyblow, looked ready to take flight, to tear themselves free, as if they, like the soul of the old woman, would like to depart.

She lay there motionless, her eyes open, seeming to await with utter indifference the death which was so close, yet so slow to come. Her breathing, sharp now, whistled a little in the contracted throat. She would die very soon and the world would hold one woman less whom nobody would miss.

When night fell Honoré came indoors. Going up to the bed, he saw that his mother was still living and he asked: "How are you?" just as he used to do when she was sick. Then he sent Mother Rapet away, telling her:

"Tomorrow at five o'clock without fail."

She repeated:

"Tomorrow, five o'clock."

. She came, in fact, at daybreak. Honoré was drinking the soup he had made for himself before going out into the fields.

The woman asked him:

"Well, has your mother gone yet?"

He replied with a cunning smile:

"She's getting on a bit better."

Then he went out.

Mother Rapet suddenly felt uneasy. She went up to the sufferer, who was lying in the same state, breathing painfully and imperceptibly, her eyes open and her clenched hands on the counterpane.

The woman saw that this might last two days, four days, even eight days; and fear gripped her miserly heart; then she was shaken by a furious anger against the trickster who had cheated her, and against this old woman who would not die.

She set to work, however, and waited and waited, her eyes fixed on the wrinkled face of Mother Bontemps.

Honoré came back to breakfast; he seemed happy, almost jovial; then he went out again. He was certainly getting in his wheat under excellent conditions.

Mother Rapet was getting irritated: each minute that went by now was stolen time, stolen money. She wanted, wanted madly, to take this mulish old woman, this obstinate and pigheaded old woman, by the neck and with a little shaking make an end of the scant, short breath that was stealing her time and her money.

Then she thought of the danger, and other ideas came into her head. She came up close to the bed and asked:

"Have you seen the devil yet?"

Mother Bontemps murmured:

"No."

Then the nurse began to talk, telling her tales to terrify the feeble soul of this dying woman.

Some minutes before one breathed one's last, the devil appeared, she said, to all sick people. He had a broom in one hand, and a saucepan on his head. He made strange noises.

If you saw him, it was all over, you had only a few seconds to live. She enumerated all those in her charge to whom the devil had appeared that year: Joséphine Loisel, Eulalie Ratier, Sophie Padagnan, Séraphine Grospied.

Mother Bontemps, disturbed at last, shook in her bed, waved her hands, trying to turn her head so that she could see to the farthest corner of the room.

Suddenly Mother Rapet disappeared from the foot of the bed. She took a sheet from the cupboard and wrapped herself in it; then she set a stew-pan on her head so that the three short curved legs stood on end like three horns. She grabbed a broom in her right hand and in her left a metal water-jug which she threw sharply in the air so that it fell down with a great noise.

It struck the floor with a terrible clatter. Then, clambering onto a chair, the nurse lifted the curtain that hung at the end of the bed and appeared, waving her arms, uttering hoarse shrieks from beneath the iron pot that hid her face, and with her broom threatening the old dying peasant woman, like the devil in a Punch and Judy show.

Mad with fear, her eyes wild, the dying woman made a superhuman effort to get up and get away from it. She managed to get her shoulders and chest out of bed, then she fell back with a great sigh. It was all over.

Mother Rapet placidly put everything back: the broom in the corner of the cupboard, the sheet inside,

the stew-pan on the stove, the water-jug on the shelf
and the chair against the wall. Then with a professional
gesture she closed the wide-staring eyes of the dead,
placed on the bed a dish, poured into it a little of the
water from the holy-water vessel, dipped in it the sprig
of yew nailed to the cupboard door and, kneeling down,
began to recite fervently the prayers for the dead which
she knew by heart, professionally.

When Honoré returned, at nightfall, he found her
praying, and his first thought was that she had cheated
him of twenty sous, for she had only spent three days
and one night, which came to five francs, instead of the
six which he owed her.

MARTIN'S GIRL

IT HAPPENED to him one Sunday after Mass. He
came out of church and was following the sunken road
that led to his house, when he found himself behind
Martin's girl, who also was on her way home.

The head of the family marched beside his daughter
with the consequential step of a prosperous farmer. Dis-
daining a smock, he wore a sort of jacket of gray cloth,
and on his head a wide-brimmed felt hat.

She, squeezed into stays that she laced up only
once a week, walked along stiffly, swinging her arms a
little, her waist compressed, broad-shouldered, her hips
swinging as she walked.

On her head she wore a flower-trimmed hat, the creation of an Yvetot milliner, that left bare all her strong, supple, rounded neck; short downy hairs, bleached by sun and open air, blew about it.

Benoist saw only her back, but her face was familiar enough to him, although he had never really looked at it.

"Dammit," he said abruptly, "she's a rare fine wench after all, is Martin's girl." He watched her walking along, filled with sudden admiration, his senses stirred. He had no need to see her face again. He kept his eyes fixed on her figure; one thought hammered in his mind, as if he had said it aloud: "Dammit, she's a rare fine wench."

Martin's girl turned to the right to enter Martin's Farm, the farm belonging to Jean Martin, her father; she turned round and looked behind her. She saw Benoist, whom she thought a very queer-looking fellow.

"Good morning, Benoist," she called.

"Good morning, lass; good morning, Martin," he answered, and walked on.

When he reached his own house, the soup was on the table. He sat down opposite his mother, beside the hired man and the boy, while the servant-girl went to draw the cider.

He ate some spoonfuls, then pushed away his plate.

"Are you sick?" his mother asked.

"No," he answered. "It feels like I had porridge in my stomach and it spoils my appetite."

He watched the others eating, every now and then breaking off a bit of bread that he carried slowly to his mouth and chewed for a long time. He was thinking of Martin's girl: "She's a rare fine wench after all." And to think he had never noticed it until this moment, and that it had come upon him like this, out of a clear sky, and so desperately that he could not eat.

He hardly touched the stew. His mother said:

"Come, Benoist, make yourself eat a morsel; it's a bit of loin, it'll do you good. When you've no appetite, you ought to make yourself eat."

He swallowed a little, then pushed his plate aside again—no, it was no better.

When the meal was over, he went off round the fields and gave the farm hand the afternoon off, promising to look to the beasts himself on the way round.

The countryside was deserted, it being the day of rest. Dotted about a clover-field, the cows lay placidly with swollen bellies, chewing the cud under the hot sun. Unyoked ploughs were waiting in the corner of a ploughed field; and the wide brown squares of up-turned earth, ready for the sowing, stretched between patches of yellow ground covered with the rotting stubble of wheat and oats recently gathered in.

An autumn wind, a dry wind, blew over the plain with the promise of a fresh evening after sunset. Benoist sat down on the edge of a ditch, rested his hat on his knees, as if he needed the air on his head, and declared aloud to the silent countryside, "A fine girl that, a fine girl."

He was still thinking about her when night came, in his bed, and in the morning, when he woke.

He was not unhappy, he was not restless: he could hardly say what his feelings were. It was something that gripped him, something that had fastened on his imagination, an idea that obsessed him and roused something like a thrill in his heart. A big fly sometimes gets shut up in a room. You hear it fly round, buzzing, and the sound obsesses and irritates. Suddenly it stops: you forget it, but all at once it begins again, forcing you to raise your head. You can neither catch it nor chase it nor kill it nor make it keep still. It settles for a brief moment, and begins droning again.

The memory of Martin's girl flitted distractedly through Benoist's mind like an imprisoned fly.

Then he was seized with desire to see her again, and walked several times past Martin's Farm. At last he caught a glimpse of her, hanging washing on a line stretched between two apple-trees.

It was warm: she had taken off everything but a short petticoat and her chemise, which revealed the curve of her body when she lifted her arms to peg out the towels.

He remained crouching under the ditch for more than an hour, even after she had gone. He went away with her image more firmly fixed in his mind than ever.

For a month his mind was filled with thoughts of her, he quivered when she was spoken of in his presence. He could not eat, and every night he sweated so that he could not sleep.

On Sunday at Mass, his eyes never left her. She noticed it, and smiled at him, flattered by his admiration.

One evening he came upon her unexpectedly on a road. She stopped when she saw him coming. Then he walked right up to her, choking with nervousness and a passion of desire, but determined to speak to her. He began, stuttering:

"Look here, my lass, this can't go on like this."

Her reply sounded as if she were making fun of him:

"What is it that can't go on, Benoist?"

He answered:

"That I think about you as often as there are hours in the day."

She rested her hands on her hips:

"I'm not making you do it."

He stammered:

"Yes, you are: I can't sleep, or rest, or eat, or anything."

She said softly:

"Well, and what would cure you?"

He stood paralyzed, his arms dangling, his eyes round, his mouth hanging open.

She poked him in the stomach, and ran away.

After the day, they met again by the ditches, in the sunken roads, or more often at dusk on the edge of a field, when he was coming home with his goats and she was driving the cows back to their shed.

He felt himself urged, driven towards her by a wild desire of heart and body. He would have liked to crush her, strangle her, devour her, absorb her into himself. And he trembled with impotent, impatient rage because she was not his completely, because they were not one and indivisible.

People were talking about them. They were said to be betrothed. In fact, he had asked her if she would be his wife, and she had answered: "Yes."

They were waiting an opportunity to speak to their parents.

Then, without warning, she stopped coming to meet him at the usual hour. He did not even see her when he prowled round the farm. He could not catch a glimpse of her at Mass on Sundays. And then one Sunday, after the sermon, the priest announced in the pulpit that he published the banns of marriage between Victoire-Adélaïde Martin and Josephin-Isidore Vallin.

Benoist felt a strange emotion in his hands, as though the blood had run out of them. His ears sang; he heard nothing more, and after a time he realized that he was crying in his missal.

He kept to his room for a month. Then he began working again.

But he was not cured, and he thought about it continually. He avoided walking along the roads that ran past the house where she lived, so that he should not see even the trees in the yard: it necessitated a wide detour, which he made morning and evening.

She had now married Vallin, the wealthiest farmer in the district. Benoist and he no longer spoke, although they had been friends since childhood.

One evening, as Benoist passed through the village square, he heard that she was pregnant. Instead of bitter suffering, the knowledge brought him, on the contrary, something like relief. It was finished now, absolutely finished. This divided them more utterly than her marriage. He really preferred it so.

Months passed, and more months. He caught occasional glimpses of her going about the village with her burdened gait. She turned red when she saw him, hung her head and quickened her step. And he turned out of his way to avoid crossing her path and meeting her eye.

But he thought wretchedly that the day would inevitably come when he would find himself face to face with her, and be compelled to speak to her. What should he say to her now, after all he had said to her in other days, holding her hands and kissing the hair which fell round her cheeks? He still thought often of their ditch-side trysts. It was a wicked thing she had done, after all her promises.

Little by little, however, his heart forgot its pain; only a gentle melancholy lingered in it. And one day, for the first time, he took again his old road past the farm where she lived. He saw the roof of her house long before he drew near. It was under that very roof that she was living with another. The apple-trees were in bloom, the cocks crowing on the dunghill. There did not seem to be a soul in the house: everyone was in the fields, hard at work on the tasks spring brought. He halted near the fence and looked into the yard. The dog was asleep in front of his kennel, three calves were going slowly, one after another, towards the pond. A plump turkey was strutting before the door, showing off before the hens with the air of an operatic star.

Benoist leaned against the post: a sudden, violent desire to weep had seized him again. But all at once he heard a cry, a cry for help. It came from the house. He stood a moment bewildered, his hands gripping the wooden bar, listening, listening. Another cry, a long-drawn, agonized cry, thrust through his ears and mind and flesh. It was she crying like this. He leaped forward, crossed the grass, pushed open the door and saw her stretched on the floor, writhing, with livid and haggard eyes, taken by the pangs of childbirth.

He stood there, then, pale and more violently trembling than she, stammering:

"Here I am, here I am, my lass."

Gasping, she answered:

"Oh, don't leave me, don't leave me, Benoist."

He stared at her, not knowing what else to say or do. Her cries began again:

"Oh! oh! it tears me! Oh! Benoist!"

And she twisted herself in an agony of pain.

All at once, Benoist was overwhelmed by a wild impulse to succour her, comfort her, take away her pain. He stooped, took her in his arms, lifted her up, carried her to her bed, and while she continued to moan, he undressed her, taking off her bodice, her skirt, her petticoat. She was gnawing her fists to keep from screaming. Then he did for her all he was used to do for beasts, for cows and sheep and mares: he helped her and received between his hands a plump, wailing child.

He washed it, wrapped it in a dish-cloth that was drying before the fire, and laid it on a pile of linen that was lying on the table to be ironed; then he went back to the mother.

He laid her on the floor again, changed the bed, and put her back in it. She stammered, "Thanks, Benoist, you're a kind soul." And she wept a few tears, as if she were regretting things a little.

As for him, he felt no love for her now, none at all. It was over. Why? How? He could not have said. The events of the last hour had cured him more effectually than ten years' absence would have done.

Exhausted and fainting, she asked:

"What is it?"

He answered calmly:

"It's a girl, and a very fine one."

They were silent again. A few moments later, the mother spoke in a weak voice:

"Show her to me, Benoist."

He went to bring the infant, and he was offering it to her as if he held the Holy Sacrament, when the door opened and Isidore Vallin appeared.

At first he did not understand; then, suddenly, realization came to him.

Benoist, filled with dismay, stammered:

"I was going past, I was just going past, when I heard her screaming, and I came in . . . here's your baby, Vallin."

Tears in his eyes, the husband stooped towards him and took the tiny morsel the other held out to him, kissed it; a moment he stood, his emotion choking him; he laid his child back on the bed and, holding out both hands to Benoist:

"Put it there, Benoist, put it there: there's nothing more for you and me to say now. We'll be friends if you're willing; eh, friends!"

And Benoist answered:

"I'm willing, I am; of course I'm willing."

TOINE

OLD TOINE was known for twenty miles around, fat Toine, Toine-ma-Fine, Antoine Mâcheblé, alias Brûlot, the innkeeper at Tournevent.

He had made famous this hamlet, buried in the depths of the valley which ran down to the sea, a poor peasant hamlet, composed of a dozen Norman houses surrounded by ditches and trees. The houses were huddled together in a ravine, covered with grass and furze, behind the curve of the hill which had given the village the name of Tournevent. As birds conceal themselves in the furrows during a storm, so the houses seemed to have sought a shelter in this hollow, shelter against the fierce salt winds of the sea, which gnawed and burned like fire, and withered and destroyed like the frosts of winter.

The whole hamlet seemed to be the property of Antoine Mâcheblé, alias Brûlot, who was, besides, often called Toine, and Toine-ma-Fine, because of a phrase which he constantly used. "My *fine* is the best in France," he would say. His *fine* was his cognac, of course. For twenty years he had soaked the countryside in his cognac, for whenever his customers said: "Well, what is it going to be, my boy?" he invariably replied: "Try a brandy, old son. It warms the insides and clears the head; there is nothing better for your health." He called everybody "old son," but he had never had a son of his own.

Ah, yes, everyone knew old Toine, the biggest man in the district, or even in the province. His little house seemed too ridiculously small to contain him, and when one saw him standing in his doorway, where he spent the greater part of every day, one wondered how he could enter his home. But he did enter, each time a customer presented himself, for Toine-ma-Fine was invited, as by right prescriptive, to levy a glass on all who drank in his house.

His café bore on its sign the legend "The Rendezvous of Friends," and old Toine was truly the friend of all the country round. People came from Fécamp and Montivilliers to see him and laugh at his stories—for this great, good-natured man could bring a smile to the most solemn face. He had a way of joking without giving offense, of winking his eye to express what he dared not utter, and of slapping his thigh in his bursts of mirth, which made one laugh in spite of oneself. And then it was a curiosity just to see him drink. He drank all that was offered him by everybody, with joy in his wicked eye, a joy which came from a double pleasure: first, the pleasure of regaling himself, and then the pleasure of heaping up money at the expense of his friends.

The local wits would ask:

"Tell us now, Toine. Why don't you drink up the sea?"

And he would reply:

"There are two objections. First, it is salty, and second, it would have to be bottled, since my paunch prevents me from stooping down to that cup."

The quarrels of Toine and his wife were Homeric. It was such a good show that one would have paid to see it. They had squabbled every day through the whole thirty years of their married life. Only, Toine was good-natured over it, while his wife was furious. She was a tall peasant woman who walked with long, stilt-like strides, her thin, flat body surmounted by the head of an ugly screech-owl. She spent her whole time rearing poultry in the little yard behind the inn, and was renowned for the success with which she fattened her fowls.

When any of the great ladies of Fécamp gave a feast to the people of quality, it was necessary to the success of the repast that it should be garnished with the celebrated fowls from Mother Toine's poultry-yard.

But she was born with a vile temper and had continued to be dissatisfied with everything. Angry with everybody, she was particularly so with her husband. She sneered at his gaiety, his popularity, his good health, and his bulk; she treated him with the utmost contempt because he got his money without working for it, and because, as she said, he ate and drank as much as ten ordinary men. Not a day passed without her declaring, in exasperated tones, "Wouldn't a hog like that be better in the sty with the pigs! He's that fat, it makes me sick in the stomach." "Wait a little, wait a little," she would shriek in his face, "we shall soon see what is going to happen! This great windbag will burst like a sack of grain!"

Toine would laugh, tap his enormous belly, and reply, "Ah, old skin-and-bones, let us see you try to make your chickens as fat as this."

And rolling up his sleeve he would show his brawny arm. "There's a wing for you!" he would cry. And the customers would strike their fists on the table and fairly writhe with joy, and stamp their feet and spit upon the floor in a delirium of delight.

The old woman would grow more furious than ever, and shout at the top of her lungs: "Just wait a bit, we shall see what will happen. You will burst like a sack of grain."

And she would rush out, maddened with rage at the laughter of the crowd of drinkers.

Toine, in fact, was a wonder to see, so fat and red and short of breath had he grown. He was one of those enormous creatures with whom Death seems to play, with tricks, and jokes, and treacherous buffooneries, making irresistibly comic the slow work of destruction. Instead of behaving as he did towards others, showing the white hairs, shrunken limbs, wrinkles, and general feebleness which makes one say with a shiver, "Heavens, how he has changed!" Death took pleasure in fattening Toine; in making a droll monster of him, in reddening his face and giving him the appearance of superhuman health; and the deformities which he inflicted on others became in Toine's case laughable and diverting instead of sinister and pitiable.

"Wait a little, wait a little," Mother Toine would mutter, as she scattered the grain about her poultry-yard, "you will see what will happen!"

II

One day, indeed, Toine had a seizure, and fell down
with a paralytic stroke. They carried the hulk to the
little chamber partitioned off at the rear of the café in
order that he might hear what was going on on the other
side of the wall, and converse with his friends, for his
brain remained clear while his enormous body was
prone and helpless. They hoped for a time that his
mighty limbs would recover some of their energy, but
this hope disappeared very soon, and Toine was forced
to pass his days and nights in his bed, which was made
up but once a week, with the help of four friends who
lifted him by his four limbs while his mattress was
turned. He continued to be cheerful, but with a different
kind of good humor; more timid, more humble, and
with the pathetic fear of a little child in the presence
of his wife, who scolded and raged all the day long.
"There he lies, the boozer, the good-for-nothing, the
idler!" she would cry. Toine would say nothing, only
wink his eye behind the old woman's back, and turn
over in bed, the only movement he was able to make.
He called this change "making a move to the north, or a
move to the south." His only entertainment now was to
listen to the conversation in the café and to join in the
talk across the wall, and when he recognized the voice
of a friend he would cry, "Hello, old son; is that you,
Célestin?"

And Célestin Maloisel would reply: "It is me, Father
Toine. How are the legs today, my boy?"

"I can't run yet, Célestin," Toine would answer, "but
I am not growing thin, either. The shell is sound."
Presently he invited his intimates into his bedroom for
company, because it pained him to see them drinking

without him. He would say, "Boys, what beats me is not to be able to have a glass. I don't care a hoot about anything else, but it's terrible not to drink."

Then the screech-owl's head of Mother Toine would appear at the window, and she would cry, "Look, look at him! that great hulking idler, who must be fed and washed and scoured like a pig!"

And when she disappeared a red-plumaged rooster sometimes perched on the window-sill, and, looking about with his round and curious eye, gave forth a shrill crow. And sometimes two or three hens flew in and scratched and pecked about the floor, attracted by the crumbs which fell from Father Toine's plate.

The friends of Toine-ma-Fine very soon deserted the café for his room, and every afternoon they gossiped around the bed of the big man. Bedridden as he was, this rascal Toine still amused them; he would have made the devil himself laugh, the jolly fellow! There were three friends who came every day: Célestin Maloisel, a tall, spare man with a body twisted like the trunk of an apple-tree; Prosper Horslaville, a little dried-up old man with a nose like a ferret, cunning and sly as a fox; and Césaire Paumelle, who never uttered a word, but enjoyed himself all the same. They brought in a board from the yard which they placed across the bed and on it they played dominoes from two o'clock in the afternoon until six. But Mother Toine soon interfered: she could not endure that her husband should amuse himself by playing dominoes in his bed, and, each time she saw the game begin, she bounced into the room in a rage, overturned the board, seized the dominoes, and carried them into the café, declaring that it was enough to feed this great lump of fat without seeing him amuse himself at the expense of hard-working people. Célestin Maloisel bent his head before the

storm, but Prosper Horslaville tried to further excite the
old woman, whose rages amused him. Seeing her one
day more exasperated than usual, he said, "Hello,
Mother Toine! Do you know what I would do if I were
in your place?"

She waited for an explanation, fixing her owl-like eyes
upon him. He continued:

"Your husband, who never leaves his bed, is as hot as
an oven. I should set him to hatching out eggs."

She remained stupefied, thinking he was jesting,
watching the thin, sly face of the peasant, who continued:

"I would put five eggs under each arm the same day
that I set the yellow hen; they would all hatch out at the
same time; and when they were out of their shells, I
would put your husband's chicks under the hen for her
to bring up. That would bring you some poultry, Mother
Toine."

The old woman was amazed. "Is it possible?" she
asked.

Prosper continued, "Why not? If one can hatch out
eggs in a warm box, one can hatch them out in a warm
bed."

She was greatly impressed with this reasoning, and
went out completely quieted down and thoughtful.

A week later she came into Toine's chamber with her
apron full of eggs, and said, "I have just put the yellow
hen to set with ten eggs under her; here are ten for you!
Be careful not to break them!"

Toine was astonished. "What do you mean?" he cried.

"I mean that you shall hatch them, good-for-nothing."

Toine laughed at first, then as she insisted he grew
angry, he resisted and obstinately refused to allow her
to put the eggs under his great arms, that his warmth
might hatch them. But the baffled old woman grew furi-

ous and declared, "You shall have not a bite to eat so long as you refuse to take them—there, we'll see what will happen!"

Toine was uneasy, but he said nothing. When he heard the clock strike twelve he called to his wife, "Hey, mother, is the soup ready?" The old woman shouted from the kitchen: "There is no dinner for you today, you lazy thing!"

He thought at first she was joking, and waited. Then he begged and prayed and swore by fits; turned himself "to the north" and "to the south," grew desperate under the pangs of hunger and the smell of the viands, and pounded on the wall with his great fists, until at last, worn out and almost famished, he allowed his wife to introduce the eggs into his bed and place them under his arms. After that he had his soup.

When his friends arrived, they believed Toine to be very ill; he seemed constrained and uneasy.

Then they began to play dominoes as formerly, but Toine appeared to take no pleasure in the game, and put forth his hand so gingerly and with such evident precaution that they suspected at once something was wrong.

"Is your arm tied?" demanded Horslaville.

Toine feebly responded, "I have a feeling of heaviness in my shoulder."

Suddenly someone entered the café, and the players paused to listen. It was the mayor and his assistant, who called for two glasses of cognac and then began to talk of the affairs of the country. As they spoke in low tones, Toine Brûlot tried to press his ear against the wall; and forgetting his eggs, he gave a sudden lunge "to the north," which resulted in his lying down on an omelet. At the oath he uttered, Mother Toine came running in, and divining the disaster she uncovered him with a jerk.

She stood a moment too enraged and breathless to speak, at the sight of the yellow poultice pasted on the flank of her husband. Then, trembling with fury, she flung herself on the paralytic and began to pound him with great force on the body, as though she were pounding her dirty linen on the banks of the river. She showered her blows upon him with the force and rapidity of a drummer beating his drum.

Toine's friends were choking with laughter, coughing, sneezing, uttering exclamations, while the frightened man parried the attacks of his wife with due precaution in order not to break the five eggs he still had on the other side.

III

Toine was conquered. He had to turn broody. He had to renounce the innocent pleasure of dominoes, to give up any effort to move, for his wife deprived him of all nourishment every time he broke an egg. He lay on his back, with his eyes fixed on the ceiling, his arms extended like wings, warming against his immense body the incipient chicks in their white shells. He spoke only in low tones as if he feared a noise as much as a movement, and he asked often about the yellow hen in the poultry-yard, who was engaged in the same task as himself.

"Did the yellow one eat last night?" he would say to his wife.

The old woman went from the hen to her husband, and from her husband to the hen, possessed and preoccupied with the little broods which were maturing in the bed and in the nest. The country people, who soon learned the story, came in, curious and serious, to get the news of Toine. They entered on tiptoe as one enters

sick-chamber, and inquired with concern: "How goes
t, Toine?"

"It's all right," he answered; "but it is so long, I get
ery hot. I feel cold shivers galloping all over my skin."

One morning his wife came in very much disturbed,
nd exclaimed, "The yellow hen has hatched seven
hicks; there were three bad eggs!"

Toine felt his heart beat. How many would he have?

"Will it be soon?" he asked, with the anguish of a
voman who is about to become a mother.

The old woman, who was tortured by the fear of
ailure, answered angrily: "I hope so!"

They waited.

The friends, seeing that Toine's time was approach-
ig, soon became uneasy themselves. They gossiped
bout it in the house, and kept all the neighbors in-
ormed of the progress of affairs. Towards three o'clock
'oine grew drowsy. He slept now half the time. He was
uddenly awakened by an unusual ticking under his
rm. He put his hand carefully to the place and seized a
ttle beast covered with yellow down, which struggled
etween his fingers. His emotion was so great that he
ried out and let go the chick, which ran across his
reast. The café was full of people. The customers
ushed into the room and circled round the bed, as if
hey were at a circus, while Mother Toine, who had ar-
ived at the first sound, carefully caught the fledgling as
t nestled in her husband's beard. No one uttered a
vord. It was a warm April day; one could hear through
he open window the clucking of the yellow hen calling
o her new-born. Toine, who perspired with emotion
nd agony, murmured, "I feel another one now under
ny left arm."

His wife plunged her great, gaunt hand under the

bed-clothes and drew forth a second chick with all the
precautions of a midwife.

The neighbors wished to see it and passed it from
hand to hand, regarding it with awe as though it were a
phenomenon. For the space of twenty minutes no more
were hatched, then four chicks came out of their shells
at the same time. This caused great excitement among
the watchers.

Toine smiled, happy at his success, and began to feel
proud of this singular paternity. Such a sight had never
been seen before. This was a droll man, truly! "That
makes six," cried Toine. "By heavens, what a christening
there will be!" and a great laugh rang out from the
public. Other people now crowded into the café and
filled the doorway, with outstretched necks and curious
eyes.

"How many has he?" they inquired.

"There are six."

Mother Toine ran with the new fledglings to the hen,
who, clucking distractedly, puffed up her feathers and
spread wide her wings to shelter her increasing flock of
little ones.

"Here comes another one!" cried Toine. He was mistaken—there were three of them. This was a triumph.
The last one broke its shell at seven o'clock in the
evening. All Toine's eggs were good! He was delivered
and, delirious with joy, he seized and kissed the frail
little creature on the back. He could have smothered it
with caresses. He wished to keep this little one in his
bed until the next day, moved by the tenderness of a
mother for this being to whom he had given life; but the
old woman carried it away, as she had done the others,
without listening to the supplications of her husband.

The spectators went home delighted, talking of the
event by the way, and Horslaville, who was the last to

leave, said, "You will invite me to the first fricassée, won't you, Toine?"

At the idea of a fricassée, Toine's face brightened and he answered:

"Certainly I will invite you, old son."

CONFESSING

THE NOON sun poured fiercely down upon the fields that lay in undulating folds around the clumps of trees that marked each farmstead. Ripe rye and yellowing wheat, pale-green oats, dark-green clover, spread a vast striped cloak, soft and rippling, over the bare body of the earth.

In the distance, on the crest of a slope, the horizon was broken by an endless line of cows, that were like soldiers at ease, some lying down, others on their feet, their great eyes blinking in the burning light, chewing the cud and grazing in a field of clover as broad as a lake.

Two women, mother and daughter, were walking with a swinging step, one behind the other, towards this regiment of cattle. Each carried two zinc pails, slung outwards from the body on the hoop of a cask; at each step the metal sent out a dazzling white flash under the sun that struck full upon it.

The women did not speak. They were on their way to milk the cows. When they arrived, each set down one of her pails and approached a cow. With a kick in the

ribs from her wooden shoe she forced the cow to struggle
to its feet. The beast rose slowly, first on its forelegs,
then with more difficulty it raised its large hind quarters,
which seemed to be weighed down by the enormous
udder of livid pendulous flesh.

The two Malivoires, mother and daughter, kneeling
beneath the animal's belly, tugged swiftly at the swollen
teat, which at each squeeze sent a slender pet of milk
into the pail. The yellowish froth mounted to the brim,
and the women went from cow to cow until they reached
the end of the long line.

As soon as they finished milking a beast, they changed
its position, giving it a fresh patch of grass on which to
graze.

Then they started on their way home, more slowly
now, weighed down by the load of milk, the mother in
front, the daughter behind.

Abruptly the daughter stopped, put down her burden,
sat on the ground, and began to cry.

Madame Malivoire, missing the sound of steps behind
her, turned round amazed.

"What's the matter with you?" she said.

Her daughter Céleste, a tall girl with bright red hair
and flaming cheeks, flecked with freckles as though
sparks of fire had fallen upon her face one day as she
worked in the sun, moaned and murmured like a beaten
child:

"I can't carry the milk any further."

Her mother looked at her suspiciously.

"What's the matter with you?" she repeated.

"It drags too heavy, I can't," replied Céleste. She had
collapsed and was lying on the ground between the
two pails, hiding her eyes in her apron.

"What's the matter with you, now?" said her mother
for the third time. The girl moaned:

"I think there's a baby on the way." And she broke into sobs.

The older woman in her turn set down her load, so amazed that she could find nothing to say. At last she stammered:

"You . . . you . . . you're going to have a baby, you idiot! How can that be?"

The Malivoires were prosperous farmers, well-off and of a certain position, widely respected, good business folk, of some importance in the district.

"I think I am, all the same," faltered Céleste.

The frightened mother looked at the weeping girl groveling at her feet. After a moment she cried:

"You're going to have a baby! A baby! Where did you get it, you slut?"

Céleste, shaken with emotion, murmured:

"I think it was in Polyte's wagon."

The old woman tried to understand, tried to imagine, who could have brought this misfortune upon her daughter. If the lad was well-off and of decent position, an arrangement might be come to. The damage could still be repaired. Céleste was not the first to be in the family way, but it was a nuisance, just the same, considering their position and the way people talked.

"And who was it, you slut?" she repeated.

Céleste, resolved to make a clean breast of it, stammered:

"I think it was Polyte."

At that Madame Malivoire, mad with rage, rushed upon her daughter and began to beat her with such fury that her hat fell off.

With great blows of the fist she struck the girl on the head, on the back, all over her body; Céleste, prostrate between the two pails, which afforded her some slight protection, shielded her face with her hands.

All the cows, disturbed by the noise of the row, had stopped grazing and turned round, staring with their great eyes. The last one mooed, stretching out its muzzle towards the women.

After beating her daughter till she was out of breath, Madame Malivoire stopped, exhausted; her spirits reviving a little, she tried to get a thorough understanding of the situation.

"—— Polyte! Lord save us, it's not possible! How could you, with a bus driver! You must have lost your wits. He must have played you a trick, the good-for-nothing!"

Céleste, still prostrate, murmured in the dust:

"I didn't pay my fare!"

This was something the old Norman woman could understand.

Every week, on Wednesday and on Saturday, Céleste went to town with the farm produce—poultry, cream, and eggs.

She started at seven with her two huge baskets on her arms, the dairy produce in one, the chickens in the other, and went down to the main road to wait for the wagon to Yvetot.

She set down her wares and sat in the ditch, while the chickens with their short pointed beaks and the ducks with their broad flat bills thrust their heads between the wicker slats and looked about them with their round, stupid, surprised eyes.

Soon the bus, a sort of yellow box with a black leather cap on top, came up, jerking and quivering with the trotting of the old white horse.

Polyte the coachman, a big, jolly fellow, stout though still young, and so burnt by sun and wind, soaked by rain, and colored with brandy that his face and neck were brick-red, cracked his whip and shouted from the distance: "Morning, Mam'selle Céleste. In good health, I hope?"

She gave him her baskets, one after the other, which he stowed in the boot; then she got in, stepping very high to reach the bus, and exposing a sturdy leg clad in a blue stocking.

Every time Polyte repeated the same joke: "Well, it's not got any thinner."

She laughed, thinking this funny.

Then he uttered a "Gee up, old girl!" which started off the thin horse. Then Céleste, reaching for her purse in the depths of her pocket, slowly took out ten sous, six for herself and four for the baskets, and handed them to Polyte over his shoulder.

He took them, saying:

"Aren't we going to have our little bit of sport today?"

And he laughed heartily, turning round towards her so as to stare at her at his ease.

She thought it a great expense, this half-franc for a journey of two miles. And when there were no coppers in her purse she felt it still more keenly; it was hard to make up her mind to part with a silver coin.

One day, as she was paying, she asked:

"You ought not ask more than six sous from a good customer like me."

He burst out laughing.

"Six sous, my beauty; why, you're worth more than that."

She insisted:

"But you make a good two francs a month out of me."

He whipped up his horse and exclaimed:

"Look here, I'm an obliging fellow! We'll call it quits for a bit of sport."

"What do you mean?" she asked innocently.

He was so amused that he laughed till he coughed

"A bit of sport is a bit of sport, damn it; a game for a lad and a lass, a dance for two without music."

She understood, blushed, and declared:

"I don't care for that sort of game, Monsieur Polyte."

But he was in no way abashed, and repeated merrily

"You'll come to it some day, my beauty, a bit of spor for a lad and a lass!"

Ever since that day he had taken to asking her, each time that she paid her fare:

"Aren't we going to have our bit of sport today?"

She, too, joked about it by this time, and replied:

"Not today, Monsieur Polyte, but Saturday, for cer tain!"

And amid peals of laughter he answered:

"Saturday, then, my beauty."

But inwardly she calculated that, during the two year that this had been going on, she had paid Polyte forty eight whole francs, and in the country forty-eight franc is not a sum which can be picked up on the roadside she also calculated that in two more years she woulc have paid nearly a hundred francs.

To such purpose she meditated that, one spring da as they jogged on alone, when he made his customar inquiry, "Aren't we going to have our bit of sport yet? she replied:

"Yes, if you like, Monsieur Polyte."

He was not at all surprised, and clambered over th back of his seat, murmuring with a complacent air:

"Come along, then. I knew you'd come to it som day."

The old white horse trotted so gently that she seeme to be dancing upon the same spot, deaf to the voic

which cried at intervals, from the depths of the vehicle:
"Gee up, old girl! Gee up, there!"

Three months later Céleste discovered that she was
going to have a child.

All this she had told her mother in a tearful voice.
Pale with fury, the old woman asked:

"Well, what did it cost?"

"Four months; that makes eight francs, doesn't it?"
replied Céleste.

At that the peasant woman's fury was utterly un-
leashed, and, falling once more upon her daughter, she
beat her a second time until she was out of breath. Then
she rose and said:

"Have you told him about the baby?"

"No, of course not."

"Why haven't you told him?"

"Because very likely he'd have made me pay for all
the free rides!"

The old woman pondered a while, then picked up her
milk-pails.

"Come on, get up, and try to walk home," she said.
After a pause she spoke again:

"And don't tell him as long as he doesn't notice anything. We'll make six or eight months' fares out of him."

Céleste, who had risen, still crying, disheveled and
swollen round the eyes, started off again with dragging
steps, murmuring:

"Of course I won't tell him."

THE RETURN

THE SEA is fretting the shore with tiny recurring waves. Small white clouds pass rapidly across the wide blue sky, swept along like birds by the swift wind; and the village, in a fold of a valley which descends to the sea, lies drowsing in the sun.

By the side of the road, at the very entrance to the village, stands the lonely dwelling of the Martin-Lévesques. It is a little fisherman's cottage with clay walls and a roof of thatch made gay with tufts of blue iris. There is a square patch of front garden the size of a pocket-handkerchief, containing onions, cabbages, parsley, and chevril, separated from the road by a hedge.

The man is out fishing, and his wife is sitting in front of the house, mending the meshes of a large brown net spread upon the wall like a gigantic spider's web. A little girl of fourteen is sitting near the gate in a cane-chair tilted back and supported against the fence; she is mending linen, miserable stuff already well darned and patched. Another girl a year younger is rocking in her arms a tiny child still too young to walk or talk, and two mites of two and three are squatting on the ground, opposite each other, digging in the earth with clumsy fingers and throwing handfuls of dust in one another's faces.

No one speaks. Only the baby that is being rocked to sleep cries incessantly in a weak, thin, small voice. A cat is asleep on the window-sill; some faded pinks at the foot of the wall make a fine patch of white blossom, over which a swarm of flies is humming.

The little girl sewing by the gate cries out abruptly: "Mother!"

"What is it?" her mother answers.

"He's here again."

Ever since the morning they have been uneasy, for a man has been prowling round the house, an old man who looks like a beggar. They saw him as they were taking their father to his boat, to see him on board. He was sitting in the ditch opposite their gate. Then, when they came back from the seashore, they saw him still staring at the house.

He looked ill and very wretched. For more than an hour he had not stirred; then, seeing that they took him for a bad character, he had got up and gone off, dragging one leg behind him.

But before long they had seen him return with his weary limp, and he had sat down again, a little farther off this time, as though to spy upon them.

The mother and the little girls were afraid. The mother was particularly uneasy, for she was by nature timid, and her husband, Lévesque, was not due back from the sea before nightfall.

Her husband's name was Lévesque, and hers was Martin, and the pair had been baptized Martin-Lévesque. This is why: her first husband had been a sailor named Martin who went every summer to the Newfoundland cod-fisheries. After two years of married life she had borne him a little daughter and was six months gone with another child, when her husband's ship, the *Two Sisters,* a three-masted barque from Dieppe, disappeared.

No news of her was ever heard, no member of the

crew returned, and she was believed lost with all hands.

For ten years Madame Martin waited for her man, having a hard struggle to bring up the two children. Then, as she was a fine, strong woman, a local fisherman named Lévesque, a widower with one son, asked her to marry him. She consented, and bore him two other children in three years.

Their life was hard and laborious. Bread was dear, and meat almost unknown in the household. Sometimes they were in debt to the baker, in the winter, during the stormy months. But the children grew up strong; the neighbors said:

"They're good folk, the Martin-Lévesques. She's a hard-working wife, and there's no better fisherman than Lévesque."

The little girl sitting by the fence went on:

"He looks as though he knew us. Perhaps he's some beggar from Épreville or Auzebosc."

But the mother was sure of the truth. No, no, he wasn't a local man, that was certain.

As he remained motionless as a log, his eyes fixed obstinately upon the cottage, Madame Martin lost her temper; fear lending her courage, she seized a spade and went out in front of the gate.

"What are you doing there?" she cried to the vagabond.

"I'm taking the air," he replied in a hoarse voice. "Am I doing you any harm?"

"What are you playing the spy for round my house?" she replied.

"I'm doing no one any harm," he answered. "Can't I sit down by the roadside?"

Not finding an answer, she went back into the house.

Slowly the day dragged by. Round about midday the

man disappeared. But near five o'clock he wandered past once more. He was not seen again that evening.

Lévesque came home at nightfall and was told of the affair.

"Some dirty rascal slinking about the place," he decided.

He went to bed with no anxiety, while his wife dreamed of this tramp who had stared at her with such strange eyes.

When dawn came a gale was blowing, and the sailor, seeing that he could not put out to sea, helped his wife to mend the nets.

About nine o'clock the eldest girl, one of Martin's children, who had gone out for some bread, ran in with a scared face, and cried:

"He's back again, mother."

Her mother felt a prick of excitement; very pale, she said to her husband:

"Go and tell him not to spy on us like this, Lévesque; it's fairly getting on my nerves."

Lévesque was a big fisherman with a brick-red face, a thick red beard, blue eyes with gleaming black pupils, and a strong neck always well wrapped up in a woolen scarf, to protect him from the wind and rain of the open sea. He went out calmly and marched up to the tramp.

And they began to talk.

The mother and children watched from the distance, trembling with excitement.

Suddenly the unknown man got up and accompanied Lévesque towards the house.

Madame Martin recoiled from him in terror. Her husband said:

"Give him a bit of bread and a mug of cider; he hasn't had a bite since the day before yesterday."

The two of them entered the cottage, followed by the woman and the children. The tramp sat down and began to eat, his head lowered before their gaze.

The mother stood and stared at him; the two eldest daughters, Martin's children, leaned against the door, one of them holding the youngest child, and stared eagerly at him. The two mites sitting among the cinders in the fireplace stopped playing with the black pot, as though to join in gaping at the stranger.

Lévesque sat down and asked him:

"Then you've come from far?"

"From the Mediterranean, from Cette."

"On foot, like that?"

"Yes. When you've no money, you must."

"Where are you going?"

"I was going here."

"Know anyone in these parts?"

"Maybe."

They were silent. He ate slowly, although ravenous, and took a sip of cider between the mouthfuls of bread. His face was worn and wrinkled, full of hollows, and he looked like a man who had suffered greatly.

Lévesque asked him abruptly:

"What's your name?"

He answered without raising his head:

"My name is Martin."

A strange shudder ran through the mother. She made a step forward as though to get a closer view of the vagabond, and remained standing in front of him, her arms hanging down and her mouth open. No one spoke another word. At last Lévesque said:

"Are you from these parts?"

"Yes, I'm from these parts."

And as he at last raised his head, his eyes met the

woman's and remained gazing at them; it was as though their glances were riveted together.

Suddenly she said in an altered voice, low and trembling:

"Is it you, husband?"

"Yes, it's me," he said slowly.

He did not move, but continued to munch his bread.

Lévesque, surprised rather than excited, stammered:

"It's you, Martin?"

"Yes, it's me," said the other simply.

"Where have you come from?" asked the second husband.

He told his story:

"From the coast of Africa. We foundered on a reef. Three of us got away, Picard, Vatinel, and me. Then we were caught by savages, who kept us twelve years. Picard and Vatinel are dead. An English traveler rescued me and brought me back to Cette. And here I am."

Madame Martin had begun to cry, hiding her face in her apron.

"What are we to do now?" said Lévesque.

"Is it you that's her husband?" asked Martin.

"Yes, it's me," replied Lévesque.

They looked at one another and were silent.

Then Martin turned to the circle of children round him and, nodding towards the two girls, asked:

"Are those mine?"

"Yes, they're yours," said Lévesque.

He did not get up; he did not kiss them. He only said:

"God, they're big!"

"What are we to do?" repeated Lévesque.

Martin, perplexed, had no idea. Finally he made up his mind:

"Whatever you say. You're a good fellow. What bothers me is the house. I've got two children, you've got three. Each has his own. As for their mother, is she yours, or shall I have her? Do as you like about her, but as for the house, that's mine; my father left it to me, I was born in it; the lawyer's got the papers about it."

Madame Martin was still crying, stifling her short gasps in the blue cloth of her apron. The two tall girls had drawn nearer and were looking uneasily at their father.

He had finished eating, and said:

"What are we to do?"

Lévesque had an idea:

"We must get the priest. He'll decide."

Martin rose, and as he went towards his wife she flung herself upon his breast, sobbing:

"It's you, husband! Martin, my poor Martin, it's you!"

She held him in her arms, suddenly stirred by a breath of the past, by an anguished rush of memories that reminded her of her youth and of her first kisses.

Martin, much affected, kissed her bonnet. The two children by the fireplace both began to cry when they heard their mother cry, and the youngest of all, in the arms of the younger Martin daughter, screamed in a shrill voice like a fife out of tune.

Lévesque stood up and waited.

"Come on," he said. "We must get it put straight."

Martin let go of his wife and, as he was looking at his two daughters, their mother said:

"You might kiss your dad."

They came up together, dry-eyed, surprised, a little frightened. He kissed them one after another, on both cheeks, with a loud, smacking kiss. The baby, seeing the stranger draw near, screamed so violently that it nearly fell into convulsions.

Then the two men went out together.

As they passed the Café du Commerce, Lévesque asked:

"How about a little drink?"

"Yes, I could do with some," declared Martin.

They went in and sat down in the room, which was still empty. Lévesque shouted:

"Hey, there, Chicot, two double brandies, and the best! It's Martin, he's come back; Martin, you know, my wife's man; Martin of the *Two Sisters*, that was lost."

The barman came up, three glasses in one hand and a pitcher of water in the other, a red-faced, podgy, pot-bellied man. In a calm voice he asked:

"Ah! So here you are, then, Martin?"

Martin answered:

"Here I am."

THE STRING

Along all the roads around Goderville the peasants and their wives were coming towards the little town, for it was market-day. The men walked with plodding steps, their bodies bent forward at each thrust of their long bowed legs. They were deformed by hard work, by the pull of the heavy plough which raises the left shoulder and twists the torso, by the reaping of the wheat which forces the knees apart to get a firm stand, by all the slow and strenuous labors of life on the farm. Their blue smocks, starched, shining as if varnished, orna-

mented with a little design in white at the neck and
wrists, puffed about their bony bodies, seemed like
balloons ready to carry them off. From each smock a
head, two arms, and two feet protruded.

Some led a cow or a calf at the end of a rope, and their
wives, walking behind the animal, whipped its haunches
with a leafy branch to hasten its progress. They carried
on their arms large wicker-baskets, out of which here
a chicken and there a duck thrust forth its head. The
women walked with a quicker, livelier step than their
husbands. Their spare, straight figures were wrapped in
a scanty little shawl, pinned over their flat bosoms, and
their heads were enveloped in a piece of white linen
tightly pressed on the hair and surmounted by a cap.

Then a wagon passed, its nag's jerky trot shaking up
and down two men seated side by side and a woman in
the bottom of the vehicle, the latter holding on to the
sides to lessen the stiff jolts.

The square of Goderville was filled with a milling
throng of human beings and animals. The horns of the
cattle, the rough-napped top-hats of the rich peasants,
and the headgear of the peasant women stood out in the
crowd. And the clamorous, shrill, shouting voices made
a continuous and savage din dominated now and again
by the robust lungs of some countryman's laugh, or the
long lowing of a cow tied to the wall of a house.

The scene smacked of the stable, the dairy and the
dung-heap, of hay and sweat, and gave forth that sharp,
unpleasant odor, human and animal, peculiar to the
people of the fields.

Maître Hauchecorne, of Bréauté, had just arrived at
Goderville. He was directing his steps toward the square,
when he perceived upon the ground a little piece of
string. Maître Hauchecorne, economical like a true
Norman, thought that everything useful ought to be

picked up, and he stooped painfully, for he suffered
from rheumatism. He took up the bit of string from the
ground and was beginning to roll it carefully when he
noticed Maître Malandain, the harness-maker, on the
threshold of his door, looking at him. They had once had
a quarrel on the subject of a halter, and they had remained on bad terms, being both good haters. Maître
Hauchecorne was seized with a sort of shame to be
seen thus by his enemy, picking a bit of string out of the
dirt. He hid his find quickly under his smock, and
slipped it into his trouser pocket; then he pretended
to be still looking on the ground for something which
he did not find, and he went towards the market, his
head thrust forward, bent double by his pain.

He was soon lost in the noisy and slowly moving
crowd, which was busy with interminable bargainings.
The peasants looked at cows, went away, came back,
perplexed, always in fear of being cheated, not daring
to decide, watching the vendor's eye, ever trying to find
the trick in the man and the flaw in the beast.

The women, having placed their great baskets at their
feet, had taken out the poultry, which lay upon the
ground, tied together by the feet, with terrified eyes
and scarlet crests.

They listened to offers, stated their prices with a dry
air and impassive face, or perhaps, suddenly deciding
on some proposed reduction, shouted to the customer
who was slowly going away: "All right, Maître Anthime,
I'll let you have it for that."

Then little by little the square was deserted, the
church bell rang out the hour of noon, and those who
lived too far away went to the different inns.

At Jourdain's the great room was full of people eating,
and the big yard was full of vehicles of all kinds, gigs,
wagons, nondescript carts, yellow with dirt, mended

and patched, some with their shafts rising to the sky like two arms, others with their shafts on the ground and their backs in the air.

Behind the diners seated at table, the immense fireplace, filled with bright flames, cast a lively heat on the backs of the row on the right. Three spits were turning on which were chickens, pigeons, and legs of mutton; and an appetizing odor of roast meat and gravy dripping over the nicely browned skin rose from the fireplace, lightening all hearts and making the mouth water.

All the aristocracy of the plough ate there, at Maître Jourdain's, tavern keeper and horse dealer, a clever fellow and well off.

The dishes were passed and emptied, as were the jugs of yellow cider. Everyone told his affairs, his purchases, and sales. They discussed the crops. The weather was favorable for the greens but rather damp for the wheat.

Suddenly the drum began to beat in the yard, before the house. Everybody rose, except a few indifferent persons, and ran to the door, or to the windows, their mouths still full, their napkins in their hands.

After the public crier had stopped beating his drum, he called in a jerky voice, speaking his phrases irregularly:

"It is hereby made known to the inhabitants of Goderville, and in general to all persons present at the market, that there was lost this morning, on the road to Benzeville, between nine and ten o'clock, a black leather pocketbook containing five hundred francs and some business papers. The finder is requested to return same to the Mayor's office or to Maître Fortuné Houlbrèque of Manneville. There will be twenty francs' reward."

Then the man went away. The heavy roll of the drum and the crier's voice were again heard at a distance.

Then they began to talk of this event discussing the chances that Maître Houlbrèque had of finding or not finding his pocketbook.

And the meal concluded. They were finishing their coffee when the chief of the gendarmes appeared upon the threshold.

He inquired:

"Is Maître Hauchecorne, of Bréauté, here?"

Maître Hauchecorne, seated at the other end of the table, replied:

"Here I am."

And the officer resumed:

"Maître Hauchecorne, will you have the goodness to accompany me to the Mayor's office? The Mayor would like to talk to you."

The peasant, surprised and disturbed, swallowed at a draught his tiny glass of brandy, rose, even more bent than in the morning, for the first steps after each rest were specially difficult, and set out, repeating: "Here I am, here I am."

The Mayor was waiting for him, seated in an armchair. He was the local lawyer, a stout, solemn man, fond of pompous phrases.

"Maître Hauchecorne," said he, "you were seen this morning picking up, on the road to Benzeville, the pocketbook lost by Maître Houlbrèque, of Manneville."

The countryman looked at the Mayor in astonishment, already terrified by this suspicion resting on him without his knowing why.

"Me? Me? I picked up the pocketbook?"

"Yes, you, yourself."

"On my word of honor, I never heard of it."

"But you were seen."

"I was seen, me? Who says he saw me?"

"Monsieur Malandain, the harness-maker."

The old man remembered, understood, and flushed with anger.

"Ah, he saw me, the clodhopper, he saw me pick up this string, here, Mayor." And rummaging in his pocket he drew out the little piece of string.

But the Mayor, incredulous, shook his head.

"You will not make me believe, Maître Hauchecorne, that Monsieur Malandain, who is a man we can believe, mistook this string for a pocketbook."

The peasant, furious, lifted his hand, spat at one side to attest his honor, repeating:

"It is nevertheless God's own truth, the sacred truth. I repeat it on my soul and my salvation."

The Mayor resumed:

"After picking up the object, you went on staring, looking a long while in the mud to see if any piece of money had fallen out."

The old fellow choked with indignation and fear.

"How anyone can tell—how anyone can tell—such lies to take away an honest man's reputation! How can anyone——"

There was no use in his protesting, nobody believed him. He was confronted with Monsieur Malandain, who repeated and maintained his affirmation. They abused each other for an hour. At his own request, Maître Hauchecorne was searched. Nothing was found on him.

Finally the Mayor, very much perplexed, discharged him with the warning that he would consult the Public Prosecutor and ask for further orders.

The news had spread. As he left the Mayor's office, the old man was surrounded and questioned with a serious or bantering curiosity, in which there was no indignation. He began to tell the story of the string. No one believed him. They laughed at him.

He went along, stopping his friends, beginning end
lessly his statement and his protestations, showing his
pockets turned inside out, to prove that he had nothing.

They said:

"Ah, you old rascal!"

And he grew angry, becoming exasperated, hot and
distressed at not being believed, not knowing what to do
and endlessly repeating himself.

Night came. He had to leave. He started on his way
with three neighbors to whom he pointed out the place
where he had picked up the bit of string; and all along
the road he spoke of his adventure.

In the evening he took a turn in the village of Bréauté,
in order to tell it to everybody. He only met with in-
credulity.

It made him ill all night.

The next day about one o'clock in the afternoon,
Marius Paumelle, a hired man in the employ of Maître
Breton, husbandman at Ymauville, returned the pocketbook and its contents to Maître Houlbrèque of Manneville.

This man claimed to have found the object in the
road; but not knowing how to read, he had carried it to
the house and given it to his employer.

The news spread through the neighborhood. Maître
Hauchecorne was informed of it. He immediately went
the circuit and began to recount his story completed by
the happy climax. He triumphed.

"What grieved me so much was not the thing itself,
as the lying. There is nothing so shameful as to be
placed under a cloud on account of a lie."

He talked of his adventure all day long, he told it on
the highway to people who were passing by, in the inn
to people who were drinking there, and to persons coming out of church the following Sunday. He stopped

strangers to tell them about it. He was calm now, and yet something disturbed him without his knowing exactly what it was. People seemed to wink at him while they listened. They did not seem convinced. He had the feeling that remarks were being made behind his back.

On Tuesday of the next week he went to the market at Goderville, urged solely by the necessity he felt of discussing the case.

Malandain, standing at his door, began to laugh on seeing him pass. Why?

He approached a farmer from Criquetot, who did not let him finish, and giving him a poke in the stomach said to his face:

"You clever rogue."

Then he turned his back on him.

Maître Hauchecorne was confused, why was he called a clever rogue?

When he was seated at the table, in Jourdain's tavern he commenced to explain "the affair."

A horse-dealer from Monvilliers called to him:

"Come, come, old sharper, that's an old trick; I know all about your piece of string!"

Hauchecorne stammered:

"But the pocketbook was found."

But the other man replied:

"That'll do to tell, pop. One man finds a thing, and another man brings it back. No one is any the wiser, so you get out of it."

The peasant stood choking. He understood. They accused him of having had the pocketbook returned by a confederate, by an accomplice.

He tried to protest. All the table began to laugh.

He could not finish his dinner and went away in the midst of jeers.

He went home ashamed and indignant, choking with

anger and confusion, the more dejected for the fact that he with his Norman cunning was capable of doing what they had accused him of, and even of boasting of it as a good trick. His innocence seemed to him, in a confused way, impossible to prove, for his sharpness was well known. And he was stricken to the heart by the injustice of the suspicion.

Then he began to recount the adventure again, enlarging his story every day, adding each time new reasons, more energetic protestations, more solemn oaths which he formulated and prepared in his hours of solitude, his whole mind given up to the story of the string. The more complicated his defense and the more subtle his argument, the less he was believed.

"Those are lying excuses," people said behind his back.

He felt it, ate his heart out over it, and wore himself out with useless efforts. He was visibly wasting away.

The wags now made him tell about the string to amuse them, as they make a soldier who has been on a campaign tell about his battles. His mind, seriously affected, began to weaken.

Towards the end of December he took to his bed.

He died early in January, and in the delirium of his death struggles he continued to protest his innocence, and to repeat his story:

"A piece of string, a piece of string—look—here it is."

IN PORT

Having left Havre on May 3, 1882, for a voyage in
Chinese waters, the three-masted sailing-ship *Notre-
Dames-des-Vents* entered Marseilles harbor on August 8, 1886, after a four years' voyage. She had discharged her original cargo in the Chinese port to which
she had been chartered, had there picked up a new
freight for Buenos Aires, and thence had shipped cargo
for Brazil.

Various other voyages, not to speak of damages, repairs, several months spent becalmed, storms that blew
her out of her course, and all the accidents, adventures
and misadventures of the sea, had detained this three-
masted Norman ship now returned to Marseilles with a
hold full of tin boxes containing American preserved
foods.

At the beginning of the voyage she had on board,
besides the captain and the mate, fourteen sailors, eight
Normans and six Bretons. At the end only five Bretons
and four Normans remained; the Breton had died at
sea; the four Normans, who had disappeared in various
circumstances, had been replaced by two Americans, a
Negro, and a Norwegian shanghaied one evening in a
Singapore den.

The great ship, sails furled, yards forming a cross
with the mast, drawn by a Marseilles tug that panted
along before her, rolled in a slight swell that died gently

away in the calm waters astern; she passed in front of
the Château d'If, then under all the gray rocks of the
roadstead over which the setting sun flung a veil of gold,
and entered the old harbor where, tied up side by side,
were gathered ships from all corners of the globe, huddled together, large and small, of all shapes and rig-
gings, like a fish-soup of ships in this too confined basin,
full of foul water, where the hulls grazed and rubbed
against each other, for all the world as if they were
pickled in salt-water liquor.

Notre-Dame-des-Vents took her place between an
Italian brig and an English schooner, which drew apart
to make way for their comrade; then, when all the
formalities of customs and harbor had been complied
with, the captain gave two-thirds of his crew shore leave
for the evening.

It was night. The lights of Marseilles were lit. In the
warmth of the summer evening, an odor of garlic-
flavored cooking hung over the noisy city, alive with the
sound of voices, rumblings, clatterings, all the gaiety of
the South.

As soon as they felt land under them, the ten men
who had been tossed for months on the sea, began to
walk very carefully, with hesitant steps, like creatures
strayed out of their element, unaccustomed to cities,
two by two in a procession.

They rolled along, taking their bearings, following
the scent down the by-streets that opened onto the harbor, their blood on fire with a hunger for love that had
grown stronger and stronger in their bodies throughout
their last sixty-six days at sea. The Normans marched
ahead, led by Célestin Duclos, a tall, shrewd, sturdy
young fellow, who captained the others whenever they
set foot on shore. He found out the best places, devised
ways and means to his liking, and refrained from risking

himself too readily in the brawls so common between sailors on shore. But when he did get involved in one, he was absolutely fearless.

After hesitating some little time between the obscure streets that ran down to the sea like sewers, from which rose a heavy smell, as it were the very breath of hovels, Célestin decided on a sort of winding passage where lighted lamps, bearing enormous numbers on their frosted colored glass, were hung out above the doors. Under the narrow arch of the doorways, women in aprons sat in cane-bottomed chairs, looking like servant-girls. They got up at their approach, took three steps to the edge of the stream that ran down the middle of the street and stood right across the path of the men who advanced slowly, singing and chuckling, excited already by the neighborhood of these prostitutes' cells.

Sometimes in the depths of a lobby a second door padded with brown leather opened abruptly, and behind it appeared a stout, half-naked woman, whose heavy thighs and plump arms were sharply outlined under a coarse, tight-fitting shift of white cotton. Her short skirt looked like a hooped girdle, and the soft flesh of her bosom, arms, and shoulders made a rosy patch against a bodice of black velvet edged with gold lace. She called to them from far off, "Are you coming in, dearies?" and sometimes came out herself to clutch one of them, pulling him towards her doorway with all her might, clinging to him like a spider dragging in a body bigger than itself. The man, excited by her touch, would resist feebly, and the others would stop to watch him, hesitating between their impulse to go in without further delay and their desire to make this appetizing stroll last a little longer. Then, after the woman had dragged the sailor to the threshold of her cell by main strength, and the whole company were about to plunge after him,

Célestin Duclos, who was a judge of such houses, would suddenly cry, "Don't go in there, Marchand, that's not the one we want."

Whereupon, obedient to this command, the man would disengage himself with violence, and the friends would fall again into line, pursued by the obscene abuse of the exasperated woman, while other women, all the way down the passage ahead of them, would come out of their doors, attracted by the noise, and pour out hoarse-voiced, enticing appeals. They went on their way, growing more and more excited, between the cajoling cries and seductive charms offered by the chorus of love's doorkeepers down the length of the street before them, and the vile curses flung after them by the chorus of despised and disappointed women behind. Now and then they met other companies of men, soldiers marching along with swords clattering against their legs, more sailors, a solitary citizen or so, a few shop assistants. Everywhere opened other narrow streets, starred with evil beacon-lights. They walked steadily through this labyrinth of hovels over the greasy cobbled streets oozing streams of foul water, between houses full of women's flesh.

At last Duclos made up his mind and, halting in front of a fairly decent-looking house, marshaled his company into it.

II

The entertainment lacked nothing! For four hours the ten sailors took their fill of love and wine. Six months' pay vanished.

They were installed lords of all they surveyed, in the big salon, staring with unfriendly eyes at the ordinary clients who sat at little tables in corners, where those of the women who were disengaged, dressed like over-grown babies or music-hall singers, ran to attend on them, and then sat down beside them.

Each man had on arrival selected his companion, whom he retained throughout the evening, for the lower orders are not promiscuous. Three tables had been dragged together, and after the first round of drinks, the procession, in two ranks and increased by as many women as there were sailors, re-formed on the staircase. The noise made by the four feet of each couple was heard for a time on the wooden steps, while this long file of lovers plunged through the narrow door that led to the bedrooms.

Then they came down again for more drinks; went up again, came down again.

Now, very nearly drunk, they began to bawl. Each man, with reddened eyes, his fancy on his knee, sang or shouted, hammering on the table with clenched fists, rolled the wine round his throat, giving full play to the beast in man. In the midst of them, Célestin Duclos, his arm round a tall red-cheeked wench who sat astride on his knee, gazed at her ardently. Not so drunk as the others—not that he had drunk any less—he could still think of more than the one thing, and more human than the rest, he tried to talk to her. His thoughts were a little elusive, slipping from his grasp, returning and disappearing before he could remember just what he had wanted to say.

He laughed, repeating:

"Then, then . . . you've been here a long time."

"Six months," replied the girl.

He appeared pleased with her, as if that were a proof of good conduct, and went on:

"Do you like this life?"

She hesitated, then spoke resignedly:

"You get along. It's no worse than anything else. Being a servant or walking the streets, they're both dirty jobs."

He seemed to approve this truth too.

"You're not from these parts?" said he.

She shook her head without speaking.

"Do you come from far?"

She nodded, still silent.

"Where from?"

She seemed to search her mind, trying to collect her memories, then she murmured:

"From Perpignan."

Again he showed great satisfaction, and said:

"That's good."

In her turn she asked him:

"You're a sailor, aren't you?"

"Yes."

"Have you come a long way?"

"Oh, yes! I've seen countries, ports, and all that."

"I suppose you've sailed round the world?"

"I dare say, more like twice than once."

Again she seemed to hesitate, searching in her mind for something forgotten, then, in a rather altered, grave voice, she said:

"You have come across a good many ships in your voyages?"

"I have that."

"Perhaps you've even come across *Notre-Dame-des-Vents?*"

He chuckled.

"No later than a week ago."

She turned pale, all the blood ebbing from her cheeks, and asked:

"Is that true, really true?"

"As true as I'm telling you."

"You're not telling me a lie?"

He lifted his hand.

"God's truth I'm not," said he.

"Then do you know whether Célestin Duclos is still with her?"

He was surprised, uneasy, and wanted to know more before replying.

"Do you know him?"

She became suspicious too.

"No, not me, it's some woman who knows him."

"One of the women here?"

"No, outside."

"In the street?"

"No."

"What woman?"

"Oh, just a woman, a woman like me."

"What's this woman want with him?"

"How should I know, what d'you think?"

They stared into each other's eyes, trying to read the thoughts behind, guessing that something serious was going to come of this.

He went on:

"Can I see this woman?"

"What would you say to her?"

"I'd say . . . I'd say . . . that I have seen Célestin Duclos."

"Is he all right?"

"As right as you or me, he's a lad."

She was silent again, collecting her thoughts, then, very slowly, asked:

"Where was she bound for, the *Notre-Dame-des-Vents?*"

"Well, to Marseilles."

She could not repress a start.

"Really?"

"Yes, really."

"Do you know Duclos?"

"Yes. I know him."

She hesitated again, then said softly:

"Good. That's good."

"What d'you want with him?"

"Listen, you can tell him . . . nothing!"

He continued to stare at her, more and more uneasy. He must know the whole story now.

"Do you know him then?"

"No," said she.

"Then what d'you want with him?"

She came to a sudden decision, got up, ran to the bar where the proprietress sat enthroned, seized a lemon, cut it open, pouring the juice into a glass, then filled up the glass with plain water and, bringing it to him, said:

"Drink this."

"Why?"

"To sober you up. After that I'll talk to you."

He drank obediently, wiped his lips with the back of his hand, and declared:

"That's all right, I'm listening to you."

"You must promise not to tell him that you have seen me, nor who told you what I am going to tell you. Swear it."

He lifted his hand, with a knowing air.

"I swear it."

"On the good God himself?"

"Yes, on the good God."

"Well, you're to tell him that his father is dead, that his mother is dead, that his brother is dead, all the three of them in the same month, of typhoid fever, in January 1883, three and a half years ago."

And now it was he who felt the blood rush through

his body, and for some moments he sat there, so overcome that he could find nothing to say in reply; then he began to have doubts and asked:

"Are you sure?"

"I'm quite sure."

"Who told it to you?"

She put her hands on his shoulders and, peering into his eyes, said:

"You swear you won't give me away?"

"I swear it."

"I'm his sister."

Her name broke involuntarily from his mouth:

"Françoise?"

She stared at him again fixedly, then, overwhelmed by a crazy fear, by a profound feeling of horror, murmured under her breath, against his mouth:

"Oh, oh, is it you, Célestin?"

They sat rigid, eyes staring into eyes.

Round them, the sailors went on shouting. The noise of glasses, fists, and heels beating in tune to the choruses, and the shrill cries of the women mingled with the uproarious songs.

He felt her against him, held close to him, warm and terrified, his sister! Then, in a whisper, afraid lest someone overhear him, so low that she herself could hardly hear:

"My God, I've done a fine thing!"

Her eyes filled with tears in an instant, and she stammered:

"It's not my fault, is it?"

But he said abruptly:

"So they're dead?"

"Yes, they're dead."

"Dad, and mother, and my brother?"

"All three in the same month, as I've just told you. I

was left alone, with nothing but what I stood up in, seeing that I owed money to the chemist and the doctor and for burying the three bodies, which I paid off with the furniture.

"After that I went as servant to old Cacheux, you know him, the cripple. I was just exactly fifteen then, seeing that you went away when I was not quite fourteen. I got into trouble with him. You're a fool when you're young. Then I went as housemaid to a solicitor; he seduced me too and set me up in a room in Havre. It wasn't long before he stopped coming; I spent three days without food and then, since I couldn't get any work, I went into a house, like many another. I've seen the world too, I have, and a dirty world at that! Rouen, Evreux, Lille, Bordeaux, Perpignan, Nice, and now here I am at Marseilles!"

Tears poured out of her eyes and her nose, wetting her cheeks, and ran down into her mouth.

She went on:

"I thought you were dead too, my poor Célestin."

He said:

"I would never have known you again, you were so little then, and now you're so big, but how was it you didn't recognize me?"

She made a despairing gesture.

"I see so many men that they all look alike to me."

He was still staring into her eyes in the grip of a confused emotion, an emotion so overwhelming that he wanted to cry like a beaten child. He still held her in his arms, sitting astride his legs, his hands spread out on the girl's back, and now by dint of staring at her, he recognized her at last, the little sister left in the country with the three she had watched die while he tossed at sea.

All at once he took her new-found face in his great sailor's paws and began to embrace her as a man embraces his flesh and blood. Then sobs, a man's terrible sobs, long-drawn surging cries, rose in his throat like the hiccups of a drunken man.

He stammered:

"To see you, to see you again, Françoise, my little Françoise. . . ."

Suddenly he leaped to his feet and began to swear in a dreadful voice, bringing his fist down on the table with such violence that the overturned glasses were shattered. He took three steps, staggered, flung out his arms and fell face downwards. He rolled on the floor, shouting, beating the ground with arms and legs, and uttering groans like the death-rattle of a man in agony.

The sailors looked at him and laughed.

"He's kind of drunk," said one.

"Put him to bed," said another; "if he goes out they'll stick him in jail."

Then, as he had money in his pockets, the proprietress offered a bed, and the other sailors, themselves so drunk that they couldn't stand, hoisted him up the narrow staircase to the bedroom of the woman who had so recently received him there, and who sat on a chair at the foot of that guilty couch, weeping over him, until morning.

THE BOURGEOISIE

A MILLION

It was a modest clerk's household. The husband, who was employed in a Government department, was conventional and painstaking, and he was always very careful in the discharge of his duties. His name was Léopold Bonnin. He was a mediocre young man who held the right opinions about everything. He had been brought up a Christian, but he was inclined to be less religious since the country had begun to move in the direction of the separation of Church and State. He would say in loud tones at the office, "I am a believer, a true believer, but I believe in God, not in the clergy." His greatest claim was that he was an honest man. He would strike his chest as he said so. And he was an honest man, in the most humdrum sense of the word. He arrived punctually at his office and left as punctually. He never idled and was always very straight in "money matters." He had married the daughter of one of his poor colleagues. His wife's aunt, however, was worth a million francs; a

123

rich man had married her for love. She had no children, which was a deep disappointment for her, and, consequently, she had no one to whom she could leave her money except her niece. This legacy was the constant preoccupation of the family. It haunted the house, and even the office. It was known that "the Bonnins would come in for a million."

The young couple were also childless, a fact which did not distress them in the least, as they were perfectly satisfied with their humdrum, narrow life. They were thrifty people, and their home was tidy and well kept. They were both placid and moderate in all things, and they firmly believed that a child would upset their lives and interfere with their habits.

They would not have gone out of the way to avoid having children; but, since Heaven had not blessed them in that respect, they thought it was no doubt for the best.

The wealthy aunt, however, was not to be consoled and was profuse with practical advice. Years ago, she had vainly tried a number of methods recommended by clairvoyants and her women friends, and since she had reached the age where all thought of offspring had to be abandoned, she had heard of many more, which she supposed to be unfailing, and which she persisted in revealing to her niece. Every now and then she would inquire, "Well, have you tried what I told you about the other day?"

Finally she died. The young people experienced a delighted relief which they sought to conceal from themselves as well as from the outside world. Often one's conscience is garbed in black while the soul sings with joy.

They were notified that a will had been deposited with a lawyer, and they went to the latter's office immediately after leaving the church.

The aunt, faithful to her lifelong idea, had bequeathed her fortune to their first-born child, with the provision that after a child was born, the income was to go to the parents until their decease. Should the young couple have no offspring within three years, the fortune was left to the poor and needy.

They were completely overwhelmed. The husband collapsed and stayed away from the office for a week. When he recovered, he resolved with sudden energy to become a parent.

He persisted in his endeavors for six months, until he was but the shadow of his former self. He remembered all the hints his aunt had given and put them into practice conscientiously, but without results. His desperate determination lent him a factitious strength, which, however, proved almost fatal.

He became hopelessly anemic. His physician threatened him with tuberculosis, and terrified him to such an extent that he forthwith resumed his peaceful habits, even more peaceful than before, and began a restorative treatment.

Broad rumors had begun to float around the office. All the clerks had heard about the disappointing will, and they made much fun over what they termed the "million franc deal."

Some ventured to give Bonnin facetious advice; while others dared to offer themselves for the accomplishment of the distressing clause. One tall fellow, especially, who had the reputation of being quite a lad and whose many affairs were notorious throughout the office, teased him constantly with veiled allusions, broad hints and the boast that he, Morel, could make him, Bonnin, inherit in about twenty minutes.

However, one day, Léopold Bonnin became suddenly infuriated, and jumping out of his chair, his quill behind his ear, he shouted, "Sir, you are a cad; if I did not respect myself, I would spit in your face."

Seconds were dispatched to the antagonists, and for days the whole department was in an uproar. They were to be found everywhere, in and out of the offices, meeting in the halls to discuss some important point and to exchange their views of the affair. Finally a document was drawn up by the four delegates and accepted by the interested parties, who gravely shook hands and mumbled a few words of apology in the presence of the departmental chief.

During the month that followed, the two men bowed ceremoniously and with affected courtesy, as became adversaries who had met on the field of honor. But one day, they happened to collide against each other in the hall, outside the office, whereupon Monsieur Bonnin inquired with dignity, "I trust I did not hurt you?" And Monsieur Morel replied, "Not in the least."

After that encounter, they saw fit to speak a few words whenever they met. And little by little they became more friendly, appreciated one another and grew to be inseparable.

But Léopold was unhappy. His wife kept taunting him with allusions, torturing him with thinly veiled sarcasm.

And the days were flitting by. A year had already elapsed since the aunt's demise. The inheritance seemed lost to them.

When sitting down to dinner Madame Bonnin would remark: "We have not very much to eat; it would be different if we were well off."

Or, when Léopold was ready to start for the office, his wife would hand him his walking-stick and observe, "If we had an income of fifty thousand francs, you would not have to kill yourself working, you poor quill-driver."

When Madame Bonnin went out on a rainy day, she would invariably murmur, "If we had a carriage, I should not be compelled to ruin my clothes on a day like this."

In fact, at all times, she seemed to blame her husband, rendering him alone responsible for the state of affairs and the loss of the fortune.

Finally, growing desperate, he took her to a well-known physician, who, after a lengthy consultation, expressed no opinion and declared he could discover nothing unusual; that similar cases were of frequent occurrence; that it was the same with bodies as with minds; that, after having seen so many couples separated through incompatibility of temper, it was not surprising to find some who were childless because of physical incompatibility. The consultation cost forty francs.

A year went by, and war was declared between the pair, incessant, bitter war, almost ferocious hatred. Madame Bonnin never stopped saying over and over again, "Isn't it dreadful to lose a fortune because one happens to have married a fool!" or "To think that if I had married another man, today I would have an income of forty thousand francs!" or again, "Some people are always in the way. They spoil everything."

In the evening, after dinner, the tension became well-nigh insufferable. One night, fearing a terrible scene, and not knowing how to ward it off, Léopold brought his friend, Frédéric Morel, with whom he had almost had a duel, home with him. Soon Morel became the friend of the household, the counselor of husband and wife.

The expiration of the delay stipulated in the will was

drawing near; only six months more and the fortune would go to the poor and needy. Little by little Léopold's attitude toward his wife changed. He, too, became aggressive, taunting, would make obscure insinuations, mentioning in a mysterious way wives of clerks who had built up their husbands' careers.

Every little while he would bring up some story of promotion that had fallen to the luck of some obscure clerk. "Little Ravinot, who was only a temporary clerk, five years ago, has been made assistant chief clerk." Then Madame Bonnin would reply, "You're certainly not the man to accomplish anything like that."

Léopold would shrug his shoulders.

"As if he did more than anyone else! He has a bright wife, that is all. She captivated the head of the department and now gets everything she wants. In this life we have to look out that we are not fooled by circumstances."

What did he really mean? What did she infer? What occurred? Each of them had a calendar on which the days which separated them from the fatal term were marked; and every week they were overcome by a sort of madness, a desperate rage, a wild exasperation, so that they felt capable of committing a crime if necessary.

And then one morning Madame Bonnin, with shining eyes and a radiant face, laid her hands on her husband's shoulders, looked at him intently, joyfully, and whispered, "I believe that I am pregnant." He experienced such a shock that he almost collapsed; and suddenly clasping his wife in his arms, he drew her down on his knee, kissed her like a beloved child, and, overwhelmed by emotion, sobbed aloud.

Two months later, doubt was no longer possible. He went with her to a physician and had the latter make out a certificate which he handed to the executor of the will. The lawyer stated that, inasmuch as the child existed, whether born or unborn, he could do nothing but bow to circumstances, and would postpone the execution of the will until the birth of the heir.

A boy was born, whom they christened Dieudonné,[1] in remembrance of the practice in royal households.

They were very rich.

One evening, when M. Bonnin came home—his friend Frédéric Morel was to dine with them—his wife remarked casually, "I have just requested our friend Frédéric never to enter this house again. He insulted me." Léopold looked at her for a second with a light of gratitude in his eyes, and then he opened his arms; she flew to him and they kissed each other tenderly, like the good, united, upright little couple that they were.

And it is worth while to hear Madame Bonnin talk about women who have transgressed for love, and those whom a great passion has led to adultery

THE CHAIR MENDER

THE DINNER given by the Marquis de Bertrans to celebrate the opening of the hunting season was drawing to a close. Eleven sportsmen, eight young women, and the district doctor were seated round the large, well-lit table covered with fruits and flowers.

---

[1] Theodore, Gift of God.

The talk fell on love, and a great discussion arose, the eternal discussion, whether one could love truly but once, or many times. They cited examples of people who had never had but one serious love; they also cited other examples of people who had loved often, violently. The men maintained in general that passion, like a malady, could strike the same person many times, and strike to kill if an obstacle appeared in its path. Although the point of view was not contestable, the women, whose opinion was founded upon literature rather than observation, affirmed that love, true love, great love, could come only once to a mortal; that it was like a thunderbolt, this love, and that a heart once touched by it remained ever after so vacant, ravaged, and burned out that no other powerful sentiment, not even a dream, could again take root.

The Marquis, having loved often, contested this belief in lively fashion:

"I tell you that a person can love many times with all his strength and all his soul. You cite people who have killed themselves for love as proof of the impossibility of a second passion. I answer that if they had not been stupid enough to commit suicide, thus eliminating all chance of another fall, they would have been healed; and they would have recommenced, again and again, until their natural death. Lovers are like drunkards— once a drunkard always a drunkard, once a lover, always a lover. It is simply a matter of temperament."

They chose the doctor as arbitrator, an old Paris physician retired to the country, and begged him to give his opinion.

To tell the truth, he had none. As the Marquis had said, it was an affair of temperament.

"For my part," the doctor said, "I have known of one

passion which lasted fifty-five years without a day of respite, and which was ended only by death."

The Marquis clapped his hands.

"That is beautiful," said a lady. "And what a dream, to be loved like that! What happiness to live fifty-five years enveloped in a deep, living affection! How happy, how pleased with life, the man must be who was adored like that!"

The doctor smiled:

"Madame," said he, "you are right on one point. The object of that love was a man. You know him; it is Chouquet, the village chemist. And as for the woman, you knew her too; it is the old itinerant chair mender, for she used to come every year to your house. But how can I make you understand the whole story?"

The enthusiasm of the women fell. A look of disgust came into their faces—as if love could only overwhelm those fine and distinguished creatures who were worthy of the interest of fashionable people.

The doctor continued:

"I was called, three months ago, to the bedside of this old woman. She was dying. She had driven into our town in the old carriage that served her for a house, drawn by the nag that you have often seen, and accompanied by her two great black dogs, her friends and guard. The priest was already there. She made us the executors of her will, and in order to explain her will, she told us the story of her life. I have never heard anything more singular or more moving.

"Her father wove cane seats and so did her mother, going from town to town. She had never known a home on earth. As a little girl, she went around ragged, covered with vermin, and dirty. They would stop beside the road at the entrance to a town, unharness the horse and let him browse; the dog would go to sleep with his nose on his paws; the child would play in the grass while the father and mother, under the shade of the elms bordering the roadside, would mend all the old chairs in the neighborhood.

"No one ever talked in this itinerant dwelling. After the necessary words had been spoken to decide who should make the tour of the houses and call out the usual, 'Chairs to mend!' they would sit down in silence to plait the straw, face to face or side by side.

"When the child strayed too far away or struck up an acquaintance with some village urchin, the angry voice of the father would call out: 'You come back here, you brat!' This was as much tenderness as she ever knew.

"When she grew bigger they sent her round to collect the worn-out chairs to be mended. Thus she would make acquaintances from place to place among the street children. Then it would be the parents of her new friends who would call out harshly to their children, 'Will you come here, you scamp! Let me catch you talking to that barefoot again!'

"Often the boys would throw stones at her. When ladies gave her a few pence she saved them carefully.

"One day—she was then eleven years old—as they were passing through this place, she met the little Chouquet boy behind the cemetery, weeping because some comrade had stolen two sous from him. The tears of this little well-to-do citizen, one of those fortunate ones who in her queer noddle she had thought always content and gay, quite upset her. She went up to him, and when she learned the cause of his trouble, she poured into his hands all her savings, seven sous, which he took quite as a matter of course, drying his tears. Then, mad with joy, she had the audacity to kiss him.

Since he was busy counting the money, he allowed her to do it. Seeing that she was not repulsed or beaten, she did the same thing again. She embraced him with all her strength and all her heart. Then she ran away.

"What could have taken place in her wretched little head after that? Did she attach herself to this little boy because she had sacrificed for him her beggar's fortune, or because it was to him that she had given her first tender kiss? The mystery is as great for the lowly as for the exalted.

"For months she dreamed of that cemetery and that boy. In the hope of seeing him again, she began to rob her parents, keeping back a sou here and there, either from a chair seat or upon the provisions which she was sent to buy.

"When she returned here she had two francs in her pocket, but she saw the chemist's son, very clean behind the big colored bottles of his father's shop, only through the window, between a red decanter and a tapeworm. She loved him there still more, charmed, aroused to ecstasy by this glory of colored water, this apotheosis of shining crystal.

"This picture became an ineffaceable memory, and when, the following year, she saw him playing marbles near the school with his comrades, she threw herself upon him, seized him in her arms, and kissed him with such violence that he began to howl with fear. Then, in order to appease him, she gave him all her money— three francs and twenty centimes, a real treasure which he looked at with bulging eyes.

"He took the money and let her caress him as much as she wished.

"During the next four years she turned over to him all her little savings, which he pocketed with a clear conscience, in exchange for kisses. Once it was thirty sous, now and then forty, and once only twelve—and she wept with grief and humiliation at this, but it had been a bad year. The last time there was a five-franc piece, a great round coin that made him laugh with content.

"She thought of nothing but him; and he now looked for her return with a certain impatience, running to meet her, which made the heart of the girl leap with joy.

"Then he disappeared. His family had sent him away to school, as she found out by skillful questioning. Thereupon she used her wits to change her parents' itinerary and make them pass through here during the holidays. She succeeded, but only after two years' guile. Then, as she had been two years without seeing him, she scarcely recognized him, so much was he changed; he was so tall and handsome in his coat with the brass buttons, so imposing. He pretended not to recognize her and passed haughtily by.

"She wept over it for two days, and after that she suffered endlessly.

"Each year she came back, passing him without daring to greet him, and without his deigning to raise his eyes to her. She loved him passionately. She said to me, 'Doctor, he is the only man I have seen on earth; I have never known that other men existed.'

"Her parents died. She continued their trade, but took with her two dogs instead of one, two terrible dogs that no one would dare challenge.

"One day on entering this town, where her heart still lay, she saw a young woman coming out of the Chouquet shop on the arm of her well-beloved. It was his wife. He was married.

"That evening she threw herself into the pond on the Town Hall square. A drunken man fished her out and took her to the pharmacy. Chouquet, came down in his dressing-gown, to revive her; and without appearing to recognize her, as he loosened her clothing and rubbed her skin, he said in a hard voice, 'Why, you are out of your head! You must not do such foolish things.'

"That was enough to cure her. He had spoken to her! She was happy for a long time.

"He wanted no remuneration for his services, although she insisted upon paying him. And all her life was spent like this. She wove and mended chair bottoms, and thought of Chouquet. Every year she saw him behind his large windows. She adopted the pretext of trading at his shop. In this way she could see him, speak to him, and still give him a little money.

"As I told you in the beginning, she died this spring. After having told me her history, she begged me to give to him she had so patiently loved all the savings of her life, because she had worked only for him, she said, fasting even, in order to save, and to be sure that he would think of her at least once after she was dead.

"She then gave me two thousand three hundred and twenty-seven francs. I allowed the priest twenty-seven for burial, and carried off the rest when she had drawn her last breath.

"Next day, I took myself to the house of the Chouquets. They had just finished breakfast, sitting opposite each other, fat and red, smelling of their pharmaceutical products, important and satisfied.

"They asked me to sit down; they offered me a glass of kirsch which I accepted; then I commenced my discourse in an emotional voice, persuaded that they were going to weep.

"When Chouquet got it into his head that this itinerant chair mender, this vagrant, had been in love with him, he bounced with indignation, as if she had robbed him of his reputation, of the esteem of honest people, of his honor, of something rare that was dearer to him than life.

"His wife, as exasperated as he, kept repeating, 'The beggar! The beggar! The beggar!' unable to find any other word.

"He got up and walked around the table with long strides, his skullcap tipped over his ear. He muttered, 'Think of it, Doctor! This is a horrible thing to happen to a man! What is to be done? Oh! if I had known this while she was alive I would have had her arrested and shut up in prison. And she wouldn't have got out, I can tell you!'

"I was stupefied by this result of my pious errand. I neither knew what to say nor what to do. But I had to go on with my mission. I said, 'She instructed me to give you all her savings, which amount to two thousand three hundred francs. As what I have told you seems to be so very disagreeable to you, perhaps it would be better that I turn this money over to the poor.'

"They stared at me, the man and the woman, too stunned to move. I drew the money from my pocket, miserable money from all countries, and of every denomination, gold and copper mixed. Then I asked, 'What have you decided?'

"Madame Chouquet spoke first. She said, 'Since it was the woman's dying wish—it seems to me that it would be difficult to refuse it.'

"The husband, somewhat confused, answered, 'We could always do something with that money for our children.'

"I remarked dryly, 'As you wish.'

"He continued, 'Yes, give it to us, since she told you to do so. We can always find a way to use it in some good cause.'

"I put down the money, bowed, and went out.

"Next day Chouquet came to me and said brusquely, 'She must have left a wagon here, that—that woman. What are you going to do with the wagon?'

" 'Nothing,' said I, 'take it if you wish.'

" 'Exactly. Just what I want. I'll make a shed of it for my kitchen-garden.'

"He was going, but I recalled him. 'She also left an old horse and her two dogs. Do you want them?'

"He stopped, surprised, 'Oh! no,' he answered, 'what could I do with them? Dispose of them as you wish.'

"Then he laughed and held out his hand, which I shook. What else could I do? In the country it will not do for the doctor and the chemist to be enemies.

"I have kept the dogs. The priest, who has a large yard, took the horse. The wagon serves Chouquet as a shed, and he has bought five railway shares with the money.

"This is the only profound love that I have met with in my life."

The doctor was silent. The Marquise, tears in her eyes, sighed, "You can't get away from it; it is only women who know how to love."

AN ADVENTURE IN PARIS

Is there any feeling in a woman stronger than curiosity? Fancy seeing, knowing, touching what one has dreamed about! What would a woman not do for that?

Once a woman's eager curiosity is aroused, she will be guilty of any folly, commit any imprudence, venture upon anything, and recoil from nothing. I speak of women who are really women, who are endowed with that triple-bottomed disposition, which appears to be reasonable and cool on the surface, but whose three secret compartments are filled as follows: The first, with female uneasiness, which is always in a state of fluttering; the next, with sly dodges always brought into play under color of complete sincerity; the sophistical and formidable wiles of seemingly straightforward women; and the last, with all those charming, improper acts, that delightful deceit, exquisite perfidy, and all those wayward qualities that drive stupidly credulous lovers to suicide, but delight other men.

The woman whose adventure I am about to relate was a little person from the provinces, who had been insipidly respectable till the moment when my story begins. Her life, which was on the surface so calm, was spent at home, with a busy husband and two children, whom she brought up in the fashion of an irreproachable mother. But her heart beat with unsatisfied curiosity and with longing for the unknown. She was continually thinking of Paris, and read the fashionable papers eagerly. The accounts of parties, of dresses, and various entertainments, excited her longing; but, above all, she was strangely agitated by those paragraphs which were full of double meaning, by those veils half raised by clever phrases which gave her a glimpse of culpable and ravishing delights. From her home in the provinces she saw in Paris an apotheosis of magnificent and corrupt luxury.

During the long nights, when she dreamed, lulled by the rhythmical snores of a husband who lay sleeping on his back by her side with a silk handkerchief tied round his head, she saw in her sleep those well-known men whose names appeared regularly on the front page of the newspapers like stars in the dark sky. She pictured to herself their lives—continual excitement, constant debauchery, orgies such as were practiced in ancient Rome, horribly voluptuous and with refinements of sensuality so complicated that she could not even imagine them.

The boulevards seemed to her a kind of abyss of human passions, and she did not doubt that the houses that lined them concealed mysteries of prodigious love. But she felt that she was growing old without having known life, except in those recurrent repellently monotonous, everyday occupations which constitute the happiness of the home. She was still pretty, for she was well preserved by a tranquil existence, like winter fruit in a cool cupboard; but she was consumed, agitated, and upset by her secret longings. She used to ask herself if she was meant to die without having experienced any of those damning, intoxicating joys, without having plunged once, just once, into that flood of Parisian voluptuousness.

By dint of much perseverance, she paved the way for a journey to Paris, found a pretext, got some relatives to invite her, and as her husband could not go with her, she went alone. As soon as she arrived, she invented a reason for remaining for some days, or rather for some nights, if necessary. She told him that she had met some friends who lived a little way out of town.

And then she set out on a voyage of discovery. She went up and down the boulevards, without seeing anything except roving and licensed vice. She looked into the large cafés, and read the Agony Column of the *Figaro*, which every morning seemed to her like a tocsin, a summons to love. But nothing put her on the

track of those orgies of actors and actresses; nothing
revealed to her those temples of debauchery which
opened, she imagined, at some magic word, like the
cave of Ali Baba or the catacombs of Rome, where the
mysteries of a persecuted religion were secretly celebrated.

Her relatives, who were quite middle-class people,
could not introduce her to any of those well-known
men of whose names her head was full; and in despair
she was thinking of returning, when chance came to
her aid. One day, as she was going along the Rue de la
Chaussée d'Antin, she stopped to look into a shop full
of those colored Japanese knickknacks which attract the
eye by their color. She was gazing at the grotesque
little ivories, the tall vases of flaming enamel, and the
curious bronzes, when she heard the shopkeeper inside
dilating, with many bows, on the value of an enormous,
pot-bellied, comical figure—which was unique, he said
—to a little, bald-headed, gray-bearded man.

At every moment, the shopkeeper repeated his customer's name, which was a celebrated one, in a voice
like a trumpet. The other customers, young women and
well-dressed gentlemen, gave a swift and furtive but
respectful glance at the celebrated writer, who was
looking admiringly at the china figure. Man and figure
were equally ugly, as ugly as two brothers who had
sprung from the same ugly mother.

"To you the price will be a thousand francs, Monsieur Varin, and that is exactly what it cost me. I should
ask anybody else fifteen hundred, but I think a great
deal of my literary and artistic customers, and have
special prices for them. They all come to me, Monsieur
Varin. Yesterday, Monsieur Busnach bought a large,
antique goblet from me, and the other day I sold two
candelabra like this (aren't they beautiful?) to Mon-

sieur Alexandre Dumas. If Monsieur Zola were to see that Japanese figure he would buy it immediately, Monsieur Varin."

The author hesitated in perplexity. He wanted the figure, but the price was above him, and he thought no more about being stared at than if he had been alone in the desert. She came in trembling, her eyes fixed shamelessly upon him, and she did not even ask herself whether he was good-looking, elegant, or young. It was Jean Varin himself, Jean Varin! After a long struggle and painful hesitation, he put the figure down onto the table.

"No, it is too expensive," he said.

The shopkeeper's eloquence redoubled. "Oh! Monsieur Varin, too expensive? It is worth two thousand francs, if it is worth a sou."

But the man of letters replied sadly, still looking at the figure with the enameled eyes, "I do not say it is not: but it is too expensive for me."

And thereupon, she, seized by a kind of mad audacity, came forward and said, "What will you charge me for the figure?"

The shopkeeper, in surprise, replied, "Fifteen hundred francs, Madame."

"I will take it."

The writer, who had not even noticed her till that moment, turned round suddenly. He looked her over from head to foot, with half-closed eyes, observantly, taking in the details like a connoisseur. She was charming, suddenly animated by the flame which had hitherto been dormant in her. And then, a woman who gives fifteen hundred francs for a knickknack is not to be met with every day.

She was overcome by a feeling of delightful delicacy, and turning to him, she said in a trembling voice:

"Excuse me, Sir; no doubt I have been rather hasty. You have probably not made up your mind."

He, however, bowed and said, "Indeed I had, Madame."

And she, filled with emotion, continued, "Well, if either today, or at any other time, you change your mind, you may have this Japanese figure. I bought it only because you seemed to like it."

He was visibly flattered, and smiled. "I should like to find out how you know who I am?" he said.

Then she told him how she admired him, and became quite eloquent as she quoted his works, and while they were talking, he rested his arms on a table and fixed his bright eyes upon her, trying to make out who and what she really was. But the shopkeeper, who was pleased to have that living puff of his goods, called out, from the other end of the shop, "Just look at this, Monsieur Varin; is it not beautiful?"

And then everyone looked round, and she almost trembled with pleasure at being seen talking so intimately with such a well-known man.

At last, however, intoxicated, as it were, by her feelings, she grew bold, like a general who is about to order an assault.

"Sir," she said, "will you do me a great, a very great pleasure? Will you allow me to offer you this comic Japanese figure, as a souvenir from a woman who admires you passionately, and whom you have seen for ten minutes."

He refused. She persisted. Still he resisted her offer, very much amused, and laughing heartily. But that only made her more obstinate, and she said, "Very well, then, I shall take it to your house immediately; where do you live?"

He refused to give her his address, but she got it

from the shopkeeper, and when she had paid for her purchase, she ran out to take a cab. The writer went after her, not wishing to accept a present from a person he did not know. He reached her just as she was getting into the cab. Getting in after her, he almost fell on top of her, as the cab gave a jolt. Then he sat down by her side, feeling very much annoyed.

It was no good for him to argue and to beg; she showed herself intractable, and when they got to the door, she stated her conditions, "I will undertake not to leave this with you," she said, "if you will promise to do all I want today." And the whole affair seemed so amusing to him that he agreed.

"What do you generally do at this time?" she asked him; and after hesitating for a few moments, he replied, "I generally go for a walk."

"Very well, then, we will go to the Bois de Boulogne!" she said, in a resolute voice, and they started.

He was obliged to tell her the names of all the well-known women they crossed, pure or impure, with every detail about them—their mode of life, their habits, their homes, and their vices; and when it was getting dusk, she said to him, "What do you do every day at this time?"

"I have some absinthe," he replied with a laugh.

"Very well, then," she went on seriously; "let us go and have some absinthe."

They went into a large café on the boulevard which he frequented, and where he met some of his colleagues, whom he introduced to her. She was half beside herself with pleasure, and kept saying to herself, "At last! At last!"

But time went on, and she asked, "Is it your dinner time?" To which he replied, "Yes."

"Then, let us go and have dinner."

When they left Bignon's after dinner, she wanted to know what he did in the evening, and looking at her fixedly, he replied, "That depends; sometimes I go to the theater."

"Very well, then, let us go to the theater."

They went to the Vaudeville with a pass, thanks to him, and, to her great pride, the whole house saw her sitting by his side in the stalls.

When the play was over, he gallantly kissed her hand, and said, "It only remains for me to thank you for this delightful day."

But she interrupted him, "What do you do at this time, every night?"

"Why—why—I go home."

She began to laugh, a little tremulous laugh: "Very well, let us go to your rooms."

They did not say anything more. She shivered occasionally from head to foot, feeling inclined to stay, and inclined to run away, but with a fixed determination, after all, to see it out to the end. She was so excited that she had to hold on to the banister as she went upstairs, and he went on ahead of her, with a lighted match in his hand.

As soon as they were in the flat, she undressed quickly and retired without saying a word. Then she waited for him, cowering against the wall. But she was as simple as it was possible for a provincial lawyer's wife to be, and he was more exacting than a pasha with thirty wives, so that they did not really get on at all.

At last, however, he went to sleep. The night passed, its silence disturbed only by the tic-toc of the clock, while she, lying motionless, thought of her conjugal nights. By the light of a Chinese lantern, she lay nearly heartbroken and stared at the little fat man lying on his back, his round stomach puffing out the bedclothes

like a balloon filled with gas. He snored with the noise of
a wheezy organ pipe, with prolonged snorts and comic
chokings. His few hairs profited by his sleep to stand
up in a very strange way, as if they were tired of
having been glued for so long to that pate whose bare-
ness they were trying to cover. And a thin stream of
saliva trickled from the corner of his half-opened mouth.

At last daylight appeared through the drawn blinds.
She got up and dressed without making any noise.
Opening the door, she made the lock creak, and he
woke up and rubbed his eyes. He was some moments
coming to himself, and then, when he remembered
what had happened, he said:

"What! Going already?"

She remained standing, in some confusion, and then
said, in a hesitant voice:

"Yes, of course; it is morning."

Then he sat up, and said, "Look here, I have something to ask you, in my turn." And as she did not reply,
he went on, "You have astonished me most confoundedly since yesterday. Be frank, and tell me why you did
it all, for upon my word I cannot understand it in the
least."

She went over to him, blushing as if she had been a
virgin, and said, "I wanted to know—what—what vice
—really was, and—well—well, it is not at all funny."

And she ran out of the room and down the stairs
into the street.

The street-cleaners were already at work, sweeping
the road, sending their brushes along the gutters, bringing together the rubbish in neat little heaps. With
movements as regular as the motion of mowers in a
meadow, they swept the refuse before them in broad
semi-circular strokes. She met them in every street, like
dancing puppets, walking automatically with a swaying

motion, and it seemed to her as if something had been swept out of her; as if her over-excited dreams had been brushed into the gutter, or down into the sewers. So she went home, out of breath and very cold, and all that she could remember was the sensation of the motion of those brooms sweeping the streets of Paris in the early morning.

When she got to her room, she threw herself onto her bed and cried.

THE LITTLE FELLOW

MONSIEUR LEMONNIER had remained a widower with one child. He had loved his wife madly, with a noble and tender love that never failed, throughout the whole of their life together. He was a good, honest fellow, simple, very simple in fact, free from selfishness and malice.

Having fallen in love with a poor neighbor, he asked for her hand and married her. He was in a fairly prosperous drapery business, was making quite a good amount of money, and did not for one moment imagine that the girl might not have accepted him for himself alone.

At all events she made him happy. He had no eyes for anybody or anything but her, thought only of her, and looked at her continually in an abandon of adoration. During meals he would commit a thousand blunders rather than look away from the beloved face; he would pour the wine into his plate and the water into the salt-cellar, and then would burst out laughing like a child, declaring:

"There, you see I love you too much; it makes me do such a lot of silly things."

And she would smile with an air of calm resignation, and then would turn away her eyes, as though embarrassed by her husband's worship, and would try to make him talk, to chat on any subject; but he would reach across the table, take her hand, and, holding it in his, would murmur:

"My little Jeanne, my dear little Jeanne."

She would end by growing vexed and exclaiming:

"Oh, do be reasonable; get on with your dinner, and let me get on with mine!"

He would utter a sigh and break off a mouthful of bread, which he would proceed slowly to munch.

For five years they had no children. Then suddenly she found herself with child. They were deliriously happy. He would never leave her during the whole of her pregnancy; to such an extent, that her maid, an old nurse who had brought her up and was given to speaking her mind to them, would sometimes thrust him out of the house and lock the door, so as to force him to take the air.

He had formed an intimate friendship with a young man who had known his wife since her childhood, and who was junior chief clerk at the Prefecture. Monsieur Duretour dined three times a week at the Lemonniers, brought flowers for Madame and sometimes took a box at the theater; and often, during dessert, the kind, affectionate Lemonnier would turn to his wife and exclaim:

"With a wife like you and a friend like him, a man is perfectly happy on earth."

She died in childbed. He nearly died too. But the sight of the child gave him courage: a little shriveled creature that moaned.

He loved the baby with a passionate and grief-stricken love, a morbid love compounded of the remembrance of death and his adoration of the dead woman. The boy was his wife's flesh, her continued being, a quintessence of her, as it were. He was her very life poured into another body; she had disappeared that he might exist. . . . And the father would embrace him frantically.

But also the child had killed her, had taken, stolen that adored existence, had fed upon it, had drunk up her share of life. . . . And Monsieur Lemonnier would replace his son in the cradle and sit down to contemplate him. He would remain there for hours, watching him, musing on a thousand sad or sweet things. Then, as the child was sleeping, he would stoop over his face and weep into his coverings.

The child grew. The father could not forego his presence for an hour; he would prowl about the nursery, take him out for walks, put on his clothes, wash him, give him his meals. His friend, Monsieur Duretour, also seemed to cherish the baby, and would embrace him with rapture, with those frenzies of affection which properly belong to the parent. He would make him leap in his arms or ride a cockhorse upon his leg, and suddenly, overturning him upon his knees, would raise his short frock and kiss the brat's fat thighs and round little calves.

"Isn't he a darling, isn't he a darling!" Monsieur Lemonnier would murmur in delight, and Monsieur Duretour would clasp the child in his arms, tickling his neck with his mustache.

Only Céleste, the old nurse, seemed to have no affection for the little one. She was vexed at his pranks and seemingly exasperated by the cajolery of the two men.

"Is that a way to bring up a child?" she would exclaim. "You'll make a perfect fool of him."

More years went by, and Jean attained the age of nine. He could scarcely read, he had been so spoiled, and he always did exactly as he liked. He had a stubborn will, a habit of obstinate resistance, and a violent temper. The father always gave way and granted him everything. Monsieur Duretour was perpetually buying and bringing for the little fellow the toys he coveted, and feeding him cakes and sweets.

On these occasions Céleste would lose her temper, and exclaim:

"It's a shame, Sir, a shame. You'll be the ruin of the child, the ruin of him, do you hear! It's got to be stopped, and stopped it shall be, yes, I promise it shall, and before long, too."

"Well, what about it, my good woman?" Monsieur Lemonnier would answer with a smile. "I'm too fond of him, I can't deny him anything. It's up to you to do your share in his upbringing."

Jean was weak and somewhat ailing. The doctor declared him to be anemic, and ordered iron, red meat, and strong broth.

But the little fellow liked nothing but cakes, and refused all other nourishment; and his father, in despair, stuffed him with cream tarts and chocolate éclairs.

One evening, as the two sat down to table alone together, Céleste brought in the soup-tureen with an assurance and an air of authority unusual in her. She abruptly took off the lid, plunged the ladle into the middle of it, and announced:

"There's broth such as I've never made before; the little fellow really must eat some, this time."

Monsieur Lemonnier, terrified, lowered his head. He saw that this was not going down well.

Céleste took up his plate, filled it herself, and set it back in front of him.

He tasted the soup and declared:

"Yes, it is excellent."

Then the servant took the little boy's plate and poured into it a whole ladleful of soup. She stepped back and waited.

Jean sniffed it, pushed away the plate, and uttered a sound of disgust. Céleste, grown pale, went swiftly up to him and, seizing the spoon full of soup, thrust it forcibly into the child's half-open mouth.

He choked, coughed, sneezed, and spat, and, yelling, grasped his glass in his fist and flung it at his nurse. It caught her full in the stomach. At that, exasperated, she took the brat's head under her arm and began to ram spoonful after spoonful of soup down his gullet. He steadily vomited it back, stamping his feet with rage, writhing, choking, and beating the air with his hands, as red as though he were dying of suffocation.

At first the father remained in such stupefaction that he made no movement at all. Then suddenly he rushed forward with the wild rage of a madman, took the servant by the shoulders, and flung her against the wall.

"Get out! . . . get out! . . . brute!" he stammered.

But with a vigorous shake she repulsed him, and with disheveled hair, her cap hanging down her back, her eyes blazing, cried:

"What's come over you now? You want to beat me because I make the child eat his soup, when you'll kill him with your spoiling!"

"Out! . . . be off with you . . . off with you, brute!" he repeated, trembling from head to foot.

Then in a rage she turned upon him, and looking him in the eye, said in a trembling voice:

"Ah! . . . You think . . . you think you're going to treat me like that, me, me? . . . But you won't! . . . And for whose sake, for whose sake? . . . For that snotty brat who isn't even your own child! No . . . not yours! . . . No! not yours! . . . not yours! . . . not yours! Why, everybody knows it, by God, except you. . . . Ask the grocer, the butcher, the baker, everyone, everyone. . . ."

She faltered, choked with anger, then was silent and stared at him.

He sat motionless, livid, his arms waving wildly. Finally he stammered in a feeble, tremulous voice, in which strong emotion still quivered:

"You say? . . . you say? . . . What did you say?"

She answered in a calmer voice:

"I say what I know, by God! What everyone knows."

He raised his two hands and, flinging himself upon her with the fury of a beast, tried to knock her down. But she was strong, in spite of her age, and agile too. She slipped through his arms and, running round the table, once more in a violent rage, screeched:

"Look at him, look at him, you fool, and see if he isn't the living image of Monsieur Duretour; look at his nose and his eyes, are *your* eyes like that? Or your nose? Or your hair? And were *hers* like that? I tell you everybody knows it, everybody, except you! You're the laughing-stock of the town! Look at him! Look at him! . . ."

She went to the door, opened it, and disappeared.

Jean, terrified, sat motionless, staring at his soup-plate.

At the end of an hour she returned, very softly, to see

what had happened. The little fellow, after having devoured the cakes, a dish of custard, and a dish of pears in syrup, was now eating jam out of a pot with his soup-spoon.

The father had gone out.

Céleste took the child, kissed him, and, with silent steps, carried him off to his room and put him to bed. Then she returned to the dining-room, cleared the table, and set everything in order, very uneasy in her mind.

No sound whatever was to be heard in the house. She went upstairs and set her ear to her master's door. He was not moving about the room. She put her eye to the keyhole. He was writing and seemed calm.

Then she went back to sit in her kitchen, so as to be ready for any circumstance, for she realized that something was in the air.

She fell asleep in her chair and did not wake until daybreak.

She did the household work, as was her custom every morning; she swept and dusted, and, at about eight o'clock, made Monsieur Lemonnier's coffee.

But she dared not take it to her master, having very little idea how she would be received; and she waited for him to ring. He did not ring. Nine o'clock went by, then ten o'clock.

Céleste, alarmed, prepared the tray, and started out of the kitchen with a beating heart. She stopped before his door and listened. Nothing was stirring. She knocked, there was no answer. So, summoning all her courage, she opened the door and went in; then, uttering a shriek, she dropped the breakfast-tray.

Monsieur Lemonnier was hanging in the middle of the room, suspended by the neck from a ring in the ceiling. His tongue protruded in ghastly fashion. The slipper had fallen off his right foot and lay on the floor; the other slipper had remained on the foot. An overturned chair lay beside the bed.

Céleste fled shrieking. The neighbors ran up. The doctor discovered that death had taken place at midnight.

A note, addressed to Monsieur Duretour, was found upon the suicide's desk. It contained this single sentence:

"I leave and entrust the little one to you."

THE NECKLACE

SHE WAS one of those pretty, attractive girls born, as though fate had blundered, into a family of artisans. She had no marriage portion, no expectations, no means of being known, understood, loved, and married by a man of wealth and distinction; and she let herself be married off to a little clerk in the Ministry of Education.

Her tastes were simple because she had never been able to afford any other, but she was as unhappy as though she had married beneath her; for women have no caste nor class, their beauty, grace, and charm serving them for birth or family. Their natural delicacy, their instinctive elegance, their nimbleness of wit, are their only mark of rank, and put the slum girl on a level with the highest lady in the land.

She suffered endlessly, feeling herself born for every

delicacy and luxury. She suffered from the shabbiness of her house, from its mean walls, worn chairs, and ugly curtains. All these things, of which other women of her class would not even have been aware, tormented and offended her. The sight of the little Breton girl who came to do her housework aroused pangs of regret and hopeless dreams in her mind. She imagined silent antechambers, heavy with Oriental tapestries, lit by torches in lofty bronze sockets, with two tall footmen in knee-breeches dozing in large armchairs, overcome by the heavy warmth of the stove. She imagined vast salons hung with antique silks, exquisite pieces of furniture supporting priceless ornaments, and small, charming, perfumed rooms, created for little parties of intimate friends, men who were famous and sought after, whose homage roused every other woman's envious longings.

When she sat down for dinner at the round table covered with a three-day-old cloth, opposite her husband, who always exclaimed, as he took the cover off the soup-tureen, "Aha! Scotch broth! What could be better?" she imagined delicate meals, gleaming silver, tapestries peopling the walls with folk of a past age and strange birds in fairy forests; she imagined exquisite viands served in marvelous dishes, murmured gallantries, listened to with an inscrutable smile while she trifled with the rosy flesh of trout or wings of asparagus chicken.

She had no clothes, no jewels, nothing. And these were the only things she loved; she felt that she was made for them. She had longed so eagerly to charm, to be desired, to be wildly attractive and sought after.

She had a rich friend, an old school friend whom she refused to visit, because she suffered so keenly each time she returned home. She would weep whole days, with grief, regret, despair, and misery.

One evening her husband came home with an exultant air, holding a large envelope in his hand.

"Here's something for you," he said.

Swiftly she tore it open and drew out a printed card on which were these words:

The Minister of Education and Madame Ramponneau request the pleasure of the company of Monsieur and Madame Loisel at the Ministry on the evening of Monday, January the 18th.

Instead of being delighted, as her husband hoped, she flung the invitation petulantly across the table, murmuring:

"What do you want me to do with this?"

"Why, darling, I thought you'd be pleased. You never go out, and this is a great occasion. I had tremendous trouble to get it. Everyone wants one; it's very select, and very few go to the clerks. You'll see all the really big people there."

She looked at him out of furious eyes, and said impatiently:

"And what do you suppose I am to wear at such an affair?"

He had not thought about it; he stammered:

"Why, the dress you go to the theater in. It looks very nice, to me. . . ."

He stopped, stupefied and utterly at a loss when he saw that his wife was beginning to cry. Two large tears ran slowly down from the corners of her eyes towards the corners of her mouth.

"What's the matter with you? What's the matter with you?" he faltered.

But with a violent effort she overcame her grief and replied calmly, wiping her wet cheeks:

"Nothing. Only I haven't a dress and so I can't go to

this party. Give your invitation to some friend whose wife will be turned out better than I shall."

He was heartbroken.

"Look here, Mathilde," he persisted. "What would be the cost of a suitable dress, which you could use on other occasions as well, something very simple?"

She thought for several seconds, reckoning up prices and also wondering how large a sum she could ask without bringing upon herself an immediate refusal and an exclamation of horror from the prudent clerk.

Finally she replied with some hesitation:

"I don't know exactly, but I think I could do it for four hundred francs."

He grew slightly pale, for this was exactly the amount he had been saving for a gun, intending to get a little shooting next summer on the plain of Nanterre with some friends who went lark-shooting there on Sundays.

Nevertheless he said, "Very well. I'll give you four hundred francs. But try to get a really nice dress with the money."

The day of the party drew near, and Madame Loisel seemed sad, uneasy and anxious. Her dress was ready, however. One evening her husband said to her:

"What's the matter with you? You've been very odd for the last three days."

"I'm utterly miserable at not having any jewels, not a single stone to wear," she replied. "I shall look absolutely like a nobody. I would almost rather not go to the party."

"Wear flowers," he said. "They're very smart at this time of the year. For ten francs you could get two or three gorgeous roses."

She was not convinced.

"No . . . there's nothing so humiliating as looking poor in the middle of a lot of rich women."

"How stupid you are!" exclaimed her husband. "Go
nd see Madame Forestier and ask her to lend you some
ewelry. You know her quite well enough for that."

She uttered a cry of delight.

"That's true. I never thought of it."

Next day she went to see her friend and told her her
rouble.

Madame Forestier went to her dressing-table, took
ıp a large box, brought it to Madame Loisel, opened it,
ınd said:

"Choose, my dear."

First she saw some bracelets, then a pearl necklace,
hen a Venetian cross in gold and gems, of exquisite
workmanship. She tried the effect of the jewels before
he mirror, hesitating, unable to make up her mind to
leave them, to give them up. She kept on asking:

"Haven't you anything else?"

"Yes. Look for yourself. I don't know what you would
like best."

Suddenly she discovered, in a black satin case, a
superb diamond necklace; her heart began to beat
covetously. Her hands trembled as she lifted it. She
fastened it round her neck, upon her high dress, and
remained in ecstasy at sight of herself.

Then, with hesitation, she asked in anguish:

"Could you lend me this, just this?"

"Yes, of course."

She flung herself on her friend's breast, embraced her
rapturously, and went away with her treasure.

The day of the party arrived. Madame Loisel was a
success. She was the prettiest woman present, elegant,
graceful, smiling, and quite beside herself with happiness. All the men stared at her, inquired her name, and
asked to be introduced. All the Under-Secretaries of

State were eager to waltz with her. The Minister noticed her.

She danced madly, ecstatically, drunk with pleasure, with no thought for anything, in the triumph of her beauty, in the pride of her success, in a cloud of happiness made up of this universal homage and admiration, of the desires she had aroused, of the completeness of a victory so dear to her feminine heart.

She left about four o'clock in the morning. Since midnight her husband had been dozing in a deserted little room, in company with three other men whose wives were having a good time.

He threw over her shoulders the garments he had brought for them to go home in, modest everyday clothes, whose poverty clashed with the beauty of the ball-dress. She was conscious of this and was anxious to hurry away, so that she should not be noticed by other women who were putting on costly furs.

Loisel restrained her.

"Wait a little. You'll catch cold in the open. I'm going to fetch a cab."

But she did not listen to him and went swiftly down the staircase. When they were out in the street they could not find a cab; they began to look for one, shouting at the drivers whom they saw passing in the distance.

They walked down towards the Seine, anxious and shivering. At last they found on the quay one of those old night-prowling carriages which are to be seen in Paris only after dark, as though ashamed of their shabbiness in the daylight.

It brought them to their door in the Rue des Martyrs, and sadly they walked up to their own apartment. This was the end, for her. As for him, he was thinking that he must be at the office at ten.

She took off the garments in which she had wrapped her shoulders, so as to see herself in all her glory before the mirror. But suddenly she uttered a cry. The necklace was no longer round her neck!

"What's the matter with you?" asked her husband, already half undressed.

She turned towards him in the utmost distress.

"I . . . I . . . I've lost Madame Forestier's necklace. . . ."

He started with astonishment.

"What! . . . Impossible!"

They searched in the folds of her dress, in the folds of the coat, in the pockets, everywhere. They could not find it.

"Are you sure that you still had it on when you came away from the ball?" he asked.

"Yes, I fingered it in the hall at the Ministry."

"But if you had lost it in the street, we should have heard it fall."

"Yes. Probably we should. Did you take the number of the cab?"

"No. You didn't notice it, did you?"

"No."

They stared at one another, dumbfounded. At last Loisel put on his clothes again.

"I'll go over all the ground we walked," he said, "and see if I can't find it."

And he went out. She remained in her evening clothes, lacking strength to get into bed, huddled on a chair, without volition or power of thought.

Her husband returned about seven. He had found nothing.

He went to the police station, to the newspapers, to offer a reward, to the cab companies, everywhere that a ray of hope impelled him.

She waited all day long, in the same state of bewilderment at this fearful catastrophe.

Loisel came home at night, his face lined and pale; he had discovered nothing.

"You must write to your friend," he said, "and tell her that you've broken the clasp of her necklace and are getting it mended. That will give us time to look about us."

She wrote at his dictation.

By the end of a week they had lost all hope.

Loisel, who had aged five years, declared:

"We must see about replacing the diamonds."

Next day they took the box which had held the necklace and went to the jeweler whose name was inside. He consulted his books.

"It was not I who sold this necklace, Madame; I must have merely supplied the clasp."

Then they went from jeweler to jeweler, searching for another necklace like the first, consulting their memories, both ill with remorse and anguish of mind.

In a shop at the Palais-Royal they found a string of diamonds which seemed to them exactly like the one they were looking for. It was worth forty thousand francs. They could have it for thirty-six thousand.

They begged the jeweler not to sell it for three days. And they arranged matters on the understanding that it would be taken back for thirty-four thousand francs, if the first one were found before the end of February.

Loisel possessed eighteen thousand francs left to him by his father. He intended to borrow the rest.

He did borrow it, a thousand from one man, five hundred from another, five louis here, three louis there. He gave notes of hand, entered into ruinous arrangenents, did business with usurers and the whole tribe of moneylenders. He mortgaged the whole remaining years of his existence, risked his signature without even knowing if he could honor it, and, appalled at the agonizing face of the future, at the black misery about to fall upon him, at the prospect of every possible physical privation and moral torture, he went to get the new necklace and put down upon the jeweler's counter thirty-six thousand francs.

When Madame Loisel took back the necklace to Madame Forestier, the latter said to her in a chilly voice: "You ought to have brought it back sooner; I might have needed it."

She did not, as her friend had feared, open the case. If she had noticed the substitution, what would she have thought? What would she have said? Would she not have taken her for a thief?

Madame Loisel began to live the ghastly life of abject poverty. From the very first she played her part heroically. This fearful debt must be paid off. She would pay it. The servant was dismissed. They changed their flat; they took a garret under the roof.

She came to know the heavy work of the house, the hateful duties of the kitchen. She washed the plates, wearing out her pink nails on the coarse pottery and the bottoms of pans. She washed the dirty linen, the shirts and dishcloths, and hung them out to dry on a cord; every morning she took the dustbin down into the street and carried up the water, stopping on each landing to get her breath. And, clad like a poor woman, she went to the fruiterer, to the grocer, to the butcher, a basket on her arm, haggling, insulted, fighting for every wretched halfpenny of her money.

Every month notes had to be paid off, others renewed, time gained.

Her husband worked in the evenings at putting straight a merchant's accounts, and often at night he did copying at five sous a page.

This life lasted ten years.

At the end of ten years everything was paid off, everything, the usurers' charges and the accumulation of superimposed interest.

Madame Loisel looked old now. She had become like all the other strong, hard, coarse women of poor households. Her hair was badly done, her skirts were awry, her hands were red. She spoke in a shrill voice, and the water slopped all over the floor when she scrubbed it. But sometimes, when her husband was at the office, she sat down by the window and thought of that evening long ago, of the ball at which she had been so beautiful and so much admired.

What would have happened if she had never lost those jewels? Who knows? Who knows? How strange life is, how fickle! How little is needed to ruin or to save!

One Sunday, as she had gone for a walk along the Champs Elysées to freshen herself after the labors of the week, she caught sight suddenly of a woman who was taking a child out for a walk. It was Madame Forestier, still young, still beautiful, still attractive.

Madame Loisel was conscious of some emotion. Should she speak to her? Yes, certainly. And now that she had paid, she would tell her all. Why not?

She went up to her.

"Good morning, Jeanne."

The other did not recognize her, and was surprised at being thus familiarly addressed by a poor woman.

"But . . . Madame . . ." she stammered. "I don't know . . . you must be making a mistake."

"No . . . I am Mathilde Loisel."

Her friend uttered a cry.

"Oh! . . . my poor Mathilde, how you have changed! . . ."

"Yes, I've had some hard times since I saw you last; and many sorrows . . . and all on your account."

"On my account! . . . How was that?"

"You remember the diamond necklace you lent me for the ball at the Ministry?"

"Yes. Well?"

"Well, I lost it."

"How could you? Why, you brought it back."

"I brought you another one just like it. And for the last ten years we have been paying for it. You realize it wasn't easy for us; we had no money. . . . Well, it's paid for at last, and I'm glad indeed."

Madame Forestier had halted.

"You say you bought a diamond necklace to replace mine?"

"Yes. Hadn't you noticed it? They were very much alike."

And she smiled in proud and innocent happiness.

Madame Forestier, deeply moved, took her two hands.

"Oh, my poor Mathilde! But mine was paste. It was worth at the very most five hundred francs! . . ."

SAVED

T HE LITTLE Marquise de Rennendon burst into the room like a bullet crashing through a window, and began to laugh before she said a word; she laughed until she cried, just as she had laughed a month before when she came to tell her friend that she had deceived the Marquis to revenge herself, for no reason but to revenge herself, and only once, because he really was too stupid and too jealous.

The little Baronne de Grangerie had put down on her vast couch the book she was reading, and she stared curiously at Annette, laughing already herself.

At last she asked:

"What have you done now?"

"Oh . . . my dear . . . my dear . . . it's too funny . . . too funny . . . think of it . . . I'm saved . . . saved . . . saved!"

"What do you mean, saved?"

"Yes, saved."

165

"From what?"

"From my husband, darling, saved! Delivered! Free!
. . . free! . . . free!"

"How are you free? In what way?"

"In what way? Divorce! Yes, divorce! I can get a
divorce."

"You're divorced?"

"No, not yet. How silly you are! You can't get divorced in three hours! But I've got evidence . . . evidence . . . evidence that he is deceiving me . . . absolutely caught in the act . . . think! . . . in the act.
. . . I can prove it. . . ."

"Oh, tell me about it. So he has deceived you?"

"Yes . . . that's to say, no . . . yes and no. Oh, I've
been clever, vastly clever. For the last three months he
has been detestable, utterly detestable, brutal, coarse,
tyrannical, simply impossible. I said to myself: This
can't go on, I must get a divorce! But how? It wasn't
easy. I tried to get him to beat me. He wouldn't. He
crossed me from morning till night, made me go out
when I didn't want to, and stay at home when I was
longing to drive in town; he made my life unbearable
from one week's end to another, but he didn't beat me.

"Then I tried to find out if he had a mistress. Yes, he
had one, but he took every precaution when he went to
visit her. It simply wasn't possible to catch them together. So, guess what I did."

"I can't guess."

"Oh, you'd never guess. I begged my brother to get
me a photograph of his girl."

"Of your husband's mistress?"

"Yes. It cost Jacques fifteen louis, the price of one
evening, from seven o'clock to twelve, dinner included,
three louis an hour. He got the photograph thrown in."

"I should have thought he could have got it cheaper by any other method, and without—without being obliged to take the original as well."

"Oh, but she's pretty. Jacques didn't mind at all. And besides, I wanted to know all sorts of physical details about her figure, her bosom, her skin, and all that."

"I don't understand."

"You will in a minute. When I found out all I wanted to know, I went to a man . . . what shall I call him? . . . a very clever man . . . you know . . . one of those men who arrange things of all . . . of all kinds . . . one of those agents who can get you detectives and accomplices . . . one of those men . . . do you understand?"

"Yes, I think so. And what did you say to him?"

"I showed him the photograph of Clarisse (she's called Clarisse) and I said, 'I want a lady's maid like this photograph. She must be pretty, graceful, neat, clean. I'll pay any price you like. If it costs me ten thousand francs, so much the worse for me. I shan't need her for more than three months.'

"The man looked most surprised. 'You want a girl with a good character, Madame?' he asked.

"I blushed and stammered, 'She must be honest about money.'

"'And what about morals?' he asked. I didn't dare answer. I could only shake my head to mean 'No.' And all at once I realized that he had a dreadful suspicion, and I lost my head and cried, 'Oh, Monsieur, it's for my husband . . . he is deceiving me . . . he's deceiving me in town . . . and I want . . . I want him to deceive me at home . . . you see . . . so that I can catch him at it.'

"Then the man burst out laughing. I saw by his face

that he was no longer suspicious of me. He even thought me rather splendid. I'd have been ready to bet that he wanted to shake hands with me on the spot.

"'I'll arrange it for you within the week, Madame,' he said. 'And if necessary we'll change the attraction. I'll guarantee success. You won't pay me until the thing's a success. . . . So this is the photograph of your husband's mistress?'

"'Yes.'

"'She's got a good figure, not so thin as she appears. And what scent?'

"I didn't understand. 'How do you mean, what scent?' I repeated.

"He smiled. 'Madame, scent is of the first importance in seducing a man; it stirs hidden memories that prepare his mind for the necessary impulse; scent works a subtle confusion in his mind, disturbs him and weakens his defense by reminding him of past pleasures. You should also try to find out what your husband usually eats when he dines with this lady. You could arrange to give him the same dishes the evening you catch him. Ah, we'll pull it off, Madame, we'll pull it off!'

"I went away delighted. I really had discovered a most intelligent man."

II

"Three days later, a tall, dark girl presented herself. She was very beautiful, with an expression at once demure and provocative, a strangely sophisticated expression. Her manner towards me was correctness itself. As I didn't know quite on what footing to put her, I called her 'Mademoiselle'; then she said, 'Oh, Madame need not call me anything but Rose.'

"'Well, Rose, you know why you are here?'

"'I know quite well, Madame.'

"'Excellent, my girl. . . . And you . . . you don't mind at all?'

"'Oh, Madame, this is the eighth divorce I've helped to arrange; I'm used to it.'

"'That's splendid. Will it take you long to bring it off?'

"'Oh, Madame, that depends entirely on the gentleman's temperament. As soon as I have seen him alone for five minutes, I shall be able to tell you with some certainty.'

"'You shall see him at once, my child. But I warn you that he's not beautiful.'

"'That doesn't matter to me, Madame. I've come between wives and some very ugly husbands before this. But I must ask Madame if she has ascertained what scent I ought to use.'

"'Yes, my good Rose . . . verbena.'

"'So much the better, Madame: I'm very fond of that scent.'

"'And perhaps Madame can also tell me if her husband's mistress wears silk.'

"'No, my child; very fine lawn trimmed with lace.'

"'Oh, she must be very smart. Silk is beginning to be so common.'

"'I quite agree with you.'

"'Very well, Madame, I'll begin my duties.'

"She did begin her duties on the spot, as if she had never done anything else in all her life.

"An hour later my husband came in. Rose didn't even look at him, but he looked at her. She was already smelling strongly of verbena. After five minutes she left the room.

"'Who's that girl?' he asked me at once.

"'That . . . oh, that's my new maid.'

"'Where did you get her?'

" 'The Baronne de Grangerie sent her to me, with an excellent recommendation.'

" 'Well, she's pretty enough.'

" 'You think so?'

" 'I do . . . for a lady's maid.'

"I was overjoyed. I was sure he was nibbling already.

"That same evening Rose said to me, 'I can now promise Madame that it won't take a fortnight. The gentleman is very easy.'

" 'Ah, you've tried already?'

" 'No, Madame, but it's obvious at a glance. Even now he'd like to put his arms round me as he walks past.'

" 'He hasn't said anything to you?'

" 'No, Madame, he has only asked my name . . . to hear the sound of my voice.'

" 'Excellent, my good Rose. Get on as quickly as you can.'

" 'Don't be afraid of that, Madame. I shall resist just long enough not to make myself cheap.'

"By the end of the week my husband hardly went to town at all. I used to see him all afternoon wandering about the house; and what was more significant than anything else of his state of mind, was that he no longer stopped me from going out. I was out all day, I was . . . to . . . to leave him free.

"On the ninth day, as Rose was undressing me, she said meekly:

" 'It's happened, Madame—this morning.'

"I was a little surprised, even a little distressed, not by the thing itself, but by the way in which she had said it to me. I stammered:

" 'And . . . and . . . it went off all right?'

" 'Oh, very well, Madame. He has been urging me for three days now, but I didn't want to give in too quickly. Perhaps Madame will tell me what time she would like the *flagrante delicto.*'

" 'Yes, my girl; let's see . . . we'll make it Friday.'

" 'Friday then, Madame. I'll not allow any more liberties until then, so as to keep Monsieur eager.'

" 'You're sure you won't fail?'

" 'Oh, yes, Madame, quite sure. I'll go on keeping Monsieur hanging, so that he'll be ready for it at any hour Madame likes to fix.'

" 'Let's say five o'clock, my good Rose.'

" 'Five o'clock, Madame; and where?'

" 'Well—in my room.'

" 'Right, in Madame's room.'

"Well, my dear, you see what I did. I went and brought papa and mamma first, and then my uncle d'Orvelin, the judge, and Monsieur Raplet, the public prosecutor, a friend of my husband's. I didn't warn them what I was going to show them. I made them all creep on tiptoe to the door of my room. I waited until five o'clock, exactly five o'clock. Oh, how my heart beat! I made the concierge come up too, so as to have one more witness. Then . . . then, the moment the clock began to strike, bang, I flung the door open. . . . Oh, oh, oh, there they were in the very middle of it, my dear! . . . Oh, what a face . . . what a face, if you had only seen his face! . . . And he turned round, the fathead. Oh, it was funny! I laughed and laughed. . . . Papa was furious and wanted to whip my husband. And the concierge, an excellent servant, helped him to dress again . . . in front of us . . . in front of us . . . he buttoned his braces for him . . . it was wildly funny. . . . As for Rose, she was perfect, quite perfect. . . . She cried . . . she cried beautifully. She's a priceless girl . . . if ever you want a girl like that, remember her!

"And here I am. . . . I came away at once to tell you all about it . . . at once—I'm free. Hurrah for divorce!"

She began to dance in the middle of the drawing-room, while the little Baronne murmured, in a voice full of dreamy disappointment:

"Why didn't you invite me to see it?"

DUCHOUX

Because the great staircase of the club was like a hot-house, Baron Mordiane came down the steps with his fur-lined overcoat open; but when the front door had closed behind him, the intense cold suddenly pierced him to the marrow, increasing his despondency. He had been losing money in the gambling rooms, besides which he had for some time been suffering from indigestion, unable any longer to eat what he fancied.

He was about to return home, when the thought of his great, bare room, his valet sleeping in the anteroom, the water singing on the gas-stove in his dressing-room, and the enormous bed, as old and gloomy as a death-bed, suddenly struck him with a chill even sharper than the frosty air.

For some years he had felt weighing on him the burden of loneliness which sometimes overwhelms old bachelors. He had been strong, active and cheerful, spending his days in sport and his evenings in amusement. Now he was growing dull, and no longer took an interest in anything. Exercise tired him, suppers and even dinners made him ill, while women bored him as much as they had once amused him.

The monotony of unvarying evenings, of the same friends met in the same place—at the club—the same card parties with their run of good and bad luck evenly balanced, the same conversation on the same topics, the same wit from the same tongues, the same jokes on the same subjects, the same scandal about the same women, all sickened him so that there were times when he thought seriously of suicide. He could no longer face this regular, aimless, and commonplace life, both frivolous and dull, and, without knowing why, he longed for peace, rest and comfort.

He did not indeed think of marrying, for he lacked the courage to face a life of depression, conjugal slavery, and that hateful coexistence of two human beings who know each other so well that every word uttered by one is anticipated by the other, and every thought, wish or opinion is immediately divined. He considered that a woman was worth attention only so long as one knew very little about her, while she was still mysterious and unfathomed, vague and perplexing. Therefore what he wanted was family life without the tyranny of family ties, in which he need spend only part of his time; and again he was haunted by the memory of his son.

For the last year he had thought of him continually, with an ever-increasing, tormenting longing to see him and make his acquaintance. The affair had taken place while he was a young man, in an atmosphere of romance and tenderness. The child had been sent to the South of France, and brought up near Marseilles, without knowing his father's name. His father had paid for his upbringing, in his infancy, in his schooldays and in the activities that followed, ending up with a substantial settlement on a suitable marriage. A trustworthy lawyer had acted as intermediary without giving away the secret.

Baron Mordiane, then, knew only that a child of his was living somewhere near Marseilles, that he was said to be intelligent and well educated, and that he had married the daughter of an architect and surveyor, whom he had succeeded in the business. He was also said to be making money.

Why should he not go and see this unknown son, without disclosing his identity—study him at first hand and see whether, in case of need, he might find a welcome refuge in his home?

He had always treated him liberally, and had made a generous settlement, which had been gratefully received. He was therefore sure of not coming into conflict with an unreasonable pride, and the idea of leaving for the South had now become an oft-recurring desire which gave him no rest. He was urged on, also, by a curious feeling of self-pity at the thought of that cheerful and comfortable home on the coast where he would find his charming, young daughter-in-law, his grandchildren ready to welcome him, and his son; all this would remind him of that brief and happy love-affair so many years ago. His only regret was his past generosity, which had assisted the young man on the road to prosperity and would prevent the father from appearing amongst them in the role of benefactor.

With these thoughts running through his mind he walked along, his head buried deep in his fur collar: his decision was quickly made. Hailing a passing cab, he drove home, and said to his valet, aroused from his sleep to open the door:

"Louis, we leave for Marseilles tomorrow evening.

We shall be there perhaps a fortnight. Make all preparations for the journey."

The train sped along the sandy banks of the Rhone, over yellow plains and through sunny villages—a country with gaunt encircling mountains in the distance.

Baron Mordiane, awakened after a night in the sleeping-car, gloomily contemplated his reflection in the little mirror in his dressing-case. The crude light of the South showed up wrinkles he had never seen before, and revealed a state of decrepitude that had passed unnoticed in the shaded light of Paris flats. Looking at the corners of his eyes, the wrinkled eyelids, bald temples and forehead, he said to himself:

"Good heavens, I am worse than faded: I look worn out!"

His desire for peace suddenly increased, and for the first time in his life he was conscious of a vague longing to take his grandchildren on his knee.

He hired a carriage in Marseilles and about one o'clock in the afternoon he stopped before a dazzling white country-house typical of the South of France, standing at the end of an avenue of plane-trees. He beamed with pleasure as he went along the avenue and said to himself:

"It's damned nice."

Suddenly a youngster of about five or six rushed from behind the shrubs and stood motionless at the end of the drive, gazing round-eyed at the visitor.

Mordiane approached and said to him:

"Good afternoon, my boy!"

The youngster made no reply.

The baron then stooped and picked him up to kiss him, but so strong was the odor of garlic coming from the child that he quickly put him down again, murmur-

ing, "Oh! he must be the gardener's son." And he went
on towards the house.

On a line in front of the door, the washing was drying, shirts, napkins, towels, aprons, and sheets, while a
display of socks hanging in rows on cords one above
another filled the whole of a window, like tiers of sausages in front of a pork-butcher's shop.

The baron called out, and a servant appeared, truly
Southern in her dirty and unkempt state, with wisps of
hair straggling across her face. Her stained skirt still retained some of its original gaudiness, suggesting a country fair or a mountebank's costume.

"Is M. Duchoux at home?" he inquired.

"You want M. Duchoux?" the servant repeated.

"Yes."

"He is in the parlor, drawing plans."

"Tell him that M. Merlin wishes to see him."

She replied in surprise, "Oh! come in, if you want
him," and shouted:

"M. Duchoux, a visitor to see you!"

The baron entered a large room darkened by half-
closed shutters, and received a vague impression of filth
and disorder.

A short, bald-headed man, standing at an untidy
table, was tracing lines on a large sheet of paper. He
stopped his work and came forward.

His open waistcoat, slackened trousers and rolled-up
shirt-sleeves showed how hot it was, and the muddy
shoes that he was wearing pointed to recent rain.

"To whom have I the honor? . . ." he asked, with
a strong Southern accent.

"I am M. Merlin. I have come to consult you about
some building land."

"Ah! yes. Certainly."

And turning towards his wife, who was knitting in the darkened room, Duchoux said:

"Clear one of the chairs, Josephine."

Mordiane saw a young woman, already showing signs of age, as provincial women of twenty-five do for want of attention and regular cleanliness, in fact, of all those precautions which form part of a woman's toilet, helping to preserve her youthful appearance, her charm and beauty up to the age of fifty. A kerchief hung over her shoulders, and her hair, which was beautifully thick and black, but was twisted up in slipshod fashion, looked as though it was seldom brushed. With her roughened hands she removed a child's dress, a knife, a piece of string, an empty flower-pot and a greasy plate from a chair, and offered it to the visitor.

He sat down, and then noticed that on the table at which Duchoux had been working, in addition to his books and papers, there were two freshly cut lettuces, a basin, a hairbrush, a napkin, a revolver, and several dirty cups.

The architect saw him glance at these, and smilingly remarked, "I am sorry that the room is rather untidy; that is the children's fault," and he drew up his chair to talk to his client.

"You are looking for a piece of land round Marseilles?"

Although he was some distance away, the baron smelt the odor of garlic which people of the South exhale as flowers do their perfume.

"Was that your son I met under the plane-trees?" Mordiane inquired.

"Yes, the second."

"You have two sons, then?"

"Three, sir, one a year," replied Duchoux, with evident pride.

The baron thought that if they all had the same perfume, their nursery must be a real conservatory. He resumed: "Yes, I should like a nice piece of ground near the sea, on a secluded beach. . . ."

Then Duchoux began to explain. He had ten, twenty, fifty, a hundred and more plots of land of that kind, at all prices and to suit all tastes. The words came in a torrent as he smiled and wagged his round, bald head in his satisfaction.

Meanwhile, the baron was bringing to mind a little woman, slight, fair, and rather sad, who used to say with such yearning, "My own beloved," that the very memory made his blood run hot in his veins. She had loved him passionately, madly, for three months; then becoming pregnant in the absence of her husband, who was Governor of a colony, she had fled into hiding, distracted by fear and despair, until the birth of the child whom Mordiane carried off one summer evening and whom they had never seen again.

She died of consumption three years later, in the colony where she had gone to rejoin her husband. It was their son who sat beside him now, who was saying with a metallic ring in his voice:

"As for this plot, sir, it is a unique opportunity. . . ."

And Mordiane remembered the other voice, light as a zephyr, murmuring:

"My own beloved; we will never part. . . ." The memory of the gentle, devoted look in those blue eyes came back to him as he watched the round, blue, but so vacant eyes of this ridiculous little man who was so like his mother, and yet. . . .

Yes, he looked more and more like her every minute; his intonation, his demeanor, his gestures were the same; he resembled her as a monkey resembles a man;

yet he was of her blood, he had many of her little habits, though distorted, irritating and revolting. The baron was in torment, haunted suddenly by that terrible, ever-growing resemblance, which enraged, maddened, and tortured him like a nightmare, or like bitter remorse.

"When can we look at this land together?" he stammered.

"Why, tomorrow, if you like."

"Yes, tomorrow. What time?"

"At one o'clock."

"Very good."

The child he had met in the avenue appeared in the door and cried:

"Father!"

No one answered him.

Mordiane stood up trembling with an intense long-ing to escape. That word "father" had struck him like a bullet. That garlicky "father," that Southern "father," was addressed to him, was meant for him. Oh! how sweet had been the perfume of his beloved of bygone days!

As Duchoux was showing him out, the baron said:

"Is this house yours?"

"Yes, sir, I bought it recently, and I am proud of it. I am fortune's child, sir, and I make no secret of it; I am proud of it. I owe nothing to anyone; I am the child of my own efforts, and I owe everything to myself."

The child, who had remained on the door-step, again cried, "Father!" the voice coming from a greater dis-tance.

Mordiane, shivering with fear, seized with panic, fled as from a great danger. "He will guess who I am," he thought to himself, "he will hug me in his arms and call me 'Father' and give me a kiss reeking of garlic."

"I shall see you tomorrow, sir."

"Tomorrow, at one o'clock."

. . .

The carriage rumbled along the white road.

"Driver, take me to the station," he shouted, while two voices seemed to ring in his ears. One of them, far away and sweet, the faint, sad voice of the dead, was saying, "My own beloved"; the other, a metallic, shrill, repellent voice, crying, "Father!" much as one shouts, "Stop him!" when a thief is in flight.

As he came into the club next evening, Count d'Etreillis said to him:

"We have not seen you for three days. Have you been ill?"

"Yes, I have not been very well. I suffer from headaches occasionally. . . ."

YVETTE

As THEY left the Café Riche, Jean de Servigny said to Léon Saval:

"We'll walk, if you don't mind. It's too fine to take a cab."

"It will suit me perfectly," answered his friend.

"It's barely eleven," continued Jean. "We shall be there long before midnight, so let us go slowly."

A restless crowd swarmed on the boulevard, the crowd which on summer nights is always to be seen there, contented and merry, walking, drinking, and talking, flowing past like a river. Here and there a café flung a brilliant splash of light on a group which sat outside, drinking at little round tables loaded with bottles and glasses, and obstructing the moving stream of passers-by. In the road the cabs, with their red, blue, and green eyes, passed swiftly across the harsh glare of the lighted front, revealing for an instant the silhouette of the thin, trotting horse, the profile of the driver on the box, and the dark, square body of the vehicle. The "Urbaine" cabs gleamed as the light caught their yellow panels.

The two friends walked slowly along, smoking their cigars. They were in evening dress, their overcoats on their arms, flowers in their buttonholes, and their hats a little on one side, with the careless tilt affected by men who have dined well and are enjoying the mild evening breeze.

Ever since their schooldays the two had been close friends, profoundly and loyally devoted to each other. Jean de Servigny, short, slim, frail, very elegant, with thinning hair, a curled mustache, bright eyes, and thin lips, was one of those night-birds who seem to have been born and bred on the boulevards; inexhaustible, though he wore a perpetual air of fatigue, vigorous despite his pallor—one of those slender Parisians to whom gymnastics, fencing, the cold plunge, and the Turkish bath have given an artificial nervous strength. He was as well known for his conviviality as for his wit, his wealth, and his love-affairs, and for that geniality, popularity, and fashionable gallantry which are the hallmark of a certain type of man.

In other ways, too, he was a true Parisian, quick-witted, skeptical, changeable, impulsive, energetic yet irresolute, capable of anything and of nothing, an egoist on principle and a philanthropist on impulse. He kept his expenditure within his income, and amused himself without ruining his health. Cold and passionate by turns, he was continually letting himself go and pulling himself up, a prey to conflicting impulses, and yielding to all of them, obeying the prompting of his instinct like any hardened pleasure-seeker whose weathercock logic bids him follow every wind and profit from any train of events, without taking the trouble to set a single one of them in motion.

His companion, Léon Saval, rich also, was one of those superb giants who impel women to turn round and stare after them in the street. He had the air of a statue come to life, of a racial type: he was like one of those models which are sent to exhibitions. Too handsome, too tall, too broad, too strong, all his faults were those of excess. He had broken innumerable hearts.

As they reached the Vaudeville, he inquired:

"Have you let this lady know that you're bringing me?"

Servigny laughed.

"Let the Marquise Obardi know! Do you let a bus-driver know in advance that you're going to get onto his bus at the corner of the boulevard?"

"Well, then, exactly who is she?" asked Saval, slightly perplexed.

"A parvenue," replied his friend, "a colossal fraud, a charming jade, sprung from Lord knows where, who appeared one day, Lord knows how, in the world of adventurers, in which she is well able to make herself prominent. Anyhow, what does it matter? They say her real name, her maiden-name—for she has remained a maiden in every sense but the true one—is Octavie Bardin, whence Obardi, retaining the first letter of the Christian name and dropping the last letter of the surname. She's an attractive woman, too, and with your physique you're certain to become her lover. You can't introduce Hercules to Messalina without something coming of it. I ought to add, by the way, that though admission to the place is as free as to a shop, you are not obliged to buy what is on sale. Love and cards are the stock-in-trade, but no one will force you to purchase either. The way out is as accessible as the way in.

"It is three years now since she took a house in the Etoile Quarter, a rather shady district, and opened it to all the scum of the Continent, which comes to Paris to display its most diverse, dangerous, and vicious accomplishments.

"I went to the house. How? I don't remember. I went, as we all go, because there's gambling, because the women are approachable and the men scoundrels. I like this crowd of decorated buccaneers, all foreign, all noble, all titled, and all, except the spies, unknown to their ambassadors. They talk of their honor on the slightest provocation, trot out their ancestors on no provocation at all, and present you with their life-histories on any provocation. They are braggarts, liars, thieves, as dangerous as their cards, as false as their names, brave because they must be, like footpads who cannot rob their victims without risking their necks. In a word, the aristocracy of the galleys.

"I adore them. They're interesting to study, interesting to meet, amusing to listen to, often witty, never commonplace like the dregs of French officialdom. Their wives too are always pretty, with a little flavor of foreign rascality, and the mystery of their past lives, half of which were probably spent in a penitentiary. Most often the women have glorious eyes and wonderful hair, the real professional physique, a grace which intoxicates, a seductive charm that drives men mad, a vicious but wholly irresistible fascination! They're the real old highway robbers, female birds of prey. And I adore them too.

"The Marquise Obardi is a perfect type of these elegant jades. A little over-ripe, but still beautiful, seductive, and feline, she's full of vice to the marrow. There's plenty of fun at her house—gambling, dancing, supper . . . all the distractions of the world, the flesh, and the devil, in fact."

"Have you been, or are you, her lover?" asked Léon Saval.

Servigny answered:

"I haven't been, am not, and never shall be. It's the daughter I go there for."

"Oh, there's a daughter, then, is there?"

"There is indeed! She's a marvel. At present she's the principal attraction. A tall, glorious creature, just the right age, eighteen, as fair as her mother is dark, always merry, always ready for fun, always laughing at the top of her voice, and dancing like a thing possessed. Who's to have her? Who has had her? No one knows. There are ten of us waiting and hoping.

"A girl like that in the hands of a woman like the Marquise is a fortune. And they don't show their hands, the rogues. No one can make it out. Perhaps they're waiting for a catch, a better one than I am. Well, I can assure you that if the chance comes my way I'll take it.

"This girl, Yvette, absolutely nonplusses me. She's a mystery. If she isn't the most finished monster of perverse ingenuity that I've ever seen, she's certainly the most extraordinary scrap of innocent girlhood to be found anywhere. She lives there among that disgraceful crew with easy and triumphant serenity, exquisitely wicked or exquisitely simple.

"She's an extraordinary girl to be the daughter of an adventuress, sprung up in that hotbed, like a beautiful plant nourished on manure. She may be the daughter of some man of high rank, a great artist or a great nobleman, a prince or a king who found himself one night in her mother's bed. No one can understand just what she is, or what she thinks about. But you will see her."

Saval burst into laughter.

"You're in love with her," he said.

"No, I am one of the competitors, which is not the same thing. By the way, I'll introduce you to my most serious rivals. But I have a real chance. I have a good start, and she regards me with favor."

"You're in love," repeated Saval.

"No, I'm not. She disturbs me, allures me, and makes me uneasy, at once attracts me and frightens me. I distrust her as I would a trap, yet I long for her with the longing of a thirsty man for a cool drink. I feel her charm, and approach it as nervously as if I were in the same room with a man suspected of being a clever thief. In her presence I feel an almost absurd inclination to believe in the possibility of her innocence, and a very reasonable distrust of her equally possible cunning. I feel that I am in contact with an abnormal being, a creature outside the laws of nature, delicious or detestable, I don't know which."

For the third time Saval declared:

"You're in love, I tell you. You speak of her with the fervor of a poet and the lyricism of a troubadour. Come now, have it out with yourself, search your heart and admit it."

"Well, it may be so, after all. At least she's always in my mind. Yes, perhaps I am in love. I think of her too much. I think of her when I'm falling asleep and when I wake up; that's fairly serious. Her image haunts me, pursues me, is with me the whole time, in front of me, round me, in me. Is it love, this physical obsession? Her face is so sharply graven in my mind that I see it the moment I shut my eyes. I don't deny that my pulses race whenever I see her. I love her, then, but in an odd fashion(I long for her passionately, yet the idea of making her my wife would seem to me a monstrous, absurd folly. I am also a little afraid of her, like a bird fascinated by a hawk. And I'm jealous of her too, jealous of all that is hidden from me in her incomprehensible heart.) I'm always asking myself: 'Is she a delightful little guttersnipe or a thoroughly bad lot?' She says things that would make a trooper blush, but so do parrots. Sometimes she's so brazenly indecent that I'm inclined to believe in her absolute purity, and sometimes her artlessness is so much too good to be true that I wonder if she ever was chaste. She provokes me and excites me like a harlot, and guards herself at the same time as though she were a virgin. She appears to love me, and laughs at me; in public she almost proclaims herself my mistress, and when we're alone together she treats me as though I were her brother or her footman.

"Sometimes I imagine that she has as many lovers as her mother. Sometimes I think that she knows nothing about life, absolutely nothing.

"And she has a passion for reading novels. At present, while waiting for a more amusing position, I am her bookseller. She calls me her librarian.

"Every week the Librairie Nouvelle sends her, from me, everything that appears; I believe she reads through the whole lot.

"It must make a strange hodgepodge in her head.

"This literary taste may account for some of her queer ways. When you see life through a maze of a thousand novels, you must get a queer impression of things and see them from an odd angle.

"As for me, I bide my time. It is certainly true that I

have never felt towards any woman as I feel towards her.

"It's equally certain that I shall never marry her.

"If she has had lovers, I shall make one more. If she has not, I shall be the first to take my seat in the train.

"It's all very simple. She can't possibly marry, ever. Who would marry the daughter of the Marquise Obardi, Octavie Bardin? Clearly, no one, for any number of reasons.

"Where could she find a husband? In society? Never; the mother's house is a public resort, and the daughter attracts the clients. One can't marry into a family like that. In the middle classes, then? Even less. Besides, the Marquise has a good head on her shoulders; she'd never give Yvette in marriage to anyone but a man of rank, and she'll never find him.

"In the lower classes, perhaps? Still less possible. There's no way out of it, then. The girl belongs neither to society nor to the middle class, nor to the lower classes, nor would marriage fit her into any one of them. She belongs, by her parentage, her birth, her upbringing, heredity, manners, habits, to the world of gilded prostitution.

"She can't escape unless she becomes a nun, which is very unlikely, seeing that her manners and tastes are already what they are. So she has only one possible profession—love. That's where she'll go, if she has not already gone. She can't escape her destiny. From being a young girl, she'll become just a—'woman.' And I should very much like to be the man who brings about the transformation.

"I am waiting. There are any number of lovers. You'll come across a Frenchman, Monsieur de Belvigne, a Russian who calls himself Prince Kravalow, and an Italian,

Chevalier Valreali. These have all definitely entered themselves in the race, and are already in training. There are also a number of camp-followers of less account.

"The Marquise is on the lookout. But I fancy she has her eye on me. She knows I'm very rich and she knows less about the others.

"Her house is the most extraordinary place of its kind that I have ever seen. You meet some very decent fellows there; we're going ourselves and we shall not be the only ones. As for the women, she has come across, or rather picked out, the choicest fruit on the professional stall. Lord knows where she found them. And she was magnificently inspired to make a point of picking women who had children of their own, daughters for choice. The result is that a greenhorn might think the house was full of respectable women!"

They had reached the Avenue des Champs Elysées. A faint breeze whispered among the leaves and was now and again wafted against their faces, like the soft breath of a giant fan swinging somewhere in the sky. Mute shadows drifted under the trees, others were visible as dark blots on the benches. And all these shadows spoke in very low tones, as though confiding important or shameful secrets.

"You cannot imagine," went on Servigny, "what a collection of fancy titles you come across in this rabbit-warren. By the way, I hope you know I'm going to introduce you as Count Saval. Saval by itself would not be at all popular, I assure you."

"No, damn it, certainly not!" cried his friend. "I'm hanged if anyone is going to think me fool enough to scrape up a comic-opera title even for 'one night only,' and for that crowd. With your leave, we'll cut that out."

Servigny laughed.

"You old idiot! Why, I've been christened Duc de Servigny. I don't know how or why it was done. I have just always been Duc de Servigny; I never made trouble about it. It's no discomfort. Why, without it I should be utterly looked down on!"

But Saval was not to be persuaded.

"You're a nobleman, you can carry it off. As for me, I shall remain, for better or worse, the only commoner in the place. That will be my mark of distinctive superiority."

But Servigny was obstinate.

"I tell you it can't be done, it absolutely cannot be done. It would be positively indecent. You would be like a rag-and-bone man at an assemblage of emperors. Leave it to me; I'll introduce you as the Viceroy of Upper Mississippi, and no one will be surprised. If you're going to go in for titles, you might as well do it with an air."

"No; I tell you again, I won't have it."

"Very well, then. I was a fool to try persuading you, for I defy you to get in without someone decorating you with a title; it's like those shops a lady can't pass without being given a bunch of violets at the door."

They turned to the right down the Rue de Berri, climbed to the upper floor of a fine modern mansion, and left their coats and sticks in the hands of four flunkeys in kneebreeches. The air was heavy with the warm festive odor of flowers, scent, and women; a ceaseless murmur of voices, loud and confused, came from the crowded rooms beyond.

A sort of master of ceremonies, a tall, straight-backed, solemn, pot-bellied man, with a face framed in white whiskers, approached the newcomers and, making a short, stiff bow, asked:

"What name, please?"

"Monsieur Saval," replied Servigny.

Whereupon the man flung open the door and in a loud voice announced to the crowd of guests:

"Monsieur le Duc de Servigny. Monsieur le Baron Saval."

The first room was full of women. The eye was filled at once by a vast vision of bare bosoms rising from billows of white lace.

The lady of the house stood talking to three friends; she turned and came forward with stately steps, grace in her bearing and a smile upon her lips.

Her low, narrow forehead was entirely hidden by masses of black, gleaming hair, thick and fleecy, encroaching even on her temples. She was tall, a little too massive, a little too plump, a little over-ripe, but very handsome, with a warm, heady, and powerful beauty. Her crown of hair, with the large black eyes beneath it, provoked entrancing dreams and made her subtly desirable. Her nose was rather thin, her mouth wide and infinitely alluring, made for speech and conquest.

But her liveliest charm lay in her voice. It sprang from her mouth like water from a spring, so easily, so lightly, so well pitched, so clear, that listening to it was sheer physical joy. It thrilled the ear to hear the smooth words pour forth with the sparkling grace of a brook bubbling from the ground, and fascinated the eye to watch the lovely, too-red lips part to give them passage.

She held out her hand to Servigny, who kissed it, and, dropping the fan that hung from a thin chain of wrought gold, she gave her other hand to Saval, saying:

"You are welcome, Baron. My house is always open to any friend of the Duke's."

Then she fixed her brilliant eyes on the giant to whom she was being introduced. On her upper lip was a faint smudge of black down, the merest shadow of a mustache, more plainly visible when she spoke. Her scent was delicious, strong and intoxicating, some American or Indian perfume.

But other guests were arriving, marquises, counts, or princes. She turned to Servigny and said, with the graciousness of a mother:

"You will find my daughter in the other room. Enjoy yourselves, gentlemen. The house is yours."

She left them in order to greet the new arrivals, giving Saval that fugitive smiling glance with which women let men know that they have found favor.

Servigny took his friend's arm.

"I'll be your pilot," he said. "Here, where we are at present, are the women; this is the Temple of the Flesh, fresh or otherwise. Bargains as good as new, or better; very superior articles at greatly reduced rates. On the left is the gambling. That is the Temple of Money. You know all about that.

"At the far end, dancing; that is the Temple of Innocence. There are displayed the offspring, if we may believe it, of the ladies you see here. Even lawful unions would be smiled on! There lies the future, the hope . . . of our nights. And there, too, are the strangest exhibits in this museum of diseased morals, the young girls whose souls are double-jointed, like the limbs of little clowns who had acrobats for parents. Let us go and see them."

He bowed to right and left, a debonair figure, scattering pretty speeches and running his rapid, expert glance over every pair of bare shoulders whose possessor he recognized.

At the far end of the second room an orchestra was playing a waltz; they stopped at the door and watched. Some fifteen couples were dancing, the men gravely, their partners with fixed smiles on their lips. Like their mothers, the girls showed a great deal of bare skin; since the bodices of some were supported only by a narrow ribbon round the upper part of the arm, there were occasional glimpses of a dark shadow under the armpits.

Suddenly a tall girl started up and crossed the room, pushing the dancers aside, her absurdly long train gathered in her left hand. She ran with the short quick steps affected by women in a crowd, and cried out:

"Ah, there's Muscade. How are you, Muscade!"

Her face was glowing with life and radiant with happiness. She had the white, golden-glowing skin which goes with auburn hair. Her forehead was loaded with a sheaf of flaming, gleaming tresses that burdened her still slender neck.

She seemed made for motion as her mother was for speech, so natural, gracious, and simple were her movements. A sense of spiritual delight and physical contentment sprang from the mere sight of her as she walked, moved, bent her head or raised her arm.

"Ah, Muscade," she repeated. "How are you, Muscade?"

Servigny shook her hand vigorously, as though she were a man, and said:

"This is my friend, Baron Saval, Mam'selle Yvette."

She greeted the newcomer, then stared at him.

"How do you do? Are you always as tall as this?"

"Oh, no, Mam'selle," answered Servigny, in the mocking tone he used to conceal his uneasiness in her presence. "He has put on his largest size today to please your mother, who likes quantity."

"Oh, very well, then," replied the girl in a serio-comic voice. "But when you come for my sake, please be a little smaller; I like the happy medium. Muscade here is about my size," and she offered him her little hand.

"Are you going to dance, Muscade?" she asked. "Let's dance this waltz."

Servigny made no answer, but with a sudden swift movement put his arm round her waist, and away they went like a whirlwind.

They danced faster than any, turning and twirling with wild abandon, so tightly clasped that they looked like one. Their bodies held upright and their legs almost motionless, it was as though they were spun round by an invisible machine hidden under their feet. They seemed tireless. One by one the other couples dropped out till they were left alone, waltzing on and on. They looked as though they no longer knew where they were or what they were doing, as though they were far away from the ballroom, in ecstasy. The band played steadily on, their eyes fixed on this bewitched pair; everyone was watching, and there was a burst of applause when at last they stopped.

She was rather flushed; her eyes were no longer frank, but strangely troubled, burning yet timid, unnaturally blue, with pupils unnaturally black.

Servigny was drunk with giddiness and leaned against a door to recover his balance.

"You have a weak head, Muscade," she said. "You don't stand it as well as I do."

He smiled his nervous smile and looked at her with hungry eyes, a savage lust in his eyes and the curve of his lips.

She continued to stand in front of the young man, her breast heaving as she regained her breath.

"Sometimes," she continued, "you look just like a cat about to make a spring. Give me your arm, and let us go find your friend."

Without a word he offered her his arm, and they crossed the large room.

Saval was no longer alone; the Marquise Obardi had joined him, and was talking of trivial things, bewitching him with her maddening voice. Gazing intently at him, she seemed to utter words very different from those on her lips, words that came from the secret places of her heart. At the sight of Servigny she smiled and, turning to him, said:

"Have you heard, my dear Duke, that I've just taken a villa at Bougival for a couple of months? Of course you'll come to see me; you'll bring your friend, won't you? I'm going down on Monday, so will you both come and dine there next Saturday, and stay the week end?"

Servigny turned sharply to Yvette. She was smiling a serene, tranquil smile, and with an air of bland assurance said:

"Of course Muscade will come to dinner on Saturday: there's no need to ask him. We shall have all kinds of fun in the country."

He fancied that he saw a vague promise in her smile, and an unwonted decision in her voice.

The Marquise thereupon raised her great black eyes to Saval's face, and said:

"And you also, Baron?"

There was nothing equivocal about her smile.

He bowed.

"I shall be only too pleased."

"We'll scandalize the neighborhood—won't we, Muscade?—and drive my admirers wild with rage," murmured Yvette, glancing, with a malice that was either candid or assured, towards the group of men who watched them from the other side of the room.

"To your heart's content, Mam'selle," replied Servigny; by way of emphasizing the intimate nature of his friendship with her, he never called her "Mademoiselle."

"Why does Mademoiselle Yvette always call my friend Servigny 'Muscade'?" asked Saval.

The girl assumed an air of innocence.

"He's like the little pea that the conjurers call 'Muscade.' You think you have your finger on it, but you never have."

"Quaint children, aren't they?" the Marquise said carelessly, obviously thinking of far other things, and not for an instant lowering her eyes from Saval's face.

"I'm not quaint, I'm frank," said Yvette angrily. "I like Muscade, and he's always leaving me; it's so annoying."

Servigny made her a low bow.

"I'll never leave you again, Mam'selle, day or night."

She made a gesture of alarm.

"Oh, no, that would never do! In the daytime, by all means, but at night you'd be in the way."

"Why?" he asked imprudently.

With calm audacity she replied:

"Because I don't expect you look so nice with your clothes off."

"What a dreadful thing to say!" exclaimed the Marquise, without appearing in the least upset. "You can't possibly be so innocent as all that."

"I entirely agree with you," added Servigny in a jesting tone.

Yvette looked rather hurt, and said haughtily:

"You have just been guilty of blatant vulgarity; you have permitted yourself far too much of that sort of thing lately."

She turned her back on him, and called out:

"Chevalier, come defend me; I have just been insulted."

A thin, dark man came slowly towards them.

"Which is the culprit?" he asked, forcing a smile.

She nodded towards Servigny.

"That's the man; but all the same I like him better than all of you put together; he's not so boring."

The Chevalier Valreali bowed.

"We do what we can. Perhaps we are not so brilliant, but we are at least as devoted."

A tall, stout man with gray whiskers and a deep voice was just leaving.

"Your servant, Mademoiselle Yvette," he said as he passed.

"Ah, it's Monsieur de Belvigne," she exclaimed, and turning to Saval, she introduced him.

"Another candidate for my favor, tall, fat, rich, and stupid. That's how I like them. He's a real field-marshal —one of those who hold the door open at restaurants. But you're taller than he is. Now what am I going to christen you? I know! I shall call you Rhodes Junior, after the colossus who must have been your father. But you two must have really interesting things to discuss, far above our heads, so good night to you."

She ran across to the orchestra, and asked them to play a quadrille.

Madame Obardi's attention seemed to be wandering.

"You're always teasing her," she said softly. "You're spoiling the child's disposition and teaching her a number of bad habits."

"Then you haven't finished her education?" he replied.

She seemed not to understand, and continued to smile benevolently.

But observing the approach of a solemn gentleman whose breast was covered with orders, she ran up to him:

"Ah, Prince, how delightful!"

Servigny took Saval's arm once more and led him away, saying:

"There's my latest serious rival, Prince Kravalow. Isn't she a glorious creature?"

"They're both glorious," replied Saval. "The mother's quite good enough for me."

Servigny bowed.

"She's yours for the asking, old chap."

The dancers elbowed them as they took their places for the quadrille, couple by couple, in two lines facing one another.

"Now let's go and watch the Greeks for a bit," said Servigny.

They entered the gambling-room.

Round each table a circle of men stood watching. There was very little conversation; sometimes a little chink of gold, thrown down on the cloth or hastily gathered up, mingled its faint metallic chime with the murmur of the players, as though the voice of gold were making itself heard amid the human voices.

The men were decorated with various orders and strange ribbons; and their diverse features all wore the same severe expression. They were more easily distinguished by their beards.

The stiff American with his horseshoe beard, the haughty Englishman with a hairy fan spread over his chest, the Spaniard with a black fleece reaching right up to his eyes, the Roman with the immense mustache bequeathed to Italy by Victor Emmanuel, the Austrian with his whiskers and clean-shaven chin, a Russian general whose lip was armed with two spears of twisted hair, Frenchmen with gay mustaches—they displayed the imaginative genius of every barber in the world.

"Aren't you going to play?" asked Servigny.

"No; what about you?"

"I never play here. Would you like to go now? We'll come back one day when it's quieter. There are too many people here today; there's nothing to be done."

"Yes, let us go."

They disappeared through a doorway which led into the hall.

As soon as they were out in the street, Servigny asked: "Well, what do you think of it all?"

"It's certainly interesting. But I like the women better than the men."

"Good Lord, yes! Those women are the best hunting in the country. Don't you agree with me that love exhales from them like the perfumes from a barber's shop? These are positively the only houses where one can really get one's money's worth. And what expert lovers they are! What artists! Have you ever eaten cakes made by a baker? They look so good, and they have no flavor at all. Well, the love of an ordinary woman always reminds me of a baker's pastry, whereas the love you get from women like the Marquise Obardi—that really is love! Oh, they can make cakes all right, can these confectioners. You have to pay them twopence halfpenny for what you would get anywhere else for a penny, that's the only thing."

"Who is paying the bills just now?" asked Saval.

Servigny shrugged his shoulders.

"I have no idea," he said. "The last I knew certainly was an English peer, but he left three months ago. At the moment she must be living on the community, on the gambling and the gamblers, very likely, for she has her whims. But it's agreed, isn't it, that we are dining with her at Bougival on Saturday? There's more freedom in the country, and I shall end by finding out what notions Yvette has in her head!"

"I ask for nothing better," replied Saval. "I'm not doing anything that day."

As they returned down the Champs Élysées, under the embattled stars, they passed a couple lying on a bench, and Servigny murmured:

"How ridiculous, yet how utterly indispensable, is this business of love! A commonplace, and an ecstasy, always the same and always different! And the clown who is paying that girl a franc is only seeking the very thing I buy for ten thousand from some Obardi who is perhaps no younger or more fascinating than that drab! What folly!"

He was silent for some minutes, then said:

"All the same, to be Yvette's first lover would not be a thing to disdain. For that I'd give . . . I'd give. . . ."

He did not make up his mind what he would give. Saval bade him good night at the corner of the Rue Royale.

II

The table had been laid on the veranda overlooking the river. Villa Printemps, the house that the Marquise Obardi had taken, stood half-way up the hillside, just where the Seine made a turn, running round in front of the garden wall and down towards Marly. Opposite the house the island of Croissy formed a background of tall trees, a mass of leafage. A long reach of the broad river was clearly visible as far as the floating café, La Grenouillère, half hidden in its branches.

Night was coming down, calm and still, after a flaming riverside sunset; one of those tranquil evenings that bring with them a vague sense of happiness. Not a breath of air stirred the branches, no gust of wind disturbed the smooth, translucent surface of the Seine. The air was warm, but not too hot; it was good to be alive. The grateful coolness of the river banks rose to the quiet sky.

The sun was disappearing behind the trees, wheeling towards other lands. The serene calm of the sleeping earth soothed the visitors' senses; under the vast quiet dome of the sky they felt the effortless surge of universal life.

The scene enchanted them when they came out of the drawing-room and sat down at the dinner-table. A tender gaiety filled their hearts; they all felt it very good to be dining in the country with that broad river and glorious sunset for scenery, and breathing that limpid, heady air.

The Marquise had taken Saval's arm, Yvette Servigny's.

These four made up the little party.

The two women were not in the least like their Parisian selves. Yvette was the more altered of the two; she spoke very little, and seemed tired and grave.

Saval hardly recognized her, and asked:

"What's the matter with you, Mademoiselle? I find you very changed since last week. You have become quite a reasonable being."

"It's the effect of the country," she answered. "I am not the same here; I feel quite strange. And besides, I never am the same two days together. Today I behave like a lunatic, tomorrow I'll be like a funeral oration; I change like the weather, I don't know why. I'm capable of absolutely anything—at the right time. There are days when I could kill people; not animals—I could never kill animals—but people, certainly; and then there are days when I cry for no reason at all. A hundred different ideas rush through my head. It depends, too, on how I feel when I get up in the morning. Every morning when I wake up I know just what I shall be like all day. Perhaps our dreams decide that sort of thing. Partly it depends on the book I have just been reading."

She was dressed in white flannel; the soft, delicate folds of material covered her from head to foot. The bodice was loose, with big pleats, and suggested, without too rigidly defining, the firm contour of her already well-formed bosom. Her slender neck rose from fold upon fold of frothy drooping lace, its warm gleaming flesh even whiter than her dress and weighed down with the heavy burden of her golden hair.

Servigny gazed at her without speaking, then said:

"You are adorable tonight, Mam'selle—I wish I could always see you like that."

"Don't propose to me, Muscade," she said, with a touch of her wonted archness. "On a day like this I should take you at your word, and that might cost you dear."

The Marquise looked happy, very happy. She was dressed severely in black; the fine folds of the gown set off the superb, massive lines of her figure. A touch of red adorned her bodice, a spray of red carnations fell from her waist and was caught up at her side, a red rose was fastened in her dark hair. There was a flame in her tonight, in her whole being, in the simple dress with the blood-red blossoms, in the glance that lingered on Saval, in her slow voice, in her rare movements.

Saval, too, was grave and preoccupied. From time to time, with a gesture familiar to him, he stroked his brown Vandyke beard; he seemed sunk in thought.

For some moments no one spoke.

"There is sometimes a saving grace in silence," said

Servigny at last, as the trout was being handed round. "One often feels nearer one's fellow-creatures when silent than when speaking; isn't that so, Marquise?"

She turned slightly towards him and replied:

"Yes, it's true. It is so sweet to think together of the same delightful thing."

Her burning gaze shifted to Saval; for a moment they remained looking into one another's eyes. There was a slight, an almost imperceptible movement under the table.

"Mam'selle Yvette," continued Servigny, "you'll make me think you're in love if you continue to behave so beautifully. Now with whom can you be in love? Let's think it out together. I leave the vulgar herd of sighing swains on one side and go straight for the principals. How about Prince Kravalow?"

At this name Yvette was roused.

"My poor dear Muscade, what *are* you thinking about? The Prince looks like a Russian in a waxworks, who has won a medal at a hairdressers' competition."

"Very well. The Prince is out of it. Perhaps you have chosen the Vicomte Pierre de Belvigne?"

This time she broke into a fit of laughter and asked:

"Can you see me hanging round Raisiné's neck"—she called him Raisiné, Malvoisie, or Argenteuil, according to the day of the week, for she nicknamed everyone—"and whispering in his ear, 'My dear little Pierre,' or 'My divine Pedro, my adored Pietro, my darling Pierrot, give your dear fat poodlehead to your darling little wifie because she wants to kiss it'?"

"Away with Number Two, then," said Servigny. "We are left with the Chevalier Valreali, whom the Marquise seems to favor."

Yvette was as much amused as before.

"What, Old Lachrymose? Why, he's a professional

mourner at the Madeleine; he follows all the high-class funerals. Whenever he looks at me I feel as though I were already dead."

"That's three. Then you've fallen hopelessly in love with Baron Saval, here present."

"With Rhodes Junior? No, he's too strong. It would feel like being in love with the Arc de Triomphe."

"Well, then, Mam'selle, it is plain that you're in love with me, for I'm the only one of your worshipers that we haven't already dealt with. I had kept myself to the end, out of modesty and prudence. It only remains for me to thank you."

"You, Muscade!" she replied with charming gaiety. "Oh, no, I like you very much . . . but I don't love you. . . . Wait, I don't want to discourage you. I don't love you yet. . . . You have a chance . . . perhaps. . . . Persevere, Muscade, be devoted, ardent, obedient, take plenty of trouble and all possible precautions, obey my lightest whims, be prepared to do anything I choose . . . and we'll see . . . later."

"But, Mam'selle, I'd rather do all this for you after than before, if you don't mind."

"After what . . . Muscade?" she asked him with the ingenuous air of a soubrette.

"Why, deuce take it, after you've shown me that you love me."

"Well, behave as though I did, and believe it if you want to."

"But, I must say. . . ."

"Be quiet, Muscade. That's enough for this time."

He made her a military salute and held his tongue.

The sun had gone down behind the island, but the sky still gleamed like a brazier, and the quiet water of the river was as though changed to blood. The sunset spilled a ruddy sheen over houses, people, the whole earth; the scarlet rose in the Marquise's hair was like a drop of crimson fallen upon her head from the clouds.

Yvette was staring into the distance; her mother laid her hand on Saval's, as though by accident. But the young girl turned around, and the Marquise quickly snatched away her hand and fumbled at the folds of her bodice.

Servigny, who was watching them, said:

"If you like, Mam'selle, we'll go for a walk presently on the island."

She was delighted with the idea.

"Oh, yes; that will be lovely; we'll go by ourselves, won't we, Muscade?"

"Yes, all by ourselves, Mam'selle."

Once more they were silent.

The calm of the wide landscape, the restful slumber of eventide weighed on their hearts, their bodies, their voices. There are rare, quiet hours when speech is almost impossible. The servants moved noiselessly about. The flaming sky burnt low; slowly night folded the earth in shadow.

"Do you propose to stay here long?" asked Saval.

"Yes," replied the Marquise, dwelling upon each word, "for just as long as I'm happy here."

As it was now too dark to see, lamps were brought. They flung across the table a strange, pale light in the hollow darkness. A rain of little flies began falling upon the cloth. They were midges, burnt as they flew over the glass chimneys of the lamps; their wings and legs singed, they powdered the table-linen, the plates, and the glasses with a gray, creeping dust. The diners swallowed them in their wine, ate them in the sauces, watched them crawling over the bread. Their faces and hands were perpetually tickled by a flying swarm of innumerable tiny insects.

The wine had constantly to be poured away, the plates covered; they took infinite precautions to protect the food they were eating. Yvette was amused at the game; Servigny carefully sheltered whatever she was raising to her lips, guarded the wine-glass and held his napkin spread out over her head like a roof. But it was too much for the fastidious nerves of the Marquise, and the meal was hastily brought to an end.

"Now let's go to the island," said Yvette, who had not forgotten Servigny's suggestion.

"Don't stay long, will you?" advised her mother languidly. "We'll come with you as far as the ferry."

They went off along the tow-path, still two and two, the young girl in front with her friend. They could hear the Marquise and Saval behind them talking very fast in very low voices. All round them was black, a thick, inky blackness. But the sky, swarming with seeds of fire, seemed to spill them out on the river, for the dark water was richly patined with stars.

By this time the frogs were croaking; along the banks their rolling, monotonous notes creaked out.

The soft voices of innumerable nightingales rose in the still air.

Yvette remarked abruptly:

"Hallo! They are no longer following us. Where are they?"

And she called, "Mother!"

There was no answer. "They can't be far away," continued the young girl. "I heard them a moment ago."

"They must have gone back," murmured Servigny. "Perhaps your mother was cold." He led her on.

A light shone in front of them; it was the inn run by one Martinet, a fisherman who also ran a tavern. At their call a man came out of the house, and they boarded a large boat moored in the grasses on the bank.

The ferryman took up his oars, and the heavy boat advanced, waking the stars slumbering on the water and rousing them to a frenzied dancing that died slowly down in their wake. They touched the other bank and stepped off under the tall trees. The coolness of the moist earth floated up under the high, thick branches that seemed to bear as many nightingales as leaves. In the distance, a piano began to play a popular waltz.

Servigny had taken Yvette's arm; very softly he slipped his hand round her waist and pressed it gently.

"What are you thinking of?" he asked.

"I? . . . Nothing, I'm so happy."

"Then you don't care for me?"

"Yes, I do, Muscade. I care for you, I care for you a great deal; only don't talk about it now. It's too beautiful here to listen to your nonsense."

He clasped her to him, though she strove, with little struggles, to free herself; through the flannel, so soft and fleecy to the touch, he could feel the warmth of her body.

"Yvette," he stammered.

"Yes; what is it?"

"It's . . . I who care for you."

"You . . . don't mean that, Muscade."

"Yes, I do; I've cared for you for a very long time."

She was still struggling to get away, striving to free her arm caught between their two bodies. They walked with difficulty, hampered by this link and by her struggles, zigzagging like a couple of drunkards.

He did not know what to say to her now, well aware that it is impossible to use to a young girl the words one would use to a mature woman; he was worried, wondering what he could do, wondering if she consented or did not understand, at his wits' end for words that would be at once tender, discreet, and unmistakable.

Every second he repeated:

"Yvette! Speak to me, Yvette!"

Suddenly he pressed an audacious kiss on her cheek. She made a little movement of withdrawal, and said in a vexed tone:

"Oh! How absurd you are. Will you leave me alone?"

Her voice revealed nothing of her thoughts and wishes; he saw that she was not too angry, and he put his lips to the nape of her neck, on the first few downy golden hairs, the adorable spot he had coveted so long. Then she struggled with all her might to get free. But he held her firmly, and placing his other hand on her shoulder, forced her head round towards him, and took from her mouth a long, maddening kiss. She slipped between his arms with a quick twist of her whole body, stooped swiftly, and having thus dexterously escaped from his embrace, vanished in the darkness with a sharp rustling of petticoats like the whir of a rising bird.

At first he remained motionless, stunned by her quickness and by her disappearance; then, hearing no further sound, he called in a low voice:

"Yvette!"

There was no answer; he began to walk on, ransacking the darkness with his eyes, searching in the bushes for the white patch that her dress must make. All was dark. He called again more loudly:

"Mam'selle Yvette!"

The nightingales were silent.

He hurried on, vaguely uneasy, calling ever louder and louder:

"Mam'selle Yvette! Mam'selle Yvette!"

Nothing! He stopped, listened. The whole island was silent; there was barely a rustle in the leaves overhead. The frogs alone kept up their sonorous croaking on the banks.

He wandered from copse to copse, going at first down the steep wooded slope of the swift main stream, then returning to the bare flat bank of the backwater. He went right up until he was opposite Bougival, then came back to the café La Grenouillère, hunting through all the thickets, constantly crying:

"Mam'selle Yvette, where are you? Answer! It is only a joke. Answer me, answer me! Don't make me hunt like this."

A distant clock began to strike. He counted the strokes; it was midnight. For two hours he had been running round the island. He thought that she had probably gone home, and, very uneasy, went back, going round by the bridge.

A servant, asleep in an armchair, was waiting in the hall. Servigny woke him and asked:

"Is it long since Mademoiselle Yvette came in? I left her out in the country, as I had to pay a call."

"Oh, yes, your Grace," the fellow replied, "Mademoiselle came in before ten."

He walked up to his room and went to bed. But he lay with his eyes open, unable to sleep. That snatched kiss had disturbed her. What did she want? he wondered. What did she think? What did she know? How pretty she was, how tormenting! His desire, blunted by the life he had led, by all the women he had known, was reawakened by this strange child, so fresh, provoking, and inexplicable.

He heard one o'clock strike, then two. He realized that he would get no sleep that night. He was hot and damp with sweat; he felt in his temples the quick thudding of his heart. He got up to open the window.

A cool breeze came in, and he drew long deep breaths of it. The night was utterly dark, silent, and still. But suddenly, in the darkness of the garden he caught sight of a speck of light, like a little piece of glowing coal. "Ah, a cigar," he thought. "It can't be anyone but Saval. Léon," he called softly.

"Is that you, Jean?" a voice answered.

"Yes. Wait, I'm coming down."

He dressed, went out, and joined his friend, who was smoking astride an iron chair.

"What are you doing at this time of night?"

"Resting up," replied Saval, and laughed.

Servigny shook his head.

"I congratulate you, my dear chap. As for me, I've run my head into a wall."

"You are telling me . . . ?"

"I am telling you . . . that Yvette is not like her mother."

"What happened? Tell me all about it."

Servigny recounted his unsuccessful efforts, then continued:

"Yes, the child really worries me. Do you realize that I haven't been able to get to sleep? What a queer thing a girl is. This one looked as simple as possible, and yet she's a complete mystery. One can understand at once a woman who has lived and loved, who knows what life is like. But with a young girl, one can't be sure of anything at all. I'm really beginning to think she's making a fool of me."

Saval rocked gently on his chair.

"Be careful, my dear chap," he said very slowly; "she'll get you to marry her. Remember the illustrious

examples in history. That was how Mademoiselle de
Montijo became Empress, and she at least came of a
decent family. Don't play the Napoleon."

"Have no fears about that," said Servigny. "I'm neither a fool, nor an emperor. One has to be one or the
other to lose one's head so completely. But, I say, are
you sleepy?"

"Not a bit."

"Come for a walk along the riverside, then."

"Very well."

They opened the gate and started off down the river
in the direction of Marly.

It was the cool hour just before dawn, the hour of
deepest sleep, deepest rest, utter quiet. Even the faint
noises of the night were silent now. The nightingales
sang no longer, the frogs had finished their croaking;
some unknown creature, a bird perhaps, broke the stillness, making a feeble sawing noise, monotonous and
regular, like the working of a machine. Servigny, who
had at times a touch of the poet and of the philosopher
too, said abruptly:

"Look here. This girl absolutely maddens me. In
arithmetic, one and one make two. In love, one and one
ought to make one, but they make two all the same. Do
you know the feeling? The wild need of absorbing a
woman into oneself, or of being absorbed into her? I
don't mean the mere physical desire to embrace her,
but the mental and spiritual torment to be one with
another human being, to open one's whole soul, one's
whole heart, to her, and to penetrate to the uttermost
depths of her mind. And never, never do you really
know her or discover all the fluctuations of her will, her
longings, her thoughts. Never can you make even the
slightest guess at the whole of the secret, the whole
mystery of the spirit come so close to you, a spirit hid-

den behind two eyes as clear as water, as transparent as though there were no secret behind them. A spirit speaks to you through a beloved mouth, a mouth that seems yours because you desire it so passionately; one by one this spirit sends you its thoughts cloaked in words, and yet it remains farther from you than the stars are from one another, farther out of reach than the stars. Strange, isn't it!"

"I do not ask so much," replied Saval. "I do not bother to look behind the eyes. I don't care much for the inside; it's the outside I care for."

"Say what you will, Yvette's a queer creature," murmured Servigny. "I wonder how she'll treat me in the morning."

As they reached the weir at Marly, they saw that the sky was paling. Cocks began to crow in the farmyards; the sound reached them slightly muffled by thick walls. A bird screeched in a park on the left, continually repeating a simple and ridiculous little cadenza.

"Time to go back," said Saval, and they turned back.

When Servigny reached his room, the horizon gleamed rosily through the open window. He pulled down the Venetian blinds and drew the heavy curtains across, got into bed, and at last he fell asleep. And all the time he dreamt of Yvette.

A curious sound awoke him. He sat up and listened, but did not hear it again. Then suddenly there came against his shutters a rattling like hail. He jumped out of bed and ran to the window; throwing it open, he saw Yvette standing on the garden-path, throwing great handfuls of gravel in his face.

She was dressed in pink and wore a broad-brimmed straw hat surmounted with a military plume; she was laughing mischievously.

"Well, Muscade, still asleep? What *can* you have been

doing last night to sleep so late? Did you have any adventures, my poor Muscade?"

"Coming, coming, Mam'selle! Just a moment, while I stick my nose into the water-jug, and I'll be down."

"Hurry up,'" she cried; "it's ten o'clock. And I've got a scheme to talk over with you, a plot we are going to carry out. Breakfast at eleven, you know."

He found her seated on a bench with a book on her knees, a novel. She took his arm with friendly familiarity, as frankly and gaily as though nothing had happened the night before, and leading him to the far end of the garden, said:

"This is my plan. We're going to disobey mamma, and you shall take me presently to the Grenouillère. I want to see it. Mamma says that decent women can't go there, but I don't care whether I can or I can't. You'll take me, Muscade, won't you? We'll have such sport with the people on the river."

The fragrance of her was delightful, but he could not discover what vague, faint scent it was that hung round her. It was not one of her mother's heavy perfumes, but a delicate fragrance in which he thought he recognized a faint whiff of iris powder and perhaps a touch of verbena.

Whence came this elusive scent—from her dress, her hair, or her skin? He was wondering about this when, as she spoke with her face very close to his, he felt her fresh breath full in his face, and found it quite as delightful. He fancied that the fleeting fragrance he had failed to recognize was the figment of his own bewitched senses, nothing but a delusive emanation from her youth and alluring grace.

"You will, won't you, Muscade?" she said. "It will be so hot after breakfast that mother won't want to go out. She's very lazy when it's hot. We'll leave her with your friend, and you shall be my escort. We'll pretend we are going to the woods. You don't know how I shall enjoy seeing the Grenouillère."

They reached the gate facing the Seine. A flood of sunlight fell on the quiet, gleaming river. A light heat-haze was lifting, the steam of evaporated water, leaving a little glittering vapor on the surface of the river. From time to time a boat went by, a light skiff or a heavy barge, and distant whistles could be heard, the short notes of the whistles on the Sunday trains that flood the country with Parisians, and the long warning notes of the steamboats passing the weir at Marly.

But a small bell rang for breakfast, and they went in.

The meal was eaten in silence. A heavy July noon beat down on the earth and oppressed the spirit. The heat was almost tangible, paralyzing both mind and body. The sluggish words would not leave their lips; every movement was an effort, as though the air had acquired the power of resistance, and was more difficult to thrust through.

Yvette alone, though silent, was animated and possessed by impatience. As soon as dessert was finished she said:

"Suppose we go for a walk in the woods. It will be perfectly delightful under the trees."

"Are you mad?" murmured the Marquise, who looked utterly exhausted. "How can one go out in weather like this?"

"Very well," replied the young girl slyly, "we'll leave you here with the Baron to keep you company. Muscade and I will scramble up the hill and sit down and read on the grass."

She turned to Servigny, saying, "That's all right, isn't it?"

"At your service, Mam'selle," he replied.

She ran off to fetch her hat. The Marquise shrugged her shoulders and sighed, "Really, she's quite mad." Indolently she held out her beautiful white hand in a gesture of profound and seductive lassitude; the Baron pressed a lingering kiss upon it.

Yvette and Servigny departed. At first they followed the river, then they crossed the bridge and went on to the island. They sat down under the willows on the bank of the main stream, for it was still too early to go to La Grenouillère.

The young girl at once took a book from her pocket and, laughing, said:

"Muscade, you're going to read to me." And she held out the volume for him to take. He made a deprecatory gesture. "I, Mam'selle? But I can't read."

"Come, now, no excuses, no arguments," she replied severely. "You're a nice lover, you are. 'Everything for nothing'—that's your motto, isn't it?"

He took the book and opened it, and was surprised to find that it was a treatise on entomology, a history of ants by an English author. He remained silent, thinking that she was making fun of him.

"Go on, read," she said.

"Is this a bet," he asked, "or just a joke?"

"Neither. I saw the book in a shop; they told me it was the best book about ants, and I thought it would be nice to hear about the lives of the little creatures and watch them running about in the grass at the same time. So read away."

She lay down face downwards at full length, her elbows resting on the ground and her cheeks cupped in her hands, her eyes fixed on the grass.

"'Without doubt,'" he read, "'the anthropoid apes are of all animals those which approach most closely to man in their anatomical structure; but if we consider the habits of ants, their organization into societies, their vast communities, the houses and roads which they construct, their custom of domesticating animals and even at times of having slaves, we shall be forced to admit that they have the right to claim a place near man on the ladder of intelligence.'"

He continued in a monotonous voice, stopping from time to time to ask, "Isn't that enough?"

She signed "no" with a shake of her head, and, having picked up a wandering ant on the point of a blade of grass she had plucked, she amused herself by making it run from one end of the stem to the other, tilting it as soon as the insect reached either end. She listened in silence and with concentrated attention to all the surprising details of the life of these frail creatures, their subterranean establishments, the way in which they bring up, keep, and feed little grubs in order to drink the liquid they secrete, just as we keep cows in our byres, their custom of domesticating little blind insects which clean their dwellings, and of going to war in order to bring back slaves to serve the victors, which the slaves do with such solicitude that the latter even lose the habit of feeding themselves.

And little by little, as though a maternal tenderness had awakened in her for this creature at once so tiny and so intelligent, Yvette let it creep over her finger, watching it with loving eyes, longing to kiss it. And as Servigny read how they live in a community, how they play together in friendly rivalry of strength and skill, the young girl, in her enthusiasm, tried to kiss the insect, which escaped from her finger and began to run over her face. She shrieked as violently as though a deadly peril threatened her, and with wild gestures she slapped at her cheek to get rid of the creature. Servigny, roaring with laughter, caught it near her hair and, at the spot where he had caught it, pressed a long kiss, from which Yvette did not recoil.

She got up, declaring, "I like that better than a novel. Now let's go to La Grenouillère."

They reached a part of the island which was laid out like a park, shaded with huge trees. Couples wandered under the lofty foliage beside the Seine, over which boats were gliding. There were girls with young men, working girls with shirt-sleeved sweethearts who carried their coats on their arms and wore their tall hats on the back of their heads, looking weary and dissipated; clerks with their families, the wives in their Sunday best, the children running round their parents like a brood of chickens. A continuous distant buzz of human voices, a dull, rumbling clamor, announced the nearness of the establishment beloved of boating parties. Suddenly it came into view, an enormous roofed barge moored to the bank, filled by a crowd of men and women who sat drinking at tables or stood up, shouting, singing, laughing, dancing, capering to the noise of a jangling piano, out of tune and as clattery as a tin can. Tall, red-haired girls, displaying before and behind them the swelling, provocative curves of breasts and hips, walked up and down with eager, inviting glances, all three parts drunk and talking obscenities. Others were dancing wildly in front of young men who were half naked, dressed only in rowing-shorts and shirts, and wearing colored jockey-caps on their heads. There was a pervading odor of sweat and face powder, the combined exhalations of perfumeries and armpits. Those who sat drinking at the tables were swallowing white and red and yellow and green liquids, screaming and yelling for no reason, yielding to a violent need to make a din, an animal instinct to fill ears and brain with noise. From time to time a swimmer dived from the roof, splashing those sitting near, who yelled at him like savages.

On the river a fleet of boats passed and repassed; long slim boats went by, propelled by the powerful strokes of bare-armed oarsmen, whose muscles worked under the tanned skin. The women in the boats, dressed in blue or red flannel, holding open sunshades, also blue or red, over their heads, made brilliant splashes of color under the burning sun. They lolled on their seats in the stern and seemed to glide on the surface of the water, motionless or drowsy. Heavier boats moved slowly past, loaded with people. A lighthearted student, bent on showing off, rowed with a windmill stroke, bumping into all the boats, whose occupants swore at him. He eventually disappeared crestfallen, after nearly drowning two swimmers, followed by the jeers of the crowd jammed on the floating café.

Yvette was radiant as she passed through this noisy, milling crowd on Servigny's arm. She seemed happy to be jostled by all and sundry, and stared at the girls with calm and friendly eyes.

"Look at that one, Muscade, what lovely hair she's got! They do seem to be enjoying themselves."

The pianist, an oarsman dressed in red, whose hat was very like a colossal straw parasol, began a waltz. Yvette promptly seized her companion by the waist and swung him off with the fury she always put into her dancing. They went on so long and with such frenzy that the whole crowd watched them. Those who were sitting drinking stood upon their tables and beat time with their feet, others smashed glasses. The pianist seemed to go mad; he banged at the ivory keys with galloping hands, gesticulating wildly with his whole body, swaying his head and its enormous covering with frantic movements.

Abruptly he stopped, slid down, and lay full length on the ground, hidden under his hat, as though dead of exhaustion. There was a burst of laughter in the café, and every one applauded. Four friends rushed up as though there had been an accident, and picking up their comrade, bore him off by all four limbs, after placing on his stomach the roof under which he sheltered his head. Another jester followed, intoning the *De Profundis,* and a procession formed behind the mock corpse. It went round all the paths in the island, collecting drinkers, strollers, indeed every one it met.

Yvette ran along enraptured, laughing heartily and talking to everyone, wild with the din and the bustle. Young men pushed against her and stared at her excitedly with eyes whose burning glances seemed to strip her naked. Servigny began to be afraid that the adventure might end unfortunately. The procession went on its way, moving faster and faster, for the four bearers had begun to race, followed by the yelling crowd. But suddenly they turned towards the bank, stopped dead at the edge, swung their comrade to and fro, and then, all letting go of him at once, they heaved him into the water. A great shout of merriment burst from every mouth, while the bewildered pianist splashed about, swearing, coughing, and spitting out water; stuck fast in the mud, he struggled to climb up the bank. His hat, which was floating down the stream, was brought back by a boat.

Yvette danced with joy and clapped her hands, saying:

"Oh, Muscade, what fun, what fun!"

Servigny, now serious, watched her, a little embarrassed and a little dismayed to see her so much at ease in these vulgar surroundings. He felt a faint disgust born of the instinct that an aristocrat rarely loses, even

in moments of utter abandon, the instinct that protects
him from unpardonable familiarities and contacts that
would be too degrading. "No one will credit you with
too much breeding, my child," he said to himself, astounded. He had an impulse to speak to her aloud as
familiarly as he always did in his thoughts, with as
little ceremony as he would have used on meeting any
woman who was common property. He no longer saw
her as different from the red-haired creatures who
brushed against them, bawling obscene words in their
harsh voices. Coarse, brief, and expressive, these words
were the current speech of the crowd; they seemed to
flit overhead, born there in the mud like flies in the
dunghill over which they hover. No one seemed
shocked or surprised; Yvette did not seem to notice
them at all.

"Muscade, I want to bathe," she said. "Let's go out
into deep water."

"At your service, ma'am," he replied.

They went to the bathing-cabin to get costumes. She
was ready first and waited for him on the bank, smiling
at all who looked at her. Then they went off side by
side in the warm water. She swam with a luxurious
abandon, caressed by the stream, quivering with a
sensual pleasure; at every stroke she raised herself as
though she were ready to leap out of the river. He
found difficulty in keeping up with her; he was out
of breath and angry at his inferiority. But she slowed
down and then turned quickly and floated, her arms
crossed, her eyes staring towards the blue sky. He gazed
at the smooth, supple line of her body as she lay there
on the surface of the river, at the rounded form and
small, firm tips of the shapely breasts revealed by her
thin, clinging garment, the curving sweetness of her
belly, the half-submerged thighs, the bare calf gleam-

ing through the water, and the small foot thrust out. He saw every line of her, as though she were deliberately displaying herself to tempt him, offering herself to him or trying to make a fool of him again. He began to desire her with a passionate ardor, every nerve on edge. Abruptly she turned round and looked at him.

"What a nice head you have," she said with a laugh.

He was hurt, irritated by her teasing, filled with the savage fury of the derided lover. He yielded to a vague desire to punish her, to avenge himself; he wanted to hurt her.

"You'd like that sort of life, would you?" he said.

"What sort?" she asked, with her most innocent air.

"Come now, no more nonsense. You know perfectly well what I mean."

"No, honestly, I don't."

"We've had enough of this comedy. Will you or won't you?"

"I don't understand you in the least."

"You're not so stupid as all that. Besides, I told you last night."

"What? I've forgotten."

"That I love you."

"You!"

"Yes, I!"

"What a lie!"

"I swear it's true."

"Prove it, then."

"I ask for nothing better."

"Well, do, then."

"You didn't say that last night."

"You didn't propose anything."

"Oh, this is absurd!"

"Besides, I am not the one to be asked."

"That's very kind of you! Who is, then?"

"Mamma, of course."

He gave way to a fit of laughter.

"Your mother? No, really, that's too much!"

She had suddenly become very serious, and, looking into his eyes, said:

"Listen, Muscade, if you really love me enough to marry me, speak to mamma first, and I'll give you my answer afterwards."

At that he lost his temper altogether, thinking that she was still playing the fool with him.

"What do you take me for, Mam'selle? An idiot like the rest of your admirers?"

She continued to gaze at him with calm, clear eyes. After a moment's hesitation she said:

"I still don't understand."

"Now look here, Yvette," he said brusquely, with a touch of rudeness and ill nature in his voice. "Let's have done with this ridiculous comedy, which has already gone on too long. You keep on playing the innocent maiden, and, believe me, the part doesn't suit you at all. You know perfectly well that there can be no question of marriage between us—but only of love. I told you I loved you—it's quite true—I repeat, I do love you. Now don't pretend not to understand, and don't treat me as though I were a fool."

They were upright in the water, face to face, supporting themselves by little movements of the hands. For some seconds more she continued motionless, as though she could not make up her mind to understand his words, then suddenly she blushed to the roots of her hair. The blood rushed in a swift tide from her neck to her ears, which turned almost purple, and without a word she fled landwards, swimming with all her strength, with hurried, powerful strokes. He could not overtake her, and the pursuit left him breathless. He saw her leave the water, pick up her wrap, and enter her cabin, without turning her head.

He took a long time to dress, very puzzled what to do, planning what to say to her, and wondering whether to apologize or persevere.

When he was ready, she had gone, alone. He returned slowly, worried and anxious. The Marquise, on Saval's arm, was strolling along the circular path round the lawn. At sight of Servigny she spoke with the careless air she had assumed on the previous evening:

"Didn't I tell you not to go out in such heat? Now Yvette has sunstroke; she's gone to lie down. She was as scarlet as a poppy, poor child, and had a frightful headache. You must have been walking full in the sun, and up to some mischief or other, Heaven knows what. You have no more sense than she has."

The young girl did not come down to dinner. When asked if she wanted something brought up to her room, she replied through the closed door that she was not hungry—she had locked herself in and wished to be left alone. The two young men left by the ten o'clock train, promising to come again the following Thursday, and the Marquise sat down by the open window and, musing, listened to the far-off sound of dance-music pounded out at La Grenouillère, vibrating in the profoundly solemn silence of night.

Inured and hardened to love by love, as a man is to riding or rowing, she nevertheless had sudden moments of tenderness which attacked her like a disease. These passions seized roughly upon her, swept through her whole being, driving her mad, exhausting her, or depressing her according to their nature, lofty, violent, dramatic, or sentimental.

She was one of those women who were created to love and to be loved. From a very humble beginning

she had climbed high through love, of which she had
made a profession almost without being aware of it:
acting by instinct, by inborn skill, she accepted money
as she accepted kisses, naturally, without distinguishing
between the two, employing her amazing intuition in
an unreasoning and utterly simple fashion, as animals,
made cunning by the struggle for life, employ theirs.
Many lovers had lain in her arms, and she had felt no
tenderness for them, but also no disgust at their embraces. She endured caresses with calm indifference, as
a traveler eats anything, because he must live. But from
time to time her heart or her flesh caught fire, and she
fell into a passion which lasted weeks or months, according to the physical and moral qualities of her lover.
These were the delicious moments of her life. She loved
with her whole soul, her whole body, with ecstatic
abandon. She threw herself into love like a suicide into
a river, and let herself be carried away, ready to die
if necessary, intoxicated, maddened, infinitely happy.
Each time she thought she had never before felt anything like it, and she would have been entirely amazed
if she had been reminded of the many different men
of whom she had dreamed passionately all night long,
gazing at the stars.

Saval had fascinated her, captured her body and soul.
She dreamed of him now, soothed by his image and
her remembrance of him, in the calm exaltation of a
joy fulfilled, of a happiness present and certain.

A noise behind her made her turn round. Yvette had
just come in, still in the same dress she had worn all
day, but pale now, and with the burning eyes that are
the mark of great weariness. She leaned on the ledge
of the open window opposite her mother.

"I've something to tell you," she said.

The Marquise, surprised, looked at her. Her love for

her daughter was selfish; she was proud of her beauty, as one is proud of wealth; she was herself still too beautiful to be jealous, too careless to make the plans she was commonly supposed to entertain, yet too cunning to be unconscious of her daughter's value.

"Yes, child," she replied, "I'm listening; what is it?"

Yvette gave her a burning look, as though to read the depths of her soul, as though to detect every emotion which her words would rouse.

"This is it. Something extraordinary happened today."

"What?"

"Monsieur de Servigny told me he loved me."

The Marquise waited, uneasy. But as Yvette said nothing more, she asked:

"How did he tell you? Explain!"

The young girl sat down by her mother's feet in a familiar coaxing attitude and, pressing her hand, said:

"He asked me to marry him."

Madame Obardi made a sudden gesture of amazement, and cried:

"Servigny? You must be mad!"

Yvette's eyes had never left her mother's face, watching sharply for her thoughts and her surprise.

"Why must I be mad?" she asked gravely. "Why should Monsieur de Servigny not marry me?"

"You must be wrong," stammered the Marquise, embarrassed; "it can't be true. You can't have heard properly—or you misunderstood him. Monsieur de Servigny is too rich to marry you, and too . . . too . . . Parisian to marry at all."

Yvette slowly rose to her feet.

"But if he loves me as he says he does?" she added.

Her mother replied somewhat impatiently:

"I thought you were old enough and knew enough

f the world not to have such ideas in your head. Servigny is a man of the world and an egoist; he will
only marry a woman of his own rank and wealth. If
he asked you to marry him . . . it means he wants
. . he wants. . . ."

The Marquise, unable to voice her suspicions, was
silent for a moment, then added:

"Now leave me alone, and go to bed."

And the young girl, as though she now knew all she
wanted, replied obediently:

"Yes, mother."

She kissed her mother's forehead and departed with
a calm step. Just as she was going out of the door, the
Marquise called her back:

"How is your sunstroke?" she asked.

"I never had one. It was what Monsieur de Servigny
said that upset me."

"We'll have another talk about it," added the Marquise. "Meanwhile, don't remain alone with him again
after this. And you may be quite sure that he won't
marry you, do you understand, and that he only wants
o . . . to compromise you."

This was the best she could do by way of expressing
her thoughts. Yvette returned to her room.

Madame Obardi began to reflect.

Having lived for years in an amorous and opulent
tranquillity, she had carefully guarded her mind from
every thought that might preoccupy, trouble, or sadden
her. She had always refused to ask herself what would
become of Yvette; there would be time enough to think
of that when difficulties arose. She knew, with her
courtesan's instinct, that her daughter could not marry
a rich and really well-born man save by an extremely
improbable piece of good fortune, one of those surprises
of love which set adventuresses upon thrones. She did

not really contemplate this possibility, being too self centered to form plans by which she herself would no be directly affected.

Yvette would doubtless follow in her mother's foot steps. She would become a light o' love; why not? Bu the Marquise had never had the courage to ask hersel when, or how, this would come about.

And now here was her daughter suddenly, withou any preparation, asking her one of those question which cannot be answered, and forcing her to take up a definite position in an affair so difficult, so delicate, so dangerous in every sense, which so profoundly troubled her conscience, the conscience that must move any mother when her daughter is involved in an affair such as this.

She had too much natural sense, a good sense tha might nod but was never quite asleep, to be deceived for one moment in Servigny's intentions, for she knew men, by personal experience, especially men of tha tribe. And so, at the first words uttered by Yvette, she had cried out, almost involuntarily:

"Servigny marry you? You must be mad!"

What had led him to use the old, old trick—he, the shrewd rake, the jaded man about town? What would he do now? And the child, how was she to be more explicitly warned or even defended? She was capable of any folly. Who would have imagined that a grown up girl like that could be so innocent, so ignorant, so unwary?

The Marquise, thoroughly perplexed and already ex hausted by her mental efforts, was utterly at a loss she found the situation truly difficult.

Weary of the whole business, she thought:

"Oh, well, I'll keep a close watch on them and ac

according to events. If necessary, I'll even talk to Serrigny; he's sensitive, and can take a hint."

She did not ask herself what she should say to him, nor what he would reply, nor what sort of agreement could be reached between them; happy at being relieved of this anxiety without having had to take a decision, she began again to dream of her adored Saval. Her glance, wandering in the night, turned to the right towards the misty radiance that hovered over Paris; with both hands she threw kisses towards the great city, swift unnumbered kisses that flew into the darkness one after another; and very softly, as though she were still speaking to Saval, she murmured:

"I love you! I love you!"

III

Yvette also could not sleep. Like her mother, she sat at the open window, resting her elbows on the sill, and tears, her first bitter tears, filled her eyes.

Till now she had lived and grown up in the heedless and serene self-confidence of happy youth. Why should she have analyzed, wondered, reflected? Why should she not have been like all young girls? Why should doubt, fear, painful suspicions have troubled her? Because she seemed to talk about every subject, because she had taken the tone, the manner, the bold speech of those around her, she had seemed to know all about everything. But she knew no more than a girl brought up in a convent; her risky phrases came from her memory, from the faculty women possess of imitation and assimilation, not from a mind sophisticated and debauched.

She talked of love in the same way that an artist's

or musician's child talks of painting and music at ten or
twelve years of age. She knew, or rather suspected, the
sort of mystery hidden behind this word—too many
jests had been whispered in her presence for her innocence to remain completely unenlightened—but how
was she to tell from this that every household was not
like the one she lived in? Her mother's hand was kissed
with apparent respect; all their friends were titled; all
were rich, or appeared to be; all spoke familiarly of
princes of the blood royal. Two kings' sons had actually
come several times to the Marquise's house. How was
she to know?

And, besides, she was by nature innocent. She did
not probe into things, she had not her mother's intuitive
judgment of other people. She lived tranquilly, too full
of the joy of life to worry about circumstances which
might have roused suspicions in people of more quiet,
more thoughtful, more secluded ways, who were less
impulsive and less radiantly joyous. And now, in a
single instant, by a few words whose brutality she had
felt without understanding, Servigny had roused in her
a sudden uneasiness, an uneasiness at first unreasoning,
and now growing into a torturing fear.

She had gone home, had fled from him like a
wounded animal; deeply wounded, indeed, by the
words she repeated to herself again and again, trying
to penetrate their farthest meaning, trying to guess their
whole implication: "You know perfectly well that there
can be no question of marriage between us—but only
of love!"

What had he meant? And why this insult? There was
something, then, some shameful secret, of which she
was ignorant. Doubtless she was the only one in ignorance of it. What was it? She was terrified, crushed, as
at the discovery of a hidden infamy, the treachery of

a friend, one of those calamities of the heart which strike at one's very reason.

She had thought, wondered, pored over it, wept, consumed with fears and suspicions. Then her young and buoyant nature calmed her, and she began to imagine an adventure, to build up an unusual and dramatic situation drawn from her remembrance of all the fanciful romances she had read. She recalled exciting changes of fortune, gloomy and heart-rending plots, and mingled them with her own story, flinging a romantic glory round the half-perceived mystery which surrounded her.

She was no longer miserable, she was wholly wrapped up in her dreams. She lifted mysterious veils, imagined improbable complications, a thousand curious and terrible ideas, attractive through their very strangeness. Was she, by any chance, the natural daughter of a prince? Had her unfortunate mother been seduced and deserted, created a marquise by a king, King Victor Emmanuel perhaps, and had she even been forced to flee from the wrath of his family?

Or was she not more probably a child abandoned by her parents, very noble and famous parents, as the fruit of a guilty love, and found by the Marquise, who had adopted her and brought her up? A hundred other notions raced through her head; she accepted or rejected them at the dictates of her fancy. She grew profoundly sorry for herself, at once very happy and very sad; above all, she was delighted at becoming the heroine of a romance with emotions to reveal, a part to act, a dignity and nobility to be upheld. And she thought of the part she would have to play in each plot she imagined. She saw it vaguely, as if she were a character in a play by Scribe or a novel by George Sand. It would be compounded of equal parts of devotion, pride, self-sacrifice, magnanimity, tenderness, and fine words. Her volatile heart almost reveled in her new situation.

She had continued till nightfall to ponder over her future course of action, wondering how to set to work to drag the truth from the Marquise.

And at the coming of night, so suitable to a tragic situation, she had thought of a trick, a quite simple yet subtle trick, for getting what she wanted; it was to tell her mother very abruptly that Servigny had asked her to marry him. At this news Madame Obardi, in her surprise, would surely let fall a word, an exclamation, that would illumine the situation for her daughter.

So Yvette had promptly put her plan into execution. She expected a burst of astonishment, protestations of affection, disclosures, accompanied by tears and every sign of emotion.

Instead, her mother had apparently not been either surprised or heartbroken, merely annoyed; from the worried and peevish tone of her reply the young girl, in whose mind every latent power of feminine cunning, wit, and knowledge were suddenly aroused, realized that it was no good insisting, that the mystery was quite other and more painful than she had imagined, and that she must discover it for herself. So she had returned to her room with a sad heart, her spirit distressed, depressed now in the apprehension of a real misfortune, without knowing how or why she was suffering such an emotion. She rested her elbows on the window-sill and wept.

She cried for a long time, not dreaming now; she made no attempt at further discovery. Little by little she was overcome with weariness, and closed her eyes. She dozed, for a few minutes, in the unrefreshing slumber of a person too exhausted to undress and get into bed; her sleep was long and fitful, rudely broken whenever her head slipped from between her hands.

She did not go to bed until the daylight gleamed, when the chill of dawn drove her from the window.

During the next day and the next, she continued melancholy and reserved. Her mind was at work ceaselessly and urgently within her; she was learning to watch, to guess, to reason. A gleam, still vague, seemed to throw a new light upon the men and events passing around her; distrust invaded her soul, distrust of everyone that she had believed in, distrust of her mother. During those two days she conjectured every conceivable supposition. She envisaged every possibility, making the most extravagant resolutions, in the impulsiveness of her volatile and unrestrained nature. On Wednesday she fixed on a plan, a whole scheme of conduct and an elaborate plan of espionage. On Thursday morning she rose with the determination to be more cunning than the most experienced detective, to be armed against all the world.

She even decided to take as her motto the two words "Myself alone," and for more than an hour she wondered how they could with best effect be engraved round her monogram and stamped on her note-paper.

Saval and Servigny arrived at ten o'clock. The young girl held out her hand with reserve, but without embarrassment, and said in a familiar, though serious, tone:

"Good morning, Muscade. How are you?"

"Pretty well, thank you, Mam'selle. And you?"

He watched her narrowly. "What game is she playing now?" he said to himself.

The Marquise having taken Saval's arm, he took Yvette's, and they began to walk in the garden, disappearing and reappearing behind the clumps of trees.

Yvette strolled with a pensive air, her eyes on the gravel path, and seemed scarcely to hear her companion's remarks, to which she made no reply.

Suddenly she asked:

"Are you really my friend, Muscade?"

"Of course, Mam'selle."

"But really, really and truly?"

"Absolutely your friend, Mam'selle, body and soul."

"Enough not to tell a lie for once, just for once?"

"Enough not even to tell one for twice, if necessary."

"Enough to tell me the whole truth, even if it's unpleasant?"

"Yes, Mam'selle."

"Well, what do you really think, really, really think, of Prince Kravalow?"

"Oh, Lord!"

"There you are, already getting ready to tell a fib."

"No, I'm searching for the words, the right words. Well, dash it, the Prince is a Russian—a real Russian, who speaks Russian, was born in Russia, and perhaps had a passport to get into France. There's nothing false about him except his name and his title."

She looked into his eyes.

"You mean he's a . . . a . . ."

He hesitated; then, making up his mind, said:

"An adventurer, Mam'selle."

"Thank you. And the Chevalier Valreali is no better, is he?"

"That's quite right."

"And Monsieur de Belvigne?"

"Ah, he's rather different. He's a gentleman, provincial of course; he's honorable . . . up to a point . . . but he's singed his wings through flying too near the candle."

"And you?"

Without hesitation he replied:

"I? Oh, I'm what's generally called a gay dog, a bachelor of good family who once had brains and frittered them away in clever chit-chat; who had health, and ruined it by playing the fool; moderate wealth, and wasted it doing nothing. All I have left is a certain experience of life, a pretty complete freedom from prejudice, a vast contempt for men, women included, a profound sense of the futility of my actions, and a wide tolerance of scoundrels in general. I still have momentary flashes of honesty, as you see, and I'm even capable of affection, as you could see if you would. With these qualities and defects I place myself at your orders, Mam'selle, body and soul, for you to dispose of at your pleasure. There!"

She did not laugh; she listened attentively, carefully scrutinizing his words and meanings.

"What do you think of the Comtesse de Lammy?" she continued.

"You must allow me to refrain from giving you my opinions on women," he said gaily.

"Not on any?"

"No, not on any."

"Then that means you must have a very low opinion of them, of all of them. Now think, aren't there any exceptions?"

He laughed with the insolent air he almost always wore and the brutal audacity that was his strength, his armor against life.

"Present company always excepted, of course," he said.

She flushed slightly, but coolly asked:

"Well, what do you think of me?"

"You want to know? Very well, then. I think you're a person of excellent sense, of considerable experience, or, if you prefer it, of great common sense; that you know very well how to mask your battery, amuse yourself at others' expense, hide your purpose, pull the strings and wait, without impatience, for the result."

"Is that all?" she asked.

"That's all," he replied.

"I'll make you alter that opinion, Muscade," she said very gravely. Then she went over to her mother, who was walking with bent head and tiny steps, with the languid gait one falls into when murmuring of things sweet and intimate. As she walked she drew designs, letters perhaps, with the tip of her sunshade, and talked to Saval without looking at him, talked long and slowly, resting on his arm, held close against his side. Yvette looked sharply at her, and a suspicion, so vague that she could not put it into words, as if it were a physical sensation only half realized, flitted across her mind as the shadow of a wind-blown cloud flits across the earth.

The bell rang for lunch.

It was silent, almost gloomy.

There was storm in the air, as the saying goes. Vast motionless clouds lay in wait on the horizon, silent and heavy, but loaded with tempest.

When they had taken their coffee on the veranda, the Marquise asked:

"Well, darling, are you going for a walk today with your friend Servigny? This is really the weather to enjoy the coolness of the woods."

Yvette threw her a rapid glance, and swiftly looked away again.

"No, mother, I'm not going out today."

The Marquise seemed disappointed.

"Do go for a little walk, child," she persisted. "It's so good for you."

"No, mother," said Yvette sharply, "I'm going to stay

in the house, and you know quite well why, because I told you the other night."

Madame Obardi had quite forgotten, consumed with her need to be alone with Saval. She blushed, fidgeted, and, distracted by her own desire, uncertain how to secure a free hour or two, stammered:

"Of course; I never thought of it. You're quite right; I don't know where my wits are wandering."

Yvette took up a piece of embroidery which she called her "charity work," busying herself with it five or six times a year, on days of utter boredom, and seated herself on a low chair beside her mother. The young men sat in deck-chairs and smoked their cigars.

The hours went by in idle conversation that flagged continually. The Marquise threw impatient glances at Saval, seeking for an excuse, any way of getting rid of her daughter. Realizing at last that she would not succeed, and not knowing what plan to adopt, she said to Servigny:

"You know, my dear Duke, that you're both going to stay the night here. Tomorrow we are going to lunch at the restaurant Fournaise, at Chatou."

He understood, smiled, and said with a bow:

"I am at your service, Marquise."

The day wore on slowly and uncomfortably, under the menace of the storm. Gradually the dinner hour approached. The lowering sky was heavy with dull, sluggish clouds. Not a breath of air was stirring.

The evening meal was eaten in silence. A sense of embarrassment and restraint, a sort of vague fear, silenced the two men and the two women.

When the table had been cleared, they remained on the veranda, speaking only at long intervals. Night was falling, a stifling night. Suddenly the horizon was torn by a great jagged flash that lit with its dazzling and pallid glare the four faces sunk in the shadows. Followed a distant noise, dull and faint, like the rumble made by a cart crossing a bridge; the heat increased, the air grew still more oppressive, the evening silence more profound.

Yvette rose.

"I'm going to bed," she said. "The storm makes me feel ill."

She bent her forehead for the Marquise to kiss, offered her hand to the two young men, and departed.

As her room was directly above the veranda, the leaves of a large chestnut-tree planted in front of the door were soon gleaming with a green light. Servigny fixed his eyes on this pale gleam in the foliage, thinking now and then that he saw a shadow pass across it. But suddenly the light went out. Madame Obardi sighed deeply.

"My daughter is in bed," she said.

Servigny rose.

"I will follow her example, Marquise, if you will allow me."

He kissed her hand and disappeared in his turn.

She remained alone with Saval, in the darkness. At once she was in his arms, clasping him, embracing him. Then, though he tried to prevent it, she knelt down in front of him, murmuring, "I want to look at you in the lightning flashes."

But Yvette, her candle blown out, had come out in bare feet on her balcony, gliding like a shadow, and was listening, tortured by a painful and confused suspicion. She could not see, being exactly over their heads on the roof of the veranda. She heard nothing but a murmur of voices, and her heart beat so violently that the thudding of it filled her ears. A window slammed overhead. So

Servigny had gone up to bed. Her mother was alone with Saval.

A second flash split the sky, and for a second the whole familiar landscape was revealed in a vivid and sinister glare. She saw the great river, the color of molten lead, like a river in some fantastic dream-country. At the same instant a voice below her said, "I love you." She heard no more; a strange shudder passed over her, her spirit was drowned in a fearful sea of trouble.

Silence, pressing, infinite, a silence that seemed the eternal silence of the grave, brooded over the world. She could not breathe, her lungs were suffocated by some unknown and horrible weight. Another flash kindled the heavens and for an instant lit up the horizon, still another followed on its heels, then another and another.

The voice she had already heard repeated more loudly: "Oh! How I love you! How I love you!" And Yvette knew the voice well; it was her mother's.

A large drop of warm water fell upon her forehead, and a slight, almost imperceptible quiver ran through the leaves, the shiver of the coming rain.

Then a tumult came hurrying from far off, a confused tumult like the noise of the wind in trees; it was the heavy shower pouring in a torrent upon the earth, the river, and the foliage. In a few minutes the water was streaming all round her, covering her, splashing her, soaking her like a bath. She did not move, thinking only of what was happening on the veranda. She heard them rise and go up to their rooms. Doors slammed inside the house. And obeying an irresistible longing for certainty, a maddening, torturing urge, the young girl ran down the stairs, softly opened the outer door, ran across the lawn under the furious downpour of rain, and hid in a clump of bushes to watch the windows.

One alone, her mother's, showed a light. And suddenly two shadows appeared on the luminous square, two shadows side by side. Then they drew closer and made only one; another flash of lightning flung a swift and dazzling jet of light upon the house-front, and she saw them embracing, their arms about one another's necks.

At that she was stunned; without thinking, without knowing what she did, she cried out with all her strength, in a piercing voice, "Mamma!" as one cries to warn another creature of deadly peril.

Her desperate cry was lost in the clatter of the rain, but the entwined pair started uneasily apart. One of the shadows disappeared, while the other tried to distinguish something in the darkness of the garden.

Fearing to be taken unawares by her mother, Yvette ran to the house, hurried upstairs, leaving a trail of water dripping from step to step, and locked herself in her room, determined to open to no one. Without taking off the soaking clothes which clung to her body, she fell upon her knees with clasped hands, imploring in her distress some superhuman protection, the mysterious help of heaven, that unknown aid we pray for in our hours of weeping and despair. Every instant the great flashes threw their livid light into the room, and she saw herself fitfully reflected in her wardrobe-mirror, with her wet hair streaming down her back, so strange a figure that she did not recognize herself.

She remained on her knees for a long time, so long that the storm passed without her noticing its departure. The rain ceased to fall, light flowed into the sky, though it was still dark with clouds, and a warm, fragrant, delicious freshness, the freshness of wet leaves and grass, drifted in at the open window. Yvette rose from her knees, took off her cold sodden clothes, without thinking at all of what she did, and got into bed. She fixed her eyes on the growing daylight, then wept again, then tried to think.

Her mother! With a lover! The shame of it! But she had read so many books in which women, even mothers, abandoned themselves in like fashion, only to rise once more to honor in the last few pages, that she was not utterly dumbfounded to find herself involved in a drama like all the dramas in the stories she read. The violence of her first misery, her first cruel bewilderment, was already slightly lessened by her confused recollection of similar situations. Her thoughts had roamed among so many tragic adventures, gracefully woven into their stories by the authors of romances, that gradually her horrible discovery began to seem the natural continuation of a novelette begun the night before.

"I will save my mother," she said to herself.

Almost calmed by this heroic resolution, she felt herself strong, great, ready upon the instant for sacrifice and combat. She thought over the means she must employ. Only one seemed good to her, and accorded with her romantic nature. And she rehearsed, like an actress before the performance, the interview she would have with her mother.

The sun had risen and the servants were up and about. The maid came in with her chocolate. Yvette had the tray set down on the table, and said:

"Tell my mother that I'm not well, that I shall stay in bed till the gentlemen leave; tell her I did not sleep last night and that I wish not to be disturbed, because I must try to sleep."

The astonished maid caught sight of the soaked dress, thrown like a rag on the carpet.

"Mademoiselle has been out, then?" she said.

"Yes, I went for a walk in the rain to clear my head."

The servant picked up the petticoats, and went out carrying them gingerly on her arm with an expression of disgust; they were dripping like the clothes of a drowned woman.

Yvette waited, well knowing that her mother would come.

The Marquise entered, having leapt out of bed at the first words of the maid, for she had endured a vague uneasiness ever since that cry of "Mamma!" pierced the darkness.

"What's the matter?" she said.

Yvette looked at her and faltered.

"I . . . I . . ."

Then, overcome by violent and sudden emotion, she began to sob.

The astonished Marquise asked again:

"What's the matter with you?"

Then, forgetting all her schemes and carefully prepared phrases, the young girl hid her face in her hands and sobbed:

"Oh, mother! Oh, mother!"

Madame Obardi remained standing by the bed, too excited to understand fully, but guessing, with that subtle instinct wherein her strength lay, almost the whole truth.

Yvette, choked with sobs, could not speak, and her mother, exasperated at last and feeling the approach of a formidable scene, asked sharply:

"Come, what's the matter with you? Tell me."

With difficulty Yvette stammered:

"Oh! last night . . . I saw . . . your window."

"Well, what then?" asked the Marquise, very pale.

Her daughter repeated, still sobbing:

"Oh, mother! Oh, mother!"

Madame Obardi, whose fear and embarrassment were

changing to anger, shrugged her shoulders and turned to go.

"I really think you must be mad. When it's all over, let me know."

But suddenly the young girl parted her hands and disclosed her tear-stained face.

"No. . . . Listen. . . . I *must* speak to you. . . . Listen. Promise me . . . we'll both go away, far away, into the country, and we'll live like peasants and no one will know what's become of us. Will you, mother? Please, please, I beg you, mother, I implore you!"

The Marquise, taken aback, stood stock still in the middle of the room. She had the hot blood of the people in her veins. Shame, maternal shame, mingled with a vague sensation of fear and the exasperation of a passionate woman whose love is threatened. She shuddered, equally ready to implore forgiveness or to fly into a rage.

"I don't understand you," she said.

"I saw you, mother," continued Yvette, "last night. . . . You must never again . . . Oh, if you knew . . . we'll both go away. . . . I'll love you so much that you'll forget. . . ."

"Listen, my child," said Madame Obardi in a trembling voice, "there are some things you don't yet understand. Well, never forget . . . never forget . . . that I forbid you . . . ever to speak to me . . . of . . . of . . . of those matters."

But the young girl caught desperately at her role of savior and went on:

"No, mother, I'm no longer a child, and I have the right to know. I know all sorts of disreputable people, adventurers, come to our house, and that that's why we are not respected; and I know more than that. Well, it mustn't be, I won't endure it. We'll go away; you can sell your jewels; we'll work if necessary, and we'll live like decent women somewhere far away. And if I manage to get married, so much the better."

Her mother looked at her out of angry black eyes, and answered:

"You're mad. Be good enough to get up and come out to lunch with the rest of us."

"No, mother. There's someone here, you know whom, whom I won't see again. He must leave this house, or I will. You must choose between us."

She was sitting up in bed, and she raised her voice, speaking like a character on the stage; at last she had entered upon the drama so long dreamed of; her grief was almost forgotten in absorption in her mission.

"You must be mad," repeated the astonished Marquise again, finding nothing else to say.

"No, mother," the young girl added, with dramatic verve, "that man leaves this house or else I go; I shall not weaken."

"And where will you go? . . . What will you do?"

"I don't know; it doesn't matter much . . . I want us to be decent women."

The repetition of that phrase "decent women" aroused in the Marquise the fury of a drab.

"Silence!" she shouted. "I won't be spoken to like that. I'm as good as any other woman, do you hear? I'm a harlot, it's true, and I'm proud of it; I'm worth a dozen of your decent women."

Yvette, overwhelmed, looked at her and stammered:

"Oh, mother!"

But the Marquise was frenzied with excitement.

"Yes, I am a harlot. What of it? If I weren't a harlot, you'd be a kitchen-maid today, as I was once, and you'd work for thirty sous a day, and you'd wash dishes, and your mistress would send you out on errands to the butcher's, d'you hear, and kick you out if you were idle; whereas here you are, idling all day long, just because I *am* a harlot. There! When you're only a poor servant-girl with fifty francs of savings, you must get away from it somehow if you don't want to rot in the workhouse; and there's only one way for women, only one way, d'you hear, when you're a servant! We can't make fortunes on the stock exchange or at high finance. We've nothing but our bodies, nothing but our bodies."

She beat her breast like a penitent at confession, and advanced towards the bed, flushed and excited:

"So much the worse for a pretty girl; she must live on her looks or grind along in poverty all her life long . . . all her life. . . . There's no alternative."

Then, returning hastily to her old idea: "And as for your decent women, do they go without? It's they who are the sluts, because they're not forced to it. They've money to live on and amuse themselves with; they have their lovers out of pure wantonness. It's they who are the sluts!"

She stood beside Yvette's bed; Yvette, utterly overcome, wanted to scream for help and run away; she was sobbing noisily, like a beaten child.

The Marquise was silent, and looked at her daughter; seeing the girl's utter despair, she was herself overcome by sorrow, remorse, tenderness, and pity; and falling upon the bed with outstretched arms, she too began to sob, murmuring:

"My poor darling, my poor darling, if you only knew how you hurt me."

And for a long time they both wept.

Then the Marquise, whose grief never lasted very long, rose to her feet and said very gently:

"Well, darling, that's how it is; it can't be helped. It can't be altered now. We have to take life as it comes."

But Yvette continued to cry; the shock had been too severe and too unexpected for her to be able to reflect upon it calmly and recover herself.

"Come, get up, and come down to breakfast, so that nothing will be noticed," said her mother.

The young girl shook her head, unable to speak; at last she said very slowly, her voice choked with sobs:

"No, mother, you know what I said; I won't change my mind. I will not leave my room till they have gone. I won't see any of those people again, never, never. If they come back, I . . . I . . . you won't see me again."

The Marquise had dried her eyes and, worn out with her emotion, murmured:

"Come now, think it over, be sensible about it." Then again, after a minute's silence: "Yes, you had better rest this morning. I'll come and see you in the afternoon."

She kissed her daughter on the forehead and went away to get dressed, quite calm again.

As soon as her mother disappeared, Yvette ran to the door and bolted it, so as to be alone, quite alone; then she began to reflect.

About eleven o'clock the maid knocked at the door and asked:

"Madame la Marquise wishes to know if you want anything, Mademoiselle, and what will you have for lunch?"

"I'm not hungry," replied Yvette; "I want to be left alone."

She stayed in bed as though she were really ill. About three o'clock there was another knock.

"Who's there?" she asked.

"It's I, darling," answered her mother's voice; "I've come to see how you are."

She hesitated. What should she do? She opened the

door and got back into bed. The Marquise came close, speaking gently, as though to an invalid.

"Well, are you feeling better? Won't you eat an egg?"

"No, thank you, nothing."

Madame Obardi had sat down beside the bed. Neither spoke for some time; then, at last, as her daughter remained immobile, her hands resting inertly on the sheets, the Marquise added:

"Aren't you going to get up?"

"Yes, presently," answered Yvette. "I've thought a great deal, mother," she continued slowly and seriously, "and this . . . this is my decision. The past is the past; let us say no more about it. But the future will be different . . . or else . . . or else I know what I shall have to do. And now let us have done with this subject."

The Marquise, who had thought that the scene was all over, felt somewhat irritated. She had had more than enough. This great goose of a girl ought to have understood long ago. But she made no answer, only repeating:

"Are you going to get up?"

"Yes, I'm ready now."

The mother acted as maid to her daughter, bringing her her stockings, her corset, and her petticoats. Then she kissed her.

"Shall we go for a walk before dinner?"

"Yes, mamma."

And they walked along the bank of the river, talking almost entirely of trivial things.

IV

Next morning Yvette went off alone to sit in the place where Servigny had read aloud the history of the ants.

"I will not leave this place," she said to herself, "until I have come to a decision."

The river ran at her feet, the swift water of the main stream; it was full of eddies and great bubbles which swirled silently past her.

She had already examined every aspect of the situation and every means of escape from it. What was she to do if her mother failed to hold scrupulously to the condition she had laid down, if she did not give up her life, her friends, everything, and take refuge with her in some distant region?

She might go alone . . . away. But whither? How? What could she live on? By working? At what? Whom should she ask for work? And the melancholy and humble life of the working girl, of the daughters of the common folk, seemed to be a little shameful and unworthy of her. She thought of becoming a governess, like the young ladies in novels, and of being loved and married by the son of the house. But for that role she should have been of noble descent, so that when an irate parent reproached her for stealing his son's heart, she could have answered proudly:

"My name is Yvette Obardi."

She could not. And besides, it was a rather commonplace, threadbare procedure.

A convent was no better. Besides, she felt no call to a religious life, having only an intermittent and fleeting piety. No one—since she was the thing she was—could save her by marrying her, she could not take help from a man, there was no possible way out, no certain resource at all.

Besides, she wanted something violent, something really great, really brave, something that would set the world an example: and she decided to die.

She came to this resolution quite suddenly, quite calmly, as though it were a question of a journey, without reflecting, without seeing what death means, without realizing that it is an end without a new beginning, a departure without a return, an eternal farewell to earth, to life.

She was attracted immediately by this desperate decision, with all the impulsiveness of a young and ardent spirit. And she pondered over the means she should employ. They all appeared to be painful and dangerous to carry out, and they seemed to demand a violence which was repulsive to her.

She soon gave up the idea of dagger or pistol, which might only wound, maim, or disfigure her, and which required a steady and practiced hand—rejected hanging as vulgar, a pauper's sort of suicide, ridiculous and ugly—and drowning because she could swim. Poison was all that remained, but which poison? Almost all are painful, and produce vomiting. She did not want to suffer, or to vomit. Then she thought of chloroform, having read in a newspaper of a young woman who suffocated herself by this means.

At once she felt something like pleasure in her resolve, a secret self-praise, a prick of vainglory. They should see what manner of woman she was!

She returned to Bougival and went to the chemist's, where she asked for a little chloroform for an aching tooth. The man, who knew her, gave her a very small phial of the drug. Then she walked over to Croissy, where she procured another little phial of poison. She got a third at Chatou, and a fourth at Rueil, and returned home late for lunch. As she was very hungry after her walk, she ate a hearty meal, with the sharp enjoyment that exercise brings.

Her mother, glad to see her excellent appetite, felt now quite confident, and said to her as they rose from the table:

"All our friends are coming to spend Sunday here.

I've invited the prince, the chevalier, and Monsieur de Belvigne."

Yvette turned slightly pale, but made no answer. She left the house almost at once, went to the railway station, and took a ticket to Paris.

Throughout the afternoon she went from chemist to chemist, buying a few drops of chloroform from each.

She returned in the evening, her pockets full of little bottles. Next day she continued her campaign, and once she was even able to buy half a pint in a single shop. She did not go out on Saturday—it was stuffy and overcast; she spent the whole of the day on the veranda, lying in a long cane-chair. She thought about nothing, filled with a placid resolution.

The next day, wishing to look her best, she put on a blue frock which suited her very well. As she viewed herself in the mirror she thought suddenly: "Tomorrow I shall be dead." A strange shudder ran through her body. "Dead! I shall not speak, I shall not think, no one will see me any more. And I shall never see all this again." She scrutinized her face carefully, as though she had never seen it before, examining, above all, the eyes, discovering a thousand aspects of herself, a secret character in her face that she did not know, astonished to see herself, as though she were face to face with a stranger, a new friend.

"It is I," she said to herself, "it is I, in that glass. How strange it is to see oneself. We should never recognize ourselves, if we had no mirrors. Everyone else would know what we looked like, but we should have no idea of it."

She took the thick plaits of her hair and laid them across her breast, gazing at her own gestures, her poses and movements.

"How pretty I am!" she thought. "Tomorrow I shall be dead, there, on my bed."

She looked at her bed, and imagined that she saw herself lying on it, white as the sheets.

Dead! In a week that face, those eyes, those cheeks, would be nothing but black rottenness, shut up in a box underground.

A frightful spasm of anguish constricted her heart.

The clear sunlight flooded the landscape, and the sweet morning air came in at the window.

She sat down and thought. Dead—it was as though the world was disappearing for her sake; but no, nothing in the world would change, not even her room. Yes, her room would stay as it was, with the same bed, the same chairs, the same dressing-table, but she would be gone forever, and no one would be sorry, except perhaps her mother.

People would say, "How pretty she was, little Yvette!" and that was all. And when she looked at her hand resting on the arm of her chair, she thought again of decay, of the black and evil-smelling corruption that her flesh would become. Again a long shudder of horror ran through her body, and she could not understand how she could disappear without the whole world coming to an end, so strong was her feeling that she herself was part of everything, of the country, of the air, of the sun, of life.

A burst of laughter came from the garden, a clamor of voices, shouts, the noisy merriment of a country-house party just beginning, and she recognized the sonorous voice of Monsieur de Belvigne, singing:

> *Je suis sous ta fenêtre,*
> *Ah! daigne enfin paraître.*

She rose without thinking and went to look out. Everyone clapped. They were all there, all five of them, with two other gentlemen she did not know.

She drew back swiftly, torn by the thought that these men had come to enjoy themselves in her mother's house, in the house of a courtesan.

The bell rang for lunch.

"I will show them how to die," she told herself.

She walked downstairs with a firm step, with something of the resolution of a Christian martyr entering the arena where the lions awaited her.

She shook hands with them, smiling pleasantly but a little haughtily. Servigny asked her:

"Are you less grumpy today, Mam'selle?"

"Today," she replied in a strange, grave voice, "I am for the wildest pleasures. I'm in my Paris mood. Take care." Then, turning to Monsieur de Belvigne: "You shall be my pet today, my little Malvoisie. After lunch I'm taking you all to the fair at Marly."

Marly fair was indeed in full swing. The two newcomers were presented to her, the Comte Tamine and the Marquis de Boiquetot.

During the meal she hardly spoke, bending every effort of will to her resolve to make merry all that afternoon, so that none might guess, so that there should be all the more surprise; they would say: "Who would have thought it? She seemed so gay, so happy! One can never tell what is going on in their heads!"

She forced herself not to think of the evening, the hour she had chosen, when they would all be on the veranda.

She drank as much wine as she could get down, to sharpen her courage, and took two small glasses of brandy; when she left the table she was flushed and a little giddy; she felt herself warmed in body and spirit, her courage high, ready for adventure.

"Off we go!" she cried.

She took Monsieur de Belvigne's arm, and arranged the order of the rest.

"Come along, you shall be my regiment. Servigny, I appoint you sergeant; you must march on the right, outside the ranks. You must make the Foreign Legion march in front, our two aliens, the prince and the chevalier, and behind them the two recruits who have joined the colors today. Quick march!"

They went off, Servigny playing an imaginary bugle, and the two new arrivals pretending to play the drum. Monsieur de Belvigne, somewhat embarrassed, said to Yvette:

"Do be a little reasonable, Mademoiselle Yvette. You'll get yourself talked about."

"It's you I'm compromising, Raisiné," she replied. "As for myself, I don't care a rap. It will be all the same tomorrow. So much the worse for you; you shouldn't go about with girls like me."

They marched through Bougival to the amazement of the people in the streets. Everyone turned round and stared; the local inhabitants came to their doors; the travelers on the little railway which runs from Rueil to Marly called out to them; the men standing on the platforms shouted:

"To the river! . . . To the river! . . ."

Yvette marched with a military step, holding Servigny by the arm, as if she were leading a prisoner. She was far from laughter; her face had an air of pale gravity, a sort of sinister impassivity. Servigny interrupted his bugle solo in order to shout orders. The prince and the chevalier were enjoying themselves hugely, judging it all vastly diverting and very witty. The two recruits played the drum steadily.

On their arrival at the fair ground they caused quite a sensation. The girls clapped, all the young folk giggled; a fat man arm-in-arm with his wife said to her enviously:

"*They're* enjoying life, they are."

Yvette caught sight of a merry-go-round, and made Belvigne mount a wooden horse on her right, while the rest of the squad clambered onto horses behind them. When their turn was over she refused to get off, making her escort remain upon the back of her childish steed for five turns running. The delighted crowd flung witticisms at them. Monsieur de Belvigne was very white when he got off, and felt sick.

Then she began careering through the stalls. She made each of the men get weighed before the eyes of a large crowd. She made them buy absurd toys, which they had to carry in their arms. The prince and the chevalier very soon had more than enough of the jest; Servigny and the two drummers alone kept up their spirits.

At last they reached the far end, and she looked at her followers with a curious expression, a glint of malice and perversity in her eyes. A strange fancy came into her head; she made them all stand in a row on the right bank overlooking the river, and said:

"Let him who loves me most throw himself into the water."

No one jumped. A crowd had formed behind them; women in white aprons gaped at them, and two soldiers in red breeches laughed stupidly.

"Then not one of you is ready to throw himself into the water at my request?" she repeated.

"So much the worse, damn it," murmured Servigny, and leapt, upright, into the river.

His fall flung drops of water right up to Yvette's feet. A murmur of surprise and amusement ran through the crowd. Then the young girl bent down, picked up a little piece of wood, and threw it into the river, crying: "Fetch it."

The young man began to swim, and seizing the floating stick in his mouth, like a dog, he brought it to land, clambered up the bank, dropped on one knee, and offered it to her.

"Good dog," she said, taking it, and patting his head.

"How can they do it?" cried a stout lady, vastly indignant.

"Nice goings-on," said another.

"Damned if I'd take a ducking for any wench," said a man.

She took Belvigne's arm again, with the cutting remark: "You're a noodle; you don't know what you've missed."

As they went home she threw resentful glances at the passers-by.

"How stupid they all look," she observed; then, raising her eyes to her companion's face, added, "and you too, for the matter of that."

Monsieur de Belvigne bowed. Turning round, she saw that the prince and the chevalier had disappeared. Servigny, wretched and soaked to the skin, was no longer playing the bugle, but walked with a melancholy air beside the two tired young men, who were not playing the drum now.

She began to laugh dryly.

"You seem to have had enough. That's what you call fun, isn't it? That's what you've come here for. I've given you your money's worth."

She walked on without another word, and suddenly Belvigne saw that she was crying.

"What's the matter?" he asked in alarm.

"Leave me alone," she murmured. "It's nothing to do with you."

But he insisted foolishly, "Now, now Mademoiselle, what is the matter with you? Has anybody hurt you?"

"Be quiet," she said irritably.

Abruptly, unable to withstand the terrible sorrow flooding her heart, she broke into such a violent fit of sobbing that she could not walk any farther. She covered her face with her hands, and gasped for breath, choking, strangled, stifled by the violence of her despair.

Belvigne stood helplessly beside her, repeating:

"I don't understand at all."

But Servigny rushed towards her. "Come along home, Mam'selle, or they'll see you crying in the street. Why do you do these silly things, if they make you so unhappy?"

He led her forward, holding her arm. But as soon as they reached the gate of the villa she ran across the garden and up to her room, and locked herself in.

She did not reappear until dinner-time; she was pale and very grave. All the rest were gay enough, however. Servigny had bought a suit of workman's clothes in the neighborhood, corduroy trousers, a flowered shirt, a jersey, and a smock, and he was talking like a peasant.

Yvette was in a fever for the ending of the meal, feeling her courage ebbing. As soon as coffee was over she went again to her room. She heard laughing voices under her window. The chevalier was telling jokes, foreign witticisms and puns, crude and not very savory. She listened in despair. Servigny, slightly drunk, was imitating a tipsy workman, and was addressing the Marquise as "Mrs. Obardi." Suddenly he said to Saval, "Hullo, Mr. Obardi." Everyone laughed.

Then Yvette made up her mind. First she took a sheet of her notepaper and wrote:

> Bougival, Sunday, 9 P.M.
> I die so that I may not become a kept woman.
> YVETTE.

Then a postscript:

> Good bye, mother, dear. Forgive me.

She sealed up the envelope, and addressed it to Madame la Marquise Obardi.

Then she moved her armchair up to the window, set a little table within reach of her hand, and placed upon it the large bottle of chloroform, with a handful of cotton-wool beside it.

An immense rose-tree in full bloom, planted near the veranda and reaching right up to her window, filled the night with little gusts of faint, sweet fragrance; for some moments she sat breathing in the perfumed air. The crescent moon swung in the dark sky, its left side gnawed away, and veiled now and again with small clouds.

"I'm going to die," thought Yvette. "I'm going to die!" Her heart, swollen with sobs, bursting with grief, choked her. She longed to cry for mercy, to be reprieved, to be loved.

Servigny's voice came up to her; he was telling a shady story, constantly interrupted by bursts of laughter. The Marquise seemed more amused than any of them; she repeated gaily: "No one can tell a story like that as well as he can."

Yvette took the bottle, uncorked it, and poured a little of the liquid onto the cotton-wool. It had a queer, pungent, sweet smell, and as she lifted the pad of cotton-wool to her lips, she swallowed the strong, irritating flavor of it, and it made her cough.

Then, closing her mouth, she began to breathe it in. She took long draughts of the deadly vapor, shutting her eyes, and compelling herself to deaden every impulse of her mind, so that she would no longer think nor realize what she was doing.

At first she felt as though her heart were swelling and expanding, as though her spirit, just now heavy and burdened with sorrow, were growing light, as light as if the weight oppressing it had been raised, lessened, removed.

A lively and pleasant sensation filled her whole body, penetrating to the tips of her fingers and toes, entering into her flesh, a hazy drunkenness, a happy delirium.

She saw that the cotton-wool was dry, and was surprised that she was not yet dead. Her senses were sharpened, intensified, and more alert. She heard every word uttered on the veranda. Prince Kravalow was relating how he had killed an Austrian general in a duel.

Far away, in the depth of the country, she heard the noises of the night; the intermittent barking of a dog, the brief croak of bullfrogs, the faint shiver of the leaves.

She took up the bottle, soaked the little piece of cotton-wool, and began again to breathe it in. For some moments she felt nothing; then the languid, delightful, secure contentment that she had felt at first took hold of her once more.

Twice she poured out more chloroform, greedy now of the physical and mental sensation, the drowsy languor in which her senses were drowning. She felt as though she no longer had bones or flesh or arms or legs. All had been gently taken from her, and she had felt nothing. The chloroform had drained away her body, leaving nothing but her brain, keener, freer, more lively, more alert than she had ever felt it before.

She remembered a thousand things she had forgotten, little details of her childhood, trifles which gave her pleasure. Her mind, suddenly endowed with an agility hitherto unknown to it, leapt from one strange idea to another, ran through a thousand adventures, wandered at random in the past, and rambled through hopes of the future. This rapid, careless process of thought filled her with sensuous delight; dreaming so, she enjoyed a divine happiness.

She still heard the voices, but could no longer distinguish the words, which seemed to her to take on another sense. Down and down she felt herself wafted, wandering in a strange and shifting fairyland.

She was on a large boat which glided through a very pleasant landscape, filled with flowers. She saw people on the banks, and these people were talking very loudly; and then she found herself on land again, without wondering how she got there, and Servigny, dressed like a prince, came to take her to a bullfight. The streets were full of people talking, and she listened to their conversations, which did not in the least surprise her, but were as though she had always known them; for through her dreamy intoxication she still heard her mother's friends laughing and chatting on the veranda.

For a time, all grew dim.

Then she awoke, deliciously sleepy, and had some difficulty in recalling herself to consciousness.

So she was not dead yet.

But she felt so rested, and in such comfort and in such peace of mind, that she was in no hurry to finish the affair. She would have liked this glorious languor to last forever.

She breathed slowly and looked at the moon facing her above the trees. Something in her soul was changed. Her thoughts were no longer those of a short while ago. The chloroform, soothing her body and mind, had assuaged her grief, and put to sleep her will to die.

Why not live? Why should she not be loved? Why should she not live happily? Everything now seemed possible, easy, sure. Everything in life was sweet, was good and charming. But because she wished to go on dreaming forever, she poured more of this dream-water onto the cotton-wool, and again began to breathe it in, occasionally removing the poison from her nostrils, so that she should not take too much, so that she should not die.

She looked at the moon, and saw a face in it, a woman's face. She began once more to roam about the country, adrift in the hazy visions of an opium dream. The face hung in the center of the sky; then it began to sing; in a well-known voice it sang the *Alleluia d'Amour*. It was the Marquise, who had just gone indoors to play the piano.

Yvette had wings now. She was flying through the night, a beautiful, clear night, over woods and rivers. She flew with vast delight, opening and beating her wings, wafted by the wind as by a caressing touch. She whirled through the air, which kissed her skin, and glided along so fast, so fast, that she had no time to see anything below her, and she found herself sitting beside a pond, with a line in her hand—she was fishing.

Something tugged at the line; she pulled it in and brought up the magnificent pearl necklace she had once desired. She was not in the least astonished at the catch, and looked at Servigny, who had appeared beside her, though she did not know how, and was fishing too; he was just landing a wooden roundabout horse.

Then once again she felt that she was waking, and heard them calling to her from below.

Her mother had said, "Blow out the candle."

Then Servigny's voice, clear and humorous, "Mam'-selle Yvette, blow out your candle."

They all took up the cry in chorus.

"Mam'selle Yvette, blow out your candle."

Again she poured chloroform onto the cotton-wool, but as she did not want to die, she kept it at some distance from her face, so that she could breathe the fresh air while filling her room with the asphyxiating odor of the narcotic, for she knew that someone would come upstairs. So she arranged herself in a charming attitude of abandonment, a mimicking of the abandon of death, and waited.

"I'm a little uneasy," said the Marquise. "The foolish child has gone to sleep leaving the candle alight on the table. I'll send Clémence up to blow it out and to shut her balcony window, which she has left wide open."

In a few moments the maid knocked at the door and called:

"Mademoiselle, Mademoiselle!"

After an interval of silence she began again, "Mademoiselle, Madame la Marquise says please will you blow out your candle and shut the window."

Again she waited, then knocked more loudly and called:

"Mademoiselle, Mademoiselle!"

As Yvette did not answer, the servant went down and told the Marquise:

"Mademoiselle has certainly gone to sleep; her door is bolted and I can't wake her."

"But surely she won't go on sleeping like that?" murmured Madame Obardi.

On Servigny's advice they all assembled under the

young girl's window and shouted in chorus: "Hip, hip, hurrah—Mam'selle Yvette!"

The cry rang out in the still night, piercing the clear moonlit air, and died away in the sleeping countryside; they heard it fade away like the noise of a train that has gone by.

As Yvette did not reply, the Marquise said:

"I hope nothing's the matter with her; I'm beginning to be alarmed."

Then Servigny snatched the red roses and the still unopened buds from the big rose-tree that grew up the wall, and began to hurl them through the window into her room. At the first which struck her, Yvette started and nearly cried out. Some fell on her dress, some in her hair, others flew over her head and landed on the bed, covering it with a rain of flowers.

Once more the Marquise cried in a choking voice:

"Come, Yvette, answer!"

"Really, it's not normal," declared Servigny. "I'll climb up by the balcony."

But the chevalier was indignant.

"Pardon me, pardon me, but that's too much of a favor, I protest; it's too good a way—and too good a time—for making a rendezvous!"

And all the others, thinking that the young girl was playing a trick on them, cried out:

"We protest. It's a put-up affair. He shan't go up, he shan't go up."

But the Marquise repeated in her agitation:

"Someone must go and see."

"She favors the duke; we are betrayed," declared the prince, with a dramatic gesture.

"Let's toss for the honor," suggested the chevalier, and took a gold hundred-franc piece from his pocket.

He began with the prince. "Tails," he called. It was heads. The prince in his turn threw the coin, saying to Saval:

"Call, please."

"Heads," called Saval.

It was tails.

The prince proceeded to put the same question to all the others. All lost. Servigny, who alone remained facing him, drawled insolently:

"Damn it, he's cheating!"

The Russian placed his hand on his heart and offered the gold coin to his rival, saying:

"Spin it yourself, my dear duke."

Servigny took it and tossed it, calling, "Heads!"

It was tails. He bowed, and pointed to the pillar of the balcony.

"Up you go, prince," he said.

But the prince was looking about him with a troubled air.

"What are you looking for?" asked the chevalier.

"I . . . I should like a . . . a ladder."

There was a general roar of laughter, and Saval came forward, saying, "We'll help you."

He lifted the man in his Herculean arms, with the advice: "Hold on to the balcony."

The prince promptly caught hold of it and, Saval letting go, he remained suspended, waving his legs. Servigny caught hold of the wildly struggling limbs that were groping for a foothold, and tugged at them with all his strength; the hands loosed their grip and the prince fell like a log onto the stomach of Monsieur de Belvigne, who was hurrying forward to help support him.

"Whose turn now?" asked Servigny, but no one offered.

"Come on, Belvigne, a little courage."

"No, thank you, my boy. I'd sooner keep my bones whole."

"Well, you then, chevalier? You should be used to scaling redoubts."

"I leave it to you, my dear duke."

"Well . . . well . . . I don't know that I'm so keen on it as all that." And Servigny walked round the pillar with a scrutinizing eye. Then he leapt, caught hold of the balcony, hauled himself up like a gymnast on the horizontal bar, and clambered over the rail.

All the spectators applauded, with uplifted faces. But he reappeared directly, crying, "Come at once! Quickly! Yvette's unconscious!"

The Marquise screamed loudly and dashed up the stairs.

The young girl, her eyes closed, lay like one dead. Her mother rushed wildly into the room and threw herself upon her.

"What is it? Tell me, what is it?" she asked.

Servigny picked up the bottle of chloroform which had fallen on the floor. "She's suffocated herself," he said. He set his ear to her heart, then added, "But she's not dead; we'll soon bring her round. Have you any ammonia here?"

"Any what . . . any what . . . sir?" said the distracted maid.

"Any sal volatile?"

"Yes, sir."

"Fetch it at once, and leave the door open, to make a draught."

The Marquise had fallen upon her knees and was sobbing. "Yvette! Yvette! My child, my little girl, my child, listen, answer me, Yvette! My child! Oh! my God, my God, what is the matter with her?"

The frightened men wandered aimlessly about the room, bringing water, towels, glasses, and vinegar.

Someone said, "She ought to be undressed."

The Marquise, who was almost out of her wits, tried to undress her daughter, but she no longer knew what she was doing. Her trembling hands fumbled uselessly at the clothing, and she moaned, "I . . . I . . . I can't, I can't."

The maid had returned with a medicine bottle; Servigny uncorked it and poured out half of its contents onto a handkerchief. He thrust it under Yvette's nose, and she choked.

"Good; she's breathing," he said. "It's nothing."

He bathed her temples, her cheeks, and her neck with the strong-smelling liquid. Then he signed to the maid to unlace the young girl, and when nothing but a petticoat was left over her chemise, he took her in his arms and carried her to the bed; he was shaken, his senses maddened by the fragrance of her half-naked body, by the touch of her flesh, and the softness of the half-seen breasts on which he pressed his lips.

When she was in bed he rose to his feet, very pale.

"She's coming to," he said; "it's nothing," for he had heard that her breathing was continuous and regular. But seeing the men's eyes fixed upon Yvette stretched across the bed, a spasm of jealous fury seized him. He went up to them, saying:

"Gentlemen, there are too many of us in this room. Be good enough to leave Monsieur Saval and myself alone with the Marquise."

His voice was sharp and authoritative. The other men left at once.

Madame Obardi had seized her lover in her arms and, with her face raised to his, was crying:

"Save her! . . . Oh, save her!"

But Servigny, who had turned round, saw a letter on the table. With a swift movement he picked it up and read the address. He guessed the whole affair at once and thought: "Perhaps the Marquise had better not know about this." And tearing open the envelope, he read at a glance the two lines which it contained:

"I die so that I may not become a kept woman.

YVETTE."

"Good bye, mother, dear. Forgive me."

"Deuce take it," he said to himself. "This needs thinking over"; and he hid the letter in his pocket. He returned to the bedside, and at once the thought came to him that the young girl had regained consciousness, but dared not show it out of shame, humiliation, and a dread of being questioned.

The Marquise had fallen on her knees and was weeping, her head resting on the foot of the bed. Suddenly she exclaimed:

"A doctor! We must have a doctor!"

But Servigny, who had been whispering to Saval, said to her:

"No, it's all right now. Just go out for a minute and I promise you that she'll be ready to kiss you when you come back."

The baron took Madame Obardi's arm and led her away. Servigny sat down beside the bed and took Yvette's hand.

"Listen to me, Mam'selle," he said.

She did not answer. She felt so happy, so comfortable, so cosy and warm that she would have liked never to move or speak again, but to live on in this state. A sense of infinite well-being possessed her, like no sensation she had ever known. The warm night air drifted into the room on a gentle, caressing breeze, and from time to time its faint breath blew sweetly across her face. It was a caress, the wind's kiss, the soft refreshing breath of a fan made of all the leaves in the wood, all the shadows of the night, all the mists of the river, and all the flowers, for the roses strewn upon the floor and the bed, and the rose-tree that clung to the balcony, mingled their languid fragrance with the healthy tang of the night breeze.

She drank in the good air, her eyes closed, her senses still half adrift in the intoxication of the drug; she no longer felt a wish to die, but a strong, imperious desire to live, to be happy, no matter how, to be loved, yes, loved.

"Mam'selle Yvette, listen to me," repeated Servigny.

She decided to open her eyes. Seeing her thus revived, he went on:

"Come now, what's all this foolishness?"

"I was so unhappy, Muscade," she murmured.

He gave her hand a benevolent squeeze.

"Well, this has been a deuce of a lot of use to you, now, hasn't it? Now promise me not to try again."

She did not answer, but made a little movement of her head, and emphasized it with a smile that he felt rather than saw.

He took from his pocket the letter he had found on the table.

"Am I to show this to your mother?" he asked.

"No," she signed with a movement of her head.

He did not know what more to say, for there seemed no way out of the situation.

—"My dear little girl," he murmured, "we must all accept our share of things, however sad. I understand your grief, and I promise. . . ."

"You're so kind . . ." she stammered.

They were silent. He looked at her. There was tenderness and surrender in her glance, and suddenly she raised her arms, as if she wished to draw him to her. He bent over her, feeling that she was calling him, and their lips met.

For a long time they stayed thus with closed eyes. But he, realizing that he was on the point of losing control, raised his head and stood up. She was smiling at him now with real tenderness, and gripping his shoulders with both hands, she tried to hold him back.

"I'm going to fetch your mother," he said.

"One more second," she murmured. "I'm so happy."

Then, after a brief interval of silence, she said very softly, so softly that he hardly heard her:

"You will love me very much, won't you?"

He knelt down by the bedside and kissed her wrist, which she held out to him.

"I adore you."

But there were footsteps at the door. He sprang up and called out in his ordinary voice, with its faint note of irony:

"You can come in. It's all over now."

The Marquise flung herself upon her daughter with open arms and embraced her frantically, covering her face with tears. Servigny, his heart full of joy and his body on fire with love, stepped out onto the balcony to breathe deeply of the cool night air, humming:

> *"Souvent femme varie;*
> *Bien fol est qui s'y fie."*

WAITER, A BOCK

Why did I go into that café on that particular evening? I do not know. It was cold; a fine rain, a flying mist, veiled the gas-lamps with a transparent fog through which the sidewalks reflected the glare that streamed from the shop-windows, lighting up the soft slush and the muddy feet of the passers-by.

I was going nowhere in particular; was simply taking a short walk after dinner. I had passed the Crédit Lyonnais, the rue Vivienne, and several other streets. I suddenly perceived a large café which was more than half full. I walked inside, with no object in view. I was not the least thirsty.

I glanced round to find a corner that was not too crowded, and went and sat down by the side of a man who seemed to me to be old, and who was smoking a cheap clay-pipe, which was as black as coal. The six or eight saucers piled up on the table in front of him indicated the number of bocks he had already absorbed. I did not look at him closely. At a glance I recognized a beer-drinker, one of those frequenters of beer-houses who come in the morning when the place opens, and do not leave till evening when it is about to close. He was dirty, bald on top of his head, with a fringe of iron-gray hair falling on the collar of his frock-coat. His clothes, which were much too large for him, appeared to have been made for him at a time when he was corpulent. Looking at him, you guessed that these trousers never held up, that he could not take ten steps without having to stop to put them straight and adjust them. Did he wear a waistcoat? The mere thought of his boots and of that which they covered filled me with horror. The frayed cuffs were perfectly black at the edges, as were his nails.

As soon as I had sat down beside him, this individual said to me in a quiet tone of voice:

"How goes it?"

I turned sharply round and scanned his features, whereupon he continued:

"I see you do not recognize me."

"No, I do not."

"Des Barrets."

I was stupefied. It was the Comte Jean des Barrets, my old school-friend.

I seized him by the hand, and was so dumbfounded that I could find nothing to say. At length I managed to stammer out:

"And you, how goes it with you?"

He responded placidly:

"I get along as best I can."

"What are you doing now?" I asked.

"You see what I am doing," he answered quite resignedly.

I felt my face getting red. I went on:

"But what do you do with your days?"

"Every day is the same," was his reply, accompanied by a thick puff of tobacco smoke.

He then tapped with a sou on the top of the marble table, to attract the attention of the waiter, and called out:

"Waiter, two bocks."

A voice in the distance repeated:

"Two bocks for number four."

Another voice, more distant still, shouted out shrilly: "Here!"

Immediately a man with a white apron appeared, carrying two bocks at a run, and spilling some of the yellow liquid on the sandy floor in his haste.

Des Barrets emptied his glass at a single draught and replaced it on the table, while he sucked in the foam that lingered on his mustache. Then he asked:

"What news?"

I really had nothing new to tell him. I stammered:

"Nothing, old man. I am in business."

In his matter-of-fact tone he said:

"Indeed, does it amuse you?"

"No, but what can I do? One must do something!"

"Why should one?"

"To have an occupation."

"What's the use of an occupation? I never do anything, as you see, nothing at all. When one has not a sou I can understand why one should work. But when one has enough to live on, what's the use? What is the good of working? Do you work for yourself, or for others? If you work for yourself, if you do it for your own amusement, that's all right; if you work for others, you are a fool."

Then, laying his pipe on the marble table, he called out anew:

"Waiter, a bock." He continued: "Talking makes me thirsty. I am not accustomed to it. Yes, I do nothing. I let things slide, and I am growing old. In dying I shall have nothing to regret. My only remembrance will be this tavern. No wife, no children, no cares, no sorrows, nothing. That is best."

He emptied the glass which had been brought him, passed his tongue over his lips, and resumed his pipe.

I looked at him in astonishment, and said:

"But you have not always been like this?"

"Oh, yes, I have; ever since I left college."

"But you can't call that living, my dear fellow; it is simply horrible. Come, you must have something to do, you must love something, you must have friends."

"No. I get up at noon, I come here, I have my lunch, I drink bocks, I remain until the evening, I have my dinner, I drink bocks. Then about half-past one in the morning, I go home to bed, because the place closes up; that annoys me more than anything. In the last ten years I have spent fully six years on this bench, in my corner; and the other four in my bed, nowhere else. I sometimes chat with the regular customers."

"But when you came to Paris what did you do at first?"

"I studied law . . . at the Café de Médicis."

"What next?"

"Next I crossed the Seine and came here."

"Why did you take the trouble?"

"Well, one cannot spend all one's life in the Latin Quarter. The students make too much noise. Now I shall not move again. Waiter, a bock."

I began to think that he was making fun of me, and I continued:

"Come now, be frank. You have been the victim of some great sorrow; some disappointment in love, no doubt! It is easy to see that you are a man who has had some trouble. How old are you?"

"I am thirty-three, but I look at least forty-five."

I looked him straight in the face. His wrinkled, ill-shaven face was the face of an old man. On the top of his head a few long hairs waved over a skin of doubtful cleanliness. He had long eyelashes, a heavy mustache, and a thick beard. Suddenly I had a kind of vision, I know not why, of a basin filled with dirty water in which all that hair had been washed. I said to him:

"You certainly look older than your age. You surely must have experienced some great sorrow."

He replied:

"I tell you that I have not. I am old because I never go out into the air. Nothing makes a man deteriorate more than café life."

I still could not believe him.

"You must surely also have got married? One could not get as bald-headed as you are without having loved greatly."

He shook his head, sending dandruff down on his collar as he did so.

"No, I have always been virtuous."

And, raising his eyes towards the chandelier which heated our heads, he said:

"If I am bald, it is the fault of the gas. It destroys the hair. Waiter, a bock. Are you not thirsty?"

"No, thank you. But you really interest me. Since when have you been so morbid? Your life is not normal, it is not natural. There is something behind all this."

"There is; and it dates from my childhood. I received a great shock when I was very young. It turned my life into darkness which will last to the end."

"What was it?"

"You want to know about it? Well, then, listen. You recall, of course, the house in which I was brought up, for you came there five or six times in the holidays. You remember that large gray building, in the middle of a great park, and the long avenues of oaks which opened to the four points of the compass. You remember my father and mother, both of them so ceremonious, solemn, and severe.

"I worshiped my mother; I was afraid of my father;

but I respected them both, accustomed as I was to see everyone bow before them. They were *Monsieur le Comte* and *Madame la Comtesse* to all the country round, and our neighbors, the Tannemares, the Ravelets, the Brennevilles, showed them the utmost consideration.

"I was then thirteen years old. I was happy, pleased with everything, as one is at that age, full of the joy of life.

"Well, towards the end of September, a few days before returning to school, as I was playing about in the shrubbery of the park, among the branches and leaves, and was about to cross a path, I saw my father and mother walking along.

"I remember it as though it were yesterday. It was a very windy day. The whole row of trees swayed beneath the gusts of wind, groaning, and seeming to utter cries—those dull, deep cries that forests give out during a storm.

"The yellow falling leaves flew away like birds, circling and falling, and then running along the path like swift animals.

"Evening came on. It was dark in the thickets. The motion of the wind and of the branches excited me, made me tear about as if I were crazy, and howl in imitation of the wolves.

"As soon as I perceived my parents, I crept furtively towards them, under the branches, in order to surprise them, as though I had been a veritable prowler. But I stopped in fear a few paces from them. My father was in a terrible passion and he was shouting:

"'Your mother is a fool; moreover, it is not a question of your mother. It is you. I tell you that I need that money, and I want you to sign this.'

"My mother replied in a firm voice:

"'I will not sign it. It is Jean's fortune. I shall keep it for him and I will not allow you to squander it on vile women as you did your own inheritance.'

"Then my father, trembling with rage, wheeled round and, seizing my mother by the throat, he began to strike her with all his force full in the face.

"My mother's hat fell off, her hair became loosened and fell over her shoulders; she tried to parry the blows, but she could not. And my father, like a madman, kept on striking her. My mother rolled over on the ground, covering her face with her hands. Then he turned her over on her back to strike her again, pulling away her hands which were covering her face.

"As for me, my friend, it seemed as though the world was coming to an end, that the eternal laws had changed. I experienced the overwhelming dread that one has in the presence of things supernatural, of irreparable disasters. My childish mind was bewildered, distracted. I began to cry with all my might, without knowing why; a prey to a fearful dread, sorrow, and astonishment. My father heard me, turned round, and, on seeing me, started towards me. I believe that he wanted to kill me, and I fled like a hunted animal, running straight ahead into the thicket.

"I ran perhaps for an hour, perhaps for two. I don't know. Darkness fell. I sank down on the grass, exhausted, and lay there dismayed, frantic with fear, and devoured by a sorrow capable of breaking forever the heart of a poor child. I was cold, hungry, perhaps. At length day broke. I was afraid to get up, to walk, to return home, to run farther, fearing to meet my father, whom I wished never to see again.

"I should probably have died of misery and of hunger at the foot of a tree if the gamekeeper had not discovered me and led me home by force.

"I found my parents looking as usual. My mother spoke to me:

"'How you frightened me, you naughty boy. I lay awake the whole night.'

"I did not answer, but began to weep. My father did not utter a single word.

"A week later I returned to school.

"Well, my friend, it was all over with me. I had seen the other side of things, the bad side. I have not been able to perceive the good side since that day. What took place in my mind, what strange phenomenon warped my ideas, I do not know. But I no longer had a taste for anything, a wish for anything, a love for anybody, a desire for anything whatever, any ambition, or any hope. And I always see my poor mother on the ground, in the park, my father beating her. My mother died some years later; my father is still alive. I have not seen him since. Waiter, a bock."

A waiter brought him his bock, which he swallowed at a gulp. But, in taking up his pipe again, trembling as he was, he broke it. "Confound it!" he said, with a gesture of annoyance. "That is a real sorrow. It will take me a month to color another!"

And he called out across the vast hall, now reeking with smoke and full of men drinking, his everlasting, "Waiter, a bock—and a new pipe."

OLD MILON

For a month past the great sun had been casting its broiling heat over the fields. Nature was unfolding radiantly beneath this shower of fire; as far as the eye could reach, the earth was green. To the ends of the horizon, the sky was blue. The Norman farms scattered over the plain looked, from the distance, like little woods enclosed in their girdle of slender beeches. From near at hand, when you opened the worm-eaten gate, it was like looking at a giant garden, for all the aged apple-trees, bony of limb like country-folk, were in flower. The rows of black, crooked, twisted old trunks in the farmyard displayed their dazzling white and pink domes under the sky. The sweet perfume of their blossoms mingled with the rich stenches of the open cow-shed and the steam of the fermenting dung-heap over-run with hens.

It was noon. The family were at dinner in the shade of the pear-tree by the door: the father, the mother, the four children, the two maids, and the three farm hands. No one was speaking. The soup was eaten, then a dish full of potatoes cooked in fat was uncovered.

From time to time a maid got up and went down to the cellar to refill the pitcher of cider.

The man, a big fellow of forty, gazed at a vine, still bare of leaves, which grew up the front of his house and ran, writhing like a snake, under the shutters, the whole length of the wall.

"The old man's vine is budding early this year," he remarked at last. "Maybe it will bear."

The woman also turned round and looked at it, without speaking.

The vine was planted on the exact spot where the old man was shot.

It was during the war of 1870. The Prussians were occupying the entire district. General Faidherbe, with the Northern Army, was putting up a stout resistance.

The Prussian Staff was quartered at this farm. The old peasant who owned it, old Milon, Pierre Milon, had taken them in and installed them as comfortably as he could.

For a month the German advance-guard had remained in the village, reconnoitering. The French were twenty-five miles away; yet every night Uhlans kept disappearing.

All the detachments of scouts, those who were sent out on picket duty, when only two or three men set out together, never returned.

They were found dead in the morning, in a field, beside a farmyard, or in a ditch. Their horses lay at the roadside, their throats cut by a saber.

These murders all appeared to be committed by the same men, who could not be discovered.

The whole district was under a reign of terror. Peasants were shot on mere denunciation, and women imprisoned; the Prussians tried to frighten the children into revealing the truth. Nothing was discovered.

But one morning old Milon was seen lying in his stable, his face slashed across.

Two disemboweled Uhlans were found about two miles away from the farm. One still held his bloodstained weapon in his hand. He had fought, had defended himself.

A court-martial was held at once in the open, in front of the farm, and the old man was brought in.

He was sixty-eight. He was small, thin, and rather crooked, with big hands like the claws of a crab. His faded, thin hair, light as a duckling's down, concealed none of the flesh on his skull. The brown, creased skin on his neck showed veins which were lost under the jaws and reappeared at the temples. He was known throughout the neighborhood as a miser and a hard man in business.

He was made to stand among four soldiers, in front of the kitchen table, which had been carried out of doors. Five officers and the colonel sat facing him.

The colonel began speaking, in French:

"Father Milon, since we have been here, we have had nothing but praise for you. You have always been obliging, and even zealous, in our service. But today a terrible charge rests upon you, and the matter must be cleared up. How did you get the wound in your face?"

The peasant did not reply.

"Your silence condemns you, Milon," continued the colonel. "But I will have an answer from you, do you hear? Do you know who killed the Uhlans who were found this morning near the Calvary?"

"It was me," said the old man in a clear voice.

Amazed, the colonel was silent for a second, staring

fixedly at the prisoner. Old Milon remained impassive, with his stupid peasant expression, his eyes lowered as though he were talking to his priest. One thing only revealed his inner distress; again and again he kept swallowing his saliva, with a visible effort, as though his throat were tightly constricted.

The man's family, his son Jean, his daughter-in-law and two grandchildren, stood ten paces back, in frightened consternation.

"Do you also know who killed the scouts in our army corps, who have been found every morning, in the district, for the past month?" went on the colonel.

"It was me," replied the old man, with the same animal impassivity.

"You killed all of them?"

"Yes, all of them; it was me."

"You alone?"

"Me alone."

"Tell me how you set about it."

This time the man seemed affected; the necessity of speaking at length visibly embarrassed him.

"How do I know?" he stammered. "I just did it like it happened."

"I warn you that you will have to tell me everything," said the colonel. "So you will do well to make up your mind to it at once. How did you begin?"

The man flung an uneasy glance at his anxious family behind him. He hesitated for an instant, then suddenly made up his mind.

"I was coming home one night, maybe ten o'clock, the day after you got here. You and your men, you'd taken more than two hundred francs' worth of my forage, with a cow and two sheep. I said to myself: 'So many times as they take fifty francs' worth of stuff, so many times I'll pay them out for it.' And I'd other things

n my mind, too; I'll tell you about them later. And then
saw one of your troopers smoking his pipe in my ditch,
behind my barn. I went and got down my scythe, and
came up very softly behind him; he never heard a
sound. And I cut off his head with one blow, with a
single blow, like an ear of wheat; he never so much as
said 'Oh!' You've only to look in the pond: you'll find
him there in a coal sack, with a stone out of the wall.

"I had my scheme. I took all his things, from boots
to cap, and hid them in the cement-kiln in Martin
Wood, behind the yard."

The old man was silent. The astounded officers gazed
at one another. The questioning went on again; and this
is what they learned:

Once the murder had been done, the man had lived
with this one idea: "Kill Prussians!" He hated them with
the cunning, desperate hatred of a peasant at once
avaricious and patriotic. He had his scheme, as he said.
He waited for a few days.

He was free to come and go, enter and depart at will,
so humble, submissive, and obliging had he shown himself to the conquerors. Every night he saw the scouts
go out; and he went out himself, one night, having
heard the name of the village for which the troopers
were bound, and having learned, thanks to the constant
presence of the soldiers, the few words of German he
needed.

He walked out of his farmyard, slipped into the
wood, reached the cement-kiln, walked to the far end
of the long gallery, and, finding the dead man's clothes
on the ground, he put them on.

Then he went prowling through the fields, crawling
along, following the embankments so as to conceal himself, stopping to listen at the faintest sound, alert as a
poacher.

When he judged that the time had come, he went near the road and hid in a hedge. He waited again. At last, at about midnight, he heard a horse's hoof ring out on the hard road. He set his ear to the ground, to make sure that only one horseman was approaching; then made ready.

The Uhlan came up at a fast trot, carrying dispatches. His eyes were on the lookout, and his ears alert. When he was no more than ten paces distant, old Milon crawled across the road, groaning: *"Hilfe! Hilfe!"* The horseman stopped, recognized a dismounted German, imagined that he was wounded, got off his horse, and went up to him, unsuspectingly. As he bent over, he received the long curved blade of the saber clean through the stomach. He fell, without a death struggle, only quivering with a few final tremors.

Then the Norman, radiant with an old peasant's silent pleasure, rose and, to please himself, cut the throat of the corpse. Then he dragged it to the ditch and threw it in.

The horse was quietly waiting for its master. Old Milon got into the saddle and galloped off across the plain.

An hour later he perceived two more Uhlans side by side, returning to their camp. He went straight towards them, again shouting: *"Hilfe! Hilfe!"* The Prussians, recognizing the uniform, let him come on without distrust. And the old man dashed between them like a cannonball, felling both, one with his saber, the other with a revolver.

Then he cut the throats of the horses, the German horses. Thereafter he went quietly back to the cement kiln and hid his horse at the end of the dark gallery. He took off the uniform, put on his mean clothes again, and going home to bed, slept till morning.

For the next four days he did not go out, as he was waiting for the end of the inquiry which had been opened; but on the fifth day he went out again and killed two more soldiers by the same stratagem.

Thenceforward he never stopped. Every night he wandered out, prowling at random, killing Prussians first in one place then another, galloping over the deserted fields, in the moonlight, a lost Uhlan, a hunter of men. Then, his task over, leaving the bodies lying in the roads behind him, the old horseman returned to hide his horse and uniform in the cement-kiln.

At about midday he would go out with an unconcerned air to take oats and water to his mount, which remained in the underground passage. He fed the beast without stint, for he demanded a great deal of work from it.

But, on the previous night, one of the men he attacked had been on his guard and had slashed the old peasant's face with his saber.

Even so, he had killed both men! He had once more returned, hidden his horse, and put on his humble clothes again; but while walking home, he had been overtaken by faintness and had crawled to the stable, unable to reach the house.

He was found there, bleeding, in the straw.

When he had ended his tale, he suddenly raised his head and stared proudly at the Prussian officers.

"Have you anything more to say?" asked the colonel, pulling his mustache.

"No, nothing more; the score is paid: I've killed sixteen of them, not one more and not one less."

"You know that you are going to die?"

"I never asked you for mercy."

"Have you been in the army?"

"Yes. I've been to the wars, in my time. And besides,

it was you that killed my father, who was a soldier under the first Emperor. Not counting that you killed my youngest son, François, last month, near Evreux. I owed you for that, and I've paid. We're quits."

The officers looked at one another.

The old man continued:

"Eight for my father, eight for my son, we're quits. I never sought a quarrel with you! I don't know you! I don't even know where you come from. And here you are at my house, ordering people about as though you were at home. I had my revenge on the others. I don't regret it."

And, drawing up his crippled body, the old man folded his arms in the attitude of a humble hero.

For a long time the Prussians whispered together. A captain, who also lost his son the month before, defended the great-hearted old peasant.

Then the colonel rose and went up to old Milon, saying, in a low voice:

"Listen, old man, there may be a way of saving your life, if you——"

But the man was not listening. His eyes were fixed upon the conquering officer, and, while the wind stirred the wisps of hair on his head, he made a frightful grimace which distorted his thin face, all seamed as it was by the saber-gash, and, swelling his chest, he spat, with all his might, full in the Prussian's face.

The furious colonel raised his hand, and for a second time the peasant spat in his face.

All the officers had risen and were shouting orders at the same time.

In less than a minute the old man, still quite impassive, was put against the wall and shot, smiling at Jean, his eldest son, his daughter-in-law, and the two little children, who stood watching, distracted with horror.

A COUP D'ÉTAT

PARIS had just had news of the disaster at Sedan. The Republic was proclaimed. All France was panting on the threshold of a delirium that lasted until after the Commune. Everybody was playing at soldier from one end of the country to the other.

Hatters became colonels and assumed the duties of generals; revolvers and daggers were displayed on large rotund paunches, enveloped in red sashes; common citizens became temporary warriors, commanding battalions of noisy volunteers and swearing like troopers to emphasize their importance.

The mere fact of bearing arms and handling guns excited people who hitherto had only handled weighing-scales, and made them formidable to the first comer, without reason. They even executed a few innocent people to prove that they knew how to kill; and, in roaming through country places as yet innocent of Prussians, they shot stray dogs, cows chewing the cud in peace, or sick horses put out to pasture. Every man believed himself called upon to play a great role in military affairs. The cafés of the smallest villages, full of tradesmen in uniform, resembled barracks or field-hospitals.

Now, the town of Canneville had not yet heard the news of the army and the Capital, but a violent agitation had been disturbing it for a month, and the rival political parties had confronted each other. The Mayor, Vicomte de Varnetot, a small, thin man already old, a Legitimist who had rallied recently to the Empire spurred by ambition, had seen rising up against him a powerful adversary in Doctor Massarel, a stout, full-blooded man, head of the Republican party in the district, venerable chief of the Masonic Lodge at the county seat, president of the Society of Agriculture, chairman of the annual Fire Department banquet, and organizer of the rural militia which was to save the country.

In two weeks he had induced sixty-three married men and fathers of families to volunteer in defense of their country, prudent farmers and merchants of the town, and he drilled them every morning on the square in front of the Town Hall.

Whenever the mayor happened to appear at the local government building, Commander Massarel, covered with pistols, sword in hand, passing proudly up and down in front of his troops, would make them shout "Long live our country!" And this, they noticed, disturbed the little Vicomte, who no doubt heard in it menace and defiance, and perhaps some odious recollection of the great Revolution.

On the morning of the fifth of September the doctor, in uniform, his revolver on the table, was giving a consultation to an old peasant couple of whom the husband had suffered with varicose veins for seven years, but had waited until his wife had the same complaint before coming to see the doctor, when the postman arrived with the newspaper.

Doctor Massarel opened it, grew pale, straightened himself abruptly and, raising his arms to heaven in gesture of exaltation, cried out with all his might, in the face of the amazed rustics:

"Long live the Republic! Long live the Republic! Long live the Republic!"

Then he dropped into his armchair weak with emotion.

When the peasant explained again that this sickness had begun with a feeling as if ants were running up and down his legs, the doctor exclaimed, "Leave me in peace. I have no time to waste on such nonsense. The Republic is proclaimed! The Emperor is a prisoner! France is saved! Long live the Republic!" And, running to the door, he bellowed, "Céleste! Quick! Céleste!"

The frightened maid hastened in. He stuttered, so rapidly did he try to speak, "My boots, my sword—my cartridge box—and—the Spanish dagger, which is on my night table. Hurry now!"

The obstinate peasant, taking advantage of the moment's silence, began again, "They became like knots that hurt me when I walked."

The exasperated doctor shouted, "Shut up, for Heaven's sake! If you had washed your feet oftener, it would not have happened." Then, seizing him by the neck, he hissed in his face, "Can't you understand that we are living in a Republic, idiot?"

But a sense of his profession calmed him suddenly, and he led the astonished old couple out of the house, repeating: "Come back tomorrow, come back tomorrow, my friends; I have no time today."

While equipping himself from head to foot, he gave another series of urgent orders to the maid:

"Run to Lieutenant Picart's and to Sub-lieutenant Pommel's and tell them that I want them here immediately. Send Torchebeuf to me, too, with his drum. Quick, now! Quick!" And when Céleste was gone, he collected his thoughts and prepared to overcome the difficulties of the situation.

The three men arrived together. They were in their working clothes. The Commander, who had expected to see them in uniform, gave a start of surprise.

"Good Lord! Haven't you heard the news? The Emperor has been taken prisoner. A Republic is proclaimed. We must take action. My position is delicate. I might almost say perilous."

He reflected for some minutes in the presence of his astonished subordinates and then continued:

"We must act without hesitation. Minutes are worth hours in times like these. Everything depends upon promptness of decision. You, Picart, go find the priest and order him to ring the bell to bring the people together, so that I may inform them. You, Torchebeuf, beat the call in every part of the district, as far as the hamlets of Gerisaie and Salmare, to assemble the militia in arms, in the square. You, Pommel, put on your uniform at once, that is, the jacket and cap. We, together are going to take possession of the Town Hall and summon M. de Varnetot to transfer his authority to me. Do you understand?"

"Yes."

"Act, then, and promptly. I will accompany you to your house, Pommel, since we are to work together."

Five minutes later, the Commandant and his subaltern, armed to the teeth, appeared in the square, just at the moment when the little Vicomte de Varnetot, wearing hunting gaiters, and with his rifle on his shoulder came along by another street, walking rapidly and followed by three gamekeepers in green jackets, each carrying a knife at his side and a gun over his shoulder.

While the doctor stopped in amazement, the four

men entered the Town Hall and the door closed behind them.

"We have been forestalled," murmured the doctor. "Now we shall have to wait for reinforcements; nothing can be done for the time being."

Lieutenant Picart reappeared. "The priest refuses to obey," said he; "he has shut himself up in the church with the beadle and the usher."

On the other side of the square, opposite the white, closed front of the Town Hall, the church, silent and somber, showed its great oak door with the wrought-iron trimmings.

Then, as the puzzled inhabitants put their heads out of the windows, or came out upon their doorsteps, the rolling of a drum was heard, and Torchebeuf suddenly appeared, beating with fury the three quick strokes of the call to arms. He crossed the square with disciplined step and disappeared along the road leading to the country.

The Commandant drew his sword, advanced alone about half-way between the two buildings where the enemy was barricaded and, waving his weapon above his head, roared at the top of his lungs, "Long live the Republic! Death to traitors!" Then he fell back beside his officers. The butcher, the baker, and the apothecary, feeling a little uncertain, put up their shutters and closed their shops. The grocery alone remained open.

Meanwhile the militiamen were gradually arriving, variously clothed, but all wearing caps with red braid, the cap constituting the whole uniform of the corps. They were armed with their old, rusty guns, guns that had hung over chimney-pieces in kitchens for thirty years, and looked rather like a detachment of foresters. When there were about thirty around him, the Commandant explained in a few words the state of affairs. Then, turning toward his general staff, he said, "Now, we must act."

While the inhabitants collected, looked on, and discussed the matter, the doctor quickly formed his plan of campaign:

"Lieutenant Picart, you advance to the windows of the Town Hall and order M. de Varnetot to surrender it to me, in the name of the Republic."

But the Lieutenant was a master-mason and refused.

"You are very clever, aren't you? Trying to make a target of me! Those fellows in there are good shots, you know. No, thanks! Execute your commissions yourself!"

The Commandant turned red. "I order you to go in the name of discipline," said he.

The Lieutenant rebelled.

"I am not going to have my face spoiled without knowing the reason why."

The notables of the village, in a group near by, began to laugh. One of them called out, "You are right, Picart, this is not the proper time." The doctor, under his breath, muttered, "Cowards!" And, placing his sword and his revolver in the hands of a soldier, he advanced with measured step, his eyes fixed on the windows, as if he expected to see the muzzle of a gun pointed at him.

When he was within a few steps of the building the doors at the two ends, affording an entrance to two schools, opened, and a flood of little creatures, boys on one side, girls on the other, poured out and began playing in the open space, chattering around the doctor like a flock of birds. He could hardly make himself heard.

As soon as they were all out, the two doors closed. The greater part of the little monkeys finally scattered, and then the Commandant called out in a loud voice:

"Monsieur de Varnetot!" A window in the upper story opened and M. de Varnetot appeared.

The Commandant began, "Sir, you are aware of the great events which have changed the system of government. The party you represent no longer exists. The side I represent now comes into power. In these sad but decisive circumstances, I summon you, in the name of the new Republic, to place in my hands the authority vested in you by the outgoing power."

M. de Varnetot replied, "Doctor Massarel, I am Mayor of Canneville, so placed by the proper authorities, and Mayor of Canneville I shall remain until my title is revoked and I am replaced by an order from my superiors. As Mayor, I am at home in the Town Hall and here I shall stay. Furthermore, just try to put me out." And he closed the window.

The Commandant returned to his troops. But, before explaining anything, measuring Lieutenant Picart from head to foot, he said:

"You are a fine fellow, you are—a goose, the disgrace of the army. I degrade you."

The Lieutenant replied, "I don't care a damn." And he went over to the group of grumbling citizens.

Then the doctor hesitated. What should he do? Make an assault? Would his men obey him? And then, was he in the right? He had a bright idea. He ran to the telegraph office opposite the Town Hall, on the other side of the square, and sent three dispatches, "To the Members of the Republican Government, at Paris"; "To the New Republican Prefect of the Seine-Inférieure, at Rouen"; "To the New Republican Sub-prefect of Dieppe."

He explained the situation fully; told of the danger which the district incurred by remaining in the hands of the monarchist mayor, offered his loyal services, asked for orders and signed his name, followed by all his titles. Then he returned to his army corps and, drawing ten francs out of his pocket, said:

"Now, my men, go and eat and drink a little something. Only, leave a detachment of ten men here, so that no one leaves the Town Hall."

Ex-Lieutenant Picart, chatting with the watchmaker, overheard this. With a sneer he remarked, "Pardon me, but if they go out, you will have a chance to go in. Otherwise, I can't see how you are to get in there!"

The doctor made no reply, but went off to lunch. In the afternoon, he placed guards all about town, as if it were threatened by a surprise. Many times he passed before the doors of the Town Hall and of the church, without noticing anything suspicious; one might have thought the two buildings were empty.

The butcher, the baker, and the apothecary reopened their shops. There was a lot of talking in the houses. If the Emperor had been taken prisoner, there must be a traitor somewhere. They did not know exactly which Republic had been restored.

Night came on. Towards nine o'clock, the doctor returned quietly and alone to the Town Hall, persuaded that his adversary had retired. And, as he was trying to force an entrance with a few blows of a pickaxe, the loud voice of a sentry demanded suddenly, "Who goes there?" Monsieur Massarel beat a retreat at top speed.

Another day dawned without any change in the situation. The militia in arms occupied the square. The inhabitants stood around them, awaiting the solution. People from neighboring villages came to look on. Finally, the doctor, realizing that his reputation was at stake, resolved to settle the thing in one way or another. He had just decided that it must be something energetic, when the door of the telegraph office opened and the little servant of the postmistress appeared, holding in her hand two papers.

First she went to the Commandant and gave him one of the dispatches; then, crossing the deserted center of the square, intimidated by so many eyes fixed upon her, with lowered head and running steps, she rapped gently at the door of the barricaded house, as if unaware that a party of armed men was concealed there.

The door opened slightly; the hand of a man received the message, and the girl returned, blushing and ready to weep, from being stared at by the whole countryside.

In vibrating tones the doctor shouted, "Silence, please." And, when the populace became quiet, he continued proudly:

"Here is a communication which I have received from the government." And raising the telegram, he read:

> Old Mayor revoked. Please attend to urgent matters. Instructions will follow.
>
> For the Sub-prefect,
> SAPIN, Councilor.

He had triumphed. His heart was beating with joy. His hands were shaking. But Picart, his old subaltern, cried out to him from a neighboring group, "That's all right; but if they in there won't get out, that piece of paper will not do you much good." M. Massarel turned pale. Supposing the others refused to get out? He would now have to take the offensive. It was not only his right, but his duty. And he looked anxiously at the Town Hall, hoping that he might see the door open and his adversary retreat. But the door remained closed. What was to be done? The crowd was increasing, surrounding the militia. People were laughing.

One thought especially tortured the doctor. If he should make an assault, he must march at the head of his men; and as, once he was killed, there would be no opposition, it would be at him, and at him alone that M. de Varnetot and the three gamekeepers would aim. And their aim was good, very good! Picart had reminded him of that.

But an idea occurred to him, and turning to Pommel, he said, "Go, quickly, and ask the chemist to lend me a napkin and a pole."

The Lieutenant hurried off. The doctor was going to make a political banner, a white one, that would, perhaps, rejoice the Legitimist heart of the old mayor.

Pommel returned with the piece of linen required, and a broom handle. With some pieces of string, they improvised a flag, which Massarel seized in both hands. Again, he advanced towards the Town Hall, bearing the standard before him. When in front of the door, he called out, "Monsieur de Varnetot!"

The door opened suddenly, and M. de Varnetot and his three gamekeepers appeared on the threshold. The doctor recoiled, instinctively. Then, he saluted his enemy courteously, and announced, almost strangled by emotion, "I have come, sir, to communicate to you the instructions I have just received."

That gentleman, without any salutation whatever, replied, "I am going to withdraw, sir, but you must understand that it is not because of fear, or in obedience to an odious government that has usurped power." And, biting off each word, he declared, "I do not wish to have the appearance of serving the Republic for a single day. That is all."

Massarel, amazed, made no reply; and M. de Varnetot, walking off at a rapid pace, disappeared around the corner, followed closely by his escort. Then the doctor, mad with pride, returned to the crowd. When he was near enough to be heard, he cried, "Hurrah! Hurrah! The Republic triumphs all along the line!"

But no emotion was manifested. The doctor tried again, "The people are free! You are free and independent! Do you understand? Be proud of your freedom!"

The listless villagers looked at him with eyes unlit by glory. In his turn, he looked at them, indignant at their indifference, seeking for some word that could make a grand impression, electrify this placid country folk and make good his mission. The inspiration came, and turning to Pommel, he said, "Lieutenant, go and get the bust of the Ex-Emperor, which is in the Municipal Council Hall, and bring it to me with a chair."

And soon the man reappeared, carrying on his right shoulder, Napoleon III in plaster, and holding in his left hand a straw-bottomed chair.

Massarel met him, took the chair, placed it on the ground, put the white image upon it, fell back a few steps and called out, in sonorous voice:

"Tyrant! At last you have fallen! Fallen in the dust and in the mire. An expiring country groaned beneath your foot. Avenging fate has struck you down. Defeat and shame cling to you. You fall conquered, a prisoner to the Prussians, and upon the ruins of the crumbling Empire the young and radiant Republic arises, picking up your broken sword."

He awaited applause. But not a shout was raised, not a hand clapped. The bewildered peasants remained silent. And the bust, with its pointed mustaches extending beyond the cheeks on each side, the bust, as motionless and well groomed as a hairdresser's sign, seemed to be looking at M. Massarel with a plaster smile, an ineffaceable and mocking smile.

They remained thus face to face, Napoleon on the

chair, the doctor in front of him about three steps away.
Suddenly the Commandant grew angry. What was to be
done? What was there that would move these people,
and bring about a definite victory of opinion? His hand
happened to rest on his hip and to come in contact there
with the butt-end of his revolver, under his red sash.
No inspiration, no further word would come. So he drew
his pistol, advanced two steps, and, taking aim, fired at
the late monarch. The bullet entered the forehead, leaving a little, black hole, like a spot, nothing more. It
made no effect. He fired a second shot, which made a
second hole; then, a third; and then, without stopping,
he emptied his revolver. Napoleon's forehead disappeared in white powder, but the eyes, the nose, and the
fine points of the mustaches remained intact. Then, the
exasperated doctor overturned the chair with a blow
of his fist and, resting a foot on the remainder of the
bust in an attitude of triumph, he turned to the flabbergasted public and shouted, "So let all tyrants perish!"

Still no enthusiasm was manifest, and as the spectators seemed to be in a kind of stupor from astonishment,
the Commandant called to the militiamen, "You may
now disperse to your homes." And he went towards his
own house with great strides, as if he were pursued.

His maid, when he appeared, told him that some
patients had been waiting in his office for three hours.
He hastened in. There were the two varicose-vein patients, who had returned at daybreak, obstinate and
patient.

The old man immediately began his explanation, "It
began by a feeling like ants running up and down my
legs."

BOULE DE SUIF

For several days in succession straggling remnants of the routed French army had been passing through the town. This was not the regular army, but a disjointed rabble, the men unshaven and dirty, their uniforms in tatters, slouching along without regimental colors, without order—worn out, broken down, incapable of thought or resolution, marching from pure habit and dropping with fatigue the moment they stopped. The majority belonged to the militia and were men of peaceful pursuits, retired from business, all sinking under the weight of their accouterments: quick-witted little militiamen as prone to terror as they were to enthusiasm, as ready to attack as they were to fly; here and there a few red trousers, remnants of a company mowed down in one of the big battles; dark-coated artillerymen, side by side with these various uniforms of the infantry, and now and then the glittering helmet of a heavily booted dragoon who followed with difficulty the march of the more light-footed soldiers of the line.

Companies of franc-tireurs, heroically named "Avengers of the Defeat," "Citizens of the Tomb," "Companions in Death," passed in their turn, looking like a horde of bandits.

Their chiefs—formerly drapers or grain-dealers, retired soap-boilers or suet-refiners, temporary heroes, created officers by reason of their wealth or the length of their mustaches, burdened with weapons, flannels, and gold lace—talked loudly, discussed plans of campaign, and gave you to understand that they were the sole support of France in her death-agony; but they were generally in terror of their own soldiers, gallows birds, most of them brave to foolhardiness, all of them given to pillage and debauchery.

Report said that the Prussians were about to enter Rouen. The National Guard, which for two months past had made the most careful reconnoiterings in the neighboring wood, even to the extent of occasionally shooting their own sentries and putting themselves in battle array if a rabbit stirred in the brushwood, had now retired to their domestic hearths; their arms, their uniforms, all the murderous apparatus with which they had been wont to strike terror into the hearts of all beholders for three leagues round, had vanished.

Finally, the last of the French soldiery crossed the Seine on their way to Pont-Audemer by Saint-Severin and Bourg-Achard; and then, last of all, came their despairing general tramping on foot between two orderlies, powerless to attempt any action with these disjointed fragments of his forces, himself utterly dazed and bewildered by the downfall of a people accustomed to victory and now so disastrously beaten in spite of its traditional bravery.

After that a profound calm, the silence of terrified suspense, fell over the city. Many a rotund bourgeois, emasculated by a lifetime of trade, awaited the arrival of the victors with anxiety, trembling lest his meat-skewers and kitchen carving-knives should come under the category of arms.

Life seemed to have come to a standstill, the shops were closed, the streets silent. From time to time an inhabitant, intimidated by their silence, would flit rapidly along the pavement, keeping close to the walls.

In this anguish of suspense, men longed for the coming of the enemy.

Towards the end of the day following the departure of the French troops, some Uhlans, appearing from goodness knows where, traversed the city hastily. A little later, a black mass descended from the direction of Sainte-Catherine, while two more invading torrents poured in over the roads from Darnetal and Boisguillaume. The advance guards of the three corps converged at the same moment into the square of the Hotel de Ville, while battalion after battalion of the German army wound through the adjacent streets, making the pavement ring under their heavy rhythmic tramp.

Orders shouted in strange and guttural tones were echoed back by the apparently dead and deserted houses, while from behind closed shutters eyes peered furtively at the conquerors, masters by right of might, of the city and the lives and fortunes of its inhabitants. The people in their darkened dwellings fell a prey to the helpless bewilderment which comes over men before the floods, the devastating upheavals of the earth, against which all wisdom and all force are unavailing. The same phenomenon occurs each time that the established order of things is overthrown, when public security is at an end, and when all that the laws of man or of nature protect is at the mercy of some blind elemental force. The earthquake burying an entire population under its falling houses; the flood that carries away the drowned body of the peasant with the carcasses of his cattle and the beams torn from his roof-tree; or the victorious army massacring those who defend their lives, and making prisoners of the rest—pillaging in the name

of the sword, and thanking God to the roar of cannon—
are so many appalling scourges which overthrow all
faith in eternal justice, all the confidence we are taught
to place in the protection of Providence and the reason
of man.

Small detachments now began knocking at the doors
and then disappearing into the houses. It was the occupation after the invasion. It now behooved the vanquished to make themselves agreeable to the victors.

After a while, the first alarms having subsided, a new
sense of tranquillity began to establish itself. In many
houses the Prussian officer shared the family meals. Not
infrequently he was a gentleman, and out of politeness
expressed his commiseration with France and his repugnance at having to take part in such a war. They were
grateful enough to him for this sentiment—besides, who
knew when they might not be glad of his protection?
By gaining his good offices one might have fewer men
to feed. And why offend a person on whom one was
utterly dependent? That would not be bravery but te-
merity, a quality of which the citizens of Rouen could
no longer be accused as in the days of those heroic de-
fenses by which the city had made itself famous. Above
all, they said, with the unassailable urbanity of the
Frenchman, it was surely permissible to be on politely
familiar terms in private, provided one held aloof from
the foreign soldier in public. In the street, therefore,
they ignored one another's existence, but once indoors
they were perfectly ready to be friendly, and each evening found the German staying longer at the family fire-
side.

The town itself gradually regained its wonted aspect.
The French inhabitants did not come out much, but
the Prussian soldiers swarmed in the streets. For the
rest, the blue hussar officers who trailed their mighty

implements of death so arrogantly over the pavement did not appear to entertain a vastly deeper grade of contempt for the simple townsfolk than did the officers of the Chasseurs who had drunk in the same cafés the year before. Nevertheless there was something in the air; something subtle and indefinable, an intolerably unfamiliar atmosphere like a widely diffused odor—the odor of invasion. It filled the private dwellings and the public places, it affected the taste of food, and gave one the impression of being on a journey, far away from home, among barbarous and dangerous tribes.

The conquerors demanded money—a great deal of money. The inhabitants paid and went on paying; for the matter of that, they were rich. But the wealthier a Normandy tradesman becomes, the more keenly he suffers at each sacrifice each time he sees the smallest particle of his fortune pass into the hands of another.

Two or three leagues beyond the town, however, following the course of the river about Croisset, Dieppedalle or Biessard, the sailors and the fishermen would often drag up the swollen corpse of some uniformed German, killed by a knife-thrust or a kick, his head smashed in by a stone, or thrown into the water from some bridge. The slime of the river bed swallowed up many a deed of vengeance, obscure, savage, and legitimate; unknown acts of heroism, silent onslaughts more perilous to the doer than battles in the light of day and without the trumpet-blasts of glory.

For hatred of the alien is always strong enough to arm some intrepid beings who are ready to die for an Idea.

At last, seeing that though the invaders had subjected the city to their inflexible discipline they had not committed any of the horrors with which rumor had credited them throughout the length of their triumphal progress, the public took courage and the commercial spirit began once more to stir in the hearts of the local tradespeople. Some of them who had grave interests at stake at Havre, then occupied by the French army, purposed trying to reach that port by going overland to Dieppe and there taking ship.

They took advantage of the influence of German officers whose acquaintance they had made, and a passport was obtained from the general in command.

Having therefore engaged a large coach with four horses for the journey, and ten persons having entered their names at the livery stable office, they resolved to start on Tuesday morning before daybreak, to avoid all public remark.

For some days already the ground had been hard with frost, and on Monday, about three o'clock in the afternoon, thick dark clouds coming up from the north brought snow, which fell steadily all evening and during the night.

At half-past four the travelers were assembled in the courtyard of the Hotel de Normandie, from whence they were to start.

They were still half asleep, their teeth chattering with cold in spite of their thick wraps. It was difficult to distinguish one from another in the darkness, their heaped-up winter clothing making them look like fat priests in long cassocks. Two of the men, however, recognized each other; they were joined by a third, and they began to talk. "I am taking my wife with me," said one. "So am I." "And I too." The first one added, "We shall not return to Rouen, and if the Prussians come to Havre we shall slip over to England."

They were all like-minded and all had the same plan.

Meanwhile there was no sign of the horses being put in. A small lantern carried by a hostler appeared from time to time out of one dark doorway only to vanish instantly into another. There was a stamping of horses' hoofs deadened by the straw of the litter, and the voice of a man speaking to the animal and cursing sounded from the depths of the stables. A faint tinkle of bells gave evidence of harnessing, and became presently a clear and continual jingle timed by the movement of the beast, now stopping, now going on again with a brisk shake, and accompanied by the dull tramp of hobnailed clogs.

A door slammed sharply. All sound ceased. The frozen travelers were silent, standing stiff and motionless. A continuous curtain of white snowflakes glistened as it fell to the ground, blotting out the shape of things, powdering everything with an icy froth; and in the utter stillness of the town, quiet and buried under its winter pall, nothing was audible but this faint, fluttering, and indefinable rustle of falling snow—more a sensation than a sound—the intermingling of ethereal atoms seeming to fill space, to cover the world.

The man reappeared with his lantern, dragging after him by a rope a dejected and unwilling horse. He pushed it against the pole, fixed the traces, and was occupied for a long time in buckling the harness, having only the use of one hand as he carried the lantern in the other. As he turned away to fetch the other horse he caught sight of the motionless group of travelers, by this time white with snow. "Why don't you get inside the carriage?" he said, "you would at least be under cover."

It had never occurred to them, and they made a rush for it. The three men packed their wives into the upper end and then got in themselves, after which other distinct and veiled forms took the remaining seats without exchanging a word.

The floor of the vehicle was covered with straw into

which the feet sank. The ladies at the end, who had brought little copper charcoal foot-warmers, proceeded to light them, and for some time discussed their merits in subdued tones, repeating to one another things which they had known all their lives.

At last, the coach having been furnished with six horses instead of four on account of the difficulties of the road, a voice outside asked, "Is everybody here?" A voice from within answered, "Yes," and they started.

The conveyance advanced slowly—slowly—the wheels sinking in the snow; the whole vehicle groaned and creaked, the horses slipped, wheezed, and smoked, and the driver's gigantic whip cracked incessantly, flying from side to side, twining and untwining like a slender snake, and cutting sharply across one or other of the six humping backs, which would thereupon straighten up with a more violent effort.

Imperceptibly the day advanced. The airy flakes which a traveler—a true-born Rouennais—likened to a shower of cotton, had ceased to fall; a dirty gray light filtered through the heavy thick clouds which served to heighten the dazzling whiteness of the landscape, where now a long line of trees crusted with icicles would appear, now a cottage with a hood of snow.

In the light of this melancholy dawn the occupants of the diligence began to examine one another curiously.

Right at the end, in the best seats, opposite to one another, dozed Madame and Monsieur Loiseau, wholesale wine merchant of the Rue Grand-Pont.

The former salesman of a master who had become bankrupt, Loiseau had bought up the stock and made his fortune. He sold very bad wine at very low prices to the small country retail dealers, and enjoyed the reputation among his friends and acquaintances of being an unmitigated rogue, a thorough Norman full of trickery and jovial humor.

His character for knavery was so well established that one evening at the Prefecture, Monsieur Tournel, a man of keen and trenchant wit, author of certain fables and songs—a local celebrity—seeing the ladies growing drowsy, proposed a game of "L'oiseau vole." [1] The pun itself flew through the prefect's reception rooms and afterwards through the town, and for a whole month called up a grin on every face in the province.

Loiseau was himself a noted wag famous for his jokes both good and bad, and nobody ever mentioned him without adding immediately, "That man, Loiseau, is simply priceless!"

He was of medium height with a balloon-like stomach and a rubicund face framed in grizzled whiskers. His wife—tall, strong, resolute, loud in voice and rapid of decision—represented order and arithmetic in the business, which he enlivened by his jollity and bustling activity.

Beside them, in a more dignified attitude as befitted his superior station, sat Monsieur Carré-Lamadon, a man of weight; an authority on cotton, proprietor of three spinning factories, officer of the Legion of Honor and member of the General Council of the *Département*. So long as the Second Empire lasted, he had remained leader of a friendly opposition, for the sole purpose of making a better thing out of it when he decided to come over to the régime which he had fought with polite weapons, to use his own expression. Madame Carré-Lamadon, who was much younger than her husband, was the consolation of all officers of good family who

---

[1] Literally, "The bird flies"—a pun on the verb voler, which means both "to fly" and "to steal."

might be quartered at the Rouen garrison. She sat there opposite to her husband, very small, very dainty, very pretty, wrapped in her furs, and staring at the lamentable interior of the vehicle with despairing eyes.

Their neighbors, the Count and Countess Hubert de Bréville, bore one of the most ancient and noble names in Normandy. The Count, an elderly gentleman of dignified appearance, did all in his power to accentuate by every artifice of the toilet his natural resemblance to Henri Quatre, who, according to a legend of the utmost glory to the family, had honored with his royal embraces a Dame de Bréville, whose husband, in consequence, had been made Count and Governor of the province.

A colleague of Monsieur Carré-Lamadon in the General Council, Count Hubert represented the Orleanist faction in the department. The history of his marriage with the daughter of a small tradesman of Nantes had always remained a mystery. But as the Countess had an air of grandeur, understood better than anyone else the art of receiving, passed even for having been beloved by one of the sons of Louis Philippe, the neighboring nobility bowed down to her, and her salon held the first place in the province, the only one which preserved the traditions of old-fashioned gallantry and to which the entrée was difficult.

The fortune of the Brévilles—all in Government bonds—was reported to yield them an income of five hundred thousand francs.

The six passengers who occupied the upper end of the conveyance represented the unearned income stratum of society, serene in the consciousness of its strength —honest well-to-do people possessed of religion and principles.

By some strange chance all the women were seated on the same side, the Countess having two Sisters of

Mercy for neighbors, wholly occupied in fingering their long rosaries and mumbling Paters and Aves. One of them was old and so deeply pitted with the smallpox that she looked as if she had received a charge of grapeshot full in the face; the other was very shadowy and frail, with a pretty unhealthy little face, a narrow consumptive chest, consumed by that devouring faith which creates martyrs and ecstatics.

Seated opposite the two nuns were a man and woman who excited a good deal of attention.

The man, who was well known, was Cornudet, "the Democrat," the terror of all respectable, law-abiding people. For twenty years he had dipped his great red beard into the beer mugs of all the democratic cafés. In the company of kindred spirits he had managed to run through a comfortable little fortune inherited from his father, a confectioner, and he looked forward with impatience to the Republic, when he should obtain the well-merited reward for so many revolutionary draughts. On the fourth of September—probably through some practical joke—he understood that he had been appointed prefect, but when he attempted to take office the clerks, who had remained sole masters of the prefecture, refused to recognize him, and he was constrained to retire. For the rest, he was a good fellow, inoffensive and willing, and had busied himself with incomparable industry in organizing the defense of the town; had had holes dug all over the plain, cut down all the young trees in the neighboring woods, scattered pitfalls up and down all the high roads, and at the threatened approach of the enemy—satisfied with his preparations—had fallen back with all haste on the town. He now considered that he would be more useful in Havre, where fresh entrenchments would soon become necessary.

The woman, one of the so-called "gay" sisterhood,

was noted for her precocious stoutness, which had gained her the nickname of "Boule de Suif"—"Butter-Ball." She was a little roly-poly creature, cushioned with fat, with podgy fingers squeezed in at the joints like rows of thick, short sausages; her skin tightly stretched and shiny, her bust enormous, and yet she was attractive and much sought after, her freshness was so pleasant. Her face was like a ruddy apple—a peony rose just burst into bloom—and out of it gazed a pair of magnificent dark eyes overshadowed by long thick lashes that deepened their blackness; and lower down, a charming little mouth, dewy to the kiss, and furnished with a row of tiny milk-white teeth. Apart from all this she was said to be a good-hearted creature, full of inestimable qualities.

No sooner was her identity recognized than a whisper ran through the ladies in which the words "prostitute" and "public scandal" were so conspicuously distinct that she raised her head and retaliated by sweeping her companions with such a bold and defiant look that deep silence instantly fell upon them, and they all cast down their eyes with the exception of Loiseau, who watched her with a kindling eye.

However, conversation was soon resumed between the three ladies, whom the presence of this "person" had suddenly rendered friendly—almost intimate. It seemed to them that they must, as it were, raise a rampart of their dignity as spouses between them and this shameless creature who made a traffic of herself; for legalized love always takes a high hand with her unlicensed sister.

The three men too, drawn to one another by a conservative instinct at sight of Cornudet, talked money in a certain tone of contempt for the impecunious. Count Hubert spoke of the damage inflicted on him by the Prussians, of the losses which would result to him from the seizing of cattle and from ruined crops, but with all the assurance of a great landed proprietor, ten times a millionaire, whom these ravages might inconvenience for the space of a year at most. Monsieur Carré-Lamadon, of great experience in the cotton industry, had taken the precaution to send six hundred thousand francs across to England as provision against a rainy day. As for Loiseau, he had made arrangements to sell all the common wines in his cellars to the French commission of supplies, consequently the government owed him a formidable sum, which he counted upon receiving at Havre.

The three exchanged rapid and amicable glances. Although differing in position they felt themselves brothers in money, and of the great freemasonry of those who possess, of those who can make the gold jingle when they put their hands in their pockets.

The coach went so slowly that by ten o'clock in the morning they had not made ten miles. The men had got out three times to climb hills on foot. They began to grow anxious, for they were to have lunched at Tôtes, and now they despaired of reaching that place before night. Everybody was on the lookout for some inn by the way. Once the vehicle stuck fast in a snowdrift, and it took two hours to get it out.

Meanwhile the pangs of hunger began to affect them severely both in mind and body, and yet not an inn, not a tavern even, was to be seen; the approach of the Prussians and the passage of the famished French troops had frightened away all trade.

The gentlemen foraged diligently for provisions in the farms by the roadside; but they failed to obtain so much as a piece of bread, for the mistrustful peasant hid all reserve stores for fear of being pillaged by the soldiers, who, having no food supplied to them, took by force everything they could lay their hands on.

Towards one o'clock Loiseau announced that he felt a very decided void in his stomach. Everybody had been suffering in the same manner for a long time, and the violent longing for food had extinguished conversation.

From time to time someone would yawn, to be almost immediately imitated by another and then each of the rest in turn, and according to their disposition, manners, or social standing, would open his mouth noisily, or modestly cover with the hand the gaping cavity from which the breath issued in a vapor.

Boule de Suif had several times stooped down as if feeling for something under her skirts. She hesitated a moment, looked at her companions, and then composedly resumed her former position. The faces were pale and drawn. Loiseau declared he would give a thousand francs for a ham. His wife made a faint movement as to protest, but restrained herself. It always affected her painfully to hear of money being thrown away, nor could she ever understand a joke upon the subject.

"To tell the truth," said the Count, "I do not feel quite myself either—how could I have omitted to think of bringing provisions?" And everybody reproached himself with the same neglect.

Cornudet, however, had a flask of rum which he offered round. It was coldly refused. Loiseau alone accepted a mouthful, and handed back the flask with thanks saying, "That's good! That warms you up and keeps the hunger off a bit." The alcohol raised his spirits somewhat, and he proposed that they should do the same as on the little ship in the song—eat the fattest of the passengers. This indirect but obvious allusion to Boule de Suif shocked the gentlefolk. Nobody responded and only Cornudet smiled. The two Sisters of Mercy had ceased to tell their beads and sat motionless, their hands buried in their wide sleeves, their eyes obstinately lowered, doubtless engaged in offering back to Heaven the sacrifice of suffering which it sent them.

At last, at three o'clock, when they were in the middle of an interminable stretch of bare country without a single village in sight, Boule de Suif, stooping hurriedly, drew from under the seat a large basket covered with a white napkin.

Out of it she took, first of all, a little china plate and a delicate silver drinking-cup, and then an immense dish, in which two whole fowls ready carved lay stiffened in their jelly. Other good things were visible in the basket: patties, fruits, pastry—in fact provisions for a three days' journey in order to be independent of inn cookery. The necks of four bottles protruded from between the parcels of food. She took the wing of a fowl and began to eat it daintily with one of those little rolls which they call "Régence" in Normandy.

Every eye was fixed upon her. As the odor of the food spread through the carriage nostrils began to quiver and mouths to water, while the jaws, just below the ears, contracted painfully. The dislike entertained by the ladies for this abandoned young woman grew savage, almost to the point of longing to murder her or at least to turn her out into the snow, her and her drinking-cup and her basket and her provisions.

Loiseau, however, was devouring the dish of chicken with his eyes. "Madame has been more prudent than we," he said. "Some people always think of everything."

She turned her head in his direction. "If you would care for any, Sir—? It is not comfortable to fast for so long."

He bowed. "By Jove!—frankly, I won't refuse. I can't

stand this any longer—the fortune of war, is it not, madame?" And with a comprehensive look he added, "In moments such as this we are only too glad to find anyone who will oblige us." He had a newspaper which he spread on his knee to save his trousers, and with the point of a knife which he always carried in his pocket he captured a drumstick all glazed with jelly, tore it with his teeth, and then proceeded to chew it with satisfaction so evident that a deep groan of distress went up from the whole party.

Upon this Boule de Suif in a gentle and humble tone invited the two Sisters to share the collation. They both accepted on the spot, and without raising their eyes began to eat very hurriedly, after stammering a few words of thanks. Nor did Cornudet refuse his neighbor's offer, and with the Sisters they formed a kind of table by spreading out newspapers on their knees.

The jaws opened and shut without a pause, biting, chewing, gulping ferociously. Loiseau, hard at work in his corner, urged his wife in a low voice to follow his example. She resisted for some time, then, after a pang which gripped her very vitals, she gave in. Whereupon her husband, rounding off his phrases, asked if their "charming fellow-traveler" would permit him to offer a little something to Madame Loiseau.

"Why, yes, certainly, Monsieur," she answered with a pleasant smile, and handed him the dish.

There was a moment of embarrassment when the first bottle of claret was uncorked—there was but the one drinking-cup. Each one wiped it before passing it to the rest. Cornudet alone, from an impulse of gallantry no doubt, placed his lips on the spot still wet from the lips of his neighbor.

Then it was that, surrounded by people who were eating, suffocated by the fragrant odor of the viands, the Count and Countess de Bréville and Monsieur and Madame Carré-Lamadon suffered the agonies of that torture which has ever been associated with the name of Tantalus. Suddenly the young wife of the cotton manufacturer gave a deep sigh. Every head turned towards her; she was as white as the snow outside, her eyes closed, her head fell forward—she had fainted. Her husband, distraught with fear, implored assistance of the whole company. All lost their heads till the elder of the two Sisters, who supported the unconscious lady, forced Boule de Suif's drinking-cup between her lips and made her swallow a few drops of wine. The pretty creature stirred, opened her eyes, smiled and then declared in an expiring voice that she felt quite well now. But to prevent her being overcome again in the same manner, the Sister induced her to drink a full cup of wine, adding, "It is simply hunger—nothing else."

At this Boule de Suif, blushing violently, looked at the four starving passengers and faltered shyly, *"Mon Dieu!* If I might make so bold as to offer the ladies and gentlemen—" She stopped short, fearing a rude rebuff.

Loiseau, however, at once threw himself into the breach. *"Parbleu!* Under such circumstances we are all companions in misfortune and bound to help each other. Come, ladies, don't stand on ceremony—take what you can get and be thankful: who knows whether we shall be able to find so much as a house where we can spend the night? At this rate we shall not reach Tôtes till tomorrow afternoon."

They still hesitated, nobody having the courage to take upon themselves the responsibility of the decisive "Yes." Finally the Count seized the bull by the horns. Adopting his grandest air, he turned with a bow to the embarrassed young woman and said, "We accept your offer with thanks, madame."

The first step only was difficult. The Rubicon once crossed, they fell to with a will. They emptied the basket, which contained, besides the provisions already mentioned: a pâté de foie gras, a lark pie, a piece of smoked tongue, some pears, a slab of gingerbread, mixed biscuits, and a cup of pickled onions and gherkins in vinegar—for, like all women, Boule de Suif adored pickles.

They could not well eat the young woman's provisions and not speak to her, so they conversed—stiffly at first, and then, seeing that she showed no signs of presuming, with less reserve. Mesdames de Bréville and Carré-Lamadon, having a great deal of *savoir vivre*, knew how to make themselves agreeable with tact and delicacy. The Countess, in particular, exhibited the amiable condescension of the extremely high-born lady whom no contact can sully, and was charming. But big Madame Loiseau, who had the soul of a gendarme, remained unmoved, speaking little and eating much.

The conversation naturally turned upon the war. They related horrible deeds committed by the Prussians and examples of the bravery of the French; all these people who were flying rendering full homage to the courage of those who remained behind. Incidents of personal experience soon followed, and Boule de Suif told, with that warmth of coloring which women of her type often employ in expressing their natural feelings, how she had come to leave Rouen.

"I thought at first I should be able to hold out," she said, "for I had plenty of provisions in my house, and would much rather feed a few soldiers than turn out of my home and go goodness knows where. But when I saw them—those Prussians—it was too much for me. They made my blood boil with rage, and I cried the whole day for shame. Oh, if I had only been a man!—

well, there! I watched them from my window—fat pigs that they were with their spiked helmets—and my servant had to hold my hands to prevent me throwing the furniture down on the top of them. Then some of them came to be quartered on me, and I flew at the throat of the first one—they are not harder to strangle than anyone else—and would have finished him too if they had not dragged me off by the hair. Of course I had to lie low after that. So as soon as I found an opportunity I left—and here I am."

Everybody congratulated her. She rose considerably in the estimation of her companions, who had not shown themselves of such valiant mettle, and listening to her tale, Cornudet smiled the benignant and approving smile of an apostle—as a priest might on hearing a devout person praise the Almighty. Democrats with long beards have the monopoly of patriotism as the men of the cassock possess that of religion. He then took up the parable in a didactic tone with the phraseology culled from the notices posted each day on the walls, and finished up with a flourish of eloquence in which he scathingly alluded to "that blackguard Badinguet." [1]

But Boule de Suif fired up at this for she was a Bonapartist. She turned upon him with scarlet cheeks and stammering with indignation, "Ah! I should just like to have seen any of you in his place! A nice mess you would have made of it! It is men of your sort that ruined him, poor man. There would be nothing for it but to leave France for good if we were governed by cowards like you!"

Cornudet, nothing daunted, preserved a disdainful and superior smile, but there was a feeling in the air that high words would soon follow, whereupon the Count interposed, and managed, not without difficulty,

---

[1] Nickname for Napoleon III.

to quiet the infuriated young woman by asserting au
thoritatively that every sincere opinion was to be re
spected. Nevertheless the Countess and the manufac
turer's wife, who nourished in their hearts the unrea
soning hatred of all well-bred people for the Republic
and at the same time that instinctive weakness of al
women for uniformed and despotic governments, fel
drawn, in spite of themselves, to this woman of the
streets who had so much sense of the fitness of thing
and whose opinions so closely resembled their own.

The basket was empty—this had not been difficul
among ten of them—they only regretted it was no
larger. The conversation was kept up for some little time
longer, although somewhat more coldly after they had
finished eating.

The night fell, the darkness grew gradually deeper
and the cold, to which digestion rendered them more
sensitive, made even Boule de Suif shiver in spite of he
fat. Madame de Bréville thereupon offered her her char
coal foot-warmer, which had been replenished severa
times since the morning; she accepted with alacrity, fo
her feet were like ice. Mesdames Carré-Lamadon and
Loiseau lent theirs to the two Sisters.

The driver had lit his lanterns, which shed a vivid
light over the cloud of vapor that hung above the steam
ing backs of the horses and over the snow at each side
of the road, that seemed to open out under the shifting
reflection of the lights.

Inside the conveyance nothing could be distinguished
any longer, but there was a sudden movement between
Boule de Suif and Cornudet, and Loiseau, peering
through the gloom, fancied he saw the man with the
beard start back quickly as if he had received a well
directed but noiseless blow.

Tiny points of light appeared upon the road ahead

It was Tôtes. The travelers had been driving for eleven
hours, which, with the four half-hours for feeding and
resting the horses, made thirteen. They entered the town
and stopped in front of the Hôtel du Commerce.

The door opened. A familiar sound caused every pas-
senger to tremble—it was the clink of a scabbard on the
stones. At the same moment a German voice called out
something.

Although the coach had stopped, nobody attempted
to get out, as though they expected to be massacred on
getting foot to the ground. The driver then appeared
holding up one of the lanterns, which suddenly illumined the vehicle to its farthest corner and revealed the
two rows of bewildered faces with their open mouths
and startled eyes wide with alarm.

Beside the driver in the full glare of the light stood a
German officer, a tall young man excessively slender and
blonde, compressed into his uniform like a girl in her
stays, and wearing, well over one ear, a flat black wax-
cloth cap like the "Boots" of an English hotel. His pre-
posterously long mustache, which was drawn out stiff
and straight, and tapered away indefinitely to each side
till it finished off in a single thread so thin that it was
impossible to say where it ended, seemed to weigh upon
the corners of his mouth and form a deep furrow in
either cheek.

In Alsatian-French and stern accents he invited the
passengers to descend, "Will you get out, gentlemen
and ladies?"

The two Sisters were the first to obey with the docility of holy women accustomed to unfaltering submission. The Count and Countess appeared next, followed
by the manufacturer and his wife, and after them
Loiseau pushing his better half in front of him. As he
set foot to the ground he remarked to the officer, more

from motives of prudence than politeness, "Good evening, Sir," to which the other with the insolence of the man in possession, vouchsafed no reply but a stare.

Boule de Suif and Cornudet, though the nearest the door, were the last to emerge—grave and haughty in face of the enemy. The buxom young woman struggled hard to command herself and be calm; the democrat tugged at his long rusty beard with a tragic and slightly trembling hand. They sought to preserve their dignity, realizing that in such encounters each one, to a certain extent, represents his country; and the two being similarly disgusted at the ready servility of their companions, she endeavored to show herself prouder than her fellow travelers who were respectable women, while he, feeling that he must set an example, continued in his attitude his mission of resistance begun by digging pitfalls in the high roads.

They entered the huge kitchen of the inn, and the German, having been presented with the passport signed by the general in command—where each traveler's name was accompanied by a personal description and a statement as to his or her profession—he proceeded to scrutinize the party for a long time, comparing the persons with the written notices.

Finally, he exclaimed unceremoniously, "That's all right," and disappeared.

They breathed again more freely. Hunger having reasserted itself, supper was ordered. It would take half an hour to prepare, so while two servants were apparently busied about it the travelers dispersed to look at their rooms. These were all together down each side of a long passage ending in a door marked "Toilet."

At last, just as they were sitting down to table, the innkeeper himself appeared. He was a former horse dealer, a stout asthmatic man with perpetual wheezing and blowings and rattlings of phlegm in his throat. His father had transmitted to him the name of Follenvie.

"Mademoiselle Elizabeth Rousset?" he said.

Boule de Suif started and turned round. "That is my name."

"Mademoiselle, the Prussian officer wants to speak to you at once."

"To me?"

"Yes, if you really are Mademoiselle Elizabeth Rousset."

She hesitated, thought for a moment, and then declared roundly, "That may be, but I'm not going."

There was a movement round about her—everybody was much exercised as to the reason of this summons. The Count came over to her.

"You may do wrong to refuse, madame, for it may entail considerable annoyance not only to yourself but to the rest of your companions. It is a fatal mistake ever to offer resistance to people who are stronger than ourselves. The step can have no possible danger for you— it is probably about some little formality that has been omitted."

One and all concurred with him, implored and urged and scolded, till they ended by convincing her; for they were all apprehensive of the results of her obstinacy.

"Well, it is only for your sakes that I am doing it!" she said at last. The Countess pressed her hand. "And we are most grateful to you."

She left the room, and the others agreed to wait for her before beginning the meal. Each one lamented that he had not been asked for instead of this hot-headed, violent young woman, and mentally prepared any number of platitudes for the event of being called in his turn.

At the end of ten minutes she returned, crimson with rage, choking, snorting—"Oh, the blackguard; the low blackguard!" she stammered.

They all crowded round her to know what had happened, but she would not say, and the Count becoming insistent, she answered with much dignity, "No, it does not concern anybody! I can't speak of it."

They then seated themselves round a great soup tureen from which steamed a smell of cabbage. In spite of this little incident the supper was a gay one. The cider, of which the Loiseaus and the two nuns partook from motives of economy, was good. The rest ordered wine and Cornudet called for beer. He had a particular way of uncorking the bottle, of making the liquid froth, of gazing at it while he tilted the glass, which he then held up between his eye and the light to enjoy the color; while he drank, his great beard, which had the tints of his favorite beverage, seemed to quiver fondly, his eyes squinting that he might not lose sight of his tankard for a moment, and altogether he had the appearance of fulfilling the sole function for which he had been born. You would have said that he established in his own mind some connection or affinity between the two great passions that monopolized his life—Ale and Revolution —and most assuredly he never tasted the one without thinking of the other.

Monsieur and Madame Follenvie dined at the farther end of the table. The husband—puffing and blowing like a locomotive—had too much cold on the chest to be able to speak and eat at the same time, but his wife never ceased talking. She described her every impression at the arrival of the Prussians and all they did and all they said, execrating them in the first place because they cost so much, and secondly because she had two sons in the army. She addressed herself chiefly to the

Countess, as it flattered her to be able to say she had conversed with a lady of quality.

She presently lowered her voice and proceeded to recount some rather delicate matters, her husband breaking in from time to time with—"You had much better hold your tongue, Madame Follenvie,"—to which she paid not the slightest attention, but went on.

"Well, madame, as I was saying—these men, they do nothing but eat potatoes and pork and pork and potatoes from morning till night. And as for their habits—! Saving your presence, they make dirt everywhere. And you should see them exercising for hours and days together out there in the fields. It's forward march and backward march, and turn this way and turn that. If they even worked in the fields or mended the roads in their own country! But, no, madame, these soldiers are no good to anybody, and the poor people have to keep them and feed them simply that they may learn how to murder. I know I am only a poor ignorant old woman, but when I see these men wearing themselves out by tramping up and down from morning till night, I cannot help saying to myself, if there are some people who make a lot of useful discoveries, why should others give themselves so much trouble to do harm? After all, isn't it an abomination to kill anybody, no matter whether they are Prussians, or English, or Poles, or French? If you revenge yourself on someone who has harmed you, that is wicked, for you are punished; but let them shoot down our sons as if they were game, and it is all right, and they give medals to the man who kills the most. No, no, I say, I shall never be able to see any rhyme or reason in that!"

"War is barbarous if one attacks an unoffending neighbor—it is a sacred duty if one defends one's country," remarked Cornudet in a declamatory tone.

The old woman drooped her head. "Yes—defending oneself, of course, that is quite another thing; but wouldn't it be better to kill all these kings who do this for their pleasure?"

Cornudet's eyes flashed. "Bravo, citizeness!" he cried.

Monsieur Carré-Lamadon was lost in thought. Although he was an ardent admirer of famous military men, the sound common sense of this peasant woman made him reflect upon the wealth which would necessarily accrue to the country if all these unemployed and consequently ruinous hands—so much unproductive force—were available for the great industrial works that would take centuries to complete.

Loiseau meanwhile had left his seat and gone over beside the innkeeper, to whom he began talking in a low voice. The fat man laughed, coughed, and spat, his unwieldy stomach shaking with mirth at his neighbor's jokes, and he bought six hogsheads of claret from him for the spring when the Prussians would have cleared out.

Supper was scarcely over when, dropping with fatigue, everybody went off to bed.

Loiseau, however, who had noticed certain things, let his wife go to bed and proceeded to glue first his ear and then his eye to the keyhole, endeavoring to penetrate what he called "the mysteries of the corridor."

After about an hour he heard a rustling, and hurrying to the keyhole, he perceived Boule de Suif looking ampler than ever in a dressing-gown of blue cashmere trimmed with white lace. She had a candle in her hand and was going towards the door at the end of the corridor. Then a door at one side opened cautiously, and when she returned after a few minutes, Cornudet in his shirtsleeves was following her. They were talking in a low voice and presently stood still; Boule de Suif apparently defending the entrance of her room with much energy. Unfortunately Loiseau was unable to hear what they said, but at last, as they raised their voices somewhat, he caught a word or two. Cornudet was insisting eagerly. "Look here," he said, "you are really very ridiculous—what difference can it make to you?"

And she with an offended air retorted, "No!—let me tell you there are moments when that sort of thing won't do; and besides—here—it would be a crying shame."

He obviously did not understand. "Why?"

At this she grew angry. "Why?" and she raised her voice still more, "you don't see why? and there are Prussians in the house—in the next room for all you know!"

He made no reply. This display of patriotic prudery evidently aroused his failing dignity, for with a brief kiss he made for his own door on tiptoe.

Loiseau, deeply thrilled and amused, executed a double shuffle in the middle of the room, donned his nightcap, slipped into the blankets where the bony figure of his spouse already reposed, and waking her with a kiss he murmured, "Do you love me, darling?"

The whole house sank to silence. But anon there arose from somewhere—it might have been the cellar, it might have been the attic—impossible to determine the direction—a rumbling—sonorous, even, regular, dull, prolonged roar as of a boiler under high pressure: Monsieur Follenvie slept.

It had been decided that they should start at eight o'clock the next morning, so they were all assembled in the kitchen by that hour; but the coach, roofed with snow, stood solitary in the middle of the courtyard without horses or driver. The latter was sought for in vain either in the stables or in the coachhouse. The men of the party then resolved to beat the country round for him, and went out accordingly. They found themselves in the public square with the church at one end, and low-roofed houses down each side in which they caught sight of Prussian soldiers. The first one they came upon was peeling potatoes; farther on another was washing out a barber's shop; while a third, bearded to the eyes, was soothing a crying child and rocking it to and fro on his knee to quiet it. The big peasant women whose men were all "with the army in the war" were ordering about their docile conquerors and showing them by signs what work they wanted done—chopping wood, grinding coffee, fetching water; one of them was even doing the washing for his hostess, a helpless old crone.

The Count, much astonished, stopped the beadle, who happened to come out of the priest's house at that moment, and asked the meaning of it all.

"Oh," replied the old church rat, "they are not at all bad. From what I hear they are not Prussians, either; they come from farther off, but where I can't say; and they have all left a wife and children at home. I am very sure their women at home are crying for their men, too, and it will all make a nice lot of misery for them as well as for us. We are not so badly off here for the moment, because they do no harm and are working just as if they were in their own homes. You see, Sir, the poor always help one another; it is the bigwigs who make the wars."

Cornudet, indignant at the friendly understanding established between the victors and the vanquished, retired from the scene, preferring to shut himself up in the inn. Loiseau of course must have his joke. "They are re-populating," he said. Monsieur Carré-Lamadon found a more fitting expression. "They are making reparations."

But the driver was nowhere to be found. At last he

was unearthed in the village café hobnobbing frater-
nally with the officer's orderly.

"Did you not have orders to have the coach ready
by eight o'clock?" the Count asked him.

"Oh, yes, but I got another order later on."

"What?"

"Not to put the horses in at all."

"Who gave you that order?"

"Why—the Prussian commandant."

"Why?"

"I don't know—you had better ask him. I am told
not to harness the horses, and so I don't harness them—
there you are."

"Did he tell you so himself?"

"No, Sir, the innkeeper brought me the message from
him."

"When was that?"

"Last night, just as I was going to bed."

The three men returned much disconcerted. They
asked for Monsieur Follenvie, but were informed by the
servant that on account of his asthma he never got up
before ten o'clock—he had even positively forbidden
them to awaken him before then except in case of fire.

Then they asked to see the officer, but that was absolutely impossible, although he lodged at the inn.

Monsieur Follenvie alone was authorized to approach
him on non-military matters. So they had to wait. The
women returned to their rooms and occupied themselves as best they could.

Cornudet installed himself in the high chimney-corner
of the kitchen, where a great fire was burning. He had
one of the little coffee-room tables brought to him and
a can of beer, and puffed away placidly at his pipe,
which enjoyed among the democrats almost equal consideration with himself, as if in serving Cornudet it

served the country also. The pipe was a superb meer-schaum, admirably colored, black as the teeth of its owner, but fragrant, curved, shining, familiar to his hand, and the natural complement to his physiognomy. He sat there motionless, his eyes fixed alternately on the flame of the hearth and the foam on the top of his tankard, and each time after drinking he passed his bony fingers with a self-satisfied gesture through his long greasy hair, while he absorbed the fringe of froth from his mustache.

Under the pretext of stretching his legs, Loiseau went out and palmed off his wines on the country retail dealers. The Count and the manufacturer talked poli-tics. They forecast the future of France, the one putting his faith in the Orleans princes, the other in an unknown savior, a hero who would come to the fore when things were at their very worst—a Du Guesclin, a Joan of Arc perhaps, or even another Napoleon I. Ah, if only the Prince Imperial were not so young! Cornudet listened to them with the smile of a man who could solve the riddle of Fate if he would. His pipe perfumed the whole kitchen with its balmy fragrance.

On the stroke of ten Monsieur Follenvie made his appearance. They instantly attacked him with ques-tions, but he had but one answer which he repeated two or three times without variation. "The officer said to me, 'Monsieur Follenvie, you will forbid them to harness the horses for these travelers tomorrow morning. They are not to leave till I give my permission. You under-stand?' That is all."

They demanded to see the officer; the Count sent up his card, on which Monsieur Carré-Lamadon added his name and all his titles. The Prussian sent word that he would admit the two men to his presence after he had lunched, that is to say, about one o'clock.

The ladies came down and they all managed to eat a little in spite of their anxiety. Boule de Suif looked quite ill and very much agitated.

They were just finishing coffee when the orderly arrived to fetch the two gentlemen.

Loiseau joined them, but when they proposed to bring Cornudet along to give more solemnity to their proceedings, he declared haughtily that nothing would induce him to enter into any communication whatsoever with the Germans, and he returned to his chimney-corner and ordered another bottle of beer.

The three men went upstairs, and were shown into the best room in the inn, where they were received by the officer lolling in an armchair, his heels on the chimney-piece, smoking a long porcelain pipe, and arrayed in a flamboyant dressing-gown, taken, no doubt, from the abandoned dwelling-house of some bourgeois of inferior taste. He did not rise, he vouchsafed them no greeting of any description, he did not even look at them—a brilliant example of the victorious military cad.

At last after some moments' waiting he said: "What do you want?"

The Count acted as spokesman.

"We wish to leave, Sir."

"No."

"May I take the liberty of asking the reason for this refusal?"

"Because I do not choose."

"With all due respect, Sir, I would draw your attention to the fact that your general gave us a permit for Dieppe, and I cannot see that we have done anything to justify your hard measures."

"I do not choose—that's all—you can go down."

They all bowed and withdrew.

The afternoon was miserable. They could make nothing of this caprice of the German's, and the most far-fetched ideas tortured their minds. The whole party remained in the kitchen engaging in endless discussions, imagining the most improbable things. Were they to be kept as hostages?—but if so, to what end?—or taken prisoners?—or asked a large ransom? This last suggestion threw them into a cold perspiration of fear. The wealthiest were seized with the worst panic and saw themselves forced, if they valued their lives, to empty bags of gold into the rapacious hands of this soldier. They racked their brains for plausible lies to dissemble their riches, to pass themselves off as poor—very poor. Loiseau pulled off his watch-chain and hid it in his pocket. As night fell their apprehensions increased. The lamp was lighted, and as there were still two hours till supper Madame Loiseau proposed a game of cards. It would be some little distraction, at any rate. The plan was accepted; even Cornudet, who had put out his pipe from motives of politeness, taking a hand.

The Count shuffled the cards, dealt, Boule de Suif won the first deal; and very soon the interest in the game allayed the fears that beset their minds. Cornudet, however, observed that the two Loiseaus were in league to cheat.

Just as they were sitting down to the evening meal Monsieur appeared and said in his husky voice, "The Prussian officer wishes to know if Mademoiselle Elizabeth Rousset has not changed her mind yet?"

Boule de Suif remained standing and turned very pale, then suddenly her face flamed and she fell into such a paroxysm of rage that she could not speak. At last she burst out, "You can tell that scoundrel—that low scum of a Prussian—that I won't—and I never will —do you hear?—never! never! never!"

The fat innkeeper retired. They instantly surrounded

Boule de Suif, questioning, entreating her to disclose the mystery of her visit. At first she refused, but presently she was carried away by her indignation: "What does he want?—what does he want?—he wants me to go to bed with him!" she shouted.

The general indignation was so violent that nobody was shocked by the words she used. Cornudet brought his beer glass down on the table with such a bang that it broke. There was a perfect babel of invective against the drunken lout, a hurricane of wrath, a union of all for resistance, as if each had been required to contribute a portion of the sacrifice demanded of her. The Count protested with disgust that these people behaved really as if they were early barbarians. The women, in particular, accorded her the most lively and affectionate sympathy. The nuns, who only appeared at meals, dropped their eyes and said nothing.

The first fury of the storm having abated, they sat down to supper, but there was little conversation and a good deal of thoughtful abstraction.

The ladies retired early; the men, while they smoked, got up a game of écarté, which Monsieur Follenvie was invited to join, as they intended pumping him skillfully as to the means that could be employed for overcoming the officer's opposition to their departure. Unfortunately, he would absorb himself wholly in his cards, and neither listened to what they said nor gave any answer to their questions, but repeated incessantly, "Play, gentlemen, play!" His attention was so deeply engaged that he forgot to spit, which caused his chest to wheeze from time to time; his wheezing lungs running through the whole gamut of asthma from notes of the profoundest bass to the shrill, hoarse crow of the young cock.

He refused to go to bed when his wife, who was dropping with sleep, came to fetch him. She therefore departed alone, for on her devolved the "day duty," and she always rose with the sun, while her husband took the "night duty," and was always ready to sit up all night with friends. He merely called out, "Mind you put my egg flip in front of the fire!" and returned to his cards. When they were convinced that there was nothing to be got out of him, they declared that it was high time to go to bed, and left him.

They were up again pretty early the next day, filled with an indefinite hope, a still keener desire to be gone, and a horror of another day to be got through in this horrible little inn.

Alas! The horses were still in the stable and the coachman remained invisible. For lack of something better to do, they sadly wandered round the carriage.

Lunch was very depressing, and a certain chilliness had sprung up with regard to Boule de Suif, for the night—which brings counsel—had somewhat modified their opinions. They were almost vexed with the girl now for not having gone to the Prussian secretly, and thus prepared a pleasant surprise for her companions in the morning. What could be simpler, and, after all, who could have been any the wiser? She might have saved appearances by telling the officer that she could not bear to see their distress any longer. It could make so very little difference to her one way or another!

But, as yet, nobody confessed to these thoughts.

In the afternoon, as they were feeling bored to extinction, the Count proposed a walk round the village. Everybody wrapped up carefully and the little party started, with the exception of Cornudet, who preferred sitting by the fire, and the two Sisters, who passed their days in the church or with the parish priest.

The cold—grown more intense each day—nipped their noses and ears viciously, and the feet hurt so that every step was anguish; but when they caught sight of the open stretch of country it appeared to them so appallingly lugubrious under its illimitable white covering that they turned back with one accord, their hearts constricted, their spirits below zero. The four ladies walked in front, the three men following a little behind.

Loiseau, who thoroughly took in the situation, suddenly broke out, "How long was this damned wench going to keep them hanging on in this hole?" The Count, courteous as ever, observed that one could not demand so painful a sacrifice of any woman—the offer must come from her. Monsieur Carré-Lamadon remarked that if—as there was every reason to believe—the French made an offensive counter-march by way of Dieppe, the collision could only take place at Tôtes. This reflection greatly alarmed the other two. "Why not escape on foot?" suggested Loiseau. The Count shrugged his shoulders. "How can you think of such a thing in this snow—and with our wives? Besides which, we should instantly be pursued, caught in ten minutes, and brought back prisoners at the mercy of these soldiers." This was incontestable—there was nothing more to be said.

The ladies talked dress, but a certain constraint seemed to have risen up among them.

All at once, at the end of the street, the officer came in sight, his tall figure, like a wasp in uniform, silhouetted against the dazzling background of snow. He was walking with his knees well apart, with that movement peculiar to the military when endeavoring to save their carefully polished boots from the mud.

In passing the ladies he bowed, but only stared contemptuously at the men, who, be it said, had the dignity not to lift their hats, though Loiseau made a faint gesture in that direction.

Boule de Suif blushed up to her eyes, and the three

married women felt it a deep humiliation to have encountered this soldier while they were in the company of the young woman he had treated so cavalierly.

The conversation then turned upon him, his general appearance, his face. Madame Carré-Lamadon, who had known a great many officers and was competent to judge of them as a connoisseur, considered this one really not half bad—she even regretted that he was not French, he would have made such a fascinating hussar, and would certainly have been much run after.

Once indoors again, they did not know what to do with themselves. Sharp words were exchanged on the most insignificant pretexts. The silent dinner did not last long, and they shortly afterwards went to bed, hoping to kill time by sleeping.

They came down next morning with jaded faces and exasperation in their hearts. The women scarcely addressed a word to Boule de Suif.

Presently the church bell began to ring; it was for a christening. Boule de Suif had a child out at nurse with some peasants near Yvetot. She did not see it once a year and never gave it a thought, but the idea of this baby that was going to be baptized filled her heart with sudden and violent tenderness for her own, and nothing would satisfy her but that she should assist at the ceremony.

No sooner was she gone than they all looked at one another and proceeded to draw up their chairs; for everybody felt that things had come to that point that something must be decided upon. Loiseau had an inspiration: they should propose to the officer to keep Boule de Suif and let the rest go.

Monsieur Follenvie undertook the mission, but returned almost immediately. The German, who had some knowledge of human nature, had simply turned him out of the room. He meant to retain the whole party so long as his desire was unsatisfied.

At this Madame Loiseau's plebeian tendencies got the better of her. "But surely we are not going to sit down calmly here and die of old age! As that is this harlot's trade, I don't see that she has any right to refuse one man more than another. Why, she took anybody she could get in Rouen, down to the very cab drivers. Yes, Madame, the coachman of the Prefecture. I know all about it. He buys his wine at our shop. And now, when it lies with her to get us out of this scrape, she pretends to be particular—the brazen hussy! For my part, I consider the officer has behaved very well! He has probably not had a chance for some time, and there were three here whom, no doubt, he would have preferred; but no —he is content to take the one who is public property. He respects married women. Remember, he is master here. He had only to say 'I will,' and he could have taken us by force with his soldiers!"

A little quiver ran through the other two women. Pretty little Madame Carré-Lamadon's eyes shone and she turned rather pale as though she already felt herself forcibly seized by the officer.

The men, who had been arguing the matter in a corner, now joined them. Loiseau, foaming with rage, was for delivering up "the hussy" bound hand and foot to the enemy. But the Count, coming of three generations of ambassadors, and gifted with the physique of the diplomatist, was on the side of skill as opposed to brute force.

"She must be persuaded," he said. Whereupon they conspired.

The women drew up closer together, voices were lowered, and the discussion became general, each one offering his or her advice. Nothing was said to shock the proprieties. The ladies, in particular, were most expert in felicitous turns of phrase, charming subtleties of speech for expressing the most ticklish things. A foreigner would have understood nothing, the language was so carefully veiled. But as the slight coating of modesty with which every woman of the world is enveloped is hardly more than skin deep, they expanded under the influence of this equivocal adventure, enjoying themselves tremendously at bottom, thoroughly in their element, dabbling in sensuality with the gusto of an epicurean cook preparing a toothsome delicacy for somebody else.

The story finally appeared to them so funny that they quite recovered their spirits. The Count indulged in some rather risky pleasantries, but so well put that they raised a responsive smile; Loiseau, in his turn, rapped out some decidedly strong jokes which nobody took in bad part, and the brutal proposition expressed by his wife swayed all their minds: "As that is her trade, why refuse one man more than another?" Little Madame Carré-Lamadon seemed even to think that in her place she would refuse this one less readily than another.

They were long in preparing the siege, as if against an invested fortress. Each one agreed upon the part they would play, the arguments they would bring forward, the maneuvers they would execute. They arranged the plan of attack, the stratagems to be employed, and the surprises of the assault for forcing this living citadel to receive the enemy within its gates. Cornudet alone held aloof, completely outside the affair.

They were so profoundly occupied with the matter in hand that they never heard Boule de Suif enter the room. But the Count breathed a low warning "Hush!" and they lifted their heads. She was there. The talk ceased abruptly, and a certain feeling of embarrassment prevented them from addressing her at first, till the Countess, more versed than the others in the duplicities of the drawing-room, asked how she had enjoyed the christening.

Still full of emotion at what she had witnessed, Boule de Suif described every detail—the people's faces, their attitudes, even the appearance of the church. It was so nice to pray now and then, she added.

Till luncheon, however, the ladies confined themselves merely to being agreeable to her in order to increase her confidence in them and her acquiescence in their counsels. But once seated at table, the attack began. It first took the form of a desultory conversation on devotion to a cause. Examples from ancient history were cited: Judith and Holofernes, and then, without any apparent connection, Lucretia and Sextus, Cleopatra admitting to her couch all the hostile generals, and reducing them to the servility of slaves. Then began a fantastic history, which had sprung up in the minds of the ignorant millionaires, in which the women of Rome were seen on their way to Capua, to rock Hannibal to sleep in their arms, and his officers along with him, and the phalanxes of the mercenaries. The women were mentioned who had arrested the course of conquerors, made of their bodies a rampart, a means of domination, a weapon; who had vanquished by their heroic embraces beings hideous or repulsive, and sacrificed their chastity to vengeance or patriotism. They even talked in veiled terms of an Englishwoman of good family who had herself inoculated with a horrible contagious disease, in order to give it to Napoleon, who was saved miraculously by a sudden indisposition at the hour of the fatal meeting.

And all this in a discreet and moderate manner, with now and then a little burst of warm enthusiasm, admirably calculated to excite emulation. To hear them you would have come to the conclusion that woman's sole mission here below was perpetually to sacrifice her person, to abandon herself continually to the caprices of the warrior.

The two Sisters appeared to be deaf to it all, sunk in profound thought. Boule de Suif said nothing.

They allowed her all the afternoon for reflection, but instead of calling her "Madame," as they had done up till now, they addressed her as "Mademoiselle"—nobody could have said exactly why—as if to send her down a step in the esteem she had gained, and force her to feel the shame of her position.

In the evening just as the soup was being brought to table Monsieur Follenvie made his appearance again with the same message as before: "The Prussian officer sends to ask Mademoiselle Elizabeth Rousset if she had not changed her mind."

"No, Sir," Boule de Suif replied curtly.

At supper the coalition weakened. Loiseau put his foot in it three times. They all racked their brains for fresh instances to the point, and found none, when the Countess, possibly without premeditation and only from a vague desire to render homage to religion, interrogated the older of the two Sisters on the main incidents in the lives of the saints. Now, several saints had committed acts which would be counted crimes in our eyes, but the Church readily pardons such misdeeds when they are accomplished for the glory of God or the benefit of our neighbors. It was a powerful argument, and the Countess took advantage of it. Then by one of those tacit agreements, those veiled complaisances in which every one who wears ecclesiastical habit excels, or perhaps simply from a happy want of intelligence, a helpful stupidity, the old nun brought formi-

dable support to the conspiracy. They had imagined her
timid; she proved herself bold, verbose, violent. She was
not troubled by any of the shilly-shallyings of casuistry,
her doctrine was like a bar of iron, her faith never
wavered, her conscience knew no scruples. She considered Abraham's sacrifice a very simple affair, for she
herself would have instantly killed father or mother at
an order from above, and nothing, she averred, could
displease the Lord if the intention were commendable.
The Countess, taking advantage of the sacred authority
of her unexpected ally, drew her on to make an edifying paraphrase, as it were, on the well-known moral
maxim: "The end justifies the means."

"Then, Sister," she inquired, "you think God approves
of every pathway that leads to Him, and pardons the
deed if the motive be a pure one?"

"Who can doubt it, Madame? An action blamable in
itself is often rendered meritorious by the impulse which
inspires it."

And she continued in the same strain, unraveling the
intricacies of the will of the Almighty, predicting His
decisions, making Him interest Himself in matters
which, of a truth, did not concern Him at all.

All this was skillfully and discreetly wrapped up, but
each word spoken by the pious woman in the big white
cap made a breach in the indignant resistance of the
courtesan. The conversation then glancing off slightly,
the woman of the rosaries went on to speak of the
religious houses of her Order, of her Superior, of herself
and her fragile little companion, her dear little Sister
St. Nicephora. They had been summoned to Havre to
nurse the hundreds of soldiers there down with smallpox. She described the condition of these poor wretches,
gave details of their disease; and while they were thus
stopped upon the road by the whim of this Prussian,

many French soldiers might die whom perhaps they could have saved. That was her specialty—nursing soldiers. She had been in the Crimea, in Italy, in Austria; and relating her campaigns, she suddenly revealed herself as one of those Sisters of the fife and drum who seem made for following the camp, picking up the wounded in the thick of battle, and better than any officer for quelling with a word the great hulking undisciplined louts—her ravaged face all pitted with innumerable holes, calling up an image of the devastations of war.

No one spoke after her for fear of spoiling the excellent effect.

Immediately after dinner they hurried to their rooms, not to reappear till pretty late the next morning.

Luncheon passed off quietly. They allowed time for the seed sown yesterday to grow and bear fruit.

In the afternoon the Countess proposed a walk, whereupon the Count, following the preconcerted arrangement, took Boule de Suif's arm and fell behind with her a little. He adopted that familiar, paternal, somewhat contemptuous tone which elderly men affect towards such girls, calling her "my dear child," talking down to her from the height of his social position and indisputable respectability.

He came to the point without further preamble. "So you prefer to keep us here exposed like yourself to all the violence which must inevitably follow a check to the Prussian arms, rather than consent to accord one of those favors you have so often dispensed in your time?"

Boule de Suif did not reply.

He then appealed to her kindness of heart, her reason, her sentiment. He knew how to remain "Monsieur le Comte," yet showing himself at the same time chivalrous, flattering—in a word, altogether amiable. He exalted the sacrifice she would be making for them, touched upon their gratitude, and with a final flash of roguishness, "Besides, my dear, he may think himself lucky—he will not find many such pretty girls as you in his own country!"

Boule de Suif said nothing and rejoined the rest of the party.

When they returned, she went straight to her room and did not come down again. The anxiety was terrible. What was she going to do? How unspeakably mortifying if she still persisted in her refusal!

The dinner-hour arrived, they waited for her in vain. Monsieur Follenvie, entering presently, announced that Mademoiselle Rousset was indisposed, and that there was consequently no need to delay supper any longer. They all pricked up their ears. The Count approached the innkeeper with a whispered "All right?"

"Yes."

For propriety's sake he said nothing to his companions, but he made them a slight sign of the head. A great sigh of relief went up from every heart, every face lit up with joy.

"*Saperlipopette!*" cried Loiseau, "I will stand champagne if there is such a thing in this establishment!"

Madame Loiseau suffered a pang of anguish when the innkeeper returned with four bottles in his hands. Everybody suddenly turned communicative and cheerful, and their hearts overflowed with prurient delight. The Count seemed all at once to become aware that Madame Carré-Lamadon was charming; the manufacturer paid compliments to the Countess. Conversation became lively, sprightly, and full of sparkle.

Suddenly Loiseau, with an anxious expression, raised his arms and shouted, "Silence!" They all stopped talk-

ing, surprised and already terrified. Then he listened
intently, motioning to them to be silent with his two
hands, and raising his eyes to the ceiling. He listened
again, and resumed in his natural voice, "It is all right.
Don't worry."

They did not understand at first, but soon a smile
spread over their faces.

A quarter of an hour later he began the same comedy,
and repeated it frequently during the evening. He pretended to be questioning someone on the floor above,
giving advice in double-meaning phrases which he drew
from his repertory as a commercial traveler. At times
he would assume an air of sadness, and sigh, "Poor girl";
or he would mutter between his teeth with a furious air:
"You swine of a Prussian!"—Sometimes, when least expected, he would shout in resonant tones: "Enough!
Enough!" adding, as though speaking to himself, "If
only we see her again; if the scoundrel does not kill
her!"

Although these jokes were in deplorable taste, they
amused every one and hurt nobody, for, like everything
else, indignation is qualified by circumstances, and the
atmosphere about them had gradually become charged
with obscene thoughts.

By the time they reached dessert the women themselves were indulging in decidedly risky witticisms.
Eyes grew bright, tongues were loosened, a good deal
of wine had been consumed. The Count, who, even in
his cups, retained his characteristic air of diplomatic
gravity, made some highly spiced comparisons on the
subject of the end of the winter season at the Pole and
the joy of ice-bound mariners at sight of an opening to
the south.

Loiseau, now in full swing, rose, and lifting high his
glass of champagne, "To our deliverance!" he cried.

Everybody started to their feet with acclamation. Even the two Sisters of Mercy, yielding to the solicitations of the ladies, consented to take a sip of the effervescing wine which they had never tasted before. They pronounced it to be very like lemonade, though the taste was finer.

"What a pity there is no piano," said Loiseau as a crowning point to the situation, "we might have finished up with a quadrille."

Cornudet had not uttered a word, nor made a sign of joining in the general hilarity; he was apparently plunged in the gravest abstractions, only pulling viciously at his great beard from time to time as if to draw it out longer than before. At last, about midnight, when the company was preparing to separate, Loiseau came stumbling over to him, and digging him in the ribs: "You seem rather down in the mouth this evening, citizen—haven't said a word."

Cornudet threw up his head angrily, and sweeping the company with a flashing and terrible look, "I tell you all that what you have done today is infamous!"

He rose, made his way to the door, exclaimed once again, "Infamous!" and vanished.

This somewhat dashed their spirits for the moment. Loiseau, nonplussed at first, soon regained his aplomb and burst into a roar of laughter. "Sour grapes, old man —sour grapes!"

The others not understanding the allusion, he proceeded to relate the "mysteries of the corridor." This was followed by an uproarious revival of gaiety. The ladies were in a frenzy of delight, the Count and Monsieur Carré-Lamadon laughed till they cried. They could not believe it.

"Do you mean to say he wanted—"

"I tell you I saw it with my own eyes."

"And she refused?"

"Because the Prussian was in the next room."

"It is incredible."

"As true as I stand here!"

The Count nearly choked; the manufacturer held both his sides.

"And you can understand that he does not quite see the joke of the thing this evening—oh, no—not at all!"

And they all three went off again, breathless, choking, sick with laughter.

After that they parted for the night. But Madame Loiseau remarked to her husband when they were alone that that little cat of a Carré-Lamadon had laughed on the wrong side of her mouth all the evening. "You know how it is with those women—they dote upon a uniform, and whether it is French or Prussian matters precious little to them. But, Lord—it seems to me a poor way of looking at things."

All night the darkness of the corridor seemed full of thrills, of slight noises, scarcely audible, the pattering of bare feet, and creaking that was almost imperceptible. Certainly nobody got to sleep until very late, for it was long before the lights ceased to shine under the doors. Champagne, they say, often has that disturbing effect; it makes one restless and wakeful.

Next morning a brilliant winter sun shone on the dazzling snow. The coach was by this time ready and waiting before the door, while a flock of white pigeons, muffled in their thick plumage, strutted solemnly in and out among the feet of the six horses, seeking what they might devour.

The driver, enveloped in his sheepskin, sat on the box smoking his pipe, and the radiant travelers were busily laying in provisions for the rest of the journey.

They had only to wait now for Boule de Suif. She appeared.

She looked agitated and downcast as she advanced timidly towards her fellow travelers, who all, with one movement, turned away their heads as if they had not seen her. The Count, with a dignified movement, took his wife by the arm and drew her away from this contaminating contact.

The poor thing stopped short, bewildered; then gathering up her courage she accosted the wife of the manufacturer with a humble "Good morning, Madame." The other merely replied with an impertinent little nod, accompanied by a stare of outraged virtue. Everybody seemed suddenly extremely busy, and they avoided her as if she had brought the plague in her skirts. They then precipitated themselves into the vehicle, where she arrived the last and by herself, and resumed in silence the seat she had occupied during the first part of the journey.

They affected not to see her, not to recognize her; only Madame Loiseau, glancing round at her with scorn and indignation, said half audibly to her husband, "It's a good thing that I am not sitting beside her!"

The heavy conveyance jolted off, and the journey was resumed.

No one spoke for the first little while. Boule de Suif did not venture to raise her eyes. She felt incensed at her companions, and at the same time deeply humiliated at having yielded to their persuasions, and let herself be sullied by the kisses of this Prussian into whose arms they had hypocritically thrust her.

The Countess was the first to break the uncomfortable silence. Turning to Madame Carré-Lamadon, she said, "You know Madame d'Etrelles, I think?"

"Oh, yes; she is a great friend of mine."

"What a charming woman!"

"Fascinating! So truly refined; very cultivated, too, and an artist to the tips of her fingers—she sings delightfully, and draws to perfection."

The manufacturer was talking to the Count, and through the rattle of the crazy windowpanes one caught a word here and there; shares—dividends—premium —settlement day—and the like. Loiseau, who had appropriated an old pack of cards from the inn, thick with the grease of the five years' rubbing on dirty tables, started a game of bezique with his wife. The two Sisters pulled up the long rosaries hanging at their waists, made the sign of the cross, and suddenly began moving their lips rapidly, faster and faster, hurrying their vague babble as if for a wager; kissing a medal from time to time, crossing themselves again, and then resuming their rapid and monotonous murmur.

Cornudet sat motionless—thinking.

At the end of the three hours' steady traveling Loiseau gathered up his cards and remarked facetiously, "It's turning hungry."

His wife then produced a parcel, which she untied, and brought out a piece of cold veal. This she cut up into thin, firm slices, and both began to eat.

"Supposing we do the same?" said the Countess, and proceeded to unpack the provisions prepared for both couples. In one of those oblong dishes with a china hare upon the cover to indicate that a roast hare lies beneath, was a succulent selection of cold viands—brown slices of juicy venison mingled with other meats. A delicious square of Gruyère cheese wrapped in newspaper still bore imprinted on its dewy surface the words "Latest News."

The two Sisters brought out a sausage smelling of

garlic, and Cornudet, plunging his hands into the vast pockets of his loose greatcoat, drew up four hard-boiled eggs from one and a big crust of bread from the other. He peeled off the shells and threw them into the straw under his feet, and proceeded to bite into the egg, dropping pieces of the yolk into his long beard, from whence they shone out like stars.

In the hurry and confusion of the morning Boule de Suif had omitted to take thought for the future, and she looked on, furious, choking with mortification, at these people all munching away so placidly. A storm of rage convulsed her, and she opened her mouth to hurl at them the torrent of abuse that rose to her lips, but she could not speak, suffocated by her indignation.

Nobody looked at her, nobody thought of her. She felt herself drowning in the flood of contempt shown towards her by these respectable scoundrels who had first sacrificed her and then cast her off like some useless and unclean thing. Then her thoughts reverted to her great basket full of good things which they had so greedily devoured—the two fowls in their glittering coat of jelly, her patties, her pears, her four bottles of claret; and her fury suddenly subsided like the breaking of an overstrung chord and she felt that she was on the verge of tears. She made the most strenuous efforts to overcome it—straightened herself up and choked back her sobs as children do, but the tears would rise. They glittered for a moment on her lashes, and presently two big drops rolled slowly over her cheeks. Others gathered in quick succession like water dripping from a rock and splashed onto the ample curve of her bosom. She sat up very straight, her eyes fixed, her face pale and rigid, hoping that nobody would notice.

But the Countess saw her and nudged her husband.

He shrugged his shoulders as much as to say, "What can you expect? It is not my fault." Madame Loiseau gave a silent chuckle of triumph and murmured, "She is crying over her shame." The two Sisters had resumed their devotions after carefully wrapping up the remnants of their sausages.

Then Cornudet, while digesting his eggs, stretched his long legs under the opposite seat, leaned back, smiled like a man who has just thought of a capital joke, and began to softly whistle the *Marseillaise*.

The faces clouded; the people's anthem seemed unpleasing to his neighbors; they became nervous—irritable—looking as if they were ready to throw back their heads and howl like dogs at the sound of a barrel organ. He was perfectly aware of this, but did not stop. From time to time he hummed a few of the words:

> *Amour sacré de la patrie,*
> *Conduis, soutiens nos bras vengeurs,*
> *Liberté, liberté chérie,*
> *Combats avec tes défenseurs!*

They drove at a much quicker pace today, the snow being harder; and all the way to Dieppe, during the long, dull hours of the journey, through all the jolting and rattling of the conveyance, in the falling shades of evening and later in the profound darkness of the carriage he continued with unabated persistency his vengeful and monotonous whistling; forcing his wearied and exasperated fellow travelers to follow the song from end to end and to remember every word that corresponded to each note.

And Boule de Suif wept on, and at times a sob which she could not repress broke out between two stanzas in the darkness.

MADNESS

THE HORLA

MAY 8. What a glorious day! I have spent the whole morning lying on the grass in front of my house, under the enormous plane-tree that forms a complete covering, shelter, and shade for it. I love this country, and I love living here because it is here I have my roots, those deep, subtle roots that hold a man to the place where his forefathers were born and died, hold him to ways of thought and habits of eating, to customs and to particular foods, to local fashions of speech, to the intonations of country voices, to the scent of the soil, the villages, and the very air itself.

I love this house of mine where I grew up. From my windows I see the Seine flowing alongside my garden, beyond the high road, almost at my door, the great, broad Seine, that runs from Rouen to Havre, covered with passing boats.

Away to the left, the great city of Rouen, with its blue roofs lies under the bristling host of Gothic belfries. They are beyond number, frail or sturdy, dominated by the iron spire of the cathedral, and filled with bells that ring out in the limpid air on fine mornings, sending me the sweet and far-off murmur of their iron tongues, a brazen song borne to me on the breeze, now louder, now softer, as it swells or dies away.

How beautiful this morning has been!

Towards eleven o'clock a long convoy of boats followed each other past my gate, behind a squat tug as small as a fly, that wheezed painfully as it vomited thick clouds of smoke.

After two English yachts, whose crimson ensign rose and fell against the sky, came a splendid Brazilian three-master, all white, gloriously clean and glittering. The sight of this ship filled me with such joy that I saluted her, I don't know why.

May 11. I have had a slight fever for the last few days; I feel ill, or rather, I feel unhappy.

Whence come these mysterious influences that change our happiness to dejection and our self-confidence to discouragement? It is as if the air, the unseen air, were full of unknowable powers whose mysterious nearness we endure. I wake full of joy, my throat swelling with a longing to sing. Why? I go down to the waterside; and suddenly, after a short walk, I come back home wretched, as if some misfortune were awaiting me there. Why? Has a chill shudder, passing lightly over my skin, shaken my nerves and darkened my spirit? Have the shapes of the clouds, or the color of the day, the ever-changing color of the visible world, troubled my mind as they slipped past my eyes? Does anyone know? Everything that surrounds us, everything that we see unseeing, everything that we brush past unknowing, everything that we touch impalpably, everything that we meet unnoticing, has on us, on the organs of our bodies, and through them on our thoughts, on our very hearts, swift, surprising, and inexplicable effects.

How deep it is, this mystery of the Invisible! We cannot fathom it with our miserable senses, with our eyes that perceive neither the too small, nor the too great, nor the too near, nor the too distant, neither the inhabitants of a star, nor the inhabitants of a drop of water . . . with our ears that deceive us, for they transmit the vibrations of the air to us as sonorous sounds. They are fairies who by a miracle transmute movement into sound, and by this metamorphosis give birth to music, and turn into song the mute quivering of Nature . . . with our smell, feebler than a dog's . . with our taste, that can only just detect the age of a wine.

If only we had other organs to work other miracles on our behalf, what things we could discover round us!

May 16. I am certainly ill. I was so well last month. I have a fever, a frightful fever, or rather, a feverish weakness that oppresses my mind as much as my body. All day and every day I suffer this frightful sense of threatened danger, this apprehension of coming ill or approaching death, this presentiment which is doubtless the warning signal of a lurking disease germinating in my blood and my flesh.

May 18. I have consulted my doctor, for I was getting no sleep. He found that my pulse is rapid, my pupils are dilated, my nerves on edge, but no alarming symptom of any kind. I am to take baths and drink bromide of potassium.

May 25. No change. My case is truly strange. As
night falls, an incomprehensible uneasiness fills me, as
if the night concealed a frightful menace for me. I
dine in haste, then I try to read; but I don't understand
the words: I can hardly make out the letters. So I walk
back and forth in my sitting-room, oppressed by a
vague fear that I cannot throw off, fear of sleeping and
fear of my bed.

About ten o'clock I go up to my room. The instant
I am inside the room I double-lock the door and shut
the windows; I am afraid . . . of what? I never dreaded
anything before. . . . I open my cupboards, I look under my bed; I listen . . . listen . . . to what? It's a
queer thing that a mere physical ailment, some disorder
in the blood perhaps, the jangling of a nerve thread,
a slight congestion, the least disturbance in the function-
ing of this living machine of ours, so imperfect and so
frail, can make a melancholic of the happiest of men
and a coward of the bravest. Then I lie down, and wait
for sleep as if I were waiting to be executed. I wait for
it, dreading its approach; my heart beats, my legs tremble; my whole body shivers in the warmth of the bedclothes, until the moment I fall suddenly on sleep, like
a man falling into deep and stagnant waters, there to
drown. I never feel it come, as I used to, this perfidious
sleep, that lurks near me, spying on me, ready to take
me by the head, shut my eyes, steal my strength.

I sleep—for a long time—two or three hours—then
a dream—no—a nightmare seizes me. I feel that I am
lying down and that I am asleep . . . I feel it and I
know it . . . and I feel too that someone approaches
me, looks at me, touches me, climbs on my bed, kneels
on my chest, takes my neck between his hands and
squeezes . . . squeezes . . . with all his might, strangling me.

I struggle madly, in the grip of the frightful helplessness that paralyzes us in dreams; I try to cry out—I can't; I try to move—I can't; panting, with the most frightful efforts, I try to turn round, to fling off this creature who is crushing and choking me—I can't do it.

And suddenly I wake up, terrified, bathed in sweat. I light a candle. I am alone.

This crisis recurs every night. When it is over I fall at last into a quiet sleep, until daybreak.

June 2. My case has grown worse still. What can be the matter with me? Bromide is useless; baths are useless. Lately, by way of wearying a body already quite exhausted, I went for a tramp in the forest of Roumare. At first I thought that the fresh air, the clear, sweet air, full of the odors of grass and trees, was pouring a new blood into my veins and a new strength into my heart. I followed a broad glade, then I turned towards Boville, by a narrow path between two ranks of immensely tall trees that flung a thick, green roof, almost black, between the sky and me.

A sudden shudder ran through me, not a shudder of cold but a strange shudder of anguish.

I quickened my pace, uneasy at being alone in this wood, unreasonably, stupidly, terrified by the profound solitude. Abruptly I felt that I was being followed, that someone was on my heels, quite close, near enough to touch me.

I swung round. I was alone. I saw behind me only the straight, open path, empty, high, terrifyingly empty; it stretched out in front of me too, as far as the eye could see, just as empty and as frightening.

I shut my eyes. Why? And I began to spin round on my heel at a great rate like a top. I almost fell; I opened my eyes again; the trees were dancing; the earth was swaying; I was forced to sit down. Then, ah! I didn't know now which way I had been walking. Strange thought! Strange! Strange thought! I knew nothing at all now. I took the right-hand way, and found myself back in the avenue that had led me into the middle of the forest.

June 3. The night has been terrible. I am going to go away for several weeks. A short journey will surely put me right.

July 2. Home again. I am cured. I have had, moreover, a delightful holiday. I visited Mont-Saint-Michel, which I didn't know.

What a vision one gets, arriving at Avranches as I did, towards dusk! The town lies on a slope, and I was taken into the public garden, at one end of the city. A cry of astonishment broke from me. An immense bay stretched before me, as far as eye could see, between spreading coasts that vanished in distant mist; and in the midst of this vast, yellow bay, under a gleaming, golden sky, a strange hill, somber and peaked, thrust up in the midst of the sands. The sun had just sunk, and on a horizon still riotous with color was etched the outline of this fantastic rock that bore on its summit a fantastic monument.

At daybreak I went out to it. The tide was low, as on the evening before, and as I drew near it, the miraculous abbey grew in height before my eyes. After several hours' walking I reached the monstrous pile of stones that supports the little city dominated by the great church. I clambered up the steep, narrow street, I entered the most wonderful Gothic dwelling made for God on this earth, as vast as a town, with innumerable low rooms hollowed out under the vaults, and high galleries

slung over slender columns. I entered this gigantic
granite jewel, as delicate as a piece of lace, pierced
everywhere by towers and airy belfries where twisting
stairways climb, towers that, into the blue sky of day,
the dark sky of night, lift strange heads bristling with
gargoyles, devils, fantastic beasts and monstrous flowers,
and are linked together by slender, carved arches.

When I stood on the top I said to the monk who
accompanied me, "What a glorious place you have here,
Father!"

"We get strong winds," he answered, and we fell into
talk as we watched the incoming sea run over the sand
and cover it with a steel cuirass.

The monk told me stories, all the old stories of this
place, legends and more legends.

One of them particularly impressed me. The people
of the district, those who lived on the Mount, declared
that at night they heard voices on the sands, followed
by the bleating of two she-goats, one that called loudly
and one softly. Unbelievers insisted that it was the crying of sea birds which sometimes sound like bleat-
ings, sometimes like human lamentations: but benighted
fishermen swore that they had met an old shepherd
wandering on the dunes, between two tides, round the
little town flung so far out of the world. No one ever
saw the head, hidden in his cloak: he led behind him a
goat with the face of a man and a she-goat with the face
of a woman, both with long white hair and speaking
incessantly, disputing in an unknown tongue, then
abruptly ceasing to chatter, and bleating with all their
strength.

"Do you believe it?" I asked the monk.

He murmured, "I don't know."

"If," I went on, "there existed on earth beings other
than ourselves, why have we not long ago learned to

know them; why have you yourself not seen them? Why have I not seen them myself?"

He answered, "Do we see the hundred-thousandth part of all that exists? Think, there's the wind, the greatest force in nature, which throws down men, shatters buildings, uproots trees, stirs up the sea into watery mountains, destroys cliffs and tosses the tall ships against the shore, the wind that kills, whistles, groans, roars—have you seen it, can you see it? Nevertheless, it exists."

Before his simple reasoning I fell silent. This man was either a seer or a fool. I should not have cared to say which; but I held my peace. What he had said, I had often thought.

July 3. I slept badly; there must be a feverish influence at work here, for my coachman suffers from the same trouble as myself. When I came home yesterday, I noticed his strange pallor.

"What's the matter with you, Jean?" I demanded.

"I can't rest these days, sir; I'm burning the candle at both ends. Since you went away, sir, I haven't been able to throw it off."

The other servants are all right, however, but I am terrified of getting caught by it again.

July 4. It has surely caught me again. My old nightmares have come back. Last night I felt someone crouching on me, his mouth on mine, drinking my life between my lips. Yes, he sucked it from my throat like a leech. Then he rose from me, replete, and I awoke, so mangled, bruised, enfeebled, that I could not move. If this goes on for many days more, I shall certainly go away again.

July 5. Have I lost my reason? What happened last night is so strange that my head reels when I think of it.

I had locked my door, as I do now every evening; then, feeling thirsty, I drank half a glass of water and I happened to notice that my carafe was filled up right to its crystal stopper.

I lay down after this and fell into one of my dreadful slumbers, from which I was jerked about two hours later by a shock more frightful than any of the others.

Imagine a man murdered in his sleep, who wakes with a knife through his lung, with the death-rattle in his throat, covered with blood, unable to breathe, and on the point of death, understanding nothing—there you have it.

When I finally recovered my sanity, I was thirsty again; I lit a candle and went towards the table where I had placed my carafe. I lifted it and held it over my glass; not a drop ran out. It was empty! It was completely empty. At first, I simply didn't understand; then all at once a frightful rush of emotion so overwhelmed me that I was forced to sit down, or rather, fell into a chair! Then I leaped up again and looked round me! Then I sat down again, lost in surprise and fear, in front of the transparent crystal. I gazed at it with a fixed stare, seeking an answer to the riddle. My hands were trembling. Had someone drunk the water? Who? I? It must have been me. Who could it have been but me? So I was a somnambulist, all unaware I was living the mysterious double life that raises the doubt whether there be not two selves in us, or whether, in moments when the spirit lies unconscious, an alien being, unknowable and unseen, inhabits the captive body that obeys this other as it obeys us, more readily than it obeys us.

Ah, who can understand my frightful agony? Who can understand the feelings of a sane, educated, thoroughly rational man, staring in abject terror through the glass of his carafe, where the water has disappeared while he slept? I remained there until daylight, not daring to go back to bed.

July 6. I am going mad. My carafe was emptied again last night—or rather, I emptied it.

But is it I? Is it I? Who can it be? Who? Oh, my God! Am I going mad? Who will save me?

July 10. I have just had astonishing proof. Listen!

On the 6th of July, before lying down in bed, I placed on my table wine, milk, water, bread, and strawberries.

Someone drank—I drank—all the water, and a little of the milk. Neither the wine, nor the bread, nor the strawberries were touched.

On the 7th of July, I made the same experiment and got the same result.

On the 8th of July, I left out the water and the milk. Nothing was touched.

Finally, on the 9th of July, I placed only the water and milk on my table, taking care to wrap the carafes in white muslin cloths and to tie down the stoppers. Then I rubbed my lips, my beard and my hands with a charcoal pencil and lay down.

The usual overpowering sleep seized me, followed shortly by the frightful wakening. I had not moved, my bed-clothes themselves bore no marks. I rushed towards my table. The cloths wrapped round the bottles remained spotless. I untied the cords, shaking with fear. All the water had been drunk! All the milk had been drunk! Oh, my God! . . .

I am leaving for Paris at once.

July 13. Paris. I suppose I lost my head during the last few days! I must have been the sport of my disordered imagination, unless I really am a somnambulist or have fallen under one of those indubitable but hitherto inexplicable influences that we call suggestions. However that may be, my disorder came very near to lunacy, and twenty-four hours in Paris have been enough to restore my balance.

Yesterday, after doing some errands and paying some visits, which breathed new life into my soul, I ended my evening at the Théâtre Français. They were presenting a play by the younger Dumas; and his alert, forceful intelligence completed my cure. There can be no doubt that loneliness is dangerous to active minds. We need round us men who think and talk. When we live alone for long periods, we people the void with phantoms.

I returned to the hotel in high spirits, walking along the boulevards. Amid the jostling of the crowd, I thought ironically on my terrors, on my hallucinations of a week ago, when I had believed, yes, believed that an invisible being dwelt in my body. How weak and shaken and speedily unbalanced is our brain immediately it is confronted by a tiny incomprehensible fact!

Instead of concluding by simply saying, "I do not understand, because the cause eludes me," at once we imagine frightening mysteries and supernatural powers.

July 14. *Bastille Day.* I walked through the streets. The rockets and the flags filled me with a childish joy. At the same time, it is very silly to be joyous on a set day by order of the government. The mob is an imbecile herd, sometimes stupidly patient, sometimes violently rebellious. You say to it, "Enjoy yourself," and it enjoys itself. You say to it, "Go and fight your neighbor." It goes to fight. You say to it, "Vote for the Emperor." It votes for the Emperor. Then you say to it, "Vote for the Republic." And it votes for the Republic.

Its rulers are as besotted; instead of obeying men they obey principles, which can only be half-baked, sterile, and false by the very fact that they are principles, that is to say, ideas reputed certain and immutable, in this world where nothing is sure, since light and sound are both illusions.

July 16. Yesterday I saw things that profoundly disturbed me.

I dined with my cousin, Mme Sablé, whose husband commands the 76th Light Horse at Limoges. At her house I met two young women, one of whom is married to a doctor, Dr. Parent, who devotes himself largely to nervous illnesses and the extraordinary discoveries that are the outcome of the recent experiments in hypnotism and suggestion.

He told us at length about the amazing results obtained by English scientists and by the doctors of the Nancy school.

The facts that he put forward struck me as so fantastic that I confessed myself utterly incredulous.

"We are," he declared, "on the point of discovering one of the most important secrets of Nature, I mean one of the most important secrets of this earth; for there are certainly others as important, away yonder, in the stars. Since man began to think, since he learned to express and record his thoughts, he has felt the almost impalpable touch of a mystery impenetrable by his clumsy and imperfect senses, and he has tried to supplement the impotence of his organic powers by the force of his intelligence. While this intelligence was still in a rudimentary stage, this haunting sense of invisible phenomena clothed itself in crudely terrifying forms. Thus are born popular theories of the supernatural, legends of wandering spirits, fairies, gnomes, ghosts. I'll add the God-myth itself, since our conceptions of the artificer-creator, to whatever religion they belong, are really the most uninspired, the most unintelligent, the most inacceptable products of the fear-clouded brain of human beings. Nothing is truer than that saying of Voltaire's: 'God has made man in His image, but man has retorted upon Him in kind.'

"But for a little over a century we have had glimpse of a new knowledge. Mesmer and others have set our feet on a fresh path, and, more specially during the last four or five years, we have really achieved surprising results."

My cousin, as incredulous as I, smiled. Dr. Parent said to her, "Shall I try to put you to sleep, Madame?"

"Yes, do."

She seated herself in an armchair, and he looked fixedly into her eyes, as if he were trying to fascinate her. As for me, I felt suddenly uneasy: my heart thumped, my throat contracted. I saw Mme Sablé's eyes grow heavy, her mouth twitch, her bosom rise and fall with her quick breathing.

Within ten minutes she was asleep.

"Go behind her," said the doctor.

I seated myself behind her. He put a visiting-card in her hand and said to her, "Here is a looking-glass: what can you see in it?"

"I see my cousin," she answered.

"What is he doing?"

"He is twisting his mustache."

"And now?"

"He is drawing a photograph from his pocket."

"Whose photograph is it?"

"His own."

She was right! This photograph had been sent me at my hotel only that very evening.

"What is he doing in the photograph?"

"He is standing, with his hat in his hand."

Evidently she saw in the card, in the piece of white pasteboard, as she would have seen in a glass.

The young women, terrified, cried, "Stop, stop, stop!"

But the doctor said authoritatively, "You will get up tomorrow at eight o'clock; you will call on your cousin at his hotel and you will beg him to lend you five thousand francs that your husband has told you to get and will ask you for on his next leave."

Then he woke her up.

On my way back to the hotel, I thought about this curious séance, and I was assailed by doubts, not of the absolutely unimpeachable good faith of my cousin, whom since our childhood I had looked upon as my sister, but of the possibility of trickery on the doctor's part. Had he concealed a looking-glass in his hand and held it before the slumbering young woman with his visiting-card? Professional conjurers do things as strange.

I had reached the hotel by now and I went to bed.

This morning, about half-past eight, I was roused by my man, who said to me:

"Mme Sablé wishes to speak to you at once, sir."

I got hurriedly into my clothes and had her shown in.

She seated herself, very agitated, her eyes downcast, and, without lifting her veil, said:

"I have a great favor to ask you, my dear cousin."

"What is it, my dear?"

"I hate to ask it of you, and yet I must. I need, desperately, five thousand francs."

"You?"

"Yes, I, or rather my husband, who has told me to get it."

I was so astounded that I stammered as I answered
her. I wondered whether she and Dr. Parent were not
actually making fun of me, whether it weren't a little
comedy they had prepared beforehand and were acting
very well.

But as I watched her closely my doubts vanished entirely. The whole affair was so distasteful to her that she
was shaking with anguish, and I saw that her throat was
quivering with sobs.

I knew that she was very rich and I added:

"What! Do you mean to say that your husband can't
get hold of five thousand francs! Come, think. Are you
sure he told you to ask me for it?"

She hesitated for a few moments as if she were making a tremendous effort to search her memory, then she
answered:

"Yes . . . yes. . . . I'm quite sure."

"Has he written to you?"

She hesitated again, reflecting. I guessed at the tortured striving of her mind. She didn't know. She only
knew that she had to borrow five thousand francs from
me for her husband. Then she plucked up courage to lie.

"Yes, he has written to me."

"But when? You didn't speak to me about it yesterday."

"I got his letter this morning."

"Can you let me see it?"

"No . . . no . . . no . . . it is very intimate . . .
too personal. . . . I've . . . I've burned it."

"Your husband must be in debt, then."

Again she hesitated, then answered:

"I don't know."

I told her abruptly:

"The fact is I can't lay my hands on five thousand
francs at the moment, my dear."

A kind of agonized wail broke from her.

"Oh, I implore you, I implore you, get it for me."

She grew dreadfully excited, clasping her hands as if she were praying to me. The tone of her voice changed as I listened: she wept, stammering, torn with grief, goaded by the irresistible command that had been laid on her.

"Oh, I implore you to get it. . . . If you knew how unhappy I am! . . . I must have it today."

I took pity on her.

"You shall have it at once, I promise you."

"Thank you, thank you," she cried. "How kind you are!"

"Do you remember," I went on, "what happened at your house yesterday evening?"

"Yes."

"Do you remember that Dr. Parent put you to sleep?"

"Yes."

"Very well, he ordered you to come this morning and borrow five thousand francs from me, and you are now obeying the suggestion."

She considered this for a moment and answered:

"Because my husband wants it."

I spent an hour trying to convince her, but I could not do so.

When she left, I ran to the doctor's house. He was just going out, and he listened to me with a smile. Then he said:

"Now do you believe?"

"I must."

"Let's go and call on your cousin."

She was already asleep on a day-bed, overwhelmed with weariness. The doctor felt her pulse, and looked at her for some time, one hand lifted towards her eyes, that slowly closed under the irresistible compulsion of his magnetic force.

When she was asleep:

"Your husband has no further need for five thousand francs. You will forget that you begged your cousin to lend it to you, and if he speaks to you about it, you will not understand."

Then he woke her up. I drew a note-case from my pocket.

"Here is what you asked me for this morning, my dear."

She was so dumbfounded that I dared not press the matter. I did, however, try to rouse her memory, but she denied it fiercely, thought I was making fun of her and at last was almost angry.

Back at the hotel. The experience disturbed me so profoundly that I could not eat lunch.

July 19. I have told several people about this adventure and been laughed at for my pains. I don't know what to think now. The wise man says: Perhaps?

July 21. I dined at Bougival, then I spent the evening at the rowing-club dance. There's no doubt that everything is a question of places and persons. To believe in the supernatural in the island of Grenouillère would be the height of folly . . . but at the top of Mont-Saint-Michel? . . . in the Indies? We are frightfully influenced by our surroundings. I am going home next week.

July 30. I have been home since yesterday. All is well.

August 2. Nothing fresh. The weather has been glorious. I spend my days watching the Seine run past.

August 4. The servants are quarreling among themselves. They declare that someone breaks the glasses in the cupboard at night. My man blames the cook, who blames the housemaid, who blames the other two. Who is the culprit? It would take a mighty clever man to find out.

August 6. This time, I am not mad. I've seen . . . I've seen . . . I've seen. . . . I can doubt no more. . . . I've seen. . . . I'm still chilled to the bone . . . still terrified to the marrow. . . . I've seen! . . .

At two o'clock, in broad daylight, I was walking in my rose-garden . . . between the autumn roses, that are just coming out.

As I paused to look at a *Géant des Batailles,* which bore three superb flowers, I saw, I distinctly saw, right under my eye, the stem of one of these roses bend as if an invisible hand had twisted it, then break as if the hand had plucked it. Then the flower rose, describing in the air the curve that an arm would have made carrying it towards a mouth, and it hung suspended in the clear air, quite alone, motionless, a terrifying scarlet splash three paces from my eyes.

I lost my head and flung myself on it, grasping at it. My fingers closed on nothing: it had disappeared. Then I was filled with a savage rage against myself; a rational, serious-minded man simply does not have such hallucinations.

But was it really a hallucination? I turned round to look for the flower and found it immediately under the bush, freshly broken off and lying between the two roses that still remained on the branch.

Then I went back to the house, my senses reeling: for I am sure now, sure as I am that day follows night, that there lives at my side an invisible being who feeds on milk and water, who can touch things, take them, move them from one place to another, is endowed therefore with a material nature, though imperceptible to our senses, and lives beside me, under my roof. . . .

August 7. I slept quietly. He drank the water from my carafe, but he did not disturb my sleep.

I wonder if I am mad. Sometimes as I walk in the blazing sunshine along the river-bank, I am filled with doubts of my sanity, not the vague doubts I have been feeling, but precise and uncompromising doubts. I have seen madmen; I have known men who were intelligent, lucid, even exceptionally clear-headed in everything in life but on one point. They talked quite clearly, easily, and profoundly about everything, until suddenly their minds ran onto the rocks of their madness and was there rent in pieces, strewn to the winds and foundered in the fearful raging sea, filled with surging waves, fogs, squalls, that we call "insanity."

I should certainly think myself mad, absolutely mad, if I were not conscious, if I were not perfectly aware of my state of mind, if I did not plumb and analyze it with such complete clearness. I assume that I must be merely a sane man troubled by hallucinations. There must be some unknown disturbance in my brain, one of those disturbances that modern physiologists are trying to observe and elucidate; and this disturbance has opened a deep gulf in my mind, in the orderly and logical working of my thoughts. Similar phenomena take place in a dream that drags us through the most unreal phantasmagoria without surprising us, because the mechanism of judgment, the controlling censor, is asleep, while the imaginative faculty wakes and works. Can one of the invisible strings that control my mental keyboard have become muted?

Sometimes, after an accident, a man loses his power to remember proper names, or verbs, or figures, or dates. The localization of all the different faculties of the mind is now proved. Is there anything surprising, therefore, in the idea that my power of examining the unreality of certain hallucinations has ceased to function in my brain just now?

I thought of all this as I walked by the side of the water. The sunlight flung a mantle of light across the river, clothing the earth with beauty, filling my thoughts with love of life, of the swallows whose swift flight is a joy to my eyes, of the riverside grasses whose whisper delights my ears.

Little by little, however, I fell prey to an inexplicable uneasiness. I felt as though some force, an occult force, were paralyzing my movements, halting me, hindering me from going farther, calling me back. I felt the kind of unhappy impulse to turn back that one feels when a beloved person has been left at home ill and one is possessed by a foreboding that the illness has taken a turn for the worse.

So, in spite of myself, I turned back, sure that I should find bad news waiting in my house, a letter or a telegram. There was nothing; and I was left more surprised and uneasy than if I had had yet another fantastic vision.

August 8. Yesterday I spent a frightful night. He did not manifest himself again, but I feel him near me, spying on me, watching me, penetrating me, dominating me, more to be feared when he hides himself thus than if he gave notice of his constant, invisible presence by supernatural phenomena.

However, I slept.

August 9. Nothing, but I am afraid.

August 10. Nothing; what will happen tomorrow?

August 11. Still nothing: I can't stay at home any longer, with this fear and these thoughts in my mind: I shall go away.

August 12. Ten o'clock in the evening. I have been wanting to go away all day. I can't. I have been wanting to carry out the easy, simple act that will set me free —go out—get into my carriage to go to Rouen—I can't. Why?

August 13. Under the affliction of certain maladies, all the resources of one's physical being seem crushed, all one's energy exhausted, one's muscles relaxed, one's bones grown as soft as flesh and one's flesh turned to water. In a strange and wretched fashion I suffer all these pains in my spiritual being. I have no strength, no courage, no control over myself, no power even to summon my will. I can no longer will; but someone wills for me—and I obey.

August 14. I am lost. Someone has taken possession of my soul and is master of it; someone orders all my acts, all my movements, all my thoughts. I am no longer anything in myself, I am only a spectator, enslaved, and terrified by all the things I do. I wish to go out. I cannot. He does not wish it; and I remain, dazed, trembling, in the armchair where he keeps me seated. I desire no more than to get up, to raise myself, so that I can think I am master of myself again. I can't do it. I am riveted to my seat; and my seat is fast to the ground, in such fashion that no force could lift us.

Then, all at once, I must, must, must go into my garden and pick strawberries and eat them. Oh, my God! my God! my God! Is there a God? If there is one, deliver me, save me, help me! Pardon me! Pity me! Have mercy on me! How I suffer! How I am tortured! How terrible this is!

August 15. Think how my poor cousin was possessed and overmastered when she came to borrow five thousand francs from me. She submitted to an alien will that had entered into her, as if it were another soul, a parasitic, tyrannical soul. Is the world coming to an end?

But what is this being, this invisible being who rules me? This unknowable creature, this wanderer from a supernatural race.

So Unseen Ones exist? Then why is it that since the world began they have never manifested themselves unmistakably, as they do to me now? I have never read of anything like the things that are happening under my roof. If I could only leave it, if I could go away, fly far away and return no more, I should be saved, but I can't.

August 16. Today I was able to escape for two hours, like a prisoner who finds the door of his cell accidentally left open. I felt that I was suddenly set free, that he had withdrawn himself. I ordered the horses to be put in the carriage as quickly as possible and I reached Rouen. Oh, what a joy it was to find myself able to tell a man, "Go to Rouen," and be obeyed!

I stopped at the library and I asked them to lend me the long treatise of Dr. Hermann Herestauss on the unseen inhabitants of the antique and modern worlds.

Then, just as I was getting back into my carriage, with the words, "To the station," on my lips, I shouted

—I didn't speak, I shouted—in a voice so loud that the passers-by turned round, "Home," and I fell, over-whelmed with misery, onto the cushions of my carriage. He had found me again and taken possession once more.

August 17. What a night! What a night! Nevertheless it seems to me that I ought to congratulate myself. I read until one o'clock in the morning. Hermann Here-stauss, a doctor of philosophy and theogony, has written an account of all the invisible beings who wander among men or have been imagined by men's minds. He describes their origins, their domains, their power. But none of them is the least like the being who haunts me. It is as if man, since he began to think, has had a fore-boding of some new being, mightier than himself, who shall succeed him in this world; and, in his terror, feel-ing him draw near, and unable to guess at the nature of this master, has created all the fantastic crowd of occult beings, dim phantoms born of fear.

Well, I read until one o'clock and then I seated myself near an open window to cool my head and my thoughts in the mild night air.

It was fine and warm. In other days how I should have loved such a night!

No moon. The stars trembled and glittered in the black depths of the sky. Who dwells in those worlds? What forms of life, what living creatures, what animals or plants do they hold? What more than we do the thinkers in those far-off universes know? What more can they do than we? What do they see that we do not know of? Perhaps one of them, some day or other, will cross the gulf of space and appear on our earth to con-quer it, just as in olden days the Normans crossed the sea to subdue weaker nations.

We are so infirm, so defenseless, so ignorant, so small,

on this grain of dust that revolves and crumbles in a drop of water.

So dreaming, I fell asleep, in the fresh evening air.

I slept for about forty minutes and opened my eyes again without moving, roused by I know not what vague and strange emotions. At first I saw nothing, then all at once I thought that the page of a book lying open on my table had turned over of itself. Not a breath of air came in at the window. I was surprised and I sat waiting. About four minutes later, I saw, I saw, yes, I saw with my own eyes another page come up and turn back on the preceding one, as if a finger had folded it back. My arm-chair was empty, seemed empty; but I realized that he was there, he, sitting in my place and reading. In one wild spring, like a maddened beast springing on his trainer, I crossed the room to seize him, crush him, kill him. But before I had reached it my seat turned right over as if he had fled before me . . . my table rocked, my lamp fell and was extinguished, and my window slammed shut as if I had surprised a malefactor who had flung himself out into the darkness, tugging at the sashes with all his force.

So he had run away; he had been afraid, afraid of me, me!

Then . . . then . . . tomorrow . . . or the day after . . . or some day . . . I should be able to get him between my fingers, and crush him to the ground. Don't dogs sometimes bite and fly at their masters' throats?

August 18. I've been thinking things over all day. Oh, yes, I'll obey him, satisfy his impulses, do his will, make myself humble, submissive, servile. He is the stronger. But an hour will come. . . .

August 19. I know now. . . . I know. . . . I know all! I have just read the following in the *Revue du Monde Scientifique:*

"A strange piece of news reaches us from Rio de Janeiro. Madness, an epidemic of madness, comparable to the contagious outbursts of dementia that attacked the peoples of Europe in the Middle Ages, is raging in our day in the district of San Paulo. The distracted inhabitants are leaving their houses, deserting their villages, abandoning their fields, declaring themselves to be pursued, possessed, and ordered about like a human herd by certain invisible but tangible beings, vampires of some kind, who feed on their vitality while they sleep, in addition to drinking milk and water, while not, apparently, touching any other form of food.

"Professor Don Pedro Henriquez, accompanied by several medical authorities, has set out for the district of San Paulo, to study on the spot the origins and the forms taken by this surprising madness, and to suggest to the Emperor such measures as appear to him most likely to restore the delirious inhabitants to sanity."

Ah! I remember, I remember the lovely Brazilian three-master that sailed past my windows on the 8th of last May, on her way up the Seine. I thought her such a bonny, white, gay boat. The Being was on board her, come from over the sea, where his race is born. He saw me. He saw my house, white like the ship, and he jumped from the vessel to the bank. Oh, my God!

Now I know, I understand. The reign of man is at an end.

He is here, whom the dawning fears of primitive peoples taught them to dread. He who was exorcized by troubled priests, evoked in the darkness of night by wizards who yet never saw him materialize, to whom the foreboding vision of the temporary masters of this world lent all the monstrous or gracious forms of gnomes, spirits, jinns, fairies, and hobgoblins. Primitive terror visualized him in the crudest forms; later wiser men have seen him more clearly. Mesmer foresaw him, and it is ten years already that doctors have made the most exact inquiries into the nature of his power, even before he had begun to exercise it himself. They have been making a plaything of this weapon of the new God, this imposition of a mysterious will on the enslaved soul of man. They called it magnetism, hypnotism, suggestion . . . anything you like. I have seen them amusing themselves with this horrible power like foolish children. Woe to us! Woe to man! He is here . . . the . . . the . . . what is his name? . . . the . . . it seems as if he were shouting his name in my ear, and I cannot hear it . . . the . . . yes . . . he is shouting it. . . . I am listening. . . . I can't hear . . . again, tell me again . . . the . . . Horla. . . . I heard . . . the Horla . . . it is he . . . the Horla . . . he is here!

Ah, the vulture ate the dove, the wolf ate the sheep; the lion devoured the sharp-horned buffalo; man slew the lion with arrow, spear, and gun; but the Horla will make of man what we have made of the horse and the cow: his thing, his servant, and his food, by the mere force of his will. Woe to us!

But sometimes the beast rebels and kills his tamer . . . I too want . . . I could . . . but I must know him, touch him, see him. Scientists say that the eye of the beast is not like ours and does not see as ours does. . . . And my eye fails to show me this newcomer who is oppressing me.

Why? Oh, the words of the monk of Mont-Saint-Michel come to my mind: "Do we see the hundred-thousandth part of all that exists? Think, there's the wind, the greatest force in Nature, which throws down men, shatters buildings, uproots trees, stirs up the sea into watery mountains, destroys cliffs and tosses the tall ships against the shore, the wind that kills, whistles, groans, roars—have you seen it, can you see it? Nevertheless, it exists."

And I considered further: my eye is so weak, so imperfect, that it does not distinguish even solid bodies if they are transparent as glass is. If a looking-glass that has no foil backing bars my path, I hurl myself against it as a bird that has got into a room breaks its head on the windowpane. How many other things deceive and mislead my eye? Then what is there surprising in its failure to see a new body that offers no resistance to the passage of light?

A new being! Why not? He must assuredly come! Why should we be the last? Why is he not seen of our eyes as are all the beings created before us? Because his form is nearer perfection, his body finer and completer than ours—ours, which is so weak, so clumsily conceived, encumbered by organs always tired, always strained like a too complex mechanism, which lives like a vegetable or a beast, drawing its substance painfully from the air, from grasses and meat, a living machine subject to sickness, deformity and corruption, drawing its breath in pain, ill-regulated, simple and fantastic, ingeniously ill-made, clumsily and delicately erected, the mere rough sketch of a being who might become intelligent and noble.

There have been so few genera created in the world, from the bivalve to man. Why not one more, when we reach the end of the period of time that separates each successive appearance of a species from that which appeared before it?

Why not one more? Why not also new kinds of trees bearing monstrous flowers, blazing with color and filling all the countryside with their perfume? Why not other elements than fire, air, earth and water? There are four, only four sources of our being! How scanty! Why not forty, four hundred, four thousand? How poor, niggardly, and brutish is life! Grudgingly given, meanly conceived, stupidly executed. Consider the grace of the elephant, the hippopotamus! The elegance of the camel!

You bid me consider the butterfly! A winged flower! I can imagine one vast as a hundred worlds, with wings for whose shape, beauty, color, and sweep I cannot find any words. But I see it . . . it goes from star to star, refreshing and perfuming them with the soft, gracious wind of its passing. And the people of the upper air watch it pass, in an ecstasy of joy!

What is the matter with me? It is he, he, the Horla, who is haunting me, filling my head with these absurdities! He is in me, he has become my soul; I will kill him.

August 19. I will kill him. I have seen him! I was sitting at my table yesterday evening, pretending to be absorbed in writing. I knew very well that he would come and prowl round me, very close to me, so close that I might be able to touch him, seize him, perhaps? And then! . . . then, I should be filled with the strength of desperation; I should have hands, knees, chest, face, teeth to strangle him, crush him, tear him, rend him.

With every sense quiveringly alert, I watched for him.

I had lit both my lamps and the eight candles on my chimney-piece, as if I thought I should be more likely to discover him by this bright light.

In front of me was my bed, an old oak four-poster; on my right, the fireplace; on my left, my door carefully shut, after I had left it open for a long time to attract him; behind me, a very tall cupboard with a mirror front, which I used every day to shave and dress by, and in which I always looked at myself from head to foot whenever I passed in front of it.

Well, I pretended to write to deceive him, because he was spying on me too; and, all at once, I felt, I was certain, that he was reading over my shoulder, that he was there, his breath on my ear.

I stood up, my hand outstretched, and turned round, so quickly that I almost fell. What do you think? . . . the room was as light as day, and I could not see myself in my looking-glass! It was empty, transparent, deep, filled with light! I was not reflected in it . . . and I was standing in front of it. I could see the wide limpid expanse of glass from top to bottom. And I stared at it with a distraught gaze: I dared not step forward, I dared not move; nevertheless I felt that he was there, whose immaterial body had swallowed up my reflection, but that he would elude me still.

How frightened I was! A moment later my reflection began to appear in the depths of the looking-glass, in a sort of mist, as if I were looking at it through water; this water seemed to flow from left to right, slowly, so that moment by moment my reflection emerged more distinctly. It was like the passing of an eclipse. The thing that was concealing me appeared to possess no sharply defined outlines, but a kind of transparent opacity that gradually cleared.

At last I could see myself from head to foot, just as I saw myself every day when I looked in the glass.

I had seen him! The horror of it is still on me, making me shudder.

August 20. Kill him—but how, since I cannot touch him? Poison? But he would see me put it in the water; and besides, would our poisons affect an immaterial body? No . . . no, they certainly would not. . . . Then how? . . . how?

August 21. I have sent for a locksmith from Rouen, and ordered him to fit my room with iron shutters, such as they have in certain hotels in Paris, to keep out robbers. He is to make me, also, a similar sort of door. Everyone thinks me a coward, but much I care for that!

.   .   .   .

September 10. Rouen, Hôtel Continental. It is done . . . it is done . . . but is he dead? My brain reels with what I have seen.

Yesterday the locksmith put up my iron shutters and my iron door, and I left everything open until midnight, although it began to get cold.

All at once I felt his presence, and I was filled with joy, a mad joy. I rose slowly to my feet, and walked about the room for a long time, so that he should suspect nothing; then I took off my boots and carelessly drew on my slippers; then I closed my iron shutters and, sauntering back towards the door, I double-locked it too. Then I walked back to the window and secured it with a padlock, putting the key in my pocket.

Suddenly I realized that he was prowling anxiously round me, he was afraid now, and commanding me to open them for him. I almost yielded: I did not yield but, leaning on the door, I set it ajar, just wide enough for me to slip out backwards; and as I am very tall my head touched the lintel. I was sure that he could not have got out and I shut him in, alone, all alone. Thank God! I had him! Then I ran downstairs; in the drawing-room which is under my room, I took both my lamps and emptied the oil all over the carpet and the furniture, everything; then I set it on fire and I fled after having double-locked the main door.

And I went and hid myself at the bottom of my garden, in a grove of laurels. How long it took, how long! Everything was dark, silent, still; not a breath of air, not a star, mountains of unseen clouds that lay heavily, how heavily, on my spirit.

I kept my gaze fixed on my house, and waited. How long it took! I was beginning to think that the fire had died out of itself, or that he, He, had put it out, when one of the lower windows fell in under the fierce breath of the fire and a flame, a great red and yellow flame, a long, curling, caressing flame, leaped up the white wall and pressed its kiss on the roof itself. A flood of light poured over trees, branches, leaves, and with that a shudder, a shudder of fear, ran through them. The birds woke; a dog howled: I thought the dawn was at hand. In a moment two more windows burst into flame and I saw that the lower half of my house was now one frightful furnace. But a cry, a frightful, piercing, agonized cry, a woman's cry, stabbed the night, and two skylights opened. I had forgotten my servants. I saw their distraught faces and their wildly waving arms. . . .

Then, frantic with horror, I began to run towards the village, shouting, "Help! help! fire! fire!" I met people already on their way to the house and I turned back with them to look at it.

By now the house was no more than a horrible and magnificent funeral pyre, a monstrous pyre lighting up the whole earth, a pyre that was consuming men, and consuming Him, Him, my prisoner, the new Being, the new Master, the Horla!

The whole roof fell in with a sudden crash, and a

volcano of flames leaped to the sky. Through all the windows open on the furnace, I saw the fiery vat, and I reflected that he was there, in this oven, dead. . . .

Dead? Perhaps? . . . His body? Perhaps that body through which light fell could not be destroyed by the methods that kill our bodies?

Suppose he is not dead? . . . Perhaps only time has power over the Invisible and Dreadful One. Why should this transparent, unknowable body, this body of the spirit, fear sickness, wounds, infirmity, premature destruction?

Premature destruction? The source of all human dread! After man, the Horla. After him who can die any day, any hour, any moment, by accidents of all kinds, comes he who can only die at his appointed day, hour and moment, when he has attained the limit of his existence.

No . . . no . . . I know, I know . . . he is not dead . . . so . . . so . . . I must kill myself, now.

Having packed her trunks, Jeanne went to the window. It was still raining. The downpour had beaten against the windowpanes and the roof all night long. It seemed as if the lowering clouds, heavy with water, had burst, emptying upon the earth, reducing it to pulp and melting it like sugar. Sudden squalls swept by in warm gusts. The roaring of overflowing gutters filled the deserted streets, in which the houses, like sponges, absorbed the moisture which penetrated inside and made the walls perspire from cellar to attic.

Jeanne, who had left the convent the day before, free for ever, at last, and ready to seize upon all the happiness of life, of which she had dreamed so long, feared her father would not start if the weather did not clear, and for the hundredth time since morning she studied the horizon.

Then she noticed that she had forgotten to put her calendar in her traveling-bag. She took from the wall the little card divided into months, which bore in the midst of a design the date of the current year, 1819, in gilt figures. She crossed off with a pencil the first four columns, drawing a line through each saint's name until she came to the second of May, the day of her leaving the convent.

A voice outside the door called, "Jeannette!" Jeanne answered, "Come in, papa." And her father appeared.

Baron Simon Jacques Le Perthuis des Vauds was a gentleman of the old order, eccentric and good-hearted. An enthusiastic disciple of Jean Jacques Rousseau, he had all the tenderness of a lover for nature, for fields, woods and animals.

An aristocrat by birth, he instinctively hated the year 1793; but, being a philosopher by temperament, and liberal by upbringing, he execrated tyranny with an inoffensive and declamatory hatred. His great strength and his great weakness was his good nature, a good nature which had no arms enough to caress, to give, to embrace, a creative good nature, diffuse and incapable of resistance, as though a nerve of his will were paralyzed; a lack of energy, almost a vice.

A man of theories, he had thought out a whole plan of education for his daughter, desiring to make her happy, good, upright, and tender. She had remained at home up to the age of twelve, when, in spite of her mother's tears, she was placed in the convent of the Sacred Heart.

He had kept her strictly shut up there, cloistered, ignorant of human affairs. He wanted her to return to him chaste, at the age of seventeen, so that he himself might steep her in a sort of bath of poetry; and in the fields, in the midst of the fruitful country, open her soul and enlighten her ignorance by the sight of artless love, of the simple tenderness of animals, of the serene laws of life.

She was leaving the convent now, radiant, full of the sources and desires of happiness, ready for all joys, for all the charming adventures which her mind had already dwelt upon in the idleness of her days, during the long nights, in the solitude of her hopes.

She was like a portrait by Paul Veronese, with her fair, shining hair, which looked as if it had colored her skin, the skin of an aristocrat, slightly tinted with pink, shaded with a light brown, a sort of pale velvet, just perceptible when the sun kissed it. Her eyes were blue, that opaque blue which is seen in Dutch china figures. Upon her left nostril she had a little beauty spot, and another to the right upon her chin, where there curled a few tiny hairs so like her skin that they could hardly be seen. She was tall, with a well-developed bosom and a supple waist. Her clear voice sounded at times too shrill, but her frank laugh spread happiness about her. Often, with a habitual gesture, she would put her two hands to her temples as if to smooth her hair.

She ran to her father and put her arms round him and kissed him. "Well, are we off?" she asked. He smiled, shook back his already white hair, which he wore rather long, and pointing towards the window said:

"How can you wish to travel in such weather?"

But she begged him, coaxing and tender, "Oh, papa, do let us go. It will clear up in the afternoon."

"But your mother will never consent to it."

"Yes, I promise you that she will. I will answer for it."

"If you succeed in persuading your mother, I am quite willing."

Jeanne hastened to the Baronne's room, for she had looked forward to this day of departure with growing impatience. Since entering the Sacred Heart she had not left Rouen, as her father would not allow any distraction before the age which he had fixed. Twice only she had been taken to Paris for a fortnight, but that was another town, and her heart was set on the country. She was going now to pass the summer on their estate of Les Peuples, an old family château situated on the cliff near Yport, and she anticipated boundless joy in the free life beside the sea. Besides, it was understood that this manor would be given to her, and that she should always live in it when she was married. The rain, which had been falling ceaselessly since the day before, was the first great sorrow of her existence.

But in three minutes she came running out of her mother's room, crying all through the house, "Papa, papa! Mamma is willing. So have them harness the horses."

The deluge was not lessening, it even seemed to be coming down twice as heavily, when the carriage was driven to the door. Jeanne was ready to get in when the Baronne came downstairs, supported on one side by her husband and on the other by a tall chambermaid, as strong and strapping as a country lad. She was a Norman woman from Caux who appeared at least twenty, although she was eighteen at the most. She was treated in the family as a second daughter, for she was Jeanne's foster-sister. Her name was Rosalie, and her principal duty consisted in guiding the steps of her mistress, who had become enormous in the last few years owing to hypertrophy of the heart, of which she was always complaining.

The Baronne, panting a good deal, reached the steps of the old house, looked at the courtyard where the water was streaming, and murmured, "It is really not wise."

With a smile her husband replied, "It is as you wish, Madame Adelaide."

As she bore the Bourbon name of Adelaide, he always preceded it by "Madame" with a slight air of mocking respect. Madame continued her progress and climbed painfully into the carriage, the springs of which bent under her weight. The Baron sat at her side and Jeanne and Rosalie took their places on the seat, with their backs to the horses.

The cook, Ludivine, brought piles of rugs, which were spread over their knees, and two baskets, which were concealed beneath the legs of the travelers; then she climbed to the box beside old Simon and wrapped herself in a great blanket which entirely covered her. The concierge and his wife came to say good-bye as they shut the carriage door, and received the last orders about the trunks which were to follow in a cart, and so they started. Old Simon, the coachman, his head bowed, his back bent under the rain, disappeared beneath his box-coat with its triple cape; the howling storm beat upon the carriage windows and inundated the roadway.

With the two horses at a rapid trot the carriage rolled quickly down to the quay, skirted the line of great ships whose masts, yards, and rigging rose up gloomily in the dripping sky, like leafless trees: then it turned into the long Mount Riboudet Boulevard.

Soon they were driving through meadows, and from time to time a weeping-willow, its branches hanging as inertly as a corpse, stood out somberly through a sheet of rain. The horses' hoofs clattered and the four wheels splashed little pools of mud.

They were silent: even their spirits seemed dampened like the earth. The old lady leaned back, pillowed her head and closed her eyes. The Baron gazed at the drenched and monotonous fields with a mournful eye. Rosalie, a parcel on her knees, was dreaming in the animal way of the common people. But Jeanne, under this tepid downpour, felt herself reviving like a plant which had been shut up and has now been restored to the air; and the density of her joy sheltered her heart from sorrow like foliage. Although she did not speak, she wanted to sing, to stretch out her hand in order to fill it with rain-water which she would drink: and she enjoyed being carried along at full trot by the horses, looking at the desolation of the landscape and feeling herself protected in the midst of this inundation. Under the pelting rain the gleaming backs of the two animals threw off a cloud of steam.

The Baronne gradually fell asleep. Her face, framed by six dangling ringlets, sank lower and lower, weakly supported by the three great billows of her chin, whose final undulations were lost in the broad ocean of her bosom. Her head, rising at each breath, fell again, her cheeks were puffed out, while from between her partly opened lips a snore issued. Her husband leaned towards her, and gently placed a little leather pocketbook in her hands, which were folded upon her broad stomach.

This touch awakened her; and she gazed at the object with dazed eyes, with the stupid expression born of interrupted dreams. The pocketbook dropped and opened. Gold coins and banknotes were scattered all over the carriage. This completely aroused her, and the gaiety of her daughter was heard in a peal of laughter.

The Baron picked up the money and placing it on her knees said, "This, dear, is all that is left of my farm at Eletot. I sold it to repair Les Peuples, where we shall live so much in future."

She counted six thousand four hundred francs and put them quietly in her pocket. It was the ninth farm thus sold out of the thirty-one which their parents had left to them. They, nevertheless, still possessed an income of about twenty thousand francs from properties which, if properly managed, would have easily yielded them thirty thousand francs a year.

As they lived simply, this income would have been sufficient if there had not been a bottomless hole always open in the house: good-natured generosity. It dried up the money in their hands as the sun dries up the water in the marshes. It flowed, fled, disappeared. How? Nobody knew. One of them frequently said to the other:

"I don't know how it is, but I have spent a hundred francs today, without buying anything much."

This lavishness was, however, one of the great pleasures of their life. They agreed on this point in a way which was both superb and touching.

Jeanne asked, "Is my castle beautiful now?"

The Baron answered gaily, "You shall see, little daughter."

Gradually the violence of the rain lessened: then there was only a sort of mist, a fine dust of whirling rain. The arch of clouds seemed to rise and to lighten: and suddenly through an unseen rift, a long slanting ray of sunshine fell upon the meadows, and the clouds having been rent asunder, the blue heights of the heavens appeared: then the rift widened like the rending of a veil, and a beautiful azure sky, clear and fathomless, spread over the world.

A fresh and gentle breath of wind was felt, like a happy sigh of the earth, and when they skirted gardens or woods they heard at times the sprightly song of a bird, drying his wings. Evening came. Everyone in the carriage was asleep except Jeanne. Twice they stopped at inns to rest the horses and give them oats and water.

The sun had set. Bells were ringing in the distance. In a little village the people were lighting the lamps;

and the sky was also lit by myriads of stars. Lighted houses appeared at intervals, piercing the darkness with points of fire; and suddenly, behind a hill, through the branches of the fir-trees, the moon rose, red, enormous, and, as it were, heavy with sleep.

It was so mild that the windows were left lowered. Jeanne, exhausted with dreaming, surfeited with happy visions, was now sleeping. At times the numbed feeling caused by remaining too long in one position made her open her eyes: then she looked out and saw the trees of a farm pass in the clear night, or perhaps some cows, lying here and there in a field, raised their heads. Then she settled in another position, and tried to recapture an interrupted dream; but the continuous rumbling of the carriage filled her ears, tired her mind, and she closed her eyes again, feeling her spirit as stiff and cramped as her body.

At last they stopped. Some men and women were standing before the carriage door with lanterns in their hands. They had arrived. Jeanne, suddenly awakened, quickly jumped out. Her father and Rosalie, lighted by a farmer, almost carried the Baronne, who was absolutely worn out, groaning in distress, and continually repeating in a weak little voice, "Ah! my God! my poor children!" She would not take anything to eat or anything to drink, but went to bed and at once fell asleep.

Jeanne and the Baron had supper together. They smiled as they looked at each other, holding hands across the table; and, both filled with childish joy, they began to inspect the restored manor.

It was one of those big, high Norman residences, both farmhouse and château, built of white stone which had turned gray, and spacious enough to hold a tribe. An immense vestibule divided the house in two and crossed it, opening its great doors on both sides. A double staircase seemed to bestride this entrance, leaving the center empty, and uniting its two flights of steps on the first floor like a bridge. On the ground floor to the right was an inordinately large drawing-room, hung with tapestries representing foliage with birds. All the furniture, upholstered in needle-point tapestry, illustrated La Fontaine's Fables: and Jeanne had a shiver of pleasure on seeing again an old chair which she had loved as a child, and which represented the story of the fox and the stork.

Beside the drawing-room were the library, filled with old books, and two other unused rooms. At the left were the dining-room with new wainscoting, the linen-room, the butler's pantry, and a little room containing a bath-tub.

A corridor ran along the whole length of the upper story, and divided it in two. The ten doors of the ten rooms opened onto this. At the very end, on the right, was Jeanne's apartment. They entered it. The Baron had just had it done up, merely having used the hangings and the furniture which were lying idle in the garret. Tapestries of a Flemish origin, and very old, peopled this place with strange characters.

But when she saw her bed, the young girl shouted with joy. At the four corners, four large oaken birds, all black and gleaming with polish, supported the bed and seemed to be its guardians. The sides represented two great garlands of carved flowers and fruits: and four finely fluted columns terminating in Corinthian capitals supported a cornice of Cupids intertwined with roses.

It stood, monumental, yet very graceful, in spite of the austerity of the wood darkened by time. The counterpane and the hangings of the canopy shone like two firmaments. They were made of antique silk of a deep blue, were starred in places by large embroidered gold lilies. When she had sufficiently admired it, Jeanne, raising her light, examined the tapestries to make out the subject.

A young nobleman and a young lady dressed in green, red, and yellow, in the strangest fashion, were conversing under a blue tree, on which white fruit was ripening. A fat rabbit of the same color was nibbling a little gray grass.

Just above the figures, at a conventional distance, one could see five little round houses with pointed roofs and, higher up, almost in the sky, a very red windmill. A flowery pattern ran through all this. The two other panels much resembled the first, except that out of the houses came four little old men clad in the Flemish fashion, and raising their arms to heaven in token of their extreme astonishment and anger.

But the last tapestry represented a drama. Near that rabbit, which was still nibbling, the young man was stretched out apparently dead. The young lady, looking at him, was piercing her bosom with a sword, and the fruits of the tree had become black. Jeanne gave up trying to understand, when she observed in a corner a diminutive little creature, which the rabbit, had he been alive, could have swallowed as easily as a blade of grass. And yet it was a lion.

Then she recognized the misfortunes of Pyramus and Thisbe, and although she smiled at the simplicity of the designs, she felt happy to be inclosed within this adventure of love, which would continually speak to her thoughts of cherished hopes, and every night this legendary love would hover over her slumbers.

All the rest of the furniture was of the most diverse styles. They were pieces which each generation leaves in the family, and which make of ancient houses a sort of museum, in which all kinds of things are mingled.

A superb Louis XIV chest of drawers, bound in shining brass, was flanked by two Louis XV armchairs, still covered with their silken bouquets. A rosewood writing-table stood opposite the mantelpiece, on which was an Empire clock under a glass globe. It was a bronze bee-hive upheld by four marble columns above a garden of gilt flowers. A slender pendulum, hanging from the hive through a long slit, swung eternally a little bee with enameled wings over this flower-bed. The dial was of painted faïence, and set in the side of the beehive. It began to strike eleven. The Baron kissed his daughter and went to his own room. Then Jeanne, with regret, went to bed.

With a last glance she ran over the room, and then extinguished her candle. But the bed, whose head alone was against the wall, had a little window on its left, through which a flood of moonlight streamed, spreading a splash of light on the floor. Reflections were cast upon the walls, pale reflections, feebly caressing the motionless figures of Pyramus and Thisbe. Through the other window, opposite her feet, Jeanne perceived a tall tree, all bathed in a soft light. She turned on her side, shut her eyes, then in a little while opened them again.

She seemed to feel still shaken by the jolting of the carriage, whose rumbling still lingered in her head. She remained quiet at first, hoping that this repose would make her finally go to sleep: but the impatience of her mind soon spread through her whole body. She had twitchings in her legs, and an increasing fever. Then she got up, and bare-footed, bare-armed, with her long nightdress, which gave her the appearance of a phantom, she crossed the little lake of light spread over the floor, opened her window, and looked out.

The night was so clear that one could see as if it were broad daylight; and the young girl recognized all that country, beloved of her early childhood. There was first, opposite her, a large lawn, yellow as butter under the nocturnal light. Two giant trees stood before the château, a plane-tree to the north, and a lime to the south. Away at the end of the great stretch of grass, a little grove terminated this domain, sheltered from the ocean gales by five rows of ancient elms, twisted, clipped, eaten away, bent like a roof by the unceasing ocean wind.

This little park was bounded on the right and left by two long avenues of extremely tall poplars, which separated the residence of the owners from the two adjacent farmhouses, one occupied by the Couillard and the other by the Martin family.

These poplars had given their name to the château. Beyond this inclosure stretched a long uncultivated plain, thick with furze, where the breeze whistled and galloped day and night. Then suddenly the rising ground descended to a cliff of a hundred meters, steep and white, bathing its foot in the ocean waves.

Jeanne gazed afar over the wide mottled surface of the sea, which seemed to slumber beneath the stars. In the sunless calm all the odors of the earth were spread abroad. A jasmine clambering about the lower windows continually exhaled its penetrating breath, which mingled with the lighter fragrance of the growing leaves. Sluggish breezes passed, bringing the strong savors of the saline air and the sticky moisture of the seaweed.

The young girl at first gave herself up to the pleasure of breathing, and the repose of the fields calmed her like a cool bath. All the animals which awake when evening comes and conceal their obscure existence in the tranquillity of the night filled the half-shadows with a silent agitation.

Large birds, which uttered no cries, fluttered through the air like dark shadows: the humming of invisible insects caressed the ear; silent races were run across the grass, heavy with dew, or the dark surface of the deserted roads. Only the melancholy frogs launched their short and monotonous notes into the air.

It seemed to Jeanne that her heart was swelling, filled with whispers like this tranquil night, feeling suddenly a thousand roving desires, similar to those nocturnal animals whose quiverings surrounded her. An affinity united her to this living poetry: and in the soft whiteness of the night she felt strange shivers run over her, the throbbing of impalpable hopes, something like a breath of happiness.

And she began to dream of love.

Love! For two years it had filled her with the increasing anxiety of its approach. Now she was free to love; she had nothing more to do but to meet *him*. What would he be like? She did not exactly know, and she did not even ask herself the question. It would be *he*, that was all.

She only knew that she would adore *him* with all her soul, and that *he* would cherish her with all *his* strength. They would take walks on evenings like this, beneath the luminous dust that falls from the stars. They would go hand in hand close together, hearing the beating of their hearts, feeling the warmth of their shoulders, mingling their love with the sweet simplicity of the summer nights, so united that by the sole power of their tenderness they would easily penetrate each other's more secret thoughts. And this would continue forever in the serenity of an indescribable affection.

It seemed to her suddenly that she felt *him* there, near her, and a vague, sensual thrill ran over her from head to foot. She pressed her arm against her breast, with an unconscious gesture, as if to clasp her dream, and upon her lips proffered to the unknown there passed something which almost made her swoon, as if the breath of spring had given her a kiss of love.

Suddenly she heard someone walking on the road, in the night, behind the château. And in an impulse of her perturbed soul, a transport of faith in the impossible, in providential chances, in divine presentiments, in the romantic combinations of fate, she thought, "If it were only *he?*" She listened eagerly to the rhythmic step of the approaching person, sure that he was going to stop at the iron gate to ask hospitality. When he had passed, she felt as sad as after some deception. But she understood the madness of her hopes and smiled at her folly.

Then, when she was calmed a little, she let her mind float on the current of more reasonable reveries, seeking to see the future, planning her existence. She would live here with *him* in their quiet château which overlooked the sea. She would doubtless have two children, a son for *him* and a daughter for herself. And she could see them running over the grass between the plane-tree and the lime, while the father and mother followed them with glances of delight, exchanging looks full of passion above their heads.

And she remained a long, long time musing thus, while the moon, completing her voyage across the heavens, was disappearing in the ocean. The air became cooler. Towards the East the horizon grew lighter. A cock crowed on the farm to the right; another answered from the farm on the left. Their hoarse cries seemed to come from very far away through the partition of the poultry houses; and the stars imperceptibly paling disappeared in the immense vault of the sky.

A little cry of a bird rose somewhere. Twitterings, timid at first, came from the leaves; then they grew bolder, became vibrating, joyous, spreading from branch to branch and from tree to tree. Jeanne suddenly perceived herself to be in a ray of light, and raising her head which she had hidden in her hands, she closed her eyes, dazzled by the splendor of the dawn.

A mountain of empurpled clouds, partly concealed beneath the great avenue of poplars, cast their hues of blood upon the awakened earth. And slowly, bursting asunder the gleaming clouds, touching with fire the trees, the plains, the ocean, all the horizon, the great flaming globe appeared.

Jeanne felt herself becoming mad with happiness. A delirious joy, an infinite tenderness before the splendor of things drowned her fluttering heart. It was her sun! Her dawn! The beginning of her life! The rising of her hopes! She stretched her arms towards the shining space, with a desire to embrace the sun; she wanted to speak, to utter something divine, like this opening of the day, but she stood paralyzed in an impotent enthusiasm. Then, resting her forehead on her hands, she felt her eyes filling with tears, and she wept deliciously.

When she raised her head the superb glory of the dawning day had disappeared. She felt soothed, a little weary, as if chilled. Without shutting the window she threw herself upon the bed, mused a few minutes more, and fell into such a profound sleep that she did not hear her father's calls at eight o'clock and only awoke when he came into her room.

He wanted to show her the improvements of the château, of *her* château. The façade which looked onto the estate was separated from the road by a great court planted with apple-trees. This road, called the parish road, running between the fields of the peasants, joined, half a league away, the main road from Havre to Fécamp.

A straight avenue ran from the wooden fence to the steps of the house. The outbuildings, small structures, made of pebbles, roofed with thatch, lined both sides of the court, along the ditches of the two farms.

The covers had been newly done over: all the woodwork had been restored, the walls repaired, the rooms repapered, and all the interior repainted. And on the weather-beaten old manor the new shutters of silver-white and the recent plastering on its great grayish façade stood out prominently. The other façade, in which was one of Jeanne's windows, looked out upon the distant sea, above the grove and the wall of elms beaten with the wind.

Jeanne and the Baron, arm-in-arm, inspected everything, not omitting a corner; they walked slowly through the long avenue of poplars which inclosed what was called the park. The grass had sprouted beneath the trees, spreading its green carpet. The grove at the end was charming, with its crooked little paths, separated by partitions of foliage. A hare suddenly started, and frightened the young girl; then it leaped the embankment and scampered off through the furze towards the cliff.

After breakfast, as Madame Adelaide, still exhausted, declared that she was going to lie down and rest, the Baron proposed to go down to Yport. They started, first passing through the hamlet of Etouvent, in which Les Peuples was situated. Three peasants saluted them as if they had always known them. They entered the sloping woods running down to the sea, as they followed a winding valley. Soon the village of Yport appeared. Women who were mending clothes, seated at the threshold of their homes, watched them pass. The sloping road, with a gutter in the middle and heaps of refuse lying about before the doors, exhaled a strong odor of brine.

The brown nets in which here and there gleaming scales remained, like small coins, were drying before the doors of the houses, whence came the sounds of numerous children swarming in one room. A few pigeons were walking along the edge of the gutter, looking for food.

Jeanne looked at all this, which seemed curious and new to her, like a scene in a theater. But suddenly, as they turned the corner of a wall, she perceived the sea, of a smooth, deep blue, stretching out of sight. They stopped opposite the beach, to look. Some sails were passing in the distance, white as the wings of birds. To the right and left rose the enormous cliff. A sort of cape stopped the view on one side, while on the other side the coastline was indefinitely prolonged until it became nothing but an imperceptible point.

A harbor and some houses appeared at the foot of one of the neighboring inlets; and tiny waves rolled with a light noise upon the shingle, making a fringe of foam upon the water. The boats of the country, hauled upon the slope of round pebbles, lay upon their sides, stretching their round cheeks, varnished with tar, to the sun. Some fishermen were getting them ready for the evening tide. A sailor approached to offer some fish, and Jeanne bought a brill, which she wanted to carry to Les Peuples herself.

Then the man offered his services if they wanted a row, repeating his name time and time again to impress it on their memories: Lastique, Joséphin Lastique. The Baron promised not to forget him, and they took the road back to the château.

As the big fish tired Jeanne, she passed her father's walking-stick through its gills. Each took one end and they went along gaily climbing the hill, chatting like two children, their foreheads to the wind and their eyes shining, while the brill, which gradually fatigued their arms, swept the grass with its fat tail.

II

A charming life of freedom began for Jeanne. She read, dreamed, and wandered about, all alone, in the neighborhood. She loitered along the woods, her mind in a dream; or perhaps she scampered down the crooked little valleys whose two sides bore a carpet of furze like a cloak of gold. Their sweet and fragrant odor, increased by the heat, intoxicated her like a perfumed wine; and to the distant sounds of the waves rolling on the beach, a billow lulled her spirit.

Lassitude occasionally made her stretch herself out on the thick grass of a hillside; and at times, when she suddenly perceived at a turn of the valley, through a grassy funnel, a triangle of blue sea sparkling in the sunshine with a sail on the horizon, there came to her inordinate joys as at the mysterious approach of happiness hovering over her.

A love of solitude seized her in the sweetness of this fresh country and in the calm of the rounded horizons, and she remained so long seated on the hilltops that the little wild rabbits gamboled at her feet.

She often ran along the cliff, caressed by the soft air of the coast, vibrating with an exquisite enjoyment in moving without fatigue, like the fish in the water or the swallows in the air. She sowed memories everywhere as seeds are cast upon the earth, memories whose roots hold till death. It seemed to her that she cast a little of her heart into every fold of these valleys.

She began to go in passionately for bathing. She swam almost out of sight, being strong and sturdy and unconscious of danger. She felt well in this cold, limpid, blue water which bore her up and rocked her to and fro.

When she was far from the shore, she floated on her back, her arms crossed upon her chest, her eyes lost in the profound azure of the sky, which the flight of a swallow quickly cleft, or the white silhouette of a sea-bird. No other sound was heard than the distant murmur of surf on the shingle, and a vague noise of the land still welling beneath the undulations of the waves, but confused and almost imperceptible. And then Jeanne righted herself in the water and, in the distraction of joy, uttered sharp cries as she struck out with both hands.

Sometimes when she ventured too far a boat went out for her. She came back to the château pale with hunger, but light, alert, with a smile on her lips and her eyes beaming with happiness.

The Baron, on his part, planned great agricultural enterprises, he wanted to make trials, to organize progress, to experiment with new implements, to acclimatize foreign varieties; and he spent part of his days in conversation with peasants who shook their heads, incredulous at his attempts. Often also he went to sea with the sailors of Yport. When he had visited the grottoes, the springs, and the rocks of the vicinity, he wanted to fish like a common sailor.

On breezy days when the filled sails made the chubby shells of the boats fly over the waves, and when over each side dragged, almost to the bottom of the sea, the long fleeing lines which schools of mackerel pursued, he held in his hand, which trembled with eagerness, the little line which vibrates as soon as a hooked fish begins to struggle.

By moonlight he would go off to bring in the nets which had been placed the night before. He loved to hear the mast creak, to breathe in the fresh and whistling squalls of the night; and after having tacked a long time, to find the buoys, guiding himself by a peak of rocks, the roof of a belfry, or the Fécamp lighthouse, he delighted to remain motionless beneath the first gleams of the rising sun, which made the slimy backs of the large fan-shaped rays and the fat stomachs of the turbots glisten on the deck of the boat.

At each repast he enthusiastically recounted his expeditions, and the Baronne in her turn told how many times she had walked through the great avenues of poplars, the one on the right, towards Couillard farm, the other one not having sufficient sun.

As she had been recommended to take exercise, she insisted on walking. As soon as the chill of the night had disappeared, she descended, leaning on Rosalie's arm, wrapped in a cloak and two shawls, with her head concealed in a black hood which was covered in addition by a red knitted scarf.

Then dragging her left foot, which was a little heavier, and which had already traced throughout the whole length of the road, one in going and the other in returning, two dusty trails, where the grass was dead, she began unceasingly to journey in a straight line from the angle of the château to the first shrubs of the grove. She had had a bench placed at each end of this track; and every five minutes she stopped, saying to the poor patient maid who assisted her, "Let us sit down, my girl, I am a little tired."

And at each stop she would leave on one of the benches, now the knitted scarf which covered her head, now one shawl and then the other, then the hood, then the cloak; and all this made at both ends of the avenue two big parcels of clothing which Rosalie would carry on her free arm when they came in to breakfast.

And in the afternoon the Baronne began in a more moderate way, with longer rests, even having a nap of an hour from time to time on a reclining-chair which was rolled outdoors for her.

She called this taking "her exercise," as she would say, "my hypertrophy."

A physician, consulted ten years previously, had spoken of hypertrophy because she had suffered from shortness of breath. Since that time this word, of whose significance she had little knowledge, had remained in her head. She obstinately made the Baron, Jeanne, and Rosalie sound her heart, which nobody could feel any more, so deeply was it covered by the adipose tissue of her chest; but she energetically refused to have herself examined by any new physician, for fear that he would discover other diseases. She spoke of "her" hypertrophy on all occasions, and so often that it seemed as if this malady was special to her, and belonged to her as something unique, over which no one else had any right.

The Baron would say, "My wife's hypertrophy" and Jeanne, "Mamma's hypertrophy," as they would have mentioned her dress, her hat, or her umbrella.

She had been very pretty in her youth and as slender as a reed. After having waltzed in the arms of every regiment of the Empire, she had read *Corinne*, which made her cry, and she had remained ever since as if that novel had left its imprint upon her.

As her figure grew stouter her soul had been seized by the most poetical impulses, and when obesity had restricted her to an easy-chair, her thoughts wandered through tender adventures of which she fancied herself the heroine. She had some favorite ones which she always recalled in her reveries, as a music-box, when wound up, interminably repeats the same air. All the languorous novels, in which captives and swallows are mentioned, infallibly filled her eyes with tears: and she liked even certain indecent songs of Béranger on account of the regretful sorrows which they expressed.

She often remained motionless for hours, abstracted in these day-dreams, and her home, Les Peuples, was infinitely pleasing to her because it furnished a frame for the romances of her soul, reminding her by the surrounding woods, by the lonely heaths and by the neighborhood of the ocean, of the books of Sir Walter Scott, which she had been reading for some months.

On rainy days she remained shut up in her room for the purpose of visiting what she called "her relics." These were all her old letters, letters from her father and mother, letters from the Baron when they were engaged, and still others. She had locked them in a mahogany writing-table, with brass spikes at the corners, and she would say in a peculiar voice: "Rosalie, my girl, bring me the drawer with the souvenirs."

The maid would open the writing-table, take out the drawer, and place it on a chair beside her mistress, who began slowly to read these letters one by one, letting a tear fall upon them from time to time.

Jeanne sometimes took the place of Rosalie, and walked with her mother, who told to her the memories of her childhood. The young girl saw herself in the stories of the past, being astonished at the similarity of their thoughts, at the kinship of their desires; for each heart imagines itself the first to have trembled thus beneath a crowd of sensations which have made the hearts of the first beings beat, and will yet make those of the last men and women palpitate.

Their slow pace followed the slowness of the story, which was sometimes interrupted for a few seconds by shortness of breath; and then Jeanne's mind, leaping over the adventures which had been begun, threw itself towards a future filled with joys, and reveled in hopes. One afternoon, as they were resting on a bench, they suddenly perceived at the end of the avenue a stout priest who was coming towards them. He greeted them with a bow while still at a distance, assumed a smiling air, bowed again when he was three feet away, and cried:

"Well, Madame la Baronne, how are we?" It was the village priest.

The Baronne, born in the century of philosophers, brought up by a father who was not very orthodox, in the days of the Revolution, did not often go to church, although she liked priests from a sort of religious instinct which women possess. She had entirely forgotten the Abbé Picot, her priest, and blushed as she saw him. She made excuses for not having anticipated his call, but the good man did not seem at all hurt; he looked at Jeanne, complimented her on her appearance, sat down, placed his three-cornered hat upon his knees, and wiped his brow. He was very stout, very red, and perspired profusely. He drew from his pocket every moment an enormous handkerchief wet with sweat, and passed it over his face and his neck, but hardly was the damp linen replaced in the hidden recesses of his robe when new beads of sweat accumulated on his skin and falling upon his soutane, which his stomach distended, marked the flying dust of the roads in little round spots.

He was jolly, a true country priest, tolerant, garrulous, and kind. He told stories, spoke of the people of the country, and did not seem to notice that his two parishioners had not yet attended service, the Baronne reconciling her indolence with her confused faith, and Jeanne too happy at being freed from the convent, where she had been satiated with pious ceremonies.

The Baron appeared. His pantheistic religion left him indifferent to dogmas. He was friendly with the Abbé, whom he had known for a long time, and kept him to dinner. The priest knew how to make himself agreeable, thanks to that unconscious astuteness which the handling of souls gives to the most mediocre men who are called by the chance of events to exercise a power over their fellows.

The Baronne paid him every attention, attracted perhaps by one of those affinities which draw similar natures together, the ruddy face and short breath of the stout man being pleasing to her puffing obesity.

Towards dessert he became filled with priestly merriment, the gaiety that follows a good meal. And suddenly he cried as if a happy idea had crossed his mind, "I have a new parishioner whom I must introduce to you, Monsieur le Vicomte de Lamare."

The Baronne, who had at the ends of her fingers all the peerage of the province, inquired:

"Is he of the family of Lamare of the Eure?"

The priest replied:

"Yes, Madame, he is the son of the Vicomte Jean de Lamare, who died last year."

Then ·Madame Adelaide, who loved the nobility above everything, asked a lot of questions, and learned that, after paying his father's debts, he had sold the family château and established himself on one of the three farms which he possessed in the commune of Etouvent. These estates represented in all an income of five or six thousand francs; but the Vicomte was economical and prudent and counted on living simply for

wo or three years in the modest cottage in order to
ave enough to cut some figure in society, to marry to
dvantage without contracting debts or mortgaging his
arms.

The priest added, "He is a charming fellow; and so
teady and quiet. But there is not much to amuse him
round here."

The Baron said, "Bring him to see us, Monsieur
'Abbé, that will amuse him from time to time." And
hen they spoke of other things.

When they entered the drawing-room, after having
aken coffee, the priest asked permission to take a stroll
n the garden, as he was in the habit of taking a little
xercise after his meals. The Baron accompanied him.
They slowly walked the length of the white façade of
he château, retracing their steps. Their shadows, one
hin and the other round and wearing a mushroom hat,
:ame and went, now before them, now behind them,
iccording as they walked towards the moon or turned
heir backs upon it. The priest chewed a sort of cigarette
vhich he had taken from his pocket. He explained its
ise with the frankness of country folk:

"This helps to make me belch, because my digestion
s a little slow."

Then suddenly looking at the sky, across which the
:lear moon was traveling, he said, "A man is never,
weary of that spectacle." And he went in to take his
leave of the ladies.

III

The following Sunday the Baronne and Jeanne went
to mass, impelled by a delicate sentiment of deference
for their priest. They waited after the service in order
to invite him for lunch on Thursday. He came out of

the sacristy with a tall elegant young man who held him
familiarly by the arm. As soon as he saw the two ladies
he made a gesture of pleased surprise and cried:

"How fortunate this is! Permit me, Madame la
Baronne and Mademoiselle Jeanne, to present your
neighbor, Monsieur le Vicomte de Lamare."

The Vicomte bowed, spoke of his long desire to make
the acquaintance of the ladies, and began to converse
easily, as a man of society who had seen life. He possessed one of those lucky faces about which women
dream and which are disagreeable to all men. His black
curly hair shaded his smooth and sunburned brow, and
two heavy eyebrows, so regular that they looked artificial, rendered deep and tender his dark eyes, whose
whites seemed a little tinged with blue.

His long and thick eyelashes lent to his glance that
passionate eloquence which creates havoc in the hearts
of haughty society ladies, and makes the girl in a bonnet
carrying a basket in the streets turn around. The languorous charm of those eyes made every one believe in
the depth of his thoughts and gave importance to his
slightest words. A thick beard, glossy and fine, concealed a chin which was a trifle too heavy. They separated after many compliments.

Two days later Monsieur de Lamare made his first
call. He arrived as they were trying a rustic bench,
placed that very morning beneath the tall plane-tree
opposite the drawing-room windows. The Baron wanted
to have another placed under the windows of the limes
to keep it company. The Baronne, who disliked sym-
metry, did not want this. The Vicomte, on being consulted, was of the Baronne's opinion. Then he spoke of
the country, which he declared very picturesque, having discovered many delightful views in his lonely
walks.

From time to time, as if by chance, his eyes met Jeanne's; and she felt a singular sensation at this brusque glance, and quickly turned away from a look in which a caressing admiration and an awakened sympathy appeared.

Monsieur de Lamare's father, who had died the preceding year, had known very well an intimate friend of Monsieur des Cultaux, the Baronne's father: and the discovery of this acquaintance started an endless conversation about family relations and dates. The Baronne accomplished great feats of memory, settling the ancestry and descendants of other families, wandering in the complicated labyrinth of genealogies without ever getting lost.

"Tell me, Vicomte, have you ever heard of the Saunoy family of Varfleur? The oldest son Gontran married a Mademoiselle de Coursil, a Coursil-Courville, and the younger son, one of my cousins, Mademoiselle de la Roche-Aubert, who was related to the Crisange family. Now Monsieur de Crisange was the intimate friend of my father and must also have known yours."

"Yes, Madame. Isn't that the Monsieur de Crisange who emigrated and whose son ruined himself?"

"Precisely. He had asked for the hand of my aunt in marriage after the death of her husband, Comte d'Eretry; but she did not want him because he took snuff. Do you know, by the way, what became of the Viloises? They left Touraine towards 1813, after reverses of fortune, to settle in Auvergne, and I haven't heard of them since."

"I believe, Madame, that the old Marquis was killed by a fall from his horse, leaving one daughter who was married to an Englishman, and another who was married to a certain Bassolle, a rich merchant, who, they say, had seduced her."

And the names learned in childhood, and retained
since then in the conversations of old relations, came
back to her. And the marriages of these families of equal
rank assumed in their minds the importance of great
public events. They spoke of people whom they had
never seen as if they were well acquainted with them;
and the other people, in other districts, spoke of them
in the same way; and they felt acquainted at a distance,
almost friends, almost relations, by the mere fact of belonging to the same class, the same caste, and of being
of equal birth.

The Baron, whose nature was rather rough, and
whose education made him differ from the beliefs and
principles of people of his set, knew little of the families
of the neighborhood. He questioned the Vicomte about
them.

Monsieur de Lamare answered, "Oh, there are not
many of the nobility in the district," in the same tone in
which he would have declared that there were not many
rabbits on the hillsides; and he gave particulars. Only
three families lived within a sufficiently short radius: the
Marquis de Coutelier, a sort of chief of the Norman aristocracy; the Vicomte and Vicomtesse de Briseville, persons of excellent family but keeping themselves rather
isolated; and, finally the Comte de Fourville, a kind of
bogey who was said to be killing his wife with sorrow
and who lived like a huntsman in his château of La
Vrillette, built near a pond. Some parvenus, who associated with each other, had bought estates here and there.
The Vicomte did not know them.

He took his leave, and his last glance was for Jeanne,
as if he addressed to her a special farewell, more cordial
and more tender. The Baronne found him charming,
and above all, very good form. The Baron remarked,
"Yes, certainly, he is a gentleman."

They invited him to dinner the following Sunday. He came quite regularly after that. He generally arrived about four o'clock in the afternoon, joining the Baronne in "her avenue" and offering her his arm to take "her exercise." When Jeanne had not gone out, she supported the Baronne on the other side, and all three walked slowly back and forth from one end of the avenue to the other. He spoke little to the young girl, but his eyes, which seemed of black velvet, often met Jeanne's eyes, which might have been made of blue agate. Very often they both went down to Yport with the Baron.

As they were on the beach one evening, old Lastique approached them, and without taking from his mouth his pipe, the absence of which would have astonished people more than the disappearance of his nose, he said:

"With that wind, Monsieur le Baron, we could easily get to Étretat and back tomorrow."

Jeanne clasped her hands: "Oh! papa, let us do it!" The Baron turned toward Monsieur de Lamare:

"Will you come, Vicomte? We will go and have lunch there." And the excursion was decided upon at once.

Jeanne was up at dawn. She waited for her father, who was slower in dressing, and they started to walk in the dew, crossing first the plain, and then the woods vibrant with the singing of birds. The Vicomte and old Lastique were seated on a capstan.

Two other sailors helped them to make a start. The men, placing their shoulders against the sides of the boat, pushed with all their strength. They advanced with difficulty over the beach. Lastique slipped some guard rollers of wood beneath the keel; then, taking up his position again, uttered in a drawling voice his interminable "Oh, yeo, ho!" intended to regulate the general effort.

But when they came to the slope the boat started, al
of a sudden, and slid down upon the round pebbles with
a great sound like a torn sail. It stopped short at the
foam of the little waves and all took their places on
board; then the two sailors who stayed on shore shoved
the boat off.

A light but steady breeze, blowing from offshore
skimmed and wrinkled the surface of the water. The sail
was hoisted, it bellied a little, and the boat started
gently, hardly rocked by the sea.

They stood off at first. Towards the horizon the pale
blue sky mingled with the ocean. Towards the shore, the
high, steep cliff cast a broad shadow at its foot, and the
sunny slopes of turf indented it at certain spots. Behind
them in the distance the brown sails were leaving the
white pier of Fécamp, and, before them a rock of
strange shape, rounded and flooded with light, looked
like an enormous elephant burying its trunk in the
waves. It was the harbor of Étretat. Jeanne, holding
the weather-board with one hand, a little dizzy with the
rocking of the waves, looked far away; and it seemed to
her that only three things were truly beautiful in creation: light, space, and water.

No one spoke. Old Lastique, who held the tiller and
the sheet, took a nip occasionally from a bottle hidden
under the seat, and unceasingly smoked his stump of a
pipe which seemed inextinguishable. There continually
rose from it a slender thread of blue smoke, while another similar one escaped from the corner of his mouth.
Yet no one ever saw the sailor light his bowl of clay,
blacker than ebony, or fill it with tobacco. Sometimes
he took it in one hand, removed it from his lips, and
from the same corner from whence issued the smoke, he
squirted into the sea a long jet of brown saliva.

The Baron, seated in the bow, looked after the sail,

taking the place of a sailor. Jeanne and the Vicomte sat side by side, both a little embarrassed. An unknown power made their eyes meet when they raised them at the same moment, as if an affinity had impelled them; for there already floated between them that subtle and vague tenderness which springs up so quickly between two young people, when the young man is not ugly and the girl is pretty. They felt happy near each other, perhaps because they were thinking of each other.

The sun was rising as if to view from a higher plane the vast sea stretched beneath it. But the sea was coquettish and clothed herself in a light mist which veiled her from its rays. It was a transparent fog, very low and golden, which did not really conceal anything, but rendered the distance softer. The orb darted its flames to melt this shining cloud; when it was in all its strength the vapor evaporated, disappeared, and the ocean, smooth as a mirror, began to glisten in the light.

Jeanne murmured with emotion: "How beautiful it is!" The Vicomte assented. The serene brilliancy of the morning awakened an echo in their hearts.

Suddenly they saw the great arches of Étretat like two legs of the cliff standing in the sea, high enough for vessels to pass under them; while a point of rock, white and sharp, rose in front of the first arch. They reached the shore, and while the Baron, getting out first, held the boat to the bank by its painter, the Vicomte took Jeanne in his arms in order to put her ashore without letting her wet her feet. Then they went up the shingle beach, side by side, both moved by this close entwining, and they suddenly overheard old Lastique say to the Baron:

"It is my opinion that they would make a fine couple."

The breakfast in a little inn near the beach was charming, and while the ocean had lulled their thoughts and their tongues and had made them silent, the break-fast table made them as talkative and garrulous as schoolboys on a holiday. The simplest things gave them endless merriment.

Old Lastique, seating himself at the table, carefully hid his lighted pipe in his cap; and they laughed at that. A fly, attracted no doubt by his red nose, kept alighting on it; and when he brushed it off, with a hand too slow to catch it, it would post itself on a muslin curtain, which many of its fellows had already specked, and seemed carefully to watch the sailor's highly colored proboscis, for it would soon again fly back to it.

At each of the flights of this insect they shouted with laughter; and when the old man, bothered by this tick-ling, muttered, "It is damned persistent," Jeanne and the Vicomte laughed till the tears came into their eyes, stifling their outbursts with their napkins.

When coffee had been served, Jeanne said, "Let us take a little walk?"

The Vicomte rose, but the Baron preferred to bask in the sun on the beach. "Go on, my children, you will find me here in an hour."

They passed in a straight line the few cottages of the place; and after going beyond a little château, which resembled a big farmhouse, they found themselves in an open valley before them.

The motion of the sea had wearied them, disturbing their ordinary equilibrium, the strong saline air made them hungry, then the food had appeased them, and the merriment had weakened them. They now had a wild longing to run madly through the fields, and Jeanne felt a humming in her ears; she was full of emo-tion from so many new and rapidly changing sensations.

A scorching sun was shining on them. On both sides of the road the ripened harvest bent under the heat.

The locusts were calling, numerous as the blades of grass, uttering everywhere in the wheat, in the rye, in the furze of the slopes, their thin, shrill cry.

No other voice was heard beneath the torrid sky, of a glittering blue, shading to yellow, as if it were about to turn red, after the manner of metals too near a fire.

Having observed a little grove further on, towards the right, they went to it. Inclosed between two slopes a narrow path stretched beneath tall trees impenetrable to the sun. A kind of moist freshness in the air was perceptible, that dampness which makes the skin shiver and penetrates the lungs. The grass had disappeared for want of sunlight, and the ground was carpeted with moss.

"Come, we can sit down there a little while," said Jeanne. Two old trees had died, and taking advantage of the opening made in the foliage a flood of light descended there, warmed the earth, awakened the germs of the grass, of the dandelions and the convolvuli, made the little white flowers, fine as a mist, bloom, and the foxgloves abound. Butterflies, bees, innumerable hornets, gnats which resembled the skeletons of flies, a thousand flying insects, some red and spotted, some of greenish hues, others black, with horns, peopled this hot and luminous recess, hidden in the cold shadows of the heavy foliage.

They sat down, their heads in the shade and their feet in the sun. They gazed at all this swarming tiny life which a ray of light caused to appear, and Jeanne kept repeating with emotion:

"How delightful it is! How delicious the country seems. There are moments when I would like to be a fly, or a butterfly to hide myself in the flowers."

They spoke of themselves, their habits and tastes, in that low, intimate tone in which confidences are told. He said that he was already disgusted with the world, tired of his futile life; it was always the same thing; there was no truth, no sincerity in it. The world! she would have liked to know it; but she was convinced beforehand that it was not equal to a country life. And the nearer their hearts seemed to be in sympathy, the more ceremoniously they called each other "Monsieur" and "Mademoiselle," the more smiling and simultaneous became their glances, and it seemed to them that a new feeling of benevolence was awakened in them, a wider sympathy, an interest in a thousand things about which they had never concerned themselves.

They went back, but the Baron had set off on foot for the Chambre des Demoiselles, a grotto in a ridge of the cliff, and they waited for him at the inn. He did not appear until five in the evening, after a long walk along the cliffs. They got into the boat. The boat went gently, scarcely seeming to make any headway, the wind blowing from behind with hardly any motion. The breeze came in slow and tepid puffs which filled the sail for a second, then let it flap limply along the mast. The opaque sea appeared dead; and the sun, worn with its labors in following its rounded path, softly approached the horizon. The lulling motion of the ocean made every one silent.

Jeanne finally said, "How I should love to travel!"

The Vicomte replied, "Yes, but it is lonely to travel by yourself; there must be at least two to exchange impressions."

She reflected a moment. "It is true—but I like to walk alone—it is delightful to dream all alone."

He looked at her intently. "Two can dream together," he said.

She lowered her eyes. Was it a hint? Possibly. She gazed at the horizon as if to discover something still further off; then she said slowly, "I should like to go to Italy—and Greece—ah! yes, Greece—and to Corsica; it must be so wild and so beautiful!" But he preferred Switzerland on account of the châlets and the lakes.

"No," she said, "I like new countries, like Corsica, or very old countries full of memories, like Greece. It must be delightful to find the traces of peoples whose history we have known since childhood, and to see places where great things have been accomplished."

The Vicomte, less romantic, declared, "As for me, England attracts me strongly; there is so much to be learned there."

Thus they talked about the universe, discussing the attractions of each country, from the poles to the equator, going into ecstasies over imaginary landscapes and the odd customs of certain peoples like the Chinese and the Laplanders; but they arrived at the conclusion that the most beautiful country in the world was France, with its temperate climate, cool in summer, mild in winter, its rich soil, its green forests, its great calm rivers, and that worship of the fine arts which has existed nowhere else since the great centuries of Athens.

Then they were silent. The sun, sinking lower, seemed to bleed; and a broad luminous track, a dazzling train of light, ran over the water from the horizon to the edge of their boat. The last puffs of wind died away; every ruffle was smoothed and the motionless sail was red. A limitless calm seemed to settle down on space, to spread silence around this conjunction of the elements; while, offering her gleaming bosom, the sea, a monstrous bride, awaited her fiery lover now descending to her. Hastening to his fall, he empurpled her with the desire of their embrace. Now he joined her; and, little by little, she devoured him. Then a fresh breeze seemed to arise; a shiver went over the surface of the water, as if the engulfed orb cast a sigh of satisfaction across the world.

The twilight was short: night fell, with its myriad stars. Old Lastique took the oars: and they all observed that the sea was phosphorescent. Jeanne and the Vicomte, side by side, watched the fitful gleams in the wake of the boat. They thought little, gazing vaguely, breathing in the beauty of the evening with a delicious contentment; and as Jeanne had one hand on the seat a finger of her neighbor touched her, as if by accident; she did not move, surprised, happy, and confused at this slight contact.

When she retired that evening, she felt strangely disturbed and so softened that everything made her wish to cry. She looked at her clock, thought that the little bee on the pendulum was beating like a heart, a friend's heart; that it was aware of her whole life, that it would accompany her joys and sorrows with this lively and regular ticking; and she stopped the gilded insect to imprint a kiss upon its wings. She would have kissed anything, no matter what. She remembered hiding in the bottom of a drawer an old doll of bygone days; she looked for it, found it with the joy a person feels on meeting dear old friends; and pressing it to her heart, she covered its painted cheeks and curly hair with kisses.

And while she held it in her arms she thought: Was *he* really the husband, promised by a thousand secret voices, whom an all-wise Providence had thus thrown across her path? Was he really the being created for her, to whom she would devote her existence? Were they the two predestined beings whose united affections should entwine, indissolubly mingle and engender *love*?

She did not, as yet, feel those tumultuous impulses of her whole being, those mad raptures, those deep stirrings which she thought were passion. It seemed to her, nevertheless, that she was beginning to fall in love, for she felt at times quite weak thinking of him; and she thought of him incessantly. His presence moved her heart; she blushed and grew pale when she met his glance and trembled when she heard his voice.

She slept very little that night. Then, from day to day, the longing for love increased. She consulted herself continually, consulted the daisies, too, and the clouds, and coins tossed in the air. One evening, her father said to her, "Make yourself pretty tomorrow morning."

She asked, "Why, papa?"

He answered, "It is a secret."

And when she came down the next morning, looking fresh in a pretty light dress, she found the drawing-room table covered with boxes of bonbons, and on a chair an enormous bouquet. A wagon entered the court-yard, bearing the inscription, "Lerat, Confectioner, Wedding Breakfasts, Fécamp," and Ludivine and a kitchen-maid were taking out from the back of the wagon big flat baskets which had an appetizing smell.

The Vicomte de Lamare appeared. His trousers were tight and strapped down under his dainty patent-leather boots which showed the smallness of his feet. His long frock-coat, fitted to his figure, was open at the bosom, showing the lace of his ruffle; and a fine neckcloth, with many folds, made him hold high his handsome dark head, with its grave and distinguished bearing. His air was unusual, that air which special dress lends to the most familiar faces. Jeanne, astonished, looked at him as if she had never seen him before; she thought him supremely the gentleman, a grand seigneur from head to foot.

He bowed smilingly, saying, "Well, my little friend, are you ready?"

She stammered, "Why, what is it?"

"You will know presently," said the Baron.

The carriage which was waiting drove up, Madame Adelaide came down from her room in festive attire, on the arm of Rosalie, who seemed so much impressed by Monsieur de Lamare's elegance that the Baron whispered:

"I say, Vicomte, I believe that our maid admires you." The Vicomte blushed to his ears, pretended not to have heard, and taking up the huge bouquet, offered it to Jeanne. She took it, more astonished than ever.

All four got into the carriage and the cook Ludivine, who brought the Baronne a cup of cold broth to sustain her strength, declared, "Truly, Madame, one would say it was a wedding."

They alighted from the carriage as they entered Yport, and as they advanced through the village, the sailors in their new clothes, the creases still showing, left their houses, bowed, shook hands with the Baron, and followed as if it were a procession. The Vicomte had offered Jeanne his arm and walked with her at the head.

When they arrived in front of the church, they stopped, and the great silver cross appeared, held straight by an acolyte preceding another boy in red and white, who carried the holy-water urn in which the sprinkler was dipping.

Then three old choristers passed, one of them limping, then the serpent, then the curé, wearing upon his fat stomach his gold-embroidered stole with its cross. He said good morning with a smile and a nod; then, with his eyes half closed, his lips moving in prayer, his biretta pulled down nearly to his nose, he followed his surpliced bodyguard towards the sea.

On the shore there was a crowd waiting around a new boat, wreathed with flowers. Its mast, sail, and rigging were covered with long streamers flapping in the breeze, and the name "Jeanne" appeared on the stern in gold letters.

Old Lastique, master of this boat built with the Baron's money, advanced to meet the procession. All the men, with one accord, took off their hats; and a row of pious women, clad in large black cloaks falling in great folds from their shoulders, knelt in a circle at the sight of the Cross.

The curé, between the two acolytes, stood at one end of the boat, while, at the other end, the three old cantors in their soiled white surplices, with stubby chins, a serious air, and their eyes on their book of chants, sang out of tune at the top of their lungs in the bright morning. Each time they stopped to take breath, the serpent continued its bellowing alone, and as he puffed out his cheeks the musician's little gray eyes disappeared, and the skin of his forehead and neck seemed to distend.

The still and transparent sea appeared to be taking part in the baptism of the boat, hardly moving, with a slight sound as of a rake scratching the shingle, its tiny waves a finger high. And the big white seagulls with widespread wings circled about in the blue heavens, flying off and returning in a curve above the heads of the kneeling crowd, as if they too desired to see what was going on.

But the chanting ceased after an Amen howled for five minutes; and the priest in an unctuous voice murmured some Latin words of which only the sonorous terminations were distinguishable. He next walked round the boat, sprinkling it with holy water, then he began to mutter the *Oremus*, standing alongside the boat opposite the sponsors, who stood motionless, hand in hand.

The Vicomte had his usual grave expression on his handsome face, but the young girl, choked by a sudden emotion, faltering, began to tremble so violently that her teeth chattered. The dream that had haunted her for some time had just taken the appearance of a reality, as if in a kind of hallucination. They had spoken of a wedding, a priest was there, surpliced men were chanting prayers; was she not being married? Did her fingers send out an electric shock, did the emotion of her heart run through her veins until it reached the heart of her companion? Did he understand, did he guess—was he, like her, seized with a sort of intoxication of love? Or else, did he know by experience that no woman could resist him?

She suddenly noticed that he was squeezing her hand, gently at first, then tighter and tighter, almost enough to break it. And without moving a muscle of his face, without anybody's perceiving it he said, yes, he certainly said, and very distinctly, "Oh, Jeanne, if you were willing, this might be our betrothal!" She bowed her head very slowly, which perhaps signified "Yes." And the priest, who was still sprinkling holy water, scattered several drops upon their fingers.

The ceremony was over. The women rose. The return was a stampede. The Cross, in the hands of the acolyte, had lost its dignity; it quickly vanished, oscillating from right to left, or perhaps dipping forward, ready to fall on anyone's nose. The priest, who no longer prayed, was hurrying behind; the cantors and the musician with the serpent had disappeared down a side-street the more quickly to doff their vestments, and the sailors hastened away in groups. The same thought, which filled their heads like the smell of a kitchen, lengthened their legs and made their mouths water. A good luncheon awaited them at Les Peuples.

The large table was spread in the courtyard under the apple-trees. Sixty people sat down; sailors and peasants.

The Baronne, in the center, had the two priests at her sides, the one from Yport and the one from the village. The Baron, opposite, was flanked by the mayor and his wife, the latter a thin countrywoman already old, who kept smiling and bowing to all around her. She had a narrow face, squeezed into her big Normandy cap, a veritable hen's head with a white crest and round eyes perpetually astonished. She ate with quick little bites as if she were pecking her plate with her nose.

Jeanne seated beside her sponsor was swimming in happiness. She saw nothing, knew nothing, and remained silent, bewildered with joy.

She asked him, "What is your Christian name?"

"Julien," he replied; "did you not know?"

But she did not reply, thinking, "How often I shall repeat that name!"

When the meal was finished they left the courtyard to the sailors and went to the other side of the château. The Baronne began to take her exercise leaning on the Baron, escorted by the two priests. Jeanne and Julien went to the wood and walked along one of the mossy paths; suddenly he seized her hands:

"Tell me," said he, "will you be my wife?"

She again bowed her head; and as he stammered, "Answer, I beg of you!" she raised her eyes towards him, very gently, and he read his answer there.

IV

The Baron came into Jeanne's room one morning before she was up, and sitting down at the foot of the bed, said:

"Monsieur le Vicomte de Lamare has asked us for your hand." She wanted to hide her face under the bedclothes.

Her father continued, "We have postponed our answer for the present." She gasped, choking with emotion.

At the end of a minute the Baron, who was smiling, added:

"We did not wish to do anything without speaking to you about it. Your mother and I are not opposed to this marriage, but nevertheless we do not want to urge you to it. You are very much richer than he is, but when the happiness of a life is concerned, we should not think too much about money. He has no relations left, so that if you marry him, it would be as if a son came into our family, while with another, it would be you, our daughter, who would go among strangers. The young man pleases us. Do you like him?"

She stammered, blushing to the roots of her hair, "I am willing, papa."

And her father, looking deep into her eyes, and still smiling, murmured, "I thought as much, Mademoiselle."

She remained in a sort of intoxication of emotion until evening, not knowing what she was doing, taking one object for another mechanically, her legs wearied without having walked. Towards six o'clock as she was sitting with her mother under the plane-tree, the Vicomte appeared.

Jeanne's heart began beating wildly. The young man approached without seeming disturbed. When he was very near, he took the Baronne's fingers and kissed them; then raising the trembling hand of the young girl, he gave it a long, tender and grateful kiss.

The radiant period of betrothal began. They talked alone in the corner of the drawing-room, or on the slope at the end of the wood before the stretch of wild land. Sometimes they walked in the Baronne's avenue, he speaking of the future, she with her eyes cast down, looking at the dusty footprints of the Baronne.

The thing once decided upon, they wanted to hasten matters. It was therefore agreed that the ceremony should take place in six weeks, on the fifteenth of August; and that the young couple should start at once on their wedding trip. Jeanne, on being consulted about the country she would like to visit, chose Corsica, where they could be more alone than in the Italian cities.

They awaited the moment fixed for their marriage without too great impatience, but wrapped in a delicious tenderness, tasting the exquisite charm of insignificant caresses, of clasped fingers, of passionate glances in which their souls seemed to mingle; and vaguely tormented by the wavering desire for a long embrace.

They decided not to invite anybody to the wedding except Mademoiselle Lison, the Baronne's sister, who lived as a lady boarder in a convent at Versailles. After the death of their father, the Baronne wanted to keep her sister with her; but the old maid, possessed by the idea that she was in everybody's way, that she was useless and troublesome, retired into one of those religious houses which rent apartments to people whose lives are sad and isolated.

She came to spend a month or two with the family from time to time. She was a small woman who spoke little, always retiring, appearing only at mealtime, and going back again to her room, where she remained shut up continually.

She had a placid and aged air, although she was only forty-two, with gentle and sad eyes, and had never counted for anything in the family. When quite little, as she was neither pretty nor naughty she was not much petted, and she stayed in corners, quiet and sweet. She had been neglected ever since. As a young girl nobody noticed her.

She was something like a shadow or a familiar object, a living piece of furniture, which people are accustomed to see every day, but about which they do not trouble themselves.

Her sister, from the habit learned in their home, looked upon her as queer, and quite insignificant. They treated her with an easy familiarity which concealed a sort of good-natured contempt.

She was called Lise, and seemed hurt by this childish and jaunty appellation. When it was clear that she would not marry, they had changed the name Lise to Lison. At Jeanne's birth she had become Aunt Lison, a poor relation, neat, frightfully timid, even with her sister and her brother-in-law, who, for all that, were fond of her, but with a vague sort of affection, made up of indifference, unconscious compassion, and natural benevolence.

Sometimes, when the Baronne was speaking of the far-off things of her youth, she said, in order to fix the date, "That was at the time of Lison's inconsiderate act."

This was never explained further; and that "inconsiderate act" remained shrouded as in a mist. One evening Lise, then twenty years old, had thrown herself into the water without anyone knowing why. Nothing in her life, in her conduct gave a hint of such folly. She had been fished out half dead, and her parents, raising their indignant hands, instead of seeking the mysterious cause of the deed, had contented themselves with speaking of the "inconsiderate act" as they spoke of the accident to the horse "Coco," which had broken his leg a little before this in a rut and had to be killed.

Since then Lise, afterwards Lison, was considered as of a very weak mind. The gentle contempt which she had inspired in her nearest relatives spread slowly through the hearts of all the persons who surrounded her. Little Jeanne herself, with that natural divination of children, paid no attention to her, never went up to kiss her in her bed, nor entered her room. Good Rosalie, who gave the room all the necessary attentions, seemed the only one to know where it was situated.

When Aunt Lison entered the dining-room for breakfast, "the child" went, from force of habit, and put up her forehead to be kissed, and that was all. If anyone wanted to speak to her, a servant was sent to look for her; and when she was not there, no one worried about her, no one ever had the notion of being disturbed at her absence and of saying, "Why, I haven't seen Aunt Lison this morning."

She held no stated place; she was one of those beings who live unknown even to their kindred, as unexplored entities, and whose death makes no gap or void in a house—one of those beings who do not know how to enter into the existence, nor into the habits, nor into the love of those who live beside them. When "Aunt Lison" was uttered, these two words aroused, so to speak, no affection in anyone's mind. It was as if one had said "the coffee-pot" or "the sugar-bowl."

She always walked with quick, silent steps; never made any noise, never ran against anything, seemed to communicate to objects the faculty of making no sound. Her hands seemed to be made of a kind of wadding, she handled everything she touched so lightly and delicately.

Aunt Lison arrived towards the middle of July, quite upset by the idea of this marriage. She brought a lot of presents which, coming from her, were almost unnoticed. On the day after her arrival no one noticed that she was there. But an extraordinary emotion was stirring within her, and she hardly took her eyes off the engaged

couple. She busied herself with the wedding outfit with
a singular energy, a feverish activity, working like a
simple seamstress in her room where no one ever came
to see her.

Every morning she presented the Baronne with handkerchiefs which she had hemmed herself, with towels
on which she had embroidered the crests, asking: "Is
that right, Adelaide?" And the Baronne, while carelessly
examining the object, would reply: "Don't take so much
trouble, my poor Lison." One evening, towards the end
of the month, after a day of sultry heat, the moon rose in
one of those clear warm nights, which disturb, soften,
exalt, and seem to arouse all the secret poetry of our
souls.

The soft breath of the fields entered the quiet drawing-room where the Baronne and her husband were languidly playing cards in the round spot of light which the
lampshade marked upon the table. Aunt Lison, seated
beside them, was knitting; and the young people, leaning at the open window, looked out into the moonlit
garden. The limes and the plane-trees cast their shadows
on the great lawn, which stretched away, pale and
gleaming, as far as the dark wood.

Irresistibly drawn by the tender charm of this night,
by this misty light in which the trees and shrubs were
bathed, Jeanne turned towards her parents and said:

"Father, we are going to take a stroll on the lawn
there, in front of the house."

The Baron replied without stopping his playing, "Go,
my children," and continued the game.

They went out and began to walk slowly over the
moonlit lawn as far as the little wood at the bottom.
Time passed without their thinking of returning. The
Baronne, who was tired, wanted to go up to her room.
"We must call the lovers," she said. The Baron cast a

glance across the big luminous garden where the two
shadows were slowly wandering.

"Leave them alone," he said, "it is so lovely outside.
Lison will wait for them, won't you, Lison?"

The old maid raised her restless eyes and answered
in her timid voice, "Certainly, I will wait for them."

The Baron helped his wife to rise, and, tired himself
by the heat of the day, said, "I am going to bed, too."
And he departed with the Baronne.

Then Aunt Lison rose in her turn and, placing her un-
finished work on the arm of the chair, her wool and her
long needle, she went to lean at the window and gazed
out at the charming night. The engaged pair walked
endlessly across the lawn from the wood to the steps,
from the steps to the wood. They held each other's
hands without speaking, as if they had gone out of
themselves, all mingled with the visible poetry which
was exhaled from the earth.

Jeanne suddenly perceived framed in the window the
silhouette of the old maid outlined by the light of the
lamp behind her. "See," she said, "there is Aunt Lison,
looking at us."

The Vicomte raised his head, and, with the indifferent
voice of one who speaks without thinking, replied:

"Yes, Aunt Lison is looking at us."

And they continued to dream, to walk slowly, to
make love.

But the dew was falling fast, and they shivered a little
from the dampness. "Let us go in," said Jeanne. And
they went in.

As they entered the drawing-room, Aunt Lison had
begun her knitting again; she had her forehead bent
over her work, and her thin fingers trembled a little as
if they had been very tired.

Jeanne approached her.

"Aunt, every one is going to bed now," she said.

The old maid turned away her eyes; they were red as if she had been weeping. The lovers paid no attention to this; but the young man suddenly saw that Jeanne's thin shoes were covered with dew. He was seized with anxiety and tenderly inquired, "Aren't your dear little feet cold?" And suddenly the aunt's fingers were seized with such a trembling that she dropped her work; the ball of yarn rolled away across the floor, and quickly hiding her face in her hands, she began to weep with great convulsive sobs.

The two lovers looked at her in astonishment, without moving. Jeanne quickly fell on her knees, and taking her aunt's hands away from her face, very much upset, asked, "What is the matter, what is the matter, Aunt Lison?"

Then the poor woman, stammering, with her voice full of tears and her body shaken with grief, replied, "It is because he asked you—'Aren't your dear l-l-l-little f-feet c-c-cold?' No one ever said anything like that to me, never—never——"

Jeanne, surprised, touched with pity, nevertheless felt like laughing at the thought of a lover lavishing tenderness on Aunt Lison; and the Vicomte turned aside in order to conceal his mirth. But the aunt suddenly rose, left her yarn on the floor and her knitting on the chair, and went without a light up the dark stairway, groping her way to her room.

Left alone, the two young people gazed at each other, amused and softened. Jeanne murmured, "Poor Aunt!" Julien replied, "She must be a little crazy, this evening." They held each other's hands and could not decide to separate, and gently, very gently, they exchanged their first kiss before the empty chair which Aunt Lison had just left.

They gave no thought the next day to the tears of the old maid. The two weeks which preceded the wedding left Jeanne calm and tranquil enough, as if she were worn out with sweet emotions. She had no time for reflection on the morning of the eventful day. She felt only a great sensation of emptiness throughout her whole body, as if her flesh, her blood, her bones, were all melted together under her skin; and she saw, as she touched various objects, that her fingers trembled a good deal.

She did not regain her self-possession until she was in the chancel of the church during the marriage ceremony.

Married! So she was married! All the things, movements, events, that had occurred since daybreak seemed to her a dream, a real dream. There are moments in which all about us seems changed; even gestures have a new meaning; there are even hours which do not seem in their ordinary place.

She felt bewildered, above all, astonished. The day before, nothing had been altered in her existence; the constant hope of her life was only becoming a little nearer, almost tangible. She had gone to sleep a young girl, she was now a married woman. She had crossed this barrier which seemed to conceal the future with its joys, its happiness of which she had dreamed so long. She felt as though a door had opened in front of her; she was about to enter into the "Hoped-For."

The ceremony was ended. They passed into the almost vacant sacristy; for no one had been invited; then they went out. As they appeared at the door of the church a formidable uproar startled the bride, and made the Baronne scream: it was a salvo of guns fired by the peasants. The firing continued until they reached Les Peuples.

A collation was served for the family, for the priest of the manor and the one from Yport, and for the husband and the witnesses selected from among the principal farmers of the neighborhood. Then a turn was taken in the garden to await dinner. The Baron, the Baronne, Aunt Lison, the Mayor, and the Abbé Picot began to stroll through the mother's avenue, while in the opposite avenue the other priest was reading his breviary and walking with long strides. From the other side of the château was heard the gaiety of the peasants, who were drinking cider beneath the apple-trees. All the country-side in its Sunday best thronged the courtyard. The lads and girls chased each other about.

Jeanne and Julien crossed through the copse, climbed the slope, and, both in silence, began to look at the sea. It was a trifle cool, although it was the middle of August; the north wind was blowing and the great sun blazed mercilessly down from the blue sky.

The young people, in order to find shelter, crossed the heath, turning to the right, wishing to reach the undulating wooded valley which descends towards Yport. As soon as they had gained the coppice no breath of wind touched them, and they left the road to take a narrow path buried in the foliage. There was hardly room for them to walk side by side, and she felt an arm sliding gently about her waist.

She said nothing, her heart quickening, her breath broken. Low branches caressed their heads; they often had to stoop in order to pass. She gathered a leaf; two ladybirds, like two frail little red shells, were hidden beneath it. Then she said, quite innocently, and a little reassured, "Look, a little family."

Julien placed his mouth to her ear and said, "This evening you will be my wife." Although she had learned

many things in her sojourn in the country, she had thus
far thought only of the poetry of love and was surprised.
His wife? Was she not that already?

Then he began to kiss her with little rapid kisses on
the temple and on the neck, where the first tresses began to grow. Startled each time by these masculine
kisses to which she was not accustomed, she instinctively withdrew her head the other way in order to
avoid them, though they delighted her. But they suddenly found themselves at the edge of the wood. She
stopped, embarrassed at being so far from home.

"What would people think? Let us return," she said.

He withdrew his arm from her waist, and, both turning, they faced each other, so near that they felt each
other's breath upon their faces, and they gazed at each
other. They gazed deep into one another's eyes with
that gaze in which two souls seem to blend. They looked
into each other's eyes, into that impenetrable "unknown"
of each other's being; they sought each other in a silent
and prolonged interrogation. What would they be to
one another? What would this life be that they were
about to begin together? What joys, what happiness, or
what disillusions were they preparing for each other in
that long, indissoluble tête-à-tête of marriage? And it
seemed to them as if they had never yet seen each other.

And suddenly Julien, placing his two hands upon his
wife's shoulders, planted full on her mouth a long kiss,
such as she had never received. It descended, that kiss,
and penetrated her very blood and marrow, giving her
such a shock that she wildly pushed Julien away with
both arms, almost falling backward as she did so.

"Let us go away from here, let us go away from
here," she faltered.

He did not reply, but he took her hands and held

them in his own. They did not exchange a word until
they reached the house. The rest of the afternoon
seemed long.

All gathered at the table at nightfall. The dinner was
simple and did not last long, contrary to Norman
custom. A sort of embarrassment paralyzed the guests.
Only the two priests, the mayor, and the four farmers
showed a little of that heavy gaiety which generally ac-
companies weddings. Apparently they had forgotten
how to laugh, when a remark of the mayor's woke them
up.

It was about nine o'clock; they were about to take
coffee. Outside, beneath the apple-trees of the first
courtyard, the *bal champêtre* was beginning. Through
the open window they could see the festivity. Lanterns
hung on the branches gave the leaves tints of verdigris.
Rustic dancers swung round, singing a wild air which
two violins and a clarinet feebly accompanied, mounted
on a large kitchen-table used as a platform. The boisterous singing of the peasants at times entirely drowned
the sound of the instruments; and the slender sound,
torn by the unrestrained voices, seemed to fall from the
air in shreds, in little fragments of scattered notes.

Two big casks surrounded by flaming torches furnished drink for the crowd. Two servants did nothing
but rinse glasses and bowls in a tub, to hold them, still
dripping with water, under the taps from which flowed
a stream of red wine or of golden cider. And the
dancers, the thirsty dancers, the older ones tranquil, the
girls perspiring, crowded around, stretching out their
arms to seize in their turn any glass that came, throwing
back their heads, and tossing down their throats the
liquid which they preferred.

On a table there were bread, butter, cheese, and

sausage. Everyone took a bite from time to time, and beneath the roof of illuminated leaves, this healthy and boisterous fête gave the bored guests in the dining-room the desire to dance also and to drink from those big barrels, while they munched a slice of bread and butter with a raw onion.

The mayor, who was keeping time with his knife, cried:

"By Jove, that is fun; it is like the wedding of Ganache."

There was a murmur of subdued laughter. But the Abbé Picot, the natural enemy of civil authority, replied, "You mean the marriage at Cana." The other did not accept the correction.

"No, Monsieur le curé, I mean what I say. When I say Ganache, I mean Ganache."

They rose and passed into the drawing-room. Then they mingled a little with the merry crowd, and soon the guests took their leave.

The Baron and Baronne quarreled in whispers. Madame Adelaide, more breathless than ever, appeared to refuse what her husband asked; finally she said, "No, my dear, I cannot. I would not know how to go about it."

The father, then, abruptly left her, and approached Jeanne: "Will you take a walk with me, my child?" he asked.

She answered, very much moved:

"If you like, papa." They went out.

As soon as they were outside, on the side towards the sea, they felt the sharp wind—one of the cold breezes of summer which already foretell autumn. Clouds were scudding through the sky, now veiling, now revealing the stars. The Baron pressed his daughter's arm against him, tenderly clasping her hand. They walked for a few minutes. He seemed undecided, disturbed. Finally he made up his mind.

"Darling, I am going to perform a difficult task, which really should fall to your mother. But as she refuses to do it, I must take her place. I am not sure of what you know of the things of life. There are mysteries which are carefully hidden from children, from girls especially, who must be kept pure in mind, irreproachably pure, up to the time when we place them in the arms of the man who is to care for their happiness. It belongs to him to lift that veil thrown over the sweet secret of life. But if no hint has been given to them, they are sometimes shocked by the somewhat brutal reality hidden behind their dreams. Hurt in their soul, hurt even in their body, they refuse their husband that which is accorded to him as an absolute right by both human and natural laws. I cannot tell you more, my darling; but do not forget that you belong wholly to your husband."

What did she know exactly? What did she guess? She began to tremble, she felt low-spirited, overcome by a painful presentiment. They went back into the house. What they saw made them stop at the drawing-room door. Madame Adelaide was sobbing on Julien's shoulder. Her noisy tears, as if blown out by a pair of bellows, seemed to come at the same time from her nose, mouth, and eyes; and the young man, amazed, was awkwardly supporting the huge woman who had thrown herself into his arms to implore him to cherish her beloved, her darling, her adored daughter.

The Baron hastened forward.

"Oh, no scenes, please; no heroics, I beg of you"; and taking his wife, made her sit down in an armchair, while she wiped away her tears. He then turned towards Jeanne.

"Now then, my dear, kiss your mother and go to bed."

Ready to cry too, she quickly kissed her parents and fled. Aunt Lison had already retired to her room.

The Baron and his wife were left alone with Julien. All three felt very awkward and could think of nothing to say; the two men in evening-dress remained standing, with averted eyes, and Madame Adelaide leant back in her armchair still shaken by sobs. The embarrassment becoming unbearable, the Baron began to speak of the trip which the young people were to take in a few days.

Jeanne, in her room, was being undressed by Rosalie, who wept like a fountain; her trembling hands could not find hooks or pins, and she seemed assuredly much more moved than her mistress. But Jeanne did not pay any attention to her maid's tears; it seemed to her that she had entered another world, had gone upon another earth, separated from all that she had known and loved. Everything in her life and thoughts seemed turned upside down, even this strange idea came to her: Did she love her husband? He suddenly seemed to her like a stranger whom she hardly knew. Three months before, she did not know that he existed, and now she was his wife. Why was this? Did people plunge into marriage as into a hole open under your feet?

When she was in her night-dress, she slipped into bed; and the cold sheets made her shiver, increasing that sensation of cold, sadness, and loneliness which had weighed upon her soul for two hours. Rosalie went away, still sobbing, and Jeanne waited. She waited, anxious, her heart oppressed, for that certain something, divined and announced in confused terms by her father, that mysterious revelation of the great secret of love.

Without her having heard anyone come up the stairs, there were three soft knocks on her door. She started

violently and did not answer. There was another knock
and then the door-handle was turned. She hid her head
under the covers as if a thief had entered the room.
Footsteps sounded softly upon the floor, and suddenly
someone touched her bed. She gave a start and uttered
a little cry, and uncovering her head, she saw Julien
standing before her, smiling as he looked at her.

"Oh! how you frightened me!" she said.

"Did you not expect me then?" he asked.

She did not reply. He was in evening-dress, with his
grave, handsome face, and she felt horribly ashamed to
be in bed thus before this man, so formally dressed.
They did not know what to say, or what to do, not
daring even to look at each other, at this serious and
decisive hour on which the intimate happiness of their
whole lives depended.

He felt vaguely perhaps, what danger this battle
offered, and what a supple self-possession and what
artful tenderness were necessary, not to offend any of
the subtle modesties, the infinite delicacies of a virginal
soul nourished on dreams. Then, very gently he took her
hand and kissed it, and kneeling at the bedside, as at an
altar, he murmured in a voice as light as a breath,
"Won't you love me?" Suddenly reassured, she raised
her head upon the pillow among the lace, and smiled.
"I love you already, dear."

He put his wife's fine little fingers in his mouth, and,
in a voice muffled by the act, he said, "Will you prove
to me that you love me?"

She answered, troubled anew, without exactly understanding what she was saying, remembering the words
of her father: "I am yours, dear." He covered her wrist
with warm kisses, and raising himself slowly, he drew
near to her face, which she began to conceal again.

Suddenly throwing one arm forward across the bed, he clasped his wife through the covers, while, slipping his other arm under the pillow, he raised it with her head, and very softly asked, "Then you will make a little place for me beside you?"

She was filled with an instinctive fear and stammered, "Oh, not yet, please."

He seemed disappointed, a little ruffled, and he rejoined in a tone still suppliant, but a little more brusque, "Why later, since it must be?" She was angry with him for saying that; but, submissive and resigned, she repeated for the second time, "I am yours, dear."

Then he disappeared suddenly into the dressing-room; and she distinctly heard his motions, with the rustling of garments being taken off, a sound of coins in his pocket, the successive falling of his shoes.

And suddenly, in his underwear and socks, he quickly crossed the floor to place his watch on the mantelpiece. Then he returned, running, to the small adjoining room, moved about a little while longer, and Jeanne turned rapidly to the other side, shutting her eyes, when she felt that he was coming. She made a movement as if to throw herself on the floor, but there quickly glided against her leg another leg, cold and hairy; and, her face in her hands, bewildered, ready to cry out with fear and terror, she cowered to the back of the bed.

Then he clasped her in his arms, although she turned her back upon him, and he voraciously kissed her neck, the floating laces of her night-cap, and the embroidered collar of her night-dress. She did not move, stiffened with a horrible anxiety, feeling a strong hand seeking for her bosom hidden between her elbows. She gasped, overwhelmed by this brutal touch; and she desired, more than ever, to escape, to run through the house, to shut herself up somewhere far from this man. He no longer stirred. She felt his warmth on her back.

Then her fright was again allayed, and she suddenly thought that she would only have to turn and embrace him.

Finally he seemed to grow impatient, and, in a grieved voice, he said, "Then you won't be my little wife?"

She murmured through her fingers, "Am I not that now?"

He answered with a shade of bad humor, "No, my dear, come, do not make fun of me."

She felt moved by the discontent in his voice, and she suddenly turned towards him to ask his forgiveness. He madly clasped her in his arms, as if starving for her, and he covered with rapid, biting, frantic kisses her whole face and the top of her throat, smothering her with caresses. She had opened her hands and remained inert under his efforts, no longer knowing what she was doing, or what he was doing, in a bewilderment which prevented her from understanding anything. But she felt a sharp, sudden pain; and she began to groan, twisting in his arms while violently he possessed her.

What happened then? She had little recollection of it for she had lost her head; it seemed to her only that he showered upon her lips a storm of little, grateful kisses. Then he must have spoken to her and she must have answered him. Then he made other attempts, which she resisted with fright, and as she struggled, she felt on his chest that thick hair which she had already felt on his leg, and she recoiled from the shock. Wearied, finally, of soliciting her without success, he remained motionless upon his back.

Then she began to think. She said to herself, despondent to the bottom of her heart, in the disillusion of an intoxication which she had dreamed to be so different, of a dear expectation destroyed, of a dead bliss, "So this is what he calls being his wife!"

And she remained a long while thus, disconsolate, her glances wandering over the tapestries of the wall, over the ancient legend of love which adorned the room.

But as Julien no longer spoke, no longer moved, she slowly turned her face towards him, and perceived that he was asleep. Asleep, with his mouth partly open and a calm countenance. Asleep! She could not believe it, feeling indignant, more outraged by this sleep than by his brutality, treated like a casual stranger.

Could he sleep on such a night? What had passed between them was, then, nothing unusual to him? Oh! she would rather have been struck, treated violently again, bruised with odious caresses until she had lost consciousness. She remained quiet, leaning on her elbow, bending towards him, listening to the light breath passing between his lips, which at times became something like a snore.

Day dawned dull at first, then clear, then pink, then brilliant. Julien opened his eyes, yawned, stretched his arms, looked at his wife, smiled, and asked, "Did you sleep well, darling?"

She perceived that he used the *tu* now, and replied with the more formal *vous*. "Oh, yes. And you?"

He said, "I, oh! very well." And turning towards her, kissed her, and then tranquilly began to talk. He developed plans for their life, with notions of economy, and that word, often recurring, astonished Jeanne. She listened to him without fully seizing the meaning of the words, looked at him, and thought of a thousand things which passed over the surface of her mind.

Eight o'clock struck. "Come, we must get up," said

he, "we should be ridiculous to stay in bed late," and he rose first. When he had finished dressing, he jauntily assisted his wife in all the small details of her toilette, not permitting Rosalie to be summoned.

As they were going out, he stopped her. "You know," said he, "that we may use the *tu* now, between ourselves. But before your parents we had better wait awhile. It will be quite natural when we come back from our wedding journey."

She did not appear except to breakfast. And the day ran on just as ordinarily as if nothing new had happened. There was simply one man the more in the house.

V

Four days later the carriage arrived which was to take them to Marseilles. After the pang of the first night, Jeanne had become accustomed to the contact of Julien, to his kisses, his tender caresses, although her repugnance to their more intimate relations had not decreased. She thought him handsome, she loved him; and again she felt herself happy and gay.

The farewells were brief and without sorrow. The Baronne alone seemed affected; and as the carriage was about to start, she placed a purse, heavy as lead, in her daughter's hand. "It is for your pocket-money as a young wife," she said. Jeanne thrust it into her pocket, and the horses dashed off.

Towards evening Julien said to her, "How much did your mother give you in that purse?" She had thought no more about it, but now she emptied it on her lap. There was a flood of gold, two thousand francs. She clapped her hands. "I will do all sorts of foolish things with it," she said, as she gathered up the money.

After a week's journey, through terrible heat, they

reached Marseilles. The next day the *Roi-Louis*, a little packet which was going to Naples and touching at Ajaccio, took them towards Corsica. Corsica! the maquis, the bandits! the mountains! the birthplace of Napoleon! It seemed to Jeanne that she had left reality, and was entering, wide awake, into a dream. Side by side on the deck of the ship, they watched the cliffs of Provence glide by. The motionless sea, of a deep azure, as if congealed and hardened in the glowing light of the sun, stretched away under an infinite sky of a still deeper, almost exaggerated blue.

"Do you remember our sail in old Lastique's boat?" she said. Instead of answering he gave her a quick kiss on the ear.

The paddles were beating the water, disturbing its heavy slumber; and astern, in a long, foamy trail, a great, faint track where the water frothed like champagne, the straight wake of the boat stretched as far as the eye could reach.

Suddenly, off the bow, only a few fathoms away, an enormous fish, a dolphin, leaped out of the water, plunged back into it head-first, and disappeared. Jeanne, quite frightened, uttered a cry, and threw herself on Julien's breast. Then she began to laugh at her terror, and watched attentively to see if the fish would not reappear. In a few seconds it leaped again, like a great mechanical toy. Then it fell back and sprang again; then there were two, then three, then six, which seemed to gambol around the heavy boat, as an escort to their huge brother, the wooden fish with the iron fins. They passed to the left, returned on the right of the ship, and now all together, now in succession, as in play, or in a gay pursuit, they threw themselves into the air with leaps which described a curve, and then dived back, one after the other.

Jeanne clapped her hands, jumping for joy, delighted at each appearance of these huge and supple swimmers. Her heart bounded with them in a mad and childish pleasure. Suddenly they disappeared. Once or twice they were seen very far off toward the open sea; then they vanished, and Jeanne felt, for a few seconds, sorry at the departure.

Evening came, a calm, radiant evening, full of light, of happy peacefulness. Not a movement in the air or on the water, and the illimitable repose of the ocean and of the sky communicated itself to their drowsy souls in which likewise no emotion stirred.

The great sun sank softly beneath the horizon, towards invisible Africa, Africa, the burning land whose ardors they already seemed to feel; but a sort of cool caress, which yet was not a breeze, lightly touched their faces when the orb had disappeared.

They did not wish to seek their stateroom, where there were all the horrible odors of a steamer; so they both stretched themselves on the deck, side by side, wrapped in their cloaks. Julien went to sleep at once; but Jeanne remained with her eyes open, agitated by the novelty of the journey. The monotonous sound of the paddles lulled her; and she looked above her at the legions of stars, so bright with a sharp light, scintillating and, as it were, moist in the pure sky of the south.

Towards morning, nevertheless, she slumbered. Noises and voices awoke her. The sailors, with their song, were cleaning up the ship. She shook her husband, who was motionless in sleep, and they rose. She drank in with exultation the savor of the salt mist, which penetrated her to the very tips of her fingers. The sea was everywhere. Nevertheless, off the bow, something gray, confused still in the growing dawn, a sort of accumulation of strange, pointed, jagged clouds, seemed to float on the waves. Then it appeared more distinct; the forms were more sharply outlined on the brightening sky; a long line of angular and fantastic mountains rose: it was Corsica, enveloped in a sort of light veil.

The sun rose behind, outlining all the projections of the peaks in black shadows; then all the summits were illumined while the rest of the island remained enshrouded in vapor.

The captain, a little dried-up, sunburned, short, shriveled man, shrunk by the harsh salt winds, appeared upon the deck, and in a voice hoarse with thirty years of command, worn by orders shouted in storms, said to Jeanne, "Do you smell it?"

There was, in fact, a strange and peculiar odor of plants and wild shrubs. The captain resumed:

"It is Corsica which smells like that, Madame; it is her own pretty woman's odor. After twenty years' absence I would recognize it five miles away. I come from there. The great man far away at St. Helena is always speaking, they say, of the odor of his native country. He is of my family." And the captain, raising his hat, saluted Corsica, saluting at the same time, across the ocean, the great imprisoned Emperor, who was of his family. Jeanne was so touched that she almost wept.

Then the sailor stretched his arm toward the horizon. "Les Sanguinaires!" he said. Julien, standing near his wife, held her by the waist, and they both looked far off to discover the indicated point. They finally descried some pyramid-shaped rocks, which the vessel soon rounded in order to enter an immense and tranquil gulf, surrounded by a number of lofty peaks whose lower slopes seemed covered with moss.

The captain pointed out this verdure. "That is the maquis," said he. Accordingly as they advanced, the circle of mountains seemed to close in behind the ship, which slowly sailed in an azure lake so transparent that they could at times see the bottom. Suddenly the city appeared, all white, at the end of the gulf, beside the billows, at the foot of the mountains.

Some little Italian boats were anchored in the harbor. Four or five lighters came prowling about the *Roi-Louis* to seek passengers for the shore. Julien, who was collecting their luggage, asked his wife in a low tone, "It is enough to give the steward twenty sous, isn't it?" For a week he had been asking that same question, and every time it annoyed her. She answered with a little impatience. "When a person is not sure of giving enough, he gives too much."

He continually disputed with the managers and waiters of the hotel, with coachmen, with the sellers of no matter what, and when, by force of quibbling, he had obtained a slight reduction, he said to Jeanne, rubbing his hands, "I don't like to be robbed."

She trembled when bills were presented, sure in advance of the remarks which he would make on each item, humiliated by this haggling, blushing to the roots of her hair under the contemptuous look of the servants who followed her husband with their glances while holding his insufficient tip in the palms of their hands. He had a discussion with the boatman who put them ashore.

The first tree which she saw was a palm! They went to a great empty hotel, at the corner of a big square, and had lunch. When they had finished dessert, just as Jeanne was rising to go for a stroll through the city, Julien, taking her in his arms, murmured tenderly in

her ear, "Suppose we lie down a little while, sweet-
heart?"

She was taken by surprise. "Go to bed? But I am
not tired."

He embraced her. "I need you. Do you understand?
It's two days——!"

She grew purple, abashed, and stammered, "Oh!
Now? But what will people think? How can you ask for
a bedroom in full daylight? Oh! Julien, I beg of you."

But he interrupted her. "I don't care what the hotel
people may say and think. You will see how little that
bothers me." And he rang the bell. She said no more,
her eyes downcast, revolted, nevertheless, in her soul
and in her flesh, by this incessant desire of her husband,
obeying only with disgust, resigned but humiliated,
seeing in this something bestial, degrading, in fine, an
obscenity. Her senses were still sleeping, and her husband treated her now as if she shared his ardors.

When the waiter arrived, Julien asked him to show
them to their room. The man, a true Corsican, hairy to
his eyes, did not understand, saying that the apartment
would be prepared for the night. Julien impatiently explained, "No, now, at once. We are tired from traveling
and we want to rest."

Then a surreptitious grin appeared on his face, and
Jeanne felt she would like to run away. When they
came downstairs again, an hour later, she dared no
longer pass in front of the people whom she met, persuaded that they would laugh and whisper behind her
back. She was angry at heart with Julien for not understanding this, for not having these little modesties, these
delicacies of instinct; and she felt a barrier, a curtain
between them, perceiving for the first time that two
persons never penetrate to each other's soul, each

other's mind, and that, entwined at times but not
mingled, they go through life side by side, the moral
being of each one of us remaining eternally alone
through life.

They stayed for three days in this little town hidden
in its blue gulf, as warm as a furnace behind its screen
of mountains, which never allow the winds to strike it.
Then an itinerary was arranged for their trip, and in
order not to be turned back by any difficult road, they
decided to hire their horses. They engaged, therefore,
two small Corsican stallions with wild eyes, thin and
tireless, and set out one morning at daybreak. A guide,
mounted on a mule, accompanied them and carried the
provisions, for inns are unknown in that wild country.

The road at first followed the gulf, but plunged later
into a shallow valley going towards the great peaks.
Often they crossed torrents which were almost dry: an
appearance of a stream still flowed beneath the stones,
like a slinking animal, and made a timid gurgle.

The uncultivated country seemed all naked. The hillsides were covered with tall grass, yellow at this hot
season. At times they met a mountaineer, either on
foot, or on a small horse, or astride a donkey about the
size of a dog. All carried loaded guns on their shoulders
—old, rusty weapons, but formidable in their hands.

The sharp perfume of the aromatic plants with which
the island is covered seemed to thicken the air; and the
road kept gently ascending amidst the long folds of the
mountains. The summits of pink or blue granite gave
tints of fairyland to the vast landscape; and on the
lower slopes forests of huge chestnut-trees looked like
green bushes, so gigantic are the undulations of the
earth in this country.

Sometimes the guide, pointing towards the steep
heights, would mention a name. Jeanne and Julien

looked, saw nothing, then finally discovered something gray, like a mass of rock fallen from the summit. It was a village, a little hamlet, hanging there, clinging like a bird's nest, almost invisible on the immense mountain.

This long journey at a slow space wearied Jeanne. "Let us canter a little," said she. And she urged her horse. Then, as she did not hear her husband galloping near her, she turned around, and began to laugh heartily at seeing him careering along, pale, holding his horse's mane, and bounding up and down most strangely. His beauty, his face, typical of a "handsome cavalier," made his awkwardness and his fear even more ridiculous. They then began to trot gently.

The road now stretched between two interminable coppices which covered the whole of the slopes like a mantle. This was the maquis, the impenetrable maquis, formed of green oaks, junipers, arbutus, mastic, alatern, heather, laurel, thyme, myrtle, and box, mingling like tresses with entwining clematis, monstrous ferns, honeysuckles, laburnum, rosemary, lavender, and briars, covering the sides of the mountains with a tangled fleece.

They were hungry. The guide rejoined them and conducted them to one of those charming springs so frequent in mountainous countries, a slender thread of water coming from a hole in the rock and flowing in a tiny canal formed by a chestnut-leaf placed there by some passer-by to lead the slight current to the mouth. Jeanne felt so happy that she could hardly restrain herself from uttering cries of joy. They started again, and began to descend, passing round the Gulf of Sagone.

Towards evening they went through Cargese, the Greek village, founded in former times by a colony of fugitives driven from their native land. Tall and lovely girls, with straight backs, long hands, slender figures, singularly graceful, formed a group about a fountain. Julien having greeted them with a "Good evening," they replied in a musical voice in the harmonious language of their abandoned country.

Arriving at Piana, they had to ask for hospitality, as in ancient times and lost regions. Jeanne shivered with pleasure while waiting for the door, at which Julien had knocked, to be opened. Oh! this was indeed traveling with all the unforeseen happenings of unexplored ways. They applied, it so happened, to a young married couple, and were received as the Patriarchs might have received guests sent by God. They slept on a corn mattress, in an old worm-eaten house. All its woodwork was punctured with holes, and threaded by long borer-worms which are devourers of wood. It rustled, seeming to live and breathe.

They departed at sunrise, but soon halted in front of a forest, a true forest of purple granite. It was one of those peaks, columns, or towers, a startling shape modeled by time, the wind, and sea-mist.

Nine hundred feet high, slender, round, twisted, crooked, misshapen, unexpected, fantastic, these surprising rocks appeared to be trees, plants, animals, monuments, men, robed monks, horned devils, huge birds, a collection of monstrosities, a nightmare procession, petrified by the fiat of some whimsical god. Jeanne no longer spoke; her heart was oppressed, and she took Julien's hand, clasping it tightly, overwhelmed with the need of loving, before all this natural beauty.

Suddenly rising out of this chaos, they discovered a new gulf entirely girdled with a blood-colored wall of red granite. These scarlet rocks were reflected in the blue water. Jeanne stammered, "Oh! Julien!" not being able to find other words, softened with admiration, her throat choking; and two tears fell from her eyes. He looked at her astonished, and asked, "What's the matter, pet?"

She wiped her cheeks, smiled, and in a slightly trembling voice, she said, "It is nothing—I am nervous—I don't know—I was affected. I am so happy that the least thing moves my heart."

He did not understand these womanly weaknesses, the shocks felt by these sensitive beings, perturbed by a mere nothing, whom an enthusiasm will move like a catastrophe, whom an impalpable sensation revolutionizes, maddens with joy, or plunges into despair. These tears seemed ridiculous to him, and entirely preoccupied with the dangerous road, he said, "You would do better to watch your horse."

By an almost impassable road they descended to the bottom of this gulf, then turned to the right to climb the somber valley of Ota. But the path proved horrible. Julien proposed trying it on foot. She asked nothing better, delighted to walk and to be alone with him after her recent emotion.

The guide went ahead with the mule and the horses, and they walked on slowly. The mountain opened, cleft from top to bottom. The path buried itself in this breach. It followed the bottom, between two prodigious walls; and a great torrent ran through this crevasse. The air was chill, the granite seemed black, and, far above, one was astonished and bewildered to see a little of the blue sky. A sudden sound made Jeanne start. She raised her eyes: an enormous bird flew from a hole; it was an eagle. Its opened wings seemed to seek the two sides of the shaft and it mounted into the azure and disappeared.

Further on, the crack in the mountain divided: the path climbed between the two ravines in zigzags.

Jeanne, light and sportive, went first, making the pebbles roll under her feet, intrepid, leaning over abysses. He followed her, a little out of breath, keeping his eyes on the ground for fear of a vertigo.

Suddenly the sun inundated them: they felt as if they had just come out of hell. They were thirsty, a damp trail guided them through a chaos of rocks to a tiny little spring running through a hollow stick put there for the use of the goatherds. A carpet of moss covered the soil round about. Jeanne kneeled to drink, and Julien did the same.

As she was enjoying the coolness of the water, he took her waist and tried to steal her place at the end of the little wooden conduit. She resisted. Their lips touched, met, and parted. In the struggle, they seized in turn the slender end of the tube and bit it in order not to let it go. And the thread of cold water, taken and left continually, broke and renewed itself, splashed their faces, necks, clothes, and hands. Little drops like pearls glistened in their hair. And kisses flowed with the stream.

Suddenly love suggested an idea to Jeanne. She filled her mouth with the clear liquid, and, her cheeks swollen like water-bottles, made Julien understand that she wanted to give him a drink from her lips. He held his mouth forward, smiling, his head thrown back, his arms open; and he drank a draught from this fountain of living flesh which filled him with a wild desire. Jeanne leaned upon him with an unwonted tenderness; her heart palpitated, her breasts heaved, her eyes seemed softened, moist with water. She murmured softly, "Julien—I—I love you," and drawing him to her, she lay back and hid her blushing face in her hands. He fell upon her, and embraced her passionately. Her breath was coming in gasps of nervous expectation, and suddenly she gave a cry, thrilled by the lightning stroke of the sensation she craved.

They were a long time in reaching the top of the mountain, she was so breathless and overpowered with lassitude, and it was evening when they reached Evisa and found the house of a relative of their guide, Paoli Palabretti. He was a man of tall figure, a little bent, with the melancholy air of a consumptive. He conducted them to their room, a gloomy room with walls of naked stone, but handsome for a country where all elegance is unknown, and he expressed, in his Corsican dialect—a mixture of French and Italian—his pleasure at receiving them. A clear voice interrupted him, and a small, dark woman, with big black eyes warmed by the sun, with a slender form, her teeth showing from her habit of laughing continually, rushed forward, kissed Jeanne, shook Julien's hand and said, "Good day, Madame; good day, Monsieur; are you well?"

She removed the hats and shawls, doing everything with one arm, for she carried the other in a sling, then she drove everybody out, saying to her husband:

"Take them for a stroll till dinner."

Monsieur Palabretti immediately obeyed, placed himself between the two young people and took them to see the village. He dragged his steps and his words, coughing frequently and repeating every five minutes, "It is the cold air of Val which has affected my lungs."

He guided them by a hidden path under enormous chestnut-trees. Suddenly he stopped, and, with a monotonous accent, said, "It was here that my cousin, Jean Rinaldi, was killed by Mathieu Lori. I was there, quite near Jean, when Mathieu appeared at ten paces from us. 'Jean,' he cried, 'don't go to Albertacce; don't go there, Jean, or I will kill you, I tell you.' I took Jean's arm, and said, 'Don't go there, Jean, he'll do it.' It was on account of a girl whom both were after, Paulina Sinacoupi. But Jean replied, 'I'll go, Mathieu; you can't prevent me.' Then Mathieu lowered his gun, before I could aim mine, and fired. Jean gave a great leap with both feet, like children skipping rope, yes, Monsieur, and fell full length upon me, so that my gun fell from my grasp and rolled as far as that chestnut there. Jean opened his mouth wide but did not speak a word, he was dead."

The young people, stupefied, looked at the tranquil witness of this crime. Jeanne asked, "And the assassin?"

Paoli Palabretti had a long fit of coughing, then he continued, "He reached the mountains. My brother killed him, the next year. You know my brother, Philippi Palabretti, the bandit."

Jeanne shivered, "Your brother a bandit?"

The placid Corsican had a gleam of pride in his eyes. "Yes, Madame, he was a celebrity, he was. He laid low six gendarmes. He was killed with Nicolas Morali, when they were surrounded in Niolo, after a six days' battle, and when they were almost dying with hunger."

Then he added with a resigned air, "It is the way of the country," in the same tone in which he said, "The air of Val is cold." Then they returned for dinner, and the little Corsican woman treated them as if she had known them for twenty years.

But an uneasiness haunted Jeanne. Would she again find in the arms of Julien that strange and impetuous shock of the senses which she had felt on the moss at the fountain? When they were alone in their room she trembled lest she should be still insensible under his kisses. But she was quickly reassured: it was her first night of love.

The next morning, at the hour of starting, she did not like to leave this humble house in which it seemed to her that a new happiness had begun for her. She drew her host's little wife into her room, and while asserting that she would not ask her to accept a present, she insisted that she must be permitted, after her return, to send her from Paris some souvenir, to which she attached an almost superstitious idea.

The young Corsican woman resisted a long while, not wanting to accept anything. Finally she consented. "Well," said she, "you may send me a small pistol, quite a small one."

Jeanne opened her eyes wide. The other added in a low tone, almost in her ear, as a person confides a sweet and intimate secret, "It is to kill my brother-in-law." And smiling she quickly unrolled the bandages which enveloped her unused arm, and showed her round white flesh, pierced quite through with a stiletto, the wound having almost healed, leaving a scar.

"If I had not been as strong as he, he would have killed me. My husband is not jealous, he knows me; and then he is ill, you know, and that calms his blood. Besides, I am an honest woman, Madame; but my brother-in-law believes everything that anyone tells him. He is jealous for my husband, and he will certainly make another attempt. Then if I had the pistol, I should be tranquil, and sure of avenging myself."

Jeanne promised to send her the weapon, kissed her new friend tenderly and continued her journey. The rest of the trip was only a dream, endless embraces and intoxicating kisses. She saw nothing, neither the landscapes, nor the places where she stopped. She saw nothing but Julien.

Then began the childish and charming play of love, the silly, delightful words of affection, the giving of tender names to all the curves and contours of their bodies where their kisses lingered. As Jeanne slept on her right side, her left breast was often exposed in the morning when she awoke. When Julien noticed this, he called that breast "Flirt," and the other "Faithful," because its rosy tip seemed more sensitive to his kisses. The passage between the two was known as "Mother's walk," because he constantly lingered there, and another more secret place was called "the road to Damascus," in memory of the Ota Valley.

On arrival at Bastia, the guide had to be paid. Julien rummaged in his pockets. Finding nothing, he said to Jeanne, "As you are not using your mother's two thousand francs, give them to me to carry for you. They will be safer in my belt; and it will prevent my having to make change." And she handed him the purse.

They reached Leghorn, visited Florence, Genoa, and all the Corniche district. One morning, when the mistral was blowing, they arrived back at Marseilles. Two months had flown since their departure from Les Peuples. It was now the fifteenth of October. Jeanne, affected by the cold wind which seemed to come from far-off Normandy, felt sad. Julien had for some time seemed changed, tired, indifferent: and she was afraid without knowing of what she was afraid.

She delayed their homeward journey four days more, not being able to make up her mind to leave this country of the sun. It seemed to her that she had just reached the acme of happiness.

Finally they started. They were to make in Paris all the purchases for their definite installation at Les Peuples; and Jeanne was anticipating delight at taking home marvels, thanks to her mother's gift; but the first thing of which she thought was the pistol promised to the young Corsican woman of Evisa.

The day after their arrival she said to Julien, "My

dear, will you please give me back mamma's money because I want to make some purchases."

He turned towards her with a displeased expression of face, "How much do you need?"

She was surprised and stammered, "Why, as much as you like."

He replied, "I am going to give you one hundred francs; be careful not to waste it."

She did not know what to say, abashed and confused. Finally she hesitatingly said, "But I gave you that money to——"

He did not let her finish. "Yes, certainly. Whether it be in your pocket or in mine makes no difference, now that we have the same purse. I don't refuse it to you, do I, since I am giving you a hundred francs?"

She took the five twenty-franc pieces without adding a word; but she dared not ask for more, and bought nothing but the pistol.

A week later they started for Les Peuples.

VI

In front of the white fence with brick pillars the family and the servants stood waiting. The post-carriage stopped, and there were long embraces. The Baronne wept. Jeanne, affected, wiped away her tears; her father walked up and down nervously. Then, while the luggage was removed, the journey was described before the drawing-room fire. Words flowed abundantly from Jeanne's lips; and all was told in half an hour, except, perhaps, some little details, forgotten in this rapid recital.

Then the young woman went to open her valises. Rosalie, deeply affected herself, assisted her. When this was finished, when the linen, the dresses, the toilette articles had been put in place, the little maid left her mistress; and Jeanne, a trifle tired, sat down. She wondered what she should do now, seeking an occupation for her mind, an employment for her hands. She had no desire to go down to the drawing-room with her mother who was dozing; and she thought of a walk; but the country seemed so dull that simply from looking at it through the window she felt a weight of melancholy.

Then she realized that she had nothing to do, that she would never again have anything to do. All her youth in the convent had been preoccupied with the future, busy with dreams. The continual agitation of her hopes, at that time, filled her hours without her feeling them pass. Then hardly had she left those austere walls, where her illusions had bloomed, when her expectation of love was immediately realized. The man whom she had hoped for, met, loved, and married in a few weeks, as people marry on these sudden resolves, took her to his arms without permitting her to reflect upon anything.

But now the sweet reality of the first days had become the daily reality, which closed the doors to the undefined hopes, to the charming disquietudes of love. Yes, waiting was finished. There was nothing more to do, neither today nor tomorrow, nor ever. She felt all that vaguely, with disillusion, with a sinking of her dreams. She rose and pressed her forehead to the cold windowpane. Then, after looking for some time at the sky where somber clouds were rolling, she decided to go out.

Were they the same fields, the same grass, the same trees as in the month of May? What had become of the sunny gaiety of the leaves and the green poetry of the lawn where the dandelions flamed, or the poppies bled, or the daisies blossomed, or the fantastic yellow butterflies hovered as if at the end of invisible strings? And that intoxication of the air charged with life, with aromas, and with fecundating atoms, existed no longer.

The avenues, washed by the continual downpour of autumn, stretched away, covered with a thick carpet of dead leaves, beneath the shivering thinness of the almost naked poplars. The slender branches trembled in the wind, still stirring some slight foliage ready to drop into space. And continually, all day long, like an incessant rain sad enough to make one weep, these last leaves, all yellow now, like big golden sous, became detached, turned, whirled, and fell.

She went as far as the grove. It was as sorrowful as the room of a dying man. The green wall which separated and hid the pretty walks was scattered. The entangled shrubs, like a lacework of fine wood, struck their thin branches against each other; and the murmur of fallen and dried leaves, which the breeze stirred, moved, and piled up in heaps, seemed the last sigh of dying agony. Some little birds hopped from place to place looking for a shelter.

Protected, nevertheless, by the thick curtain of elms, placed as an advance-guard against the sea winds, the lime and the plane-tree, still covered with their summer attire, seemed clad, one in red velvet and the other in orange silk, tinted thus by the first cold days according to the nature of their sap.

Jeanne walked up and down the Baronne's avenue with slow steps, along the line of the Couillard farm. Something weighed upon her, like a presentiment of the long weariness of the monotonous life which was beginning for her.

Then she seated herself on the slope where Julien

had for the first time spoken to her of love; and she remained there, musing, almost without thinking, with a pining heart, with a longing to go to sleep in order to forget the sadness of this day.

Suddenly she perceived a seagull, soaring through the sky, borne upon the breeze; and she called to mind that eagle, which she had seen, there in Corsica, in the gloomy vale of Ota. She felt in her heart the sharp shock which is given by the memory of something sweet but forever finished; and she suddenly seemed to see the radiant island with its wild perfume, its sun which ripened the oranges and the citrons, its pink-topped mountains, its azure gulfs and its ravines where torrents rushed.

Then the damp and harsh landscape which surrounded her, with the dismal falling of the leaves and the gray clouds driven before the wind, enveloped her in such a depth of desolation that she went back into the house in order to avoid sobbing outright.

Her mother, torpid before the fireplace, was napping, accustomed to the melancholy of the days, and not feeling it any longer. The Baron and Julien had gone for a walk that they might talk over their affairs. And night came, casting a gloomy shadow through the vast drawing-room, which was lighted by the flickering reflections of the fire. Outside, through the windows, a remnant of daylight still made visible the unkempt landscape of the season, and the grayish sky looked as if it had been rubbed in mud.

The Baron soon appeared, followed by Julien. When he entered the darkened room, he rang, crying, "Quick, quick, some lights! It is gloomy here." And he sat down in front of the fireplace. While his damp feet smoked near the coals, and the mud, dried by the heat, fell from the soles of his boots, he rubbed his hand gaily. "I believe," he said, "that it is going to freeze; the sky is lighting to the north; there is a full moon this evening, and the frost will bite hard tonight."

Then turning towards his daughter, he said, "Well, child, are you contented to be back in your own country, your own house, with the old folk?"

This simple question upset Jeanne. She threw herself into her father's arms, her eyes filled with tears, and kissed him nervously, as if to ask his pardon; for, in spite of the efforts of her heart to be gay, she felt overwhelmed with sadness. She thought of all the joy which she had promised herself on returning to her parents; and she was astonished at this coldness which paralyzed her tenderness. She felt like one who has thought a good deal, while far away, of people beloved—people mixed up with one's daily life—and who feels, upon finding them again, a sort of check on the affections until such time as the bonds of the former common life are renewed.

The dinner was long; there was little conversation. Julien seemed to have forgotten his wife. In the drawing-room, afterwards, she let herself doze by the fire opposite the Baronne, who slept outright. Jeanne, awakened a moment later by the voices of the two men who were engaged in a discussion, wondered, as she tried to rouse her energies, if she also were going to be seized by the dull lethargy of habits which nothing interrupts.

The flames of the fireplace, soft and reddish through the day, became lively, bright, and crackling. They threw sudden gleams on the faded chair-covers, on the fox and the stork, on the melancholy heron, on the grasshopper and the ant.

The Baron drew near, smiling and holding his open hands to the live brands, "Ah, ah! the fire is burning well, this evening. It is freezing, my children." Then he placed his hands on Jeanne's shoulder, and said, pointing at the fire, "You see, daughter, this is the best thing in the world; the home, the hearth with one's own gathered round. Nothing equals that. But it is bedtime; you must be very tired, children."

When Jeanne had gone up to her room, she wondered how two returnings to the same place, which she thought she loved, could be so different. Why did she feel as if bruised? Why should this house, this dear country, all that which up to the present time made her heart thrill, seem today so heartbreaking?

But her glance suddenly fell on the clock. The little bee still swung from left to right, and from right to left, with the same rapid and continuous motion, above the vermilion flowers. Suddenly Jeanne felt an impulse of affection, moved even to tears before this little machine which seemed alive, which sang to her the hour and palpitated like a heart. She certainly had not been so moved in kissing her father and mother. The heart has mysteries which no reasoning can penetrate.

For the first time since her marriage she was alone in bed, Julien, under the pretext of fatigue, having taken another bedroom. It had been arranged, for that matter, that each should have his or her own. She was a long time getting to sleep, astonished at no longer feeling anyone at her side, unaccustomed to sleeping alone and annoyed by the harsh north wind which beat against the roof. She was awakened in the morning by a great light which bathed the foot of her bed. The windowpanes, thick with frost, were reddened as if the whole horizon were on fire.

Wrapping herself in a large dressing-gown, she ran to the window and opened it. An icy breeze, healthful and sharp, made her skin tingle with a piercing cold which brought the tears to her eyes; and in the midst of a purple sky a great sun appeared behind the trees, shining and puffed like the face of a drunken man. The earth, covered with white frost, hard and dry now, creaked beneath the tread of the farm people. In that single night, all the unstripped branches of the poplar-trees had been denuded; and beyond the waste land appeared the great, greenish line of the waves all strewn with white trails.

The plane-tree and the lime were quickly stripped by the blasts. At each passing of the icy wind the clouds of leaves detached by the sudden frost were scattered in the air like a flight of birds. Jeanne dressed herself, went out, and, for something to do, started to see the farmers.

The Martins welcomed the mistress of the house, and kissed her on both cheeks; then they urged her to drink a little glass of cordial, and then she went to the other farm. The Couillards opened their arms to her; the mistress of the house pecked her on the ears, and she had to drink a little glass of black-currant wine. After this she went back to breakfast.

The day passed like the preceding one, cold instead of damp. And the other days of the week resembled these two; and all the weeks of the month resembled the first week. Little by little, however, her longing for far-off countries grew weaker. Habit placed a coating of resignation over her life like the chalky deposit which limestone springs leave upon objects. And a certain interest in the thousand insignificant things of daily existence, a care for the simple and trifling regular occupations, sprang up again in her heart.

There developed in her a species of meditative melancholy, a vague disenchantment with life. What did she require? What did she desire? She knew not. No social ambition possessed her: no thirst for pleasures, no inclination even towards possible joys; what were they,

for that matter? Just as the old armchairs of the drawing-room faded in time, everything gradually lost its
color in her eyes, everything lost its ancient character,
or took on a pale and dull hue.

Her relations with Julien had completely changed.
He seemed quite another person since the return from
their wedding journey, like an actor who has played his
part and reassumes his ordinary character. He hardly
noticed her, or even spoke to her; all trace of love had
suddenly disappeared, and the nights were few when he
entered her room.

He had taken charge of the fortune and of the house,
altered the leases, harassed the peasants, curtailed the
expenses, and, having put on the bearing of a gentleman farmer, had lost the polish and the elegance of the
betrothed young man. He never discarded an old velvet
hunting-coat adorned with brass buttons, which he had
found in his wardrobe, although it was stained with
spots; and influenced by the negligence of those who
have no longer the desire to please, he had ceased to
shave himself, so that his long, badly trimmed beard
disfigured him incredibly. His hands were no longer
cared for; and after each meal he drank four or five
glasses of brandy.

Jeanne having tried tender reproaches, he had answered her so shortly, "Let me alone, won't you?" that
she did not venture any more advice. She had resigned
herself to these changes in a way which astonished herself. He had become a stranger to her, a stranger whose
soul and heart were closed to her. She often thought
about it, wondering how it was that after having thus
met, loved, and married in a glow of tenderness, they
should suddenly find themselves almost as unknown to
each other as if they had never slept side by side.

And how was it that she did not suffer more from his

abandonment? Was life like this? Had they deceived themselves? Was there nothing more for her in the future? If Julien had remained handsome, well-groomed, and seductive as of old, would she perhaps have suffered much more?

It was decided that, after New Year, the newly married couple should be left to themselves, that her father and mother would go to their house in Rouen for a few months. The young people were to spend the winter at Les Peuples so as to become familiar with the surroundings in which they would have to spend their whole life. Besides, they had neighbors, the Brisevilles, the Couteliers, and the Fourvilles, to whom Julien was to introduce his wife. They could not visit them, as they had not yet been able to get the painter to come and change the coat of arms on the family carriage. The old carriage had been ceded by the Baron to his son-in-law and under no consideration would Julien go out in it until the arms of the De Lamares had been quartered with those of the Perthuis des Vauds.

Now there was only one man in the whole province who made a specialty of coats of arms, a painter from Bolbec, named Bataille, who was naturally in great request among all the Normandy aristocracy; so Julien had to wait for some time before he could secure his services.

At last, one December morning just as they were finishing lunch at Les Peuples, they saw a man, with a box on his back, open the gate and come up the path; it was Bataille. He was shown into the dining-room, and lunch was served to him just as if he had been a gentleman, for his constant intercourse with the provincial aristocracy, his knowledge of the coats of arms, their mottoes and signification, made him a sort of herald with whom no gentleman need be ashamed to shake hands.

Pencils and paper were brought, and while Bataille ate his lunch, the Baron and Julien made sketches of their escutcheons with all the quarters. The Baronne, always delighted when anything of this sort was discussed, gave her advice, and even Jeanne took part in the conversation, as if it aroused some interest in her. Bataille, without interrupting his lunch, occasionally gave an opinion, took the pencil to make a sketch of his idea, quoted examples, described all the aristocratic carriages in Normandy, and seemed to scatter an atmosphere of nobility all around him. He was a little man with thin gray hair and paint-daubed hands which smelt of oil. It was said that he had once committed a grave offense against public morality, but the esteem in which he was held by all the titled families had long ago effaced this stain on his character.

As soon as the painter had finished his coffee he was taken to the coach-house and the carriage was uncovered. Bataille looked at it, gave an idea of the size he thought the shield ought to be, and then, after the others had again given their opinions, he began his work. In spite of the cold the Baronne ordered a chair and a foot-warmer to be brought out for her that she might sit and watch the painter. Soon she began to talk to him, asking him about the marriages and births and deaths of which she had not yet heard, and adding these fresh details to the genealogical trees which she already knew by heart. Beside her, astride a chair, sat Julien, smoking a pipe and occasionally spitting on the ground as he watched the painting of his crest.

Old Simon passed on his way to the garden, and he too stopped in to examine the work. The arrival of Bataille having been noised about the two farms, the good wives soon made their appearance and standing on each side of the Baronne, they went into raptures, saying, "It does take a clever man to arrange a thing like that!"

The escutcheons on the two doors could not be completed until about eleven o'clock the next morning. Everybody was present and the carriage was brought outside so that the effect might be better judged. It was perfect. Bataille was complimented and went on his way again, with his box on his back. The Baron, his wife, Jeanne, and Julien all agreed that Bataille was a clever man, and might have become a great artist, if circumstances had been favorable.

By way of economy Julien had effected changes which necessitated certain modifications. The old coachman had become the gardener; Julien having decided to drive himself. He had sold the carriage horses so as not to be obliged to feed them. As someone was needed for the stable, he had made a groom out of Marius, the little cowkeeper. Then, in order to procure horses, he introduced a clause in the lease of the Couillards and Martins, compelling each of them to furnish him with a horse on a certain day of the month designated by him, and in return he exempted them from their tribute of poultry.

The Couillards had brought a great, yellow-haired nag, and the Martins a small white, long-haired animal; the two horses were harnessed, and Marius, buried in an old livery of Simon's, brought the carriage round to the door. Julien, who was spruce, and in tight-fitting clothes, would have looked a little like his old, elegant self, if his long beard had not made him look common. He inspected the horses, the carriage, and the little groom, and thought they looked very well, the only thing of any importance in his eyes being the new coat of arms. The Baronne came downstairs on her husband's arm, got in, and had some cushions put behind her back; then came Jeanne. She laughed first at the strange pair of horses. The white one, she said, was the grandson of the yellow. Her laughter increased when she saw Marius with his face buried under his cockaded hat (which his nose alone prevented from slipping down to his chin) and his hands lost in his ample sleeves, and the skirts of his coat coming right down to his feet, which were encased in enormous boots; but when she saw him obliged to throw his head right back before he could see anything, and raise his knee at each step as though he were going to take a river in his stride, and move like a blind man when he had an order given him, she gave a shout of laughter. The Baron turned round, looked for a moment at the little fellow who stood looking so confused in his big clothes, and then he too was overcome with laughter, and, hardly able to speak, called out to his wife:

"Lo-lo-look at Ma-Marius! Does-doesn't he look fun-funny?"

The Baronne leaned out of the carriage-window, and, catching sight of Marius, she was shaken by such a fit of laughter that the carriage moved up and down on its springs as if it were jolting over some deep ruts.

"What on earth is there to laugh at like that?" said Julien, his face pale with anger. "You must be perfect idiots, all of you."

Jeanne sat down on the steps, holding her sides and quite unable to contain herself; the Baron followed her example, and, inside the carriage, convulsive sneezes and a sort of continual clucking intimated that the Baronne was suffocating with laughter. At last Marius's coat began to shake; no doubt, he understood the cause of all this mirth, and he giggled himself, beneath his big hat. Julien rushed towards him in a rage; he gave him a box on the ear which knocked the boy's hat off and sent it rolling onto the grass; then, turning to the Baron, he said, in a voice that trembled with anger:

"I think you ought to be the last one to laugh. Whose fault is it that you are ruined? We should not be like this if you had not squandered your fortune and thrown away your money right and left."

All the laughter stopped abruptly, but no one spoke. Jeanne, ready to cry now, quietly took her place beside her mother. The Baron, without a word, sat down opposite, and Julien got up on the box, after lifting up the crying boy, whose cheek was beginning to swell. The long drive was performed in silence, for they all felt awkward and unable to converse on ordinary topics. They could only think of the incident that had just happened, and, rather than broach such a painful subject, they preferred to sit in dull silence.

To the irregular trot of the two horses the carriage went along past the farmyards, startling the black fowls and sending them to the hedges for refuge, and sometimes a yelping dog followed for a little while and then ran back to his kennel with bristling hair, turning round every now and then to send another bark after the carriage. A lad in muddy sabots was slouching along with his hands in his pockets, his blouse blown out by the wind and his long lazy legs dragging one after the other, and as he stood on one side for the carriage to pass, he awkwardly pulled off his cap, showing his lank hair plastered down on his head. Between each farm lay meadows, with other farms dotted here and there in the distance. Finally they turned up an avenue of firs which bordered the road. Here the carriage leaned on one side as it passed over the deep ruts, and the Baronne began to give little screams. At the end of the avenue there was a white gate which was shut. Marius jumped down to open it, and then they drove round an immense lawn and drew up before a high, gloomy-looking house which had all its shutters closed.

The hall-door opened, and an old, semi-paralyzed servant (in a red and black striped waistcoat, over which was tied an apron) limped sideways down the steps; after asking the visitors' names he showed them into a large drawing-room, and drew up the closed Venetian blinds. The furniture was all covered up, and the clock and candelabra were enveloped in white cloths; the room smelt moldy, and its damp, cold atmosphere seemed to chill one to the very heart. The visitors sat down and waited. Footsteps could be heard on the floor above, hurrying along in an unusual bustle, for the owners of the house had been taken unawares and were changing their clothes as quickly as possible; a bell rang several times and then they could hear more footsteps on the stairs. The Baronne, feeling thoroughly cold, began to sneeze frequently; Julien walked up and down the room, Jeanne was gloomy and sat by her mother, while the Baron stood scowling with his back against the marble mantelpiece.

At last a door opened, and the Vicomte and Vicomtesse de Briseville appeared. They were a little, thin couple of an uncertain age, of mincing gait, both very formal and rather embarrassed. The Vicomtesse wore a flowered silk gown and a cap trimmed with ribbons, and spoke in a sharp, quick voice. Her husband was in a tight frock-coat; his hair looked as if it had been waxed, and his nose, his eyes, his long teeth and his coat, which was evidently his best one, all shone as if they had been polished with the greatest care. He returned his visitors' bow with a bend of the knees.

When the ordinary complimentary phrases had been exchanged, no one knew what to say next, so they all politely expressed their pleasure at making this new acquaintance and hoped it would be a lasting one; for, living as they did in the country all the year round, an occasional visit made an agreeable change. The icy air of the drawing-room froze the very marrow of their bones, and the Baronne was seized by a fit of coughing, interrupted at intervals by a sneeze. The Baron rose to go.

"You are not going to leave us already? Pray, stay a little longer," said the Brisevilles.

But Jeanne followed her father's example in spite of all the signs made her by Julien, who thought they were leaving too soon. The Vicomtesse would have rung to order the Baron's carriage, but the bell was out of order, so the Vicomte went to find a servant. He soon returned, to say that the horses had been taken out, and put in the stables. They had to wait. Every one tried to find some subject of conversation; the rainy winter was discussed, and Jeanne, who could not prevent herself shivering, try as she would, asked if their hosts did not find it very dull living alone all the year round. Such a question astounded the Brisevilles. Their time was always fully occupied, what with writing long letters to their numerous aristocratic relations and pompously discussing the most trivial matters, for in all their useless, petty occupations, they were as formally polite to each other as they would have been to utter strangers. Beneath the high ceiling, blackened with age, of the huge drawing-room, uninhabited and wrapped in cloths, the old couple, so small, so clean, so formal, looked to Jeanne like preserve of aristocrats. At last the carriage, with its two ill-matched steeds, drew up before the door, but Marius was nowhere to be seen; he had gone for a walk in the fields, thinking he would not be wanted again until the evening. Julien, in a great rage, left word for him to be sent after them on foot, and, after a great many bows and compliments, they started for Les Peuples again.

As soon as they were fairly off, Jeanne and the Baron, in spite of the uncomfortable feeling that Julien's ill-temper had caused, began to laugh and joke about the Brisevilles' ways and tones. The Baron imitated the husband and Jeanne the wife, and the Baronne, feeling a little hurt in her reverence for aristocracy, said to them:

"You should not joke in that way. I'm sure the Brisevilles are very well-bred people, and they belong to excellent families."

They stopped laughing for a time, out of respect for the Baronne's feelings, but every now and then Jeanne would catch her father's eye, and then they began again. The Baron would make a very stiff bow, and say in a solemn voice:

"Your château at Les Peuples must be very cold, Madame, with the sea-breeze blowing on it all day long."

Then Jeanne put on a very prim look, and said with a smirk, moving her head all the time like a duck on the water:

"Oh, Monsieur, I have plenty to fill up my time. You see we have so many relations to whom letters must be written, and M. de Briseville leaves all correspondence to me, as his time is taken up with the religious history of Normandy that he is writing in collaboration with the Abbé Pelle."

The Baronne could not help smiling, but she repeated, in a half-vexed, half-amused tone:

"It isn't right to laugh at people of our own rank like that."

All at once the carriage came to a standstill, and Julien called out to someone on the road behind; Jeanne and the Baron leaned out of the windows, and saw some singular creature, rolling, rather than running, towards them. Hindered by the floating skirts of his coat, unable to see for his hat, which kept slipping over his eyes, his sleeves waving like the sails of a windmill, splashing through the puddles, stumbling over every large stone in his way, hastening, jumping, covered with mud, Marius was running after the carriage as fast as his legs could carry him. As soon as he came up Julien leaned down, caught hold of him by the coat collar, and lifted him up on the box-seat; then, dropping the reins, he began to pommel the boy's hat, which at once slipped down to his shoulders. Inside the hat, which sounded as if it had been a drum, Marius yelled at the top of his voice, but it was in vain that he struggled and tried to jump down, for his master held him firmly with one hand while he beat him with the other.

"Papa! oh, papa!" gasped Jeanne; and the Baronne, filled with indignation, seized her husband's arm, and exclaimed, "Stop him, Jacques, stop him!" The Baron suddenly let down the front window, and, catching hold of the Vicomte's sleeve:

"Are you going to stop beating that child?" he said in a voice that trembled with anger.

Julien turned round in astonishment.

"But don't you see what a state the little wretch has got his livery into?"

"What does that matter to me?" exclaimed the Baron, with his head between the two. "You shall not be so rough with him."

Julien got angry.

"Kindly leave me alone," he said; "it's nothing to do with you"; and he raised his hand to strike the lad again.

The Baron caught hold of his son-in-law's wrist, and flung his uplifted hand heavily down against the wood-work of the seat, crying:

"If you don't stop that, I'll get out and soon make you."

He spoke in so determined a tone that the Vicomte's rage suddenly vanished, and, shrugging his shoulders, he whipped up the horses, and the carriage moved on again. The two women sat still, pale with fright, and the beating of the Baronne's heart could be distinctly heard. At dinner that evening Julien was more agreeable than usual, and behaved as if nothing had happened. Jeanne, her father, and Madame Adelaide easily forgave, and, touched by his good temper, they joined in his gaiety with a feeling of relief. When Jeanne mentioned the Brisevilles, her husband even made a joke about them, though he quickly added:

"But one can see at once that they are gentlefolk."

No more visits were paid, as everyone dreaded any reference to Marius, but they were going to send cards to their neighbors on New Year's day, and then wait to call on them until the first warm days of spring.

Christmas came, and the priest, the mayor, and his wife came to dinner. They were invited again on New Year's day, and their two visits formed the only break in the monotonous days. The Baron and Baronne were to leave Les Peuples on the ninth of January; Jeanne wanted them to stay longer, but Julien did not second her invitation, so in view of his son-in-law's increasing coldness the Baron ordered the post-chaise to be sent from Rouen. The evening before they went away was clear and frosty, and as they had finished packing, Jeanne and her father walked down to Yport, for they had not been there since Jeanne's return from Corsica.

They went across the wood where she had walked on her wedding-day, clinging close to him whose companion she was henceforth to be, where she had received his first kiss, and had caught her first glimpse of that sensual love which was not fully revealed to her till that day in the valley of Ota when she had drunk her husband's kisses with the water.

There were no leaves, no climbing plants, in the copse now, only the rustling of the branches, and that dry, crackling noise that seems to fill the bare woods in winter.

They reached the little village and went along the empty, silent streets, which smelt of fish and of seaweed. The big brown nets were drying before the doors, or stretched out on the shingle as of old. The cold, gray sea, with its eternal roar of foam, was receding, and in the direction of Fécamp the green rocks at the foot of the cliff could be seen. And all along the beach the big boats lay on their sides looking like huge dead fish.

As night drew on, the fishermen, walking heavily in their big sea-boots, began to come down on the shingle in groups, their necks well wrapped up in woolen scarfs, and carrying a liter of brandy in one hand, and the boat-lantern in the other. They busied themselves round the boats, putting on board, with true Normandy slowness, their nets, their buoys, a big loaf, a jar of butter, and the bottle of brandy and a glass. Then they pushed off the boats, which went down the beach with a harsh noise, then rushed through the surf, balanced themselves on the crest of a wave for a few seconds, spread their brown wings and disappeared into the night, with their little lights shining at the bottom of the masts. The sailors' wives, their big bony frames shown off by their thin dresses, stayed until the last fisherman had gone off, and then went back to the hushed village, where their noisy voices roused the sleeping echoes of the gloomy streets.

The Baron and Jeanne stood watching these men go off into the darkness, as they went off every night, risking their lives to keep themselves from starving, and yet gaining so little that they could never afford to eat meat.

"What a terrible, beautiful thing is the ocean!" said the Baron. "How many lives are at this very moment in danger on it, and yet how exquisite it looks now, with the shadows falling over it! Doesn't it, Jeannette?"

"This is not so pretty as the Mediterranean," she answered with a weak smile.

"The Mediterranean!" exclaimed her father scornfully. "Why, the Mediterranean's nothing but oil or sugared water, the blue water of a washtub, while this sea is terrific with its crests of foam and its wild waves. And think of those men who have just gone off on it, and who are already out of sight."

Jeanne gave in.

"Yes, perhaps you are right," she said with a sigh, for the word "Mediterranean" had sent a pang through her heart, and turned her thoughts to those faraway countries where all her dreams lay buried.

Father and daughter did not go back through the wood, but walked along the road, going slowly uphill; they walked in silence, for both were saddened by the thought of the morrow's parting. As they passed the farmhouses, they could smell the crushed apples—that scent of new cider which pervades all Normandy at this time of the year—or the strong odor of cows and the healthy, warm smell of a dunghill. The dwelling-houses could be distinguished by their little lighted windows.

It seemed to Jeanne that her soul was expanding, that

she was understanding invisible things, and these tiny lights, scattered over the country, made her think of the loneliness of human creatures, and how everything tends to separate and tear them away from those they love.

"Life is not always gay," she said in tones of resignation.

The Baron sighed.

"That is true, my child," he replied; "but we cannot help it."

The next day the Baron and Baronne went away, leaving Jeanne and Julien alone.

VII

Cards now became part of the young couple's existence. Every day after lunch Jeanne played several games of bezique with her husband, while he smoked his pipe and drank six or eight glasses of brandy. Then Jeanne went upstairs to her bedroom, and, sitting by the window, worked at a petticoat flounce she was embroidering, while the wind and rain beat against the panes. When tired she looked out at the foamy, restless sea, gazed at it for a few minutes, and then took up her work again.

She had nothing else to do, for Julien had taken the entire management of the house into his hands, that he might thoroughly satisfy his longing for authority and his mania for economy. He was exceedingly stingy; he never gave tips, never allowed any food that was not strictly necessary. Every morning, ever since she had been at Les Peuples, the baker had made Jeanne a little Normandy cake, but Julien cut off this expense, and Jeanne had to content herself with toast.

Wishing to avoid all arguments and quarrels, she never made any remark, but each fresh proof of her husband's avarice hurt her like the prick of a needle. It seemed so petty, so odious to her, brought up as she had been in a family where money was never thought of any importance. How often she had heard her mother say, "Money is made to be spent"; but now Julien kept saying to her, "Will you never be cured of throwing money away?" Whenever he could manage to reduce a salary or a bill by a few pence he would slip the money into his pocket, saying, with a smile:

"Little streams make big rivers."

Jeanne would sometimes find herself dreaming as she used to do before she was married. She would gradually stop working, and with her hands lying idle in her lap and her eyes fixed on space, she built castles in the air as if she were a young girl again. But the voice of Julien, giving an order to old Simon, would call her back to the realities of life, and she would take up her work, thinking, "Ah, that is all over and done with now," and a tear would fall on her fingers as they pushed the needle through the stuff.

Rosalie, who used to be so gay and lively, always singing snatches of songs as she went about her work, gradually changed also. Her plump and round cheeks had fallen in and lost their brightened color, and her skin was muddy and dark. Jeanne would often ask, "Are you ill, my girl?" But the little maid always answered with a faint blush, "No, Madame," and got away as quickly as she could. Instead of tripping along as she had always done, she now dragged herself painfully from room to room, and seemed not even to care how she looked, for the peddlers in vain spread out their ribbons and corsets and bottles of scent before her; she never bought anything from them now. And the huge house sounded empty, while the rain stained its front with long gray streams.

At the end of January, the snow came. From afar great heavy clouds came across the dark sea from the north, and there was a heavy fall of snow. In one night the whole plain was whitened, and, in the morning the trees looked as if a mantle of frozen foam had been cast over them.

Julien, in his high boots, and his face unshaven, passed his time in the ditch between the wood and the plain, watching for the migrating birds. Every now and then his shots would break the frozen silence of the fields, and hordes of black crows flew from the trees in terror. Jeanne, tired of staying indoors, would go out on the steps of the house. Sounds of life came from a distance, echoing over the still sleep of the livid and sad fields of snow. Then she heard nothing but the faraway murmur of the waves and the soft continual rustle of the falling snow. And the snow piled up ceaselessly under the rain of this light thick moss.

On one of these cold, white mornings she was sitting by her bedroom fire, while Rosalie, who looked worse and worse every day, was slowly making her bed. All at once Jeanne heard a sigh of pain behind her. Without turning her head, she asked:

"What is the matter with you?"

The maid answered as she always did:

"Nothing, Madame," but her voice seemed to die away as she spoke.

Jeanne had left off thinking about her, when she suddenly noticed that she could not hear the girl moving. She called, "Rosalie!"

There was no answer. Then she thought that the maid must have gone quietly out of the room without her hearing her, and she cried in a louder tone; "Rosalie!" Again she received no answer, and she was just stretching out her hand to ring the bell, when she heard a low moan close beside her. She started up in terror.

Rosalie was sitting on the floor with her back against the bed, her legs stretched stiffly out, her face livid, and her eyes staring straight before her. Jeanne rushed to her side.

"Oh, Rosalie! What is the matter? what is it?" she asked in afright.

The maid did not answer a word or make a movement, but fixed her wild eyes on her mistress and gasped for breath, as if tortured by some excruciating pain. Then, stiffening every muscle in her body, and stifling a cry of anguish between her clenched teeth, she slipped down on her back, and all at once, something stirred underneath her dress, which clung tightly round her legs. Jeanne heard a strange, gushing noise, something like the death-rattle of someone who is suffocating, and then came a long low wail of pain; it was the first cry of suffering of a child entering the world.

The sound came as a revelation to her, and, suddenly losing her head, she rushed to the top of the stairs, crying:

"Julien! Julien!"

"What do you want?" he answered, from below.

She gasped out, "It's Rosalie who—who——" but before she could say any more Julien was rushing up the stairs two at a time; he dashed into the bedroom, raised the girl's clothes, and there lay a hideous little atom of humanity, wrinkled, whining, rigid and sticky, which was moving between two bare legs. He got up with an evil look on his face, and pushed his distracted wife out of the room, saying:

"This is no place for you. Go away and send me Ludivine and old Simon."

Jeanne went down to the kitchen trembling all over, and then, afraid to go upstairs again, she went into the drawing-room, where a fire was never lighted, now her parents were away, and waited anxiously for news. Soon she saw Simon run out of the house, and come back five minutes after with Widow Dentu, the village midwife. Next she heard a noise on the stairs which sounded as if they were carrying a body, then Julien came to tell her that she could go back to her room. She was trembling as if she had just witnessed some terrible accident. She sat down again in front of her fire, and then asked:

"How is she?"

Julien, apparently in a great rage, was walking about the room in a preoccupied, nervous way. He did not answer his wife for some moments, but at last he asked, stopping in his walk:

"Well, what do you mean to do with this girl?"

Jeanne looked at her husband as if she did not understand his question.

"What do you mean?" she said. "I don't know; how should I?"

"Well, anyhow, we can't keep that child in the house," he cried, angrily.

Jeanne looked very perplexed, and sat in silence for some time. At last she said:

"But, my dear, we could put it out to nurse somewhere?"

He hardly let her finish her sentence.

"And who'll pay for it? Will you?"

"But surely the father will take care of it," she said, after another long silence. "And if he marries Rosalie, everything will be all right."

"The father!" answered Julien, roughly; "the father! Do you know who is the father? Of course you don't. Very well, then!"

Jeanne, who was moved, took courage. "But he certainly will not forsake the girl; it would be such a cowardly thing to do. We will ask her his name, and go and see him and force him to give some account of himself."

Julien had become calmer, and was again walking about the room.

"My dear girl," he replied, "I don't believe she will tell you the man's name, or me either. Besides, suppose he wouldn't marry her? You must see that we can't keep a girl and her illegitimate child in our house."

But Jeanne would only repeat, doggedly:

"Then the man must be a villain; but we will find out who he is, and then he will have us to deal with instead of that poor girl."

Julien got very red.

"But until we know who he is?" he asked.

She did not know what to propose, so she asked Julien what he thought was the best thing to do. He gave his opinion very promptly.

"Oh, I should give her some money, and let her and her brat go to the devil."

That made Jeanne very indignant.

"That shall never be done," she declared; "Rosalie is my foster-sister, and we have grown up together. She has erred, it is true, but I will never turn her out of doors for that, and, if there is no other way out of the difficulty, I will bring up the child myself."

"And we should have a nice reputation, shouldn't we, with our name and connections?" burst out Julien. "People would say that we encouraged vice, and sheltered prostitutes, and respectable people would never come near us. Why, what can you be thinking of? You must be mad!"

"I will never have Rosalie turned out," she repeated, quietly. "If you will not keep her here, my mother will take her back again. But we are sure to find out the name of the father."

At that, he went out of the room, too angry to talk to her any longer, and as he banged the door after him he cried:

"Women are fools with their absurd notions!"

In the afternoon Jeanne went up to see the invalid. She was lying in bed, wide awake, and the Widow Dentu was rocking the child in her arms. As soon as she saw her mistress Rosalie began to sob violently, and when Jeanne wanted to kiss her, she turned away and hid her face under the bedclothes. The nurse interfered and drew down the sheet, and then Rosalie made no further resistance, though the tears still ran down her cheeks.

The room was very cold, for there was only a small fire in the grate, and the child was crying. Jeanne did not dare make any reference to the little one, for fear of causing another burst of tears, but she held Rosalie's hand and kept repeating mechanically:

"It will be all right. It will be all right."

The poor girl glanced shyly at the nurse from time to time; the child's cries seemed to pierce her heart, and sobs still escaped from her occasionally, though she forced herself to swallow her tears. Jeanne kissed her again, and whispered in her ear: "We'll take good care of it, you may be sure of that," and then ran quickly out of the room, for Rosalie's tears were beginning to flow again.

After that, Jeanne went up every day to see the invalid, and every day Rosalie burst into tears when her mistress came into the room. The child was put out to nurse, and Julien would hardly speak to his wife, as if he were very angry with her for refusing to dismiss the maid. One day he returned to the subject, but Jeanne drew out a letter from her mother in which the Baronne said that if they would not keep Rosalie at Les Peuples she was to be sent on to Rouen directly.

"Your mother's as great a fool as you are," cried Julien; but he did not say anything more about sending Rosalie away, and a fortnight later the maid was able to get up and perform her duties again.

One morning Jeanne made her sit down, and holding both her hands in hers:

"Now, then, Rosalie, tell me all about it," she said, looking her straight in the face.

Rosalie began to tremble.

"All about what, Madame?" she said, timidly.

"Who is the father of your child?" asked Jeanne.

Then a terrible despair seized the maid and she struggled to disengage her hands from her mistress's grasp, to hide her face in them. But Jeanne kissed her, in spite of her struggles, and tried to console her.

"It is true you have been weak," she said, "but you are not the first to whom such a misfortune has happened, and, if only the father of the child marries you, no one will think anything more about it; we would employ him, and he could live here with you."

Rosalie moaned as if she were being tortured, and tried to get her hands free that she might run away.

"I can quite understand how ashamed you feel," went on Jeanne, "but you see that I am not angry, and that I speak kindly to you. I wish to know this man's name for your own good, for I fear, from your grief, that he means to abandon you, and I want to prevent that. Julien will see him, and we will make him marry you, and we shall employ you both; we will see that he makes you happy."

This time Rosalie made so vigorous an effort that she

succeeded in wrenching her hands away from her mistress, and she rushed from the room as if she were mad.

"I have tried to make Rosalie tell me her seducer's name," said Jeanne to her husband at dinner that evening, "but I did not succeed in doing so. Try and see if she will tell you, that we may force the wretch to marry her."

"There, don't let me hear any more about all that," he said angrily. "You wanted to keep this girl, and you have done so, but don't bother me about her."

He seemed still more irritable since Rosalie's confinement than he had been before. He had got into the habit of shouting at his wife, whenever he spoke to her, as if he were always angry, while she, on the contrary, spoke softly, and did everything to avoid a quarrel; but she often cried when she was alone in her room at night. In spite of his bad temper, Julien had resumed the marital duties he had so neglected since his wedding tour, and it was seldom now that he let three nights pass without accompanying his wife to her room.

Rosalie soon got quite well again, and with better health came better spirits, but she always seemed frightened and haunted by some strange dread. She ran away on two other occasions, when Jeanne again tried to question her. Julien suddenly became better tempered, and his young wife began to cherish vague hopes, and to regain a little of her former gaiety; but she often felt very unwell, though she never said anything about it.

The thaw had not set in. For five weeks a sky without a cloud by day, and strewn by night with stars that looked like frost, so cold was the firmament, gazed down upon the solid, hard, glistening carpet of snow. Standing alone in their square courtyards, behind the great frosted trees, the farms seemed dead beneath their snowy shrouds. Neither men nor cattle could go out, and the only sign of life about the homesteads and cottages was the smoke that went straight up from the chimneys into the frosty air.

The grass, the hedges and the wall of elms seemed killed by the cold. From time to time the trees cracked, as if the fibers of their branches were separating beneath the bark, and sometimes a big branch would break off and fall to the ground, its sap frozen and dried up by the intense cold.

Jeanne longed for a return of the warm breezes, attributing to the terrible severity of the weather all the vague suffering she experienced. Sometimes the very idea of food disgusted her, and she could eat nothing; sometimes her pulse beat wildly; at other times she vomited after every meal, unable to digest the little she did eat. Her strained nerves were always on the rack and she lived in a constant and intolerable state of nervous excitement.

One evening, when the thermometer was sinking still lower, Julien shivered as he left the dinner table (for the dining-room was never sufficiently heated, so careful was he over the wood) and rubbed his hands together.

"It will be nice to sleep together tonight, won't it, darling?" he whispered. He gave one of his old good-tempered laughs and Jeanne threw her arms round his neck, but she felt so ill, so nervous, and she had such aching pains that evening, that, with her lips close to his, she begged him to let her sleep alone.

"I feel so ill tonight," she said, "but I am sure to be better tomorrow."

"Just as you please, my dear," he answered. "If you are ill, you must take care of yourself." And he began to talk of something else.

Jeanne went to bed early. Julien, for a wonder,

ordered a fire to be lighted in her bedroom; and when the servant came to tell him that it was "burning up," he kissed his wife on the forehead and said good night.

The whole house seemed to feel the cold, and the walls made little cracking noises as if they were shivering. Jeanne lay in bed shaking with cold; twice she got up to put more logs on the fire, and to pile her petticoats and dresses on the bed, but nothing seemed to make her any warmer. Her feet were numb, and she had twitchings in her calves and thighs which made her toss and turn restlessly from side to side. Her teeth chattered, her hands trembled, her heart beat so slowly that sometimes it seemed to stop altogether; and she gasped for breath as if she could not draw the air into her lungs.

As the cold crept higher and higher up her limbs, she was seized with a terrible fear. She had never felt like this before; life seemed to be gradually slipping away from her, and she thought each breath she drew would be her last.

"I am going to die! I am going to die!" she thought; and, in her terror, she jumped out of bed, and rang for Rosalie, waited and rang again, and again waited for an answer, shuddering and half-frozen. The maid did not come. Probably she was sunk in that first sleep that is so hard to disturb, and Jeanne, almost beside herself with fear, rushed out to the landing with bare feet. She went noiselessly up the dark stairs, felt for Rosalie's door, opened it, and called "Rosalie!" then went into the room, stumbled against the bed, passed her hands over it, and found it empty and quite cold, as if no one had slept in it that night.

"Surely she cannot have gone out in such weather as this," she thought.

Her heart began to beat so violently that it almost

suffocated her, and she went downstairs to rouse Julien, her legs giving way under her as she walked. She burst open her husband's door, and hurried across the room, spurred on by the idea that she was going to die and by the desire to see him again before she lost consciousness.

By the light of the dying fire she saw Rosalie's head on the pillow beside her husband's. At her cry they both started up. She stood still for a second, horrified at this discovery. Then she fled to her room, as Julien called frantically, "Jeanne!" A fear possessed her of seeing him, of hearing his voice, of listening to his excuses, his lies, of meeting him face to face, and she rushed out again, and down the stairs. She ran in the darkness, at the risk of falling down the steps and breaking a leg on the stones. She ran on, filled with the desire to flee, to know nothing, to see nobody.

On the last step she sat down, still in her night-dress and with bare feet, unable to think, unable to reason, her head in a whirl. Julien had jumped out of bed, and was hastily dressing himself. She started up to escape from him. He came downstairs, crying, "Jeanne, do listen!"

No, she would not listen; he should not degrade her by his touch. She dashed into the dining-room as if a murderer were pursuing her, looked round for a hiding-place or some dark corner where she might conceal herself, and then crouched down under the table. The door opened, and Julien came in with a light in his hand, still calling, "Jeanne!" She started off again like a hunted hare, tore into the kitchen, round which she ran twice like some wild animal at bay, then, as he was getting nearer and nearer to her, she suddenly flung open the garden door, and rushed out into the night.

Her bare legs sank into the snow up to her knees, and

this icy contact gave her desperate strength. Although she had nothing on but her night-dress she did not feel the bitter cold. She felt nothing, for her mental anguish was so great that it numbed her body, and she ran on and on, looking as white as the snow-covered earth.

She ran down the main avenue, through the copse, across the ditch and out onto the plain.

There was no moon, the stars were shining like sparks of fire in the black sky; but the plain was light with a dull whiteness, and lay in infinite silence.

Jeanne walked quickly, hardly breathing, not knowing, not thinking of anything. She suddenly stopped on the edge of the cliff. She stopped short, instinctively, and crouched down, bereft of thought and of will-power.

In the abyss before her the silent, invisible sea exhaled the salt odor of its wrack at low tide.

She remained thus some time, her mind as inert as her body; then, all at once, she began to tremble, to tremble violently, like a sail shaken by the wind. Her arms, her hands, her feet, impelled by an invisible force, throbbed, pulsated wildly, and her consciousness awakened abruptly, sharp and poignant.

Old memories passed before her mental vision: the sail with him in old Lastique's boat, their conversation, the dawn of their love; the christening of the boat. Then her thoughts went still farther back till they reached the night of her arrival at Les Peuples—the night she had spent in happy dreams. And now, now! Her life was ruined; she had had all her pleasure; there were no joys, no happiness, in store for her; and she could see the terrible future with all its tortures, its deceptions, and despair. Surely it would be better to die now, at once.

She heard a voice in the distance crying:

"This way! This way! Here are her footmarks!" It was Julien looking for her.

Oh! she could not, she would not, see him again! Never again! From the abyss before her came the faint sound of the waves as they broke on the rocks. She stood up to throw herself over the cliff, and in a despairing farewell to life, she moaned out that last cry of the dying—the word that the soldier gasps out as he lies wounded to death on the battlefield—"Mother!"

Then the thought of how her mother would sob when she heard of her daughter's death, and how her father would kneel in agony beside her mangled corpse, flashed across her mind, and in that one second she realized all the bitterness of their grief. She fell feebly back on the snow, and she did not move when Julien and old Simon came up, with Marius behind them holding a lantern. They drew her back by the arm, so near the edge of the cliff was she; and they did with her what they liked, for she could not move a muscle. She knew that they carried her indoors, that she was put to bed, and rubbed with hot flannels, and then she was conscious of nothing more.

A nightmare—but was it a nightmare?—haunted her. She thought she was in bed in her own room; it was broad daylight, but she could not get up, though she did not know why she could not. She heard a noise on the boards—a scratching, rustling noise—and all at once a little gray mouse ran over the sheet. Then another one appeared, and another which came running towards her chest. Jeanne was not frightened; she wanted to take hold of the little animal, and put out her hand towards it, but she could not catch it.

Then came more mice—ten, twenty, hundreds, thousands, sprang up on all sides. They ran up the bedposts, and along the tapestry, and covered the whole bed. They got under the clothes, and Jeanne could feel them gliding over her skin, tickling her legs, running up and down her body. She could see them coming from the foot of the bed to get inside and creep close to her breast, but when she struggled and stretched out her hands to catch one, she always clutched the air. Then she got angry, and cried out, and wanted to run away; she fancied someone held her down, and that strong arms were thrown around her to prevent her moving, but she could not see anyone. She had no idea of the time that all this lasted; she only knew that it seemed a very long while.

At last she became conscious again. She was tired and aching, but better. She felt very, very weak. She looked round, and did not feel at all surprised to see her mother sitting by her bedside with a stout man whom she did not know. She had forgotten how old she was, and thought she was a little child again, for her memory was entirely gone.

"See, she is conscious," said the stout man.

The Baronne began to cry, and the big man said:

"Come, come, Madame; I assure you there is no longer any danger, but you must not talk to her; just let her sleep."

It seemed to Jeanne that she lay for a long time in a doze, which became a heavy sleep if she tried to think of anything. She had a vague idea that the past contained something dreadful, and she was content to lie still without trying to recall anything to her memory. But one day, when she opened her eyes, she saw Julien standing beside the bed, and the curtain which hid everything from her was suddenly drawn aside; she remembered what had happened.

She threw back the clothes and sprang out of bed to

escape from her husband; but as soon as her feet touched the floor she fell to the ground, for she was too weak to stand. Julien hastened to her assistance, but when he attempted to raise her, she shrieked and rolled from side to side to avoid the contact of his hands. The door opened, and Aunt Lison and the Widow Dentu hurried in, closely followed by the Baron and his wife, the latter gasping for breath.

They put Jeanne to bed again, and she closed her eyes and pretended to be asleep that she might think undisturbed. Her mother and aunt busied themselves around her, saying from time to time:

"Do you know us now, Jeanne, dear?"

She pretended not to hear them, and made no answer; and in the evening they went away, leaving her to the care of the nurse. She could not sleep all that night, for she was painfully trying to connect the incidents she could remember, one with another; but there seemed to be gaps in her memory, great blanks where nothing was recorded. Little by little, after long efforts, however, all the facts came back to her, and she pondered over them obstinately. She must have been very ill, or her mother and Aunt Lison and the Baron would not have been sent for; but what had Julien said? Did her parents know everything? And where was Rosalie?

What was she to do? What? An idea occurred to her to go back to Rouen with her father and mother. She would be a widow, that was all.

Then she waited and listened to all that went on around her, but she did not let anyone see that she understood everything and had recovered her full senses. She was glad of this return of her reason, and was patient and cunning. Towards evening, when no one but the Baronne was in her room, Jeanne whispered softly: "Mother, dear!"

She was surprised to hear how changed her own voice was, but the Baronne took her hands, exclaiming:

"My child! my dear little Jeanne! Do you know me, my pet?"

"Yes, mother. But you mustn't cry; I want to talk to you seriously. Did Julien tell you why I ran out into the snow?"

"Yes, my darling. You have had a very dangerous fever."

"That was not the reason, mamma; I had the fever afterwards. Hasn't he told you why I tried to run away, and what was the cause of the fever?"

"No, dear."

"It was because I found Rosalie in his bed."

The Baronne thought she was still delirious, and tried to soothe her.

"There, there, my darling; lie down and try to go to sleep."

But Jeanne continued, obstinately:

"I am not talking nonsense now, mamma dear, though I dare say I have been lately," she said. "I felt very ill one night, and I got up and went to Julien's room; there I saw Rosalie lying beside him. My grief nearly drove me mad, and I ran out into the snow, meaning to throw myself over the cliff."

"Yes, darling, you have been ill; very ill indeed," answered the Baronne.

"It wasn't that, mamma. I found Rosalie in Julien's bed, and I will not stay with him any longer. You shall take me back to Rouen with you."

The doctor had told the Baronne to let Jeanne have her own way in everything, so she answered:

"Very well, my pet."

Jeanne began to lose patience.

"I see you don't believe me," she said pettishly. "Go and find papa; perhaps he'll manage to understand that I am speaking the truth."

The Baronne rose slowly to her feet, dragged herself out of the room with the aid of two sticks, and came back in a few minutes with the Baron. They sat down by the bedside, and Jeanne began to speak in her weak voice. She spoke quite coherently, and she told them all about Julien's odd ways, his harshness, his avarice, and, lastly, his infidelity.

The Baron could see that her mind was not wandering, but he hardly knew what to say or think. He affectionately took her hand, as he used to do when she was a child and he told her fairy-tales to send her to sleep.

"Listen, my dear," he said. "We must not do anything rashly. Don't let us say anything till we have thought it well over. Will you promise me to try and bear with your husband until we have decided what is best to be done?"

"Very well," she answered; "but I will not stay here after I get well."

Then she added, in a whisper, "Where is Rosalie now?"

"You shall not see her any more," replied the Baron.

But she persisted. "Where is she? I want to know."

He owned that she was still in the house, but he declared she should go at once.

Directly he left Jeanne's room, his heart full of pity for his child and indignation against her husband, the Baron went to find Julien, and said to him sternly:

"Monsieur, I have come to ask for an explanation of your behavior to my daughter. You have not only been

false to her, but you have deceived her with your servant, which makes your conduct doubly infamous."

Julien pretended to be innocent, denied everything,
swore, and called Heaven to witness his denial. What
proof was there? Wasn't Jeanne mad? Was she not just
recovering from brain fever? And had she not rushed
out in the snow one night at the beginning of her illness,
in a fit of delirium? And how could her statement be
believed when, on the very night that she said she had
surprised her maid in her husband's bed, she was dashing over the house nearly naked?

He got very angry, and threatened the Baron with
an action if he did not withdraw his accusation; and
the Baron, confused by this indignant denial, began to
make excuses and to beg his son-in-law's pardon; but
Julien refused to take his outstretched hand.

Jeanne did not seem vexed when she heard what her
husband had said.

"He is telling a lie, papa," she said, quietly; "but we
will force him to own the truth."

For two days she lay silent, turning over all sorts of
things in her mind; on the third morning she asked for
Rosalie. The Baron refused to let the maid go up and
told Jeanne that she had left. But Jeanne insisted on
seeing her, and said:

"Send someone to fetch her, then."

When the doctor came she was very excited because they would not let her see the maid, and they
told him what was the matter. Jeanne burst into tears
and almost shrieked, "I will see her! I will see her!"

The doctor took her hand and said in a low voice:

"Calm yourself, Madame. Any violent emotion might
have very serious results just now, for you are pregnant."

She was astonished, as though she had been struck,

and at once she fancied she could feel a movement within her, and she lay still, paying no attention to what was being said, buried in thought. She could not sleep that night; it seemed so strange to think that within her was another life, and she felt sorry because it was Julien's child, and full of fears lest it should resemble its father.

The next morning she sent for the Baron.

"Papa, dear," she said, "I have made up my mind to know the whole truth; especially now. You hear, I *will* know it, and you know, you must let me do as I like, because of my condition. Now listen; go and fetch the priest; he must be here to make Rosalie tell the truth. Then, as soon as he is here, you must send her up to me, and you and mamma must come too; but, whatever you do, don't let Julien know what is going on."

The priest came about an hour afterwards. He was fatter than ever, and panted quite as much as the Baronne. He sat down in an armchair, his paunch hanging between his legs, and began joking, while he wiped his forehead with his checked handkerchief from sheer habit.

"Well, Madame, I don't think we are either of us getting thinner; in my opinion we make a very handsome pair." Then turning to the invalid, he said, "Ah, ah! my young lady, I hear we're soon to have a christening, and that it won't be the christening of a boat either, this time, ha, ha, ha!" Then he went on in a grave voice, "It will be one more defender for the country, or"—after a short silence—"another good wife and mother like you, Madame," with a bow to the Baronne.

The door flew open and there stood Rosalie, crying, struggling, and refusing to move, while the Baron tried to push her in. At last he gave her a sudden shake, and threw her into the room with a jerk, and she stood in the middle of the floor, with her face in her hands, sobbing violently. As soon as she saw her Jeanne started up as white as a sheet, and her heart could be seen beating under her thin night-dress. It was some time before she could speak, but at last she gasped out:

"There—there—is no—need for me to—question you. Your confusion in my presence—is—is quite sufficient—proof—of your guilt."

She stopped for a few moments for want of breath, and then went on again:

"But I wish to know all. I have sent for the priest, so you understand you will have to answer as if you were at confession."

Rosalie had not moved and she almost shrieked between her clenched hands. The Baron, losing all patience with her, seized her hands, drew them roughly from her face and threw her on her knees beside the bed, saying:

"Why don't you say something? Answer."

She crouched down on the ground in the position in which Mary Magdalene is generally depicted; her cap was on one side, her apron on the floor, and as soon as her hands were free she again buried her face in them.

"Come, come, my girl," said the priest, "we don't want to do you any harm, but we must know exactly what has happened. Now listen to what is asked you and answer truthfully."

Jeanne was leaning over the side of the bed, looking at the girl.

"Is it not true that I found you in Julien's bed?" she asked.

"Yes, Madame," moaned out Rosalie through her fingers.

At that the Baronne burst into choking tears also, and her convulsive sobs accompanied Rosalie's.

"How long had that gone on?" asked Jeanne, her eyes fixed on the maid.

"Ever since he came here," stammered Rosalie.

"Since he came here," repeated Jeanne, hardly understanding what the words meant. "Do you mean since—since the spring?"

"Yes, Madame."

"Since he first came to the house?"

"Yes, Madame."

As if the questions were stifling her, Jeanne asked rapidly:

"But how did it happen? How did he ask you? How did he have you? What did he say? When did you give yourself to him? How could you do such a thing?"

Rosalie, taking her hands from her face and speaking as if the words were forced from her by an irresistible desire to talk and to tell all. "I dunno. The day he dined here for the first time, he came up to my room. He had hidden in the garret and I durstn't cry out for fear of what everyone would say. He got into my bed, and I dunno how it was or what I did, but he did just as he liked with me. I never said nothin' about it because I thought he was nice."

"But your—your child? Is it his?" cried Jeanne.

"Yes, Madame," answered Rosalie, between her sobs. Then neither said anything more, and the silence was only broken by the Baronne's and Rosalie's sobs.

Jeanne was overwhelmed and the tears rose to her eyes, and flowed noiselessly down her cheeks. So her maid's child had the same father as her own! All her anger had evaporated and in its place was a dull, gloomy, deep despair. After a short silence she said in a softer, tearful voice:

"After we returned from—from our wedding trip— when did he begin again?"

"The—the night you came back," answered the maid, who was now almost lying on the floor.

Each word wrung Jeanne's heart. He had actually left her for this girl the very night of their return to Les Peuples! That, then, was why he had let her sleep alone. She had heard enough now; she did not want to know anything more, and she cried to the girl:

"Go away! go away!"

As Rosalie, overcome by her emotion, did not move, she called to her father:

"Take her away! Carry her out of the room!"

But the priest, who had said nothing up to now, thought the time had come for a little discourse.

"You have behaved very wickedly," he said to Rosalie, "very wickedly indeed, and the good God will not easily forgive you. Think of the punishment which awaits you if you do not live a better life henceforth. Now you are young is the time to train yourself in good ways. No doubt Madame will do something for you, and we shall be able to find you a husband——"

He would have gone on like this for a long time had not the Baron seized Rosalie by the shoulders, dragged her to the door and thrown her into the passage like a bundle of clothes.

When he came back, looking whiter even than his daughter, the priest began again:

"Well, you know, all the girls round here are the same. It is a very bad state of things, but it can't be helped, and we must make a little allowance for the weakness of human nature. They never marry until they are pregnant; never, Madame. One might almost call it a local custom," he added, with a smile. Then he went on indignantly, "Even the children are the same. Only last year I found a little boy and girl from my class in the cemetery together. I told their parents, and what do you think they replied, 'Well, father, we didn't teach it them; we can't help it.' So you see, your maid has only done like the others——"

"The maid!" interrupted the Baron, trembling with excitement. "The maid! What do I care about her? It's Julien's conduct which I think so abominable, and I shall certainly take my daughter away with me." He walked up and down the room, getting more and more angry with every step he took. "It is infamous, the way he has deceived my daughter, infamous! He's a wretch, a villain, and I will tell him so to his face. I'll horsewhip him within an inch of his life."

The priest was slowly enjoying a pinch of snuff as he sat beside the Baronne, and thinking how he could make peace. "Come now, between ourselves he has only done like everyone else. I am quite sure you don't know many husbands who are faithful to their wives, do you now?" And he added in a sly, good-natured way, "I bet you, yourself, have played your little games; you can't say conscientiously that you haven't, I know. Why, of course you have!" The Baron had stopped, flabbergasted, in front of the priest, who went on, "And who knows but what you have made the acquaintance of some little maid just like Rosalie. I tell you every man is the same. And your escapades didn't make your wife unhappy, or lessen your affection for her; did they?"

The Baron stood still in confusion. It was true indeed that he had done the same himself, and not only once or twice, but as often as he had got the chance; his wife's presence in the house had never made any difference, when the servants were pretty. And was he a villain because of that? Then why should he judge Julien's conduct so severely when he had never thought that any fault could be found with his own?

Though her tears were hardly dried, the idea of her husband's pranks brought a slight smile to the Baronne's lip, for she was one of those good-natured, tender-hearted, sentimental women to whom love adventures are an essential part of existence.

Jeanne lay back exhausted, thinking, with open unseeing eyes, of all this painful episode. The expression that had wounded her most in Rosalie's confession was, "I never said anything about it because I thought he was nice." She, his wife, had also thought him "nice," and that was the sole reason why she had united herself to him for life, had given up every other hope, every other project to join her destiny to his. She had plunged into marriage, into this pit from which there was no escape, into all this misery, this grief, this despair, simply because, like Rosalie, she had thought him nice.

The door was flung violently open and Julien came in, looking perfectly wild with rage. He had seen Rosalie moaning on the landing, and guessing that she had been forced to speak, he had come to see what was going on; but at the sight of the priest he was taken thoroughly aback.

"What is it? What is the matter?" he asked, in a voice which trembled in spite of his efforts to make it sound calm.

The Baron, who had been so violent just before, dared say nothing after the priest's argument, in case his son-in-law should quote his own example; the Baronne only wept more bitterly than before, and Jeanne raised herself on her hands and looked steadily at this man who was causing her so much sorrow. Her breath came and went quickly, but she managed to answer:

"The matter is that we know all about your shameful conduct ever since—ever since the day you first came here; we know that—that—Rosalie's child is yours—like—like mine, and that they will be—brothers."

Her grief became so poignant at this thought that she hid herself under the bedclothes and sobbed bitterly. Julien stood open-mouthed, not knowing what to say or do. The priest again interposed.

"Come, come, my dear young lady," he said, "you mustn't give way like that. See now, be reasonable."

He rose, went to the bedside, and laid his cool hand on this despairing woman's forehead. His simple touch seemed to soothe her wonderfully; she felt calmer at once, as if the large hand of this peasant accustomed to gestures of absolution and sympathy, had borne with it some strange, peace-giving power.

The good man remained standing and resumed, "Madame, we must always forgive. You are borne down by a great grief, but God, in His mercy, has also sent you a great joy, since He has permitted you to have hopes of becoming a mother. This child will console you for all your trouble and it is in its name that I implore, that I adjure, you to forgive M. Julien. It will be a fresh tie between you, a pledge of your husband's future fidelity. Can you withdraw your affection from the man whose seed you bear within you?"

She made no answer. She was broken, aching and exhausted now, without strength for anger or vengeance. Her nerves were thoroughly unstrung, and she clung to life but by a very slender thread.

The Baronne, to whom resentment seemed utterly impossible and whose mind was simply incapable of bearing any prolonged strain, said in a low tone:

"Come, Jeanne!"

The priest drew Julien close to the bed and placed his hand in his wife's, giving it a little tap as if to make the union more complete. Then, dropping his professional pulpit tone, he said with a satisfied air:

"There! that's done. Believe me, it is better so."

The two hands, united thus for an instant, loosed their clasp directly. Julien, not daring to embrace Jeanne, kissed his mother-in-law, then turned on his heel, took the Baron (who, in his heart, was not sorry that everything had finished so quietly) by the arm, and drew him from the room to go and smoke a cigar.

Then the tired invalid went to sleep and the Baronne and the priest began to chat in low tones. He talked of what had just occurred and proceeded to explain his ideas on the subject, while the Baronne assented to everything he said with a nod.

"Very well, then, it's understood," he said, in conclusion. "You give the girl the farm at Barville and I will undertake to find her a good, honest husband. Oh, you may be sure that with twenty thousand francs we shall not want candidates for her hand. We shall merely have difficulty in choosing amongst so many."

The Baronne was smiling happily now, while two tears still lingered on her cheeks, though their moist track had already dried.

"Barville is worth twenty thousand francs, at the very least," she said; "and you understand that it is to be settled on the child though the parents will have it as long as they live."

Then the priest shook hands with the Baronne, and rose to go.

"Don't get up, Madame, don't get up," he exclaimed. "I know too well myself what a step means."

As he went out he met Aunt Lison coming to see her patient. She did not notice anything: no one told her anything, and, as usual, she heard nothing.

VIII

Rosalie had left the house, and the time of Jeanne's confinement was drawing near. The sorrow she had gone through had taken away all pleasure from the thought of becoming a mother, and she waited for the child's birth without any impatience or curiosity, her mind entirely filled with her presentiment of coming evils.

Spring was close at hand. The bare trees still trembled in the cold wind, but, in the damp grass of the ditches, the yellow primroses were already showing among the decaying autumn leaves. The commons, the farmyards and the sodden fields exhaled a damp odor, as of fermentation, and little green leaves peeped out of the brown earth and glistened in the sun.

A big, strongly built woman had been engaged in Rosalie's place, and she now supported the Baronne in her dreary walks along the avenue, where the track made by her foot was always damp and muddy.

Jeanne, low-spirited and in constant pain, leaned on her father's arm when she went out, while on her other side walked Aunt Lison, fussy and uneasy, holding her niece's hand, and thinking nervously of this mystery that she would never know. They would all walk for hours without speaking a word, and, while they were out, Julien went all over the country on horseback, for he had suddenly become very fond of riding.

Nothing came to disturb their dull existence. The Baron, his wife, and the Vicomte, paid a visit to the Fourvilles, whom Julien seemed to know very well, though no one knew exactly how the acquaintance had begun, and another duty call was paid to the Brisevilles, who were still in retirement in their sleepy manor.

One afternoon, about four o'clock, two people on horseback trotted up to the courtyard in front of the château. Julien rushed into his wife's room in great excitement.

"Make haste and go down," he exclaimed. "Here are the Fourvilles. They have come simply to make a neighborly call as they know the condition you are in. Say I am out but that I shall be in soon. I am just going to clean myself up a bit."

Jeanne, much surprised, went downstairs. A pale, pretty young woman with a sad face, dreamy eyes, and lusterless, fair hair, looking as though the sunlight had never kissed it, quietly introduced her husband, a kind of giant or ogre with a large red mustache. She added, "We have several times had the pleasure of meeting M. de Lamare. We heard from him how ill you were, and we would not put off coming to see you as neighbors, without any ceremony. You see that we came on horseback. I also had the pleasure the other day of a visit from your mother, and the Baron."

She spoke with perfect ease, familiar but refined. Jeanne was charmed, and fell in love with her at once. "This is a friend," she thought.

The Comte de Fourville, on the contrary, seemed like a bear in the drawing-room. As soon as he was seated, he placed his hat on the chair next him, did not know what to do with his hands, placed them on his knees, then on the arms of the chair, and finally crossed his fingers as if in prayer.

Suddenly Julien entered the room. Jeanne was amazed and did not recognize him. He was shaved. He looked handsome, elegant, and attractive as on the day of their betrothal. He shook the hairy paw of the

Comte, who seemed to have wakened up on his arrival, kissed the hand of the Comtesse, whose ivory cheeks colored slightly while her eyelids quivered.

He began to speak; he was charming as in former days. His large eyes, the mirrors of love, had become tender again. And his hair, lately so dull and unkempt, had regained its soft, glossy wave, with the use of a hairbrush and perfumed oil.

At the moment when the Fourvilles were taking their leave the Comtesse, turning towards him, said: "Would you like to take a ride on Thursday, dear Vicomte?"

As he bowed and murmured, "Why, certainly, Madame," she took Jeanne's hand and said in a sympathetic and affectionate tone, with a cordial smile: "Oh! when you are well, we will all three gallop about the country. It will be delightful. What do you say?"

With an easy gesture she held up her riding skirt, looking like a Centaur, and then jumped into the saddle with the lightness of a bird, while her husband, after bowing awkwardly, mounted his big Norman steed. As they disappeared outside the gate, Julien, who seemed charmed, exclaimed, "What delightful people! Those are friends who may be useful to us."

Jeanne, pleased also without knowing why, replied, "The little Comtesse is charming; I feel that I shall love her, but the husband looks like a brute. Where did you meet them?"

He rubbed his hands together good-humoredly. "I met them by chance at the Brisevilles'. The husband seems a little rough. He cares for nothing but hunting, but he is a real nobleman for all that."

Nothing else happened until the end of July. Then, one Tuesday evening, as they were all sitting under the plane-tree beside a little table, on which stood two liqueur-glasses and a decanter of brandy, Jeanne suddenly turned very white and put both her hands to her side with a cry. A sharp pain had shot through her and at once died away. In about ten minutes came another one, hardly so severe but of longer duration than the first. Her father and husband almost carried her indoors, for the short distance between the plane-tree and her room seemed miles to her; she could not stifle her moans, and, overpowered by an intolerable sense of heaviness and weight, she implored them to let her sit down and rest.

The child was not expected until September but, in case of accident, a horse was harnessed and old Simon galloped off for the doctor. He came about midnight and at once recognized the signs of a premature confinement. The actual pain had a little diminished, but Jeanne felt an awful deathly faintness, and she thought she was going to die, for Death is sometimes so close that his icy breath can almost be felt.

The room was full of people. The Baronne lay back in an armchair gasping for breath; the Baron ran hither and thither, bringing all manner of things, consulting the doctor, and completely losing his head; Julien walked up and down looking very troubled, but feeling quite calm, and the Widow Dentu, whom nothing could surprise or startle, stood at the foot of the bed with an expression on her face suited to the occasion.

Nurse, midwife, and watcher of the dead, equally ready to welcome the new-born infant, to receive its first cry, to immerse it in its first bath and to wrap it in its first covering, or to hear the last word, the last death-rattle, the last moan of the dying, to clothe them in their last garment, to sponge their wasted bodies with vinegar, to wrap them in the winding-sheet, the Widow Dentu had become utterly indifferent to any of the chances accompanying a birth or a death. Ludivine, the cook, and Aunt Lison remained discreetly hidden behind the hall door.

Every now and then Jeanne gave a low moan. For two hours it seemed as if the event were far off; but about daybreak the pains recommenced violently and soon became terrible. As the involuntary cries of anguish burst through her clenched teeth, Jeanne thought of Rosalie who had hardly even suffered or moaned, and whose bastard child had been born without any pain or torture. In her wretched, troubled mind she drew comparisons between her maid and herself, and she cursed God whom, until now, she had believed just. She thought in angry astonishment of how fate favors the wicked, and of the unpardonable lies of those who hold forth inducements to be upright and good.

Sometimes the agony was so great that she could think of nothing else, her suffering absorbing all her strength, her reason, her consciousness. In the intervals of relief her eyes were fixed on Julien, and then she was filled with a mental anguish as she thought of the day her maid had fallen at the foot of this very bed with her new-born child—the brother of the infant that was now causing her such terrible pain. She remembered perfectly every gesture, every look, every word of her husband as he stood beside the maid, and now she could see in him, as though his movements betrayed his thoughts, the same irritation, the same indifference to her suffering as he had felt for Rosalie's; the same selfish carelessness of a man whom the idea of paternity irritates.

She was seized by an excruciating pain, a spasm so agonizing that she thought, "I am going to die! I am dying!" And her soul was filled with a furious hatred; she felt she must curse this man who was the cause of all her agony, and this child which was killing her.

She strained every muscle in a supreme effort to rid herself of this awful burden, and then it felt as if her whole inside were pouring away from her, and her suffering suddenly became less.

The nurse and the doctor bent over her and were touching her. They took something away; and she heard the choking noise she had heard once before, and then the low cry of pain, the feeble whine of the new-born child filled her ears and seemed to enter her poor, exhausted body till it reached her very soul; and, in an unconscious movement she tried to hold out her arms.

She was filled with a sudden joy, an impulse towards a new happiness just unfolded. In one second she had been delivered, soothed and made happier than she had ever been before, and her mind and body revived as she realized she was a mother.

She wanted to see her child. It had not any hair or nails, for it had come before its time, but when she saw this human larva move its limbs and open its mouth, and cry, and when she touched this wrinkled, grimacing, living monster, her heart overflowed with happiness, and she knew that she was saved, guaranteed against despair, that there she had something she could love to the exclusion of all else.

From that time her child was her only care. She suddenly became a fanatical mother, all the more idolizing because she had been so deceived in her love and disappointed in her hopes. She insisted on having the cot close to her bed, and, when she could get up, she sat by the window whole days rocking the cradle. She was jealous of the wet-nurse, and when the hungry baby held out its arms towards the big blue-veined breast, and seized the brown wrinkled nipple in its greedy lips, she would watch the placid peasant woman, pale and trembling, with a desire to snatch away her son, and strike and scratch the breast from which he drank so eagerly.

She embroidered fine robes for him herself, of most elaborate elegance. He was surrounded by a cloud of lace and wore the handsomest caps. The only thing she could talk about was the baby's clothes, and she was always interrupting a conversation to hold up a band, or bib, or some especially pretty ribbon for admiration, for she took no notice of what was being said around her as she went into ecstasies over scraps of linen, twisting and turning them in her hands, and holding them up to see better. Then suddenly she would say:

"Don't you think he will look lovely in that?"

The Baron and his wife smiled at this excess of tenderness, but Julien, whose habitual routine had been interfered with and his overweening importance diminished by the arrival of this noisy and all-powerful tyrant, unconsciously jealous of this mite of a man who had usurped his place in the house, kept on saying angrily and impatiently, "How wearisome she is with her brat!"

She became so obsessed by this affection that she would pass the entire night beside the cradle, watching the child asleep. As she was becoming exhausted by this morbid life, taking no rest, growing weaker and thinner and beginning to cough, the doctor ordered the child to be taken from her. She got angry, wept, implored, but they were deaf to her entreaties. His nurse took him every evening, and each night his mother would rise, and in her bare feet go to the door, listen at the keyhole to see that he was sleeping quietly, did not wake up and wanted nothing.

Julien found her there one night as he was coming in late from dining at the Fourvilles, and after that she was locked into her room every evening to compel her to stay in bed.

The christening took place about the end of August. The Baron was the godfather and Aunt Lison godmother. The child was baptized Pierre Simon Paul—Paul for everyday use. At the beginning of September Aunt Lison went quietly away, and her absence was as unnoticed as her presence had been.

One evening, after dinner, the priest called. He seemed embarrassed and had an air of mystery about him, and, after a few commonplace remarks, he asked the Baron and Baronne if he could speak to them in private for a few moments. They all three walked slowly down the avenue talking eagerly as they went, while Julien, feeling uneasy and irritated at this secrecy, was left behind with Jeanne. He offered to accompany the priest when he went away, and they walked off towards the church where the angelus was ringing. It was a cool, almost cold, evening, and the others soon went into the drawing-room. They were all dozing a little when Julien suddenly returned, red in the face and looking most indignant. Before he was well in the room, and without considering whether Jeanne was there or not, he shouted:

"Upon my soul you must be mad to go and give twenty thousand francs to that girl!"

They were all taken too much by surprise to make any answer, and he went on, bellowing with rage, "I can't understand how you can be such fools! But I suppose you will keep on till we haven't a sou left!"

The Baron, recovering himself a little, tried to check his son-in-law:

"Be quiet!" he exclaimed. "Don't you see that your wife is in the room?"

"I don't care a damn!" answered Julien, stamping his

foot. "Besides, she knows all about it. It is a theft to her disadvantage."

Jeanne had listened to her husband in amazement. "Whatever is the matter?" she stammered.

Then Julien turned to her, expecting her to side with him, as the loss of money would affect her also. He told her in a few words of the plan to arrange a marriage for Rosalie, and the gift of the farm at Barville, which was worth twenty thousand francs at the very least. And he kept on repeating:

"Your parents must be mad, my dear, raving mad! Twenty thousand francs! Twenty thousand francs! They can't be in their right senses! Twenty thousand francs for a bastard!"

Jeanne listened to him quite calmly, astonished herself to find that she felt neither anger nor sorrow at his meanness, but she was perfectly indifferent now to everything which did not concern her child. The Baron was choking with anger, and at last he burst out, with a stamp of the foot:

"Think of what you are saying. Really, this is too much! Whose fault is it that this girl has to have a dowry? Who is her child's father? No doubt you would abandon her altogether if you had your way!"

Julien gazed at the Baron for a few moments in silent surprise at this violence. Then he went on more quietly:

"But fifteen hundred francs would have been ample to give her. They all have children before they marry, so what does it matter whom they have them by? And then, if you give Rosalie a farm worth twenty thousand francs, apart from the injustice to us, everybody will see at once what has happened. You might, at least, have thought of what is due to our name and position."

He spoke in a calm, cool way as if he were sure of his logic and the strength of his argument. The Baron, disconcerted by this fresh view of the matter, could find nothing to say in reply, and Julien, feeling his advantage, added:

"But fortunately, nothing is settled. I know the man who is going to marry her and he is an honest fellow with whom everything can yet be satisfactorily arranged. I will see to the matter myself."

With that he went out of the room, wishing to avoid any further discussion, and taking the silence with which his words were received to mean acquiescence.

As soon as the door had closed after his son-in-law, the Baron exclaimed:

"Oh, this is more than I can stand!"

Jeanne, catching sight of her father's horrified expression, burst into a clear laugh which rang out as it used to do whenever she had seen something very funny:

"Papa, papa!" she cried. "Did you hear the tone in which he said 'twenty thousand francs!'"

The Baronne, whose smiles lay as near the surface as her tears, quivered with laughter as she thought of her son-in-law's furious face, and his indignant exclamations and determined attempt to prevent this money, which was not his, being given to the girl he had seduced. Rendered happy by the good humor of Jeanne, finally the Baron caught the contagion and they all three laughed till they ached, as in the happy days of old. When they were a little calmer, Jeanne said:

"It is very funny, but really I don't seem to mind in the least what he says or does now. I look upon him quite as a stranger, and I can hardly believe I am his wife. You see I am able to laugh at his—his want of delicacy." And without knowing why, all three kissed, smiling and close to tears.

Two days later, after lunch, when Julien had gone out for a ride, a tall, young fellow of about two- or five-

and-twenty, dressed in a brand-new blue blouse, which hung in stiff folds, with puffed sleeves fastened at the wrists, climbed stealthily over the fence, as if he had been hiding there all the morning, crept along the Couillards' ditch, and went round to the other side of the château where Jeanne and her father and mother were sitting under the plane-tree. He took off his cap when he saw them and bowed awkwardly as he came towards them, and, when he was within speaking distance, mumbled:

"Your servant, Monsieur le Baron, Madame and company." Then, as no one said anything to him he introduced himself as "Désiré Lecoq."

This name failing to explain his presence, the Baron asked:

"What do you want?"

The peasant was very disconcerted when he found he had to state his business. He hesitated, stammered, cast his eyes from the cap he held in his hands to the château roof and back again:

"His Reverence has said somethin' to me about this business——" then, fearing to say too much and thus injure his own interests, he stopped short.

"What business?" asked the Baron. "I don't know what you mean."

"About your maid—Rosalie," said the man in a low voice.

Jeanne, guessing what he had come about, got up and went away with her child in her arms.

"Come here," said the Baron, pointing to the chair his daughter had just left.

The peasant took the seat with a "Thank you, kindly," and then waited as if he had nothing whatever to say. After a considerable pause, he thought he had better say

something, so he looked up to the blue sky and remarked:

"What fine weather for this time of year to be sure.
It'll help on the crops finely." And then he again re-
lapsed into silence.

The Baron began to get impatient.

"Then you are going to marry Rosalie?" he said in a
dry tone, going straight to the point.

Immediately the man became uneasy, all the crafty,
suspicious nature of the Normandy peasant on the alert.
He answered quickly but cautiously:

"That depends. Perhaps I am and perhaps I ain't,
that depends."

All this beating about the bush irritated the Baron.

"Confound it! Can't you give a straightforward answer? Have you come to say you will marry the girl
or not?"

The man was perplexed and kept his eyes fixed on
his feet.

"If it's as His Reverence says," he replied, "I'll have
her; but if it's as M. Julien says, I won't."

"What did M. Julien tell you?"

"M'sieu Julien told me as how I'd have fifteen hundred francs; but His Reverence told me as how I'd have
twenty thousand. I'll have her for twenty thousand, but
I won't for fifteen hundred."

The Baronne was tickled by the perplexed look on
the yokel's face and began to shake with laughter as she
sat in her armchair. Her gaiety surprised the peasant,
who looked at her suspiciously out of the corner of his
eye as he waited for an answer.

The Baron who did not like all this haggling, cut it
short.

"I have told M. le curé that you shall have the farm

at Barville, which is worth twenty thousand francs, for life, and then it is to become the child's. That is all I have to say on the matter. Now is your answer yes or no?"

The man smiled with an air of humility and satisfaction, and became suddenly loquacious:

"Oh, then, I don't say no, that was the only thing that pulled me up. When His Reverence said somethin' to me about it in the first place, I said yes at once, 'specially as it was to oblige you who'd be sure to pay me back for it, as I says to myself. Ain't it always the way, and doesn't one good turn always deserve another? But M. Julien comes up, and then it was only fifteen hundred francs. Then I says to myself, 'I must find out the rights o' this' and so I came here. Of course I b'lieved your word, sir, but I wanted to find out o' the rights o' the case. Short reck'nings make long friends, don't they, sir?"

To stop him, the Baron asked:

"When will you marry her?"

The peasant became frightened directly and embarrassed. Finally he said hesitatingly:

"Couldn't I have it put down in writin' first?"

"Why, bless my soul, isn't the marriage-contract good enough for you?" exclaimed the Baron, now really angry.

"But until I get that I should like it wrote down on paper," persisted the peasant. "Havin' it down on paper never does no harm."

"Give a plain answer, now at once," said the Baron, rising to put an end to the interview. "If you don't choose to marry the girl, say so. I know someone else who would be glad of the chance."

The idea of twenty thousand francs slipping from his hands into someone else's startled the peasant out of his cautiousness, and he at once decided to say "yes."

He made up his mind, and held out his hand as if he were concluding the purchase of a cow.

"Put it there, sir. It's done, and there's no going back from the bargain."

The Baron took his hand and then shouted, "Ludivine." The cook appeared at the window.

"Bring a bottle of wine."

They drank to the bargain that had been concluded, and the peasant went off in an easier frame of mind.

Nothing was said about this visit to Julien. The marriage-contract was drawn up in secret; then, once the banns were published, the marriage took place on a Monday morning. A neighbor carried the child to the church behind the bride and bridegroom, as an omen of good luck. None of the country people were surprised, and every one thought Désiré Lecoq very fortunate. He was born lucky, said the peasants with a malicious smile, without resentment.

Julien made a terrible scene, which cut short the stay of his parents-in-law at Les Peuples. Jeanne saw them leave without very deep regret, for Paul had become for her an inexhaustible source of happiness.

IX

Jeanne having now completely recovered from her confinement, they determined to return the Fourvilles' visit, and also to call on the Marquis de Coutelier. Julien had just bought another carriage at a sale, a phaeton. It needed only one horse, so they could go out twice a month.

It was harnessed one bright day in December, and after driving for two hours across the Normandy plains they began to go down a little valley, whose sloping sides were covered with trees, while the level ground at the bottom was cultivated. The ploughed fields were followed by meadows, the meadows by a fen covered with tall reeds, all dried up at this season, which waved in the wind like yellow ribbons. Then the valley took a sharp turn and the Château de la Vrillette came in sight. It was built between a wooded slope on the one side and a large lake on the other, the water stretching from the château wall to the tall fir-trees which covered the opposite slope of the valley.

They had to pass over an old drawbridge and under a vast Louis XIII archway to reach the courtyard in front of a handsome building of the same period as the archway, with brick frames round the windows and slated turrets. Julien pointed out all the different beauties of the mansion to Jeanne as if he were thoroughly acquainted with every nook and corner of it. He did the honors, going into raptures over its beauty:

"Just look at that archway! Isn't such a place superb? On the other side of the house, which looks onto the lake, there is a magnificent flight of steps leading right down to the water. Four boats are moored at the bottom of the steps, two for the Comte and two for the Comtesse. Down there on the right, where you can see that row of poplars, the lake ends and the river, which runs to Fécamp, rises. The place abounds in wild fowl, and the Comte passes all his time shooting. Ah! it is indeed a lordly residence."

The hall-door opened and the pale Comtesse came to meet her visitors with a smile on her face. She wore a trailing dress like a chatelaine of olden days. She looked like some beautiful Lady of the Lake born to inhabit this noble manor.

Four out of the eight drawing-room windows looked onto the lake, and the gloomy fir-trees which covered the opposite slope. The somber green made the lake look deep, austere, and dismal, and when the wind blew the moaning of the trees seemed like the voice of the swamp.

The Comtesse took both Jeanne's hands in hers as if she had known her since childhood, placed her in a seat and then drew a low chair beside her for herself, while Julien, who had regained all his old refinement during the last five months, smiled and chatted in a tender, familiar way. The Comtesse and he talked about the rides they had had together. She laughed a little at his bad horsemanship, and called him "The Tottering Knight," and he too laughed, calling her in return "The Amazon Queen."

A gun went off just under the window, and Jeanne gave a little cry. It was the Comte shooting teal. His wife at once called him in. There was the splash of oars, the grating of a boat against the stone steps and then the Comte came in, a huge figure in high boots, followed by two dripping dogs of a reddish hue, like himself, which lay down on the carpet before the door.

He seemed more at his ease in his own house, and was delighted to see the visitors. He ordered more wood for the fire, and Madeira and biscuits to be brought.

"Of course you will dine with us," he exclaimed.

Jeanne, who never ceased thinking of her child, refused the invitation, and as he pressed her to stay and she still persisted in her refusal, Julien made a movement of impatience. Then afraid of arousing her husband's quarrelsome temper, she consented to stay, though the idea of not seeing Paul till the next day was torture to her.

It was a delightful afternoon. First of all the visitors were taken to see the springs which flowed from the foot of a moss-covered rock into a crystal basin of water which bubbled as if it were boiling, and then they went in a boat among the dry reeds, where paths of water had been formed by cutting down the rushes.

The Comte rowed, his two dogs sitting one on each side of him with their noses in the air, and each vigorous stroke of the oars lifted the boat half out of the water and sent it rapidly on its way. Jeanne occasionally let her hand trail in the water, enjoying the icy coolness, which penetrated from her fingers to her heart. Julien and the Comtesse, well wrapped up in rugs, sat in the stern of the boat, smiling eternally as people do whose happiness is complete.

The evening drew on, and with it the icy, northerly wind came over the withered reeds. The sun had disappeared behind the firs, and it made one cold only to look at the crimson sky, covered with tiny, red, fantastically shaped clouds.

They all went into the big drawing-room where an enormous fire was blazing. At the very threshold one felt an atmosphere of warmth and comfort, and the Comte gaily lifted up his wife in his strong arms like a child, and gave her two hearty kisses on her cheeks.

Jeanne could not help smiling at this good-natured giant; whose mustaches gave him the appearance of an ogre. "What wrong impressions of people one forms every day," she thought; and, almost involuntarily, she glanced at Julien. He was standing in the doorway, his eyes fixed on the Comte and his face very pale. His expression frightened her and, going up to him, she asked:

"What is the matter? are you ill?"

"There's nothing the matter with me," he answered, churlishly. "Leave me alone. I only feel cold."

When they went into the dining-room the Comte begged permission for his dogs to come in. They came and sat one on each side of their master, who every minute threw them some scrap of food, and tickled their silky ears. The animals stretched out their heads, and wagged their tails, quivering with pleasure.

After dinner, when Jeanne and Julien were preparing to go, the Comte insisted on their staying to see some fishing by torchlight. They and the Comtesse stood on the steps leading down to the lake, while the Comte got into his boat with a servant carrying a lighted torch and a net. The night was clear and bracing beneath a sky sown with gold. The torch cast strange trembling reflections over the water, its dancing glimmers lighting up the reeds and illuminating the curtain of firs. Suddenly, as the boat turned round, an enormous fantastic shadow was thrown on the background of the illumined wood. It was the shadow of a man, but the head rose above the trees and was lost against the dark sky, while the feet seemed to be down in the lake. This huge creature raised its arms as if it would grasp the stars. The arms rose suddenly and fell again, and the splash of water was heard.

The boat tacked a little, and the gigantic shadow seemed to run along the wood, which was lighted up as the torch moved with the boat; then it was lost in the darkness, then reappeared on the château wall, smaller, but more distinct; and the loud voice of the Comte was heard exclaiming:

"Gilberte, I have caught eight!"

The oars splashed, and the enormous shadow remained standing in the same place on the wall, but gradually it became thinner and shorter; the head seemed to sink lower and the body to get narrower, and when M. de Fourville came up the steps, followed by the servant carrying the torch, it was reduced to

his exact proportions, and faithfully copied all his movements. In the net he had eight big fish, which were still
quivering.

As Jeanne and Julien were driving home, well
wrapped up in cloaks and rugs which the Fourvilles
had lent them, she said, almost involuntarily:

"What a good-hearted man that giant is!"

"Yes," answered Julien, who was drowsy; "but he
does not always restrain his affection before people."

A week later they called on the Couteliers, who were
supposed to be the highest family in the province, and
whose estate lay near the town of Cany. The new château, built in the reign of Louis XIV, lay in a magnificent park, entirely surrounded by walls, and the ruins
of the old château could be seen from the higher parts
of the grounds.

A liveried servant showed the visitors into a large,
handsome room. In the middle of the floor an enormous
Sèvres vase stood on a column, and in the pedestal,
under glass, was the king's autograph letter, offering
this royal gift to the Marquis Léopold Hervé Joseph
Germer de Varneville de Rollebosc de Coutelier. Jeanne
and Julien were looking at this regal present when the
Marquis and Marquise came in.

The Marquise, who was powdered, thought her rank
constrained her to be amiable, and her desire to appear
condescending made her affected. Her husband was a
big man, with white hair brushed straight up all over
his head, and a haughtiness in his voice, in all his movements, in his every attitude, which plainly showed his
importance. They were ceremonious people whose
minds, whose feelings, whose words alike seemed
stilted.

They both talked on without waiting for an answer,
smiled with an air of indifference, and behaved as if

they were accomplishing a duty imposed upon them by their superior birth in receiving the smaller nobles of the province with such politeness. Jeanne and Julien tried to make themselves agreeable, though they felt ill at ease, and when the time came to conclude their visit they hardly knew how to retire, though they did not want to stay any longer. However, the Marquise, herself, ended the visit naturally and simply by stopping short the conversation, like a queen ending an audience.

"I don't think we will call on anyone else, unless you want to," said Julien, as they were going back. "The Fourvilles are quite as many friends as I want."

And Jeanne agreed with him.

December slowly passed, that dark month, a gloomy gap at the end of the year. The confined life of the previous winter began again, but Jeanne did not feel dull; her thoughts were too full of Paul, whom Julien looked at surreptitiously with an uneasy, dissatisfied air. She would hold him in her arms, covering him with those passionate kisses which mothers lavish on their children, then offering the baby's face to his father:

"Why don't you kiss him?" she would say. "You hardly seem to love him."

Julien would just touch the infant's smooth forehead with his lips, holding his body as far away as possible, as if he were afraid of the little hands touching him in their aimless movements. Then he would go quickly out of the room, almost as though the child disgusted him.

The mayor, the doctor, and the priest came to dinner occasionally, and sometimes the Fourvilles, with whom they had become very intimate. The Comte seemed to worship Paul. He nursed the child on his knees during the whole of their visits, sometimes holding him the whole afternoon. He touched him delicately with his huge hands. He would tickle the child's nose with the ends of his long mustaches, and then suddenly cover his face with kisses almost as passionate as a mother's. It was the great sorrow of his life that he had no children.

March was bright, dry, and almost mild. The Comtesse Gilberte again proposed that they should all four go for some rides together, and Jeanne, a little tired of the long, weary evenings and the dull, monotonous days, was only too pleased at the idea and agreed to it at once. And for a week she amused herself making her riding habit. Then they commenced their rides.

They always rode two and two, the Comtesse and Julien leading the way, and the Comte and Jeanne about a hundred feet behind. The latter couple talked quietly, like two friends, as they rode along, for, each attracted by the other's straightforward ways and kindly heart, they had become fast friends. The others talked in whispers alternated by noisy bursts of laughter, and looked into each other's eyes to read there the things their lips did not utter, and often they would break into a gallop, as if impelled by a desire to escape away, far away.

Sometimes it seemed as if something irritated Gilberte. Her sharp tones would be borne on the breeze to the ears of the couple loitering behind, and the Comte would say to Jeanne, with a smile:

"My wife does not always get out of bed on the right side."

One evening, as they were returning home, the Comtesse began to spur her mare, and then pull her in with sudden jerks on the rein.

"Take care, or she'll run away with you," said Julien two or three times.

"So much the worse for me; it's nothing to do with

you," she replied, in such cold, hard tones that the clear words rang out over the fields as if they were actually floating in the air.

The mare reared, kicked, and foamed at the mouth, and the Comte cried out anxiously:

"Do take care what you are doing, Gilberte!"

Then, in a fit of defiance, for she was in one of those nervous moods that nothing can check, she brought her whip heavily down between the animal's ears. It reared, beat the air with its forelegs for a moment, then, with a tremendous bound, set off over the plain at the top of its speed. First it crossed a meadow, then some ploughed fields, kicking up the damp, heavy soil behind it, and going at such a speed that in a few moments the others could hardly distinguish the Comtesse from her horse.

Julien stood stock still, crying: "Madame! Madame!" The Comte gave a groan, and, bending down over his powerful steed, galloped after his wife. He encouraged his steed with voice and hand, urged it on with whip and spur, and it seemed as though he carried the big animal between his legs, and raised it from the ground at every leap it took. The horse went at an inconceivable speed, keeping a straight line regardless of all obstacles; and Jeanne could see the two outlines of the husband and wife diminish and fade in the distance, till they vanished altogether, like two birds chasing each other till they are lost to sight beyond the horizon.

Julien walked his horse up to his wife, murmuring angrily: "She is mad today." And they both went off after their friends, who were hidden in a dip in the plain. In about a quarter of an hour they saw them coming back, and soon they came up to them.

The Comte, looking red, hot, happy, and triumphant, was leading his wife's horse. She was very pale; her features looked drawn and contracted, and she leaned on her husband's shoulder as if she were going to faint. That day Jeanne understood how madly the Comte loved his wife.

All through the following month the Comtesse was merrier than she had ever been before. She came to Les Peuples as often as she could, and was always laughing and jumping up to kiss Jeanne. She seemed to have found some unknown source of happiness, and her husband simply worshiped her now, following her about with his eyes and seeking every pretext for touching her hand or her dress in an increase of passionate affection.

"We are happy now," he said, one evening, to Jeanne. "Gilberte has never been so nice as she is now; nothing seems to vex her or make her angry. Until lately I was never quite sure that she loved me, but now I know she does."

Julien had changed for the better also; he had become gay and good-tempered, and their friendship seemed to have brought peace and happiness to both families.

The spring was exceptionally early and warm. From the mild mornings until the calm, warm evenings, the sun helped the earth to germinate. There was a sudden and powerful burgeoning of all life simultaneously, one of those irresistible bursts of sap, that ardor of rebirth which nature sometimes shows in favored years when the world seems to have grown young again.

Jeanne felt a vague excitement in the presence of this fermentation of life. She would be suddenly moved by a little flower in the grass. She gave way to a sweet melancholy and spent hours languidly dreaming. All the tender incidents of her first hours of love came back to her. Not that any renewal of affection for her hus-

band stirred her heart; *that* had been completely destroyed; destroyed forever; but her whole body, fanned
by the breezes, filled with the perfume of spring, was
troubled, as if drawn by an invisible and tender appeal.
She liked to be alone, and in the warm sunshine, to
enjoy these vague, peaceful sensations which aroused
no thoughts.

One morning as she was thus dreaming, suddenly
she saw in her mind that sunlit space in the little wood
near Étretat where for the first time she had felt thrilled
by the presence of the man who loved her then, where
he had for the first time timidly hinted at his hopes,
and where she had believed that she was going to
realize the radiant future of her dreams. She thought
she should like to make a romantic, superstitious pilgrimage to the wood, and she felt as if a visit to that
spot would in some way alter the course of her life.

Julien had gone out at daybreak, she did not know
whither, so she ordered the Martins' little white horse,
which she sometimes rode, to be saddled, and set off.

It was one of those calm days when there is not a
leaf nor a blade of grass stirring. Everything seemed
motionless for all eternity, as though the wind were
dead, even the insects seemed to have disappeared. A
burning, steady heat descended from the sun in a
golden mist, and Jeanne walked her horse along, enjoying the stillness, and every now and then looking
up at a tiny white cloud, like a speck of cotton, a flake
of vapor forgotten there in the midst of the bright
blue sky. She went down into the valley leading to the
sea, between the two great arches which are called the
gates of Étretat, and went slowly towards the wood.

The sunlight poured down through the foliage which
as yet was not very thick, and Jeanne wandered along
the little paths unable to find the spot where she had

sat with Julien. She turned into a long alley and, at the other end of it, saw two saddle-horses fastened to a tree; she recognized them at once; they were Gilberte's and Julien's. Tired of being alone and pleased at this unexpected meeting, she trotted quickly up to them, and when she reached the two animals, which were waiting quietly as if accustomed to stand like this, she called aloud. There was no answer.

On the trampled grass lay a woman's glove and two whips. They had evidently sat down and then gone farther on, leaving the horses tied to the tree. She waited fifteen or twenty minutes surprised and wondering what they could be doing. As she had got off her horse, she leaned against the trunk of a tree and stood quite motionless. Without seeing her two little birds flew down onto the grass close by her. One of them hopped round the other, fluttering his outstretched wings, and chirping and nodding his little head; all at once they coupled. Jeanne watched them, as surprised as if she had never known of such a thing before; then she thought: "Oh, of course! It is springtime."

Then came another thought—a suspicion. She looked again at the glove, the whips, and the two horses standing riderless; then she sprang on her horse with an intense longing to leave this place. She started back to Les Peuples at a gallop. Her brain was busy reasoning, connecting different incidents and thinking it all out.

How was it that she had never noticed anything, had never guessed this before? How was it that Julien's frequent absence from home, his return to his former elegance, his better temper had told her nothing? Now she understood Gilberte's nervous irritability, her exaggerated affection for herself and the bliss in which she had appeared to be living lately, and which had so pleased the Comte.

She pulled up her horse to a walking pace, for she wanted to think calmly, and the quick movement confused her ideas. After the first shock she became almost indifferent; she felt neither jealousy nor hatred, only contempt. She did not think about Julien at all, for nothing that he could do would have astonished her, but the twofold treachery of the Comtesse, her friend, revolted her. So every one was treacherous, and untrue and faithless! Her eyes filled with tears, for sometimes one weeps over an illusion as bitterly as over the death of a friend. She resolved to pretend she knew nothing. Her heart would be dead to every one but Paul and her parents, but she would bear a smiling face.

When she reached home she caught up her son in her arms, carried him to her room and pressed her lips to his face again and again, and for a whole hour she played with and caressed him.

Julien came in to dinner. He was charming and good-humored and full of great intentions.

"Won't your father and mother come and stay with us this year?" he said.

She was so grateful for this kindness that she almost pardoned what she had seen in the wood. She longed to see the two people she loved best after Paul, and she passed the whole evening in writing to them and urging them to come as soon as possible.

They wrote to say they would come on the twentieth of May; it was then the seventh and she awaited their arrival with intense impatience. Besides her natural affection, she felt a renewed desire to have near her two honest hearts, to talk freely to decent people innocent of vileness, whose life and every action, thought, and desire had always been upright and pure. She felt she stood alone in her honesty among all this guilt. She had learned to dissimulate her feelings, to meet the Comtesse with an outstretched hand and a smiling face, but her sense of desolation increased, of contempt for her fellow-men. Every day some village scandal reached her ears which filled her with still greater disgust and scorn for human frailty.

The Couillards' daughter had just had a child and was therefore going to be married. The Martins' servant, who was an orphan, a little girl only fifteen years old, who lived near, and a widow, a lame, poverty-stricken woman who was so horribly dirty that she had been nicknamed La Crotte, were all pregnant; and one was continually hearing of another pregnancy, or of the misconduct of some girl, some married woman with a family, or of some rich and respected farmer.

This warm spring seemed to revive the passions of mankind as it revived the plants; and to Jeanne, whose senses were dead, and whose wounded heart and romantic soul were alone stirred by the warm springtide breezes, and who only dreamed of the poetic side of love, these bestial desires were revolting and hateful. The mating of human couples irritated her as something contrary to the laws of nature, and she was angry with Gilberte, not for having robbed her of her husband, but for having bespattered herself with this filth. She was not of the same class as the peasants, who could not resist their brutal desires; then how could she have fallen like these brutes?

The very day that her parents were to arrive, Julien increased his wife's disgust by telling her laughingly, as though it were something quite natural and very funny, that the baker having heard a noise in his oven the day before, which was not baking day, had gone to see what it was, and instead of finding the stray cat he expected to see, had surprised his wife, "who was certainly not putting bread into the oven." "The baker closed the mouth of the oven," went on Julien, "and they would have been suffocated if the baker's little boy, who had seen his mother go into the oven with the blacksmith, had not told the neighbors what was going on." Julien laughed as he added, "That will give a nice flavor to the bread. It is just like a tale of La Fontaine's."

For some time after that Jeanne could not touch bread.

When the post-chaise drew up before the door with the Baron's smiling face looking out of the window, the young woman felt a profound emotion fill her whole being, a violent burst of affection such as she had never felt before; but when she saw her mother she was shocked and almost fainted. The Baronne looked ten years older than when she had left Les Peuples six months before. Her huge, flabby cheeks were suffused with blood, her eyes had a glazed look, and she could not move a step unless she was supported on either side; her shortness of breath was now a wheezing and she breathed with such difficulty that it hurt one to hear her.

The Baron, who had seen her every day, had not noticed the change, and if she had complained or said her breathing and the heavy feeling about her heart were getting worse, he had answered:

"Oh, no, my dear. You have always been like this."

Jeanne went to her own room and cried bitterly when she had taken her parents upstairs. Then she went to her father and, throwing herself in his arms, said, with her eyes still full of tears:

"Oh, how changed mother is! What is the matter with her? Do tell me what is the matter with her?"

"Do you think she is changed?" asked the Baron in

surprise. "It must be your fancy. You know I have been with her all this time, and to me she seems just the same as she has always been; she is not any worse."

"Your mother is in a bad way," said Julien to his wife that evening. "I don't think she's good for much now." And when Jeanne burst into tears, he lost his patience.

"Oh, good gracious! I don't say that she is dangerously ill. You always exaggerate. She is changed, that's all; it's only natural at her age."

In a week Jeanne had got accustomed to her mother's altered appearance and thought no more about it, thrusting her fears from her, as people always do put aside their fears and cares, with an instinctive and natural, though selfish, dislike of anything unpleasant.

The Baronne, unable to walk, only went out for about half an hour every day. When she had gone once up and down "her" avenue, she could not move another step and asked to be allowed to sit down on "her" seat. Some days she could not walk even to the end, and would say:

"Let us stop; my hypertrophy is too much for me today."

She never laughed as she used to; things which, the year before, would have sent her into fits of laughter, only brought a faint smile to her lips now. Her eyesight was still excellent, and she passed her time in reading *Corinne* and Lamartine's *Meditations* over again, and in going through her "Souvenir drawer." She would empty on her knees the old letters, which were so dear to her heart, place the drawer on a chair beside her, look slowly over each "relic," and then put it back in its place. When she was quite alone she kissed some of the letters as she might have kissed the hair of some loved one who was dead.

Jeanne, coming into the room suddenly, sometimes found her in tears.

"What is the matter, mamma, dear?" she would ask.

"My relics have upset me," the Baronne would answer, with a long-drawn sigh. "They stir up pleasant memories which are all over now, and make me think of people whom I had almost forgotten. I seem to see them, to hear their voices, and it makes me sad. You will feel the same, later on."

If the Baron came in and found them talking like this, he would say:

"Jeanne, my dear, if you take my advice, you will burn all your letters—those from your mother, mine, everyone's. There is nothing more painful than to plunge into the memories of one's youth when one is old."

But Jeanne also kept all her old letters to form a "relic-box," although she differed from her mother in everything else, obeying the hereditary instinct for dreaming sentimentality.

A few days after his arrival, business called the Baron away again. The Baronne soon began to get better, and Jeanne, forgetting Julien's infidelity and Gilberte's treachery, was almost perfectly happy. The weather was splendid. Mild, starlit nights followed the soft evenings, and glorious days began with dazzling sunrises. The fields were covered with bright, sweet-smelling flowers, and the vast calm sea glittered in the sun from morning till night.

One afternoon Jeanne went into the fields with Paul in her arms. She felt an exquisite gladness as she looked now at her son, now at the flowery grass by the roadside, and every minute she pressed her baby closely to her and kissed him. Then, caressed by some sweet country perfume, she felt like swooning, annihilated by infinite happiness. Then she thought of her child's future. What would he be? Sometimes she hoped he would become a great man, famous and powerful. Sometimes she felt she would rather he remained with her, passing his life in tender devotion to his mother and unknown to the world. When she loved him with her selfish mother's heart, she wished him to remain simply her son; but when she listened to her passionate reason she hoped he would become something of importance in the world.

She sat down at the edge of a ditch and studied the child's face as if she had never really looked at it before. It seemed so strange to think that this little baby would grow up, and walk with manly strides, that these soft cheeks would become bearded, and the feeble murmur change to a deep-toned voice.

Someone called her, and, looking up, she saw Marius running towards her. Thinking he had come to announce some visitor, she got up, feeling vexed at being disturbed. The boy was running as fast as his legs could carry him.

"Madame!" he cried, when he was near enough to be heard. "Madame la Baronne is very ill."

She felt as if a douche of cold water had been poured down her spine, and ran back, her head in a whirl. From a distance she could see a little crowd standing under the plane-tree. She rushed forward and when the group opened she saw her mother on the ground, her head supported by two pillows, her face black, her eyes closed, and her chest, which for the last twenty years had heaved so tumultuously, motionless. The child's nurse was standing there; she took him from his mother's arms, and carried him away.

"How did it happen? What made her fall?" asked

Jeanne, looking up with haggard eyes. "Send for the doctor immediately."

As she turned she saw the priest, who had heard about it somehow or other. He at once offered his services, and, turning up his sleeves, began to rub the Baronne with eau de Cologne and vinegar; but this had no effect.

"She ought to be undressed and put to bed," said the priest.

The farmer, Joseph Couillard, old Simon and Ludivine were there, and with the Abbé's assistance they tried to lift the Baronne, but when they lifted her, her head fell backwards, and her dress, which they were grasping, gave way, her huge body was so heavy and hard to move. Jeanne shrieked with horror. They had to lay the huge, flabby body on the ground.

They had to bring an armchair from the drawing-room and when they had placed her in it, they could at last carry her. They went slowly up the stone steps and then upstairs. When they reached the bedroom they placed her on the bed. The cook was undressing her as best she could when the Widow Dentu came in, as if, like the priest, she had "smelt death," as the servants said. Joseph Couillard hurried off for the doctor, and the priest was going to fetch the holy oil, when the nurse whispered in his ear:

"You needn't trouble to go, Monsieur le curé. I have seen too much of death not to know that she is gone."

Jeanne, in desperation, begged them to tell her what she could do, what remedies they had better apply. The priest thought that anyhow he might pronounce an absolution, and for two hours they watched beside the lifeless, livid body, Jeanne, racked with anguish and grief, sobbing aloud as she knelt beside the bed. When the door opened to admit the doctor, she thought that with him came safety and consolation and hope, and she rushed to meet him, trying to tell him, in a voice broken with sobs, all the details of the catastrophe.

"She was walking—as she did every day—and she seemed quite well, better even—than usual. She had eaten some soup and two eggs for lunch, and—quite suddenly, without any warning she fell—and turned black, as she is now; she has not moved since, and we have—tried everything to restore her to consciousness —everything——"

She stopped abruptly for she saw the nurse making a sign to the doctor to intimate that it was all over. Then she refused to understand the gesture, and went on anxiously:

"Is it anything serious? Do you think there is any danger?"

He answered at last:

"I very much fear that—that life is extinct. Be brave and try to bear up."

Jeanne opened her arms, and threw herself on her mother's body. Julien came in. He made no sign of grief or pity, but stood looking simply vexed; he had been taken too much by surprise to at once assume an expression of sorrow.

"I expected it," he whispered. "I knew she could not live long."

He drew out his handkerchief, wiped his eyes, knelt down and crossed himself as he mumbled something, then rose and attempted to raise his wife. She was clinging to the corpse, almost lying on it as she passionately kissed it; they had to drag her away for she was nearly mad with grief.

She was allowed to go back after an hour. Then every shadow of hope vanished, and the room had been ar-

ranged as a death chamber. Julien and the priest were
standing near one of the windows, talking in whispers.
The Widow Dentu was seated comfortably in an armchair, as one accustomed to watching by corpses, who
feels at home in a house where death has entered, and
she seemed to be already dozing. Night was falling.
The priest went to meet Jeanne as she came into the
room, and taking both her hands in his, he poured an
unctuous stream of pious consolation into this inconsolable heart. He spoke of the dead woman in sacerdotal
phrases, and, with the assumed sadness of the priest for
whom death is a windfall, he offered to pass the night
in prayers beside the body.

But Jeanne refused this offer as well as she could for
her tears. She wanted to be alone, quite alone, with her
mother this last night.

"That cannot be," interposed Julien; "we will watch
beside her together."

She shook her head, unable to speak for some moments; then she said:

"She was my mother, and I want to watch beside her
alone."

"Let her do as she wants," whispered the doctor;
"the nurse can stay in the next room," and Julien and
the priest, thinking of their night's rest, gave in.

Then the Abbé Picot knelt down, prayed for a few
moments, then rose and went out of the room, saying,
"She was a saintly woman," in the same tone as he
always said, "Dominus vobiscum."

"Won't you have some dinner?" asked the Vicomte
in a perfectly ordinary voice.

Jeanne, not thinking he was speaking to her, made no
answer.

"You would feel much better if you would eat something," he went on again.

"Let someone go for papa, directly," she answered distractedly; and he went out of the room to dispatch a mounted messenger to Rouen.

She remained in a sort of stupor of grief, as if she were waiting to give way to her passion of regret until she should be alone with her mother. The room became filled with shadows. The Widow Dentu moved noiselessly about, finding and arranging things in the dark, with the silent movement of a sick-nurse. Then she lit two candles which she placed at the head of the bed on a small table covered with a white cloth. Jeanne seemed unconscious of everything; she was waiting until she should be alone.

When he had dined, Julien came upstairs again and asked for the second time:

"Won't you have something to eat?"

His wife shook her head, and he sat down looking more resigned than sad, and did not say anything more. They all three sat apart from one another; the nurse dropped off to sleep every now and then, snored for a little while, then awoke with a start. After some time Julien rose and went over to his wife.

"Do you still want to be left alone?" he asked.

She involuntarily seized his hand in hers. "Oh, yes; do leave me."

He kissed her on the forehead, whispered, "I shall come and see you from time to time," then went away with the Widow Dentu, who wheeled her armchair into the next room.

Jeanne closed the door and opened both windows wide. A warm breeze, laden with the sweet smell of the hay, blew into the room, and on the lawn, which had been mown the day before, she could see the heaps of dry grass lying in the moonlight. This pleasant sensation hurt her, striking her as an irony. She returned to the bed, took one of the cold, still hands, and gazed at her mother.

She was no longer swollen as she was at the time of the attack. Now she seemed to be asleep, sleeping more peacefully than ever before, and the pale flame of the candles, stirred by the wind, changed the shadows on the face every moment as though it moved and she were alive again. Jeanne looked at her hungrily, and from the depths of her childhood memories arose. She remembered her mother's visits to the convent parlor, the way she used to hold out the bag of cakes to her; she thought of all her little ways, her affectionate words, the way she used to move, the wrinkles that came round her eyes when she laughed, the deep sigh she always heaved when she sat down, and all her little, daily habits, and as she stood gazing at the dead body she kept repeating, almost mechanically, "She is dead; she is dead," until at last she realized all the horror of that word.

The woman who was lying there—mamma—little mother—Madame Adelaide, was dead! She would never move, never speak, never laugh, never sit opposite her husband at the dinner-table again, never say, "Good morning, Jeannette." She was dead. She would be enclosed in a coffin, placed beneath the ground, and that would be the end; they would never see her again. It could not be possible! What! She would have no mother!

This dear, familiar face, the first her eyes had seen, the first she had ever loved, this great reservoir of affection, this unique being, her mother, whose share of her heart was greater than that of all other human beings—she was gone. She had only a few hours left to look at her face, motionless and unconscious; then nothing, nothing more, only a memory.

And she fell on her knees in a paroxysm of despair, her hands clutching the sheet, her face buried in the covers as she cried in a heart-rending tone, "Oh, mamma, my poor mamma!" Then feeling that she was losing her reason as she had done on the night when she fled across the snow, she rose and ran to the window to drink in the fresh air—the air which had not passed over the corpse or the bed on which it lay. The new-mown hay, the trees, the waste land and the distant sea lay peacefully sleeping in the tender moonlight. Something of this sweet calm entered into Jeanne, and she began to weep slowly. Then she went back to her seat by the bed-side and held her mother's dead hand in hers, as if she were watching by a sick-bed. Attracted by the lighted candles, a big, winged insect had entered through the open window and was flying about the room, dashing against the wall at every moment like a ball. Disturbed by its droning flight Jeanne looked up to see where it was, but she could only see its shadow moving over the white ceiling.

She ceased to hear it, and then, she noticed the regular ticking of the clock and another fainter noise, or rather an almost imperceptible rustling. It was the ticking of her mother's watch, which had been forgotten when her dress had been taken off and thrown at the foot of the bed. Suddenly a vague contrast between this little piece of mechanism still moving, while her mother lay dead, sent a fresh pang of anguish through her heart. She looked at the time. It was hardly half-past ten, and as she thought of the long night to come, she was seized with a horrible dread.

Other memories came back to her, those of her own life—of Rosalie, of Gilberte—of the bitter disillusionment of her heart. Life contained nothing but misery and pain, misfortune and death; there was nothing true, nothing honest, everything caused suffering and tears. Where could repose and happiness be found? In another existence, no doubt, when the soul had been delivered from its earthly trials. The soul! Her thoughts turned to this unfathomable mystery, seizing at once upon poetic theories which were immediately upset by others no less unreal. Where was her mother's soul now, the soul which had forsaken this still, cold body? Perhaps it was far away, floating in space. Where? Was it wandering like some invisible bird freed from its cage? Had it returned to God, or was it scattered among the new germs of creation? It might be very near; perhaps in this very room, hovering around the inanimate body it had left, and at this thought Jeanne fancied she felt a breath, as if a spirit had passed by her. She was frightened, horribly frightened, so that she dared not move, nor breathe, nor turn round to look behind her, her heart beating wildly as in a nightmare.

At that moment the invisible insect again commenced its flight around the room, knocking against the walls. Jeanne trembled from head to foot, then, as she recognized the buzzing she felt a little reassured, and rose and looked around. Her eyes fell on the escritoire with the sphinxes' heads, the guardian of the "relics." As she looked at it a tender and curious thought came to her mind. It was to read over in this last watch, as though they were a prayer-book, the old letters that her mother loved. It seemed to her that she was about to perform a delicate and sacred, a really filial duty, which would give pleasure to little mother in the other world.

It was the correspondence of her grandfather and grandmother, whom she had never known. She wanted her hands to join theirs across the corpse of their daughter, to join them on this funeral night, as if they, too, were suffering, and form a mysterious chain of affection between those who had died so long ago and the woman who had but just joined them, and her child who was still on earth.

She got up and pulled down the lid of the little desk, and took from the lowest drawer about ten small packets of faded paper, carefully tied up and ranged in order. A refinement of sentimentality prompted her to place them all on the bed in the Baronne's arms; then she began to read.

They were old-fashioned letters with the perfume of another century about them, such as one finds in old family desks. The first commenced, "My dearest"; another "My little darling"; then came some beginning "My pet"—"My beloved daughter," then "My dear child"—"My dear Adelaide"—"My dear daughter," varying as the letters had been addressed to the child, the young girl, and, later on, to the young wife. They were all full of foolish, loving phrases, and news about a thousand insignificant, homely events, which, to a stranger, would have seemed too trivial to mention: "Father has influenza; Hortense has burnt her finger; Croquerat, the cat, is dead; the fir-tree which stood on the right-hand side of the gate has been cut down; mother lost her prayer-book as she was coming home from church, she thinks someone must have stolen it," and they talked about people whom Jeanne had never known, but whose names she vaguely remembered hearing in her childhood.

She was touched by these simple details which seemed to reveal all her mother's past life and the inmost secrets of her heart to her. She looked at the corpse as it lay there, and suddenly she began to read the letters aloud, as though to console and gladden the dead woman; and the still corpse seemed happy. One by one she threw the letters on the foot of the bed, resolving to place them all in her mother's coffin as if they were flowers.

She untied another packet. These were in another handwriting, and began, "I cannot live without your kisses. I love you madly."

There was nothing more, not even a signature. She turned the paper over, unable to understand it. It was addressed clearly enough to "Madame la Baronne Le Perthuis des Vauds."

She opened the next. "Come tonight as soon as he has gone out. We shall have at least one hour together. I adore you."

Another: "I have passed a night of anguish, longing for you in vain. I fancied you in my arms, your mouth quivering beneath mine, your eyes looking into my eyes. And then I could have dashed myself from the window, as I thought that, at that very moment, you were sleeping beside him, that he could love you when he wished."

Jeanne was perfectly bewildered. What did that mean? To whom, for whom, from whom were these words of love?

She went on reading, coming across fresh impassioned declarations, appointments with warnings as to prudence, and always at the end the six words: "Be sure to burn this letter!"

At last she came to an ordinary note, merely accepting an invitation to dinner; it was signed "Paul d'Ennemare," and was in the same writing. He was the man of whom the Baron still spoke as "Poor old Paul," and whose wife had been the Baronne's dearest friend!

Then into Jeanne's mind came a suspicion which at once changed to a certainty—he had been her mother's lover! With a sudden gesture of loathing, she threw from her all these odious letters, as she would have shaken off some venomous reptile, and, running to the window, she wept bitterly, with cries that racked her breast in spite of her. All her strength seemed to have left her; she sank on the ground, and, hiding her face in the curtains to stifle her moans, she sobbed in an agony of despair. She would have crouched there the whole night if the sound of someone moving in the next room had not made her start to her feet. Perhaps it was her father! And all these letters were lying on the bed and on the floor! He had only to come in and open one, and he would know all!

She seized all the old, yellow papers—her grandparent's epistles, the love-letters, those she had not unfolded, those that were still lying in the drawer—and threw them all into the fireplace. Then she took one of the candles which were burning on the little table, and set fire to this heap of paper. A bright flame sprang up at once, lighting up the room, the bed and the corpse with a bright, flickering light and casting on the white bed-curtain a dark, trembling shadow of the rigid face and huge body beneath the sheet.

When there was nothing left but a heap of ashes in the bottom of the grate, Jeanne went and sat by the open window, as though now she dared not sit by the corpse. She began to cry again, and, hiding her face in her hands, she moaned out in heartbroken tones, "Oh, poor mamma! Poor mamma!"

Then a terrible thought came to her. Suppose her mother, by some strange chance, was not dead; suppose she was only in a trance-like sleep and should suddenly rise and speak! Would not the knowledge of this horrible secret lessen her love for her mother? Should she be able to kiss her with the same respect, and regard her with the same esteem as before? No! She knew it would be impossible; and the thought almost broke her heart.

The night wore on; the stars were fading, and a cool

breeze sprang up. The moon was slowly sinking towards the sea, over which she was shedding her pearly light, and the memory of that other night she had passed at the window, the night of her return to Les Peuples, came back to Jeanne. Ah! how far away that was! How changed everything was, and what a different future lay before her! Over the sky crept a tinge of pink, a joyous, lovely, enchanting pink. She looked at it in surprise, as at some phenomenon, this radiant break of day, and asked herself if it were possible that, on a planet where such dawns were found, there should be neither joy nor happiness.

A noise at the door made her start. It was Julien. "Well," he said, "are you not very tired?"

She murmured, "No," happy at being no longer alone. "Go and rest now," he said. She kissed her mother, a long, sad kiss; then she went to her room.

That day passed in attending to those melancholy duties that always surround a death; the Baron came in the evening, and cried a great deal. The next day the funeral took place. After she had pressed her lips to the clammy forehead for the last time, performed the final duties, and seen the coffin fastened down, Jeanne retired. The mourners were expected.

Gilberte arrived first, and threw herself into her friend's arms, sobbing violently. From the windows the carriages could be seen turning by the railings and driving up, and voices were heard in the hall. The room gradually filled with women in mourning, with whom Jeanne was not acquainted; then the Marquise de Coutelier and the Vicomtesse de Briseville arrived, and went up to her and kissed her. She suddenly perceived that Aunt Lison was in the room, and she gave her such an affectionate embrace, that the old maid was nearly overcome. Julien came in dressed in deep mourning; he seemed very busy and very pleased that all these people had come. He whispered some question to his wife about the arrangements, and added in a low tone:

"It will be a very grand funeral; all the best families are here."

Then he went away again, bowing gravely to the ladies.

Aunt Lison and the Comtesse Gilberte stayed with Jeanne while the burial was taking place. The Comtesse repeatedly kissed her, murmuring, "Poor darling, poor darling," and when the Comte de Fourville came to take his wife home, he wept as if he had lost his own mother.

X

The next few days were very sad, those dull days in a house which seems empty because of the absence of a loved one who has gone forever, those days of suffering renewed each time one's hand encounters objects which the dead person constantly used. Every moment a memory strikes the heart and bruises it. There is the empty chair, the umbrella still standing in the hall, the glass which the maid has not yet washed. In every room there is something lying; the scissors, an odd glove, the book whose pages are dog-eared from the touch of fingers now stiff, the numberless other objects, which, insignificant in themselves, become a source of sharp pain because they recall so vividly a thousand little details, and one longs to flee anywhere else, to escape from this haunted house. But one must stay because others are there who remain and also suffer.

In addition, Jeanne was crushed by the pain of her discovery. The thought of it oppressed her and her wounded heart did not heal. The terrible secret increased her sense of desolation tenfold, for her confidence had been shattered with her only remaining belief.

Her father soon went away, to find relief from the grief which was deadening all his faculties in change of air and change of scene.

The old house, which witnessed every now and then the disappearance of one of its masters, resumed its quiet, regular existence.

Then Paul fell ill, and Jeanne nearly went mad. She remained for twelve days unable to sleep and scarcely touching food. The boy got well, but there remained the thought that he might die. What should she do if he did? What would become of her? Gradually there came a vague longing for another child, and soon she could think of nothing else, entirely possessed by her old desire to have about her a boy and a girl, and it became an obsession. But since Rosalie had been sent away, she had lived quite apart from Julien, and at the present moment it seemed utterly impossible to renew their former relations. Julien's affections were centered elsewhere; she knew that; and the mere thought of having to submit to his caresses again made her shudder with disgust.

Still, she would have overcome her repugnance, so tormented was she by the desire for another child, but she did not know how to resume their marital relations. She would have died rather than let her husband guess what was in her thoughts, and he never seemed to dream of approaching her now. Perhaps she would have given up the idea had not each night the vision of a daughter playing with Paul under the plane-tree appeared to her. Sometimes she felt she *must* get up and silently join her husband in his room; twice, in fact, she did glide to his door, but each time she came back, without having turned the handle, her heart beating with shame.

The Baron was away, her mother was dead, and now Jeanne had no one she could consult, to whom she could confide this delicate secret. She made up her mind, at last, to tell the Abbé Picot her difficulty, under the seal of confession. She went to him one day and found him in his little garden, reading his breviary among the fruit-trees. She talked to him for a few minutes about one thing and another, then she faltered, with a blush. "Monsieur l'Abbé, I want to confess."

He put on his spectacles to look at her better, for he was astonished. "I don't think you can have any very heavy sins on your conscience," he said, with a laugh.

"No, but I want to ask your advice on a subject so— so painful to enter upon, that I dare not talk about it in an ordinary way," she replied, now thoroughly confused.

He dropped his jovial manner at once and assumed his priestly air.

"Very well, my daughter, come to the confessional, and I will hear you there."

But she suddenly felt a scruple at talking of such things in the quietness of an empty church.

"No, Monsieur le curé—after all—if you will let me —I can tell you here what I want to say. See, we will go and sit in your little arbor over there."

As they walked slowly over to the arbor she tried to find the words in which she could best begin. They sat down, and she commenced, as if she were confessing, "Father," then hesitated, said again, "Father," then stopped altogether, too ashamed to continue.

The priest crossed his hands over his stomach and

waited for her to go on. "Well, my daughter," he said, perceiving her embarrassment, "you seem afraid to say what it is; come now, be brave."

"Father, I want to have another child," she said abruptly, like a coward throwing himself headlong into the danger he dreads.

The priest, hardly understanding what she meant, made no answer, and she tried to explain herself, but, in her confusion, she was at a loss for words.

"I am quite alone in life now; my father and my husband do not agree; my mother is dead, and—and—the other day I almost lost my son," she whispered with a shudder. "What would have become of me if he had died?"

She was silent. The priest looked at her in bewilderment.

"There, there; come to the point," he said.

"I want to have another child," she repeated.

He was used to the coarse pleasantries of the peasants, who did not mind what they said before him, and he answered, with a smile and a knowing shake of the head, "Well, it seems to me that depends entirely on you."

She raised her clear eyes to his and said, hesitatingly:

"But—but—don't you understand that since—since that trouble with—the—maid—my husband and I live —quite apart."

Accustomed as he was to the promiscuity and easy morals of the peasants, this revelation astonished him. Then he thought he could guess what the young wife really wanted, and he looked at her out of the corner of his eye, pitying her, and sympathizing with her distress.

"Yes, yes, I know exactly what you mean. I can quite understand that you should find your—your widowhood hard to bear. You are young, healthy, and it is only natural; very natural."

He began to smile, carried away by the Rabelaisian temper of the country priest. "Besides, the Church allows these feelings, sometimes," he went on, gently tapping Jeanne's hands. "What are we told? That carnal desires may be satisfied lawfully in wedlock only. Well, you are married, are you not? You know what that means."

She, in her turn, had not at first understood what his words implied, but when his meaning dawned on her, her face became crimson, and her eyes filled with tears.

"Oh! Monsieur le curé, what do you mean? What do you think? I assure you—I assure——" and she could not continue for her sobs.

Her emotion surprised him, and he tried to console her.

"There, there," he said; "I did not mean to pain you. I was only joking, and there's no harm in a joke between decent people. But leave it all in my hands, and I will speak to M. Julien."

She did not know what to say. She wished, now, that she could refuse his help, for she feared his want of tact would only increase her difficulties, but she did not dare say anything.

"Thank you, Monsieur le curé," she stammered; and then hurried away.

A week passed. She lived in an agony of doubts and fears. Then one evening, Julien watched her curiously all through dinner, with a certain smile on his lips, which she knew in his playful moods. He evinced towards her a gallantry which was faintly tinged with irony. After dinner they walked up and down the Baronne's avenue, and he whispered in her ear:

"Then we are going to be friends again?"

She made no answer, and kept her eyes fixed on the ground where there was a straight line, hardly visible now, as the grass had grown. It was the line traced by the Baronne's foot, which was gradually being effaced, just as her memory was fading, and Jeanne's heart felt swelling and bursting with grief; she seemed so lonely, so separated from everybody.

"For my part, I am only too pleased," continued Julien. "I was afraid of displeasing you."

The sun was setting; the air was mild. Jeanne longed to weep, to rest her head on some loving heart, and there whisper her sorrows. A sob rose in her throat. She threw herself into Julien's arms and wept. He looked at her head in surprise, unable to see her face, and he dropped a condescending kiss upon her hair, thinking she still loved him. Then they went indoors in silence and he followed her to her room and spent the night with her.

To him this renewal of their former relations was a duty, though hardly an unpleasant one, while she submitted to his embraces as a disgusting, painful necessity, and resolved to put an end to them forever, as soon as she was again pregnant. Soon, however, she found that her husband's caresses were not as they used to be; they may have been more refined, they certainly were not so complete. He treated her like a careful lover, instead of an easy husband. She was astonished, observed him and soon discovered that his caresses always stopped before conception was possible.

"Why do you not give yourself up to me as you used to do?" she whispered one night, her lips close to his.

"To keep you out of the family way, of course," he answered with a chuckle.

She started.

"Don't you wish for any more children, then?" she asked.

His amazement was so great, that, for a moment, he was silent; then:

"Eh? What do you say?" he exclaimed. "Are you in your right senses? Another child? I should think not, indeed! We've already got one too many, squalling and costing money, and bothering everybody. Another child! No, thank you!"

She clasped him in her arms, pressed her lips to his and murmured:

"Oh! I entreat you, make me a mother once more."

"Don't be so foolish," he replied, angrily. "Pray don't let me hear any more of this nonsense."

She said no more, but she resolved to trick him into giving her the happiness she desired. She tried to prolong her kisses, and threw her arms passionately around him, pressing him to her, and pretending a delirium of love she was very far from feeling. She tried every means to make him lose control over himself, but she never once succeeded.

Tormented more and more by her desire, driven to extremities, and ready to do or dare anything to gain her ends, she went again to the Abbé Picot. She found him just finishing lunch, with his face crimson, as he always had palpitation of the heart after eating. He looked up as she came in, and, anxious to hear the result of his mediation:

"Well?" he exclaimed.

"My husband does not want any more children," she answered at once without any of the hesitation or shamefaced timidity she had shown before.

The priest got very interested, and turned towards

her, ready to hear once more of those secrets of wedded life, the revelation of which made the task of confessing so pleasant to him.

"How is that?" he asked.

In spite of her determination to tell him all, Jeanne hardly knew how to explain herself.

"He—he refuses—to make me a mother."

The priest understood at once; it was not the first time he had heard of such things, but he asked for all the details, and enjoyed them as a hungry man would a feast. Then he reflected for a few moments, and in calm tones, as if he were speaking of a good harvest, he drew up a plan of campaign, settling every detail.

"My dear child, the only thing you can do is to make your husband believe you are pregnant; then he will cease his precautions, and you will become so in reality."

Jeanne blushed to the roots of her hair, but, determined to be ready for every emergency, she argued:

"But—suppose he should not believe me?"

The priest knew too well the ins and outs of human nature not to have an answer for that.

"Tell everybody you are pregnant. When he sees that every one else believes it, he will soon believe it himself. You will be doing no wrong," he added, to quiet his conscience for advising this deception; "the Church does not permit any connection between man and woman, except for the purpose of procreation."

Jeanne followed the priest's artful device, and, a fortnight later, told Julien she thought she was pregnant. He started up.

"It isn't possible! You can't be!"

She gave him her reasons for thinking so.

"Bah!" he answered. "You wait a little while."

Every morning he asked, "Well?" but she always replied, "No, not yet; I am very much mistaken if I am not pregnant."

He also began to think so, and his surprise was only equaled by his annoyance.

"Well, I can't understand it," was all he could say. "I'll be hanged if I know how it can have happened."

At the end of a month she began to tell people the news, but she said nothing about it to the Comtesse Gilberte, for she felt an old feeling of delicacy in mentioning it to her. At the very first suspicion of his wife's pregnancy, Julien had ceased to touch her, then, angrily thinking, "Well, at any rate, this brat wasn't wanted," he made up his mind to make the best of it, and recommenced his visits to his wife's room. Everything happened as the priest had predicted, and Jeanne became pregnant. Then, in a transport of joy, she took a vow of eternal chastity as a token of her rapturous gratitude to the distant divinity she adored, and henceforth closed her door to her husband.

She again felt almost happy, astonished at the ease with which her grief over the death of her mother had calmed down. She thought she was inconsolable, and now after barely two months that wound was healing, and all that remained was merely a vague melancholy, like the shadow of a great sorrow resting over her life. It seemed impossible that any other catastrophe could happen now; her children would grow up and love her; her old age would be calm and happy without her husband.

Towards the end of September the Abbé Picot came to the château, in a new cassock which had only one week's stains upon it, to introduce his successor, the Abbé Tolbiac. The latter was small, thin, and very young, with hollow, black-encircled eyes which betokened the depth and violence of his feelings, and a decisive way of speaking. The Abbé Picot had been appointed Dean of Goderville. Jeanne felt very sad at the thought of his departure; he was connected, in her thoughts, with all the chief events of her life, for he had married her, christened Paul, and buried the Baronne. She liked him because he was always so good-tempered and unaffected, and she could not imagine Etouvent without the Abbé Picot's fat figure trotting past the farms. He himself did not seem greatly rejoiced at his promotion.

"I have been here eighteen years," he said, "and it grieves me to go to another place. Oh! this living is not worth much, I know, and as for the people—well, the men have no more religion than they ought to have, the women are not so moral as they might be, and the girls never dream of being married in church, until they have visited the shrine of Notre Dame du Gros Ventre, and orange blossoms are not worth much in these parts; still I love the place."

The new priest had been fidgeting impatiently during this speech, and his face had turned very red.

"I shall soon have all that changed," he said, abruptly, as soon as the other priest had finished speaking; and he looked like an angry child in his worn but spotless cassock, so thin and small was he.

The Abbé Picot looked at him sideways, as he always did when anything amused him.

"Listen," he said. "You will have to chain up your parishioners if you want to prevent that sort of thing; and I don't believe even that would be any good."

"We shall see," answered the little priest in a cutting tone.

The old priest smiled and slowly took a pinch of snuff.

"Age and experience will alter your views; you will only estrange the last of the faithful. Folk believe hereabouts, but they do what they like. Beware. When I see a girl come to mass with a waist bigger than it ought to be, I say to myself—'Well, she is going to bring me another parishioner'—and I try to marry her off. You can't prevent them from going wrong, but you can find out the father of the child and prevent him forsaking the mother. Marry them, marry them, and don't trouble yourself about anything else."

"We will not argue on this point, for we should never agree," answered the new priest, a little roughly; and the Abbé Picot again began to express his regret at leaving the village, and the sea which he could see from his windows, and the little funnel-shaped valleys, where he went to read his breviary and where he could see the boats in the distance. Then the two priests rose to go, and the Abbé Picot kissed Jeanne, who nearly cried.

A week afterwards, the Abbé Tolbiac called again. He spoke of the reforms he was bringing about as if he were a prince taking possession of his kingdom. He begged the Vicomtesse to communicate on all feast days, and to attend mass regularly on Sundays.

"You and I are at the head of the parish," he said, "and we ought to rule it, and always set it a good example; but, if we wish to have any influence, we must be united. If the Church and the Château support each other, the cottage will fear and obey us."

Jeanne's religion was simply a matter of sentiment; she had merely the dreamy faith that a woman never quite loses, and if she performed any religious duties at all it was only because she had been so used to them at the convent, for the Baron's carping philosophy had long ago overthrown all her convictions. The Abbé had always been contented with the little she did do, and never scolded her. But when his successor did not see her at church on the previous Sunday, he had hastened to the château to question and reprimand her. She did not wish to quarrel with him, so she promised, inwardly resolving to go regularly only for a few weeks, out of good nature.

Little by little, however, she fell into the habit of frequenting the church, and, in a short time, she was entirely under the influence of the delicate-looking, zealous and strong-willed priest. His ardor and enthusiasm appealed to her love of mysticism, and he seemed to make the chord of religious poetry, which she possessed in common with every woman, vibrate within her. His rigid austerity, his contempt for luxury and sensuality, his disdain for the things that usually occupy the thoughts of men, his love of God, his youthful, intolerant inexperience, his scathing words, his inflexible will made Jeanne compare him, in her mind, to the early martyrs; and she, who had already suffered so much, whose eyes had been so rudely opened to the deceptions of life, let herself be completely ruled by the rigid fanaticism of this boy who was the minister of Heaven. He led her to the feet of Christ the Consoler, teaching her how the holy joys of religion could alleviate all her sorrows, and as she knelt in the confessional, she humbled herself and felt little and weak before this priest, who looked about fifteen years old.

Soon he was detested by the whole countryside. With no pity for his own weaknesses, he showed a violent intolerance for those of others. The thing above all others that roused his anger and indignation was—love. He denounced it from the pulpit in crude terms, as is the practice of the Church, thundering out terrible judgments against concupiscence over the heads of his rustic audience; and, as the pictures he portrayed in his fury persistently haunted his mind, he trembled with rage and stamped his foot in anger. The grown-up girls and the young fellows cast sidelong glances at each other across the aisle; and the old peasants, who liked to joke about such matters, expressed their disapproval of the little priest's intolerance as they walked back to their farms after service with their wives in black capes and their sons in blue blouses. The whole countryside was in an uproar.

The priest's severity and the harsh penances he inflicted at confession were rumored about, and, as he obstinately refused to grant absolution to the girls whose chastity was not immaculate, smiles accompanied the whispers. When, at the holy festivals, several of the youths and girls stayed in their seats instead of going to communicate with the others, most of the congregation laughed outright as they looked at them. He began to watch for lovers like a keeper on the lookout for poachers, and on moonlit nights, he hunted up the couples along the ditches, behind the barns and among the clumps of rushes on the hillsides. One night he came upon two who did not cease their love-making even in his presence; they were strolling along a ditch filled with stones, with their arms round one another, kissing each other as they walked.

"Will you stop that, you rascals?" cried the priest.

"You mind yer own business, Father," replied the lad, turning round. "This ain't no business of yours."

Then the priest picked up some stones and threw them at the couple as he might have done at stray dogs, and they both ran off, laughing. The next Sunday the priest mentioned them by name before the whole congregation. All the young fellows soon ceased to attend mass.

The priest dined at the château every Thursday, but he very often went there on other days to talk to his penitent. Jeanne became as ardent and as enthusiastic as he, as she discussed supernatural things, using the old and complicated arsenal of religious controversy. They would both walk along the Baronne's avenue talking of Christ and the Apostles, of the Virgin Mary and of the Fathers of the Church as if they had really known them. Sometimes they stopped their walk to ask each other profound questions, which made them wander off into mystical divagations, and she would lose herself in cloudy, poetic arguments, while he, being more exact, would reason like a lawyer possessed with the mania of proving the possibility of squaring the circle.

Julien treated the new priest with great respect. "That's the sort of a priest I like," he was continually saying. "Half-measures don't do for him," and he zealously set a good example by frequently confessing and communicating. Hardly a day passed now without the Vicomte going to the Fourvilles, either to shoot with the Comte, who could not do without him, or to ride with the Comtesse regardless of rain and bad weather.

"They are riding-mad," remarked the Comte; "but the exercise does my wife good."

The Baron returned about the middle of November. He was changed, aged, faded, filled with a deep sadness which had taken possession of his mind. His love for his daughter seemed to have gained in strength, as if these few months of dreary loneliness had aggravated his need of affection, confidence and tenderness. Jeanne told him nothing about her new ideas, her intimacy with the Abbé Tolbiac, or her religious enthusiasm, but the first time he saw the priest he felt an invincible dislike for him, and when his daughter asked him in the evening, "Well, what do you think of him?"

"He is like an inquisitor!" he answered. "He seems to me a very dangerous man."

When the Baron learned from the peasants, whose friend he was, about the young priest's harshness and bigotry and the sort of war of persecution he waged against natural laws and instincts, his dislike changed to a violent hatred. He, the Baron, belonged to the school of philosophers who worship nature; to him it seemed something touching when he saw two animals unite, and he was always ready to fall on his knees before the sort of pantheistic God he worshiped; but he shrank from the Catholic conception of a God, of bourgeois instincts, Jesuitical wrath and tyrannical revenge; a God, in fact, who seemed less to him than that boundless omnipotent nature, which is at once life, light, earth, thought, plant, rock, man, air, animal, planet, god and insect, because it is creation, stronger than human will and vaster than reason; that nature which produces all things without aim, without reason, or limit, in every shape and form throughout the universe, according to the exigencies of chance, and the presence of heat, to foster planetary life. Nature contained the germ of everything, and she brought forth life and thought, as trees bear flowers and fruit.

To him, therefore, reproduction was a great law of Nature, and to be respected as the sacred and divine act which accomplished the constant though unexpressed will of this Universal Being; and he at once began a campaign from farm to farm against this intolerant priest who opposed the laws of life. It grieved Jeanne to the heart, and she prayed to the Lord, and implored her father, but he always answered:

"It is everyone's right and duty to fight against such men, for they are not like human creatures. They are not human," he repeated, shaking his long white hair. "They understand nothing of life, and they move in a harmful dream; they are contrary to Nature." And he pronounced "contrary to Nature" as if he were uttering a curse.

The priest had at once recognized in him an enemy, and, as he wished to remain master of the château and its young mistress, he temporized, feeling sure of victory in the end. By chance he had discovered the love affair of Julien and Gilberte, and his one idea was to break it off by no matter what means. He came to see Jeanne one day, and, after a long talk on the mystery of life, he asked her to unite with him in fighting against and destroying the wickedness which was in her own family, and to save two souls which were in danger. She asked him what he meant.

"The hour has not yet come," he replied; "but I will see you again soon," and with that he abruptly left her.

The winter was drawing to an end, a "rotten" winter, as the country people say, damp and mild. He came again in a few days and spoke in vague terms of a disgraceful connection between people whose conduct ought to be irreproachable. It was the duty, he said, of those who were aware of what was going on, to use every means to put an end to it. He used all sorts of lofty arguments, and then, taking Jeanne's hand, adjured her to open her eyes, to understand and to help him.

This time Jeanne saw what he meant, but terrified at the thought of all the trouble that might be brought to her home, which was now so peaceful, she pretended not to know to what he was alluding. Then he hesitated no longer, but spoke in terms there could be no misunderstanding.

"I am going to perform a very painful duty, but I cannot leave it undone. The office I hold forbids me to leave you in ignorance of the sin you can prevent. Learn that your husband cherishes a criminal affection for Madame de Fourville."

Jeanne bent her head in feeble resignation.

"What do you intend to do?" asked the priest.

"What can I do?" she murmured.

"Throw yourself in the way as an obstacle to this guilty love," he answered, violently.

She began to cry, and said in a broken voice:

"But he has deceived me before with a servant; he wouldn't listen to me; he doesn't love me now; he ill-treats me if I manifest any desire that does not please him, so what can I do?"

The priest, without making any direct answer, exclaimed:

"Then you bow before this sin! You submit to it! You consent to it! There is adultery under your own roof, and you tolerate it! The crime is being perpetrated before your eyes, and you refuse to see it! Are you a Christian woman? Are you a wife and a mother?"

"What would you have me do?" she sobbed.

"Anything rather than allow this sin to continue," he replied. "Anything, I tell you. Leave him. Flee from this house which has been defiled."

"But I have no money," she replied. "And I am not brave now as I used to be. Besides, how can I leave without any proofs of what you are saying? I have not the right to do so."

The priest rose to his feet, quivering with indignation.

"You are listening to the dictates of your cowardice, Madame. I thought you were a different woman, but you are unworthy of God's mercy."

She fell on her knees:

"Oh! Do not abandon me, I implore you. Advise me what to do."

"Open M. de Fourville's eyes," he said, shortly. "It is his duty to end this liaison."

She was seized with terror at this advice.

"But he would kill them. And should I turn informer? Oh, not that! Never, never!"

He raised his hand as if to curse her, his whole soul stirred with anger.

"Live on in your shame and in your wickedness, for you are more guilty than they are. You are the wife who condones her husband's sin! My place is no longer here."

He turned to go, trembling all over with wrath. She followed him distractedly, ready to give in, and beginning to promise; but he would not listen to her and strode rapidly along, furiously shaking his big blue umbrella which was nearly as high as himself. He saw Julien standing near the gate, superintending the pruning of some trees, so he turned off to the left to reach the road by way of the Couillards' farm, and as he walked he kept saying to Jeanne:

"Leave me, Madame. I have nothing further to say to you."

Right in his road, in the middle of the farmyard, a group of children, those of the house and some neighbor's children, were standing around the kennel of Mirza, the dog, looking curiously at something with silent and concentrated attention. In the midst of them stood the Baron, his hands behind his back, also looking on with curiosity. One would have taken him for a schoolmaster. When he saw the priest approaching, he moved away so as not to have to meet him and speak to him.

Jeanne said entreatingly, "Give me a few days, then return. I will tell you what I have been able to do, what I have arranged, and we can talk it over together."

By that time they had almost reached the group of children and the priest went to see what it was that was interesting them so deeply. It was the dog whelping; five little pups were already crawling round the mother, who gently licked them as she painfully lay on her side before the kennel, and just as the priest looked over the children's heads, a spasm seized the animal and a sixth appeared. When they saw it, all the youngsters clapped their hands with joy, crying:

"There's another! There's another!"

To them it was simply a perfectly pure and natural amusement, and they watched these pups being born as they might have watched the apples falling from a tree.

The Abbé Tolbiac stood still for a moment in horrified surprise, then, giving way to his passion, he raised his umbrella and began to rain down blows on the children's heads. The startled urchins ran off as fast as they could go, and he found himself left alone with the dog, which was painfully trying to rise. Before she could stand up, he knocked her back again, and began to hit her madly with all his strength. The animal moaned pitifully as she writhed under these blows, from which there was no escape, as she was chained up. He broke his umbrella. Then, as his hands were empty, he jumped on her, and stamped and crushed her underfoot in a perfect frenzy of anger. Another pup was born beneath his feet before he dispatched the mother with a last furious kick, and then the mangled body lay quivering in the midst of the whining pups, which were awkwardly groping for their mother's teats. Jeanne had run away, but the priest suddenly felt himself seized by the throat, a blow knocked his hat off, and the enraged Baron carried him to the fence and threw him out into the road.

When M. le Perthuis turned round, he saw his daughter kneeling in the midst of the pups, sobbing as she picked them up and put them in her skirt. He strode up to her gesticulating wildly.

"There!" he exclaimed. "There's your saintly fellow! What do you think of him now?"

The noise had brought the farm people to the spot, and they all stood round, gazing at the mangled dog.

"Could one have believed that a man would be so cruel as that!" said Couillard's wife.

Jeanne picked up the pups, saying she would bring them up by hand. They tried to give them some milk, but three died the next day. Then old Simon went all over the neighborhood trying to find a foster-mother for the others; he could not get a dog, but he brought back a cat, asserting that she would do as well. Three more pups were killed, and the seventh was given to this nurse of a different race, who took to it directly, and lay down on her side to suckle it. That it might not exhaust its foster-mother the pup was weaned a fortnight later, and Jeanne undertook to feed it herself with a feeding-bottle; she had named it Toto, but the Baron rechristened it, and called it Massacre.

The priest did not return, but the next Sunday he hurled curses, threats and imprecations against the château, denouncing it as a plague-spot which ought to be removed, and going on to anathematize the Baron, who laughed at him, and to make veiled, half-timid allusions to Julien's latest amour. The Vicomte was annoyed at this, but he did not dare say anything for fear of giving rise to a scandal; and the priest continued to call down vengeance, in every sermon, and to foretell that the hour of the Lord was at hand, and that He would strike down His enemies. Julien wrote a decided, though respectful, letter to the archbishop, and the Abbé Tolbiac, finding himself threatened with disgrace, ceased his denunciations. He began to take long solitary walks; often he was to be met striding along the roads with an ardent, excited look on his face. Gilberte and Julien were always seeing him when they were out riding, sometimes in the distance, on the other side of a common, or on the edge of the cliff, sometimes close at hand, reading his breviary in a narrow valley they were just about to pass through; they always turned another way to avoid passing him. Spring had come, enflaming their hearts with fresh desires, and urging them to seek each other's embraces in any secluded spot to which their rides might lead them; but the leaves were only budding, the grass was still damp from the rains of winter, and they could not, as in the height of summer, hide themselves amidst the undergrowth of the woods. Lately, they had generally sheltered their caresses within a movable shepherd's hut which had been left since autumn, on the very top of the Vaucotte Hill. It stood all alone on the edge of the precipitous descent to the valley, five hundred yards above the cliff. There they felt quite secure, for they overlooked the whole of the surrounding country, and their horses, fastened to the shafts, waited until their masters were satiated with love.

One evening as they were leaving the hut, they saw the Abbé Tolbiac sitting on the hillside, nearly hidden by the rushes.

"We must leave our horses in that ravine, another time," said Julien; "in case they should tell our whereabouts," and thenceforth they always tied their horses up in a kind of recess in the valley, which was hidden by bushes.

Another evening, they were both returning to La Vrillette where they were to dine with the Comte, when they met the priest coming out of the château. He bowed, without looking them in the face, and stood on one side to let them pass. For the moment his visit made them uneasy, but their anxiety was soon dispelled.

Jeanne was sitting by the fire reading, one windy afternoon at the beginning of May, when she suddenly saw the Comte de Fourville running towards the château at such a rate as to make her fear an accident had happened. She hastened downstairs to meet him, and when she saw him close, she thought he must have gone mad. He had on his shooting-jacket and a big fur cap, which he generally only wore on his own grounds, and he was so pale that his red mustaches, which, as a rule, hardly showed against his ruddy face, looked the color of flame. His eyes were haggard and stared vacantly or rolled from side to side.

"My wife is here, isn't she?" he gasped.

"No," answered Jeanne, too frightened to think of what she was saying; "I have not seen her at all today."

He sat down, as if his legs had no longer strength to support him, and, taking off his cap, he mechanically passed his handkerchief several times across his forehead; then he started to his feet, and went towards Jeanne with outstretched hands, and mouth open to speak and tell her of his terrible grief. But suddenly he stopped short, and fixing his eyes on her, murmured, as if he were delirious, "But it is your husband—you also ——" and breaking off abruptly, he rushed out towards the sea.

Jeanne ran after him, calling him and imploring him to stop. "He knows all!" she thought, in terror. "What will he do? Oh, pray heaven he may not find them."

She could not reach him and he did not listen to her. He ran straight on without any hesitation, sure of his objective. He leaped across the ditch, and was rapidly striding across the reeds towards the cliff. Jeanne stood on the slope planted with trees, and watched him as long as he was in sight; then, when she could see him no longer, she went indoors again, tortured with fear and anxiety.

He had turned to the right and started to run. Threatening waves overspread the sea, big black clouds were scudding along madly, passing on and followed by others, each of them coming down in a furious downpour. The wind whistled, moaned, laid the grass and the young crops low, and carried away big white birds that looked like specks of foam, bearing them far into the land. The rain, which came in gusts, beat in the Comte's face and drenched his cheeks and mustaches, and the tumult of the elements seemed to fill his heart as well as his ears. There, straight before him in the distance, lay the Vaucotte valley, and between it and him stood a shepherd's hut, with two horses tied to the shafts, beside an empty sheeprun.

What had they to fear in such a storm?

As soon as he caught sight of the animals, the Comte threw himself flat on the ground, and dragged himself along on his hands and knees, his hairy cap and mud-stained clothes making him look like some monstrous animal. He crawled to the lonely hut and, in case its occupants should see him through the cracks in the planks, he hid himself beneath it. The horses had seen him and were pawing the ground. He slowly cut the reins, by which they were fastened, with a knife that he held open in his hand, and, as a fresh gust of wind swept by, the two animals cantered off, their backs stung by the hail which lashed against the sloping roof of the shepherd's cot, and made the frail abode tremble on its wheels.

Then the Comte rose to his knees, put his eye to the

slit at the bottom of the door, looked inside. He did not move and seemed to be waiting for something. Some time passed thus, and then he suddenly leaped to his feet, covered with mire from head to foot. Furiously he fastened the bolt, which secured the shelter on the outside, and seizing the shafts, he shook the hut as if he would have broken it to atoms. After a moment he began to drag it along—exerting the strength of a bull, and bending nearly double in his tremendous effort—and it was towards the almost perpendicular slope to the valley that he dragged the caravan and its human occupants. The latter were shouting and trying to burst open the door, in their ignorance of what had happened.

At the extreme edge of the slope, the Comte let go the hut, and it at once begun to run down the hill. Its speed increasing as it went, it moved quicker and quicker; its shafts bumped along the ground and it leaped over and dashed against obstacles as if it were alive. It bounded over the head of an old beggar who was crouching in a ditch, and, as it passed, the man heard frightful cries issuing from within. Suddenly one of the wheels was torn off, and the hut turned over on its side, and began to roll over and over like a ball, or like some house uprooted from its foundations and hurled from the summit of a mountain. When it reached the edge of the last ravine it took a final leap, and after describing a curve, fell to the bottom, and smashed like an eggshell.

Directly it had dashed upon the rocks at the bottom of the ravine, the old beggar, who had seen it falling, began to make his way down through the brambles. He did not go straight to the shattered hut, but, like the cautious rustic that he was, went to announce the accident at the nearest farmhouse. The farm people ran to the spot, raised the wreckage, and found two bodies, bruised, mangled and bleeding. The man's forehead was split open, and his face crushed; the woman's jaw was almost separated from her head, and their broken limbs were as soft as if there had not been a bone beneath the flesh. Still the farmers could recognize them, and they began to make all sorts of conjectures as to the cause of the accident.

"What could they have been doin' in the cabin?" said a woman.

The old beggar replied that apparently they had taken refuge from the weather, and that the high wind had overturned the hut, and blown it down the precipice. He added that he himself was going to take shelter in it when he saw the horses fastened to the shafts and concluded that the place was already occupied.

"If it hadn't been for that I should have been where they are now," he said with an air of self-congratulation.

"Perhaps it would have been all the better if you had been," said someone.

"Why would it have been better?" exclaimed the beggar in a great rage. " 'Cause I'm poor and they're rich? Look at them now!" he said, pointing to the two corpses with his crooked stick, as he stood trembling and ragged, with the water dripping from him, his battered hat, his matted beard, and his long, unkempt hair. "We're all equal when we're dead."

The group had grown bigger, and the peasants stood round with a frightened, cowardly look on their faces. After a discussion as to what they had better do, it was finally decided to carry the bodies back to their homes, in the hope of getting a reward. Two carts were got ready, and then a fresh difficulty arose; some thought it would be quite enough to place straw at the bottom of the carts, and others thought it would look better to put mattresses.

"But the mattresses would be soaked with blood," cried the woman who had spoken before. "They'd have to be washed with *eau de javelle*."

"The château people'll pay for that," said a jolly-faced farmer. "The more damage is done, the more it will cost."

That decided the matter, and the two carts, perched on high wheels without springs, set off, one to the right, the other to the left, jolting and shaking over the huge ruts the remains of these two beings who had so often been clasped in each other's arms, but who would never meet again.

As soon as the Comte had seen the hut rolling down the steep slope, he had fled away through the rain and the wind, and had run on and on across the country like a madman. He ran for several hours, across roads, over banks, and through hedges, and, at nightfall, he found himself at his own château. The servants were anxiously awaiting his return, and hastened to tell him that the two horses had just returned riderless, for Julien's had followed the other one.

M. de Fourville staggered back. "Some accident must have happened to them," he said in broken tones. "Let everyone go and look for them."

He started off again himself, but, as soon as he was out of sight, he hid behind a bush, and watched the road along which the woman he still loved so dearly would be brought dead or dying, or perhaps maimed and disfigured for life. In a little while a cart passed by, bearing a strange load; it drew up before the château gates, then passed through them. Yes, he knew it was she; but the dread of hearing the horrible truth forced him to stay in his hiding-place, and he crouched down like a hare, trembling at the faintest rustle.

He waited for an hour—perhaps two—and yet the

cart did not come back again. He was persuaded that his wife was dying, and the thought of seeing her, of meeting her eyes was such a torture to him, that, seized with a sudden fear of being discovered and compelled to witness her death, he again set off running, and did not stop till he was hidden in the midst of a wood. Then he thought that perhaps she needed help and that there was no one to take care of her as he could, and he sped back in mad haste.

As he was going into the house, he met his gardener.

"Well?" he cried, excitedly.

The man dared not answer the truth.

"Is she dead?" almost yelled M. de Fourville.

"Yes, Monsieur le Comte," stammered the servant.

He experienced an intense relief at the answer; all his agitation left him, and he went quietly and firmly up the steps.

In the meantime, the other cart had arrived at Les Peuples. Jeanne saw it in the distance, and guessing that a corpse lay upon the mattress, understood at once what had happened; the shock was so great that she fell to the ground unconscious. When she came to herself again she found her father supporting her head, and bathing her forehead with vinegar.

"Do you know——?" he asked hesitatingly.

"Yes, father," she whispered, trying to rise; but she was in such pain that she was forced to sink back again.

That evening she gave birth to a dead child—a girl.

She did not see or hear anything of Julien's funeral. In a few days she was conscious that Aunt Lison had returned and, in the midst of the feverish nightmares by which she was haunted, she strove to recall when, and under what circumstances, the old maid had last left Les Peuples. But even in her lucid moments she could not remember, and she could only feel sure she had seen her since her mother's death.

XI

Jeanne was confined to her room for three months and everyone despaired of her life. Then, very gradually, health and strength returned to her. Her father and Aunt Lison had come to live at the château, and they nursed her day and night. The shock she had sustained had entirely upset her nervous system; she started at the least noise, and the slightest emotion caused her to go off into long swoons. She had never asked the details of Julien's death. Why should she? Did she not already know enough? Everyone except herself thought it had been an accident, and she never revealed to anyone the terrible secret of her husband's adultery, and of the Comte's sudden, fearful visit the day of the catastrophe.

And now she was filled with tender, sweet, and melancholy recollections of the brief evidences of love shown her by her husband. She constantly thrilled at unexpected memories of him, and she seemed to see him as he was when they were betrothed and as she had known him in the hours of passion born beneath the sunlight in Corsica. All his faults diminished, all his harshness vanished, his very infidelities appeared less glaring in the widening separation of the closed tomb. And Jeanne, pervaded by a sort of posthumous gratitude for this man who had held her in his arms, forgave all the suffering he had caused her, to remember only moments of happiness they had passed together. Then, as time went on and month followed month, covering all her grief and reminiscences with forgetfulness, she devoted herself entirely to her son.

He became the idol, the one thought of the three beings who surrounded him, and he ruled as a despot. A kind of jealousy even arose among his slaves. Jeanne watched with anxiety the big kisses he gave his grandfather after a ride on his knee, and Aunt Lison, neglected by him as she had been by everyone else, and treated often like a servant by this little tyrant, who could scarcely speak as yet, would go to her room and weep as she compared the slight affection he showed her with the kisses he gave his mother and the Baron.

Two peaceful, uneventful years were passed thus in devoted attention to the child; then, at the beginning of the third winter, it was arranged that they should all go to Rouen until the spring. But they had hardly arrived at the damp, old house before Paul had such a severe attack of bronchitis that pleurisy was feared. His distracted mother was convinced that no other air but that of Les Peuples agreed with him, and they all went back there as soon as he was well.

Then came a series of quiet, monotonous years. They spent all their time with the child, in the nursery, or the drawing-room, or the garden, continually going into raptures over the way he lisped, or with his funny sayings and doings. Jeanne lovingly called him "Paulet," and, when he tried to repeat the word, he made them all laugh by pronouncing it "Poulet," for he could not speak plainly. The nickname "Poulet" clung to him, and henceforth he was never called anything else. He grew very quickly, and one of the chief amusements of his "three mothers," as the Baron called them, was to measure his height. On the wainscoting, by the drawing-room door, was a series of marks made with a penknife, showing how much the boy had grown every month, and these marks, which were called "Poulet's ladder," were of great importance in everyone's eyes.

Then a new personage played an important part in the household—the dog Massacre, which Jeanne had neglected since all her attention had been centered in her son. Ludivine fed him, and he lived quite alone, and always on the chain, in an old barrel in front of the stables. Paul noticed him one morning, and at once wanted to go and kiss him. With many precautions he was taken there. The dog made a great fuss over the child, who cried when he was taken away, so Massacre was unchained, and henceforth lived in the house. He became Paul's inseparable friend and companion; they played together, and lay down side by side on the carpet to go to sleep, and soon Massacre shared the bed of his playfellow, who would not let the dog leave him. Jeanne lamented sometimes over the fleas, and Aunt Lison felt angry with the dog for absorbing so much of the child's affection, affection for which she longed, and which, it seemed to her, this animal had stolen.

At long intervals visits were exchanged with the Brisevilles and the Couteliers, but the mayor and the doctor were the only regular visitors at the château.

Jeanne no longer went to church since the killing of the dog, and the suspicions the priest had instilled into her mind about the time of Julien's and Gilberte's horrible death had roused her indignation against the God who could have such ministers. From time to time the Abbé Tolbiac inveighed in outspoken terms against the château, which, he said, was inhabited by the Spirit of Evil, the Spirit of Everlasting Rebellion, the Spirit of Error and of Lies, the Spirit of Iniquity, the Spirit of Corruption and Impurity; it was by all these names that he alluded to the Baron.

The church was deserted, and when he happened to walk past any fields in which the ploughmen were at work, the men never ceased their task to speak to him, or turned to touch their hats. He acquired the reputation of being a wizard because he cast out the devil from a woman who was possessed, and the peasants believed he knew words to dispel charms, which, according to him, were merely pranks of Satan. He laid his hands on cows that gave blue milk, or whose tails were twisted in a circle, and discovered the whereabouts of things which had been lost, by means of a mysterious incantation. He devoted his narrow, fanatical mind to the study of all the ecclesiastical books in which he could find accounts of the devil's apparitions upon earth, or descriptions of his resources and stratagems, and the various ways in which he manifested his power and exercised his influence.

Believing himself specially called to combat this invisible, harmful Power, the priest had learned all the forms given in religious manuals to exorcise the devil. He fancied Satan lurked in every shadow, and the phrase *Sicut leo rugiens circuit, quoerens quem devoret* was continually on his lips. People began to be afraid of his strange power; even his fellow-clergy, ignorant country priests to whom Beelzebub was an article of their faith, and who, perplexed by the minute directions for the rites to be observed in case of any manifestations of the Evil One's power, at last confounded religion with magic, regarded the Abbé Tolbiac as somewhat of a wizard, and respected him as much for the supernatural power he was supposed to possess as for the irreproachable austerity of his life.

He never bowed to Jeanne when he met her, and such a state of things worried and grieved Aunt Lison, whose timid old maid's mind could not understand how anyone could systematically stay away from church. Everyone took it for granted that she was religious and confessed and communicated at proper intervals, and no one ever tried to find out what her views on religion really were. Whenever she was quite alone with Paul, Lison talked to him, in whispers, about God. The child listened to her with a faint degree of interest when she related the miracles which had been performed in the old times, and, when she told him he must love God, very, very dearly, he sometimes asked:

"Where is He, auntie?"

She would point upwards and answer, "Up there, above the sky, Poulet; but you must not say anything about it," for she was afraid of the Baron. One day, however, Poulet startled her by asserting, "God is everywhere, but he is not in church," and she found he had been talking to his grandfather about his aunt's mysterious revelations.

Paul was now ten years old; his mother looked forty. He was strong, noisy, and boldly climbed the trees, but his education had, so far, been sadly neglected. He disliked lessons, would never settle down to them, and, if ever the Baron managed to keep him reading a little longer than usual, Jeanne would interfere, saying:

"Let him go and play, now. He is so young, you must not tire him."

In her eyes he was still an infant, of six months or a year, and she hardly noticed that he walked, ran, and talked like a little man. She lived in constant anxiety lest he should fall, or catch cold or overheat himself while playing, or overload his stomach, or not eat as much as his growth demanded.

When the boy was twelve years old a great difficulty arose about his first communion. Lise went to Jeanne's room one morning, and pointed out to her that the child could not be permitted to go any longer without religious instruction, and without performing the sim-

plest sacred duties. She called every argument to her
aid, and gave a thousand reasons for the necessity of
what she was urging, dwelling chiefly upon the danger
of scandal. The mother was disturbed, undecided and
hesitating, and she replied that Paul could very well go
on as he was for a little longer. A month later, when
Jeanne called on the Vicomtesse de Briseville, she
chanced to say:

"I suppose it will be Paul's first communion this year."

"Yes, Madame," answered Jeanne, taken unawares.

These few words decided her, and, without saying
anything about it to her father, she asked Lise to take
the child to the catechism class. Everything went on
smoothly for a month; then Poulet came back, one evening, with a sore throat, and the next day he began to
cough. His frightened mother questioned him as to the
cause of his cold and he told her that he had not behaved very well in class, so the priest had sent him
to wait at the door of the church, where there was a
draught from the porch, until the end of the lesson.
After that Jeanne kept him at home, and taught him
the elements of religion herself; but the Abbé Tolbiac
refused to admit him to communion, in spite of all
Lison's entreaties, alleging, as his reason, that the boy
had not been properly prepared.

The following year he refused him again, and the
Baron was so exasperated that he said plainly there
was no need for Paul to believe in such foolery as this
absurd symbol of transubstantiation to become a good
and honest man. So it was resolved to bring the boy
up in the Christian faith, but not in the Catholic
Church, and that he should decide his religion for himself when he reached his majority.

A short time afterwards, Jeanne called on the Brisevilles and received no visit in return. Knowing how

punctilious they were in all matter of etiquette, she felt very much surprised at the omission, until the Marquise de Coutelier haughtily told her the reason of this neglect. Aware that her husband's rank and wealth made her the queen of the Normandy aristocracy, the Marquise ruled in queen-like fashion, showing herself gracious or severe as occasion demanded. She never hesitated to speak as she thought, and reproved, or congratulated, or corrected whenever she thought fit. When Jeanne called on her she addressed a few icy words to her visitor, then said in a cold tone, "Society divides itself naturally into two classes: those who believe in God, and those who do not. The former, however lowly they may be, are our friends and equals; with the latter we can have nothing to do."

Jeanne felt that she was being attacked and replied:

"But cannot one believe in God without attending church?"

"No, Madame. Believers go to pray to God in His church, as they would go to visit their friends at their houses."

"God is everywhere, Madame, and not only in the churches," answered Jeanne, feeling very hurt. "I believe in His goodness and mercy from the bottom of my heart, but when there are certain priests between Him and me, I can no longer realize His presence."

"The priest is the standard-bearer of the Church, Madame," said the Marquise, rising, "and whoever does not follow that flag is as much our enemy as the Church's."

Jeanne had risen also. "You believe in the God of a sect, Madame," she replied, quivering with indignation. "I believe in the God whom every upright man reveres"; and, with a bow, she left.

Among themselves the peasants also blamed Jeanne

for not sending Poulet to his first communion. They themselves did not go to mass, and never took the sacrament, or at least, only at Easter when the Church formally commanded it; but when it came to the children, that was a different matter, and not one of them would have dared to bring a child up outside the common faith, for, after all, "religion is religion."

Jeanne was quite conscious of this disapproval, and her soul revolted at all these compromises, these arrangements with one's conscience, these universal fears of everything, this great cowardice lurking in every heart, and showing itself under the mask of righteousness.

The Baron undertook to direct Paul's studies, and began to instruct him in Latin. The boy's mother had but one word to say on the subject, "Whatever you do, don't tire him," and, while lessons were going on, she would anxiously hang round the door of the schoolroom, which her father had forbidden her to enter, because, at every moment, she interrupted his teaching to ask, "You're sure your feet are not cold, Poulet?" or "Your head does not ache, does it, Poulet?" or to admonish the master with, "Don't make him talk so much, he will have a sore throat."

As soon as lessons were over the boy went into the garden with his mother and aunt. They were all very fond of gardening, and took great pleasure and interest in planting young trees in springtime, in watching the seeds they had sown come up and blossom, and in cutting down branches, flowers for nosegays. Paul devoted himself chiefly to raising salad plants. He had the entire care of four big beds in the kitchen garden, and there he cultivated lettuce, endive, Cos-lettuce, mustard-cress, and every other known kind of salad. He dug, watered, weeded, and planted, and made his two mothers work like day laborers, and for hours together they knelt on the beds, soiling their hands and dresses as they planted the seedlings in the holes they made with their forefingers in the mold.

Poulet was growing up, he was almost fifteen; and the highest mark on the drawing-room wall was five feet from the ground, but in mind he was still an ignorant, foolish child, for he had no opportunity of expanding his intellect, confined as he was to the society of these two women and the good-tempered old man who was so far behind the times. At last one evening the Baron said it was time for the boy to go to school. Aunt Lison withdrew into a dark corner in horror at the idea, and Jeanne began to sob.

"Why does he want to know so much?" she replied. "We will bring him up to be a gentleman farmer, to devote himself to the cultivation of his property, as so many noblemen do, and he will pass his life happily in this house, where we have lived before him and where we shall die. What more can he want?"

The Baron shook his head.

"What answer will you make if he comes to you when he is twenty-five, and says, 'I am nothing, and I know nothing through your fault, your selfish love. I feel incapable of working or of becoming anyone now, and yet I know I was not intended to lead the dull, pleasureless life to which your shortsighted affection has condemned me.'"

Jeanne turned to her son with the tears rolling down her cheeks.

"Oh, Poulet, you will never reproach me for having loved you too much, will you?"

"No, mamma," promised the boy in surprise.

"You swear you will not?"

"Yes, mamma."

"You want to stay here, don't you?"

"Yes, mamma."

"Jeanne, you have no right to dispose of his life in that way," said the Baron sternly. "Such conduct is cowardly—almost criminal. You are sacrificing your child to your own personal happiness."

Jeanne hid her face in her hands, while her sobs came in quick succession.

"I have been so unhappy—so unhappy," she murmured, through her tears. "And now my son has brought peace and rest into my life, you want to take him from me. What will become of me—if I am left—all alone now?"

Her father went and sat down by her side. "And am I no one, Jeanne?" he asked, taking her in his arms. She threw her arms round his neck, and kissed him fondly. Then in a voice still choked with tears and sobs:

"Yes, perhaps you are right, papa, dear," she answered; "and I was foolish; but I have had so much sorrow. I am quite willing for him to go to school now."

Then Poulet, who hardly understood what was going to be done with him, began to cry too, and his three mothers kissed and coaxed him and told him to be brave. They all went up to bed with heavy hearts, and even the Baron wept when he was alone in his own room, though he had controlled his emotion downstairs. It was resolved to send Paul to school at Havre at the beginning of the next term, and during the summer he was more spoiled than ever. His mother moaned as she thought of the approaching separation and she got ready as many clothes for the boy as if he had been about to start on a ten years' journey.

One October morning, after a sleepless night, the two women and the Baron went off with Poulet in the landau. They had already paid a visit to fix upon the bed he was to have in the dormitory and the seat he was to occupy in class, and Jeanne and Aunt Lison passed the whole day in unpacking his things and arranging them in the little chest of drawers. As the latter would not contain a quarter of what she had brought, Jeanne went to the headmaster to ask if the boy could not have another. The bursar was sent for, and he said that so much linen and so many clothes were simply in the way, instead of being of any use, and that the rules of the house forbade him to allow another chest of drawers. The aggrieved mother made up her mind to hire a room in a little hotel close by, and to ask the landlord himself to take Poulet all he wanted, directly the child found himself in need of anything.

They all went on the pier for the rest of the afternoon and watched the ships entering and leaving the harbor. Gloomy night descended on the city, which gradually lit up. They went to a restaurant for dinner. But they were not hungry, and the dishes were placed before them and removed almost untouched as they sat looking at each other with tearful eyes. After dinner they walked slowly back to the school. Boys of all ages were arriving on every side, some accompanied by their parents, others by servants. A great many were crying, and the big dim courtyard was filled with the sound of tears.

Jeanne and Poulet clung to each other, while Aunt Lison stood, quite forgotten, in the background, with her face buried in her handkerchief. The Baron felt he too was giving way, so he hastened the farewells, and took his daughter from the school. The landau was waiting at the door, and they drove back through the night to Les Peuples. An occasional sob was heard in the darkness.

Jeanne wept the whole of the following day, and on the next she ordered the phaeton and drove over to Havre. Poulet seemed to have got over the separation already; it was the first time he had ever had any companions of his own age, and, as he sat beside his mother, he fidgeted on his chair and longed to run out and play. Every other day Jeanne went to see him, and on Sundays took him out. She felt as though she had not energy enough to leave the school between the recreation hours. She waited in the parlor, while the classes were going on, until Poulet could come to her again. At last the headmaster asked her to come and see him, and begged her not to come so often. She did not take any notice of his request, and he warned her that if she still persisted in preventing her son from enjoying his play hours, and in interrupting his work, he would be obliged to dismiss him from the school. He also sent a note to the Baron, to the same effect, and thenceforth Jeanne was always kept in sight of Les Peuples, like a prisoner. She looked forward to the holidays with more impatience than her son. She was in a constant state of nervous anxiety, and began to take long walks about the country, with Massacre as her only companion, and would stay out of doors all day long, dreamily musing. Sometimes she sat on the cliff the whole afternoon watching the sea; sometimes she walked across the wood to Yport, thinking, as she went, of former walks whose memory haunted her. How far, far away was the time when she had gone over this country as a young girl, full of dreams.

Every time she saw her son, it seemed to her as if they had been separated for ten years; for every month he became more of a man, and every month she became more aged. Her father looked like her brother, and

Aunt Lison, who had been quite faded when she was twenty-five, and had never seemed to get older since, might have been taken for her elder sister.

Poulet did not study very hard; he spent two years in the fourth form, managed to get through the third by the skin of his teeth, then spent two more in the second, and was nearly twenty when he reached the rhetoric class. He had grown into a tall, fair youth, with whiskered cheeks and a budding mustache. He came over to Les Peuples every Sunday now, instead of his mother going to see him; and as he had been taking riding lessons for some time past, he hired a horse and accomplished the journey from Havre in two hours.

Jeanne started out early in the morning to go and meet him on the road, and with her went Aunt Lison and the Baron, who was beginning to stoop, and who walked like a little old man, with his hands clasped behind his back as if to prevent himself from pitching forward on his face. The three walked slowly along, sometimes sitting down by the wayside to rest, and all the while straining their eyes to catch the first glimpse of the rider. As soon as he appeared, looking like a black speck on the white road, they waved their handkerchiefs, and he at once put his horse to the gallop, and came up like a whirlwind, frightening his mother and Aunt Lison, and making his grandfather exclaim, "Bravo!" in the admiration of impotent old age.

Although Paul was a head taller than his mother, she always treated him as if he were a child and still asked him, as in former years, "Your feet are not cold, are they, Poulet?" If he went out of doors, after lunch, to smoke a cigarette, she opened the window to cry, "Oh, don't go out without a hat, you will catch cold in your head"; and when, at night, he mounted his horse to return, she could hardly contain herself for nervousness.

"Do not ride too quickly, Poulet, dear," she would say. "Think of your poor mother, who would go mad if anything happened to you, and be careful."

One Saturday morning she received a letter from Paul to say he could not come to Les Peuples as usual, the following day, as he had been invited to a party got up by some of his college friends. The whole of Sunday Jeanne was tortured by a presentiment of evil, and when Thursday came she was unable to bear her suspense any longer, and went over to Havre.

He seemed changed, though she could hardly tell in what way. He seemed more spirited, and his words and tones were more manly.

"By the way, mamma, we are going to have another party, and I shall not come to Les Peuples next Sunday, as you have come to see me today," he said, all at once, as if it were the most natural thing in the world.

She felt as much surprised and stunned as if he had told her he was going to America; then, when she was again able to speak:

"Oh, Poulet," she exclaimed, "what is the matter with you? Tell me what is going on."

He laughed and gave her a kiss.

"Why, nothing at all, mamma. I am only going to enjoy myself with some friends, as everyone does at my age."

She made no reply, but when she was alone in the carriage, her head was filled with new and strange ideas. She had not recognized her Poulet, her little Poulet, as of old; she perceived for the first time that he was grown up, that he was no longer hers, that henceforth he was going to live his own life, independently of the old people. To her he seemed to have changed entirely in a day. What! Was this strong, bearded, firm-willed lad her son, her little child, who used to make her help him to plant his lettuces?

For three months Paul only came to see his relatives at very long intervals, and even when he was there, it was only too plain that he longed to get away again as soon as possible, and that, each evening, he tried to leave an hour earlier. Jeanne imagined all sorts of things, while the Baron tried to console her by saying, "There, let him alone; the boy is twenty years old, you know."

One morning, a shabbily dressed old man, who spoke with a German accent, asked for "Matame la Vicomtesse." He was shown in, and, after a great many ceremonious bows, pulled out a dirty pocketbook saying:

"I have a little paper for you," and then unfolded and held out a greasy scrap of paper.

Jeanne read it over twice, looked at the Jew, read it over again, then asked:

"What does it mean?"

"I will tell you," replied the man obsequiously. "Your son wanted a little money, and, as I know what a good mother you are, I lent him just a little to go on with."

Jeanne was trembling. "But why did he not come to me for it?"

The Jew entered into a long explanation about a gambling debt which had had to be paid on a certain morning before midday, that no one would lend Paul anything as he was not yet of age, and that his "honor would have been compromised," if he, the Jew, had not "rendered this little service" to the young man. Jeanne wanted to send for the Baron, but her emotion seemed to have paralyzed her, and she could not rise from her seat.

"Would you be kind enough to ring?" she said to the moneylender, at last.

He feared some trick, and hesitated for a moment.

"If I inconvenience you, I will call again," he stammered.

She answered him by a shake of the head, and when he had rung they waited in silence for the Baron. The latter at once understood the situation. The bill was for fifteen hundred francs. He paid the Jew a thousand, saying to him with a significant stare:

"Don't let me see you here again," and the man thanked him, bowed, and went away.

The grandfather and the mother at once went over to Havre, but when they arrived at the college they learned that Paul had not been there for a month. The principal had received four letters, apparently from Jeanne, the first telling him that his pupil was ill, the others to say how he was getting on, and each letter was accompanied by a doctor's certificate; of course they were all forged. They were overwhelmed and sat there staring at each other. The principal, feeling very sorry for them, took them to the police, and they slept at a hotel that night.

The next day Paul was discovered at the house of a fast woman. His mother and grandfather took him back with them to Les Peuples, and the whole way not a word was exchanged. Jeanne hid her face in her handkerchief and cried, and Paul looked out of the window with an air of indifference.

Before the end of the week they found out that, during the last three months, Paul had contracted debts to the amount of fifteen thousand francs, but the creditors had not shown themselves, because they knew the boy would soon be of age. Poulet was asked for no explanation, as his relations hoped to reform him by kindness. He was pampered and caressed in every way; the choicest dishes were prepared for him, and, as it was springtime, a boat was hired for him at Yport, in spite of Jeanne's nervousness, that he might go sailing whenever he liked. He was not allowed to have a horse, for fear he should ride to Havre. He became idle, irritable and brutal, at times. The Baron grieved over his neglected studies, and even Jeanne, much as she dreaded to be parted from him again, began to wonder what was to be done with him.

One evening he did not come home. It was found, on inquiry, that he had gone out in a boat with two sailors, and his distracted mother hurried down to Yport, without stopping even to put anything over her head. On the beach she found a few men awaiting the return of the boat, and out on the sea was a little swaying light, which was drawing nearer and nearer to the shore. The boat came in, but Paul was not on board; he had ordered the men to take him to Havre, and had landed there.

The police sought him in vain; he was nowhere to be found, and the woman who had hidden him once before, had sold all her furniture, paid the rent, and disappeared also, without leaving any trace behind her. In Paul's room at Les Peuples two letters were found from this creature, who seemed madly in love with him, saying that she had obtained the necessary money for a journey to England. The three inmates of the château lived on, gloomy and despairing, through all this mental torture. Jeanne's hair, which had been gray before, was now quite white, and she sometimes asked herself what

she could have done, that Fate should so mercilessly
pursue her. One day she received the following letter
from the Abbé Tolbiac:

MADAME,

The hand of God has been laid heavily upon you.
You have refused to give your son to Him, and He
has delivered him over to a prostitute. Will you not
profit by this lesson from heaven? God's mercy is infinite, and perhaps He will pardon you if you throw
yourself at His feet. I am His humble servant, and I
will open His door to you when you come and knock.

Jeanne sat for a long time with this letter lying open
on her knees. Perhaps, after all, the priest's words were
true; and all her religious doubts and uncertainties returned to harass her mind. Was it possible that God
could be vindictive and jealous like men? But if He was
not jealous, He would no longer be feared and loved,
and, no doubt, it was that we might better know Him,
that He manifested Himself to men, as influenced by
the same feeling as themselves. Then she felt the fear,
the cowardly dread, which urges those who hesitate
and doubt to seek the safety of the Church, and one
evening, when it was dark, she stealthily ran to the
presbytery, and knelt at the feet of the fragile-looking
priest to solicit absolution. He only promised her a
semi-pardon, as God could not shower all His favors
on a house which sheltered such a man as the Baron.
"Still, you will soon receive a proof of the divine mercy,"
said the priest.

Two days later, Jeanne did indeed receive a letter
from her son, and in the excess of her grief, she looked
upon it as the forerunner of the consolation promised
by the priest. The letter ran thus:

My Dear Mother,

Do not be uneasy about me. I am in London, and in good health, but in great need of money. We have not a sou, and some days we have to go without anything to eat. She who is with me, and whom I love with all my heart, has spent all she had, some five thousand francs, that she might remain with me, and you will, of course, understand that I am bound in honor to discharge my debt to her at the very first opportunity. I shall soon be of age, but it would be very good of you if you would advance me fifteen thousand francs of what I inherit from papa; it would relieve me from great embarrassments.

Good-bye, mother dear; much love to grandfather, Aunt Lison and yourself. I hope to see you soon again. Your son,

Vicomte Paul de Lamare

He had written to her! Then he had not forgotten her! She did not stop to think that it was simply to ask her for money; he had none and some should be sent him; what did money matter? He had written to her!

She ran to show the letter to the Baron, the tears streaming from her eyes. Aunt Lison was called, and, word by word, they read over this letter which spoke of their loved one, and lingered over every sentence. Jeanne, transported from the deepest despair to a kind of intoxication of joy, began to take Paul's part.

"Now he has written, he will come back," she said. "I am sure he will come back."

"Still he left us for this creature," said the Baron, who was calm enough to reason; "and he must love her better than he does us, since he did not hesitate in his choice between her and his home."

The words sent a sudden pang of anguish through

Jeanne's heart, and within her sprang up the fierce, deadly hatred of a jealous mother against the woman who had robbed her of her son. Until then her every thought had been for Paul, and she had hardly realized that this creature was the cause of all his errors; but the Baron's argument had suddenly brought this rival vividly to her mind, had revealed her fatal power, and she felt that between this woman and herself there must be a determined, bitter warfare. And she also felt that she would rather lose her son than share him with another; and all her joy vanished.

The fifteen thousand francs were sent, and for five months nothing more was heard of Paul. At the end of that time a lawyer came to the château to see about his inheritance. Jeanne and the Baron acceded to all his demands without any dispute, even giving up the money to which the mother had a right for her life-time, and when he returned to Paris, Paul found himself the possessor of a hundred and twenty thousand francs. During the next six months only four short letters were received from him, giving news of his doings in a few, concise sentences, and ending with formal protestations of affection.

"I am not idle," he said. "I have obtained a post in connection with the Stock Exchange, and I hope some day to see my dear relations at Les Peuples."

He never mentioned his mistress, but his silence was more significant than if he had written four pages about her; and, in these icy letters, Jeanne could feel this woman hidden, the implacable, eternal enemy of every mother—the harlot.

The three lonely people discussed what could be done to save Paul, but they could think of nothing. They would have gone to Paris, but they knew that would be no good.

"We must let this passion wear itself out," said the Baron; "sooner or later he will return to us of his own accord." And the mournful days dragged on.

Jeanne and Lison got into the habit of going to church together without letting the Baron know; and a long time passed without any news from Paul. Then, one morning they received a desperate letter which terrified them.

My Dear Mother,

I am lost; I shall have no resource left but to blow out my brains if you do not help me. A speculation which held out every hope of success has turned out badly, and I owe eighty-five thousand francs. It means dishonor, ruin, the destruction of all my future, if I do not pay, and, I say again, rather than survive the disgrace I will blow my brains out. I should, perhaps, have done so already, had it not been for the brave and hopeful words of a woman, whose name I never mention to you, but who is the good genius of my life.

I send you my very best love, dear mother. Good-bye, perhaps forever.

Paul

Enclosed in the letter was a bundle of business papers giving the details of this unfortunate speculation. The Baron answered by return post that they would help as much as they could. Then he went to Havre to get legal advice, mortgaged some property and forwarded the money to Paul. The young man wrote back three cheerful letters full of passionate affection, and said they might expect him almost immediately. But he did not come, and another year passed away.

Jeanne and the Baron were on the point of starting

for Paris, to find him and make one last effort to persuade him to return, when they received a few lines saying he was again in London, starting a steamboat company which was to trade under the name of "Paul Delamare & Co." "My fortune is assured, perhaps great wealth. At any rate I risk nothing, and you must at once see the advantages of the scheme. When I see you again, I shall be well up in the world; there is nothing like trade for making money, nowadays."

Three months later, the steamboat company went bankrupt, and the manager was prosecuted for falsifying the books. Jeanne had a hysterical fit which lasted several hours, and then took to her bed. The Baron went to Havre, made every inquiry, saw lawyers, men of business, solicitors, and sheriffs, and found that the Delamare Company had failed for two hundred and fifty thousand francs. He again mortgaged his property, and borrowed a large sum on Les Peuples and the two adjoining farms. One evening he was going through some final formalities in a lawyer's office, when he suddenly fell to the ground in an apoplectic fit. A mounted messenger was at once dispatched to Jeanne, but her father died before she could arrive. She took him back to Les Peuples, so overcome that her grief was a stupor rather than a pain. But the Abbé Tolbiac refused to allow the body to be interred with any sacred rites, in spite of all the entreaties of the two women, so the burial took place at night without any ceremony whatever.

Paul, who was still hiding in England, heard of his grandfather's death through the liquidators of the company, and wrote to say he should have come before, but he had only just heard the sad news. He concluded, "Now you have rescued me from my difficulties, mother dear, I shall return to France, and shall at once come to see you."

Jeanne lived in such a state of depression that she appeared not to understand anything more.

Towards the end of that winter Aunt Lison, who was now sixty-eight, had a severe attack of bronchitis, which turned to inflammation of the lungs, and the old maid quietly expired.

"I will ask the good God to take pity on you, my poor little Jeanne," were the last words she uttered.

Jeanne followed her to the grave, saw the earth fall on the coffin, and then sank to the ground, longing for death to take her also, that she might cease to think and to suffer. As she fell, a big, strong peasant woman caught her in her arms and carried her away as if she had been a child. When they got back to the château Jeanne let herself be put to bed by this stranger, who handled her so tenderly and firmly, and at once fell asleep, for she had spent the last five nights watching beside the old maid, and she was thoroughly exhausted by sorrow and fatigue. It was the middle of the night when she again opened her eyes. A nightlamp was burning on the mantelpiece, and in the armchair lay a woman asleep. Jeanne did not know who she was, and, leaning over the side of the bed, she tried to make out her features by the glimmering light of the wick floating in a glass filled with oil. She fancied she had seen this face before, but she could not remember when or where.

The woman was quietly sleeping, her head drooping on one shoulder, her cap lying on the ground. She was forty or forty-five years of age, a strong, red-faced, square-shouldered, powerful woman, with hair that was turning gray. Her big hands were hanging on each side of the chair. Jeanne stared at her, her mind in that troubled state of awakening from the feverish sleep that follows great misfortunes. Surely she had seen that face! Was it a long time ago or quite recently? She could not remember, and this idea disturbed and irritated her. She softly got out of bed, and went on tiptoe to see the sleeping woman nearer. It was the peasant who had caught her in her arms in the cemetery, and had afterwards put her to bed; she vaguely remembered this. But surely she had known her in former times, under other circumstances? And yet perhaps the face was only familiar to her because she had seen it that day in the cemetery. Still how was it that the woman was sleeping here?

Just then the stranger opened her eyes and saw Jeanne standing beside her. She started up, and they stood face to face, so close together that they touched each other.

"How is it that you're out of bed?" said the peasant; "you'll make yourself ill, getting up at this time of night. Go back to bed again."

"Who are you?" asked Jeanne.

The woman made no answer, but picked Jeanne up and carried her back to bed with the strength of a man. She gently laid her down, and, as she bent over her, she suddenly began to cover her cheeks, her hair, her eyes with violent kisses, while the tears streamed from her eyes.

"My poor mistress! Mam'selle Jeanne, my poor mistress! Don't you know me?" she sobbed.

"Rosalie, my girl!" cried Jeanne, throwing her arms round the woman's neck and kissing her; and, clasped in each other's arms they mingled their tears and sobs together.

Rosalie dried her eyes the first. "Come now," she said, "you must be good and not catch cold."

She picked up the clothes, tucked up the bed and put the pillow back under the head of her former mistress, who lay choking with emotion as the memories of days that were past and gone rushed back to her mind.

"How is it you have come back, my poor girl?" she asked.

"Do you think I was going to leave you to live all alone now?" answered Rosalie.

"Light a candle and let me look at you," went on Jeanne.

Rosalie placed a light on the table by the bedside, and for a long time they gazed at each other in silence.

"I should never have known you again," murmured Jeanne, holding out her hand to her old servant. "I should never have recognized you. You have altered very much, though not so much as I have."

"Yes, you have changed, Madame Jeanne, and more than you ought to have done," answered Rosalie, as she looked at this thin, faded, white-haired woman, whom she had left young and beautiful; "but you must remember it's twenty-four years since we have seen one another."

"Well, have you been happy?" asked Jeanne after a long pause.

"Oh, yes—yes, Madame. I haven't had much to grumble at; I've been happier than you—that's certain. The only thing that I've always regretted is that I didn't stop here——" She broke off abruptly, finding she had unthinkingly touched upon the very subject she wished to avoid.

"Well, you know, Rosalie, one cannot have everything one wants," replied Jeanne gently; "and now you, too, are a widow, are you not?" Then her voice trembled, as she went on, "Have you any—any other children?"

"No, Madame."

"And what is your—your son? Are you satisfied with him?"

"Yes, Madame; he's a good lad, and a hard worker. He married about six months ago, and he is going to have the farm; now I have come back to you."

"Then you will not leave me again?" murmured Jeanne.

"No fear, Madame," answered Rosalie in a rough tone. "I've arranged all about that."

And for some time nothing more was said.

Jeanne could not help comparing Rosalie's life with her own, but she had become quite resigned to the cruelty and injustice of Fate, and she felt no bitterness.

"Was your husband kind to you?"

"Oh, yes, Madame; he was a good, industrious fellow, and managed to put by a good deal. He died of consumption."

Then Jeanne sat up in bed, filled with a desire to hear more.

"Tell me all about your life, and everything that has happened to you," she said. "I feel as if it would do me good to hear it."

Rosalie drew up a chair, sat down, and began to talk about herself, her house, her friends, entering into all the little details in which country people delight, describing her farmyard, laughing sometimes over things which made her think of the happy times that were over, and gradually raising her voice as she went on, like a woman accustomed to commands. She wound up by saying:

"Oh, I'm well off now; I needn't be afraid of anything. But I owe it all to you," she added in a lower, faltering voice; "and now I've come back I'm not going to take any wages. No! I won't! So, if you don't choose to have me on those terms, I shall go away again."

"But you do not mean to serve me for nothing?" said Jeanne.

"Yes, I do, Madame. Money! You give me money! Why, I've almost as much as you have yourself. Do you know how much you will have after all these loans and mortgages have been cleared off, and you have paid all the interest you have let run on and increase? You don't know, do you? Well, then, let me tell you that you haven't ten thousand francs a year; not ten thousand. But I'm going to put everything straight, and pretty soon, too."

She had again raised her voice, for the thought of the ruin which hung over the house, and the way in which the interest money had been neglected roused her anger and indignation. A faint, sad smile which passed over her mistress's face angered her still more, and she cried:

"You ought not to laugh at it, Madame. People are good for nothing without money."

Jeanne took both the servant's hands in hers.

"I have never had any luck," she said slowly, as if she could think of nothing else. "Everything has gone the wrong way with me. My whole life has been ruined by a cruel fate."

"You must not talk like that, Madame," said Rosalie, shaking her head. "You made an unhappy marriage, that's all. But people oughtn't to marry before they know anything about their future husbands."

They went on talking about themselves and their past loves like two old friends, and when the day dawned they were still talking.

XII

Within a week Rosalie had everything and everybody in the château under her control, and even Jeanne yielded passive obedience. She was very weak now, and her legs dragged along as the Baronne's used to do. She went out on the arm of her maid, who guided her slowly, scolded her, and soothed her with brusque words of affection, as if she were a sick child. Their conversation was always about bygone times, of which Jeanne talked with tears in her eyes, and Rosalie in the calm, quiet way of an impassive peasant.

The old servant returned several times to the question of the interest that was owing, and demanded the papers which Jeanne, ignorant of all business matters, had hidden away that Rosalie might not know of Paul's misdoings. Next Rosalie went over to Fécamp each day for a week to get everything explained to her by a lawyer whom she knew; then one evening, after she had put her mistress to bed, she sat down beside her and said abruptly: "Now you're in bed, Madame, we will have a little talk."

She told Jeanne exactly how matters stood, and that when every claim had been settled she, Jeanne, would have about seven or eight thousand francs a year; not a penny more.

"Well, Rosalie," answered Jeanne, "I know I shall not live to be very old, and I shall have enough until I die."

"Very likely you will, Madame," replied Rosalie, getting angry; "but how about M. Paul? Don't you mean to leave him anything?"

Jeanne shuddered. "Pray, don't ever speak to me about him; I cannot bear to think of him."

"Yes, but I want to talk to you about him, because you don't look at things in the right light, Madame Jeanne. He may be doing all sorts of foolish things now, but he won't always behave the same. He'll marry and then he'll want money to educate his children and to bring them up properly. Now listen to what I am going to say; you must sell Les Peuples——"

But Jeanne started up in bed.

"Sell Les Peuples! How can you think of such a thing? No! I will never sell it!"

Rosalie was not in the least put out.

"But I say you will, Madame, simply because you must."

Then she explained her plans and her calculations. She had already found a purchaser for Les Peuples and the two adjoining farms, and when they had been sold Jeanne would still have four farms at Saint Léonard, which, freed from the mortgages, would bring in about eight thousand three hundred francs a year. Thirteen hundred francs would have to go for the keeping up and repairing of the property; then seven thousand would remain, out of which five thousand would be taken for yearly income, and two thousand would be set aside as an insurance fund.

"Everything else is gone, so there's an end of it," said Rosalie. "But, in future, I shall keep the money, and M. Paul sha'n't have another penny from you. He'd take your last farthing."

"But if he has nothing to eat?" murmured Jeanne, who was quietly weeping.

"He can come to us if he's hungry; there'll always be victuals and a bed for him. He'd never have got into trouble if you hadn't given him any money the first time he asked for some."

"But he was in debt; he would have been dishonored."

"And don't you think he'll get into debt just the same when you've no more money to give him? You have paid his debts up to now, so well and good; but you won't pay any more, I can tell you. And now, good night, Madame."

And away she went.

The idea of selling Les Peuples and leaving the house where she had passed her whole life threw Jeanne into a state of extreme agitation, and she lay awake the whole night. "I shall never be able to go away from here," she said, when Rosalie came into the room next morning.

"You'll have to, all the same, Madame," answered the maid with rising temper. "The lawyer is coming presently with the man who wants to buy the château, and, if you don't sell it, you won't have a blade of grass to call your own in four years' time."

"Oh, I cannot! I cannot!" moaned Jeanne.

But an hour afterwards came a letter from Paul asking for ten thousand francs. What was to be done? Jeanne did not know, and, in her distress, she consulted Rosalie, who shrugged her shoulders, and observed:

"What did I tell you, Madame? Oh, you'd both of you have been in a nice muddle if I hadn't come back."

Then, giving in to the servant, Jeanne wrote back:

My Dear Son,

I cannot help you any more; you have ruined me, and I am even obliged to sell Les Peuples. But I shall always have a home for you whenever you choose to return to your poor old mother, who has suffered so cruelly through you.

JEANNE

When the lawyer came with M. Jeoffrin, who was a retired sugar baker, Jeanne herself received them, and invited them to go all over the house and grounds. Then a month after this visit, she signed the deed of sale, and bought, at the same time, a little villa in the hamlet of Batteville, standing on the Montivilliers high road, near Goderville.

Then she walked up and down all alone until evening, in little mother's avenue, with a sore heart and troubled mind, bidding distracted and sobbing farewells to the landscape, the trees, the rustic bench under the plane-tree, to all those things she knew so well and that seemed to have become part of her vision and her soul, the grove, the mound overlooking the plain, where she had so often sat, and from where she had seen the Comte de Fourville running towards the sea on that terrible day of Julien's death, to an old elm whose upper branches were missing, against which she had often leaned, and to all this familiar garden spot.

Rosalie came out and took her by the arm to make her come into the house.

A tall young peasant of twenty-five was waiting outside the door. He greeted her in a friendly manner as if he had known her for some time, "Good day, Madame Jeanne. I hope you are well. Mother told me to come and help you move. I would like to know what you are going to take away, seeing that I shall do it from time to time so as not to interfere with my farm work."

It was her maid's son, Julien's son, Paul's brother. She felt as if her heart had stopped beating; and yet she would have liked to embrace this young fellow.

She looked at him, trying to find some resemblance to her husband or to her son. He was ruddy, vigorous, with fair hair and his mother's blue eyes. And yet he looked like Julien. In what way? How? She could not have told, but there was something like him in the whole look of his face.

"I should be very much obliged if you could show me the things now," continued the lad.

But she did not know herself yet what she should be able to take, her new house was so small, and she asked him to come again in a week's time.

For some time the removal occupied Jeanne's thoughts, and made a change, though a sad one, in her dull, hopeless life. She went from room to room seeking the pieces of furniture which were associated in her mind with various events in her life, the furniture which becomes, in time, part of our lives—almost of ourselves —to which sad and happy memories are attached, dates in our history, and which have been the silent companions of our pleasant and gloomy hours, have grown old and worn with us, whose coverings are torn in places and burst, whose joints are shaky, whose colors are faded.

As agitated as if the decisions she were making had been of capital importance, Jeanne chose, one by one, the things she should take with her, often hesitating, and altering her mind at every moment, as she stood unable to decide the respective merits of two armchairs, or of some old escritoire and a still older work-table. She opened and searched every drawer, and tried to remember facts, and when at last she made up her mind and said, "Yes, I shall take this," the article she had decided upon was taken downstairs and put into the dining-room. She wished to keep the whole of her bedroom furniture, the bed, the tapestry, the clock— everything, and she also took a few of the drawing-room chairs, choosing those with the designs she had always liked ever since her childhood—the fox and the stork, the fox and the crow, the ant and the grasshopper, and the melancholy heron.

One day, as she was wandering all over this house she should so soon have to leave, Jeanne went up into the garret. She was amazed: there lay articles of furniture of every description, some broken, others only soiled, others again stored away simply because they no longer pleased, because fresh things had been bought and put in their places. She recognized a hundred little odds and ends which used to be downstairs and had disappeared without her noticing their absence—things of no value which she had often used, insignificant little articles, which had stood fifteen years before her eyes and had never attracted her attention, but which now—suddenly discovered in the lumber-room, lying side by side with other things older still and which she could quite distinctly remember seeing when she first returned from the convent—became as precious in her eyes as if they had been forgotten witnesses, or friends that had been found again. As she looked at them she felt as she might have done if people she had known a long time, who had never revealed themselves, had suddenly begun one evening to talk interminably, and to reveal a soul she had never dreamed they possessed.

As she went from one thing to another, and remembered little incidents in connection with them, her heart felt as if it would break. "Why, this is the china cup I cracked a few days before I was married, and here is mamma's little lantern, and the cane papa broke trying to open the wooden gate the rain had swollen."

Besides all these familiar objects there were a great many things she had never seen before, which had belonged to her grandparents or her great-grandparents. Covered with dust they looked like sad, forsaken exiles from another century, their history and adventures forever lost, for there was no one living now who had known those who had chosen, bought and treasured them, or who had seen the hands which had so often touched them or the eyes which had found such pleasure in looking at them. Jeanne touched them, and turned them about, her fingers leaving their traces on the thick dust; and she stayed for a long, long time amidst these old things in the garret, which was dimly lighted by a little skylight.

She tried to find other things with associations to them, and very carefully she examined some three-legged chairs, a copper warming-pan, a dented foot-warmer, which she thought she remembered, and all the other worn-out household utensils. Then she put all the things she thought she should like to take away together, and going downstairs, sent Rosalie up to fetch them. The latter indignantly refused to bring down "such rubbish," but Jeanne, though she hardly ever showed any will of her own now, would have her own way this time, and the servant had to obey.

One morning young Denis Lecoq, Julien's son, came with his cart to take away the first lot of things, and Rosalie went off with him to look after the unloading, and to see that the furniture was put into the right rooms.

When she was alone Jeanne began to visit every room in the château, and to kiss in a transport of passionate sorrow and regret everything that she was forced to leave behind her—the big white birds in the drawing-room tapestry, the old candlesticks, anything and everything that came in her way. She went from room to room, half mad with grief, and the tears streaming from her eyes, and, when she had gone all over the house, she went out to "say good bye" to the sea. It was the end of September, and the dull yellowish waves stretched away as far as the eye could reach, under the lowering gray sky which hung over the world. For a long, long while Jeanne stood on the cliff, her thoughts running on all her sorrows and troubles, and it was not till night drew on that she went indoors. In that day she had gone through as much suffering as she had ever passed through in her greatest griefs.

Rosalie had returned enchanted with the new house, declaring that it was much livelier than this big barn of a place that was not even on a main road, but Jeanne wept the whole evening.

Now they knew the château was sold the farmers showed Jeanne barely the respect that was due to her, and, though they hardly knew why, among themselves they always spoke of her as "that lunatic." Perhaps, with their brute-like instinct, they perceived her unhealthy and increasing sentimentality, her morbid reveries, and the disordered and pitiful state of her mind which so much sorrow and affliction had unhinged.

Happening to go through the stables the day before her departure, a growl made her start. It was Massacre, whose existence she had entirely forgotten. Long past the age at which dogs generally die, he had become blind and paralyzed, and dragged out his life on a bed of straw, looked after by Ludivine, who never forgot him. Jeanne took him up in her arms, kissed him and carried him into the house. As fat as a pig, he could hardly creep along, his legs were so stiff, and he barked like a child's wooden toy-dog.

At length the last day dawned. Jeanne had passed the night in Julien's old room, as all the furniture had been moved out of hers, and when she rose she felt as tired and exhausted as if she had just been running a long distance.

In the courtyard stood a cart on which the remainder of the furniture and the trunks were already loaded. Another two-wheeled carriage was standing behind ready to take Rosalie and her mistress. Ludivine and old Simon were to stay at the château until its new owner arrived, and then they were going to their relatives, Jeanne having given them a small pension. Besides this they had their savings. They were now very old, garrulous and unfit for service. Marius had married and left the château long ago.

About eight o'clock a fine, cold rain, driven by the wind from the sea, began to fall, and already the leaves were falling. The cart had to be covered over with tarpaulins. Some steaming cups of coffee stood on the kitchen-table, and Jeanne sat down and slowly drank hers up; then rising:

"Let us go," she said.

She began to put on her hat and shawl, while Rosalie put on her galoshes. A great lump rose in her throat, and she whispered:

"Rosalie, do you remember how it rained the day we left Rouen to come here?"

She broke off abruptly, pressed her hands to her heart, and fell backwards in a sort of fit. For more than an hour she lay as if she were dead, then, when she opened her eyes, she was seized with convulsions and burst into tears. Gradually she became calmer, but this attack had left her so weak that she could not rise to her feet. Rosalie, fearing another attack if they did not get her away at once, went for her son, and between them, they carried her to the gig, and placed her on the leather-covered seat. The old servant got up beside her, wrapped up her legs, threw a thick cloak over her shoulders, then, opening an umbrella over her head, cried:

"Make haste, and let's get off, Denis."

The young man climbed up beside his mother, sat down with one leg right outside the gig, for want of room, and started off his horse at a quick, jerky trot, which shook the two women from side to side. As they turned the corner of the village, they saw someone walking up and down the road; it was the Abbé Tolbiac, apparently waiting to see their departure. He was holding up his cassock with one hand to keep it out of the wet, regardless of showing his thin legs which were encased in black stockings, and his huge, muddy boots. When he saw the carriage coming he stopped, and stood on one side to let it pass. Jeanne looked down to avoid meeting his eyes, while Rosalie, who had heard all about him, furiously muttered: "You brute, you brute!" and seizing her son's hand, "give him a cut with the whip!" she exclaimed. The young man, just as they were passing the Abbé, suddenly let the wheel of the gig drop into a deep rut, as it was going at full speed. There was a splash, and the priest was covered with mud from head to foot. Rosalie was delighted, and turning round, she shook her fist at the priest as he stood wiping himself down with his big handkerchief.

They went on for five minutes, when Jeanne suddenly cried: "Oh, we have forgotten Massacre!" Denis pulled up, gave Rosalie the reins to hold, and jumped down to run and fetch the dog. Finally the young man came back with the big, mangy, shapeless animal in his arms and placed him in the gig between the two women.

XIII

Two hours later the carriage stopped in front of a little brick house, standing by the high road in the middle of an orchard planted with pear-trees. Four latticework arbors covered with honeysuckle and clematis stood at the four corners of the garden, which was planted with vegetables, and laid out in little beds with narrow paths bordered with fruit-trees running between them, and both garden and orchard were entirely surrounded by a thick-set hedge which was separated by a field from the next farm. About thirty yards lower down the road was a forge, and the nearest houses were a mile away. The view looked out over the plain of Caux with farms scattered here and there, half-hidden by the four double rows of big trees which surrounded the orchards.

Jeanne wanted to rest as soon as they arrived, but Rosalie, wishing to keep her from thinking, would not let her do so. The carpenter from Goderville had come to help them put the place in order, and they all began to arrange the furniture which was already there, without waiting for the last cartload, which might be delayed. It was a big job and involved much thought and argument. Then the cart arrived in an hour's time, and had to be unloaded in the rain. When night fell the house was in a state of utter disorder, and all the rooms were full of things piled anyhow, one on top of another. Jeanne was tired out and fell asleep as soon as her head touched the pillow.

The next few days there was so much to do that she had no time to fret; in fact, she even found a certain pleasure in making her new home pretty, for all the time she was working she thought that her son would one day come and live there. The tapestry from her old bedroom was hung in the dining-room, which was also to serve as a drawing-room, and Jeanne took especial pains over the arrangement of one of the rooms on the first floor, which in her own mind she had already named "Poulet's room"; she was to have the other one on that floor, and Rosalie was to sleep upstairs next to the garret. The little house, thus tastefully arranged, looked pretty, and at first Jeanne was pleased with it, although she was haunted by the feeling that there was something missing, though she could not tell what.

One morning a clerk came over from the notary at Fécamp with the three thousand six hundred francs, the price at which an upholsterer had valued the furniture left at Les Peuples. Jeanne felt a thrill of pleasure as she took the money, and as soon as the man had gone she put on her hat and hurried off to Goderville to send Paul this unlooked-for sum as quickly as possible. But as she was hastening along the road she met Rosalie coming back from market; the maid suspected that something had happened, though she did not at once guess the truth. She soon found it out, however, for Jeanne could not hide anything from her, and placing her basket on the ground to give way to her wrath at her ease, she put her hands on her hips and scolded Jeanne at the top of her voice; then she took hold of her mistress with her right hand and her basket with her left and walked on again towards the house in a great passion. As soon as they were indoors Rosalie ordered the money to be given into her care, and Jeanne gave it to her, with the exception of the six hundred francs which she said nothing about; but this trick was soon detected by the now suspicious servant and Jeanne had to give it all up. However, Rosalie consented to these odd hundreds being sent to the young man, who in a few days wrote to thank his mother for the money. "You have done me a great service, mother dear," he said, "for we were reduced to utter want."

Jeanne, however, could not get accustomed to Batteville. She felt she could not breathe as she used to and she felt more alone and forsaken than ever. She would often walk as far as the village of Verneuil and come back through Trois-Mares, but as soon as she was home she started up to go out again as if she had forgotten to go to the very place to which she had meant to walk. The same thing happened time after time and she could not understand where it was she longed to go; one evening, however, she unconsciously uttered a sentence which at once revealed to her the secret of her restlessness. "Oh! how I long to see the ocean," she said as she sat down to dinner.

The sea! That was what she missed. Her neighbor for twenty-five years. The sea with its salt breezes, its roar, its tempests, its strong odors; the sea, which she could see every morning from her window at Les Peuples, which she inhaled day and night, and which, unconsciously, she had come to love like a human being.

Massacre, too, was very uneasy. The very evening of his arrival at the new house he had installed himself under the kitchen-dresser and no one could get him to move out. There he lay all day long, never stirring, except to turn himself over with a smothered grunt, but as soon as it was dark he got up and dragged himself towards the garden door, grazing himself against the wall as he went. After he had stayed out of doors a few minutes he came in again, and sat down before the stove, which was still warm, and as soon as Jeanne and Rosalie had gone to bed, he began to howl. The whole night long he howled, in a pitiful, deplorable way, sometimes ceasing for an hour, only to recommence in a still more doleful tone. A barrel was put outside the house and he was tied up to it, but he howled just the same out of doors as in, and as he was old and almost dying, he was brought back to the kitchen again.

It was impossible for Jeanne to sleep, for the whole night she could hear the old dog moaning and scratching as he tried to get used to this new house, knowing well it was not his old home. Nothing would quiet him; his eyes were dim and it seemed as if the knowledge of his infirmity made him keep still while everyone else was awake and downstairs, and at night he wandered restlessly about until daybreak, as if he only dared to move in the darkness which makes all beings sightless for the time. It was an intense relief to everyone when one morning he was found dead.

Winter wore on, and Jeanne gave way more and more to an insuperable hopelessness; it was no longer a keen, heart-rending grief that she felt, but a dull, gloomy melancholy. There was nothing to rouse her from it, no one came to see her, and the road which passed before her door was almost deserted. Sometimes a gig passed by driven by a red-faced man whose blouse, blown out by the wind, looked like a blue balloon, and sometimes a cart crawled past, or a peasant and his wife could be seen coming from the distance, growing larger and larger as they approached the house and then diminishing again when they had passed it, till they looked like two insects at the end of the long white line, which stretched as far as the eye could reach, rising and falling with the undulation of the earth. When the grass again sprang up, a little girl in a short dress passed the gate every morning with two thin cows, which browsed along the side of the road, and in the evening she returned, taking, as in the morning, ten steps every minute as she followed the animals.

Every night Jeanne dreamt that she was back at Les Peuples. She thought she was there with her father and mother and Aunt Lison, as in the old times. Again she accomplished the old, forgotten duties and supported Madame Adelaide as she walked in her avenue; and each time she awoke she burst into tears.

Paul was continually in her thoughts, and she wondered what he was doing, if he were well and if he ever thought of her. She revolved all these painful thoughts in her mind as she walked along the low-lying roads between the farms, and what was more torture to her than anything else was the fierce jealousy of the woman who had deprived her of her son. It was this hatred alone which restrained her from taking any steps towards finding Paul and trying to see him. She could imagine her son's mistress confronting her at the door and asking, "What is your business here, Madame?" and her self-respect would not permit her to run the risk of such an encounter. In the haughty pride of a chaste and spotless woman, who had never stooped to listen to temptation, she became still more bitter against the base and cowardly actions of a man enslaved by the filthy practices of carnal love, which degrades even the heart. The whole of humanity seemed to her unclean as she thought of the obscene secrets of the senses, of the caresses which debase, and of all the mysteries which surround the attraction of the sexes.

Another spring and summer passed away, and when the autumn came again with its rainy days, its dull, gray skies, its heavy clouds, Jeanne felt so weary of the life she was leading that she determined to make a supreme attempt to regain possession of her Poulet. Surely the young man's passion must have cooled by this time, and she wrote him a touching, pitiful letter:

My Dear Child,

I entreat you to return to me. Think how I am left, lonely, aged, and ill, the whole year with only a servant. I am living now in a little house by the roadside and it is very miserable for me, but if you were here everything would seem different. You are all I have in the world, and I have not seen you for seven years. You will never know how unhappy I have been and how my every thought was centered in you. You were my life, my soul, my only hope, my only love, and you are away from me, you have forsaken me.

Oh! come back, my darling Poulet, come back, and let me hold you in my arms again; come back to your old mother who so longs to see you.

JEANNE

A few days later came the following reply:

MY DEAR MOTHER,

I should only be too glad to come and see you, but I have not a penny; send me some money and I will come. I had myself been thinking of coming to speak to you about a plan which, if carried out, would permit me to do as you desire.

I shall never be able to repay the disinterested affection of the woman who has shared all my troubles, but I can at least make a public recognition of her faithful love and devotion. Her behavior is all you could desire; she is well-educated and well-read and you cannot imagine what a comfort she has been to me. I should be a brute if I did not make her some recompense, and I ask your permission to marry her. Then we could all live together in your new house, and you would forgive my follies. I am convinced that you would give your consent at once, if you knew her; I assure you she is very ladylike and quiet, and I know you would like her. As for me, I could not live without her.

I shall await your reply with every impatience, dear mother. We both send you much love. Your son,

VICOMTE PAUL DE LAMARE

Jeanne was stunned. As she sat with the letter on her knees, she could see so plainly through the designs of this woman who had not once let Paul return to his friends, but had always kept him at her side while she patiently waited until his mother should give in and consent to anything and everything in the irresistible desire of having her son with her again; and it was with bitter pain that she thought of how Paul obstinately persisted in preferring this creature to herself. "He does not love me, he does not love me," she murmured over and over again.

"Now, he wants to marry her," she said, when Rosalie came in.

The servant started.

"Oh! Madame, you surely will not consent to it. M. Paul can't marry such a hussy."

All the pride in Jeanne's nature rose in revolt at the thought, and though she was bowed down with grief, she replied, decidedly:

"No, Rosalie, never. But since he won't come here I will go to him, and we will see which of us two will win."

She wrote at once to Paul to prepare him for her visit and to arrange to meet him elsewhere than in the house he was living with that baggage. Then while she awaited his reply, she began to make all her preparations for the journey, and Rosalie began to pack her mistress's underwear and clothes in an old trunk.

"You haven't a single thing to put on," exclaimed the servant, as she was folding up an old dress she used to wear in the country. "I won't have you go with such clothes; you'd be a disgrace to everyone, and the Parisian ladies would take you for a servant."

Jeanne let her have her own way, and they both went to Goderville and chose some green checked material, which they left with the dressmaker to be made up. Then they went to see Maître Roussel the lawyer, who spent a fortnight in Paris every year; it was twenty-eight years since Jeanne had been to the capital. He gave them a great deal of advice about crossing the roads and the way to avoid being robbed, saying that the safest plan was to carry only just as much money as was necessary in their pockets and to sew the rest in the lining of their clothes; then he talked for a long time about the restaurants where the charges were moderate, and mentioned two or three to which ladies could go, and he recommended Jeanne to stay at the Hôtel de Normandie, which was near the railway station. He always stayed there himself, and she could say he had sent her. There had been a railway between Paris and Havre for the last six years, but Jeanne, absorbed in her sorrows, had never seen one of these steam-engines of which every one was talking, and which were revolutionizing the whole country.

The days passed on, but there came no answer from Paul. She waited a week, a fortnight. Every morning Jeanne had gone along the road to meet the postman, and had asked, in a voice which she could not keep steady:

"You have nothing for me today, Père Malandain?" And the man always replied in a voice roughened by all kinds of weather, "No, nothing yet, *ma bonne dame.*"

Fully persuaded that it was that woman who was preventing Paul from answering, Jeanne determined not to wait any longer, but to start at once. She wanted to take Rosalie with her, but the maid would not go because of increasing the expense of the journey, and she only allowed her mistress to take three hundred francs with her.

"If you want any more money," she said, "write to

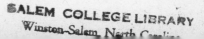

me, and I'll tell the lawyer to forward you some; but if I give you any more now, Monsieur Paul will get it all from you."

Then one December morning, Denis Lecoq's cart came to take them both to the railway station, for Rosalie was going to accompany her mistress as far as that. When they reached the station, they found out first how much the tickets were, then, when the trunk had been labeled and the ticket bought, they stood watching the rails, both too much occupied in wondering what the train would be like to think of the sad cause of this journey. At last a distant whistle made them look round, and they saw a large, black machine approaching, which came up with a terrible noise, dragging after it a long chain of little rolling houses. A porter opened the door of one of these little huts, and Jeanne kissed Rosalie and got in.

"*Au revoir*, Madame. I hope you will have a pleasant journey, and will soon be back again."

"*Au revoir*, Rosalie."

There was another whistle, and the string of carriages moved slowly off, gradually going faster and faster, till they reached a terrific speed. In Jeanne's carriage there were only two other passengers, who were both asleep, in two corners, and she sat and watched the fields and farms and villages rush past. She was frightened at the speed at which she was going, and the feeling came over her that she was entering a new phase of life, and was being hurried towards a very different world from that in which she had spent her peaceful girlhood and her monotonous life.

It was evening when she reached Paris. A porter took her trunk, and she followed closely at his heels, sometimes almost running for fear of losing sight of him, and feeling frightened as she was pushed about by the swaying crowd through which she did not know how to make her way.

"I was recommended here by M. Roussel," she hastened to say when she was in the hotel office.

The landlady, a big stolid-looking woman, was sitting at the desk.

"Who is M. Roussel?" she asked.

"The lawyer from Goderville, who stays here every year," replied Jeanne, in surprise.

"Very likely he does," responded the big woman, "but I don't know him. Do you want a room?"

"Yes, Madame."

A waiter shouldered the luggage and led the way upstairs.

Jeanne followed, feeling very low-spirited and depressed, and sitting down at a little table, she ordered some soup and the wing of a chicken to be sent up to her, for she had had nothing to eat since daybreak. She thought of how she had passed through this same town on her return from her wedding tour, as she ate her supper by the miserable light of one candle, and of how Julien had then first shown himself in his true character. But she was young then and brave and hopeful; now she felt old, shy, and full of fears, and the least thing worried and frightened her.

When she had finished her supper, she went to the window and watched the crowded street. She would have liked to go out but she dared not. She thought she would be sure to lose herself, so she went to bed, putting out her candle. But she had hardly yet got over the bustle of the journey, and that, and the noise and the sensation of being in a strange place, kept her awake. The hours passed on, and the noises outside gradually ceased, but still she could not sleep, for she was accustomed to the sound, peaceful sleep of the country, which is so different from the semi-repose of a great city. She was used to the calm, deep sleep of the country which pervades everything, men, beasts, and plants. Here she was conscious of a sort of restlessness all around her; the murmur of voices reached her ears, and every now and then a board creaked, a door shut, or a bell rang. She was just dozing off, about two o'clock in the morning, when a woman suddenly began to scream in a neighboring room. Jeanne started up in bed, and next she thought she heard a man laughing. As dawn approached she became more and more anxious to see Paul, and as soon as it was light, she got up and dressed.

He lived in the Rue du Sauvage, and she meant to follow Rosalie's advice about spending as little as possible, and walked there. It was a fine day, though the wind was keen, and there were a great many people hurrying along the pavements. Jeanne walked along the street as quickly as she could. When she reached the other end, she was to turn to the right, then to the left; then she would come to a square, where she was to ask again. She could not find the square, and a baker from whom she inquired the way gave her different directions altogether. She started on again, missed the way, wandered about, and in trying to follow other directions, lost herself entirely. She walked on and on, and was just going to hail a cab when she saw the Seine. Then she decided to walk along the quays, and in about an hour she reached the dark, dirty lane called Rue du Sauvage.

When she came to the number she was seeking, she was so excited that she stood before the door unable to move another step. Poulet was there, in that house! Her hands and knees trembled violently, and it was some moments before she could enter and walk along the passage to the concierge's quarters.

"Will you go and tell M. Paul de Lamare that an old lady friend of his mother's is waiting to see him?" she said, slipping a piece of money into the man's hand.

"He does not live here now, Madame," answered the concierge.

A shudder went over her. She faltered:

"Ah! Where—where is he living now?"

"I do not know."

She felt stunned, as though she were about to fall, and it was some time before she could speak again.

"When did he leave?" she asked at last, controlling herself by a violent effort.

The man was quite ready to tell her all he knew.

"About a fortnight ago," he replied. "They just walked out of the house one evening and didn't come back. They owed all over the neighborhood, so you can understand that they didn't leave any address."

Tongues of flame were dancing before Jeanne's eyes, as if a gun were being fired off close to her face; but she had one fixed idea in her mind: she wanted to find Poulet, and that upheld her and made her stand there as if she were calmly thinking.

"Then he did not say anything when he left?"

"No, nothing at all; they went away to get out of paying their debts."

"But he will have to send for his letters."

"He'll send a good many times before he gets them, then; besides, they didn't have ten in a twelvemonth, though I took them up one two days before they left."

That must have been the one she sent.

"Listen," she said, hastily. "I am his mother, and I have come to look for him. Here are ten francs for yourself. If you hear anything from or about him, let me know at once at the Hôtel de Normandie, Rue du Havre, and you shall be well paid for your trouble."

"You may depend upon me, Madame," answered the concierge; and Jeanne went away.

She hastened along the streets as if she were bent on an important mission, but she was not looking or caring whither she was going. She walked close to the walls, pushed and buffeted by errand-boys and porters; crossed the roads, regardless of the vehicles and the shouts of the drivers; stumbled against the curbstones, which she did not see; and hurried on and on, unconscious of everything and everyone. At last she found herself in a garden, and she felt so weary that she sat down on a seat. She sat there a long while, apparently unaware that the tears were running down her cheeks, and that the passers-by were stopping to look at her. At last the bitter cold made her rise to go, but her legs would hardly carry her, so weak and exhausted was she. She would have liked some soup, but she dared not go into a restaurant, for she knew people could see she was in trouble, and it made her feel timid and ashamed. When she passed one she would stop a moment at the door, look inside, and see all the people sitting at the tables eating, and then go on again, saying to herself, "I will go into the next one"; but when she came to the next her courage always failed her again. In the end she went into a baker's shop, and bought a little crescent-shaped roll, which she ate as she went along. She was very thirsty, but she did not know where to go to get anything to drink, so she went without.

She passed under the arch, and found herself in another garden surrounded by arcades, and she recognized the Palais Royal. Her walk in the sun had made her warm again, so she sat down for another hour or two. A crowd of people poured into the gardens—an elegant crowd composed of beautiful women and wealthy men,

who only lived for dress and pleasure, and who chatted
and smiled and bowed as they sauntered along. Feeling
ill at ease amidst this brilliant throng, Jeanne rose to go
away; but suddenly the thought struck her that perhaps
she might meet Paul here, and she began to walk from
end to end of the gardens, with hasty, furtive steps,
carefully scanning every face she met.

Soon she saw that people turned to look and laugh at
her, and she hurried away, thinking it was her odd appearance and her green-checked dress, which Rosalie
had chosen and had made up, that attracted everyone's
attention and smiles. She hardly dared ask her way, but
she did at last venture, and when she had reached her
hotel, she passed the rest of the day sitting on a chair
at the foot of the bed. In the evening she dined off some
soup and a little meat, as on the day before, and then
undressed and went to bed, performing all the duties of
her toilet quite mechanically, from sheer habit.

The next morning she went to the police department
to ask them to find her child. They told her they could
not promise her anything, but that they would attend to
the matter. After she had left the police station, she wandered about the streets, hoping that she might come
across him, and she felt more friendless and forsaken
among the busy crowds than she did in the midst of the
lonely country.

When she had returned to the hotel in the evening,
she was told that a man from M. Paul had asked for her,
and was coming again the next day. All the blood in her
body seemed suddenly to rush to her heart and she
could not close her eyes all night. Perhaps it was Paul
himself! Yes, it must be so, although his appearance did
not tally with the description the hotel people had given
of the man who had called, and when, about nine

o'clock in the morning, there came a knock at her door, she cried, "Come in!" expecting her son to rush into her arms held open to receive him.

But it was a stranger who entered—a stranger who began to apologize for disturbing her and to explain that he had come about some money Paul owed him. As he spoke she felt herself beginning to cry, and she tried to hide her tears from the man by wiping them away with the end of her finger as soon as they reached the corners of her eyes. The man had heard of her arrival from the concierge at the Rue du Sauvage, and as he could not find Paul he had come to his mother. He held out a paper, which Jeanne mechanically took; she saw "90 francs" written on it, and she drew out the money and paid the man. She did not go out at all that day, and the next morning more creditors appeared. She gave them all the money she had left, except twenty francs, and wrote and told Rosalie how she was situated.

Until her servant's answer came she passed the days in wandering aimlessly about the streets. She did not know what to do or how to kill the long, miserable hours; there was no one who knew of her troubles, or to whom she could go for sympathy, and her one desire was to get away from this city and to return to her little house beside the lonely road, where, a few days before, she had felt she could not bear to live because it was so dull and lonely. Now she was sure she could live nowhere else but in that little home where all her mournful habits had taken root.

At last, one evening, she found a letter from Rosalie awaiting her with two hundred francs enclosed.

"Come back as soon as possible, Madame Jeanne," wrote the maid, "for I shall send you nothing more. As for M. Paul, I will go and fetch him myself the next time we hear anything from him.—With best respects, your servant,

ROSALIE."

And Jeanne started back to Batteville one bitterly cold, snowy morning.

XIV

After her return from Paris, Jeanne would not go out or take any interest in anything. She rose at the same hour every morning, looked out of the window to see what sort of day it was, then went downstairs and sat before the fire in the dining-room. She would sit there for days at a time, perfectly still with her eyes fixed on the flames while she thought of all the sorrows she had passed through. The little room grew darker and darker, but she never moved, except to put more wood on the fire, and when Rosalie brought in the lamp she cried:

"Come, Madame Jeanne, you must stir about a bit, or you won't be able to eat any dinner again this evening."

Often she was worried by thoughts which she could not dismiss from her mind, and she allowed herself to be tormented by the veriest trifles, for the most insignificant matters appeared of the greatest importance to her diseased mind. She lived in the memories of the past, and she would think for hours together of her girlhood and her wedding tour in Corsica. The wild scenery that she had long forgotten suddenly appeared before her in the fire, and she could recall every detail, every event, every face connected with the island. The features of Jean Ravoli, the guide, haunted her, and sometimes she fancied she could even hear his voice.

At other times she thought of the peaceful years of Paul's childhood—of how he used to make her tend the salad plants, and of how she and Aunt Lison used to kneel on the ground, each trying to outdo the other to please the boy, and rear the greater number of plants.

Her lips would form the words, "Poulet, my little Poulet," as if she were talking to him, and she would cease to muse, and try for hours to write in the air the letters which formed her son's name, with her outstretched finger. Slowly she traced them before the fire, fancying she could see them, and, thinking she had made a mistake, she began the word over and over again, forcing herself to write the whole name though her arm trembled with fatigue. At last she would become so nervous that she mixed up the letters, and formed other words, and had to give it up.

She had all the manias and fancies which beset those who lead a solitary life, and it irritated her to the last degree to see the slightest change in the arrangement of the furniture. Rosalie often made her go out with her along the road, but after twenty minutes or so Jeanne would say, "I am tired out, Rosalie," and would sit down by the roadside. Soon movement of any kind became distasteful to her, and she stayed in bed as late as she could. Ever since childhood she had always been in the habit of jumping out of bed as soon as she had drunk her *café au lait*. She was particularly fond of her morning coffee, and she would have missed it more than anything. She always waited for Rosalie to bring it with an impatience that had a touch of sensuality in it, and as soon as the cup was placed on the bedside table she sat up, and emptied it, somewhat greedily. Then she at once threw back the bedclothes and began to dress. But gradually she fell into the habit of dreaming a few moments after she had placed the empty cup back in the saucer, and from that she soon began to lie down again, and at last she stayed in bed every day until

Rosalie came back in a temper and dressed her almost by force.

She had no longer the slightest will of her own. Whenever her servant asked her advice, or put any question to her, or wanted to know her opinion, she always answered, "Do as you like, Rosalie." So firmly did she believe herself pursued by a persistent ill-luck that she became as great a fatalist as an Oriental, and she was so accustomed to seeing her dreams unfulfilled, and her hopes disappointed, that she did not dare undertake anything fresh, and hesitated for days before she commenced the simplest task, so persuaded was she that whatever she touched would be sure to go wrong.

"I don't think anyone could have had more misfortune than I have had all my life," she was always saying.

"How would it be if you had to work for your living, and if you were obliged to get up every morning at six o'clock to go and do a hard day's work?" Rosalie would exclaim. "That's what a great many people have to do, and then when they get too old to work, they die of want."

"But my son has deserted me, and I am all alone," Jeanne would reply.

That enraged Rosalie.

"And what if he has? How about those whose children have to do their military service, or settle in America?" (America, in her eyes, was an undefined country whither people went to make their fortune, and whence they never returned.) "Children always leave their parents sooner or later; old and young people aren't meant to stay together. And then, what if he were dead?" she would finish up savagely, and her mistress could say nothing after that.

Jeanne got a little stronger when the first warm days

of spring came, but she only took advantage of her better health to bury herself still deeper in her gloomy thoughts.

She went up to the garret one morning to look for something, and, while she was there, happened to open a box full of old calendars which had been kept according to the custom of some country people.

It seemed as if she had found the past years themselves, and she was filled with emotion as she looked at the pile of square pieces of cardboard. They were of all sizes, big and little, and she took them every one down to the dining-room and began to lay them out on the table in the right order of years. Suddenly she picked up the very first one—the one she had taken with her from the convent to Les Peuples. For a long time she gazed at it with its dates which she had crossed out the day she had left Rouen, the day after leaving the convent, and she began to shed slow, bitter tears—the weak, pitiful tears of an aged woman—as she looked at these cards spread out before her on the table, and which represented all her wretched life.

Then the thought struck her that by means of these calendars she could recall all that she had ever done, and giving way to the idea, she at once devoted herself to the task of retracing the past. She pinned all the cards, which had grown yellow with age, up on the wall, and then spent hours before one or another of them, thinking, "What did I do in that month?"

She had put a mark beside all the important dates in her life, and sometimes, by means of linking together and adding one to the other, all the little circumstances which had preceded and followed a great event, she succeeded in remembering a whole month. By dint of concentrated attention, and efforts of will and of memory, she retraced nearly the whole of her first two years at Les Peuples, recalling without much difficulty this faraway period of her life, for it seemed to stand out in relief. But the following years were shrouded in a sort of fog and seemed to run one into another, and sometimes she pored over a calendar for hours without being able to remember whether it was even in that year that such and such a thing happened. She would go slowly round the dining-room looking at these images of past years, which, to her, were as pictures of an ascent to Calvary, until one of them arrested her attention and then she would sit gazing at it all the rest of the day, absorbed in her recollections.

Soon the sap began to rise in the trees; the seeds were springing up, the leaves were budding and the air was filled with the faint, sweet smell of the apple blossoms which made the orchards a glowing mass of pink. As summer approached Jeanne became very restless. She could not keep still; she went in and out twenty times a day, and, as she rambled along past the farms, she worked herself into a perfect fever of regret.

A daisy half hidden in the grass, a sunbeam falling through the leaves, or the reflection of the sky in a splash of water in a rut was enough to agitate and affect her, for their sight brought back a kind of echo of the emotions she had felt when, as a young girl, she had wandered dreamily through the fields; and though now there was nothing to which she could look forward, the soft yet exhilarating air sent the same thrill through her as when all her life had lain before her. But this pleasure was not unalloyed with pain, and it seemed as if the universal joy of the awakening world could now only impart a delight which was half sorrow to her grief-crushed soul and withered heart. Everything around her seemed to have changed. Surely the sun was hardly so warm as in her youth, the sky so deep a blue, the grass so fresh a green? And the flowers, paler and less sweet, could no longer arouse within her the exquisite ecstasies of delight as of old. On certain days she was filled with such a sense of well-being that she found herself dreaming and hoping again; for, however cruel Fate may be, is it possible to give way to utter despair when the sun shines and the sky is blue?

She went on aimlessly, for hours and hours, straight in front of her, urged on and on by her inward excitement, and sometimes she would suddenly stop and sit down by the roadside to think of her troubles. Why had she not been loved like other women? Why had even the simple pleasures of an uneventful existence been refused her?

Sometimes, again forgetting for a moment that she was old, that there was no longer any pleasure in store for her, and that, with the exception of a few more lonely years, her life was over and done, she would build all sorts of castles in the air and make plans for such a happy future, just as she had done when she was sixteen. Then, suddenly remembering the bitter reality, she would get up again, feeling as if a heavy load had fallen upon her, and return home, murmuring:

"Oh, you old fool! You old fool!"

Now Rosalie was always saying to her:

"Do keep still, Madame. What on earth makes you want to run about so?"

"I can't help it," Jeanne would reply sadly. "I am like Massacre before he died."

One morning Rosalie went into her mistress's room earlier than usual.

"Make haste and drink up your coffee," she said as she placed the cup on the table. "Denis is waiting to take us to Les Peuples. I have to go over there on business."

Jeanne was so excited that she thought she would have fainted, and, as she dressed herself with trembling fingers, she could hardly believe she was going to see her dear home once more.

Overhead was a bright, blue sky, and, as they went along, Denis's pony would every now and then break into a gallop out of sheer good humor. When they reached Etouvent, Jeanne could hardly breathe, her heart beat so quickly, and when she saw the brick pillars beside the château gate, she exclaimed, "Oh," two or three times in a low voice, as if she were in the presence of something which stirred her very soul, and she could not help herself.

They put up the horse at the Couillards' farm, and, when Rosalie and her son went to attend to their business, the farmer asked Jeanne if she would like to go over the château, as the owner was away, and gave her the key.

She went off alone, and when she found herself opposite the old manor she stood still to look at it. The outside had not been touched since she had left. All the shutters were closed, and the sunbeams were dancing on the gray walls of the big, weatherbeaten building. A little piece of wood fell on her dress, she looked up and saw that it had fallen from the plane-tree, and she went up to the big tree and stroked its pale, smooth bark as if it had been alive. Her foot touched a piece of rotten wood lying in the grass; it was the last fragment of the seat on which she had so often sat with her loved ones —the seat which had been put up the very day of Julien's first visit to the château.

Then she went to the hall-door. She had some difficulty in opening it as the key was rusty and would not turn, but at last the lock gave way, and the door itself only required a slight push before it swung back. The first thing Jeanne did was to run up to her own room. It had been hung with a light paper and she hardly knew it again, but when she opened one of the windows and looked out, she was moved almost to tears as she saw again the scene she loved so well—the thicket, the elms, the heath, and the sea covered with brown sails which, at this distance, looked as if they were motionless.

Then she went all over the big, empty house. She saw the familiar stains on the walls. She stopped to look at a little hole in the plaster which the Baron had made with his cane, for he used to make a few thrusts at the wall whenever he passed this spot, in memory of the fencing bouts he had had in his youth. In her mother's bedroom she found a small gold-headed pin stuck in the wall behind the door, in a dark corner near the bed. She had stuck it there a long while ago (she remembered it now), and had looked everywhere for it since, but it had never been found; and she kissed it and took it with her as a priceless relic.

She went into every room, recognizing the almost invisible spots and marks on the hangings which had not been changed, and again noting the odd forms and faces which the imagination so often traces in the designs of the furniture coverings, the carvings of mantelpieces and the shadows on soiled ceilings. She walked through the vast, silent château as noiselessly as if she were in a cemetery; all her life was interred there.

She went down to the drawing-room. The closed shutters made it very dark, and it was a few moments before she could distinguish anything; then as her eyes became accustomed to the darkness, she gradually made out the tapestry with the birds on it. Two armchairs stood before the fireplace, looking as if they had just been vacated, and the very smell of the room—a smell that had always been peculiar to it, as each human being has his, a smell which could be perceived at once, and yet was vague like all the faint perfumes of old rooms—brought the memories crowding to Jeanne's mind.

Her breath came quickly as she stood with her eyes fixed on the two chairs, inhaling this perfume of the past; and, all at once, in a sudden hallucination occasioned by her thoughts, she fancied she saw—she did see—her father and mother with their feet on the fender as she had so often seen them before. She drew back in terror, stumbling against the door-frame, and clung to it for support, still keeping her eyes fixed on the armchairs. The vision disappeared and for some minutes she stood horror-stricken; then she slowly regained possession of herself and turned to fly, afraid that she was going mad. Her eyes fell on the wainscoting against which she was leaning and she saw Poulet's ladder. There were all the faint marks traced on the wall at unequal intervals and the figures which had been cut with a penknife to indicate the month, and the child's age and growth. In some places there was the Baron's big writing, in others her own, a little smaller, in others again Aunt Lison's, which was a little shaky. She could see the boy standing there now, with his fair hair and his little forehead pressed against the wall to have his height measured, while the Baron exclaimed, "Jeanne, he has grown half an inch in six weeks," and she began to kiss the wainscoting in a frenzy of love.

Then she heard Rosalie's voice outside, calling, "Madame Jeanne! Madame Jeanne! lunch is waiting," and she went out with her head in a whirl. She felt unable to understand anything that was said to her. She ate what was placed before her, listened to what was being said without realizing the sense of the words, answered the farmers' wives when they inquired after her health, passively received their kisses and kissed the cheeks which were offered to her, and then got into the chaise again.

When she could no longer see the high roof of the château through the trees, something within her seemed to break, and she felt that she had just said good bye to her old home forever.

They went straight back to Batteville, and as she was going indoors Jeanne saw something white under the door; it was a letter which the postman had slipped there during their absence. She at once recognized Paul's handwriting and tore open the envelope in an agony of anxiety. He wrote:

My Dear Mother,

I have not written before because I did not want to bring you to Paris on a fruitless errand, for I have always been meaning to come and see you myself. At the present moment I am in great trouble and difficulty. My wife gave birth to a little girl three days ago, and now she is dying and I have not a penny. I do not know what to do with the child; the concierge is trying to nourish it with a feeding-bottle as best she can, but I fear I shall lose it. Could you not take it? I cannot send it to a wet-nurse as I have no money, and I absolutely do not know what to do. Pray answer by return of post.

Your loving son,

Paul

Jeanne dropped on a chair with hardly enough strength left to call Rosalie. The maid came and they read the letter over again together, and then sat looking at each other in silence.

"I'll go and fetch the child myself, Madame," said Rosalie at last. "We can't leave it to die."

"Very well, my girl, go," answered Jeanne.

"Put on your hat, Madame," said the maid, after a pause, "and we will go and see the lawyer at Goderville. If that woman is going to die, M. Paul must marry her for the sake of the child."

Jeanne put on her hat without a word. Her heart was overflowing with joy, but she would not have allowed anyone to see it for the world, for it was one of those detestable joys in which people can revel in their hearts, but of which they are, nevertheless, ashamed; her son's mistress was going to die.

The lawyer gave Rosalie detailed instructions which the servant made him repeat two or three times; then, when she was sure she knew exactly what to do, she said:

"Don't you fear; I'll see it's all right now." And she started for Paris that very night.

Jeanne passed two days in such an agony of mind that she could fix her thoughts on nothing. The third morning she received a line from Rosalie, merely saying she was coming back by that evening's train; nothing more; and about three o'clock, Jeanne sent round to a neighbor to ask him if he would drive her to the Beuzeville railway station to meet her servant.

She stood on the platform, her eyes fixed on the straight rails, which seemed to run off and meet far away on the horizon. Every now and then she would look at the clock. Ten minutes more—five minutes—two —and at last the train was due, though as yet nothing was visible on the line. Then, all at once, she saw a cloud of white smoke, and underneath it a black speck which got rapidly larger and larger. The big engine came into the station, snorting and slackening its speed, and Jeanne looked eagerly into every window as the carriages went past her.

The doors opened and several people got out—

peasants in blouses, farmers' wives with baskets on their arms, a few gentlemen in soft hats—and at last Rosalie appeared, carrying what looked like a bundle of linen in her arms. Jeanne would have stepped forward to meet her, but all strength seemed to have left her legs and she feared she would fall if she moved. The maid saw her and came up in her ordinary, calm way.

"Good day, Madame; here I am again, though I've had some bother to get along."

"Well?" gasped Jeanne.

"Well," answered Rosalie, "she died last night. They were married and here's the baby," and she held out the child, which could not be seen for its wraps. Jeanne mechanically took it, and they left the station and got into the carriage which was waiting.

"M. Paul is coming directly after the funeral. I suppose he'll be here tomorrow, by this train."

"Paul——" murmured Jeanne, and then stopped without saying anything more.

The sun was sinking towards the horizon, bathing in a glow of light the green fields, which were flecked here and there with golden colza flowers and blood-red poppies, and over the quiet earth, full of sap, fell an infinite peace.

The chaise was going at a quick pace, the peasant clicking his tongue to urge on the horse. Jeanne looked straight up into the sky, which seemed to be cut asunder by the circular flight of swallows that looked like rockets.

All at once she became conscious of a soft warmth, the warmth of life, which was making itself felt through her skirts, penetrating her legs and her whole body; it was the heat from the tiny being sleeping on her knees. She was filled with a great emotion. She suddenly drew back the covering from the child she had not yet seen, her son's daughter. As the light fell on its face the little creature opened its blue eyes, and moved its lips, and then Jeanne hugged it close to her, and, raising it in her arms, began to cover it with kisses.

"Come, come, Madame Jeanne, have done," said Rosalie, in sharp, though good-tempered tones; "you'll make the child cry."

Then she added, as if in reply to her own thoughts:

"Life, after all, is never so good nor so bad as people think."

PERSONAL WRITINGS

ON THE WATER

[This diary contains no story and no very thrilling adventure. While cruising along the Mediterranean coast last spring I amused myself by writing down every day what I saw and what I thought. What I saw was water, sun, clouds, and rocks—I have nothing else to tell about; and my thoughts were mere nothings such as were suggested by the cradling of the waves as they lulled me and bore me along. G. M.]

April 6th

MY SKIPPER Bernard is lean and lithe, remarkably clean, careful and prudent. Bearded up to the eyes, he has a frank look and a kindly voice. He is devoted and trustworthy. But everything makes him anxious on board; a sudden swell that foretells a breeze out at sea, a long cloud over the Esterel range announcing a wind to westward, even a rising barometer, for that may indicate a squall from the east. Like every good sailor, he is eternally watchful and eternally concerned to keep the boat spotless: he will rub up the brasses the moment a drop of water has splashed them.

His brother-in-law, Raymond, is a strong fellow, swarthy and mustached, indefatigable and bold, as loyal and devoted as Bernard, but calmer, less variable and nervous, more resigned to the surprises and the treachery of the sea. Bernard, Raymond, and the barometer are sometimes in contradiction with each other; they perform an amusing comedy with three characters, of which one, the best informed, is dumb.

"You know, Sir, we're sailing well," said Bernard.

We had sailed through the gulf of La Salis, cleared La Garoupe, and were approaching Cape Gros, a flat low rock stretching out almost on a level with the water. Now, the whole Alpine mountain range rose up, a monster wave threatening the sea, a granite wave capped with snow, where each pointed tip looks like a dash of spray motionless and frozen. Behind this ice the sun was up, shedding over it the light of its molten silver rays. Directly after, as we rounded the Antibes headland, we discovered the Lerins Isles, and behind them the tortuous outline of the Esterel. The Esterel is the stage scenery of Cannes, a lovely keepsake kind of mountain of faintest blue, elegantly outlined in a coquettish and yet artistic style, washed in water-colors on a theatrical sky by a good-natured Creator for the express purpose of serving as model for English lady landscape painters, and as a subject of admiration for consumptive or idle Royal Highnesses. . . .

The sun now radiant, overspreads the earth, making the walls of the houses sparkle from afar like scattered snow while it brushes the sea with a light varnish of luminous blue.

Little by little, taking advantage of the faintest breath, of those caresses of the air which one can hardly feel on the skin, but to which nevertheless lively and well-trimmed yachts respond in still waters, we sail beyond the last point of the headland, and the whole gulf of Juan, with the squadron at its center, lies before us. From afar, the ironclads look like rocks, islets, and reefs covered with dead trees. The smoke of a train runs along the shore between Cannes and Juan-les-Pins, which may one day become the prettiest place on the whole coast.

Three tartans with their lateen sails, one red and the other two white, are detained in the channel between the island of Sainte Marguerite and the mainland.

All is still, the soft and warm calm of a morning's springtide in the South; and already it seems to me as if I had left weeks ago, months ago, years ago, the busy chattering world. The intoxication of solitude swells within me, the sweet delight of a rest that nothing will disturb, neither an importunate letter nor the bark of my dog. I cannot be sent for, invited, carried off, overwhelmed by smiles or harassed by civilities. I am alone, really alone, really free. The smoke of the train runs along the seaside while I float in a winged home that is rocked and cradled; pretty as a bird, tiny as a nest, softer than a hammock, wandering over the waters at the caprice of the wind, independent and free. To attend to me and sail my boat, I have two sailors at my call, and books and provisions for a fortnight.

A whole fortnight without having to speak a word, what joy! . . .

Cannes, April 7th

People gather together at Cannes because they love Imperial and Royal Highnesses, and the Highnesses are at home here. In default of the kingdoms of which they have been dispossessed, they reign peacefully in the salons of the faithful. Great and small, poor and rich, sad and gay, all kinds of royalty are to be found here, according to one's taste. In general they are modest, they strive to please, and they show in their intercourse with humbler mortals a delicacy and affability that is hardly ever found in our own political representatives, those princes of the ballot. But though it is true that the Princes, the poor homeless Princes without subjects or civil list, who come to live in this town of flowers and fashion, affect simplicity and do not lay themselves open to ridicule, the same cannot be said of the worshipers of Highnesses. The devout circle round their idols with an eagerness at once religious and comical; and directly they are deprived of one, they fly off in quest of another, as though their mouths could only open to say "Monseigneur" or "her Highness," and speak in the third person. They cannot be with you five minutes without telling you what the Princess replied, what the Grand Duke said; the outing planned with the one, the witty saying of the other. One feels, one sees, one guesses that they frequent no other society than that of persons of royal blood, and if they deign to speak to you, it is only in order to inform you exactly of what takes place on these heights. . . .

But why laugh and be astonished at the harmless and innocent mania of the elegant admirers of Princes, when we meet in Paris fifty different races of hero-worshipers who are every bit as ridiculous.

Whoever has a salon must needs have some celebrities to show off in it, and a hunt is organized to secure them. There is hardly a woman in society who is not anxious to have her artist or her artists; and she will give dinners for them in order that the whole world may know that her's is a clever set.

Among the great men most sought after by women, old and young, are most assuredly the musicians. Some houses possess a complete collection of them, particularly as these artists possess the inestimable advantage of being useful at the evening parties. It must be said, however, that a hostess who is ambitious to show off a musician with a really great reputation, must content herself with only one at a time: two will refuse to appear together in the same drawing-room. Meanwhile, there is not a meanness of which any leader of society is not capable, in order to embellish her salon with a celebrated composer. The delicate attentions usually employed to secure a painter or a mere literary man, become quite inadequate when the subject is a tradesman in sound. For him, allurements and praise hitherto unknown are employed. His hands are kissed like those of a king, he is worshiped as a god, when he has deigned to execute his *Regina Coeli*. A hair of his beard is worn in a ring; a button torn from his sleeve in a violent movement of his arm as he plays, becomes a medal, a sacred medal hung on the bosom at the end of a gold chain.

Painters are less in demand, although still rather sought after. They are not so divine and more Bohemian. Their manners are less courteous, and above all not sufficiently sublime. They often replace inspiration by broad jests and silly puns. They carry with them too much of the aroma of the studio. Those who, by dint of watchfulness, have managed to get rid of it, only exchange one odor for another, that of affectation. And then they are a fickle, light, and bragging lot. No one is certain of keeping them long, whereas the musician builds his nest in the family circle.

Of late years, the literary man has been in fashion. He presents many great advantages: he talks, he talks a great deal, his conversation suits every kind of public, and as his profession is to be intelligent, he can be listened to and admired in all security.

The woman who is possessed with the mania for having a literary man at her house (as one might have a parrot whose chatter should attract all the neighboring concierges), has to choose between a poet and a novelist. There is more spontaneity about the novelist. Poets are more sentimental, novelists more positive. It is a matter of taste and constitution. The poet has more charm, the novelist has often more wit. But the novelist presents dangers that are not met with in the poet: he pries, pillages, and makes capital of all he sees. With him there is no tranquillity, no certainty that he will not, some day, strip you bare in the pages of a book. . . .

How blinded and intoxicated we must be by our foolish pride, to fancy ourselves anything more than animals slightly superior to other animals. Listen to them, the fools, seated round the table! They are talking! Talking with gentle confiding ingenuousness and they imagine that they are exchanging ideas. What ideas? They say where they have been walking: "It was a pretty walk, but rather cold coming home:" "The cooking is not too bad, though hotel food is always rather spicy." They tell you what they have done, what they like, what they believe.

I see the deformity of their souls as a monstrous foetus in a jar of alcohol. I assist at the slow birth of the commonplace sayings they constantly repeat; I watch the words as they drop from the granary of stupidity into their imbecile mouths, and from their mouths into the inert atmosphere which bears them to my ears. Who can deny that their ideas, their noblest, most solemn, most respected ideas, constitute unimpeachable proof of the omnipotence of human stupidity—eternal, universal, indestructible stupidity?

All of man's conceptions of God, that fumbling deity whose first tries at creation are such failures that he must needs recreate them, that deity who spies on our secrets and notes them down, that god who is in turn policeman, Jesuit, lawyer, gardener and who is conceived now in armor, now in robes, now in wooden shoes; all the denials of God's existence based upon terrestrial logic, the arguments for and against, the history of religious beliefs, of schisms, heresies, philosophies, the affirmations as well as the doubts, the childishness of the theories, the ferocious and bloody violence of the originators of theological hypotheses, the utter chaos of their disputes—in short, every miserable effort of this wretchedly impotent being, man, impotent in conception, in imagination, in knowledge—everything proves that man was put on this absurdly small earth for the sole purpose of eating, drinking, manufacturing children and little songs, and killing his kind by way of pastime.

Happy are those whom life satisfies, who are amused and content. They do exist—men and women who are easily pleased, who are delighted with everything. They love the sun and the rain, the snow and the fog; they love festivities and they love the calm of their homes; they love all they see, all they do, all they say, all they hear.

Such people lead either a tranquil life, quiet and satisfied amid their offspring, or an agitated one, filled with pleasures and distraction. In neither case are their lives dull. Life, for them, is an amusing kind of play, in which they are themselves the actors; an excellent and varied show, which, though it offers nothing unexpected, thoroughly delights them.

Other men, however, who run through at a glance the narrow circle of human satisfactions, remain dismayed before the emptiness of happiness, the monotony and poverty of earthly joys. As soon as they have reached thirty years of age all is ended for them. What have they to expect? Nothing now can interest them; they have made the round of our meager pleasures.

Happy are those who know not the loathsome weariness of the same acts constantly repeated; happy are those who have the strength to begin again each day the same task, with the same gestures, amid the same furniture, in front of the same horizon, under the same sky, to go out into the same streets, where they meet the same faces and the same animals. Happy are those who do not perceive with unutterable disgust that nothing changes, and that all is boredom.

We must indeed be a slow and shallow-minded race to be so easily pleased and satisfied with what is. How is it that the earthly audience has not yet called out, "Curtain!" has not yet demanded a second act, with other pleasures, other plants, other planets, other inventions, other adventures?

Is it possible no one has yet felt a loathing for the sameness of the human face, of the animals which by their unvarying instincts, transmitted in their seed from the first to the last of their race, seem to be but living machinery; a hatred of landscapes eternally the same, and of pleasures never varied?

Console yourself, it is said, by the love of science and art. But is it not evident that we are always shut up in ourselves, without ever being able to get out of ourselves; forever condemned to drag the chains of our wingless dream?

All the progress obtained by our cerebral effort consists in the ascertainment of material facts by means of instruments ridiculously imperfect, which however make up in a certain degree for the inefficiency of our organs. Every twenty years, some unhappy inquirer, who generally dies in the attempt, discovers that the atmosphere contains a gas hitherto unknown, that an imponderable, inexplicable, unqualifiable force can be obtained by rubbing a piece of wax on cloth; that amongst the innumerable unknown stars, there is one that has not yet been noticed in the immediate vicinity of another, which had not only been observed, but even designated by name for many years. What matter?

Our diseases are due to microbes? Very well. But where do those microbes come from? And the diseases of these invisible ones? And the suns, whence do they come from?

We know nothing, we understand nothing, we can do nothing, we imagine nothing, we are shut up, imprisoned in ourselves. And there are people who marvel at the genius of humanity!

Art? Painting consists in reproducing with coloring matter monotonous landscapes, which seldom resemble nature; in delineating men, and striving without ever succeeding, to attain the aspect of living beings. Obstinately and uselessly one struggles to imitate what is; and the result is a motionless and dumb copy of the actions of life, which is barely comprehensible even to the educated eye that the painter has sought to attract.

Wherefore such efforts? Wherefore such a vain imitation? Wherefore this trivial reproduction of things in themselves so dull? How petty!

Poets do with words what painters try to do with colors. Again, wherefore?

When one has read four of the most talented, the most ingenious authors, it is idle to open another. And nothing more can be learned. Poets exhaust themselves in sterile labor. For since mankind does not change, their useless art is immutable. Ever since our poor minds first awoke, man has been the same; his sentiments, his beliefs, his sensations have been the same. He has neither advanced nor retrograded; he has never stirred. Of what use is it to me to learn what I think, to see myself portrayed in the trivial adventures of a novel?

Ah! if poets could vanquish space, explore the planets, discover other worlds, other beings; if they could vary unceasingly for my mind the nature and form of things, convey me constantly through a changeful and surprising Unknown, open for me mysterious vistas on unexpected and marvelous horizons, I would read them night and day. But poets, impotent as they are, can but change the place of a word, and show me my own image, as painters do. Of what use is all this?

Man's thought does not advance. Each time that it attains its never remote and never to be exceeded limits, it goes round and round in a circle, like a horse in a circus, like a fly shut up in a bottle, fluttering and dashing itself against the sides.

And yet, for want of a better occupation, thought is always a solace, when one lives alone.

On this little boat rocked by the sea, this boat that a wave could fill and upset, I know, I feel, how true it is that nothing we know exists, for the earth which floats in empty space is even more isolated, more lost than this skiff on the billows. Their importance is the same, their destiny will be accomplished. And I rejoice at understanding the nothingness of the belief and the vanity of the hopes which our insectlike pride has begotten. . . .

At the mere mention of the word war, I am seized with a sense of bewilderment, as though I heard of witchcraft, of the Inquisition, of some far distant thing, ended long ago, abominable and monstrous; against all natural law.

When we talk of cannibals, we smile proudly and proclaim our superiority over the savages. Which are the savages, the true savages? Those who fight to eat the vanquished, or those who fight to kill and only to kill? . . .

A clever artist in such matters, a genius of slaughter, Moltke, replied one day to some peace delegates, in the following extraordinary words:

"War is holy and of divine institution: it is one of the sacred laws of nature; it keeps alive in men all the great and noble sentiments, honor, disinterestedness, virtue, courage; in a word, it prevents men from falling into hideous materialism."

Therefore to collect a herd of some four hundred thousand men, march day and night without respite, to think of nothing, study nothing, learn nothing, read nothing, be of no earthly use to anyone; to lie down in the mire, live like brutes in a continual stupor of mind, pillage towns, burn villages, ruin nations; then, meeting another similar agglomeration of human flesh, rush upon it, shed lakes of blood, cover plains with bruised flesh mingled with muddy and bloody earth; pile up heaps of slain; have arms and legs blown off, brains scattered, and perish at the corner of some field while your parents, your wife and children are dying of hunger; this is what we are to call not falling into hideous materialism!

Soldiers are the scourges of the earth. We struggle against nature and ignorance, against obstacles of all kinds in order to lessen the hardships of our miserable existence. Men, benefactors, scholars wear out their lives toiling, seeking what may assist, what may help, what may solace their brethren. Eager in their useful work, they pile up discovery on discovery, enlarge the human mind, extend science, add something each day to the stock of human knowledge, to the welfare, the comfort, the strength of their country. Suddenly war is declared; and in six months the generals have destroyed the efforts of twenty years' patience and genius. And this is what is called, not falling into hideous materialism.

We have seen war. We have seen men maddened and reverted to their brute estate, killing for mere pleasure, killing out of terror, out of bravado, out of sheer ostentation. Then when right no longer exists, when law is dead, when all notion of justice has disappeared, we have seen men ruthlessly shot down, innocent beings who, picked up along the road, had become objects of suspicion simply because they were afraid. We have seen dogs as they lay chained up at their master's gate, killed in order to try a new revolver; we have seen cows riddled with bullets as they lay in the fields, without reason, for the fun of firing off guns.

And this is what is called, not falling into hideous materialism. To invade a country, to kill the man who defends his home on the plea that he wears a smock and has no forage cap on his head, to burn down the houses of the poor creatures who are without bread, to steal furniture, drink wine found in cellars, violate women found in the streets, burn up gunpowder and leave behind misery and cholera—this is what is called, not falling into hideous materialism.

What have they ever done to show their intelligence, these valiant warriors? Nothing. What have they invented? Guns and cannon. That is all.

The inventor of the wheelbarrow did more for humanity by the simple and practical idea of fitting a wheel between two poles, than the inventor of modern fortifications.

What remains of Greece? Books and marble. Is she great by what she conquered, or by what she produced? Was it the invasion of the Persians that prevented her from falling into hideous materialism? Was it the invasion of the barbarians that saved Rome and regenerated her? Did Napoleon continue the great intellectual movement begun by the philosophers of the eighteenth century?

Since governments assume the right of death over their peoples, there is nothing astonishing in a people sometimes assuming the right of death over governments. The people defend themselves. They are right. No one has an absolute right to govern others. It can only be done for the good of those who are governed. Whoever governs must consider it as much his duty to avoid war, as it is the duty of the captain of a vessel to avoid shipwreck.

When a captain has lost his ship, he is judged and condemned if found guilty of negligence or even of incapacity. Why should not governments be judged after the declaration of every war? If the people understood this, if they took the law into their own hands against the murdering powers, if they refused to allow themselves to be killed without reason, if they used their weapons against those who sent them off to slaughter, war would indeed be a dead letter. But that day will never dawn. . . .

Agay, April 8th

Ay, verily, I do feel on certain days such a horror of all that is, that I long for death. The invariable monotony of landscapes, faces and thoughts, becomes an intensely acute suffering. The meanness of the universe astonishes and revolts me, the littleness of all things fills me with disgust, and I am overwhelmed by the platitude of human beings.

At other times, on the contrary, I enjoy everything as an animal does. Though my spirit, restless, agitated, hypertrophied by work, may bound onward to hopes that are not those of our race, and then after having realized that all is vanity, may fall back into a contempt for all that is, my animal body at least, is enraptured with all the intoxication of life. Like the birds, I love the sky, like the prowling wolf, the forest; I delight in rocky heights, like a chamois; the thick grass, I love to roll in and gallop over like a horse, and, like a fish, I revel in the clear waters. I feel thrilling within me the sensations of all the different species of animals, of all their instincts, of all the confused longings of inferior creatures. I love the earth as they do, not as other men do; I love it without admiring it, without poetry, without exultation. With a deep and animal attachment, contemptible yet holy, I love all that lives, all that grows, all that we see. All this leaves my spirit calm and excites only my eyes and my heart: the days, the nights, the rivers, the seas, the storms, the woods, the hues of dawn, the glance of woman and her very touch.

The gentle ripple of water on the sandy shore, or on the rocky granite affects and moves me, and the joy that fills me as I feel myself driven forward by the wind, and carried along by the waves, proceeds from the abandonment of myself to the natural forces of creation, proceeds from my return to a primitive state.

When the weather is beautiful as it is today, I feel in my veins the blood of the lascivious and vagabond fauns of olden times. I am no longer the brother of mankind, but the brother of all creatures and all nature.

April 10th

No sooner had I lain down than I felt sleep was impossible, and I remained lying on my back with my eyes closed, my thoughts on the alert, and all my nerves quivering. Not a motion, not a sound, near or far; nothing could be heard but the breathing of the two sailors through the thin bulkhead.

Suddenly, something grated. What was it? I know not. Some block in the rigging, no doubt; but the sound —tender, plaintive, and mournful—sent a thrill through me; then nothing more. An infinite silence seemed to spread from the earth to the stars; nothing more—not a breath, not a ripple on the water, not a vibration of the yacht, nothing; and then again the slight and unidentifiable moan began again. It seemed to me as I listened, as though a jagged blade were sawing at my heart. . . .

What was it? It was the voice ringing with reproaches which tortures our soul, clamoring ceaselessly, obscure, painful, harassing; a voice unappeasable and mysterious, which will not be ignored; ferocious in its reproaches for what we have done, as well as for what we have left undone; the voice of remorse and useless regrets for the days gone by and the women unloved; for the joys that were vain and the hopes that are dead; the voice of the past, of all that has disappointed us, has fled and vanished forever; the voice of what we have not, nor shall ever attain; the small shrill voice which ever proclaims the failure of our life, the uselessness of our efforts, the impotence of our minds, the weakness of our flesh.

Ah! I have coveted all, and delighted in nothing. I should have required the vitality of a whole race, the varying intelligence, all the faculties, all the powers scattered among all beings, and thousands of existences in reserve; for I bear within myself every desire and every curiosity, and I am compelled to see all, and grasp nothing.

From whence, therefore, arises this anguish over living, since to the generality of men life brings only satisfaction? Wherefore this unknown torture, which preys upon me? Why should I not know the reality of pleasure, expectation, and possession?

It is because I carry within me that second sight, which is at the same time the power and despair of writers. I write because I understand and suffer from all that is, because I know it too well, and above all, because without being able to enjoy it, I contemplate it inwardly in the mirror of my thoughts.

Let no one envy, but rather pity us, for in the following manner does the literary man differ from his fellow creatures.

For him no simple feeling exists. All that he sees, his joys, his pleasures, his suffering, his despair, all instantaneously become subjects of observation. In spite of all, in spite of himself, he analyzes everything—hearts, faces, gestures, intonations. As soon as he has seen, whatever it may be, he must know the wherefore. He has not a spark of enthusiasm, not a cry, not a kiss that is spontaneous, not one instantaneous action done merely because it must be done, unconsciously, without reflection, without understanding, without noting it down afterwards.

If he suffers, he notes down his suffering, and files it away in his memory; he says to himself as he leaves the cemetery where he has left the being he has loved most in the world: "It is curious what I felt; it was like an intoxication of pain," etc. And then he recalls all the details, the attitude of those near him, the incongruous gestures of feigned grief, the insincere faces, and a thousand little insignificant trifles noted by the artist as observer—the sign of the cross made by an old woman leading a child, a ray of light through a window, a dog that crossed the funeral procession, the effect of the hearse under the tall yew trees in the cemetery, the face of the undertaker and its muscular contractions, the strain of the four men who lowered the coffin into the grave, a thousand things in fact that a poor fellow suffering with all his heart, soul, and strength, would never have noticed.

He has seen all, noticed all, remembered all, in spite of himself, because he is first of all a literary man, and his intellect is constructed in such a manner that the reverberation in him is much more vivid, more natural, so to speak, than the first shock, the echo more sonorous than the original sound.

He seems to have two souls, one that notes, explains, comments upon each sensation of the other—the other being the natural soul common to all men. He lives condemned to be the mere reflection of himself and others; condemned to look on and watch himself feel, act, love, think, suffer, and never be free like the rest of mankind; simply, genially, frankly, without analyzing his own soul after every joy and every agony. . . .

I can remember dark days, in which my heart was so lacerated by things I had only caught sight of for a second, that the memory of those visions has remained within me like grievous wounds.

One morning, in the Avenue de l'Opéra, in the midst of a stirring and joyous crowd, intoxicated with the sunlight of the month of May, I suddenly caught sight of a creature (what else can I call her?), an old woman bent double, dressed in tatters that had been garments, with an old straw bonnet stripped of its former ornaments, the ribbons and flowers having disappeared in times immemorial. She went by, dragging her feet along so painfully, that I felt in my heart, as much as she did, more than she could, the aching pain of each of her steps. Two sticks supported her. She passed along without seeing anyone, indifferent to all—to the noise, the crowd, the carriages and the sun. Where was she going? She carried something in a paper parcel hanging by a string. What was it? Bread? . . .

Her skirt, her rag of a skirt hardly holding to her dilapidated body, draggled over the pavement. And there was a mind in that creature! A mind? No, but fearful, incessant, harassing suffering! Oh, the misery of the aged without bread, the aged without hope, without children, without money, with nothing to look forward to but death; do we ever think of it? Do we ever think of the aged famished creatures in the garrets? Do we think of the tears shed by those dimmed eyes, once bright, joyous, full of happy emotion?

Another time, it was raining, I was alone, shooting on the plains of Normandy, plodding through the deep-ploughed fields of greasy mud, that melted and slipped under my feet. From time to time, a partridge overtaken, hiding behind a clod of earth, flew off heavily through the downpour. The report of my gun, smothered by the sheet of water that fell from the skies, hardly sounded louder than the crack of a whip, and the gray bird fell, its feathers bespattered with blood.

I felt sad unto tears, tears as plentiful as the showers that were weeping over the world and over me; my heart was filled with sadness and I was overcome with fatigue, so that I could hardly raise my feet, heavily coated as they were with the clay soil. I was returning home when I saw in the middle of the fields, the doctor's gig following a crossroad.

The low black carriage was passing along, covered

by its round hood and drawn by a brown horse, like an omen of death wandering through the country on this sinister day. Suddenly, it pulled up, the doctor's head made its appearance, and he called out:

"Here."

I went towards him, and he said: "Will you help me with a case of diphtheria? I am all alone, and I want someone to hold the woman while I take out the false membrane from her throat."

"I'll come with you," I replied, and I got into his carriage. . . .

We reached the farm. The doctor fastened his horse to the bough of an apple-tree before the door, and we went in. A strong smell of sickness and damp, of fever and mold, of hospital and cellar greeted our nostrils as we entered. In this gray and dismal house, fireless and without sign of life, it was bitterly cold; the swampy chill of a marsh. The clock had stopped; the rain fell down into the great fireplace, where the hens had scattered the ashes, and we heard in a dark corner the noise of a pair of bellows, husky and rapid. It was the breathing of the child. The mother, stretched out in a kind of large wooden box, the peasant's bed, and covered with old rags and old clothes, seemed to rest quietly. She turned her head slightly towards us.

The doctor inquired, "Have you got a candle?"

She answered in a low depressed tone, "In the cupboard."

He took the light, and led me to the farther end of the room towards the little girl's crib.

The child lay panting, with emaciated cheeks, glistening eyes, and tangled hair, a pitiable sight. At each breath, deep hollows could be seen in her thin strained neck. Stretched out on her back, she clutched convulsively with both hands the rags that covered her, and directly she caught sight of us, she turned her face away and hid herself in the straw.

I took hold of her shoulders, and the doctor, forcing her to open her mouth, pulled out of her throat a long white strip of skin, which seemed to me as dry as a bit of leather.

Her breathing immediately became easier, and she drank a little. The mother raising herself on her elbow watched us. She stammered: "Is it done?"

"Yes, it's done."

"Are we going to be left all alone?"

A terror, a terrible terror shook her voice, the terror of solitude, of loneliness, of darkness, of the death that she felt so near to her.

I answered, "No, my good woman, I will stay till the doctor sends you a nurse."

And turning towards the doctor, I added, "Send old mother Mauduit; I will pay her."

"Very well, I'll send her at once."

He shook my hand, and went out; and I heard his gig drive off, over the damp road.

I was left alone with the two dying creatures.

My dog Paf had lain down in front of the empty hearth, and this reminded me that a little fire would be good for us all. I therefore went out to seek for wood and straw, and soon a bright flame lit up the whole room and the bed of the sick child, who was again gasping for breath.

I sat down and stretched out my legs in front of the fire.

The rain was beating against the windowpanes, the wind rattled over the roof. I heard the short, hard wheezing breath of the two creatures and the breathing of my dog who sighed with pleasure, curled up before the bright fireplace.

Life! Life! What is it? These two unhappy creatures, who had always slept on straw, eaten black bread, suffered every kind of misery, were about to die. What had they done? The father was dead, the son was dead. The poor souls had always passed for honest folk, had been liked and esteemed as simple and worthy people.

I watched my steaming boots and my sleeping dog, and there arose within me a shameful and sensual pleasure as I compared my lot with that of these slaves.

The little girl seemed to choke, and suddenly the grating sound became an intolerable suffering to me, lacerating me like a dagger which at each stroke penetrated my heart.

I went towards her. "Do you want a drink?" I said.

She moved her head to say yes, and I poured a few drops of water down her throat, but she could not swallow them.

The mother, who was quieter, had turned round to look at her child; and all at once a feeling of dread took possession of me, a sinister dread that passed over me like the touch of some invisible monster. Where was I? I no longer knew. Was I dreaming? What horrible nightmare was this?

Is it true that such things happen? That one dies like this? And I glanced into all the dark corners of the cottage, as though I expected to see crouching in some obscure corner, a hideous, unmentionable, terrifying thing, the thing which lies in wait for the lives of men, and kills, devours, crushes, strangles them; the thing that delights in red blood, in eyes glittering with fever, in wrinkles and scars, white hair and decay.

The fire was dying out. I threw some more wood on it and warmed my back, shuddering in every limb. At least, I hoped to die in a clean room; with doctors round my bed and medicines on the table! And these people had been all alone for twenty-four hours in this wretched hovel, without a fire, stretched on the straw with the death rattle in their throats! At last I heard the trot of a horse and the sound of wheels; and the nurse came in coolly, pleased at finding some work to do, and showing little surprise at the sight of such misery.

I left her some money and fled with my dog; I fled like a malefactor, running away in the rain with the rattle of those two throats still ringing in my ears—running towards my warm home where my servants were awaiting me and preparing my good dinner.

But I shall never forget that scene, nor many other dreadful things that make me loathe this world.

What would I not give, at times, to be allowed not to think, not to feel, to live like a brute in a warm, clear atmosphere, in a country mellow with golden light, devoid of the raw, crude tones of verdure, a country of the East where I might sleep without weariness, and wake without care, where restlessness is not anxiety, where love is free from anguish and existence is not a burden. . . .

A sick headache, the dreadful pain that racks in a way no torture could equal, shatters the head, drives one crazy, bewilders the mind and scatters the memory like dust before the wind; a sick headache had laid hold of me, and I was perforce obliged to lie down in my bunk with a bottle of ether under my nostrils.

After a few minutes, I fancied I heard a vague murmur which soon became a kind of buzzing, and it seemed as if all the interior of my body became light, as light as air, as though it were melting into vapor.

Then followed a numbness of spirit, a drowsy, comfortable state, in spite of the persisting pain, which, however, ceased to be acute. It was now a pain that one could consent to bear, and not any longer the terrible tearing agony against which the whole tortured body rises in protest.

Soon the strange and delightful sensation of vacuum I had in my chest spread to my limbs, which in their turn became light, light as though flesh and bone had melted away and skin only remained; just enough skin to permit of my feeling the sweetness of life and enjoying my repose. Now I found that I no longer suffered. Pain had disappeared, melted, vanished in air. And I heard voices, four voices, two dialogues, without understanding the words. At times they were but indistinct sounds, at other times a word or two reached me. I soon recognized that this was but the accentuated buzzing of my own ears. I was not sleeping, I was awake, I understood, I felt, I reasoned with a clearness, a penetration and power which were quite extraordinary; I felt a joyousness of spirit, a strange intoxication as a result of the tenfold increase of my mental faculties.

It was not a dream like that created by hashish, nor the sickly visions produced by opium; it was a prodigious keenness of reasoning, a new manner of seeing, of judging, of estimating things and life, with the absolute consciousness, the certitude that this view was the true one.

And the old symbol of the Scriptures, suddenly came back to my mind. It seemed to me that I had tasted of the tree of life, that all mystery was unveiled, so strongly did I feel the power of this new, strange, and irrefutable logic. And numberless arguments, reasonings, proofs, rose up in my mind, to be, however, immediately upset by some proof, some reasoning, some argument yet more powerful. My brain had become a battlefield of ideas. I was a superior being, armed with an invincible intelligence, and I enjoyed prodigious happiness in the sensation of my power.

This state lasted a long, long time. I continued to inhale the fumes of ether. Suddenly, I perceived that the bottle was empty. And I again began to suffer.

For ten hours I endured this torture for which there is no remedy. Then I fell asleep, and the next day, brisk as after convalescence, having written these few pages, I left for Saint-Raphael.

Saint-Raphael, April 11th

A large crowd was gathered in front of the church. Someone was being married. A priest was authorizing in Latin, with pontifical gravity, the solemn and comical act which so disturbs mankind, bringing with it so much mirth, suffering, and tears. According to custom, the families had invited all their relatives and friends to the funereal service of a young girl's innocence, to listen to the piously indecorous ecclesiastical admonitions, preceding those of the mother, and to the public benediction, bestowed on that which is otherwise so carefully veiled.

And the whole countryside, full of broad jokes, moved by the greedy and idle curiosity that draws the common herd to such a scene, had come there to see how the bride and bridegroom would comport themselves. I mingled with the crowd, and watched it.

Good heavens, how ugly men are! For at least the hundredth time I noticed, in the midst of this festive scene, that of all races, the human race is the most hideous. The air was pervaded by the odor of the people, the nauseous, sickening odor of unclean bodies, greasy hair, and garlic, that odor of garlic exhaled by the people of the South through nose, mouth, and skin.

Certainly men are every day as ugly, and smell as

obnoxious, but our eyes are accustomed to the sight of them; our nostrils are used to their odor; and we fail to distinguish, unless we have been spared for some time the sight and stink of them. . . .

How often have I observed that the intelligence expands and grows loftier when we live alone, and that it becomes meaner and lower when we again mingle with other men. The contact, the opinions floating in the air, all that is said, all that one is compelled to listen to, to hear, to answer, acts upon the mind. A flow and ebb of ideas goes from head to head, from house to house, from street to street, from town to town, from nation to nation, and a level is established, an average of intellect is created, by all large agglomerations of individuals.

The inherent qualities of intellectual initiative, of free will, of wise reflection and even of sagacity, belonging to any individual being, generally disappear the moment that being is brought in contact with a large number of other beings. . . .

What I say about crowds applies to all society, and he who would carefully preserve the absolute integrity of his thought, the proud independence of his opinion, and look at life, humanity, and the universe as an impartial observer free from prejudice and from preconceived belief and fear, must absolutely live apart from all social relations; for human stupidity is so contagious, that he will be unable to frequent his fellow creatures, even see them, or listen to them, without being, in spite of himself, influenced on all sides by their conversations, their ideas, their superstitions, their traditions, their prejudices, which by their customs, laws, and surprisingly hypocritical and cowardly code of morality, will surely contaminate him. . . .

Saint-Tropez, April 12th

As I went into the hotel for breakfast, an alarmingly big packet of letters and papers was handed to me, and my heart sank as at the prospect of some misfortune. I have a fear and a hatred of letters; they are bonds. Those little squares of paper bearing my name, seem to give out a clank of chains as I tear them open—of chains linking me to living creatures I have known or know.

Each one inquires, although written by different hands: "Where are you? What are you doing? Why disappear in this way, without telling us where you are going? With whom are you hiding?" Another adds: "How can you expect people to care for you, if you run away in this fashion from your friends? It is positively wounding to their feelings."

Well then, don't attach yourselves to me! Will no one endeavor to understand affection, without joining thereto a notion of possession and of despotism. It would seem as if social ties could not exist without entailing obligations, susceptibilities, and a certain amount of subserviency. From the moment one has smiled upon the attentions of a stranger, that stranger has a hold upon you, is inquisitive about your movements, and reproaches you with neglecting him. If we get as far as friendship, then each one imagines himself to have certain claims; intercourse becomes a duty, and the bonds which unite us seem to end in slip-knots which draw tighter. This affectionate solicitude, this suspicious jealousy, eager to control and to cling, on the part of beings who have met casually, and who fancy themselves linked together because they have proved to be mutually agreeable, arises solely from the harassing fear of solitude, which haunts mankind upon this earth.

Each of us, feeling the void around him, the unfathomable depth in which his heart beats, his thoughts struggle, wanders on like a madman with open arms and eager lips, seeking some other being to embrace. And embrace he does, to the right, to the left, at haphazard, without knowing, without looking, without understanding that he may not feel alone. He seems to say, from the moment he has shaken hands: "Now, you belong to me a little. You owe me some part of yourself, of your life, of your thoughts, of your time." And that is why so many people believe themselves to be friends, who know nothing whatever of each other; so many start off hand in hand, heart to heart, without having really had one good look at one another. They must care for someone, in order not to be alone, their affections must be expended in friendship or in love; some vent must be found for it incessantly. And they talk of affection, swear it, become enthusiastic over it, pour their whole heart into some unknown heart found only the evening before, all their soul into some chance soul with a face that has pleased. And from this haste to become united arise all the surprises, mistakes, misunderstandings, and dramas of life.

Just as we remain lonely and alone, notwithstanding all our efforts, so in like manner we remain free, notwithstanding all our ties.

No one, ever, belongs to another. Half unconsciously we lend ourselves to the coquettish or passionate comedy of possession, but no one really gives himself—his ego—to another human being. Man, exasperated by this imperious need to be the master of someone, instituted tyranny, slavery, and marriage. He can kill, torture, imprison; but the human will inevitably escapes him, even when it has for a few moments consented to submission. . . .

I was breakfasting at the end of a long table, in the Hotel Bailli de Suffren, and still occupied with the perusal of my letters and papers, when I was disturbed by the noisy conversation of some half-dozen men, seated at the other end.

They were commercial travelers. They talked on every subject with assurance, with contempt, in an airy, chaffing, authoritative manner, and they gave me the clearest, the sharpest feeling of what constitutes the true French spirit; that is to say, the average of the intelligence, logic, sense, and wit of France. One of them, a great fellow with a shock of red hair, wore the military medal, as well as the life-saver's medal—a fine fellow. Another, a fat little roly-poly, made puns ceaselessly and laughed at his own wit till his sides ached, even before the others had time to understand his jokes. Another man with close-cut hair was reorganizing the army and the administration of justice, reforming the laws and the constitution, sketching out an ideal republic to suit his own views as a traveler in the wine trade. Two others, side by side, were amusing each other thoroughly with the narrative of their conquests—adventures in back parlors of shops and triumphs over chambermaids.

And in them I saw France personified, the witty, versatile, brave, and gallant France of tradition. These men were types of the race; vulgar types, it is true, but which have to be poetized only a little, to make them into the Frenchman as history—that lying and imaginative jade—shows him to us.

And it is really an amusing race, by reason of certain very special qualities, which one finds absolutely nowhere else. First and foremost is their versatility, which so agreeably diversifies both their customs and their institutions. It is this that makes the history of their country resemble some surprising tale of adventure that is constantly "to be continued in the next number," full of the most unexpected events, tragic, comic, terrible, grotesque. One may be angry or indignant over it, according to one's way of thinking, but it is none the less certain that no history in the world is more amusing and more stirring than theirs.

From the point of view of pure art—and why should one not admit this special and disinterested point of view, in politics as well as in literature?—French history remains without a rival. What can be more engaging and more surprising than events in France in the eighteenth century?

What will tomorrow bring forth? This expectation of the unforeseen is, after all, very charming. Everything is possible in France, both the most wildly improbable drolleries and the most tragic adventures.

What could surprise the French? When a country has produced a Joan of Arc, and a Napoleon, it may well be considered miraculous ground.

And then the French love women: they love them well, with passion, with airy grace, and with respect. Their gallantry cannot be compared to anything in any other country.

He who has preserved in his heart the flame of gallantry which burned in earlier centuries, surrounds women with a tenderness at once profound, gentle, sensitive, and vigilant. He loves everything that belongs to them, everything that comes from them, everything that they are, everything they do. He loves their toilette, their knickknacks, their candor, their little perfidies, their lies, and their dainty ways. He loves them all, rich as well as poor, the young and even the old, the dark, the fair, the fat, the thin. He feels himself at ease with them and among them. There he could remain indefinitely, without fatigue, without boredom, happy in the mere fact of being in their presence. . . .

It is by them, and for them, that the Frenchman has learned to talk, and to display the ready wit which distinguishes him.

To talk! How shall we define it? It is the art of never seeming wearisome; of knowing how to invest every trifle with interest, to charm no matter what be the subject, to fascinate with absolutely nothing.

How can one describe the airy butterfly-touch upon things by supple words, the running fire of wit, the dainty flitting of ideas, which should all go to compose conversation?

The Frenchman is the only being in the world who has this subtle sense of wit, and he alone thoroughly enjoys and comprehends it. His wit is a mere flash and yet it abides—whether the current joke or the profound penetration that characterizes the national literature.

That which is truly innate in the French in the broadest sense of the word, that vast breath of irony or gaiety which has animated the nation from the moment it could think or speak, lives in the pungent raciness of Montaigne and Rabelais, the irony of Voltaire and Beaumarchais and Saint-Simon, in the inextinguishable laughter of Molière.

The brilliant sally, the neat epigram, is the small change of this wit. And nevertheless, it is one aspect of it, a characteristic trait of the national intelligence and one of its keenest charms. It is this that makes the skeptical gaiety of Paris life, the careless cheerfulness of their manners and customs. It is part and parcel of the social amenity of the French.

ESSAY ON THE NOVEL

I DO NOT intend in these pages to put in a plea for this little novel.[1] On the contrary, the ideas I shall try to set forth will rather involve a criticism of the class of psychological analysis which I have undertaken in *Pierre et Jean.*

I propose to treat of the novel in general.

I am not the only writer who finds himself taken to task in the same terms each time he brings out a new book. Among many laudatory phrases, I invariably meet with this observation, penned by the same critics: "The greatest fault of this book is that it is not, strictly speaking, a novel."

The same form might be adopted in reply:

"The greatest fault of the writer who does me the honor to review me is that he is not a critic."

For what are, in fact, the essential characteristics of a critic?

He must set aside preconceived notions, prejudices of "school," or partisanship for any category of artists, and appreciate, distinguish, and explain the most antagonistic tendencies and the most dissimilar temperaments, recognizing and accepting the most varied efforts of art.

Now the critic who, after reading *Manon Lescaut,*

---

[1] *This essay was published in the guise of a preface to Maupassant's novel,* Pierre et Jean.

Paul et Virginie, Don Quixote, Les Liaisons dangereuses,
Werther, Elective Affinities, Clarissa Harlowe, Émile,
Candide, Cinq-Mars, René, Les Trois Mousquetaires,
Mauprat, Le Père Goriot, La Cousine Bette, Colomba,
Le Rouge et le Noir, Mademoiselle de Maupin, Notre-
Dame de Paris, Salammbô, Madame Bovary, Adolphe,
Monsieur de Camors, L'Assommoir, Sapho, etc., still
can be so bold as to write: "This or that is, or is not, a
novel," seems to me to be gifted with a perspicacity
strangely akin to incompetence. Such a critic commonly
understands by a novel a more or less improbable narrative of adventure, elaborated after the fashion of a
play for the stage, in three acts, of which the first contains the exposition, the second the action, and the third
the climax or denouement.

This method of construction is perfectly admissible,
but on condition that all others are accepted on equal
terms.

Are there any rules for the making of a novel, which
must be observed, or else the tale given another name?
If *Don Quixote* is a novel, then is *Le Rouge et le Noir*
a novel? If *Monte Cristo* is a novel, is *L'Assommoir*?
Can any conclusive comparison be drawn between
Goethe's *Elective Affinities,* Dumas's *The Three Mus-*
keteers, Flaubert's *Madame Bovary,* Octave Feuillet's
Monsieur de Camors, and Zola's *Germinal*? Which of
them all is a novel? What are these famous rules? Where
did they originate? Who laid them down? In virtue of
what principle, of what authority, and of what reasoning?

And yet, it would appear, these critics know in some
positive and indisputable way what constitutes a novel,
and what distinguishes it from other tales which are not
novels. What this amounts to is that, without being pro-
ducers themselves, they are enrolled under a school, and

that, like the novelists themselves, they reject all work which is conceived and executed outside the pale of their esthetics.

An intelligent critic ought, on the contrary, to seek out everything which least resembles the novels already written, and urge young authors as much as possible to try fresh paths.

All writers, Victor Hugo as much as Monsieur Zola, have insistently claimed the absolute and incontrovertible right to compose—that is to say, to imagine, or observe—in accordance with their individual conception of art. Talent is the product of originality, which is a special manner of thinking, seeing, understanding, and judging. Now the critic who assumes that "the novel" can be defined in conformity with the ideas he has based on the novels he prefers, and that certain immutable rules of construction can be laid down, will always find himself at war with the artistic temperament of a writer who introduces a new manner of work. A critic really worthy of the name ought to be an analyst, devoid of preferences or passions; like an expert in pictures, he should simply estimate the artistic value of the object of art submitted to him. His intelligence, open to everything, must so far supersede his individuality as to leave him free to discover and praise books which as a man he may not like, but which as a judge he must duly appreciate.

But critics, for the most part, are only readers; whence it comes that they almost always find fault with us on wrong grounds, or compliment us without reserve or measure.

The reader, who demands of a book solely that it should satisfy the natural tendencies of his own mind, asks the writer to respond to his predominant taste, and he invariably praises a work or a passage which appeals to his imagination, which may be idealistic, gay, licentious, melancholy, dreamy, or positive, as "striking" or "well written."

The public, in short, is composed of various groups, who call out to us:

"Comfort me."

"Amuse me."

"Sadden me."

"Touch me."

"Make me dream."

"Make me laugh."

"Make me shudder."

"Make me weep."

"Make me think."

Only a few chosen spirits say to the artist:

"Give me something fine in any form which may suit you best, according to your own temperament."

The artist makes the attempt; succeeds or fails.

The critic ought to judge the result only in relation to the nature of the attempt; he has no right to concern himself about tendencies. This has been said a thousand times already; it will always need repeating.

Now, after a succession of literary schools which have given us deformed, superhuman, poetical, pathetic, charming, or magnificent pictures of life, a realistic or naturalistic school has arisen, which asserts that it shows us the truth, the whole truth, and nothing but the truth.

We must accept with equal interest these different theories of art, and we must judge the works which are their outcome solely from the point of view of artistic value, with an a priori acceptance of the general notions which gave birth to each. To dispute the author's right to produce a poetical work or a realistic work, is to endeavor to coerce his temperament, to take exception to his originality, to forbid him to use the eyes and wits bestowed on him by Nature. To blame him for seeing things as beautiful or ugly, as mean or epic, as gracious or sinister, is to reproach him for not himself being made on this or that pattern, and for having eyes which do not see exactly as ours see.

Leave him free to conceive of things as he pleases, provided he is an artist. Let us rise to poetic heights to judge an idealist, and then prove to him that his dream is commonplace, ordinary, not mad or magnificent enough. But if we judge a naturalistic writer, let us show him wherein the truth of life differs from the truth in his book.

It is evident that schools so widely different must have adopted diametrically opposite processes in composition.

The novelist who transforms truth—immutable, uncompromising, and displeasing as it is—to extract from it an exceptional and delightful adventure, must necessarily manipulate events without an exaggerated respect for probability, molding them to his will, dressing and arranging them so as to attract, excite, or affect the reader. The scheme of his novel is no more than a series of ingenious combinations skillfully leading to the issue. The incidents are planned and graduated up to the culminating point and effect of the conclusion, which is the crowning and inevitable result, satisfying the curiosity aroused from the first, closing the interest, and ending the story so completely that we have no further wish to know what happened thereafter to the most engaging actors in it.

The novelist who, on the other hand, proposes to give us an accurate picture of life, must carefully eschew any concatenation of events which might seem exceptional. His aim is not to tell a story, to amuse us or to appeal to our feelings, but to compel us to reflect, and to understand the occult and deeper meaning of events. By dint of seeing and meditating, he has come to regard the world, facts, men, and things in a way peculiar to himself, which is the outcome of the sum total of his studious observation. It is this personal view of the world which he strives to communicate to us by reproducing it in a book. To make the spectacle of life as moving to us as it has been to him, he must bring it before our eyes with scrupulous exactitude. Hence he must construct his work with such skill, such hidden art and such seeming simplicity, that it is impossible to detect and sketch the plan, or discern the writer's purpose.

Instead of manipulating an adventure and working it out in such a way as to make it interesting to the last, he will take his actor or actors at a certain period of their lives, and lead them by natural stages to the next point. In this way he will show how men's minds are modified by the influence of their environment, or how their passions and sentiments are evolved; how they love or hate, how they struggle in every sphere of society, and how their interests clash—social interests, pecuniary interests, family interests, political interests. The skill of his plan will not consist in emotional power or charm, in an attractive opening or a stirring climax, but in the happy grouping of small but constant facts from which the final purpose of the work may be discerned. If within three hundred pages he depicts ten years of a life so as to show what its individual and characteristic significance may have been in the midst of all the other human beings who surrounded it, he must know how to eliminate from among the numberless trivial incidents of daily life all which do not serve his end, and how to set in a special light all those which might have remained invisible to less clear-sighted observers, and which give his book significance and value as a whole.

It is intelligible that this method of construction, so unlike the old manner which was patent to all, must often disconcert the critics, and that they will not all detect the subtle and secret wires—almost invisibly fine —which certain modern artists use instead of the one string formerly known as the "plot."

In a word, while the novelist of yesterday preferred to relate the crises of life, the acute phases of the mind and heart, the novelist of today writes the history of the heart, soul, and intellect in their normal condition. To achieve the effect he aims at—that is to say, the sense of simple reality—and to point the artistic lesson he endeavors to draw from it—that is to say, a revelation of the real nature of his contemporaries and associates—he must bring forward no facts that are not of an irrefutable and eternal verity.

But even when we place ourselves at the same point of view as these realistic artists, we may discuss and dispute their theory, which seems to be comprehensively stated in these words: "The whole truth and nothing but the truth." Since the end they have in view is to bring out the philosophy of certain constant and current facts, they must often correct events in favor of probability and to the detriment of truth; for *le vrai peut quelquefois n'être pas le vraisemblable.* (Truth may sometimes not seem probable.)

The realist, if he is an artist, will endeavor not to show us a commonplace photograph of life, but to give us a presentment of it which shall be more complete, more striking, more cogent than reality itself. To tell everything is out of the question; it would require at least a volume for each day to enumerate the endless, insignificant incidents which crowd our existence. A choice must be made—and this is the first blow to the theory of "the whole truth."

Life, moreover, is composed of the most dissimilar things, the most unforeseen, the most contradictory, the most incongruous; it is merciless, without sequence or connection, full of inexplicable, illogical, and contradictory catastrophes, such as can only be classed as miscellaneous facts. This is why the artist, having chosen his subject, can select only such characteristic details as are of use to it, from this life overladen with chances and trifles, and must reject everything else, everything irrelevant.

To give an instance from among a thousand: The number of persons who, every day, meet with an accidental death, all over the world, is very considerable. But how can we bring a tile down on the head of an important character, or fling him under the wheels of a vehicle in the middle of a story, under the pretext that accident must have its due?

Again, life makes no distinction of treatment; events are sometimes hurried on, sometimes left to linger indefinitely. Art, on the contrary, consists in the employment of foresight and elaboration, in arranging skillful and ingenious transitions, in setting essential events in a strong light, simply by the craft of composition, and giving other things the degree of relief proportionate to their importance, in order to produce a convincing sense of the special truth to be conveyed.

"Truth" consists, then, in producing a complete illusion of the truth by following the common logic of facts and not by transcribing them pell-mell, as they succeed each other.

Whence I conclude that the skilled Realists should rather call themselves Illusionists.

How childish it is, indeed, to believe in this reality, since to each of us the truth is in his own mind, his own organs! Our different eyes and ears, taste and smell, create as many truths as there are human beings on earth. And our brains, informed by those organs, according to their different impressions, apprehend, analyze, and decide as differently as if each of us were a being of an alien race. Each of us, then, has simply his own illusion of the world—poetical, sentimental, cheerful, melancholy, foul, or gloomy, according to his nature. And the writer has no other mission than faithfully to reproduce this illusion, with all the elaborations of art which he may have learned and have at his command. The illusion of beauty—which is merely a convention invented by man! The illusion of ugliness—which is a matter of varying opinion! The illusion of truth—never immutable! The illusion of depravity—which fascinates so many minds! Great artists are those who can make other men see their own particular illusion.

Thus it is wrong to quarrel with any theory, since each is simply the outcome, in generalizations, of a special temperament analyzing itself.

Two of these theories in particular have been frequently discussed and set up in opposition to each other instead of being admitted on an equal footing: that of the purely analytical novel, and that of the objective novel.

The partisans of analysis require the writer to devote himself to indicating the most detailed evolutions of a soul, and all the most secret motives of our every action, giving but a quite secondary importance to the action in itself. It is but the goal, a simple milestone, the excuse for the book. According to them, these works, at once exact and visionary, in which imagination merges into observation, are to be written after the fashion of a

philosopher's treatise on psychology, seeking out causes
in their remotest origin, telling the why and wherefore
of every impulse, and detecting every reaction of the
soul's movements under the promptings of interests,
passion, or instinct.

The partisans of objectivity—odious word—aiming,
on the contrary, at giving us an exact presentment of all
that happens in life, carefully avoid all complicated explanations, all disquisitions on motive, and confine themselves to letting persons and events pass before our eyes.
In their opinion, psychology should be concealed in the
book, as it is in reality, under the facts of existence.

The novel conceived of on these lines gains in interest; there is more movement in the narrative, more color,
more of the stir of life.

Hence, instead of giving long explanations of the
state of mind of an actor in the tale, the objective writer
tries to discover the act or gesture which that state of
mind must inevitably lead to in that character, under
certain given circumstances. And he makes him so conduct himself from one end of the volume to the other
that all his acts, all his movements, shall be the expression of his inmost nature, of all his thoughts, and all his
impulses or hesitancies. Thus they conceal psychology
instead of flaunting it; they use it as the skeleton of the
work, just as the invisible bony framework is the skeleton of the human body. The artist who paints our portrait does not display our bones.

To me it seems that the novel executed on this principle gains in sincerity. It is more probable, for one
thing, for the persons we see moving about us do not
divulge to us the motives from which they act.

We must also take into account the fact that even if
by close observation of men and women we can so
exactly ascertain their characters as to predict their be-

havior under almost any circumstances, if we can say decisively, "Such a man, of such a temperament, in such a case, will do this or that," yet it does not follow that we could lay a finger, one by one, on all the secret evolutions of his mind—which is not our own; all the mysterious pleadings of his instincts—which are not the same as ours; all the mingled promptings of his nature—in which the organs, nerves, blood, and flesh are different from ours.

However great the genius of a gentle, sensitive man, guiltless of passion and devoted to science and work, he never can so completely transfuse himself into the body of a dashing, sensual, and violent man, of exuberant vitality, torn by every desire or even by every vice, as to understand and delineate the inmost impulses and sensations of a being so unlike himself, even though he may very adequately foresee and relate all the acts of his life.

In short, the man who writes pure psychology can do no more than put himself in the place of all his puppets in the various situations in which he places them. It is impossible that he should change his organs, which are the sole intermediary between external life and ourselves, which constrain us by their perceptions, circumscribe our sensibilities, and create in each of us a soul essentially dissimilar to all those about us. Our vision and knowledge of the world and our ideas of life are acquired by the aid of our senses, and we can but transfer them partially to all the characters whose secret and unknown nature we propose to reveal. Thus it is always ourselves that we disclose in the body of a king or an assassin, a robber or an honest man, a courtesan, a nun, a young girl, or a market-woman; for we are compelled to put the problem in this personal form: "If *I* were a king, a murderer, a prostitute, a nun, or a market-woman, what should *I* do, what should *I* think, how should *I* act?" We can vary our characters only by altering the age, the sex, the social position, and all the circumstances of life, of that ego which Nature has in fact enclosed in an insurmountable barrier of organs of sense. Skill consists in not betraying this ego to the reader, under the various masks which we employ to cover it.

Still, though on the point of absolute exactitude pure psychological analysis is impregnable, it can nevertheless produce works of art as fine as any other method of work.

Now, today, we have the Symbolists. And why not? Their artistic dream is a worthy one; and they have this especially interesting feature: that they know and proclaim the extreme difficulty of art.

And, indeed, a man must be very daring or foolish to write at all nowadays. After so many and such various masters of the craft, of such multifarious genius, what remains to be done that has not been done, or what to say that has not been said? Which of us can boast of having written a page, a phrase, which is not to be found— or something very like it—in some other book? When we read, we who are so soaked in French literature that our whole body seems, as it were, a mere compound of words, do we ever light on a line, a thought, which is not familiar to us, or of which we have not had at least some vague forecast?

The man who only tries to amuse his public by familiar methods, writes confidently, in his candid mediocrity, works intended only for the ignorant and idle crowd. But those who are conscious of the weight of centuries of past literature, whom nothing satisfies, whom everything disgusts because they dream of something better, to whom the bloom is off everything, who are always impressed with the uselessness, the commonness of their own achievements—these come to regard literary art as a thing unattainable and mysterious, scarcely revealed save in a few pages by the greatest masters.

A few lines of poetry, a few phrases suddenly discovered, thrill us to the heart like a startling revelation; but the lines which follow are just like all other verse, the further flow of prose is like all other prose.

Men of genius, no doubt, escape this anguish and torment because they bear within themselves an irresistible creative power. They do not sit in judgment on themselves. The rest of us, who are no more than persevering and conscious workers, can only contend against invincible discouragement by unremitting effort.

Two men, by their simple and lucid teaching, gave me the strength to try again and again: Louis Bouilhet and Gustave Flaubert.

If I here speak of myself in connection with them, it is because their counsels, as summed up in a few lines, may prove useful to some young writers less self-confident than most literary beginners.

Bouilhet, whom I first came to know somewhat intimately about two years before I gained the friendship of Flaubert, by dint of telling me that a hundred lines—or less—if they are without a flaw and contain the very essence of the talent and originality of even a second-rate man, are enough to establish an artist's reputation, made me understand that persistent toil and a thorough knowledge of the craft might, in some happy hour of lucidity, power, and enthusiasm, by the fortunate occurrence of a subject in perfect concord with the tendency of our mind, lead to the production of a single work, short but as perfect as we can make it. Then I learned to see that the best-known writers have hardly ever left us more than one such volume; and that what is needful above all else is to have the good fortune to hit upon and discern, amid the multifarious matter which offers itself for selection, the subject which will absorb all our faculties, all that is of worth in us, all our artistic power.

At a later date, Flaubert, whom I had occasionally met, took a fancy to me. I ventured to show him a few attempts. He read them kindly and replied, "I cannot tell whether you will have any talent. What you have brought me proves a certain intelligence; but never forget this, young man: talent—as Buffon says—is nothing but long patience. Work."

I worked; and I often went to see him, feeling that he liked me, for he had taken to calling me, in jest, his disciple. For seven years I wrote verses, I wrote tales, I even wrote a villainous play. Nothing of this remains. The master read it all; then, the next Sunday while we lunched together, he would give me his criticisms, driving into me by degrees two or three principles which sum up the drift of his long and patient exhortations: "If you have any originality," said he, "the essential point is, bring it out; if you have none, you must acquire it.

"Talent is long patience.

"You must scrutinize whatever you want to express, so long, and so attentively, as to enable you to find some aspect of it which no one has yet seen and expressed. There is an unexplored side to everything, because we are wont never to use our eyes but with the memory of what others before us have thought of the things we see. The smallest thing has something unknown in it; we must find it. To describe a blazing fire, a tree on a plain, we must stand face to face with that fire or that tree, till to us they are wholly unlike any other fire or tree. Thus we may become original."

Then, having established the truth that there are not in the whole world two grains of sand, two flies, two hands, or two noses absolutely alike, he would make me describe in a few sentences some person or object, in such a way as to define it exactly, and distinguish it from every other of the same race or species.

"When you pass a grocer sitting in his doorway," he would say, "a concierge smoking his pipe, or a cab-stand, show me that grocer and that concierge, their attitude and their whole physical aspect, including, as indicated by the skill of the portrait, their whole moral nature, in such a way that I shall never mistake them for any other grocer or concierge; and by a single word give me to understand wherein one cab-horse differs from fifty others before or behind it."

I have explained his ideas of style at greater length in another place; they are closely connected with the theory of observation I have just laid down.

Whatever the thing we wish to say, there is but one word to express it, but one verb to give it movement, but one adjective to qualify it. We must seek till we find this noun, this verb, and this adjective, and never be content with approximations, never allow ourselves to play tricks, even happy ones, or have recourse to sleights of language to avoid a difficulty. The subtlest things may be rendered and suggested by applying the hint conveyed in Boileau's line: *"D'un mot mis en sa place enseigna le pouvoir."* ("He taught the power of a word put in the right place.")

The eccentric, complicated, multifarious, and outlandish words which are put upon us nowadays in the name of artistic writing are unnecessary for the formulations of every shade of thought; but every modification of the value of a word by the place it fills must be distinguished with extreme clearness. Give us fewer nouns, verbs, and adjectives, with almost inscrutable shades of meaning, and a greater variety of phrases, more variously constructed, ingeniously divided, full of sonority and cunning rhythm. Let us strive to be first-class stylists rather than collectors of rare words.

It is in fact more difficult to bend a sentence to one's will, to make it express everything—even what it does not say—to fill it full of implications, of covert and inexplicit suggestions, than to invent new expressions, or seek out in old and forgotten books all those which have fallen into disuse and lost their meaning, so that to us they are as a dead language.

The French tongue, indeed, is a pure stream, which affected writers never could and never can trouble. Each age has flung into the limpid waters its fashions, its pretentious archaisms and euphuisms, but nothing has remained on the surface of these futile attempts and impotent efforts. It is the nature of the language to be clear, logical, and vigorous. It does not lend itself to weakness, obscurity, or corruption.

Those who describe without duly heeding abstract terms, those who make rain and hail fall on the *cleanliness* of windowpanes, may throw stones at the simplicity of their brothers of the pen. The stones may indeed hit their brothers, who have a body, but will never hurt simplicity—which has none.

LA GUILLETTE, ETRETAT,
    September, 1887.

SELECTED CORRESPONDENCE
(Translated by the Editor)

TO HIS MOTHER

Yvetot, 2 May 1864

We won't know our marks until this afternoon and I am beginning my letter this morning.

I have just found out that we won't know our marks until tomorrow, Tuesday, because the Superior is in Rouen today. We have only one case of measles left. I'm afraid I'm not going to win my Racine. I thought we had five Latin compositions still to do, but there is only one, and two Greek. I don't understand anything in that miserable language so I have no hope of any good coming of the Greek. As for the translations into French, on which our marks will be announced tomorrow, I think I'll come out all right. We shan't have to do any more composition for nearly three weeks. I shan't write you again before school closes, so let's be clear about this: we won't get home till seven in the evening. If cousin Germer is back, you can come over with my aunt, who is taking a carriage, and you can stay as late as you like without having to think about trains or spending the night here. Write me to say what you decide. What will you do?

Well, here comes the rain. We've been asking for it

long enough. I'd like to know when summer is supposed to begin by the calendar.

How is Henri? Does he still have the same friends? Do you know if Germer will be back soon? Is he better? I hope he's had a long enough vacation: he needn't complain.

You'll say that I can wait to mention this, but if it's all the same to you, instead of the dance you promised me when the long vacation begins, I'd rather have a small dinner. Or if it's all the same to you, give me half the money the dance would cost you, because it could go towards the boat I want to buy. I haven't been able to think of anything else since I came back to school, I mean not since Easter vacation but since I came back from the long vacation. I don't want to buy one of those boats they sell to people from Paris, they're not worth anything; but I know a customs guard who will sell me a fishing boat, all round on the bottom. If I don't win a prize I hope I'll get an honorable mention at least.

I haven't time to go on with my letter today, dear Mamma.

Tuesday

I am second in Latin translation, so I'm back again in the first group. I just missed being first: two professors liked my composition as well as the boy's who was first. But I'm second, that makes thirty sous you owe me, and grandma thirty, so I have three francs coming to me. But there is only one more composition so I won't be able to win my Racine; but will you give it to me if I win one or two honorable mentions?

Best love to you, dear Mamma and to Hervé too.

1870

I sent the Havre stagecoach driver to give you news of me, dear Mother, but fearing that he may not do it, I am writing this note.

I retreated with our routed army. I was nearly captured. I went from the advance post to the rear guard to carry orders from the quartermaster depot to the General. I covered thirty-seven miles on foot. After having walked and run with orders all the previous night I slept on a rock in an icy cellar.

Good bye. Fuller details tomorrow. I send you all my love and love to Hervé too. Remember me to everybody and greetings to Josephe.

Paris, Saturday (1870)

I am writing you again today because in two days communications between Paris and the rest of France will be cut off. The Prussians are moving on Paris by forced marches. The outcome of the war is of course not in doubt. The Prussians are lost. They realize it fully and their sole hope is to seize Paris in a sudden attack; but we, here, are ready to receive them.

As for me, I am not yet sleeping at Vincennes and am in no hurry to find a bed there. If there is to be a siege I prefer Paris to the old fort in which we are lodged at Vincennes—a fort the Prussians will demolish with their cannon. My father is on my trail. He insists that I must go into the Quartermaster Corps and he gives me the most earnest and comical advice on how to avoid accidents. To hear him you would think I ought to get a job as guard of the Paris sewers as the surest means of escaping the shelling. Robert will be in the front line at Saint-Maur. The militia have been issued with muskets and they are holding up bravely. Médrinal has written to ask that I lend him my Lefaucheux rifle.

I shall reply that I have promised it to my cousin Germer. Yesterday, Mme. Denisane having given me a ticket to the Opera, I heard *The Dumb Girl (of Portici).* It is very pretty.

Faure-Dujarrie, who is a great friend of the Quartermaster General, has offered to do everything in his power to get me the softest possible job. He has already seen the General and goes back again tomorrow. I shall be much better off in an office than in camp—though you never see anybody at Headquarters, communications with the army having grown very difficult.

Good bye, dear Mother, my best love to you and to Hervé too. Remember me to Josephe. Father sends greetings.

P.S. I am terribly bored. When I go back to the Q.M. everything will be all right. Médrinal may have my other rifle.

24 September 1872

You see that I am writing you promptly, but the truth is I cannot wait any longer to write. I feel so lost, so isolated, so *demoralized,* that I am forced to beg a few pages of you. I am afraid of the coming winter, I feel lonely, and my long solitary evenings are sometimes terrible. Often, when I sit at my writing table with my melancholy lamp burning, my anguish is so sharp that I don't know to whom to turn. Last winter, in such moments, I would often say to myself that you too must have gone through frightfully gloomy times during the long cold December and January evenings. My monotonous existence has started again, and there will be three months of this. L.F. cannot dine with me tonight; he is dining out, and it annoys me, for we could have chatted together.

A little while ago, by way of distraction, I wrote something in the manner of the *Monday Tales* (of Alphonse Daudet). I am sending it to you. Of course I attach no importance to it: the thing was dashed off in a quarter of an hour. Still, I wish that you would send it back, for I may be able to do something with it. There are a few ungrammatical sentences which I shall correct when I work the thing up. I wish I could be carried back two weeks. How short the time is! How little time there is for us to see each other and talk of things! And once a holiday is over, one says to oneself: "But how can it be? I've only just got here. I haven't talked to anybody yet."

Good bye, dear Mother. I send you my best love, and love to Hervé too.

Paris, 30 October 1874

. . . Try to find me subjects for short stories. During the day, at the Ministry, I could work at them a little. My plays take up all my evenings. I shall try to get them printed in some newspaper or other.

Wednesday (1874)

. . . Now I shall tell you an adventure that happened the other day. Going through the rue Notre Dame de Lorette I saw a crowd and went over to it. It had gathered round a workman who was furiously beating a boy of about ten years. I saw red, seized him by the collar, and marched him off to the police station in the rue Bréda. There, after making sure that the boy was the man's son, the police informed me that I was poking my nose into matters that did not concern me, that a father had the right to punish his son when the child was disobedient—and in short I was properly told off. And do you know why? Because if the matter had been taken up, the report would have had to mention that the man had been arrested by a private citizen, wherefore the police commissioner would have ticked off the policemen at that particular station for not being on the job when the thing took place. . . .

8 March 1875

. . . Some friends and I are going to perform an *absolutely lewd* play[1] in Leloir's studio. Flaubert and Turgeniev will be present. Needless to say, we have written the play ourselves. . . .

Paris, 3 September 1875

So my holiday is over, dear Mother, and how short it was! I wait eleven long months for the fortnight that is my only pleasure of the year; and the days go by so quickly that I wonder where they can have gone. Is it possible that I really went to Etretat and spent two weeks there? It seems to me that I never left the Ministry, and am still waiting to begin my vacation—which ended this morning. What made leaving sadder than ever, this time, was that I worried very much over the absolute solitude in which you will live this winter; I can see the long evenings that you will spend alone, musing sadly on people far away, dreaming dreams from which you will emerge ill and despondent. And often, I am sure, when I shall be working alone in my room, during those endless winter evenings, it will seem to me that I can see you sitting in your low chair, star-

---

[1] *The broad farce in question, which dealt with the experiences of a pair of newlyweds who took a room in a brothel under the impression that it was a hotel, was called "At the Sign of the Rose Petal—Turkish House."*

ing fixedly into the fire as people do whose thoughts are far away.

Today, despite the terrible heat and a blue sky, I feel the coming of winter for the first time. I've just come in from a glance at the Tuileries Gardens: the trees are leafless, and a sudden gust of ice and snow seemed to sweep over me as I looked at them. I thought of lamps being lit at three in the afternoon, the rain beating on the windowpanes, the horrible cold—and all that going on for months and months.

How wonderful it would be to live in a country where the sun always shone!

It is wrong of me to write whatever comes into my head, like this. You are already inclined enough to look on the dark side of things without me saddening you by my lamentations. But it is hard to laugh when one doesn't feel like laughing, and I assure you that I do not feel like it.

Paris, Monday, 20 September 1875

I received your letter this morning, dearest Mother, and since I have a little free time today I shall answer it immediately.

But first I must tell you what I did yesterday, especially as I had a *perfectly wonderful* outing.

I left Saturday evening by train for Saint-Rémy, a village twenty miles from Paris, near Chevreuse. My friend M., a painter and a great hiker, was my companion. From Saint-Rémy we walked to Chevreuse, where we dined, after which we took a stroll. Then we went to bed. Yesterday, at five in the morning, we got up. We went first to have a look at the ruins of the Chevreuse château, which are picturesque and are situated on an elevation dominating the valley. There (sorry about these details) we bought some sausage, ham, two pounds of bread, cheese, and a glass, and we started out. The valley is pretty, with charming prospects and remarkably luxuriant vegetation, but I must confess that I had looked forward to something better. Then we went off to Cernay, for people had extolled to me its dales, filled with little waterfalls. On the way I saw something that made me think of Zola's Paradou Gardens—a park, or rather an immense chaos of verdure where there was not a clearing to be seen, not a single prospect deliberately laid out. We followed a wall for *more than two miles* without coming to the end of it; and when we asked an old woman to whom this marvelous estate belonged, she answered with a haughty indignant air, "Sir, everybody knows that this is the estate of the Duc de Luynes." Yet it was natural that we should ask, for we knew we were a good three miles from the (duke's) château of Dampierre. The park, therefore, is at least three miles across!

We reached Cernay and went down into the valley, where I was really overwhelmed by the marvelous beauty of the countryside. I saw before me an adorable little glen at the bottom of which lay a pond planted with reeds. We went down into the wood and reached the waterfalls. I doubt that the famous Frascati Gardens you've told me about so often, are as handsome as this valley. Imagine, first, a wood with oaks of incredible girth and height; over our heads an arch of leaves; all round us red and gray rocks as big as houses; and a stream leaping from rock to rock, winding to left and to right. I thought of certain descriptions in Tasso's *Jerusalem Delivered*. We went on past pond after pond over a distance of several miles in a sort of fairyland, following the curve of a wooded hill where now and again the trees would suddenly give way to great gray rocks that jutted up through the ground on all sides. For nearly two hours we never saw a house nor met a human soul; we wandered, scouting as we went, and we were obliged to drink out of the stream while we ate our frugal lunch. The last pond, smaller than the rest, was surrounded by a curtain of pine trees: it was as dark and desolate as the others had been bright and gay. Finally, we got to Fargis [*sic* for Auffargis]. From Fargis we went along the frightful highway to Trappes, and had a look at St. Quentin's Pond. There is something else again! Imagine an immense plain, an endless sheet of water two miles long, reeds along its banks, and hundreds of moor-hens, with dozens of sportsmen on the banks. The fowl stare at the sportsmen, the sportsmen stare at the fowl. Every minute or two, a rifle shot, intended for one of the foolish birds that has ventured too near the banks: instantly, a boy jumps into the water and brings back the victim.

We came back through Versailles, then Port-Marly, and finally at half-past nine in the evening, Chatou, where we were to meet some friends. We had been walking since five in the morning and had covered fifteen leagues, or if you prefer 37½ miles—about 70,000 steps. Our feet were like jelly.

The whole day long I had been obsessed: I was hot, I was covered with dust, and I said to myself: "A swim in the sea would be wonderful." During the only ugly part of our walk (from Auffargis to Trappes) we had been pelted by rain. It had been fine up to then, but after the rain it was fine again until seven in the evening when another shower fell. The weather has cleared up and it is very hot today. I believe that soon we shall have our summers in December and our winters in July. Probably we shall be able to go sea-bathing this year

till the end of October. Are there still many people at
Etretat? I am just the lad not to think well of a supper by moonlight on Antifer Beach—I don't think!

TO ROBERT PINCHON[1]

Paris, 11 March 1876

I received your letter and shed tender tears over it.
Instantly, I thought I must take up a collection or organize a lottery for your benefit, or beg Farcey to devote
one night's receipts to you so that you can join us here.
I know that all Paris and the suburbs will respond to
my appeal.

As for me, I am not doing anything about the theater
just now. Theater managers are simply not worth working for. It's quite true that they think our plays are
amusing; but they don't produce them. Personally, I'd
rather they thought the plays poor and put them on.
Which is one way of letting you know that Raymond
Deslandes thinks my play, *Répétition,* too subtle for his
Vaudeville Theatre. As a matter of fact, I haven't done
much work. My heart was giving me a lot of trouble;
I went to see a doctor; he prescribed complete rest, no
staying up late, and a treatment of bromide of potassium and digitalis. *The treatment was totally unsuccessful,* wherefore they put me on arsenic, iodine of potassium, and tincture of colchicum. *The treatment was
totally unsuccessful,* wherefore my doctor sent me to a
specialist, to the master of masters, to Dr. Potain himself. Potain declared that there was absolutely nothing
the matter with my heart itself, but that I had the
beginnings of nicotine poisoning. This diagnosis so affected me that I swallowed all my pipes in order not

---

[1] A boyhood friend.

to see them again. But my heart beats as violently as ever—though of course it is only two weeks since I stopped smoking.

I have done a piece of verse[1] which will win for me, over night, the reputation of one of the greatest of poets. It will appear on the 20th in *la République des Lettres,* if the owner-editor does not read it, for the man is a ferocious Catholic and my piece, chaste in language, is as lewd and immoral as story and image can make it. Flaubert was enthusiastic about it and suggested that I send it to Catulle Mendès, managing editor of that paper. Mendès was completely bowled over and will try to print it, despite his proprietor. He has read it to several of the Parnassian group of poets, it is being talked about, and last Saturday, at a literary dinner attended by Zola, it appears that men who do not know me talked about me for an hour. Zola listened without saying a word. Mendès has introduced me to several of the Parnassians who complimented me effusively. It's a bit broad for publication, this tale of two young people who kill themselves with too much you know what. I wonder if, like the illustrious Barbey d'Aurevilly, I shall be haled into court over it.

My short story, "In a Rowboat," is to appear soon in *l'Officiel,* and my "Adventure of Little Pierre" very likely in *l'Opinion Nationale.* Here is why I say "very likely": the paper accepted my story, promised to publish it, and then at the last minute, out of a perfectly natural scruple, sent to ask if I had expected to be paid for it. I replied that I had, indubitably. Whereupon the editor said that he had not quite intended to pay me. With which I declared that I quite intended, in that case, to take my story back and submit it elsewhere.

---

[1] "Au bord de l'eau," *published* 20 *March* 1876 *in* la République des Lettres.

With which he begged me to wait long enough for them to decide what they finally intended, so that for the moment *l'Opinion* has left me without itself [without an opinion].

TO CATULLE MENDÈS

Paris (1876)

Here, my dear Mendès, are the reasons why I have decided not to become a Free Mason.

First, the moment a man joins any association—and particularly one of those associations which, quite inoffensively, choose to call themselves secret societies—he becomes subject to certain rules, or he promises certain things; he puts on a halter; and however lightly the halter may weigh, it is still something of a nuisance. *I had rather pay my bootmaker than be his equal.*

Secondly, if the thing became known—and it would become known, for I am not the kind of person who could join a society of decent people and then try to conceal the fact, as if there were something shameful about it—I should be automatically outlawed by almost the whole of my family; which would be superfluous, to say the least, and would in actual fact be extremely prejudicial to my interests. Out of selfishness, wickedness, or eclecticism, I want not to be bound to any political party whatever; to any religion, to any sect, to any school. I want never to belong to any association that professes a particular doctrine, nor to bow before any dogma, any primacy, any principle—and this only in order to retain the right to speak ill of them. I want to be free to attack all the gods and battalions without anyone's being able to say that there was a time when I had burnt incense before one of them, or handled a pike in the ranks of another of them. This gives me, besides, the right to fight for my friends, whatever be the flag flown by my friends.

You will say that this is foreseeing a very distant future; but I am fearful of the least little chain—whether the chain of an idea or the chain of a woman. Threads become cables before we realize it. . . .

TO GUSTAVE FLAUBERT

Paris, 10 December 1877

I've wanted for a long time to write to you, beloved master, but politics (!) has stood in the way. Politics makes it impossible for me to work, go out, think, or write. I am like those indifferent people who suddenly become the most passionate people, like those pacifists who suddenly turn belligerent. Paris has been seized by a burning fever, and I have caught the fever. Everything is at a standstill, in suspense, as if about to crumple; I have stopped smiling and am angry for good. The irritation one feels over the rascally tactics of these sordid fellows is so intense, continual, and keen, that a man can't think about anything else; it follows one like a cloud of mosquitoes—to one's desk, into a woman's arms. Patience flees before the criminal imbecility of this cretin.[1] Think of it! A general who once won a battle thanks to the fortunate conjunction of his stupidity and the hazards of luck, and who has since lost two historic battles in the course of trying to repeat by himself the maneuver which luck alone had executed the first time; a general who has the right to call himself Duke of Magenta, Grand Duke of Reichshoffen,

---

[1] *Marshal MacMahon, first President of the Third French Republic.*

and Archduke of Sedan, now, on pretext that the government of imbeciles by men of intelligence constituted a public danger, ruins the poor (whom else can one ruin?), puts a stop to all intellectual work in the nation, irritates peace-loving citizens, and pricks civil war awake as if it were one of those miserable bulls they drive mad in the Spanish arenas.

I seem to have got very rhetorical—well, what of it? I demand the abolition of the governing class, of that rabble of fine gentlemen who frolic in the skirts of that dumb old street-walker called good society. They stick their fingers in her what-d'you-call-'em and mutter that society is in danger, is threatened by freedom of thought. Well, I now believe that [the Terror of] 1793 was too easy on them; that the Septembrists were merciful fellows; that Marat was a lamb, Danton a white rabbit, and Robespierre a cooing dove. Since the old governing class is as intelligent today as it was then, we ought to wipe out the governing class today as was done then, drowning these fine cretinish gentlemen together with their fine whorish ladies. O Radicals, though you may have nothing more than Republican notions in the place of brains, deliver us from saviors and generals whose heads contain nothing but drivel and holy water.

It's a week now since I have done a stroke of work, so exasperated have I been by the buzzing round me of the machinations of these detestable pedants.

TO EMILE ZOLA

Paris, 2 July 1878

I had just been to call on you when I came home and found your letter (having gone straight from the country to the Ministry this morning). I hadn't written you because there are too many things I must explain to you. I saw a number of people at Poissy; here is what I was able to find out about the boats and the builders there.

The man you went to see is probably named Baudu or Dallemagne (and I may have got both names wrong). Both are thieves and you must not believe what they tell you. Don't turn over so much as a boat-hook to them. All the boats at Poissy, whether owned by locals or by Parisians, were built at Bougival, Chatou, Argenteuil, or Asnières.

As for the skiffs, they are simply what is known everywhere as a fisherman's wherry. If you bought one of those monuments you would have to re-sell it right away: men who work at the trade can make these boats move—slowly—by the expenditure of considerable strength. When, as this year, the current of the Seine runs swiftly, it is impossible for any but an expert in the handling of these boats to move as much as one hundred yards upstream.

The boat generally used for family outings is called the light Norwegian. I saw four pretty ones, the work of well-known boat-builders, who want from 260 to 450 francs for them. I have decided that there is no reason for you to go to Wauthelet or Philippe, whose prices are in general higher than these. At Argenteuil someone offered to build one for two hundred francs, but you would have to wait at least three weeks for delivery. I have got to go to Asnières one of these days: I shall see Picot as well as Chambellan: their prices are usually fair.

I found a boat of the type called "duck-shooter," five meters long and 1 m. 35 wide, that I can assure you is a sound vessel. There is no sapwood in her timbers, the boat handles easily, and she is a pleasure to the eye.

Her drawbacks are those of every boat of this type: being specially built for fishing and shooting, she isn't so suitable for family parties as the light Norwegian is. She will hold only four people, whereas a Norwegian of the same length will take five or six—though it would be harder to handle. She has two pairs of light flexible oars. She is brand new. You can go anywhere in this kind of craft, and can row upstream without trouble. It's the kind that amateur fishermen generally choose. The price is 170 francs and I believe you could always re-sell the boat without incurring a loss.

What do you want me to do about it?

P.S. If you decide on the duck-shooter, the builder will put a fresh coat of paint on her before delivery. The boat being new, the first two coats are not enough, and have already been absorbed by the timbers. This coat of paint is of course included in the price of 170 francs mentioned.

TO GUSTAVE FLAUBERT

Paris, 21 August 1878

I have not written you, my dear Master, because I am completely done in, mentally and morally. For three weeks, night after night, I have tried to work, and I haven't written a decent page. Not one. Wherefore I have sunk little by little into a dark pit of discouragement and despondency, and I shall have a hard time climbing out of it. After putting in seven hours a day of office work, I can't straighten up sufficiently to throw off all the weariness that falls on my spirit. I have even tried doing a few articles for the *Gaulois* in order to make a little extra money. I haven't been able. I can't seem to make a start. I could weep over my sheet of paper. Added to which, everything seems to be going badly. My mother, who went back to Etretat two months ago, is not in the least better. Her heart is in bad shape and she has had some very disturbing fainting spells. She is so weakened that she doesn't even write me any more: I am lucky to get a note once a fortnight, that she dictates to the gardener. . . .

How is it that Zola has not yet been decorated, despite M. Bardoux's promise? [1] As a matter of fact, people are talking, because the press had announced that Zola was already decorated. I have promised to spend a Sunday with him soon: I'm curious to hear what he has to say about it. I'm sure he is greatly embarrassed. He has no need of a decoration.

I met Turgeniev a few days before he went off to Russia and found him despondent and restless. His heart had been bothering him and he had decided to see a doctor. The doctor told him that his left ventricle was in bad condition. It would seem that everybody's heart was giving out.

As for me, my hair is still falling out. The doctors now think there is nothing syphilitic in my case, but that I have a constitutional rheumatism which began by attacking the stomach and the heart and has now attacked the skin. They make me take steam baths, which up to now have induced no change. But this treatment, together with the bitter decoctions, syrups, and mineral waters prescribed, has eaten up the little money I had saved up for my summer. Well, that's one result achieved, anyway. I hope, for the confusion of the doctors, that it will be the only one. . . .

---

[1] *Bardoux, an acquaintance of Flaubert, and Minister of Education and Fine Arts, was to have awarded the Cross of the Legion of Honor to Zola.*

TO GEORGES CHARPENTIER[1]

Paris, 28 August 1878

You allowed me to hope, last winter, that you might be induced to spend a day with me this summer in a region that you frequented in the old days. Next Sunday is carnival day at the village of Bezons, and I think it will be pretty funny, since the inhabitants of the place (who cannot stand me) are in my view very comical. I am asking Hennique, Céard, and Huysmans, as well as a few oarsmen of both sexes, the men among them not too stupid, the ladies not too ugly.

I have no novel to submit to you, nor has any of my friends: consequently, you have nothing to fear from us. I hope that all these inducements will persuade you to join us.

TO GUSTAVE FLAUBERT

September 1878

Yesterday, I made a clean copy of my *Histoire du vieux temps,* with all the changes you suggested, and cut out five pages of the beginning. Last night, I read the play to my friend Fontaine, who thought I had cut out too much. He said it had become a proverb rather than a play written according to the usual rules, that I had taken out things which would perhaps have been applauded, and that, from this point of view, there was almost no action in the play. For my part, I think the changes and cuts are all to the good. What do you think? The play now moves faster. I hope (if the play

---

[1] A publisher.

is accepted) that the Count's monologue won't bore the audience. It seems to me that I cannot make any cuts here without ruining it altogether. I have thought it over, and if I had it to do over again, I wouldn't make it any shorter.

With this I am again sending you *la Demande* since you were good enough to agree to submit both plays at the same time. I didn't think it worth while to re-copy it, for the manuscript is very legible despite a few lines scratched out here and there. . . .

Paris, 4 November 1878

I went this morning, my very dear Master, to see M. Bardoux's secretary. I had been invited by letter to call on him. He told me that, on your recommendation, M. Bardoux had instructed him to see if he could do anything for me; but that as the Minister had not been able to remember either what it was I wanted, or what I was doing, he had sent for me to have this information.

I explained my situation to him, and he promised to look into the matter. However, he thought it would be difficult to get me a salary equal to what I have at the Ministry of the Navy; he would see, nevertheless.

You see, therefore, that the chances are dubious. I now receive 2,000 francs a year. In addition, my father allows me 600 francs a year, and this is to stop when my father leaves his post, which he will do four years hence. I may be raised to 2,400 francs at the end of this year, and I cannot possibly take less at the Ministry of Education. As it is, I can hardly make both ends meet after taking care of my rent, my tailor, my boot-maker, the cleaning woman, the laundress, and my food. Out of 216 francs a month, there is left to me twelve or fifteen francs with which to play the young

man about town. I think that a laborer is better off than
I am, since he has about the same income and fewer
obligatory expenses. I don't mention this often, because
it is embarrassing; but I wanted you to know what my
situation was in the event that I was offered 1,800 or
2,000 francs at the Ministry of Education. . . .

[*Correspondence on the subject of Maupassant's
transfer from an obscure section of the Ministry of the
Navy, where for seven years he had been doing routine
work, to the private secretariat of the Minister of Education and Fine Arts, where he would achieve a certain
degree of personal standing, as well as engage in more
interesting work, began between Maupassant and Flaubert in September 1878. Maupassant wrote persistently
on this subject and finally attained his aim. L. G.*]

26 December (1878)

These days have been a scramble, my very dear Master, and I haven't been able to write to you. I am finally
installed in a handsome office, with windows on a garden; but I still have the feeling that all this is temporary.
They have promised me a permanent appointment at
1,800 francs per annum (which I am in a hurry to see
confirmed) and have assured me that in the event of
the Cabinet falling, part of the usual Cabinet allowance
will be added without fail to my salary.

So long as M. Bardoux continues in office, the pecuniary arrangement is wonderful. I shall have 1,800 francs
as salary, 1,000 francs as Cabinet allowance, and at least
500 francs as bonus. But if the Cabinet falls—none of
this.

I haven't yet seen the Minister, but I see M. Charmes
often. He has been of great service to me, and can still

be. I have a job; now it is up to me to make it really mine and to get promoted quickly while the thing is still possible. Incidentally, I have no time at all of my own. I get in at nine and leave at 6:30. I have two hours for lunch. But all this will change as soon as I am on the Civil Service List.

I am treated with great consideration. The departmental directors are deferential and the bureau chiefs worship me. The others are a bit standoffish, including my colleagues; I believe they think me too simpleminded. I see things comic, comic, comic; other things sad, sad, sad: in a word, everybody is stupid, stupid, stupid, here as everywhere else. . . .

One annoying thing: the Minister's staff are obliged to be on duty Sundays till noon. I believe I shall still be able to find time to work, though; for as soon as I learn the routine, the office work will go swiftly: it isn't hard.

Paris, 18 February 1879

Just a hasty scrawl, my dear Master, for I am up to the ears in work. Besides, my play opens tomorrow night, and I have a job to do, distributing the author's seats. I hope the play will not be too poor.[1]

I shall try to come to see you in Normandy, but I can't answer for my success. This is why: When I was in the Ministry of the Navy, I had a railway card that allowed me to travel at twenty-five per cent of the cost of the ticket. Rouen and return was a matter of only nine francs. Now, in second class, it costs me about thirty-six francs—which is a lot for a man who spends an average of four francs a day. (Besides, the chief

---

[1] The one-act play, *Histoire du vieux temps*, displaying two characters, two armchairs, and a fireplace, opened on the 19th February 1879 at the Troisième Théâtre Français, Place du Château d'Eau.

of the *claque*, the prompter, and the stagehand are costing me sixty francs, and this for a play that will not bring me in a penny. That's stiff!)

However, I'll see what my finances permit at the end of the month. I hope that I shall be able to spend a day with you, for I want to and need to very much.

TO MADAME BRAINNE[1]

1 April 1879

You cannot imagine how sad I am each Wednesday when I see that it is again going to be impossible for me to come to see you. I leave the Ministry every evening at six because I am obliged to stay until the Minister has signed and sent back all the letters written for him in my department; and when, by chance, I do find that I can get away earlier, it is never on a day that suits.

However, unless the whole sky comes down upon me, I shall certainly dine with you on Monday and lay at your feet, with my regrets and excuses, the homage of the most devoted and most unhappy sentiments of a prince whom public business never ceases to separate from a queen he would wish never to be parted from.

Permit me, Madame, to kiss your finger-tips.

TO GUSTAVE FLAUBERT

Paris, 24 April 1879

I shall always be a victim of the civil service, my dear master. I have tried for a week to write to you, and

---

[1] A *family friend and friend of Flaubert, to whom Maupassant dedicated Une Vie.*

have only now been able to find a half hour. I have very pleasant relations with Charmes, my chief; we are almost on a footing of equality; he has allotted me a very handsome office; but—I belong to him; he unloads half his work on me; I trot and scribble from morn till night; I am a thing obedient to an electric bell; in a word, I have no more free time here than I had at the Naval Ministry. The advantage is that the work is not so dull and the personal relations are pleasant. The afternoon of my little play, Charmes said, "It's quite clear that we are going to have to leave you time to do your own work. Don't worry, we'll arrange that." Arrange it, will he? The fact is, I'm useful to him and he takes advantage of me. I wanted him to think well of me, and I have succeeded only too well.

As for your affair[1] I told you that they would offer you 5,000 francs a year, and they will offer you this; but you know how much time it takes to get the least little thing done. And this is a big thing, since the whole system of grants-in-aid is being overhauled in order to ensure that the grants shall be distributed equitably. There are six hundred men of letters now receiving government aid. Many of them earn or possess 8,000 to 10,000 francs a year of their own; they don't need the grants, and I suppose will be deprived of them. But your case has been decided, yours and Leconte de Lisle's. (He now receives 1,600 francs a year and is to be raised to 2,000.)

What do you think about Zola? I think he is absolutely mad. Have you seen his article on Victor Hugo? His article on the contemporary poets? His pamphlet en-

---

[1] Flaubert had lost a good deal of money through the bankruptcy of his brother-in-law, Commanville. His friends, being worried, had taken steps to obtain for him a post as honorary librarian at the Mazarin Library, which would bring him a sort of pension.

titled "Literature and the Republic"? "The Republic will be naturalistic or it will not be!" "I am nothing but a scientist." (Nothing but a scientist: what modesty!) "Social research . . . the human document." Formulas and formulas. Henceforth we shall see subtitles like this: "A novel according to the naturalistic formula." I am nothing but a scientist. Colossal! And nobody thinks it's funny.

I look forward impatiently to seeing you. I am bored. I am a little under the weather. My circulation is poor and the doctors constantly repeat, "Exercise! Take exercise!" Whereas I have time only for work. It makes me foul-tempered.

Paris, 2 December 1879

Herewith, my dear Master, the letter I received from Mme. Adam.[1] The reason she gives for not publishing my poem ["la Vénus rustique"] is certainly no more than a subterfuge.

I went yesterday to see her. She gave me back my manuscript and we chatted for a few minutes. Out of mere politeness, as it seemed to me, she asked me to write a piece expressly for her, of the type and the length written by Theuriet—his "Ploughman," for example. What she wants is that verse published by her shall be written in the spirit of her review. She said, "We have a reading public that we must bear with and satisfy; whose tastes we are obliged to guess and to

---

[1] Juliette Lamber Adam, editor of the *Nouvelle Revue*, left useful memoirs of the early years of the Third French Republic. She gathered round her a group whose initial aim was revenge for the defeat of France by the Prussians, and which became in every sense fervently nationalist. Paul Déroulède, mentioned in the same letter, was one of the most powerful publicists of this group and the author of nationalistic verses of wide popularity.

know. I am myself, at this moment, going through a sort of apprenticeship."

Always, always in our country, the journalist strives to debase himself to the level of the public, instead of trying to make the public understand things that are on a higher level. I agree, of course, that it is no trouble to stoop, and it is a good deal of trouble to render the public intelligent.

I shall send the great lady, in a few days, a poem of three pages—which is the limit she puts upon inspiration. In this way, I shall not appear vexed and she will be able to let me know clearly whether or not she wants to print my verse. I gather from what she said that the poets she prefers are Déroulède and Theuriet; and she seemed to be saying to me: "Imitate them and you will become one of us." Meanwhile, I must say that she received me very graciously. She asked me to write to you, not daring to write herself.

I am hard at work on my short story on the people of Rouen and the war. I'll have to carry a gun hereafter when I go through Rouen.

Paris, 5 January 1880

My very dear Master, I see that you have forgotten what I told you when I was last at Le Croisset, about our volume of stories, and I write to explain the thing.

Zola published a story on the war, entitled "The Attack on the Mill," first in Russia and then here, in *la Reforme*. Huysmans brought out another war story, "Sack A-back," at Brussels. Céard had meanwhile sent a strange and very violent story about the siege of Paris, called "The Bloodletting," to the Russian review for which he is Paris correspondent. When Zola heard about their stories he remarked that, together with his story, they would make up an interesting book—devoid of jingoism and expressing a good deal of originality in the respective points of view. At the same time he suggested that Alexis, Hennique, and I each write a story to complete the collection. For us, the advantage is that Zola's name will sell the book, and each of us will get a hundred or two hundred francs out of it. We started right in. Charpentier now has all the manuscripts and will publish the volume on the 1st March.

In bringing out this book we had no anti-patriotic intent; in fact, we had no particular intent at all. We simply sought, each of us, to strike a truthful note about the war, to strip it of the kind of jingoism preached by Déroulède, and to get rid of the fraudulent enthusiasm which up to now has seemed to be considered a necessary ingredient in every tale that concerned a pair of red pants and a musket. Generals, instead of being perfect mathematical geniuses bubbling over with noble sentiments and making generous heartfelt gestures, are simple mediocre creatures like the rest—except that they wear stars and arrange to have men killed out of plain stupidity, without intending any harm. This entire good faith that marks our judgment of military phenomena makes our book appear a bit unusual; and our deliberate detachment in discussing subjects which everybody else writes about with passion will enrage the bourgeoisie a thousand times more than a frontal attack would do. The book will not be anti-patriotic; it will simply be true. What I say of the people of Rouen, for example, is far from the whole truth, even.

As for my volume of verse, I told Charpentier about it, but he hasn't seen the manuscript as yet. I am very much afraid of the slow pace at which he moves. Fortunately, he is getting deeper and deeper into money troubles. (He hasn't paid Huysmans the 8,000 francs he owes him, and has given him only 400 francs on account.)

My Minister has decorated me with the ribbon of Officer of the Academy. I am not impressed.

No other news. I sent some verse to Mme. Adam about five weeks ago, for her review. She has not acknowledged it. Clearly, she prefers Déroulède.

January 1880

I went to see Mme. Commanville[1] but she was ill and I was not allowed in. It's quite true that I should have gone sooner, but how could I? I rarely get away from the Ministry before six. It is really impossible for me to go calling. People get angry, but there is nothing for it. The families I know most intimately are hurt. And yet they ought to realize how difficult, how encumbered, how complicated life is for a poor wretch who spends until six o'clock in an office then starts in immediately to work on other things. A visit after dinner means the loss of a whole evening—not to mention that there is every chance that the people you go to see will be out. Then there is another reason. I was at work both on my story and on my volume of verse, for both had to be ready this month. I had dropped everything, really everything, to finish them. And when you have only three or four hours a day to do the thing you love, when you are in the obsessive grip of a piece of work just started, people ought to forgive you for letting six weeks go by without calling. But ladies never understand these things. I have been disconsolate about Mme. Brainne, too. These two months past she has been vexed with me because I stayed away—making scenes, even

---

[1] *Flaubert's sister, Caroline, for whom he had a particularly tender affection.*

calling me names; and yet hers is a house I was able to go to, for it had been agreed that I could arrive for dinner and leave immediately after. We would talk at table, then I would disappear. She is such a thoughtful woman that in the end she allowed me to pay this sort of call, which left me my whole evening for work. As a matter of fact, I haven't seen a single member of my family since last October. Well, I'll go back to Mme. Commanville's in a few days, and I shall try to still her anger.

TO IVAN TURGENIEV

Paris, 25 May 1880

I am still overwhelmed by the blow, and the dear great shade follows me everywhere. His voice haunts me; his phrases come back to me; the absence of his tenderness has created a kind of void round me.

On Saturday, the 8th May, at 3:30 in the afternoon, I received a telegram in town from Mme. Commanville which read, "Flaubert stricken by apoplexy. Case hopeless. Leaving at six o'clock." At six, I met the Commanvilles at the railway station; but, having stopped a moment at my flat between the Ministry and the railway station, I found there two telegrams from Rouen which told me that he was dead. We made the awful journey up during the night, plunged in a dark and cruel sorrow. At Le Croisset we found him lying on his bed, very little changed except that the apoplexy had swollen his neck with black blood. There we were told certain details. He had been in good health just before and was happy at the thought that he was coming to the end of his novel (*Bouvard et Pécuchet*). He was to have gone to Paris on the 9th May and had been looking forward to amusing himself, "having," as he put it, "hidden a little stake in a pot." The stake was not big, it had not been earned by literature. He had dined very well on Friday and had spent the evening reading Corneille aloud with his friend and physician, Fortin. He slept till eight o'clock on Saturday morning, took a leisurely bath, got dressed, and read the morning post. It was then that, feeling a little uncomfortable, he called out for his servant. As she was slow coming upstairs, he shouted to her through the window to get hold of Dr. Fortin, who, a moment before, had left by boat. When the servant reached his room she found him standing in a kind of daze, but not in the least worried. He said to her, "I believe I am going to faint, or something. Good thing it's happening today; it would be a nuisance if it happened tomorrow in the railway carriage." He himself uncorked a bottle of eau de cologne, rubbed his forehead with it, and let himself down on a deep divan, murmuring: "Rouen. . . . We're not far from Rouen. . . . Hellot . . . I know them, the Hellots." He fell back all purple, his fists clenched, his face swollen with blood, stricken when he had not the faintest thought of death in mind.

His last words have been interpreted by the press as relating to old Victor Hugo who lives on the Avenue d'Eylau. It seems to me incontestable that what they meant was, "Go to Rouen, we are not far from Rouen. Bring back Dr. Hellot. I know the Hellots."

I spent three days with him. Georges Pouchet and Dr. Fortin and I buried him. We bore him on Tuesday morning to the cemetery from which Le Croisset is clearly visible—that great bend in the Seine and the house he so much loved.

The days when we think ourselves happy cannot cancel out a day like that one.

Many friends came up from Paris for the funeral,

young men especially, all the young men, even those nobody knows; but Victor Hugo was not present, nor Renan, Taine, Maxime Du Camp, Frédéric Baudry, Dumas, Augier, Vacquerie, etc.

There you have the story, my dear Master and Friend; but I shall have more to tell you. We shall take up the matter of the novel as soon as the heirs have settled the estate. Your help will be necessary from every point of view.

On the day the blow fell I wrote a note to Mme. Viardot [1] asking her to let you know, for I did not have your address in Russia. I wanted very much that this news reach you through a friend rather than through the press.

[With Flaubert's death and the publication of "Boule de Suif" a period ends in Maupassant's life. He is no longer an apprentice, but an acknowledged master. But simultaneously with the coming of success, his health begins to deteriorate, and his zest for life begins to die. L. G.]

TO HIS MOTHER

Etretat, Tuesday (January 1881)

I write to you on the corner of the little table in our parlor. The two dogs are very thin, but gay and well: they are lying at my feet. Matho disturbs me ceaselessly by rubbing against my leg. Daphne is completely cured. As for me, I sneeze, blow my nose, invaded by a fearful cold in the head I caught traveling all night in a temperature five below freezing, and I cannot get warm in

---

[1] The celebrated singer, Pauline Viardot-Garcia, with whom Turgeniev was for years in love, and who was a sister of an even greater singer, la Malibran.

this frozen house. The cold wind whistles under the doors, the lamp dies, the lively chimney-fire lights me up—a fire that grills the face without warming the room. All the old things are about me, dreary, harrowing; no sound comes from the dead village, blanketed in winter. I cannot hear the sea.

The cold is owing more to the loneliness of my life than to the loneliness of this house. I have the feeling that the whole world has lost its way, and the void in which I live begins to weigh heavily upon me. Yet in the midst of the general stampede my brain operates lucidly, precisely, dazzling me with the eternal Nothingness. That sounds like something written by old Hugo, but it would take a long time for me to express my idea clearly and in precise language. Which proves to me once again that romantic bombast is the result of mere laziness in writing. . . .

I have almost finished my story about the prostitutes and the First Communion. I think it is at least as good as "Boule de Suif," if not better.

TO KISTEMAECKERS[1]

Menton, 7 May 1882

I have received your letter and am replying to it immediately.

First, my thanks for the 200 francs enclosed. Added to the 300 remitted to me in Paris, this makes 500 francs. You may wait until you make a trip to Paris to remit the balance of twenty-five francs outstanding.

Impossible to dine with you on the 11th. My mother is still too ill for me to leave that early. I shall therefore not be in Paris before the 20th.

---

[1] *A Belgian publisher.*

It is true that I forgot the critics you mention, as well as Banville, who will do the article for *Gil Blas* and Maizeroy will do one for the *Gaulois*. Do not send a copy of the book [*Mademoiselle Fifi*] to Vallès: I'll give him one when I see him. I don't know Fouquier's private address: send his copy to *XIXe Siècle*. M. Yung lives at 46, rue de Rennes. We also forgot Robert de Bonnières (who signs himself "Janus" in the *Figaro*).

Please let me know how much I shall have to pay for the copies I may require in excess of the twenty-five author's copies; and let Marpon know that he is to deliver such copies to me at the price agreed between us.

I answer for the sale of the book at the Librairie Nouvelle [bookshop]. You'll see. The clerks there are named Achille Heymann, Ménard, and Reboul. (I am not sure about the spelling of the last man's name, which is why I have not sent you inscribed copies for them.) It is essential that we give a copy to each of the clerks at the Librairie Nouvelle. I shall go in myself to inscribe their copies. That bookshop alone sold 900 copies of *la Maison Tellier*. No newspaper can match the publicity we get through those three clerks.

TO GEORGES CHARPENTIER

28 November 1882

I was somewhat astonished that right after my conversation with M. Gaullet I should receive from you the draft contract which you felt inspired to send me.

What strange notion has suddenly impelled you to wish to engage in a contract with me—considering that up to now you never thought of such a thing? I offered you my book [*Des Vers*]: you accepted the poems without mentioning the word contract. It was published without that word ever coming into our conversation. Three years have gone by without our raising and discussing the idea of a contract, and suddenly you send me two copies of a document bearing a tax stamp.

I am resolved, as a matter of principle, never to sign a definitive contract. Incidentally, the arrangements under which M. Havard publishes me are purely oral. But if I were to sign a contract with you I should do so on the terms that govern the publication of my books by others. Here they are:

Royalty of 40 centimes a copy on the first 2,000 copies.

Royalty of 1 franc a copy in excess of 2,000 copies.

At the end of six years I become free to dispose of my books as I please.

I retain the right to bring out illustrated or de luxe editions of my books whenever I please and with any publisher of my choice.

These terms have thus far proved very advantageous to me, and I am not disposed to amend them. . . .

TO A PUBLISHER[1]

4 December 1882

I have been unable to answer your letter sooner because the little free time that I possess made it difficult for me to give thought to your questions. Here are the terms on which I can deal with you:

One volume containing ten to fifteen stories, that is, 150 pages of your illustrated format. De luxe edition of 500 copies—2,000 francs, of which 1,000 on delivery of

---

[1] Probably Monnier, who published Clair de Lune in 1884.

manuscript and 1,000 francs on day of publication. You to have the exclusive right of publication of these stories for five years.

As for your projected *Love Through the Ages,* I had rather not contribute to it for several reasons, the simplest being that it would be most unpleasant for me to appear in a volume signed by several names. Besides, I should be obliged to ask a large sum.

I sell a novel to a newspaper for 8,000 francs. The Russian translation (before publication in France) brings me in 2,000 francs. Generally speaking, a long story, on the same terms, brings me in at least 1,500 francs. Assuming another 1,500 francs as the share earned by the same long story in a volume containing three others (M. Havard pays me a royalty of one franc for each copy sold at three francs fifty centimes), we arrive at a minimum of three thousand francs. And I would still prefer not to contribute to *Love Through the Ages,* even though you gave me 3,000 francs in advance.

TO EDMOND DESCHAUMES

10 February 1883

I have already invited you by letter to remove my name from the cover of your magazine, *le Chat Noir.* Today I learn that at the Newspapermen's Ball a special number was distributed in which I continue to be identified as a member of your board. Continued thus despite my protest, your joke is in very bad taste; and since it is insulting to me, it is bound to make me regret relations with you which are so absolutely devoid of courtesy on your part.

I therefore inform you that this letter has been written and posted in the presence of witnesses, and that I have

taken steps to ensure that I shall laugh last about the
attitude adopted towards me.

TO ROUVÈYRE[1]

(June 1883)

I find your two letters on my return from Rouen. Although the volume was placed on sale yesterday, I am
sending you the publicity note you ask for, which may
still be of use to you:

"Rouvèyre and Bloud have placed on sale a new book
by Guy de Maupassant, *les Contes de la Bécasse*. What
particularly distinguishes this latest work by the author
of *la Maison Tellier* and *Une Vie* is its gaiety and its
amusing irony. The first story in the volume, "Ce
Cochon de Morin," will certainly take its place beside
"Boule de Suif." And the stories that follow contain a
wide sampling of the author's good-humored mockery.
Only two or three of them introduce a dramatic note
into the collection."

TO LEON FONTAINE[2]

Rouen, Hotel du Mans,
Wednesday (June 1883)

Did you get the letter by which I informed you that I
had left five hundred francs with my father to pay for
my bit of land? I asked also what I still owed you, net of
the eighty-six francs I paid Fournaise for you in connection with the bill for 226 francs sent to me.

I am in harness—from nine to ten daily. That is the

---

[1] A publisher.
[2] A friend of his youth.

sum of my service to the Government. I write my letters
at the Ministry, after which I am free till the next day. I
am not complaining. . . .

TO BARON LUDOVIC DE VAUX[1]

Paris (November 1883)

Thank you for warning me. Don't let the paragraph
appear. It was me all right at Triel, but I did not have a
negresse blanche with me, I had two *blanches* with me.
You know one of them by name, the one I ran into by
chance when I got there. Incidentally, a paragraph you
wrote some time ago got me into serious trouble. When
what you write concerns only me, I don't mind a bit;
but this involved a woman, and it nearly turned out
disastrously. I'll tell you all about it when I see you.

Of course I can easily say something about your book
in the *Gaulois*, but do you mean *Tireurs de Pistolet* or a
new book? I am just up from Etretat and don't know
what has been going on.

TO COUNTESS POTOCKA

Cannes, 13 March 1884

. . . What am I up to? I am confoundedly bored.
Everything stultifies me—the people I see and the monotonous round of events that occur. Little wit in circles
called fashionable; little intelligence; little anything. A
resounding name and a lot of money just are not enough.
These people make me think of bad paintings in gilded
frames. But I declare that Princess Mathilde (Bonaparte)

---

[1] *Writer of a society gossip column in* Gil Blas.

is a phenomenon of wit, gaiety, distinction, and graciousness—compared to the Duchesse de Chartres.

When you get a good look at universal suffrage and the people it gives us, you want to machine-gun the voters and guillotine their representatives. But when you get a good look at the princes who might be governing us, you simply become an anarchist. Of course they're decent, simple folk, filled with infantile cheeriness, stricken with infantiasis; but what brains! What monologues! What thoughts! What concerns! Oh, I shall certainly never be a courtier. I'll tell you what the Great do to me. They fill me with a feeling of exceeding pride that I never felt before. They make me think it is I who am the Prince while they are little children who haven't yet got beyond their Sunday School lessons.

Fortunately, there are other men in the world to fill you with the contrary sensation, the wonderful sensation of humility in the presence of Thought triumphant. I have just re-read Diderot. What a genius! And how much greater he still is than the rest of us! How that prodigious intelligence operates so clearly, so easily, penetrating to the heart of the most obscure, the most distant, the highest things! I don't know why I always think of Diderot when chatting with the Duc de Chartres.

And when I think that the Prince of Wales is inferior to the Orleans princes, that the King of Spain and the Russian Emperor are inferior to the Prince of Wales, and that the King of Italy is still lower in the scale than his cousins of Spain and Russia, I stand aghast before the organization of human society. . . .

[In March 1884, a Russian girl of brilliant gifts, in the exercise of which she was impeded by the tuberculosis

*which killed her at the age of twenty-six, initiated a brief
correspondence with Maupassant. She signed her first
letter "R.D.G., Poste Restante, Madeleine P.O. Station,
Paris." The purpose of the correspondence, as she wrote
later to Edmond de Goncourt, was to find a man of
letters to whom she could bequeath the diary she had
been keeping. That diary, the* Journal of Marie Bashkirtseff, *was published after her death, translated into English (among other languages), and widely read. Marie
Bashkirtseff's letters are given below, together with Maupassant's replies.* L. G.]

FROM ''R.D.G.''
TO GUY DE MAUPASSANT

(March 1884)

I read your works almost with happiness. You worship Nature, and out of Nature's verities you fashion a
truly sublime poetry. You stir us, meanwhile, by touches
of feeling so profoundly human that we recognize ourselves in your pages and therefore feel for you an affection that is egotistical. Is this mere phrase-making? Be
tolerant: it is sincerely meant.

Of course I should like to say fine and striking things
to you, but it is rather difficult to bring out such things
straight off. I regret this all the more as you are sufficiently remarkable to inspire one with romantic dreams
of becoming the confidante of your beautiful soul—assuming, of course that your soul is beautiful. If it is not,
and if you don't go in for that sort of thing, I am sorry
—sorry mainly for you; besides which I shall have to set
you down in my mind as a literary hack and let it go at
that.

For a whole year I have been on the point of writing to you. Each time I thought I might be overrating you, and that it was perhaps not worth the effort. Two days ago, however, when I saw suddenly in the *Gaulois* that someone had honored you with a flattering epistle, and that you had asked for the person's address in order to answer it, I became jealous on the spot, your literary merits dazzled me anew, and—here I am.

Let me warn you immediately that I shall never drop my incognito so far as you are concerned. I do not wish to see you, even from a distance. Who knows, but that your looks might not please me? All I know of you is that you are young and that you are not married—two essential points, even for worship at a distance. But I must tell you that I am charming: this pleasant thought will stimulate you to answer my letter. It seems to me that if I were a man I should wish to hold no communication, even epistolary, with a dried-up old maid from England, whatever Miss Hastings[1] might say about that.

FROM GUY DE MAUPASSANT TO "R.D.G."

Cannes (March 1884)

My letter, Madame, will assuredly not be what you expect. I want first to thank you for your compliments and for your graciousness in writing to me. And now we can have a talk, like sensible people.

You wish to become my confidante? By what right? I do not know you. Why should I tell you, whom I do not know, whose mind, inclinations, and so on may clash

---

[1] "Miss Hastings" is a character in a story of the same name by Maupassant.

with my own intellectual bent, that which I can say aloud, in intimacy, to the women who are my friends? If I did, would I not prove myself a superficial fellow and an unfaithful friend?

What can mystery add to the charm that exists in correspondence? Does not the sweetness of affection between man and woman (I mean chaste affection) come mainly from the pleasure of seeing each other, chatting while looking at one another, and recalling, as one writes to a friend, her features while they float between the sheet of paper and our eyes?

How can one write intimate things, things summoned from the depths of oneself, to a person whose physical being, whose glance, smile, hair are all unknown to one? How can I possibly be interested in saying to you, "I did so-and-so today," knowing that what I say can bring to your mind only vaguely interesting images, since you do not know me?

You spoke of a letter I received recently from an anonymous correspondent: the writer was a man who was seeking my advice, that was all. I revert to the subject of anonymous letters from women: in the past two or three years I have had fifty or sixty such letters. How am I to choose (as you suggest) a confidante of my soul among those women? When, as in simple bourgeois society, a woman agrees to show herself and make herself acquainted with a man, relations of friendship and trust can be established. Why should a man neglect the charming women he knows in favor of a friend who may be charming but who remains anonymous—which is to say, remains a person who might well be unpleasant either to the eye or to the mind? I am afraid that all this is not very gallant; but if I were to throw myself at your feet would you believe that I could be constant in my mental affections?

FROM ''R.D.G.''
TO GUY DE MAUPASSANT

(March 1884)

Your letter, Sir, did not surprise me, and I did not entirely look forward to what you seem to think. For one thing, I did not ask to be made your confidante—that would have been a little too simple-minded; and if you have the time to re-read my letter you will see that you failed to take the trouble of appreciating the ironical and disparaging tone in which I spoke of myself.

You are good enough to reassure me that your *Gaulois* correspondent was a man. I thank you for that reassurance, but as my jealousy was altogether of a spiritual nature, it hardly matters.

To answer me by confiding in me would, you say, be idiotic, considering that you do not know me? Sir, would it shock you if I said to you without warning that King Henry the Fourth was dead? As a matter of fact, since you seem to think that I asked for your confidence by return post, for you to answer by unburdening yourself a little would have been a very witty fashion of amusing yourself at my expense. Had I been you, I should have done so, for I am sometimes very gay—although I am often sad enough to dream of exchanging confidences by letter with an unknown philosopher and sharing his impressions of the carnival.

Your last *Gaulois* article was extremely well done and deeply felt: those two columns were worth the three readings I gave them. On the other hand, what a piece of hack writing is that story of the old mother who avenges herself on the Prussians (the story published at about the time you were reading my letter).

As for the charm conferred by mystery, it seems to me a matter of taste. Obviously, the idea does not amuse you at all; but that it amuses me very much I admit in all sincerity, as I do the childish delight with which I received your letter, such as it was. Actually, if mystery does not amuse you, it is because not one of your sixty correspondents was able to arouse your interest, that is all; and though I have not been able to strike the right chord, either, I am too reasonable to bear you any ill-will on that account.

Only sixty? I should have supposed you besieged by a greater number. Did you answer them all?

It may be that my turn of mind does not accord with yours. You are undoubtedly hard to please. Nevertheless, I imagine that I know you (this is the effect novelists produce on scatterbrained women). And yet you are probably right.

Because I write to you with the utmost frankness (out of the feeling mentioned above), you may perhaps think me a sentimental young person, or even a woman in search of an adventure. That would annoy me very much. Make no excuses, therefore, for your want of romance, gallantry, and so on.

Really, I wrote you a very dull letter. Does that mean —to my very great regret, if it does—that we must stop writing to each other? Unless, of course, I decide some day to prove to you that I do not deserve to be tagged no. 61. As for your reasoning, it was sound, but it was aimed at a nonexistent target. I forgive you for it as I forgive you for the erasures and for the story of the old woman and the Prussians. Be happy!

Incidentally, if all you needed was a word of description to induce you to disclose to me the beauties of your ancient and unintuitive soul, perhaps this will do: Fair hair, medium height, born sometime between 1812 and

1863. Intellectually—no, I should seem to be boasting and you would know at once that I was from Marseilles.

Please forgive the blots, erasures, &c.; but I have already re-copied my letter three times.

FROM GUY DE MAUPASSANT TO "R.D.G."

Cannes (March 1884)

Yes, Madame, a second letter. It astonishes me. Very likely I feel a vague desire to write impertinently to you. Since I do not know you, the thing is permissible. Actually, I write to you because I am confoundedly bored.

You reproach me with singing an old song in my old woman and the Prussians; but all songs are old. To sing old refrains is all I do; it is all I know how to do. All ideas, all writing, all discussion, all beliefs are old refrains. And isn't writing to an anonymous woman itself an old story and a childish one? Actually, for me to write to you is silly. You know me more or less, you know what you are up to, and whom you are writing to: this or that has been said about me, and either it matters or it doesn't matter. Even if you happen not to have met any one of my acquaintance (which is wide), you've read articles about me that mentioned my appearance, that spoke of my personality. In short, you, being sure of what you are doing, are having fun. But am I?

I agree that you may be a young and charming woman whose hands I should be delighted to kiss. But you may also be an old hag brought up on the novels of Eugène Sue. You may be an old lady's companion, pedantic and as dry as a broomstick. By the way, are you thin? Not too, I hope. I should be miserable to think that I had a skinny correspondent. I am suspicious of everything about anonymous women, for I was once caught out most foolishly. A whole girls' school carried on a correspondence with me by the pen of a sub-mistress, and my replies went from hand to hand during class. The ruse was funny and made me laugh when I was told of it—by the sub-mistress herself.

Are you in society? Sentimental, or merely romantic? Or are you bored, and amusing yourself with me? In any case, I am certainly not the man you are after. There isn't a copper's worth of poetry in me. I am indifferent to everything, and I spend two thirds of my time being profoundly bored. The third third I spend writing lines which I sell as dearly as possible while regretting that I have to practice the abominable trade to which I owe the honor of having been chosen—mentally—by you.

There, if you like, are confidences! What do you say to them, Madame?

You must think me very unceremonious, and for that I ask your pardon. Writing to you, I feel as if I were going towards an unlighted underground passage, afraid at every step of tumbling into a hole. I feel about with my stick.

What perfume do you use? Are you very fond of food? What do your ears look like? Tell me the color of your eyes. Are you fond of music? I shan't ask if you are married, for if you are, you will say "no," and if you are not, you'll say "yes."

FROM "R.D.G." TO GUY DE MAUPASSANT

(March 1884)

So you are horribly bored! Ah, cruel man, you say that in order to leave me no illusion concerning that to which

I owe the honor of your letter—which, in fact, reached me at an opportune moment and gave me much pleasure.

It is true that I am enjoying this correspondence, but it is not true that I know you as well as all that. I swear that I do not even know your complexion or your height. As for your private character, I know only as much as I can gather from the lines you favor me with, and only then after taking account of quite a bit of calculation and affectation. Actually, for a ponderous naturalist you are not so stupid, and my answer would fill a volume if vanity did not restrain me. I must not let you think that all my energy is expended on this.

First, let us settle the business of hack-writing—which may take a little time, since you pour it out so fast. On the whole, you are right. But art consists precisely in getting us to swallow old tales, in charming us with them eternally, as Nature charms with her eternal sun, her ancient earth, her men built all on the same lines and all animated by the same feelings. But—and then there are the composers, who have only a few notes to work with; and the painters, who dispose of only a few colors. . . . But you know all this as well as I do, and you are pulling my leg. Honored, I'm sure.

Hack work! Old stuff! Your old peasant woman and her Prussians remind me of Jeanne d'Arc as a subject for painting. Are you really sure that a *clever fellow* (is that the word?) couldn't find something new and touching in them?

As a weekly chronicle, your letters do pretty well. What else shall I say of them? You, with your old stories about the miseries of your profession! You take me for a housewife who takes you for a poet, and you go to great lengths to educate me. George Sand boasted of writing for money before you did; and the laborious Flaubert has moaned to us of his travail. A pity that the pangs he suffered should be passed on to his readers! Balzac made no such complaint, but was always full of enthusiasm for his work. As for Montesquieu, if I may venture to put it this way, his taste for study was so keen that, as it was the source of his fame, so it was also the source of his happiness (as the sub-mistress of your girls' school would say). And as for selling dear, that's as it should be; for there was never any shining glory without gold, as the Jew, Baahrou, says. (He was a contemporary of Job, mentioned in the *Fragments* edited by the learned Spitzbube, of Berlin.) Besides, everything profits by a good setting—beauty, genius, even religion. Did not God Himself come down to give directions to His servant, Moses, concerning the ornaments of the Tabernacle, explaining to him that the cherubim on either side were to be of gold and of *exquisite workmanship?*

Bored, are you? And you look upon everything with indifference. And there is not a spark of poetry in your nature. Well, you don't succeed in frightening me one bit. I can imagine what you are like. You must have a great belly. Your waistcoat is of some indeterminate color and is too short for you. You wear it with the bottom button undone. And even so, you interest me. What I cannot understand is that you should be bored. I myself am sometimes despondent, discouraged, furious; but bored? Never!

You are not the man I am looking for? I am not looking for anyone. It is my view that for a woman of character, men ought to be mere accessories. As for the dried-up old maid, the hag, heavens! here she comes: "Will you be good enough to tell me what he looks like?"

Well, I shall answer your questions, and with perfect frankness, for I do not like to take advantage of the simple-mindedness of a man of genius who dozes off after dinner over his cigar. Am I thin? Oh, no; but neither am I stout. Worldly, sentimental, romantic? But what do you mean? It seems to me that there is room for all these things in the same person, everything depending on the moment, the occasion, the circumstances. I am an opportunist, and peculiarly susceptible to mental contagion. It could happen that I found myself as lacking in poetry as you are. What perfume do I use?—Virtue. *Vulgo,* none. Yes, I am fond of food; or, rather, I have a fastidious appetite. My ears are small, not very well shaped, but pretty. Eyes gray. Yes, I love music, but am probably not so good a pianist as your schoolmistress.

Does my docility make you glad? If so, undo another button of your waistcoat and think of me when twilight falls. If not—so much the worse for me. I think I have given you a good deal in exchange for your pretended confidences.

May I ask who are your favorite composers and painters?

And how if I were a man?

[This letter was accompanied by a sketch showing a fat man sitting in an armchair under a palm tree, by the sea. A table, a bock, and a cigar. L. G.]

FROM GUY DE MAUPASSANT
TO "R.D.G."

3 *April 1884*

Madame, I am just back from a fortnight in Paris, and as I had forgotten at Cannes the cabalistic signs that constitute your postal address, I was not able to write until now. Besides which your letter frightened me, you know. Why, you cite, one after the other, and without the slightest warning, George Sand, Flaubert, Balzac, Montesquieu, the Jew Baahrou, Job, the learned Spitz-bube of Berlin, and Moses! I know you now, O beautiful Mask! You are a fourth form professor at the Lycée Louis-le-Grand, and you won't mind if I say that I had pretty well guessed it, for your writing-paper smells vaguely of snuff. I shall cease therefore to be gallant (was I?), and shall treat you as an academic fellow, by which I mean an enemy. Aha! cunning old fox, old school usher, old worm-i'-the-vellum! You'll try to pass yourself off as a pretty young woman, will you? After which you'll send me your treatises on Art and Nature so that I may recommend them to some review for publication, and write in praise of them? What luck that I didn't let you know I was coming up to Paris! I should have had a call one fine day from a threadbare old fellow who would have put his hat down on the floor and drawn forth a roll of manuscript tied with a bit of string, and would have said, "Sir, I am the lady who—"

Well, Sir Professor, despite all this I shall answer one or two of your questions. Let me begin by thanking you for the gracious details you give me concerning your person and your tastes. Thank you also for the portrait of me you sketched. My word, it's a good likeness—except for a few mistakes:

1. Less belly.

2. Never smoke.

3. Drink no beer, wine, or spirits—nothing but water, wherefore beatitude over a bock is not my favorite pose. Most often I sit cross-legged on a divan.

Who is my favorite painter? Millet. Composer? I can't abide music. Actually, I prefer a pretty woman to all the arts. I put a good dinner, a real dinner—the rare dinner—almost as high as a pretty woman.

There, Sir Professor, you have my profession of faith.

I consider that when we have a real passion, a fundamental passion, we should let it fill our lives, sacrifice all other passions to it—which is what I do. I had two passions. One had to be sacrificed. I sacrificed food. I have become as abstemious as a camel, and so hard to please that I no longer know what to eat.

Do you want another tidbit? I have won heavy bets as oarsman, swimmer, and cross-country walker.

Now that I have given you all these confidences, Sir Usher, tell me about yourself, your wife (for you are married), and your children. Have you a daughter? If so, keep me in mind, I beg you.

FROM ''R.D.G.''
TO GUY DE MAUPASSANT

(April 1884)

Unfortunate disciple of Zola! But this is enchanting! If there were any justice in the world, you would agree with me. Not only is it great fun, but it seems to me that it contains potentialities of pleasure, of really interesting things, if only we were absolutely sincere. For where, after all, is the man or woman with whom we can be totally and unreservedly open, with whom we do not have to be somewhat on our guard? Whereas, absolute beings. . . . Oh, to belong to no nation, no class; to be unique! Such a person would be capable of Shakespearean breadth of expression.

A truce to mystification. Since you now know the whole truth, I shall not hide anything from you any longer. Yes, I have the honor to be a schoolmaster, as you say; and I shall prove it to you by eight pages of lecture. Since I am too clever to bring you rolls of manuscript tied up in visible string, I shall serve you up my doctrine in small doses.

I took advantage of the leisure afforded by Holy Week to re-read your complete works. There are no two ways about it, you are quite a lad. I had never read you in bulk like this, at one fell swoop, wherefore my impression of you is spontaneous. My impression is—there's enough in your work to turn all my pupils topsy-turvy and send a shiver through all the convents of Christendom. It happens that I am not in the least prudish; but I am astounded, yes, Sir, astounded, by the intensity with which your nature inclines you to the sentiment that M. Alexandre Dumas the Younger calls *l'Amour.* If this became an obsession with you, it would be a pity, for you are very gifted and your peasant tales are well put together.

I know that you have written *Une Vie,* and that that novel is marked by a strong impress of distaste, despondency, and discouragement. This feeling, which induces us to forgive you other things, is manifested from time to time in your stories and leads one to believe that you are a superior person, and life makes you suffer. That is what broke my heart. But your moaning, I imagine, was merely a repetition of Flaubert.

That's how it is, is it? We are a lot of worthy rascals and you are a very comical fellow (now do you see the advantage of anonymity?), with your solitude and your long-haired characters. Love is still the bait with which you lure a world of readers. Dear, dear! Gil Blas, where art thou? It was after reading one of your articles that I read Zola's "Attack on the Mill." I seemed to have walked into a great sweet-smelling wood where birds were singing. "Never had a broader peace settled down upon a lovelier spot in nature." The masterly sentence is like the famous aria in the last act of *l'Africaine.*

I was forgetting that you abhor music. I expect that people have played nothing but pedantic music for you. Well. . . . Fortunately, your book isn't written yet, the book in which you will write about a woman—yes, my dear Sir—a woman, and not a succession of violent exercises. Don't forget that though you may win a race, that merely makes you the equal of a horse; and however noble the animal may be, it remains, my dear young man, a horse. You may perhaps allow an old Latinist to recommend the passage in Sallust that begins, *Omnes hominis qui sese student praeterari.* . . . I shall order my daughter Anastasia to grind at it. One never knows, you may perhaps settle down yet.

Food and women! Look here, my young friend, these things spell debauchery, and a schoolmaster can hardly follow you on that burning ground.

No music and no tobacco, good Lord!

Millet is a good painter. But you say Millet the way a bourgeois would say Raphael. I advise you to look at a little modern chap whose name is Bastien-Lepage. You will find him exhibited in the rue de Sèze.

Just how old are you?

Do you seriously prefer pretty women to all the arts? You are making fun of me.

Forgive the incoherence of this scrappy letter and do not leave me too long without a reply. With which, O Eater of Women, I greet you . . . and sign myself, in holy terror,

Joseph Savantin.

FROM GUY DE MAUPASSANT
TO "R.D.G."

(April 1884)

My dear Joseph, is not this the moral of your letter? Since we do not know each other, let us not hesitate to say what we think and to speak frankly, like a couple of old cronies. So be it. I'll set you the example by going all out.

Do you know that for a schoolmaster who is in charge of innocent children, you said some harsh things to me? What, is there no modesty in you at all? None in your reading, your treatises, your words, your actions? What? I thought so.

So you really believe that things interest me? And that I don't care a hang about the public? My poor Joseph, there is not a man under the sun who is as world-weary as I am. Nothing seems to me worth the effort or the fatigue of a single gesture. I am endlessly bored, restlessly bored, hopelessly bored because there is nothing that I desire and nothing that I look forward to. As for regretting what I have no power to change, I shall wait to do that when I am doddering. And since we are being frank with each other, I shall say that this is my last letter, because I've had about enough of this. Why should I go on writing to you? It doesn't entertain me. It doesn't promise me any future pleasure. Why, then? I have no desire to know you. I am sure that you are ugly; and besides, I think I've sent you autographs enough as it is. Do you know that they fetch from ten to twenty sous a piece, depending on the contents? You must have at least two twenty-sou letters, lucky dog!

And besides, I believe I'll get out of Paris again, for the place bores me more than any other does. I'll go for a change to Etretat, specially as this is a time of year when I can be alone there. I like being alone, for then I am able to be bored without talking about it.

You ask what my age really is. Having been born on the 5th August 1850, I am not quite thirty-four years old. Does that satisfy you? Aren't you going to ask for a photograph, now? I warn you that I'll not send you one.

Yes, I am fond of pretty women; but there are days when I loathe them.

Farewell, Joseph, my lad. Our acquaintance has turned out very brief, very incomplete. What do you expect? It's probably much better that we never got a look at one another's mugs.

FROM ''R.D.G.''
TO GUY DE MAUPASSANT

(April 1884)

I am now going to tell you something incredible, particularly in your view, and which, coming after the event, is of only historical significance. It is that I too had enough of it. By the time of your third letter my enthusiasm had cooled. Satiety, probably.

The fact is, I prize only those things that are out of my reach. You will say I ought therefore prize you, now. Yes, almost.

Why did I ever write to you at all? Well. . . . You wake up one fine morning and you say to yourself that you are a marvelous creature surrounded by idiots. You groan at the thought of so many pearls thrown before so many swine. "Suppose I write to some famous man, to some man worthy of understanding me?" It would be fun, it would be romantic, and—who knows?—after a

certain number of letters I shall perhaps have made a
new friend in this extraordinary way. You wonder who
the man is to be; and you choose—you.

A correspondence like ours can be successful subject
to two conditions. One of them is a *limitless* admiration
on the part of the anonymous letter writer. Such an admiration creates a current of sympathy which leads the
person to write in a way that infallibly touches and
interests the famous man. This condition does not exist.
I chose you in the hope of ending by conceiving a limitless admiration for you, since I began by assuming what
you now tell me, that you are relatively very young. For
that reason I started deliberately by whipping myself
into a state of enthusiasm about you; and I ended by
saying "unbecoming" and even rude things to you (as
you may have deigned to notice). We have reached a
point, as you say, where I may as well confess that your
odious letter caused me to spend a very wretched day.

I feel as deeply hurt as if the offense were real—
which is absurd.

Good bye, with pleasure.

If you still have them, send me back my autographs.
As for yours, I have already sold them in America at a
fabulous price.

FROM GUY DE MAUPASSANT
TO ''R.D.G.''

Etretat, 12 April (1884)

Madame, can it be that I have hurt you? Do not deny
it. I am delighted. And I ask your pardon very humbly.

I said to myself, "Who is she?" First she wrote me a
sentimental letter, a dreamy letter, the letter of an emo-

tional person. That is a pose common to harlots. Is she a harlot? Many anonymous letter-writers are harlots.

Whereupon, Madame, I replied on a note of skepticism. You were quicker than I, and your penultimate letter contained strange things. As a matter of fact, I couldn't make up my mind about the kind of person you were at all. I kept saying to myself: "Is it a lady in a mask amusing herself, or is it some female scamp?"

Do you know how to find out if a woman at the Opera Ball is a lady? You tickle her. Harlots are used to it: they say simply, "Cut it out!" Ladies get angry. I squeezed you, very improperly, I admit. And you got angry. Now I beg your pardon, the more so as a sentence in your letter hurt me deeply. You say: "Your odious letter made me spend a very wretched day." (It was not the word "odious" that hurt.) You will have to guess the subtle reasons that could afflict me so much at the idea of having caused a woman I do not even know to spend a miserable day. And now believe if you can that I am neither as much of a bounder or a skeptic or a brute as I made myself out to be. Despite myself, I am suspicious of all mystery and anonymity, human and divine.

How do you expect me to write sincerely to a person, to X, who writes to me anonymously, who may be one of my enemies (I have some), or may be a practical joker? With masked men, I am obliged to wear a mask. Turn about is fair play. And yet, by a ruse, I have been able to peep into a little corner of your nature. Forgive me again.

I kiss the unknown hand that wrote to me.

FROM ''R.D.G.''
TO GUY DE MAUPASSANT

(April 1884)

In writing to you again I ruin myself forever in your
eyes. But that is a matter of indifference to me; and
besides, I write to avenge myself—oh, merely by telling
you the result of your ruse to discover what kind of person I was.

I was positively afraid to send to the post office, imagining a thousand foolish things. *That man* will probably end our correspondence by . . . out of consideration for your modesty I say no more. As I opened the
envelope I imagined every possible thing so as not to be
startled. I was, nevertheless, but agreeably so.

Devant les doux accents d'un noble repentir,
Me faut-il donc, seigneur, cesser de vous haïr? [1]

Unless, indeed, this be another ruse. "Flattered at
being taken for a lady of fashion, she will try to play
this part—after having brought into existence a human
document which I don't mind explaining on these
grounds." If this were the case, why should I have been
angry? Perhaps because there is no conclusive proof that
I was, dear Sir. Well, good bye. I forgive you, if it means
anything to you, because I am ill. And as that is a rare
thing with me, I am very gentle with myself, with all the
world, with you who managed to make yourself so extremely disagreeable to me. I am the less loath to deny
it as you will in any case believe what you please.

How shall I prove to you that I am neither playing a

---

[1] *Must I cease, my Lord, to hate you because of the gentle tone
of your noble repentance?*

part nor your enemy? And why should I? Impossible, of course, to swear to you that we were made to understand each other. You are not my equal. I am sorry about that. Nothing would give me greater pleasure than to be able to acknowledge your superiority—yours or anyone else's.

So that I could have some one to talk to. Your last article was interesting, and I should even like—concerning the matter of girls—to ask you a question. But. . . .

A silly delicate remark in your letter set me ruminating. You were unhappy at the thought of having given me pain. That is either silly or sweet. Sweet, I should say. You may make fun of me, I don't care. Yes, that remark indicates a slight attack of romanticism *à la Stendhal*, nothing more. But do not let it upset you; you will not die of it this time.

Good night.

FROM GUY DE MAUPASSANT TO ''R.D.G.''

(late April 1884)

I have just spent ten days at sea, which is why I have not answered sooner. I am back in Paris for four weeks before going away for the summer.

Clearly, Madame, you are not satisfied; and in order that your irritation shall be unmistakable, you declare that I am an inferior person.

Oh, Madame, if you knew me you would know that I make no great claims either to mental or artistic quality. At bottom, I am indifferent to both. Everything in life— men, women, events—has about equal value in my eyes. There you have my profession of faith; and I shall add something which you will not believe: I set no greater store by myself than by others. Everything is divisible into boredom, farce, and misery.

You say that, by writing to me, you ruin yourself forever in my eyes. Why is that? You have had the very rare grace to confess to me that you were wounded by my letter, and to admit it in a manner that was irritated, simple, frank, and charming. That touched and moved me. I made my excuses and told you my reasons. You replied again very nicely, but without yielding; showing benevolence, almost, but mingled still with irritation. What more natural?

Oh, I know that I shall now inspire deep mistrust in you. That can't be helped. Don't you want us to meet? We learn more about a person by listening to them talk for five minutes than in writing to them for ten years. How does it happen that you do not know any of the people I know? For when I am in Paris I go out every evening. Tell me whose house I am to go to, and I shall go. If I look to you too disagreeable, you will not need to reveal yourself. But do not have any illusions concerning me. I am neither handsome, nor distinguished, nor eccentric. Still, I shouldn't think that would matter to you. Do you go into Orleanist, or Republican, or Bonapartist society?

Perhaps you would like to keep me waiting in a church, a museum, or the street? In that case I should lay down conditions so as to be sure not to find myself waiting for a woman who did not turn up.

What do you say to an evening at the theater—without revealing yourself unless you choose. I should tell you what box I was in, and should go with friends. You would not tell me the number of your box. Next day you could, if you wished, write me a note of farewell. Am I not more magnanimous than the French Guard at Fontenoy?

FROM "R.D.G."
TO GUY DE MAUPASSANT

(late April or early May 1844)

I understand your suspicion. It is very unlikely that a respectable woman who is both young and pretty should spend her time writing to you. Is that it? But, Sir—but I was about to forget that all is over between us. My opinion is that you are mistaken; and it is very good of me to tell you so, for I shall cease thereby to be interesting to you, if I ever was. Let me put myself in your place: An unknown appears on my horizon: if the adventure is easy, it holds no attraction for me; if impossible, it would be futile and a bore to engage in it.

For my part, I have not the good fortune to dwell between extremes, and I do not mind saying so in this matter-of-fact fashion, since we have made up. What I find amusing is that whenever I tell you the plain truth, you imagine that I am trying to deceive you.

Although I am a red republican, I do not go into republican society. Not because I do not wish to meet you.

Do you have no desire for a little romance in the midst of the materialism of your Paris life? A spiritual friendship? I do not refuse to meet you; I shall even arrange to do so without giving you warning. It might make you look foolish if you knew that you were being scrutinized, and we must avoid that. Your terrestrial envelope is a matter of indifference to me, true; but is mine to you? Assume that you had the bad taste not to think me wonderful; do you think I should be glad of that, whatever my intentions? I don't say but that some day—I even count upon surprising you a bit that day. Meanwhile, if it bores you, let us stop writing. I reserve to myself the privilege of resuming my letters whenever any atrocity comes into my head.

You are suspicious of me: naturally. Well, I am going to propose to you exactly what a woman of the people would propose in order that you may convince yourself that I am not a woman of the people. But you must not laugh.

Go to a clairvoyant. Let him smell my letter. He will then tell you my age, the color of my hair, my background, and the rest. After which you will write to report what he revealed to you.

"Humbug, stupidity, nonsense!" you say. Of course it is. I do not deny that. But in my case it is because I desire great things which I have not achieved—yet. And the same must be true of you.

I am not so simple-minded as to ask you what your secret aspirations are, despite the fact that my illness has revived in me the childish naïveté of the old Japanese naturalist in a Louis XV wig!

And you think that after our letters nothing would be simpler than for you to come forward and say, "It's me"!

I assure you, that would annoy me beyond measure.

It is said that you admire only strong-minded women with dark hair. Is that true?

We, see each other? Let me charm you by . . . my literature, you who have had such success in charming by yours.

[*This was the last letter that passed between them.*
L. G.]

TO OCTAVE MIRBEAU

Paris (1886)

What has come over you that you raise hob with me like this? I don't mind being jawed; what I do mind is that you suspect me of seeking publicity in connection with something that is more of a nuisance than you can believe.

I have had in my hands five promissory notes signed with my name by the man whom I am trying desperately to have arrested. I should like to know what you would do in my place. All I know about him is his name, his age, and his description. I have more than a hundred witnesses who have seen him operate and have mistaken him for me—not to mention that in many towns in the South people are certain that it is I who am the crook!

The prosecutor's office knows all about the man and his family. What more shall I say? It seems to me that, considering what our relations have been up to now, you might have tried to find out if the story was true or false before expressing what is no more than a suspicion on your part. I have the file on the man, and the proofs, if you care to see them. . . .

TO AN UNIDENTIFIED WOMAN

Tunis, 19 December 1887

I have been thinking longingly of you since last night. An insane desire to see you again, to see you right away, suddenly filled my heart. Now I should like to cross the sea, cross the mountains, go through cities just to put my hand on your shoulder, to inhale the perfume of your

hair. Don't you feel my longing hovering round you—
this desire come from afar to seek you out, this desire
imploring you in the silence of the night?

Most of all I want to see your eyes again, your gentle
eyes. Why do our first thoughts of the woman we love
go to her eyes? How they haunt us, how happy or miserable they can make us, those bright little enigmas so deep
and so fathomless, those little blots of blue or black or
green which, though their shape and color remain un-
changed, can express love or indifference or hate, the
sweetness that soothes and the terror that freezes, better
than the most copious flow of words and the most expressive gestures!

I shall leave Africa in a few weeks. I shall see you
again. You will come to me, will you not, my beloved?
You will meet me? . . .

TO LUCIE LEPOITTEVIN

Tunis, 3 January (1888)

Forgive me, my dear cousin, for waiting so long before
answering your friendly letter; but I haven't time even
to write a note. I take trips, jot down notes, finish my
novel, and am writing a travel book; and when night
comes I am good for nothing. I have been asked to go
to Fez with the new ambassador, who is off to present
his credentials to the Sultan. Very few Europeans have
made this trip.

I assure you that you are wrong to suspect me of indifference. Since you doubt it, I hope to be able to show
you that you are mistaken.

Will you do me the favor of having the enclosed
check cashed and paying my rent with it? You may send

anybody at all with the money, provided it isn't a thief you send.

I have been working, and I go on working like a tribe of black demons, black slaves, rather. But I have few headaches here. . . .

TO THE CHIEF EDITOR OF THE
Gaulois (ARTHUR MEYER)

January 1888

Yesterday, the *Figaro* published in its literary supplement an essay by me on the contemporary novel in which I quoted Flaubert as attributing to Chateaubriand an aphorism that was written by Buffon. This stupid error is mine, not Flaubert's. . . . The reason why I address this correction to you, and not to the paper which published the article, is that I am entering suit against that paper for having made numerous cuts in the said essay without my permission, with the result that the sense of the essay is completely altered. I am not suing the *Figaro* because of its crude and mystifying treatment of me, but because I am concerned to proclaim once again the absolute right of the author to defend his thought, whatever it may be worth, against any type of manhandling of it. . . .[1]

TO HIS MOTHER

Paris, May 1888

Since my return, my time has been spent in errands, visits, and solicitations, so that I haven't yet been able

---

[1] *The essay in question was published as a preface to Maupassant's novel,* Pierre et Jean. *Suit against the Figaro was withdrawn shortly after publication of this letter in the Gaulois.*

to settle down to work. As a matter of fact, I expect to go to Etretat after a bit to be sure that nothing foolish has gone on there. My law suit is indefinitely postponed and will make me new enemies. The *Figaro's* lawyer, Lachaud, who had been ill for some time, is now partly paralyzed, and his brain is beginning to soften, they say—so that Straus, my lawyer, and I are rather embarrassed. Nevertheless, we intend to summon the *Figaro* either to oblige Lachaud to plead (a difficult business) or to get another lawyer.

Aside from this there is no news. The weather has been mild and damp, and we get rain from time to time: sunshine alternates with mud. I am working without pressure on my new novel (*Fort comme la mort*) and I find it very difficult, so much is it a matter of shading, of things suggested rather than said straight out. It won't be a long novel, actually. I want it to flash across the reader's mind like a vision of life—tender, terrible, despairing.

We are in the midst of a slump in bookselling. Nobody buys books any more. I believe that the cheap reprints and the numerous series of books at forty centimes are killing the (3 fr. 50) novel. Bookshops display nothing and sell nothing except these little reprints. . . .

Let me know if you want me to send any books to you: I'll pick out the least dull among those that are sent to me. I know you don't read much, but you may want to skim the pages. It worries me a great deal that you should be so much alone, so tormented, so ill. I am always thinking what I can do to amuse you. It isn't easy.

TO AN UNIDENTIFIED JOURNALIST

July 1888

I had hoped against hope that I should not be mentioned in the list of those who have declined the Cross of the Legion of Honor. Your article proves that I was wrong to nurse this hope. Indeed, I have read a bit of gossip and received letters which indicate that there has been much ado about the matter. I am not responsible for that, and I have no notion who could have spread the erroneous rumor that is going round.

I was not offered the Cross. I was asked merely what I should respond if the Government took it into its head to offer it to me. I answered that in my view it was ill-bred to refuse a distinction which was so respectable and so widely sought after; but I begged not to be offered it myself, and that the Government be asked to forget about me.

I have always said (my friends will bear me out) that I wished not to participate in any honorifics and dignities. As for my reasons, one will do, I imagine. I object to the establishment of an official hierarchy in the world of letters. If there were no degrees in the Legion of Honor, I should understand it better; but those grades constitute a scale of merit that is really too fantastic. . . . Edmond de Goncourt, for example, whose high distinction and influence upon contemporary literature are uncontestable, is still a Knight of the Legion of Honor. The higher ranks, I dare say, are reserved for his pupils.

TO V. HAVARD

Etretat, 20 September 1888

. . . I am not at all well. In the past two months I have not done an hour's work. I leave tomorrow for Aix-les-Bains to see if I can get rid of the frightful headaches from which I suffer.

TO AN UNIDENTIFIED WRITER

Aix-les-Bains (September 1888)

Your second letter has followed me to Aix-les-Bains where I have just arrived after a long journey. I am greatly embarrassed to know how to reply to you, for I cannot do any work at this moment and have not been able to do any for more than eight months because of the state of my health. For this reason I am not able to go over your plan and can only say, work it out by yourself, as you think best.

TO COUNTESS POTOCKA

[Following a visit to his brother Hervé, interned at the time in a private asylum at Lyons. L. G.]

(1889)

. . . He tore my heart, and I have never in my life suffered so much. When I had to go, and when they had refused to allow him to accompany me to the train, he began to moan so horribly that I couldn't restrain my tears as I gazed at that man condemned by Nature to die, that man who will never leave his prison, who will never again see his mother. . . . He knows that there is something frightful, irreparable, in him, but he doesn't know what it is. . . . Oh, man's poor body, man's poor mind, what a filthy thing, what a horrible thing to have created! If I believed in the God of your religions I should feel such limitless horror of him. . . .

If my brother dies before my mother does, I think I shall go mad myself for thinking how the poor creature will suffer. The poor woman! How crushed, hammered, pulverized she has been without respite since the day of her marriage. . . .

TO DR. GEORGES DAREMBERG

Cannes, November 1889

Thank you for your friendly invitation; but though I shall be back in Paris on Friday next, I cannot profit by it, for I am ill, and the nature of my illness requires that I follow a rigorous diet. . . . I had terrible hemorrhages for six days in Florence and was forced to return in haste to Cannes. Since then I must have a few defectively healed scabs in the abdomen, which is as knotty as a sack of potatoes. Walking is most painful to me. You can imagine what I am allowed to eat and drink.

TO HIS LANDLORD (M. NORMANT)

Paris (January 1890)

I am afraid that it will be entirely impossible for me to go on living in the apartment you let me. In any case, a doctor's orders, which I have had notarized, requires me to leave it instantly: I am off to the South where I hope I may recover from the very serious nervous condition brought about by two weeks of insomnia due to the night work of the baker whose shop is beneath my apartment. I had told you in advance that since my nerves were delicate and sleep was difficult for me, I would not take the rooms if the noise of that industry could be heard at night in my bedroom. You replied that I had nothing to fear, that it was impossible to hear the baker at work, that the ovens were in a sub-cellar, two levels below the street. The truth is that one can hear the sounds and movements of men at work from the bedroom upstairs as if the ovens were in the next room. I am going to have this fact certified by witnesses.

I have been deceived. . . .

TO OLLENDORFF

17 March 1890

. . . As for the volume you are publishing, you may be sure that "l'Inutile beauté" is worth a hundred of "Champ d'oliviers." The latter will tickle the sensibilities of the bourgeoisie; but bourgeois sensibilities are all nerves and no judgment. "L'Inutile beauté" is the finest story I have ever written. It is a mere symbol. Bear in mind your enthusiasm over *Mont Oriol*, a novel I never liked and which is no great shakes. Send me proofs to Paris as quickly as possible. My eyes are very bad, and I read proof very slowly. . . .

TO HIS MOTHER

20 May 1890

This letter will be very short, for my eyes are now well rested and I can work. I had to stop Bouchard's treatments entirely: they set my nerves on edge and in that way attacked my eyesight. I don't know whom to go to. My friend Grancher is advising me. He prescribes the waters at Plombières (where, in fact, Bouchard would like me to go), mountain air, and a warm climate. I am paralyzed by the thought of moving in July. I'll be along to see you in a few days. . . .

My new apartment will be very pretty, with this sole disadvantage that the dressing-room is too small and poorly arranged. The pretty room that was to have been my dressing-room had to be given up to my valet, François, so that he could be near me in the night; for the doctor has prescribed cupping the whole length of my spinal column in the event of insomnia accompanied by nightmares. Cupping relaxes me instantly, and is so light that I can take it again in the morning. Actually, what I have is Norman rheumatism, intensified and generalized throughout my system, so that it paralyzes all my functions. My optic mechanism reacts to every state of my stomach and intestines. And for this, Plombières is the only known remedy.

TO GEORGES CHARPENTIER

Paris, May 1890

I tried to see you last Tuesday upon learning that a painter whose name I don't know has taken the liberty of doing an etching of me and exhibiting it at the Salon without either informing me or obtaining my permission, and that the portrait is being reproduced in your new edition of *les Soirées de Médan*. You cannot be unaware that I have always refused to permit the sketching, exposition, or sale of any portrait or photograph of myself. . . .

I am merely endeavoring to settle this matter in friendly fashion, and I ask that my reply come by the bearer, for I am meeting my lawyer this afternoon. Here is what I demand:

You will furnish me the exact figure of the number of copies of the *Soirées de Médan* which you have printed, so that I may compare it with the number of portraits destroyed. Those etchings will be removed from all the copies of the book in stock. Thereafter, those copies will be exchanged against the copies held at present by the booksellers. The latter will be handled in the same manner. All the etchings will be removed from the books and will be delivered either to me or to my lawyer, M. Jacob, 4, Faubourg Montmartre, where they will be counted.

If this arrangement is not accepted, I shall this very day go to law.

TO AN UNIDENTIFIED WOMAN

(1890)

. . . If I were free to speak I should release all the desolate, repressed, unexploded thoughts that lie in the depths of my being. I feel them swelling inside me, poisoning me like bile in the bilious. But if one day I could spit them up, they might perhaps evaporate and

—who knows?—my heart might ever afterwards be gay and glad. I have so many inner bruises that the ideas in my head cannot stir without making me scream. Why? Why? Dr. Dumas would say I had a poor digestion. I think, however, that I have a poor vainglorious conscience-stricken heart, a human heart, a heart people laugh at; but which beats and aches, and makes my head ache too. I have the soul of a Latin, a threadbare soul. And then there are days when I do not think like this, but I suffer nevertheless, for I am of the thin-skinned— though I never tell people that, never show it, but dissemble it very successfully, I think. Doubtless people think me one of the most indifferent men in the world. What I am is skeptical, which is not the same thing— skeptical, because I see clearly. And my eyes say to my heart: Go hide somewhere, old man, you are grotesque. And my heart hides.

TO HIS MOTHER

Paris, 7 July 1880

. . . I shall send you a lot of reviews of *Notre Coeur* as soon as I have thanked the reviewers for them. Publication in the *Revue des Deux Mondes* has after all hurt the sale of the book. The big booksellers in Paris tell me that six out of ten of their regular customers read the novel in the review and will not buy the book. Another disadvantage is this: All the talk about the novel went on while it was running in the review; and that talk, which was immense, is now over. Nevertheless, sales have been good, though they are slowing up. I think it will outsell *Fort comme la mort*, which has done 32,000. Generally speaking, the publication of *Notre Coeur* in the review was a good thing. Now the special category of readers who subscribe to that review know me and will buy me later. I have gained readers by this.

28 February 1891

. . . My health is not flourishing. My eyes are still in the same state and I am certain that the cause is brain fatigue, or rather nervous fatigue of the brain; for after half an hour's work my thoughts are in a jumble and my brain and eyes both grow foggy and the mere act of writing becomes hard for me, my hand refuses to move as my mind directs it. I went through all this while writing *Fort comme la mort*. I rest my eyes for two whole days, after which I can see perfectly again. But I am overworked by the business of revising the play[1] and by thinking of (a new novel) *l'Angelus*, which is not getting on at all.

My doctor, Professor Robin, who is a member of the Academy, is not worried. He says, "There are serious disorders and we shall have to find a remedy; but there is no grave trouble."

Paris, 14 March 1891

Don't fret too much about my health. I think that my eyes and brain are simply weary, and that the abominable winter we've had has made a frozen plant of me. I look well and have no more stomach pains. What I chiefly need is air and quiet.

About my nervous state, I consulted a man who is said to be very much better than Charcot. . . . He examined me thoroughly, listened to my story, and said: "You have had all the symptoms of neurasthenia (Char-

---

[1] A play, Musotte, was made from a story, "l'Enfant," by Maupassant and a collaborator.

cot's word for what used to be known as hysteria). It comes of intellectual overwork: half the men of letters and stockbrokers are in your condition. A matter of nerves, first frayed by your rowing, then by your brain work; nothing but nerves in your case. The physical constitution is excellent and will last you a long time—with a spot of nuisance now and then. Hygiene, baths, a warm and quiet place to spend the summer, a long rest —alone, in peace. I am not worried about you."

He told Landolt and Cazalis the same things about me. He is called Dr. Dejerine. But I am crippled with neuralgia due to Normandy—the Seine and my shabby lodgings. Heat is the only thing that helps.

The play is doing well. Full houses every night. Four companies will be touring the provinces. Contracts with Rouen, Lyons, Bordeaux, Lille. Abroad, the play will be done at Brussels, Berlin, Vienna, in Italy, Portugal, Sweden, Denmark, and at St. Petersburg. Foreign rights don't bring much money, but what publicity!

I have the influenza, but it has been clearing up these two days past. It was very mild.

26 March 1891

My trip South is again put off for a few days—because of my teeth. Treatment is very important because it is likely that the condition of my right eye may be bound up with that of the root of the tooth just below. I know there is not a decent dentist in Nice. The matter of the eye is so important that I cannot afford to neglect it. I am so sorry, for I was all ready to leave.

The weather here is frightful. Snow is still swirling in the air, the thermometer goes down every night to two or three degrees of frost—it's awful. My influenza is pretty bad. What a horrible thing influenza is!

. . . The doctor has forbidden me to have the other tooth extracted, saying that the pain will stop as soon as the cavity has healed over. So long as the jaw is exposed to the air I shall have eye trouble and sinus accompanied by the usual neuralgia. He is now hastening the closing of the cavity by electric treatments, and I am sure that he will advance the work of Nature by three months. . . .

"What you need" (the doctor said) "is a long and complete rest. I speak to you as if you were my son. What you tell me of your plans will not do. What are you going to do? In the first place, you must get away from Paris as soon as I shall have finished treating your mouth. Don't go back to Nice: it's an enervating place, and in summer the port is an inferno." I spoke of my boat. He said: "I know the boat. She is very pretty. A pretty plaything for a lad in good health on an outing with his friends. But it is no place for a man like you, weary in body and mind, to rest. . . . I want you *isolated* in a *very healthy* region, doing nothing, thinking of nothing, taking no medicines of any kind. Nothing but cold water."

I am waiting for good weather, and then I shall leave. I'll spend a few days at Nice, and then take to my boat, with walking trips along the coast.

My teeth are not entirely well, but they will be. The abscess is dry and healed. I can leave now. . . . The influenza has come back. First it took me in the chest; and when I thought myself cured it took me in the nasal passages and the throat. And when I believed I was finally rid of it, it seized hold of my head, my megrims,

ny eye, my memory. A change of air will certainly set
ne up quickly, for I am neither thin (actually I have
gained) nor weak, but simply stupefied.

TO AN UNIDENTIFIED WOMAN

(no date)

. . . My mind moves through dark valleys that lead
I know not where. They succeed one another, they flow
into one another, long, deep, impossible to emerge out
of. I come out of one only to find myself in another, and
I cannot foretell what there will be at the end of the
last. I am afraid lest weariness induce me later not to
continue along this senseless route. . . .

TO HIS MOTHER

(Paris 1891)

Just a few lines, for Grancher has forbidden me to
write because writing brings on contractions of the eye
which are to be avoided until I am well again.

I continue to get better, as I told you. Not that I have
recovered, but I am putting on flesh, my face is full
again. The bouts of neuralgia in the jaw, and of insomnia, are gone. I began to get better the moment I
arrived, and have made constant progress. Grancher
thinks I should stay on here another two or three weeks,
and get back my strength. He said: "In Paris you have a
large airy apartment ten minutes away from the Bois de
Boulogne. In spite of which you go off, in summer, of all
seasons, to a town full of dust, with blinding sun in its
streets, and no countryside at all. I want you either in

greenery or at sea. Try your boat: it will constitute an excellent cure; but if you settle down in Nice you'll certainly have a relapse." . . .

TO DR. HENRY CAZALIS

Vasenex, near Divonne (June 1891)
. . . I don't believe I shall knock about much longer like this, whether at sea or on shore, more and more sick every day in body and brain. I am at Divonne which I shall be leaving because of the constant storms, the rains, and the humidity. I am at the end of my strength and haven't slept in four months.

Divonne (1891)
. . . I have such headaches, headaches of which I was cured two years ago, that I take two grams of antipyrene a day. I am going mad in this place: I can't write a line. . . . There are days when I damn well feel like shooting myself. I can't read. Every letter I write makes me ache with pain. . . .

TO HIS LAWYER (M. JACOB)

5 December 1891
. . . This is the substance of the story:
I wrote a tale called "le Testament" which appears in the volume entitled *Contes de la Bécasse*. Somebody used it as the scenario for a long idiotic novel, written in English. The result is plagiarism, to begin with; in addition to which my name appears as the author of a book the subject of which was stolen from me. The names of all my characters are used, but at a period in

time ten years before they appear in my story, and the whole job is so clumsily done that I cannot permit it to go on.

Please answer by return post, for the situation is very difficult.

Cannes, 5 December 1891

Herewith the letter I have written to Theodore Child, Paris representative of the American publishers, H—— & B——, with whom I am on the best of terms. I am so ill that I fear I shall die in a few days of the treatments I am forced to follow. See Mr. Child right away and hand him the letter as soon as you have read it. You will put a copy of the letter in your files.

[*The letter to Theodore Child follows.*]

"Sir, I am entering suit in America for literary piracy committed against me by *The Star*, of New York. The authorities require that I shall deposit a bond *judicatum soldi* of $250.00 and that some one in New York agree to act for me.

"If Messers. H—— & B——, who are experienced in these matters, and in things literary in their country, will be good enough to follow the case in my name, I shall be glad to indemnify them, and I shall guarantee the bond in question by depositing an equivalent sum with you, the deposit to remain in your hands until the case has been settled.

"H—— & B—— would thus be rendering me a handsome service.

"The Court claims that it is unacquainted with my name and that I am probably some cheap, little-known, and poorly remunerated writer. Messers. H—— & B—— are in a position to correct this impression. It was I who restored a pronounced taste for the short story and the novelette in France. My books have been translated throughout the world, have been sold in great numbers, and [I am] paid the highest rates ever attained. French newspapers pay me one franc a line for my novels and five hundred francs for each short story. You yourself are aware of this.

"The number of editions of my books is among the greatest, being second only to those of Zola. I shall send you in a few days an almost complete list of my works, as well as a list of articles about me.

"Write to the American publishers, please, and be sure to see my lawyer, who is to be found at 4, Faubourg Montmartre."

(?26 December 1891)

I am dying. I believe I shall be dead in two days. Busy yourself with my affairs and get in touch with my man of business at Cannes, M. Colle.

This is my farewell that I am sending you.

TO DR. HENRY CAZALIS

Cannes (no date)

I am ABSOLUTELY LOST. I AM EVEN DYING. I have softening of the brain as a result of salt-water swabbings of my nasal passages. In my brain there is a saline fermentation going on and every night my brains run out through my nose and mouth in a sticky paste. THIS IS IMMINENT DEATH AND I AM MAD. My head roars like a drum. FAREWELL, FRIEND, YOU WILL NEVER SEE ME AGAIN.